Men and Decisions

LEWIS L. STRAUSS

MEN AND DECISIONS

DOUBLEDAY & COMPANY, INC. Garden City, New York, 1962

The excerpts from *Crusade in Europe,* by Dwight D. Eisenhower, copyright 1948, Doubleday & Company, Inc., are used with the permission of the publishers.

Material was taken from *Japan Subdued,* by Herbert Feis, with permission from Princeton University Press, copyright © 1961.

The excerpts from the memoirs of Harry S. Truman have been taken from Vol. I, *Years of Decisions,* Doubleday & Company, Inc., copyright © 1955, Time, Inc., and from Vol. II, *Years of Trial and Hope,* Doubleday & Company, Inc., copyright © 1956, Time, Inc.

The articles by Dr. Robert F. Bacher and Dr. Hans A. Bethe are reprinted with permission. Copyright © 1950, © 1959 by Scientific American, Inc. All rights reserved.

The articles by Dr. Edward Teller and Dr. Harold C. Urey are reprinted with permission from the *Bulletin of the Atomic Scientists,* 935 East 60th Street, Chicago, Ill., copyright 1950 by the Educational Foundation for Nuclear Science, Inc., Chicago.

"Politics Defeats Mr. Strauss" appeared as an editorial, June 20, 1959, reprinted with permission of the New York *Times.*

TO ALICE

We have made many decisions in order to become what we are. . . . At the beginning of our period we decided for *freedom*. It was a right decision; it created something new and great in history. . . . And now, in the old age of our period, the quest to sacrifice freedom for security splits every nation and the whole world with really daemonic power. We have decided for *means* to control nature and society. We have created them, and we have brought about something new and great in the history of all mankind. But we have excluded ends. We have never been ready to answer the question, "For what?" And now, when we approach old age, the means claim to be the ends; our tools have become our masters, and the most powerful of them have become a threat to our very existence.

PAUL TILLICH, *The Shaking of the Foundations*

Foreword

A boy brought up in the South—especially in Virginia—is surrounded
by a climate of history. Washington and Jefferson, Lee and Jackson
were not legendary to me. Conquered peoples cannot celebrate victories, but they compensate by venerating their heroes. As a boy, I knew
men who had known Robert E. Lee and Jeb Stuart and Beauregard
and Pickett, men who had talked with them and fought beside them.
Hundreds of veterans in gray uniforms lived in the Old Soldiers Home
and came to watch our ball games in the fields nearby or sat and talked
with us by the hour. Thomas Jefferson had drawn the plans of the
classic building in Capitol Square, and I had played as a child in the
shade of its walls. The home of Chief Justice John Marshall stood un-
altered in the corner of the high-school yard. Even the Revolutionary
War did not seem as remote to me as World War I does to my children;
the War Between the States was simply "The War." In the Virginia of
my youth, history was pervasive and familiar—and important.

Thus, when at 21 I had the extraordinary good fortune to become
private secretary to Herbert Hoover, it was clear that to have a hand
in feeding the hungry and clothing the naked in Belgium and Northern
France was to have a hand in history.

Its dramatic aspects appealed to an idealism not yet abraded by the
events of the years which were to follow. Feeling privileged to witness
history being made by men who were humanitarians in a world which
barbarism was threatening to overwhelm, I simply resolved to record
events and later to put my recollections at the disposal of men whose
profession is the compilation of history.

This, I assumed, could be done at the end of my experiences with
Mr. Hoover. That day, happily, has not come. In order to earn a living,
I was compelled to leave his staff in the autumn of 1919. The friendship with him, however, which, following the death of my father, became almost filial, has endured. There has been scarcely a month in the

half a thousand months which have elapsed that I have not visited him, and our correspondence has grown to be voluminous.

This book, then, logically begins with those events and times in which I saw history being made by Mr. Hoover's decisions. As the years passed and experience increased, there were times when opportunity offered or occasion required judgments of my own. These, too, I have attempted to record faithfully without the palliation or the editing of hindsight, having no desire but to contribute to the record of our times the truth as I saw it. Recognizing that others may have seen the same events in a different light or from a different point of viewing, I make no claim for clear vision in those instances where subsequent history appears to have sustained my decisions, and I hope for tolerance in those instances where I was wrong.

In the main, however, this is intended to be a book about other men —men under whom I served or with whom I worked in business and in government, the decisions they made, and the effects of some of those decisions upon our world.

Contents

List of Illustrations

Men and Decisions

I

First Decisions

Originally, this book was to be without autobiographical content. Appearing as both reporter and participant as the events and decisions were recorded, I found this resolve difficult and, finally, impractical. Since the vertical pronoun has progressively intruded, the reader, having no acquaintance with my background and beliefs, would be handicapped in evaluating some of the narrative. It may be well to begin, therefore, with the outline of a self-portrait, without benefit of cosmetic repair.

In all likelihood I owe my life to decisions by three grandparents in the 1830s and 1840s to leave Austria and Germany and make their homes in a land of freedom. (One grandmother was born in Baltimore.) My maternal grandfather had completed his service in the army of Emperor Franz Joseph, his papers indicating *"sehr gut gefuhrt"*—a "good conduct" discharge, it would appear. The other grandfather emigrated at eighteen, settled in Culpeper, Virginia, raised a large family, as a Confederate was taken prisoner and lost both eyes near the end of the war. Of my generation's forebears who elected to remain in Central Europe, most were put to death along with their children by Hitler and his imitators.

My parents taught me that the right to live in the social order established by the Founding Fathers is so priceless a privilege that no sacrifice to preserve it is too great. It seems to me that, however trite it may be, I ought to begin a memoir with that acknowledgment.

From the age of sixteen until twenty, I was a traveling salesman—in the vernacular, a "drummer"—selling shoes at wholesale to merchants in the Carolinas, Georgia, and West Virginia.

It was hard work, physically hard. The tools of the trade were two trunks of sample shoes, each trunk holding eight trays. These had to be unpacked and repacked numbers of times each day. As train schedules were inconvenient and many small communities were served by only one or two stops each day, much of the traveling was done in two-horse hacks hired from a livery stable. That institution has all but disappeared, but in those days there were several in every town. Automobiles were uncommon and most of the roads too poor for anything as temperamental as the early cars.

Getting into the coal mining towns in the narrow valleys of the West Virginia Alleghenies was impossible, however, except by rail, and then by walking the crossties between mine commissaries, lugging a case of samples in each hand. The commissions were good, but I can remember thinking that I would not want a son of mine to follow in my footsteps.

Calling on a merchant for the first time, I used to introduce myself by saying, "I am a son of the vice-president of Fleishman Morris & Company in Richmond, Virginia, and I would like to show you our line of fine shoes." It never occurred to me how this must have sounded, until one occasion when I had driven miles over the sand roads east of the Atlantic Coast Line railroad, to see a storekeeper in a little place called Chinquapin. He ran a big commissary, the only one for miles around. When I opened with the introduction, the merchant looked at me and then replied, "Well, sir, I must say that this is a great honor. Imagine it, you, the son of an honest-to-goodness vice-president, coming all the way back into the sticks to see common people like us. Come on up here," he called to his clerks, "come on up here and meet a big man from Richmond." By this time, like Alice in Wonderland, I had shrunk to about two inches, and must have shown it. He pulled my leg a little more and then said, "Well, Son, I can see you are a new one. Show me your samples." He bought a sizable order and was a loyal customer as long as I traveled and a friend as long as he lived. That was forty-seven years ago. His name was G. B. D. Parker.

There was another customer in a little North Carolina town bisected by the Seaboard Airline Railroad. The "depot" was about three hundred yards from his store. One day the afternoon "cannon-ball express" unloaded my two trunks on a baggage truck and me on the platform, and, as it was late, I could not find a hack to move them to my customer's store. I told him of my predicament and said I would get them there in the morning. "How much you going to pay to get them moved?" he asked. I replied that I would pay, perhaps, a dollar. "Then pay me," he said. Whereupon he went to the station and pulled the baggage truck down the street to his store. He was a man at least three times my age. I never forgot that lesson, either.

As I observed the Sabbath by not working on Saturdays and since most of my customers did not work on Sundays, I had two days each week for study. One of my uncles, who had become wealthy and who lived in New York, would visit the less affluent members of the family in Richmond. On these occasions he would reason with me on the folly of wasting one day out of each week. He assured me that my stubbornness in this respect would doom me to failure in business. By luck, plus a burning desire to prove him wrong, I was able to lead the sales force.

When in small towns where there was no Jewish congregation, I read my prayers alone on the Sabbath and then "read law" in casebooks loaned me by a friend, the late John Garland Pollard, who later was Governor of Virginia. I also traveled with the Latin classics and enjoyed being able to read them without too great difficulty. This was due to a high-school teacher, Clement C. Reed, who had made Latin come alive. I believe this would be more generally the case if students routinely began the study of Latin with Virgil rather than with Caesar and Cicero.

In cities where there was a Jewish congregation, such as Wilmington, North Carolina, Columbia or Sumter, South Carolina, I attended services, and on occasion, when the rabbi was away or ill, I was called upon to read. Having had experience as a lay reader in Richmond, I was able to discharge this duty to the great satisfaction of my parents. In this manner I gained the friendship of some remarkable scholars such as the late Rabbi Mendelssohn of Wilmington, North Carolina, and his son, a mathematician, who later served the Army as a cryptographer in World War I and made a historic contribution to the cracking of enemy codes.

The main incentive for hard work was to accumulate enough money to be able to go to college and study physics. I had won a scholarship on graduation from high school, but for family reasons did not take advantage of it. By 1916, when I was twenty, I had saved about twenty thousand dollars and felt in sight of my goal. That I never did get to college is unfortunately evident enough, though the reason will appear as this account continues. The precise moment my interest in physics began is sharp in my memory.

As a result of a boyhood battle, I had damaged a front tooth and had to be taken to a dentist. In order to keep me amused while he went about making an amalgam or whatever dentists did in those days, he gave me a saucer of mercury. He also had a tuning fork and I found that quite beautiful waves could be produced on the surface of the mercury with the vibrating fork. When the dentist saw what I was doing, he fastened two small wires to the tines of the fork and, setting it vibrating, suggested that the points of the wires be touched to the mercury. There to my astonishment and delight was the first "standing wave" I had ever seen.

As I grew older I read whatever I could find on wave mechanics and radiation. By the time we were studying Millikan and Gale's *First Course in Physics* in high school, it was already clear that, more than anything else in the universe, the world of physics was the most exciting. The ideal life would be to have enough money to build and equip a laboratory and to work in it to learn the secrets of nature and to expand the frontiers of knowledge. It would cost a lot of money, but, with the overconfidence of youth, that seemed no great obstacle.

Many years later one of the authors of that textbook, Dr. Robert A. Millikan, became a friend. In the intervening years he had won the Nobel prize for his discoveries in the field of radiation. In the edition of his textbook which I had studied at John Marshall High School, the whole subject of radiation covered only three pages. There was a memorable concluding paragraph:

> J. J. Thompson estimates that enough energy is stored in one gram of hydrogen to raise a million tons through one hundred yards. It is not improbable that it is the transformation of this sub-atomic energy into heat which is maintaining the temperature of the sun. The most vitally interesting question which the physics of the future has to face is: Is it possible for man to gain control of this tremendous store of sub-atomic energy and to use it for his own ends? Such a result does not now seem likely or even possible; and yet the transformations which the study of physics has wrought in the world within a hundred years were once just as incredible as this.

The book in which those prophetic words appear was written in 1906. Only the previous year, Albert Einstein, an obscure young patent-office clerk, had published his now famous theorem in a German scientific journal. It had been only ten years since the work of Becquerel and the Curies. I still have the textbook, somewhat dog-eared, and on a weekend at my farm, in 1938, Dr. Millikan came across it in my library and left a note on its flyleaf:

To Lewis L. Strauss. This was my first attempt (1906) to get across a bit of the history and the method of science . . .[1]

Robert A. Millikan
1938

That year, 1938, was the year before "fission," four years before the "controlled chain reaction," and seven years before "Hiroshima." Millikan was then president of the California Institute of Technology. He died in 1953, at the age of eighty-five, but even in his eighties, he was one of the youngest men I knew.

The great war had begun in 1914 with the German invasion of Belgium and had been in progress for nearly two and a half years by the winter of 1916–17. There was little excitement about it in the South where I was at work, although there was some prosperity as a result of it. Cotton prices were good and mules were being bought up at high figures to haul the guns and caissons of the Allied armies. Here and there a few volunteers were joining up to fly for the Royal Air Force or to drive ambulances for the Red Cross. It seemed very far away to me.

There was one aspect of the war, however, of which we were generally aware—the plight of Belgium and Northern France. Through the newspapers, people were beginning to be familiar with the name of Herbert C. Hoover. It was understood that he was a successful mining engineer who had been pressed into service by Ambassador Walter Hines Page in London. His job was to get Americans who had been stranded in Europe by the war back to their homes. Apparently he had done so well at this assignment that, when starvation began in Belgium and Northern France, the Ambassador had again turned to Mr. Hoover for help.

There was a story to the effect that when he set about sending the marooned Americans home, he had advanced his own money for their passage, in many cases relying on good faith to be repaid. He had also engaged his own fortune to get the first shiploads of food to be sent to Belgium. Here, obviously, was a man of courage and action and of faith in his fellow men. He had called upon the women of America to collect clothing to be baled and sent to him for distribution to the destitute in the occupied countries. An operation on so large a scale, which today seems a natural reaction to distress in any part of the world, was at that time a pioneering idea. As a result, hundreds of good women, my mother among them, their hearts moved by the suffering of the innocent victims of war, engaged in the collection of warm clothing and blankets from their families and friends. These were sent to this mining-engineer-turned-humanitarian.

Early in 1917, the Richmond *Times-Dispatch* carried the item that President Wilson had sent for Mr. Hoover to come to Washington to discuss further relief operations and the management of food production and distribution in the United States so that waste might be eliminated, prices controlled, and production increased. The President's aim was to send more food to England and France. German submarines were increasingly successful in sinking food cargoes. England and France were severely rationing their food, and neither country had any reserves. Reading these reports, my mother was sure that Mr. Hoover was the man to do something about it. That evening she said to me, "When he gets there, why don't you go up and help him?"

It was the interval between seasons in the shoe business and I had a few weeks on my hands. I also had my savings and could volunteer to work without pay, as the press reported that Mr. Hoover was doing. When the news of his arrival appeared in the papers, I took the train to Washington and with some difficulty located Mr. Herbert Clark Hoover in the New Willard Hotel. It was the beginning of an association which, as this is written, has lasted for forty-four years.

II

A Man of Decision

Although Washington is only 112 miles north of Richmond by rail, I had never been there until a day in February 1917. My first call was at the office of Senator Martin, the Senior Senator from Virginia, and, though not acquainted with the Senator, I hoped that he might give me an introduction to Mr. Hoover. I got as far as the Senator's secretary, Mr. Merkling, who heard my request and said that "nothing could be easier." Thereupon he swiveled around and typed out a letter to Mr. Hoover, from which it appeared that I was a greatly valued friend of long standing. Then, picking up his pen, he signed the letter "Thomas J. Martin." It was my first experience with this kind of accommodation for constituents, which is a well-established Washington institution. As a result, I still have that letter and was properly grateful for it, but felt too embarrassed to use it; it seemed at the time to involve me as participant in a misrepresentation. The fact that such letters were run of the mill was soon to become familiar.

There was difficulty in locating Mr. Hoover. It was a surprise to find that many people had never heard of him. His name appeared to be a great deal more familiar back in Richmond, Virginia, than it was in Washington. Finally, it seemed that the most direct method would be to try the hotels. In those days the New Willard was the largest and most opulent. Luck was with me—Mr. Hoover was registered there—and after I knocked on the door of his suite, it was opened by his secretary, a young Englishman. He had been expecting a messenger from the White House and was both disappointed and annoyed to find me, whom he took for a reporter. When he learned that my purpose was to see Mr. Hoover, the secretary replied that his chief was busy. I said I would wait. The secretary allowed that I might have to wait all day—"the Chief" was *very* busy. I said something to indicate that time was of no consequence, took a seat near the door, and began reading a copy of *Nature* which I had in my coat pocket.

In a short while, Mr. Hoover entered from his adjoining office. He was wearing a hat and overcoat and was on his way to an appointment. I recognized him from his photographs, and, seeing that his secretary did not intend to introduce me, I stepped up, gave my name, and said that I would like to work for him, adding that I had understood that he was accepting no salary for his services and that I would be happy to work for two months under the same arrangement. As I completed that long sentence, he looked at me with a puzzled smile and asked, "When do you want to start?" "Right now," I replied. "Take off your coat," he said, and left. These ten words were the only exchange I had with him for a matter of weeks.

His secretary did the perfectly human thing. Presented with an assistant not of his selection, he decided to make me sick of my bargain. In the course of the next few days, however, he was himself so overworked and I was able to relieve him of so much detail that he broke down and proposed that we should be friends and try to make a go of it.

Within days, the food control organization began to grow. New volunteers arrived on the scene. Most of them were the heads of their businesses in sugar refining, flour milling, meat packing, and other food industries. Nutrition experts, writers, statisticians, and lawyers also joined the staff. We moved from the Willard into the old Gordon Hotel at 16th and K streets, which has since been trampled by progress. From makeshift offices we expanded finally into a spanking-new office building erected in a swampy area near the river known as "foggy-bottom" and now the permanent location of many executive agencies. Our headquarters was built by John Reed Kilpatrick, later famous as the president of Madison Square Garden in New York. The building itself was the first of a horrible proliferation of "temporaries" which marred Washington for years. It was a wooden framework sheathed with wire lath, stuccoed on the outside, and had wallboard inside partitions. Its estimated life was "three or four years at most," by which time it was expected that the war in Europe would be over and that the building would not have to be torn down, but, like the one hoss shay, would fall apart. As a matter of fact, it remained in continuous use until it was pulled down in 1953, thirty-four years later, and I was to see it again on another duty. There was a large ornamental plaster seal of the Food Administration over the main entrance to the building, and as the contractor knocked the walls to pieces, I had the ornament salvaged and sent to Mr. Hoover's museum in Palo Alto as a memento of the wartime decisions in those offices.

While we were still in the Willard, it was my habit to get to the office very early. Coming in one morning and finding me the only person there, Mr. Hoover stopped at my desk and said, "I have an idea that if we chart the prices of wheat and flour for the three prewar years to date we will find that it looks like this," at which he held out his right hand with his index and second fingers separated. "Plot it for me," he directed, as he closed the door of his office. I don't believe he recognized me as the new office boy.

Making a note of what he had said, I drew a sketch of his gesture but without the slightest idea of what it was intended to convey. Following that, I spent the rest of the day in the Library of Congress compiling wheat and flour quotations from a trade journal, *The Northwestern Miller*, and from Department of Agriculture publications. To my surprise, I discovered that there were several different kinds of both flour and wheat and that they were quoted at the opening, the high and the low, and the closing for each day. Because of my ignorance I did an unnecessary amount of averaging. By nightfall I had many columns of figures, but no curves. Determined that Mr. Hoover should have the results in the morning, I found a stationery shop which carried graph paper in rolls. By this time it was after closing hours, but the proprietor opened his shop again and he and his son unrolled the paper on the counter, and as they read the figures from my tables I plotted them. It was in the small hours of the morning when we finished.

The completed chart, when it was finally unrolled back in the office, had to be thumbtacked to the cornice. It ran down the wall, and the bottom six inches curled up on the floor in front of the baseboard. But the curves made apparent to me what Mr. Hoover had meant by his gesture. They ran along roughly parallel during the three prewar years. Beginning with the war, however, both wheat and flour began to rise and continued to rise, but the rise in the price of flour was far steeper. Clearly, it not only reflected the rise in the price of wheat, but showed that another factor was increasing the cost of bread beyond the rise in cost of its main ingredient. This, as it developed, was an increased profit margin taken by the processor and distributor.

The following morning, Mr. Hoover came in, walked over to my chart, and looked at it for about half a minute. All he said was, "I thought so," and disappeared into his office.

On the preceding day the private secretary had left. The next day his

duties were assigned to me on a temporary basis. Later I learned from
Edgar Rickard, who as Mr. Hoover's close friend from his mining days
had come to Washington to be his assistant, that some days earlier the
Chief had commented favorably on a memorandum I had prepared for
use by the Senators who were leading the fight for the food control bill.
Its opponents argued that it was an unconstitutional assumption of
power by the federal government and that not even a state of war could
justify it. There were some expressions in speeches and letters written by
Lincoln on the theme of the centralization of power as a war measure.
They seemed to me to fit the existing circumstances. For example, in
1861 Lincoln had asked, "Is there in all republics this inherent and
fatal weakness? Must a government be too strong for the liberties of its
people or too weak to maintain its own existence? So viewing the issue
no choice was left but to call on the power of the government and so
resist its destruction by force for its preservation." In a letter in 1864,
he had written, "I feel that measures otherwise unconstitutional might
become lawful by becoming indispensable to the preservation of the
Constitution through the preservation of the Nation." George Washington also was on record on our side of the issue. There was a letter in
which the first President had written, "Let rigorous measures be
adopted; . . . to punish speculation, forestall extortioners, to promote
public and private economy." Rickard said that the Senators to whom
he had given the memorandum had used it with some effect and that
Mr. Hoover had been aware of it.

The months of organizing the Food Administration were a new departure. It was Mr. Hoover's habit not only to begin work early, but
to work late hours, and, as the subjects under discussion—legislative
and economic—were strange to me, I read every night until the words
ran together, studying the memoranda addressed to him during the
day by members of the Cabinet or by the heads of the divisions into
which the Food Administration was being organized. There was nothing
secret in these communications and the whole security problem with
which I was to become familiar thirty years later was not dreamed of.
It was only necessary to observe the rudimentary precaution of locking
one's desk on leaving the office at night so that papers did not blow
away.

One morning, however, I arrived to find that my locked desk had
been jimmied open, and the tool with which the outrage had been
perpetrated—a pair of bent desk shears—lay at the scene of the crime.
A hurried examination showed that nothing was missing, and a few

minutes later the mystery was solved when Mr. Hoover arrived and apologized for wrecking the desk. He explained that during the evening he had come back to read some correspondence with Congressman Asbury F. Lever which was in my keeping and he had not wanted to wait until morning. "So," he said, "I had to break in."

The Lever Act, which established the Food Administration, was successfully shepherded through the Congress, but not without meeting bitter opposition. The most aggressive and unreasonable opponent was Senator Reed of Missouri. He used every means available in his privileged status to embarrass both President Wilson and Mr. Hoover. His speeches were intemperate and often inaccurate. By remarks to reporters, new currency was given to long since exploded charges that Mr. Hoover had made personal profits from Belgian relief; that spoiled and poisonous food had been fed to the Belgians; and that several of Hoover's principal aides and even Mr. Hoover himself were British subjects and, in consequence, more Anglophile than American in their sympathies. Because of these provocations, several young hotheads in the lower echelons of the Food Administration concluded that it would be a patriotic act to risk their careers by shanghaiing the Senator, holding him in some secure place until the end of the war, and then to release him and throw themselves on the mercy of the courts. I learned of this folly in time to throw cold water on it. Kidnaping a Senator would have made fantastic headlines. In later years, I had sympathy with its motivation if not its judgment.

The group of men who responded to Mr. Hoover's call to help organize wartime activities included many whose careers were afterward closely allied with his. A number later made records in public service, in business, and in academic pursuits. All of them drew inspiration from Hoover's ideals and many have made public acknowledgment of that fact. Robert A. Taft, an early recruit with whom I was to be closely associated in later years, became the Republican leader of the Senate and a close contender for the presidential nomination in 1952; Frederick C. Walcott represented his State of Connecticut in the Senate; H. Alexander Smith was for many years Senior Senator from New Jersey; Joseph P. Cotton became Under Secretary of State; Christian Herter became governor of Massachusetts and Secretary of State. There were many others who became university presidents, governors of states, editors, business executives, and useful citizens in less conspicuous roles. By June 1917, the Food Administration was fully staffed and under way.

The American public had responded enthusiastically to Mr. Hoover's exhortation to reduce consumption and increase production of all foods. Support came from all quarters and every section. Former President Theodore Roosevelt, who had been refused active military duty, wrote from his home at Sagamore Hill to let Mr. Hoover know that he was making speeches around the country on the duties of Americans in the war. His letter was typical of the co-operation Mr. Hoover was receiving. It ended with these words:

> Without food for ourselves and our allies this war cannot be won. We must prove the efficiency of our democracy both by increasing the amount of foodstuffs we produce, and also by saving from our own supply the food it is necessary to furnish our allies. You ask us to make what is an utterly trivial sacrifice compared to the sacrifices made by the whole populations in the countries to which we are allied, and made also by our sons and brothers who have gone abroad to risk everything, including life itself, for our honor and for the welfare of all mankind. We follow you loyally in all you do to promote the great purposes you have in view.

There had been a partial crop failure in 1916 and 1917 and the outlook for provisioning our allies was further dimmed by the alarming success of German submarine warfare. In April of 1917, the month we entered the war, the losses had been 850,000 tons of merchant shipping. The best that we were able to do was to reduce this figure to about 500,000 tons a month between April and August, since, prior to August, ships had sailed unescorted in spite of vigorous protest by Admiral Sims, who commanded U.S. naval operations in European waters. Admiral Sims had advocated convoying the cargo and troop ships with naval vessels, but his repeated proposals had fallen upon deaf ears. He made a convinced advocate of Mr. Hoover, however, who successfully urged the program on President Wilson and Colonel E. M. House, his closest advisor.* But for the adoption of the convoy system, there is little doubt that even the enormous increase in American food production which took place in 1918 would not have sufficed to feed both the allied populations and the American Expeditionary Force. Furthermore, the transport of two million men to France could not have been accomplished without grave losses.

* The relationship between the President and Colonel House was unique. There is a draft cable in the writer's possession prepared for Mr. Wilson's signature on which House has simply written: "I would sign this if I were you," followed by "Okeh. W.W.," in the President's autograph.

In order to increase food production, the prices of wheat and hogs were fixed. (In 1920 Mr. Hoover was to write that "the last three years have confirmed me in a constitutional objection to price fixing in any form.") The Lever Act provided this price-fixing authority to the Food Administrator, and price assurances enabled the American farmers to extend their operations beyond conservative limits without fear of bankruptcy. The price of $2.25 per bushel, which was established for wheat, and $15 (later $17.50) per hundredweight for hogs also effectively pegged the prices of subsidiary grains and meats. As a result foodstuffs began to pour in a great flood from the farms, to the processors and to the ports, and the reserves filled enormous warehouses. These reserves were providentially ready to replace the losses of food stocks which fell into the hands of the Germans in the spring of 1918. Following the collapse of imperial Russia and the Bolshevik treaty with Germany at Brest-Litovsk, the Germans were able to throw their entire might against the Western Front, breaking the line held by the British Fifth Army. The food stockpiled behind the British front became the spoils of the advancing German armies.

At this low point in morale, Mr. Hoover decided to visit the European theater to confer with the prime ministers, military commanders, and food administrators of the Allies. The politics which seems to plague all alliances had worked, together with food shortages, to generate friction and even personal bitterness between the Allied food controllers in Europe. The French and Italians were complaining that the British had adopted a "lion's share" policy because British bread was unrationed and stocks of bread cereals amounting to over a million tons were stockpiled in England. The French meanwhile were doling out bread on a daily ration with less than a twenty-thousand-ton wheat reserve on hand. There had been bread riots in four French cities. Italy had hardly any wheat at all and, as the Italian food staff excitedly emphasized, they were a cereal-habituated people. The British defended their better position by pointing to the special vulnerability of England to submarine blockade, which made it more imperative for them than for a Continental nation to stockpile an adequate reserve.

Since Britain controlled most of the shipping, there was not much the French and Italians could do but expostulate. They were mad clear through and asserted that it was unfair for one ally to lay up a surplus while two others were hungry. Mr. Hoover decided to see if he could compose the differences, which had not yet broken into the open but threatened to do so.

We sailed on July 11 on the S.S. *Olympic*. There was little to suggest that the great ship was the last word in luxury liners, for she carried six thousand troops in her passenger spaces. Literally every foot of space was occupied, and the crowding was like six full days in the subway at the rush hour. But the inconveniences which were most burdensome were the regulations that life preservers, in those days the permanently stuffed variety, had to be worn at all times and complete blackout had to be observed. A ship with her portholes sealed, carrying six thousand perspiring men in the month of July, in the Gulf Stream develops a special interior climate of its own. There were some expressions to the effect that a submarine attack would be welcome.

On reaching London, Mr. Hoover was given the enthusiastic reception to which his accomplishments since 1914 entitled him. The Allied food controllers (at that time they were Clynes for Great Britain, Boret for France, and Crespi for Italy) came to meet him. At a dinner in honor of the Allied food controllers, Prime Minister Lloyd George delivered the address of welcome.

Following the usual toasts to the health of King George, President Wilson, President Poincaré, and King Victor Emmanuel, Lloyd George suddenly discovered that he could not remember the names of the French and Italian food controllers (there had been a high rate of turnover in that office in each Allied country). After a painful span of seconds while unavailingly searching his memory, the Prime Minister had to reach for the printed program and read the names from it. It seems amusing only in retrospect, for all present squirmed through the interminable ten seconds of embarrassment with him. Quickly recovering his aplomb and turning to Mr. Hoover, Lloyd George observed, "It seems to me, Mr. Hoover, that you represent not only the United States but also Merciful Providence. We are no longer aliens, foreigners to one another; we now disagree with the same violence and facility as if we were members of the same cabinet." The laughter which followed saved the evening. Then, turning to the others, the Prime Minister added, "Disagreement, gentlemen, is the only road to agreement, whereas in my experience, a premature settlement is the sure path to inevitable discord." A premature food settlement had been made by the Allies in 1916, and discord had ensued. Mr. Hoover's task was to find a road to a sound agreement.

Signor Crespi, rising to his full height, something less than five feet, said that, although Italy had suffered more than any of the other Allies for shortage of food and also as a result of German and Austrian military successes, it was his wish to see the food situation so handled that on the advent of peace "large stocks of provisions may be available for the starved and driven people of the enemy countries." I saw Mr. Hoover turn to look at him with an expression of mingled surprise and admiration, for Crespi had already lost a son at the front.

The meetings with the food controllers were successful. An Allied Food Council was set up, of which Mr. Hoover was named chairman, and an agreement was reached as to the tonnage of food, clothing, and medical supplies required on a monthly basis from the United States and the share each ally was to receive.

Everything in diplomacy seems to begin or end, often both, with ceremonial eating and drinking, even when the issue is the shortage of food. There was a grand banquet given by the Lord Mayor of London at the Mansion House. The Lord Mayor, at the head of the receiving line, wore his robe of office, and his sheriffs with sword and mace and the other accouterments of medieval pomp were incredibly resplendent, especially for a small-town boy to see. The American guests included practically everyone on the staffs of the war agencies in London, and as we all passed down the line to be presented, our names were announced loudly by a major-domo in livery. Following this we shook the Lord Mayor's hand and made way for the next guest. Preceding me in line was Hugh Gibson, one of the outstanding diplomats of our day. He was fun-loving and gay and at that time attached to Mr. Hoover's staff, having been first secretary of our legation in Brussels until we entered the war. Gibson had first come to public notice in his effort to save the life of Nurse Edith Cavell, who was executed by the German High Command in Belgium. Observing that I was popeyed at all the magnificence and ceremony, Hugh asked how I liked it. I said I was trying to take it all in because nothing like it would ever happen to me a second time. "It could happen a second time right now," he said. "Let's go back to the end of the line and be presented to his nibs all over again." We did, and in due course were announced to the Lord Mayor again. The major-domo who was making the announcements mechanically never turned a hair, but I thought I detected a look in the Lord Mayor's eyes as though trying to recall where he had met the two of us before.

* * *

In a small book on aviation purchased when I was a boy and written shortly after Louis Blériot had flown across the English Channel, the author speculated on the possible future uses of aircraft. He ventured the opinion that they would be employed in wars as scouts, perhaps, to determine the location of enemy forces. He added that they could *conceivably* be used to drop explosives, or fire, on enemy cities, but concluded comfortingly, "That, of course, would never be allowed." The change in public sanctions in so short a time is not a pleasant thought.

The assumption by a more civilized era that noncombatants had certain rights which were always to be respected was dispelled by the Germans when Zeppelins bombed London and other open cities indiscriminately and without accomplishing any important military objective. This precedent breached a convention as old as the Age of Chivalry, when wars were conducted between men who mutually accepted certain unwritten standards of conduct, among them that the deliberate killing of noncombatants was barbaric.

London was not bombed while we were there, and we experienced our first bombing only after the food controllers' conferences were concluded. Before we left for Paris, Mr. Hoover received an invitation to visit King Albert of the Belgians and Queen Elisabeth. They were living at La Panne, a small seaside resort north of Dunkerque on a little triangle off the coast which was all that remained of Belgium free of German occupation. The King, a soldier in character as well as appearance, would not conduct his government from exile so long as any Belgian soil remained for him to stand upon.

Accordingly, we sailed from Folkestone one summer afternoon and were received on our arrival across the Channel at Boulogne by the British officer in command of the port. He had only just returned from the Near East and wore a tropical uniform complete with topee. We had dinner with him and his staff and were put up in a small hotel a short distance from his headquarters. That evening just as our party was about to turn in, there was an *alerte*. A few German planes came over and almost immediately the sky was filled with the probing fingers of searchlights and bursts of shrapnel from antiaircraft batteries. There was an occasional bomb detonation at a distance. The fragments of shrapnel falling in the streets and rattling on the roof tiles appeared to be more hazardous than the danger from the bombs, so we began to watch the fireworks from a balcony sheltered by another balcony above us. The hotel staff and other, more experienced guests prudently repaired to the basement.

Mr. Hoover pointed out to our group that where we were standing there was a steel beam which was a part of the structure of the building, and that unless there was a direct hit we were about as safe as if we had taken cover. "Let's watch the show," he said. "We might be better off here than going down in the cellar and battling with the rats." While we watched, however, there was a deafening explosion nearby, followed by a great burst of flame and billows of smoke. The concussion shattered the glass of the french doors and a fragment struck Mr. Hoover, cutting his hand. The wound was bloody but superficial, and no further damage was done to us or the hotel, but when the raid was over, we learned that the particular bomb which had seemed to fall near us had been a direct hit on a pile of ammunition at the pier where we had landed. British headquarters was nearby. The colonel who had been our host at dinner that evening and other members of his staff were casualties.

We left the following morning in cars sent to Boulogne by the Belgians and motored north, following the coast, passing through Calais, which seemed almost deserted, and Dunkerque, which was to figure so dramatically in another war twenty-three years later. As we neared La Panne, we began to detour around shell holes which in places had obliterated the highway. These were the result of gunfire from German destroyers which cruised down the Channel and fired at coast installations or even took pot shots at vehicles on the road. (The little Belgian Princess, Marie José, collected shell fragments on the beach and gave each of us one for a keepsake.)

King Albert received us dressed in the field uniform of a Belgian general, and the Queen wore a white nurse's uniform. Besides the Princess, Crown Prince Leopold and his brother Charles were also present. Leopold, a private in the Belgian Army, had just returned from the front lines. He was too young for service, but had insisted upon his father's consent to visit the front, which at that time, in the Belgian sector, was relatively quiet. We had a spartan meal, and afterward Queen Elisabeth made photographs of us in the small garden. Several weeks later she sent to each of us an album with a collection of the prints.

Mr. Hoover's purpose in going to France was primarily to see General Pershing, whose headquarters were at Chaumont. On reaching Paris, however, the French insisted on their share of honors for Mr. Hoover. Accordingly, there was a reception at the Hôtel de Ville, signatures to be placed in the Golden Book, and speeches of welcome. That particular variety of oratory is punishment enough when brief and one can be physically at ease, but there were six speeches on that occasion, all delivered and received while standing.

Shortly before our arrival, German ordnance specialists at the Krupp works had constructed a gun, popularly known in Paris as "Big Bertha" (an uncompliment to Frau Krupp). It was located some considerable distance behind the German lines, its exact position then unknown, but it was able to lob shells over the French lines all the way to Paris. Because of atmospheric variations and perhaps wear on the grooves and lands of the rifling, there was no accuracy in range, with the result that on some days the projectiles dropped well outside of Paris and into the cabbage patches of the suburbs. At other times they were distressingly on target. During the day, the shells fell with such regularity that at the number of minutes past the hour when one was due, conversation would come to a halt and everyone would glance at his watch and await the sound of the explosion, distant or near, after which talk would be resumed where it had left off, and life would go on. The actual damage, except in a tragic instance when a number of children were killed in a school, was never considerable, but Paris was pock-marked with houses or other buildings with one side demolished, since these projectiles fell almost vertically from a high trajectory. There is something almost indecent in seeing a house with a wall thus removed, its room exposed, beds, baths, clothes closets—like an untidy dollhouse open on one side. The indiscriminate barbarity of such a weapon did far more to infuriate Parisians than to damage their morale.

We saw the real effects of war at Reims, Soissons, Château Thierry, and St. Mihiel. The battle of Belleau Wood had been fought shortly before we arrived, and the fresh graves of our Marines were still marked only by helmets or rifles thrust bayonet down in the raw earth. Our casualties had been 7820 killed and wounded in that bloody battle. All about these battlefields was the unbelievable broadcast of military hardware—burned-out tanks, cannons, great piles of brass shell cases, heaps of the wicker baskets the Germans used for carrying the shells for their guns, helmets and equipment, our own and German—mostly German.

The French bread of the period was dark and coarse because of foreign material added to stretch the flour supply. The French family generally bought its bread each day from the baker, and control of consumption was imposed at that point. Each person received a bread card about four by six inches, divided on one side into squares numbered with the days of the month. The holder surrendered a square each day when he bought his loaf. The back of the card was used for some message from a public figure intended to inspire martial fervor, or belt-tightening, or subscriptions to war loans. Mr. Hoover was asked to contribute a message for the next month's bread card. He passed the assignment to me and I wrote it. When the ration card appeared a month later I could only wish that the earth would open and swallow me. The Hoover message appeared in my handwriting, for the French had reproduced it in facsimile under the mistaken impression that it was Mr. Hoover's holograph. And as if that was not enough, there was a misspelled word in it over my version of Hoover's signature.

Mr. Hoover was too preoccupied or too charitable to notice it. Hugh Gibson, Sidney Mitchell, and other good friends, however, got much mileage from my discomfiture. Someone sent a copy of the card to Roland Boyden, a Boston lawyer, who was attached to the Food Administration in Washington, whereupon he wrote me to call attention to the fact that, as the historian Gibbon recorded it, the Roman Emperor Carinus was so indolent that he even employed a secretary charged with the sole duty of signing the Emperor's name. Boyden suggested that I should "tell the Chief he might also get one who can spell." I sent him an appropriate answer which, fortunately, has been lost to history.

After we returned to Washington and in anticipation of the end of hostilities, the President sent for Mr. Hoover and asked him to make plans for transforming the Food Administration into an agency of relief and reconstruction for all of Europe. Mr. Hoover had suggested this to Colonel House in the course of several communications in the summer of 1918. Accordingly, on November 17, six days after the Armistice, we were again on the *Olympic*. The group on this voyage included Dr. Alonzo Taylor, the great expert of that day in the field of nutrition; Robert A. Taft, as legal adviser; and Julius Barnes, who was president of the U. S. Grain Corporation, a subsidiary of the Food Administration.

Shortly before we sailed there was an event which had embarrassing consequences. Frederic R. Coudert, a prominent New York attorney and friend of both Mr. Hoover and President Wilson, requested a statement from Mr. Hoover endorsing the election of a Congress which would be loyal to the President. Mr. Coudert passed his request through me, and I presented it to Mr. Hoover with a draft I had prepared. Heavily preoccupied with preparations for the great task which lay ahead in Europe, Mr. Hoover improved the draft and signed the letter.

His statement gave expression to what he viewed as our aims in the war: first, the surrender of Germany; second, the establishment of a representative government in that country as some sort of an assurance to world peace in future; and finally, the healing of the world's wounds. He concluded with a sentence to the effect that the President, as the acknowledged leader of the world, *deserved support* in order to succeed with these objectives.

The letter was dated November 2. President Wilson had himself appealed for the election of a Democratic Congress a week earlier. This action by the President proved to be a tactical mistake, for it was misrepresented as a slur on the character of Republican patriotism in the war and it provided the President's opponents with an issue which until then they had lacked. Largely because of it, the Democrats lost control of both the House and the Senate. Mr. Hoover's statement brought down on his head a fulmination by the Chairman of the Republican National Committee, and the incident was recalled when his name was brought forward for the Republican nomination in 1920. Mr. Hoover never blamed me for my part in the incident, though blame would have been justified, for I had failed in this instance to protect him from Mr. Coudert's request, as I might have done.

Other Republicans besides Mr. Hoover had been appointed to important posts in the war administration and had given loyal service to the President and to the country. On the other hand, some of the leading obstructionists were Democrats. Chief among these was Senator Reed of Missouri, whose opposition to the Lever Bill, the legislation creating the Food Administration, has been mentioned. He also hindered the operation of the Food Administration and very nearly hamstrung the feeding of the Allied armies and populations during the war. President Wilson's error in making a personal issue of partisan support at this particular moment in history and his consequent defeat may very well have weakened his influence in Paris. And if so, his decision, though on what appeared so clearly to be a domestic issue, nevertheless contributed to the eventual weakness of the League of Nations. On that assumption it can be regarded as a decision which set back the whole prospect of international peace. Wilson's attorney general, Thomas W. Gregory, noted in his diary[1] that he felt Mr. Wilson's appeal for a Democratic Congress was "un-Wilsonian" and the "product of extreme weariness at the end of a long session when the President's nerves were taut and his intellectual sentinels were not on the lookout for danger."

Mr. Hoover's relations with the wartime President under whom he loyally served and his deference to the President's political decision have been recorded by Mr. Hoover in his book *The Ordeal of Woodrow Wilson*. This extraordinary volume is not only unique as being the only work by an ex-President of the United States about another ex-President, it also contains a number of hitherto unpublished exchanges between the men whose common awareness of the judgment of history was a unifying link.

By early October 1918, it was apparent that the collapse of the Central Powers was not far off. An important strategic contribution to the successful conclusion of the war was Mr. Hoover's ability to apply a tourniquet to the arteries of food supplied to Germany by her neutral neighbors. This was effected by rationing the neutrals so that they could not export food across their frontiers into Germany without going hungry themselves. The procedure required precise calculations and when put into operation produced a situation in the German cities which was so marked that troops home on leave could see that the will to win had deserted the civil population. In consequence also, even German troops in the front lines were on short rations.

Mr. Hoover was painfully aware that the primary sufferers were children, since he had seen for himself that adults reduced for a time even to a starvation diet could quickly recoup their health, whereas with children the damage could be far more lasting. Therefore, he planned that immediately upon surrender cargoes of food should be rushed to the children in the vanquished countries. In order to see that the food was not appropriated by the army and the adult population, it was to be distributed to children as a first priority through schools and soup kitchens. Accordingly, ships were loaded at American ports with flour, meats, and fats, and sailing orders were issued prior to the Armistice. Indeed, on November 11, 1918, when after four years the guns were silent, a number of these ships were approaching Continental waters with cargoes consigned to the ports of Hamburg and Bremen.

At first, Prime Minister Lloyd George took a dim view of this operation, as did Prime Minister Clemenceau. It is easier to be critical of their attitude than to recapture the state of mind in those days. Germany had begun the war. It had cost millions of lives and much treasure, and there was a substantial body of British and French sentiment which felt little compassion for those whose rulers had brought so much death and sorrow into the world. Clemenceau was quoted as saying that despite German losses there were still "twenty million Germans too many." The prospect of starvation for a whole generation was viewed with equanimity in many quarters—as being unpleasant but salutary.

The British first advised Mr. Hoover that the food ships would not be allowed through the blockade. We were in London at the time and he attempted to persuade members of the Cabinet of the unwisdom of that course. He pointed out that in a world at peace it would be necessary that no wounds be left to fester. He said that the American people would find it impossible to go along with a policy which would be equivalent to "kicking a man when he is down." As he was unable to make any progress with Lloyd George, at least at that juncture, Mr. Hoover decided on a showdown. He announced that he had ordered the skippers of the ships to proceed to their destinations and that they were unarmed. "The only way you can stop them," he added, "will be to sink them." This was, of course, a bluff, but it worked, and no attempt was made to halt the movement. There were, of course, many British friends of Mr. Hoover who were completely in accord with his program, and this proved to be true of the British press and public in general.

Recognition and gratitude for Hoover's work in this instance were also mixed with strange antithesis. Twenty-two years after the feeding of Germany, he was charged with having "continued the food blockade of Germany for many months" after World War I. The late Elmer Davis made that claim in a radio program on August 10, 1940. In response to a telegram giving him the facts that Hoover had started cargoes across the Atlantic in anticipation of the Armistice and routed to ports through which the populations of the Central Powers could be fed, Mr. Davis said that the story had come up shortly before he went on the air and "with no time to investigate." It was not corrected.

As early as June 13, 1918, Colonel House suggested to President Wilson that Mr. Hoover should be temporarily relieved as Food Administrator and be sent to Russia to head a nonmilitary intervention which would be primarily concerned with the alleviation of starvation in that country. The President must have encouraged this suggestion, and on June 17, at the Colonel's invitation, Mr. Hoover traveled from Washington to Magnolia, Massachusetts, where House was living, to discuss it. Mr. Hoover was willing to undertake any assignment which the President as Commander in Chief delegated to him, but he pointed out that, in a condition where the allies were supporting military operations against the Bolsheviks in Siberia, it was unlikely that the Russians would be receptive to a friendly approach on their western front. He felt that the Russians would be more likely to suspect a Trojan horse than a sincere evidence of humanitarianism.

No more was heard of the subject until spring of the following year, when, though the war was over, the Russian food situation, in both production and transport, had further deteriorated. Reports of wide-spread starvation, even of cannibalism in some villages, were reaching our headquarters in Paris by February of 1919.

In November 1918, just before we sailed for Europe, President Wilson had suggested to Mr. Hoover that he should consult Justice Brandeis, for the President greatly respected the views of Justice Brandeis on political and economic affairs in Russia. There was no man in the United States, however, who was more familiar with Russia than Mr. Hoover himself. For years before the war his mining interests in Siberia had been important and he had traveled Russia extensively. Justice Brandeis knew this, though the President was perhaps unaware of it. We were rushed with preparations for departure, and Mr. Hoover asked me to see the Justice in his stead. I called on the great jurist at his apartment and later prepared a memorandum of the conversation for Mr. Hoover, of which the following is an excerpt:

Justice Brandeis believes that thus far we have misunderstood the Russian people and very much underestimated the situation. None of the Commissions which we have sent to Russia has, in his opinion, accomplished the least fragment of tangible results and, in fact, he has some misgivings as to whether they have not been harmful to our prestige among the masses and confusing to individual Russians who may be earnestly trying to discover a way toward stabilization and recovery. Neither military nor diplomatic missions are, in his opinion, capable of bringing the proper help and he believes what is needed is an *economic mission* which would offer its services in an attempt to promote economic recovery and heal the wounds which the transportation and production structures of the empire have suffered as a result of war and revolution.

He distrusts the ability and the disinterestedness of the Kerensky group as well as certain cliques of Russian ex-diplomats in Washington, London and Paris. These groups, he believes, are probably czarist and autocrats at heart. He does not credit a large part of the information which has come to us concerning the present regime, feeling that it may be largely inspired by the group just mentioned. The present government, he feels, should nevertheless be dealt with in the utmost caution until its intentions are clear and until we are convinced of its honesty.

The urgency of the Russian question, and the fact that upon its settlement rests inevitably the proper functioning of economic interdependence in Europe, indicates to him the necessity that it should be the first matter to be settled by the Powers at the forthcoming Conference at Paris. Any delay in facing the situation will postpone the restoration of normal world conditions and will allow the focus of the disorganization to fester and spread.

If by "disorganization" one understands "Communism," the soundness of this advice and its prophetic character are clear, for the Russian situation was not "the first matter to be settled" at the Paris Conference and, in fact, was not dealt with at all save in the ineffective manner exemplified by the Nansen episode (page 31).

As I took leave of Justice Brandeis* on the November afternoon in 1918, he asked me to keep in touch with him by writing occasionally, and this I promised to do. At irregular intervals, I sent him a sort of newsletter from London or Paris or wherever there was the opportunity to write. One of the letters to the Justice was taken to Washington by Captain Walter Lippman, who had briefly shared my apartment at Hôtel Crillon, the headquarters of the American Peace Delegation. That letter, written in January 1919, turned up in 1959 in connection with the Senate hearing on my nomination to be a member of President Eisenhower's Cabinet. The letter dealt with Poland.

At the time it was written, relatively peaceful conditions obtained in Poland, at least on the surface. Marshal Pilsudski, the Polish strong man, had formed a coalition with Roman Dmowski, the leading politician of the period, and his supporters. They had made the odd choice of Ignace Paderewski, the famous concert pianist, to become Prime Minister. Dr. Vernon Kellogg reported from Warsaw, however, that there were sounds of shooting every night in the ghetto. Finally, in one city, thirty-seven men and women, all of them Jews, had been shot by ruffians posing as police. The unfortunate victims had been attending a meeting in a synagogue to arrange for the allocation of food supplies

---

* Justice Brandeis, incidentally, was an original supporter of Mr. Hoover for the presidency. When it appeared possible that Hoover would be nominated in 1920, Brandeis wrote to Norman Hapgood, "I'm one-hundred per cent for him [Hoover]." In a letter to his brother, Alfred Brandeis, who had worked in the Enforcement Division of the Food Administration, Justice Brandeis expressed his regret that the nomination had gone to Harding instead of to Hoover. He characterized it as "a sad story of American political irresponsibility." In another letter, the Justice had described Mr. Hoover as "the biggest figure injected into Washington by the war." For reasons unknown to me, the Justice accepted the general Democratic attitude of opposition to Mr. Hoover after the Republican party nominated him eight years later.

sent from the United States by the Joint Distribution Committee. The murderers had burst into the meeting, dragged their miserable victims into the street, and killed them with a machine gun.

I showed the report to Mr. Hoover, and, on his authority, asked Paderewski to come to the office. The Prime Minister arrived wearing a top hat perched precariously on his leonine mane of yellow hair. He carefully placed the hat on a chair in the waiting room, and at any other time the disaster that ensued would have provided some hilarity. Our office orderly, who was eager but incredibly clumsy, inadvertently sat on the hat, with catastrophic results.

At Mr. Hoover's instruction, I told Mr. Paderewski that the relief supplies to Poland from the United States were contributed in greatest part by private citizens, many of whom were Americans of Jewish faith, and they could not be expected to continue to give unless pogroms were stopped immediately and those responsible for the outrages brought to justice.

Mr. Paderewski gave his promise that order would be restored, and, indeed, we had no further reports of anything as terrible as the Pinsk massacre. (At Mr. Hoover's suggestion, President Wilson appointed a board under the chairmanship of Henry Morgenthau, Sr., which visited Poland and made a study of the relations between the Polish Government and the several ethnic minorities in that country. The presence of this American mission and of other American representatives who were more or less permanently stationed in the new republic was salutary.)

My letter to Justice Brandeis was related to this situation and told him that I had arranged for two young Army officers,* who had been assigned to our staff by General Pershing, to be sent to Poland as observers. I said that I had known these men in private life, and that they would report the truth as they saw it. Forty years later the letter, taken from the papers of Justice Brandeis, was reproduced and circulated to Senators as the basis of a charge that I had used my position improperly to aid my coreligionists. The facts that the letter had been written when I was twenty-two years old and under the circumstances I have related, that my interest was not only human and proper but also had the concurrence of Mr. Hoover, were of course, not mentioned by the characters who peddled the letter. I should add that the matter

---

* They were James H. Becker and Robert Byfield. They worked with Maurice Pate, another young American officer who has been continuously engaged in relief activities ever since and now heads UNICEF (United Nations International Children's Emergency Fund).

was brought to my attention by several Senators and that I have no reason to believe that it influenced the vote of any Senator.

President Wilson had also solicited Mr. Hoover's views on a proposal which had been made to him to the effect that Japan, as one of the Allies, should be given carte blanche to move into Siberia, by force if necessary. Mr. Hoover's reaction to this idea was that the population expansion in Japan, plus her desire to make the Eastern Siberian seaboard secure against the subsequent launching of any Russian hostilities against Japan, would mean that if the Japanese ever got into Siberia they would be there to stay. In consequence of his advice, Wilson made a decision that the Japanese should not go in. An American expeditionary force was sent to Siberia and, like the army of the Duke of York in the nursery rhyme, marched in and marched out again without accomplishing anything and in many ways was one of the most unusual American military expeditions in history.

We had reached London within days of the Armistice and were quartered at the Ritz Hotel. A few hours after our arrival a telegram was delivered from the Rotterdam office of the Commission for Relief in Belgium:

> In order to go into the question of making arrangements for the provision of foodstuffs in Germany, Minister Baron Von der Lancken and Dr. Rieth would like to meet Mr. Hoover as soon as possible in The Hague or any other place to be indicated by him.

These two gentlemen had been representatives of the German Government with whom Mr. Hoover had to deal in Belgium. They had placed innumerable roadblocks in the way of the relief operation and had made themselves thoroughly despised. Mr. Hoover wrote at the bottom of the message, "You can describe two and a half years of arrogance toward ourselves and cruelty to the Belgians in any language you choose so long as you tell the pair personally to go to hell with my compliments. When we negotiate with the Germans it will not be with that pair." A proper secretary would have allowed for his chief to blow off steam and would then have paraphrased the message, but I was so delighted with it that it was transmitted unexpurgated. No more was heard from those particular intermediaries. In all the years I have known Mr. Hoover, I have heard him use profanity on fewer occasions than I could number on my hand, and he does not admire the use of it by others. Rarity made it the more effective.

When we reached Paris, the Armistice enthusiasm had reached a crescendo. President Wilson himself arrived on December 15, thus establishing an unhappy precedent for presidential involvement in international negotiations outside of the United States. His decision was to prove calamitous both to his objectives and to his health. Mr. Hoover, I am sure, knew that in spite of his intelligence Mr. Wilson was without experience in the labyrinth of European diplomacy and was therefore at a great disadvantage. Lloyd George and Clemenceau played up to Wilson's moral principles on minor issues and callously undercut him on other matters when it served their purposes. His first thrombosis occurred while he was in Paris, and the record indicates that he appeared to resign himself more and more to concessions on subjects which violated principles laid down in the famous Fourteen Points. His reliance appeared to be upon the League of Nations, which, once it came into existence, would be capable of righting all wrongs. Upon that aim evidently he concentrated his hopes.

I saw President Wilson only three times during the period between December 1918 and the day when the treaty was signed at Versailles. He was most considerate on those occasions, a trait I early found to characterize great men in dealing with subordinates very low on the totem pole. I was simply a message bearer on these occasions. I had written to the President once in early 1917 on a personal matter and had received a reply, apparently typed by himself. Mr. Hoover has written that President Wilson spoke favorably of me to him.[2] I had not imagined ever being the subject of conversation between them. But certainly I admired the President. I suffered with him during trials to which he was subjected in Paris and the martyrdom after his return to Washington, which Mr. Hoover has so feelingly chronicled. I was proud to be named a trustee of the foundation which cares for the Wilson birthplace in Staunton, Virginia.

Some years ago, my wife, searching for a Wilson letter as a gift for me and hoping to discover one in holograph (they are difficult to find; he used his portable typewriter as other men do the pen), found a letter written on April 13, 1885. In it a youthful Wilson states his aim in life:

> . . . I trust that with restored health, I shall be able to realize my ambition to do honest work in thinking and writing. Through prudent physical administration I hope to aid myself in getting into the heart of that governmental administration which it is my purpose first to understand myself and then to assist the reading public in understanding.

He was one of the favored few among men to have realized so much of an ambition which had crystallized early in his career.

* * *

As indicated earlier, President Wilson recognized that after the defeat of Germany the problem posed by the emergence of Bolshevism in Russia was the most serious of all. With the first informal meetings in Paris in late November of 1918, the Russian question became an ominous presence at the council table. Mr. Hoover once likened it to Banquo's ghost. The American objective was to find a peaceful way of penetrating the barrier to communication which had already been drawn across Europe by the Bolshevik Revolution. (More than a quarter of a century elapsed before Churchill described that barrier as an "Iron Curtain.")

On the other hand, the British and the French had more energetic plans. They expected that in any case the Communist regime would be short-lived and that its demise could be accelerated by military assistance to Russians of the old regime. There were four active commanders of anti-Bolshevik forces, Generals Denikin, Wrangel, Yudenich, and Admiral Kolchak. Their forces were widely separated—Kolchak in Siberia and the others separated by the expanse of European Russia. All were being supplied with arms and food by the Allies. We had been persuaded to move a small American force into Archangel, apparently on reasoning similar to that which prompted the dispatch of the American expeditionary force to Siberia. Our strongest desire, in early 1919, however, was disengagement.

At this time also, reports began to leak out of Russia concerning a tragic condition among the people as a result of war and crop failure. A young American who had been assistant to Secretary of State Lansing and to Colonel House and who, in later years, became Ambassador to France, William C. Bullitt, was sent to Russia by Wilson in early February of 1919. He returned with a firsthand report of the acute distress he had found there. Every man, woman, and child in Moscow and Petrograd, he said, was suffering from starvation. "Mortality is particularly high among new-born children whose mothers cannot suckle them, among newly delivered mothers and among the aged . . . diphtheria, typhus and small-pox are epidemic." This report, confirming the intelligence reaching Mr. Hoover from his own representatives, led directly to a significant episode and to one of the most fateful decisions in modern history—a decision which had its effect on the lives of millions of human beings and which has not yet run its course. The decision was affected in early 1919 by a man who has been more or less forgotten except by historians and who was relatively obscure in a period when the stage presences of Wilson, Lloyd George, Clemenceau, and Orlando monopolized the limelight. The man was Stéphen Pichon, the French Minister for Foreign Affairs.

Bullitt's mission to Russia had extraordinary consequences. He was a trained and conscientious observer and a meticulous reporter. His trip, while unpublicized, had been made with the full knowledge of Lloyd George. Nevertheless, when Bullitt returned with his recommendations and a proposal, they were never formally submitted to the Allied Council of Ministers by the American delegation, and Lloyd George, on the floor of the House of Commons, responding to a question by a member of Parliament, denied knowledge of Bullitt (whom he had seen both before and after the mission). In fact, on his return from Russia, Bullitt had breakfasted with Lloyd George and had handed to him in the presence of Philip Kerr, the Prime Minister's secretary, a copy of the proposals the Russians had given him to take back to the Big Four in Paris. Lloyd George's response to the parliamentary question is a model of parliamentary double talk:

> Constantly there are men coming and going to Russia of all nationalities and they all come back with their tales of Russia . . . There was some suggestion that a young American had come back from Russia with a communication . . . If the President of the United States had attached any value to it, he would have brought it before the Conference and he certainly did not.

The British Prime Minister was an adroit politician in domestic affairs and naïve in others. For one thing, he apparently did not understand the atheistic background of Marxist philosophy which had produced the Communist revolution. At a meeting of the "Council of Ten" on January 16, 1919, Lloyd George proposed to invite all the different governments, including the Communist regime, to what he described as "A Truce of God."*

Mr. Winston Churchill, who was then in the war cabinet and whose influence had only been slightly dimmed by the disaster at Gallipoli, appeared before a meeting of the Big Four—Wilson, Lloyd George, Clemenceau and Orlando—a month later and practically demanded

---

* This suggestion eventually did result in an invitation to the Soviets to a conference at Prinkipo which aborted.

an invasion of Russia by the Allies. This produced some consternation among the delegates, and two days later, at a meeting of the Council of Ten in Pichon's office at the Quai d'Orsay, the notes of the conversations quoted Lloyd George to the effect that, if a military enterprise were started against the Bolsheviki, there might well be a soviet in London.

At the same meeting, President Wilson made a revealing observation in his appraisal of Bolshevism. He indicated that he believed there would be more public antipathy to the brutality of Bolshevism if it were not for the common belief that large vested interests dominated the political and economic world. While there might be talk that this evil was in process of slow change, he continued, the general body of men had grown impatient. There were many men in the United States, he believed, who represented large vested interests, yet saw the necessity for reforms and desired something to be worked out at the Peace Conference which would provide opportunity for the individual greater than the world had ever known. The President noted that the whole world was disturbed by this question *before* the Bolsheviks came to power, and he added that he would not be surprised to find that the reason why British and U.S. troops were disinclined to enter Russia to fight the Bolsheviks was that they were not at all sure that if they put down Bolshevism they would not be re-establishing the ancient order.

Bullitt's report highlighted the unsatisfactory condition of our troops at Archangel and the necessity for their early withdrawal. He had also brought back with him the text of a draft proposal. He had met with Lenin, who had assured him that if the Allies would make the proposal by April 10, 1919, the Russians would accept its terms. Widespread starvation was exerting the pressure.

One paragraph in the draft proposal is of particular interest in the light of subsequent events.

> Nationals of the Allied and associated countries and of the other countries above named to have the right of free entry into the Soviet Republics of Russia; also the right of sojourn and of circulation and full security, provided they do not interfere in the domestic politics of the Soviet Republics.

Some weeks earlier Mr. Hoover had developed the idea that, because of the desperate shortage of food in the Soviet cities, there was a good chance to save lives by ending hostilities. Though the World War was officially over, there were isolated and sporadic engagements of partisans. The Communists were being engaged on three fronts by the forces of Admiral Kolchak and Generals Denikin and Yudenich. Allied forces also threatened from the base at Archangel. Accordingly, Mr. Hoover opened a correspondence with President Wilson on this subject and proposed that a neutral person "of international reputation for probity and ability" should be encouraged to set up a feeding operation in Russia which would be based upon the experience of the Commission for Relief in Belgium. It will be recalled that the C.R.B., as it was known, had operated with great success under Hoover's supervision when we were neutrals, from 1914 to 1917.

Mr. Hoover concluded his letter by stating that this plan did not involve "any recognition or relationship between the allies and the Bolshevik murderers now in control." President Wilson at a meeting of the Council of Ten on January 21 had gone on record as opposing recognition of the Bolsheviks and had stated that he thought even a partial recognition would strengthen their position. However, he welcomed Mr. Hoover's plan because it did afford the possibility of a period of tranquillity along the frontiers of Europe and, as Mr. Hoover had stated, "would save an immensity of helpless human life and would save our country from further entanglements."

The plan was at least a faint hope. Casting about for the proper individual to operate it, Mr. Hoover decided that Fridtjof Nansen, the famous arctic explorer, was his man, and invited him to come to Paris. Hoover's requirements were for a neutral with a world-wide reputation in some field remote from politics. Dr. Nansen filled this picture perfectly. He required some coaxing but eventually responded.

Nansen was an extraordinary personality. Though not above average size, he somehow conveyed an impression of colossal physique. His features looked as if roughhewn from the rocky cliffs of one of his native fjords, and he wore a droopy gray mustache reminiscent of the White Knight in Tenniel's illustrations for *Through the Looking Glass*. As a young man, he had electrified the imagination of the world as a polar explorer in the days before transpolar flights by commercial aircraft were even dreamed of. He was no mean artist and an exceptionally talented writer. His illustrated accounts of his expeditions were widely popular in the last decade of the nineteenth century and the first of this one. He came to occupy a place in public affection such as a later generation was to accord to Charles A. Lindbergh. After he heard Mr. Hoover's project, his imagination took fire, and the great enthusiasm which was his characteristic was brought to bear on its problems. A letter was drafted for him to send to the Big Four in which the proposal was formally outlined.

There were many cooks in the preparation of that letter. It was designed to preserve some of the ground that had been tentatively gained by the Bullitt mission, though in its final form Bullitt felt that the letter had thrown these gains overboard. In any event, on the evening of April 3, we prepared identical letters addressed to President Wilson, and to Prime Ministers Lloyd George, Clemenceau, and Orlando, and they were signed by Dr. Nansen.

At the same time a reply from the Big Four to Nansen had been drafted, the idea being that it would be the principal substance of a radiogram to be flashed to Lenin from the Eiffel Tower, France's most powerful radio station. This reply, which was the heart of the matter, had the most careful editing and was once more rewritten by Mr. Hoover. We completed it late on the evening of April 9, and, the secretaries having gone home, I typed it on my Corona and took it to Gilbert Close, who was confidential secretary to President Wilson. It lay on the President's desk for several days. Other things seemed more pressing. The President liked to describe himself as having a "one-track mind" and he was fully occupied with Germany at this juncture and could not spare attention for Russia.

There were private discussions among the Big Four before the letter was signed, and it became known that Lloyd George questioned a relief operation in Russia for a variety of reasons. The notes of a conversation of the Council of Ten in January record that he invited attention "to a doubt expressed by certain of the delegates of the British Dominions as to whether there would be enough food to go around should an attempt be made to feed all allied countries and enemy countries and Russia also. The expenditure of so much food would inevitably have the effect of raising food prices in allied countries and so create discontent and Bolshevism." (Incidentally, it was at this meeting, so far I can discover, that the policy of "containment" was first stated. Signor Orlando, the Italian delegate, conceding that Bolshevism constituted a grave danger to all Europe, noted that in order to prevent a "contagious epidemic" from spreading, it was sound policy to establish a "cordon sanitaire." He suggested that if similar measures were taken against Bolshevism it might be overcome, since to isolate it meant vanquishing it.)

Lloyd George, however, subsequently modified his views and informed the Council of Ten that his information confirmed the report that two-thirds of Bolshevist Russia was starving and that the "people who will die are just the people that we desire to protect. It will not result in the starvation of the Bolsheviks. It will simply mean the death of our friends."

As there had been no action by the Big Four on the Nansen letter, Mr. Hoover suspected that perhaps the French were dragging their feet. He attempted to smoke this out by calling on Pichon at the Quai d'Orsay, asking him point blank what he thought of Nansen's proposal. Mr. Hoover explained that it would result in a committee of neutrals going to Russia and the effective freezing of the frontiers as they existed, all in consideration of receiving food. Pichon replied that such a program would necessarily end all assistance to Admiral Kolchak and General Denikin as well as to the Allied expeditions at Archangel and Murmansk and would merely stabilize the Bolshevik government. He added that payment for the food which would be shipped to Russia would still further depreciate the ruble, thus diminishing the Russian supply of gold and platinum. In that connection, he requested that Mr. Hoover not forget that France had an investment of twenty billion francs in Russia. As Mr. Hoover related this part of the conversation on his return, he had some difficulty in limiting himself to diplomatic language. He replied to Pichon that he could not see that this last consideration mattered much as long as the gold and platinum supply was in the hands of the Communists, who were not going to repay their debts to the French in any case, and that Mr. Pichon had best wake up to that fact. Forty-two years and many foreign ministers later, the situation of the debt is unchanged.

Stiffening Pichon's position was the fact that at about this time the Bolshevik forces operating against Kolchak had been briefly deprived of supplies by an abortive agricultural revolt and, as a result, Kolchak's army was able to make a hundred-mile advance. When this news reached Paris, there was rejoicing, and the impression was widespread that within two weeks Kolchak would be in Moscow and the Soviet Government would be in flight. This prospect not only hardened the resolution of those who were opposed to the relief operation on political grounds, but it also made others feel that any such enterprise would be overrun and trampled by an inevitable military juggernaut.

Two days after this meeting, Pichon presented a memorandum to the Council of Ministers which in the traditional circumlocution of a diplomatic rejection began with a statement that, *"in principle,"* Dr. Nansen's proposal "can only be received with sympathy by the French Government which shares this humane attitude." This was followed, however, by several pages of conditions on which French acquiescence would be contingent. One condition reserved to Admiral Kolchak and General Denikin the right to continue their operations on the ground that to do otherwise "would be an intervention in the internal policy of Russia."

Eventually, on April 17, the letter to Dr. Nansen was signed, although the date on my draft was left unchanged (April 3). Indeed, the draft was not even retyped, and the signatures of V. E. Orlando, D. Lloyd George, Woodrow Wilson, and G. Clemenceau (in that order) were written at the foot of the same letter I had handed to Close two weeks earlier. The exchange of letters now read as follows:

Paris, April 3, 1919

My dear Mr. President:

The present food situation in Russia, where hundreds of thousands of people are dying monthly from sheer starvation and disease, is one of the problems now uppermost in all men's minds. As it appears that no solution of this food and disease question has so far been reached in any direction, I would like to make a suggestion from a neutral point of view for the alleviation of this gigantic misery, on purely humanitarian grounds.

It would appear to me possible to organize a purely humanitarian Commission for the provisioning of Russia, the foodstuffs and medical supplies to be paid for perhaps to some considerable extent by Russia itself, the justice of distribution to be guaranteed by such a Commission, the membership of the Commission to be comprised of Norwegian, Swedish, and possibly Dutch, Danish and Swiss nationalities. It does not appear that the existing authorities in Russia would refuse the intervention of such a Commission of wholly non-political order, devoted solely to the humanitarian purpose of saving life. If thus organized upon the lines of the Belgian Relief Commission, it would raise no question of political recognition or negotiations between the Allies with the existing authorities in Russia.

I recognize keenly the large political issues involved, and I would be glad to know under what conditions you would approve such an enterprise and whether such Commission could look for actual support in finance, shipping and food and medical supplies from the United States Government.

I am addressing a similar note to Messrs. Orlando, Clemenceau and Lloyd-George.

Believe me, my dear Mr. President,

Yours most respectfully,
/s/ Fridtjof Nansen

His Excellency,
The President,
11, Place des Etats-Unis,
Paris.

Paris, April 9, 1919

Dear Sir:

The misery and suffering in Russia described in your letter of April 3rd appeals to the sympathies of all peoples. It is shocking to humanity that millions of men, women and children lack the food and the necessities which make life endurable.

The Governments and peoples whom we represent would be glad to cooperate, without thought of political, military or financial advantage, in any proposal which would relieve this situation in Russia. It seems to us that such a Commission as you propose would offer a practical means of achieving the beneficent results you have in view, and could not, either in its conception or its operation, be considered as having any other aim than the "humanitarian purpose of saving life".

There are great difficulties to be overcome, political difficulties, owing to the existing situation in Russia, and difficulties of supply and transport. But if the existing local governments of Russia are as willing as the governments and peoples whom we represent to see succor and relief given to the stricken peoples of Russia, no political obstacle will remain. There will remain, however, the difficulties of supply, finance and transport which we have mentioned, and also the problem of distribution in Russia itself. The problem of supply we can ourselves hope to solve, in connection with the advice and cooperation of such a Commission as you propose. The problem of finance would seem to us to fall upon the Russian authorities. The problem of transport of supplies to Russia we can hope to meet with the assistance of your own and other Neutral Governments whose interest should be as great as our own and whose losses have been far less. The problems of transport in Russia and of distribution can be solved only by the people of Russia themselves, with the assistance, advice and supervision of your Commission.

Subject to such supervision, the problem of distribution should be solely under the control of the people of Russia themselves. The people in each locality should be given, as under the regime of the Belgian Relief Commission, the fullest opportunity to advise your Commission upon the methods and the personnel by which their community is to be relieved. In no other circumstances could it be believed that the purpose of this relief was humanitarian, and not political, under no other conditions could it be certain that the hungry would be fed.

That such a course would involve cessation of all hostilities within definitive lines in the territory of Russia is obvious. And the cessation of hostilities would, necessarily, involve a complete suspension of the transfer of troops and military material of all sorts to and within Russian territory. Indeed, relief to Russia which did not mean a return to a state of peace would be futile, and would be impossible to consider.

Under such conditions as we have outlined, we believe that your plan could be successfully carried into effect, and we should be prepared to give it our full support.

> /s/ V. E. Orlando
> /s/ D. Lloyd George
> /s/ Woodrow Wilson
> /s/ G. Clemenceau

Doctor Fridtjof Nansen
Paris

With the reply of the Big Four in hand we set about preparing the communication to Lenin. It quoted his letter to the Big Four, their reply, and concluded with this paragraph:

I would be glad to hear from you in this matter at your earliest convenience. I may add that the neutral organization which I propose offers its services in this case without any remuneration whatever; but of course its expenditures in the purchase and transportation of supplies must be met by the Soviet Government.

Dr. Nansen signed the completed message, which was sent on the same day to the French radio for transmission. But days passed with no reply, or even an acknowledgment from Moscow. The message presumably had been radioed on April 17. Mr. Hoover's suspicions were aroused and the message was privately sent to The Hague and broadcast by the Dutch radio. The Russians acknowledged its receipt from that source on May 4. On May 10 a reply was received by the

Eiffel Tower radio station. It was addressed to Dr. Nansen and was signed "Tchicherin, Peoples Commissary for Foreign Affairs." It was not delivered to Dr. Nansen at that time, but was picked up by a radio station of the Danes and by them forwarded to Nansen in Paris. Some days after that a copy was delivered by the Eiffel Tower station.

The reply was long-winded. It began with a pointed reference to the fact that Dr. Nansen's message of April 17 had arrived on May 4 by way of the Netherlands wireless; thanked him for his interest in the well-being of the Russian people; damned the associated and "so-called neutral powers" for the blockade; and accepted Nansen's proposals "in principle." Tchicherin, however, then proceeded to express his suspicion of military intervention under the cover of relief; blamed the frustration of the Prinkipo conference on the great powers; alleged that atrocities had been perpetrated by the White Russian forces; and finally, after three pages of bluster, concluded:

> We will welcome each proposal from your side made to us in the spirit of your letter sent by you to the Council of Four on April 3rd. To those wholly nonbelligerent proposals we respond most gratefully. We thank you most heartily for your good intentions and we are ready to give you every possibility of controlling the realization of such a humanitarian scheme. We will of course cover all the expenses of this work . . . We would suggest that you take the necessary steps to enable delegates of our government to meet you and your collaborators abroad and to discuss these questions and we wish you kindly to indicate the date and place for this conference . . . and what guarantees can be obtained for the free passage of our delegation through countries held by the entente.

In spite of the language condemning the Allies and other objectionable paragraphs, it was clear that the Soviets were ready, even anxious, to come to terms. By this time, however, the French had decided to forget the whole affair—the Big Four had other fish to fry— and the project died on the vine. With it died an unknown but large number of human beings. This was, first, because of the famine. A second and lasting consequence was the lost opportunity to implement other aspects of the Bullitt proposals.*

* Mr. Bullitt resigned from the American Delegation to the Peace Commission on May 17, 1919, a month to the day after the Big Four had agreed to Nansen's proposal, although his resignation had no announced connection with that fact. His letter of resignation reads interestingly in the light of later events. He wrote in part: "It is my conviction that the present League of Nations will be powerless

When a second and greater Russian famine occurred and was relieved by food from the United States in the early 1920s, the Soviet by then had fully established its control of communication and the Iron Curtain had been drawn from north to south across the continent of Europe. The abortive enterprise in which Dr. Nansen had been enlisted fortunately did not discourage him from continuing his humanitarian activities. I do not know whether he ever returned to polar exploration, but certainly for the remainder of his life he was active in international organizations concerned with the relief and resettlement of refugees. We had one further activity in common.

In the course of the operation of Mr. Hoover's responsibility as Director General of Relief for Europe, it was necessary to have a large number of Americans, both civilian and Army officers, moving about throughout Europe and the Middle East. Most of these men had crossed the Atlantic during the war wearing uniforms and had no passports. If there was one thing ingrained in the petty bureaucrat who presided at European frontiers, regardless of nationality, it was insistence upon and respect for an engraved passport, complete with photograph and seal, illegible signatures and rubber-stamped visas. With some appreciation of this, I arranged for a Paris print shop to turn out a supply of florid documents with a large red seal impressively affixed. At the foot of the page was added a flamboyant signature as illegible as those in the drawings Steinberg has since made famous. I had the privilege of issuing the first such passport to myself, signed by myself, authorizing myself to travel. (Years later when I was charged with "wearing two hats" I remembered when I had truly done so.) All of those passports were honored without question, throughout Europe, and our veterans still keep them as mementos, some with many pages of visas attached. A number of these documents were issued at the request of Dr. Nansen for his people, and upon leaving Europe I turned the "Passport Office" over to him. For many years the "Nansen Passport" was the principal travel document of so-called stateless individuals. For all I know, they are still being issued. I hope they have improved on the original format.

From our offices on the Avenue Montaigne, a large operation was managed—telecommunications, shipping, rail transport, and coal mining—in addition to the paramount task of importing and distributing

to prevent these wars and that the United States will be involved in them by the obligations undertaken in the Covenant of the League and in the special understanding of France."

hundreds of thousands of tons of food. One wall of the office was covered by a map of the Atlantic and Mediterranean sea lanes. Hundreds of small burgees bearing the names of ships and pointing either east or west to indicate the heading upon which the ship was sailing were pinned to the map and moved daily so that Mr. Hoover was provided with a graphic view of the flow of supplies from the United States to all the Atlantic and Mediterranean ports, which with his special gift of rapid visual comprehension he could take in, at a glance.

One interesting cable exchange is typical of that period. Admiral Sims had cabled Mr. Hoover:

IN REFERENCE TO CERTAIN SHIPS OPERATED BY THE NAVY FORMERLY IN ARMY SERVICE AND NOW IN SERVICE FOOD ADMINISTRATION WILL IT BE SATISFACTORY TO YOU TO HAVE ME DETERMINE WHEN CHARGES AGAINST ARMY SHOULD CEASE AND CHARGES AGAINST FOOD ADMINISTRATION COMMENCE.

SIMS

and Hoover replied:

YES, REMEMBERING THAT WE ARE IN THE BUSINESS OF TRYING TO SAVE THE LIVES OF ALLIED WOMEN AND CHILDREN ON A BUDGET OF $20 MILLION A MONTH WHILE THEY ARE IN THE KILLING BUSINESS ON A BUDGET OF $2 BILLION A MONTH.

HOOVER

There were also in the Mediterranean at that time a considerable number of our naval vessels, principally destroyers. They ran a sort of shuttle operation between ports on the Adriatic and Aegean seas. In making these short cruises, it had become apparent to some unknown financial genius in one of these crews that the paper currency of the former Austro-Hungarian Empire was still in use in the now dismembered parts of that nation and had different values in the different new countries. Following his profitable lead, the more enterprising seamen became expert arbitragers and substantial profits were accumulated. They were paper profits in a very real sense, as there had been no hard money in the area for years. The practice spread until one day a squadron arrived in Trieste with nearly every man's ditty bag crammed with paper kronen. Unhappily, the news had not reached the new financiers that all old-empire kronen had been called in to be stamped before a certain date in order to be valid thereafter. As this had occurred while the ships were on maneuvers, the currency was worthless. Next morning the harbor was covered with the confetti of paper money and the tide floated it away together with dreams of riches and easy profits.

Confidence in paper currency was not limited to sailors. The Germans had issued enormous amounts of paper money in occupied Belgium, and upon the defeat of Germany the Belgian Government went to the expense of calling in the marks that were in circulation, exchanging Belgian francs for them. The huge accumulation of paper money of the Reich which resulted was then carefully stored in a large warehouse in Brussels. Continuous armed guard was maintained against the day when the Germans would be forced to redeem every last mark in hard cash. The day, of course, never arrived, and I have often wondered when and by whom it was finally decided that it was no longer necessary to mount guard over bales of waste paper.

Although the Armistice "cease fire" had been signed on November 11, 1918, most of the details of surrender were left for subsequent settlement. These details involved such matters as the disposition of German shipping (German ocean-going tonnage was substantially intact); division of the war chest, which still contained a large store of gold; surrender of foreign securities, and a multitude of other items. Accordingly, there were conferences at Spa and Treves and a final negotiation and agreement at Brussels on March 14, 1919. Mr. Hoover was the principal American delegate to this Final Armistice Convention, the others being Hugh Gibson, as diplomatic adviser, Henry M. Robinson for shipping, Thomas W. Lamont for finance, and myself for food. The German delegation was composed of Edler von Braun and some eight or ten others, including, in the interests of confusion (or so it seemed to me), a Herr von Strauss. The British delegation of high-ranking officers and civilians was led by a retired and very senior admiral, Sir Rosslyn Wemyss, who was still fighting the war and who now at last had the Germans under his guns.

In the preliminary conference with the British on the preceding day, March 13, Mr. Hoover had made a strong representation for formally ending the blockade of Germany, which, technically, was still in force and through which we had periodic difficulty in getting our food cargoes, although the war had ended unofficially four months earlier. When Mr. Hoover and Admiral Wemyss were introduced in the lobby of the Metropole Hotel where the conference was to take place, the admiral, without preliminaries, said, "Young man, I don't see why you American chaps want to feed those bloody Germans," to which

Mr. Hoover replied, "Old man, we can't understand why you British chaps want to starve women and children after they are licked."

The Belgian delegation was lead by Emile Francqui, president of the great Belgian bank of the Société Generale. He had been one of Mr. Hoover's right-hand men during the days of the Commission for Relief in Belgium. He and the other Belgian delegates had been subjected to so many indignities by the Germans during the occupation years that they could scarcely contain their joy now that the tables were turned and it was the Germans who were coming hat in hand. The building in which the German delegation was quartered was kept under military guard by the Belgians, and the sentries appeared to be changed at least as frequently as each quarter hour. Hugh Gibson explained that the purpose was to give every Belgian soldier an opportunity to stand guard over his former jailers.

As we left Paris to go to Brussels for the Final Armistice Convention, Melville Stone, then head of the Associated Press, asked if I would report the conference for the AP. The resulting dispatch, which was printed in American papers on the fifteenth, tells the story as it appeared to me. No "conflict of interest" was involved by this sortie into journalism, as the AP did not pay for the essay. Rereading it now, forty-two years later, I can see that it would have been difficult to put any value on the composition.

The results of the conference, however, went somewhat beyond the points in my dispatch. For instance, the agreement permitted the Germans to fish in the Baltic and to buy fish from other nationals who might fish in the North Sea, concessions literally wrung from Admiral Wemyss by hours of argument. The German gold reserve turned out to amount to nearly forty-five million dollars, which was handed over to the British and the French. We took none of it. Our people audited it, however, and found that the treasure consisted to a large extent of gold Napoleons which the Germans had exacted from the French in 1870. Henry Robinson arranged to exchange some American gold dollars, ounce for ounce, for the French gold pieces, and we each bought a souvenir. Also in the horde there were a quantity of Turkish gold pounds and Russian gold rubles. The Germans further agreed to hand over all their merchant tonnage for the transport of food. Because of an incurable addiction to the collecting of mementos, my fountain pen was available when the Final Armistice Agreement was ready to be signed and, since the pen was my property, I kept it.

Thus ended the blockade, but many years were to elapse before the effects of that feature of the postwar period would be forgotten.

The telecommunication system in Europe was placed in the hands of Signal Corps officers released to Mr. Hoover for that purpose by General Pershing. In fact, without the co-operation shown by General Pershing in providing military personnel for all sorts of assignments and the very high caliber of the men so detailed the whole operation would have been impossible. There was never before in Europe, and perhaps there has not been since, a communication system so completely integrated and smoothly functioning.

Every day—indeed several times each day—at the central office of the Director General of the Supreme Economic Council on the Avenue Montaigne, we received telegraphic intelligence on every economic and political factor in Europe. This was provided without the use of codes, yet by a very simple expedient was as secure as the nature of the information warranted. The average American has a large vocabulary of slang originating in the worlds of sport, business, and journalism. Using this slang, we were able to send messages in the "clear" which could be read by censors or even the merely curious at any of the European relay stations through which the messages passed, and yet would be incomprehensible to anyone except Americans. There was amusement on occasion when we knew that our European opposite numbers had intercepted a dispatch and were wrestling with the problem of decipherment.

For instance, in Austria the Hapsburg dynasty was represented by the Archduke Joseph, whose retirement had become the assigned objective of Captain T. T. C. Gregory, an American officer in charge in the region. When one morning a telegram from Vienna was laid on my desk reading, "ARCHIE ON THE CARPET 7:00 P.M. WENT THROUGH THE HOOP AT 7:05 P.M.," it never occurred to me for a moment that the text was susceptible of any other interpretation than that reported in the press two days later. The Archduke was on the skids. With the message paraphrased into more conventional language, Mr. Hoover asked me to take it to Clemenceau but suggested that the original version go along also, recognizing that the old "Tiger of France," having been a newspaper reporter in New York, might be entertained by the system. Months later when Mr. Hoover called on Clemenceau to pay his respects before returning to the United States, Clemenceau took the original telegram from a desk drawer. He told Mr. Hoover that he kept it with him because it was one of the few flashes of entertainment that had come to light in the attempts of the preceding years to make the world over.

The high hopes which had brought President Wilson to Europe and which had animated Mr. Hoover and those who came with him were chilled by facts with which they collided. As we had been in the war so short a time ourselves, our losses had been small by comparison with the cost in lives and fortunes of our allies. The temperate treatment of the vanquished, which to us seemed appropriate and logical, appeared soft and unrealistic to the Allies. Their statesmen were men who saw their governments in debt to the tune of billions of dollars, millions of their people out of work, and scores of thousands of maimed veterans in every town who would have to be supported for the rest of their lives. The French and Belgians looked at the rubble of their ruined cities and blamed Germany for the war and its aftermath, as well they might. They were determined to have reparations and especially to see the punishment of certain individual Germans as personified by the Kaiser.

These attitudes were forced upon the Allied negotiators in Paris by popular demand at home. Lloyd George, who experimented with every conceivable slogan in his campaign speeches for re-election, found that the one which evoked the most universal response, and the one upon which he finally concentrated, was "Hang the Kaiser." The American Peace Delegation viewed all of this with a sort of Olympian detachment at first. It had to be confronted later.

There was still another problem, which came as something of a shock. This was the discovery that while the Allies had many differences among themselves, they were completely united in the reasoning that, having come into the war late, the United States ought not object to paying for it. A proposal was advanced by the leading economist of the day, John Maynard Keynes, to the effect that reparations should be financed by an issue of bonds to be sold to the American public, with the Central Powers servicing the loan but with the United States as the guarantor. As a matter of fact, under the subsequent Dawes and Young plans, scores of millions of dollars of bonds were marketed in the United States. In effect, at the investor level, we did pay much of the reparations.

One of the most serious difficulties which arose between the Allies and ourselves was an apparent decision of the food controllers to break the price of food in the United States. So much time has elapsed since this occurred that there can be no harm in relating this episode, which barely missed having serious consequences to Anglo-American relations and catastrophic results on American agriculture.

As previously noted, in order to stimulate food production so that food would be available for shipment to the Allies, we had stabilized our prices for cereals and animal proteins. This action enormously increased American production of wheat, corn, and hogs. The established prices were somewhat lower than the prices to which speculation and partial crop failures had driven these items before our entry into the war, but the stimulus to production came from guaranties of stability. These guaranties were both moral and legal obligations to the American farmer.

It occurred to certain of the Allied statesmen that they held a formidable lever with which to reduce the cost of their food imports from the United States. This simply involved the cancellation of their contracts to purchase from us specified quantities of foodstuffs for delivery at special dates. The contracts were in fact unenforceable, and since that part of our surplus represented by fats and dairy products was perishable, the Allied food controllers had the American farmers at their mercy. Wheat could be stored, but most of the surplus corn production was represented by pork products into which it had been converted, and these required cold storage. With our accelerated food production, we had available about sixty days of storage capacity of all sorts.

In the period September 1918 to March 1919, American farmers had actually raised and sent to market twenty-six million hogs. This production exceeded our domestic consumption by nearly half a billion pounds a month. Hog prices are tied to cattle prices. If there were no more storage capacity available and we could not ship to Europe, the packers would have to stop buying hogs and cattle; the prices of hogs *and* cattle would fall, and all feed grains in turn would reflect the collapse. Thousands of country banks had made loans to farmers as a wartime duty to enable them to increase production. The farmer-borrowers would have to default and the country banks would fail.

It was not the termination of hostilities which had precipitated the Allied decision to cancel the contracts. Indeed, more than a month after the Armistice, the Allied Meats and Fats Executive confirmed orders which would have absorbed about one-quarter of a billion pounds of pork and dairy products each month. This would have left enough of a surplus with which to feed the people in the Central Powers once the blockade was lifted. Mr. Hoover proposed to ship this surplus to the neutrals surrounding the Central Powers, since the former were in a position to accept the barter transactions which at that time were all that the Germans could offer. They had potash and dyestuffs to exchange, which were not in competition with the manufacturers of the neutrals.

But maintenance of the Allied blockade appears to have been part of the plan to keep the pressure on our price levels. It was essential to the scheme that we should find ourselves compelled to sell our surplus because we could not hold on to it, and for whatever the Allies were willing to pay. The blockade was lifted tentatively on December 22, and then, a week later, without notice was reimposed. On the same day—it could have been a coincidence—the Allied representatives of the Meats and Fats Executive met in London and flatly canceled all their American orders. The Allied Wheat Executive simultaneously notified Mr. Hoover that they had canceled their written contract to take a hundred million bushels of wheat monthly from January to March. The Wheat Executive contended that, although not stated in the text, it was intended that the contract was to terminate with the war. The Meats and Fats Executive simply canceled with no excuse.

The situation was desperate. Mr. Hoover sent Joseph P. Cotton to London to see if anything could be done. Cotton, who had been the director of the Meats and Fats Division of the Food Administration (he later became Hoover's Under Secretary of State), had a deserved reputation for both directness and persuasiveness. On his arrival, he was told that the Allies were already overstocked. He arranged for a private spot check which proved that statement to be in error. Allied food stocks were then in fact below normal. Cotton's protests and exhortations having no apparent effect, Mr. Hoover notified the neutral countries that the orders they had placed would be filled irrespective of the blockade, and Admiral Benson, who was at that time in charge of Naval Operations, assured Mr. Hoover that, if necessary, the Navy would escort our food cargoes through the blockade.

This show of determination made any step as drastic as blockade-running unnecessary. The opposition began to come apart. First the food controllers in France and Italy repudiated the action of the Meats and Fats Executive and reinstated their individual orders. Mr. Hoover also arranged for the Belgian Relief Commission to buy extra food in the certain knowledge that the Belgians would need it, and the U. S. Grain Corporation bought surplus fats and wheat and shipped them to neutral ports in Europe, consigned to Mr. Hoover personally. These shipments proved to be providentially timed when the degree of starvation in the liberated countries began to come to light. Mr. Hoover's decision to defy the blockade resulted in no incidents, disaster to the American farm economy was averted, and no harsh things were said in the press.

There was a useful aspect to this otherwise depressing spectacle, for it provided leverage to complete the demolition of the blockade. This had been accomplished by March of 1919 at the Final Armistice Convention, as mentioned earlier, but, with the realization that starvation waits for no man and that Communism was knocking at the door of Western Europe, Mr. Hoover had ordered ships loaded with food to be dispatched to Copenhagen, Amsterdam, Antwerp, and Rotterdam. When they were unloaded and the cargoes had been stored in those ports, the ships returned for more. At one time we had in excess of a billion pounds of fat and a hundred million bushels of wheat stored in those ports, all of it on Mr. Hoover's personal obligation for an amount exceeding five hundred million dollars. He had made a decision to feed the starving in Europe or to go gloriously broke. I was once curious to learn who had inspired Operation Cancellation, which so fortunately failed in its objective and which might have poisoned the relationships among the Allies for a generation. Now I no longer want to know.

* * *

A collection of incidents, tragic, amusing, or inspiring, which occurred in some of the remoter areas in which the Director General of Relief operated would fill volumes. Accounts of many of them are preserved in the Hoover Archives at Stanford University and at the Hoover Museum and Library in West Branch, Iowa, his birthplace. This anecdote is typical. While the Peace Conference was in session, a multitude of little wars were being fought at many points on the map. One broke out in Dalmatia. We had a feeding operation scheduled there and one of the junior American Army officers assigned to it requested permission to come to Paris to make an urgent report. After hearing it, I took him in to see Mr. Hoover.

Under his command, he said, he had two food trucks and two American soldiers as drivers. On a mountain road near Cattaro, they had found themselves under cross fire by partisans on both sides in one of these "little wars." The Lieutenant had parked his two trucks out of harm's way, disposed the two privates behind shelter, and then with a white flag made contact with the general of the nearest army. He had then vigorously expressed his indignation that the Armistice was being violated by hostilities. He found that general entirely receptive to the idea of calling the war off.

The Lieutenant then made his way over the mountain trails to the headquarters of the opposing army, where he found the other commanding general equally disposed to accept an armistice. Since, however, neither side would surrender to the other, the resourceful American Lieutenant drew up a document for each general to sign, surrendering his army to the United States of America. When it came to the point of actual signature, the Lieutenant got cold feet. He realized that he might be involving his country in something beyond his depth and he therefore made a quick alteration in the document and the two generals and their armies surrendered to "one Herbert Hoover, U. S. Food Administrator." The Lieutenant also remembered Yorktown and so he demanded their swords, and, recalling the magnanimity of Grant at Appomattox, he allowed the two armies to keep everything except their machine guns and artillery.

But this was not all. Being short of labor to unload a food ship in the harbor, the Lieutenant offered a wage of flour and bacon if the two armies would act as stevedores. They immediately accepted, whereupon he put his two soldiers, each a private, in command of an army. One army worked the day shift and one the night shift. Probably no ship before or since has been unloaded in such record time.

The reason for the Lieutenant's telephone call from Cattaro was that he had an attack of conscience about using Mr. Hoover's name without authority. He came to Paris to make a clean breast of it and take the consequences. Mr. Hoover said the important question was to state what he had done with the swords. The Lieutenant said that he had brought them along, so Mr. Hoover made a deal with him. "You give me one, you retain the other, and we'll keep the whole affair between us." And then, turning to me, Mr. Hoover added, "See if you can get this 'general' a week's leave in Paris and a button."

Mr. Hoover always referred to foreign decorations as "buttons." He regarded the prevailing passion for the acquisition of these distinctions as something less than meritorious. He did not forbid the acceptance of such rewards by members of his staff and appeared to be moderately pleased when an Allied country expressed its gratitude in this manner. For himself, however, Mr. Hoover had long ago decided not to accept such awards and had declined the honors when they were offered to him. This was not universally known, and on one morning in 1917, Jules Jusserand, the popular French Ambassador to the United States, asked for an appointment and came to my office carrying a large leather box. He favored me with a glimpse of its interior, where, reposing in cushioned splendor, was the insignia of the Grand Cordon of the Legion of Honor. I was able to inform Mr. Hoover of the purpose of the Ambassador's visit, and so skillfully was that meeting conducted by Mr. Hoover and so perceptive was the diplomat that the interview ran along pleasantly without any reference whatever to the decoration. Mr. Hoover, as far as I know, is not yet carried on the rolls of the Grand Chancellor of the Legion.

The Belgians awarded their highest honors to a number of Mr. Hoover's subordinates. With this in mind and the fact of his attitude toward decorations, they set about the creation for him of a new and unique distinction. The inspiration as worked out required an act of the Belgian Parliament and a royal decree, but thus there was created a preferment never awarded before or since. King Albert, in a letter written in his own hand, thereupon informed Mr. Hoover that henceforth he would be known as "The Friend of the Belgian People." Mr. Hoover always kept his emotions under strict control, but as he read that letter I could see that he was deeply touched.

The Treaty of Versailles was signed on June 28, 1919. It was a great day in Paris, but the exuberance of the Armistice was not repeated. A few copies of the treaty became available a day or two earlier, and I was lucky enough to obtain one on which the signatures of Wilson, Lloyd George, Clemenceau, and Orlando were later obligingly appended as a memento. I very much wanted to witness the drama of the signing by the Allied and German delegates, but the pass I rated was good only for admission to the park of the château and, far from authorizing entrance to the Hall of Mirrors, where the ceremony was to occur, did not even entitle its holder to cross the threshold of the palace itself. Fortunately, a war correspondent of legend, the late Floyd Gibbons, proved to be a resourceful friend. Floyd's working clothes were a sort of uniform—but of an unidentifiable army—a chest full of campaign ribbons, and a rakish black patch over one eye. "Rely on it," he told me, "*we* are going to get in." His first step was to buy two packs of Pall Mall cigarettes. In those days the brand came in a stiff pasteboard box in an official-looking scarlet color with gilt lettering and the British and American seals embossed in gold in the upper corners. Floyd cut out the tops of the boxes so that they could be held in the hand like a pass. Equipped with these impressive testimonials to our importance and with dead-pan assurance, we flashed the passes and brushed past the sentries and guards, some of whom I thought even slapped their rifles in salute as we passed in. I did not risk looking back. Once inside, we became separated and I never did get an unobstructed view of the signing, but I did reach a point from which I could see Floyd, well up front among the mighty, where a man of his initiative obviously belonged.

With the signing of the Treaty of Versailles and the demobilization of the Peace Conference, there was great anxiety on the part of the American staff, especially the military, many of whom had been in Europe since 1917, to return home. The process of recovery and the re-establishment of services had proceeded in most countries beyond any prediction that might have been made in view of the disorganization of nine months before. Mr. Hoover devised a plan to establish economic, financial, and transportation advisers in the several countries. These men were Americans, but were employees of the appropriate ministries in those countries. With this enterprise functioning, our Paris headquarters closed in September of 1919.

* * *

A minor matter of a personal nature had followed the signature of the Treaty of Versailles and the organization of the League of Nations. Under a ground rule established, the organizing countries did not nominate their own nationals for staff positions in the League. Sir Eric Drummond, the first Secretary General, was proposed, I understood, by the United States, while the Under Secretary General, Dr. Raymond Fosdick, was proposed by Great Britain. A cablegram from Sir Eric Drummond arrived addressed to me in Paris.

HIS MAJESTY'S GOVERNMENT PLEASED TO PROPOSE YOU FOR APPOINTMENT AS COMPTROLLER GENERAL, LEAGUE OF NATIONS, SALARY 2,000 POUNDS. PLEASE RESPOND EARLIEST. REGARDS. DRUMMOND.

It is still possible to recapture some of the elation inspired by that message. I was twenty-three at the time and my feeling was certainly largely tainted by vanity. I knew that it was a privilege to be a part of the organization which was to crystallize the dream of President Wilson, that "the war to end war" which had been fought would mean permanent peace. And picturing myself returning to Richmond to visit my parents and the notion that teachers and former classmates would be properly impressed with my exalted status were heady. I realized, of course, that the job that was offered was a sort of glorified office manager.

The figure of two thousand pounds was equivalent to about ten thousand dollars in those days, and did not strike me as excessive because my earnings had exceeded that during each of the two years before coming to work with Mr. Hoover. It was those earnings which had enabled me to indulge in the vanity of imitating Mr. Hoover in declining compensation from the Government.

Prior to the receipt of the cable from Sir Eric Drummond, I had met Mortimer Schiff in Paris. Mr. Schiff was the only son of Jacob H. Schiff, of New York, and was a partner of the international banking firm of Kuhn, Loeb & Co. He had come to Paris on a mission for the American Red Cross. He asked me whether I would care to come to work for his firm at the end of my duties with Mr. Hoover. I discussed the subject with Oscar Straus. Mr. Straus, a former Ambassador of the United States to Turkey and Secretary of Commerce and Labor in the cabinet of Theodore Roosevelt, had come to Paris representing an independent organization of the League to Enforce Peace, which he had organized together with ex-President Taft and Elihu Root. I had been invited by Mr. and Mrs. Straus to live in their apartment in Paris and I was very fond of them and set great store by Mr. Straus's judgment. He had counseled me to accept the invitation from Mr. Schiff, pointing out that banking could be a constructive profession, that it was very well rewarded, and that the means it provided enabled those who succeeded at it to engage in good works. Accordingly, Mr. Schiff having returned to New York, there was an exchange of letters in which I had agreed to come to work for his institution.

The offer from the League of Nations presented a dilemma. There was no doubt that Mr. Schiff would scarcely hold me to the undertaking, yet I felt bound in honor. I had also written to my friend Justice Brandeis, and he had replied to say that he had hopes of a career of public service for me but that if I entered the investment banking business I might as well abandon any notion that I would ever be eligible for public office. I knew that I could resolve the dilemma by putting the issue before my father back in Virginia. There was, of course, no air mail in those days, and I waited impatiently while the steamer carried my letter across the Atlantic, counting the days that it would take before it reached my father's hands. His reply was prompt and laconic. My family has always been parsimonious in the composition of telegrams. Some men save paper clips and string, others by force of habit turn off the lights in a room they are leaving. My father could not tolerate excess cable wordage at twenty-five cents a word. His telegram simply said:

DON'T BE DARN FOOL. LOVE

($1.25) I got the general idea.

His advice was not a Delphic riddle to me. I sat down at my Corona and wrote to Sir Eric Drummond to express my gratitude for having been considered and my regret that a commitment previously made would keep me from the pleasure of association with him in the great enterprise upon which he was about to embark. With the letter when I posted it went the Walter Mitty-type dream of glory, briefly enjoyed, of a career in statesmanship. Now more than ever, I was dedicated to the idea of making my way in the world of business.

I returned ahead of Mr. Hoover to keep the long-deferred commitment to report for work at the offices of Kuhn, Loeb & Co., and sailed from Brest on the S.S. *Finland* with Sergeant Everett Somers, who had been my efficient and overworked assistant in Paris. We landed in New York on September 19. Before I left Paris, Mr. Hoover called me into his office and handed me an envelope with the injunction that I was not to read it until I had gotten home. "You can consider it as 'sealed orders,'" he said. It contained a two-page letter in his own hand which was an endorsement beyond my deserts.[3]

The universal popularity of Mr. Hoover on his return from Europe was a phenomenon probably unique in American history. He was the choice of the great majority of the nation's editors for the next presidential nomination. This was in the days before "scientific polling" as it is currently conducted, and there is no way of confirming my belief that the vast majority of Americans of both parties regarded him as the ablest figure then in the public eye. Mr. Hoover did not regard himself as available. Months before, he had begun to look back with nostalgia to his years as a consulting engineer and had written to President Wilson, while in Paris, to say that four years of public service as well as practical separation from his family left him but one desire, which was to return to the practice of his profession. This expression of his intentions had been touched off by an attack in the Senate on a bill to appropriate one hundred million dollars for the relief of starvation under Mr. Hoover's direction. Senators Reed, Gore, Penrose, and Borah, who were most active in opposition to the proposal, had made the issue personal by criticism of Mr. Hoover. It was not his first experience with political mudslinging, and certainly not to be the last, but his recollections of private life seemed more attractive as its prospect grew remoter.

Friends importuned him, however, and he was persuaded at least not to oppose their efforts to secure the Republican nomination for him. A committee formed for the purpose was composed of amateurs whose eagerness and enthusiasm were matched only by their total lack of political experience. They gladly took upon themselves the organization of a preconvention campaign to pledge delegates. Totally unaware of their naïveté in the rough-and-tumble of intraparty politics, most of them remained confident of success right up to the final roll call at the Republican Convention in 1920 in Chicago, which nominated Warren G. Harding. They might as well have remained at home. Mr. Hoover himself was under no illusions and told me so.

Shortly after his election, President Harding invited Mr. Hoover to join his cabinet. This was a tribute solely to Mr. Hoover's public stature, for there was no past connection between the President-elect and the man who was to be his Secretary of Commerce. Indeed during the period between the nomination and Election Day, Mr. Hoover had occasion to admonish the candidate on the most serious issue of the day.

In his speech accepting the nomination, Senator Harding had used ambiguous language concerning his attitude toward the League of Nations. His statement permitted interpretation as an abandonment both of the Treaty of Versailles and of the Covenant of the League. Opponents of these instruments were quick to assert that this was precisely what Harding had meant, the Republican platform to the contrary notwithstanding. Senator Hiram Johnson, the irreconcilable foe of international action for peace, and a frustrated contender for the nomination Harding had won, hailed the acceptance speech as clear evidence of Harding's anti-League position, though the Senate Foreign Relations Committee (of which Harding had been a member) had recommended the substance of the provisions expressed in the treaty. Mr. Harding also had given an earlier interview to David Lawrence, which seemed to align him with the supporters of the League, but, following Senator Johnson's statement, he did nothing to clear the air.

Mr. Hoover felt very strongly on the subject and, holding his own political future of small consequence, addressed a message to the President-elect. It was couched, not diplomatically, but in the language of an engineer about to return to his job. He described Senator Johnson's intrepretation of Harding's speech as an overwhelming shock to the conscience of a great section of Republican voters. The ideals which were to be repudiated he described, prophetically, as "the only hope of a real attempt to prevent another war! . . . Abandonment of the League," he said, "would be a surrender to the worst forces in American public life." He invited the attention of Mr. Harding to the fact that Lenin, in his last address, had aligned Bolshevism with the opponents of the League. Finally Mr. Hoover warned of the defection of a large part of the progressive vote and called upon Mr. Harding to show statesmanship. This was hardly calculated to ingratiate him with the candidate, but it obviously did not alter Mr. Harding's resolve to have Mr. Hoover in his cabinet.

During Mr. Hoover's service in the cabinets of Harding and Coolidge, my contacts with him were less frequent. The banking business absorbed my interest and my time. I was succeeded as his assistant by Christian A. Herter, who had been secretary of the U. S. Peace Commission in Paris in 1918–19, where he had impressed everyone by his ability and intelligence. He served Mr. Hoover with distinction during the period when the Department of Commerce was raised to a degree of usefulness to the economy which it had never before attained. Mr. Herter later entered politics, served as a member of the House of Representatives, as Governor of the State of Massachusetts and was appointed Under Secretary of State, and later Secretary, by President Eisenhower.

In early 1928, President Coolidge was completing his second term in the White House. There was widespread speculation as to whether he would seek another term, as had Theodore Roosevelt, and on the same interpretation, i.e., that the term in which he had succeeded Harding had been incomplete. Some of Mr. Coolidge's close friends allowed it to become known that he expected the nomination and indeed desired it. Mr. Hoover's friends again hoped to see him nominated for the presidency. Those who had unsuccessfully worked to that end in 1920, if not wiser, were by now more experienced. Mr. Hoover, however, sternly discouraged any such efforts.

In the spring of 1928, Mr. Herter came to see me to say that in 1912, when Theodore Roosevelt's candidacy for a third term was a very active topic, a round robin had been addressed to W. Murray Crane of Dalton, the Republican National Committeeman for Massachusetts. This document had been signed by most of the local politicians of the state and it condemned the idea of a third term for Colonel Roosevelt in very strong language. Among the signers was a young politician by the name of Calvin Coolidge. The original of the round robin, with Mr. Coolidge's signature still as fresh as paint, had been carefully preserved by another of the signers against a day when it would be useful. This day, he felt, had now dawned and his foresight would be rewarded. It appeared that the original document was for sale and the modest asking price a mere

$25,000. Tempting as it would be to be able to quote Mr. Coolidge himself on the principle of a third term, the price was high. Moreover, Mr. Hoover had told us in no uncertain terms that he was *not* a candidate and would not consider the subject until Mr. Coolidge had made his own intentions plain. We realized that it could embarrass Mr. Hoover if his friends took any step which might appear to edge the President into a decision.

As a compromise between caution and a desire to have the document ("just in case") I made a small offer for it. The holder refused to sell. Not long after, the press carried the news that President Coolidge from his vacation resort in the Black Hills had issued the famous announcement "I do not choose to run." The fall in value of the round robin was precipitate; its owner promptly offered it at a substantial reduction. I could not resist the impulse to reply, "I do not choose to buy."

Before sailing for Europe in November 1918, there had been a meeting in Mr. Hoover's office attended by Harry A. Garfield, Bernard Baruch, and Vance McCormick to decide what should be done after the war with the four emergency organizations, the War Trade Board, the War Industries Board, the Fuel Administration and the Food Administration. There had been considerable agitation that they should become permanent agencies of the Government. The four conferees reached unanimous agreement that from the date of the Armistice (which had not then occurred) all these departments should gradually withdraw the restrictions they had imposed on commerce so that business might return to conditions as near normal as possible, having respect to the liquidation of military requirements.

Mr. Hoover, in particular, felt that a reduction of the activities of the Food Administration should begin at once. The intense regulation of trade imposed by the Food Administration had been vitally necessary in order to eliminate the profiteering and speculation which had been widespread before our entry into the war. The success of the controls, however, had been largely based on voluntary acquiescence by the several trades and a considerable part of the policing of the controls had been dependent on voluntary agreement and action. Mr. Hoover recognized that this would be difficult to maintain in peace. He also had concluded that excessive regulation dampens individual initiative and was undesirable for that reason. In effect, he had decided that the Food Administration Act ought to lapse with the coming of peace.

Therefore, upon his return to the United States, in the autumn of

1919, his lieutenants on his instruction were well along with the liquidation of the Food Administration and its several subsidiaries, such as the United States Grain Corporation, and Mr. Hoover did not settle in Washington, but established his headquarters at 42 Broadway in New York City, where his overseas relief activities were centered. Since my office was at the corner of William and Pine streets, only a few blocks distant, and as I was an officer of several foundations which he had established, there was occasion at frequent intervals for me to travel between our offices. These trips invariably took me past the corner of Broad and Wall streets between the old Treasury Building and the offices of J. P. Morgan & Co.

On one day, September 16, 1920, I had traversed this route to call on Mr. Hoover and introduce Dr. Harry Plotz, a young physician who had achieved fame as the discoverer of the organism of typhus, one of the diseases which had plagued our relief operations in Europe and Asia Minor. Plotz made an interesting report on conditions in the Ukraine, and as we were about to leave, Mr. Hoover asked me to remain for discussion of a matter on which he had to reach a decision. To this, I very possibly owe my life, for we had been talking for only a few more minutes when there was a tremendous explosion which shook the windows and sounded as though it had been directly outside the building. We paused for only a moment, as the sound of blasting was not then uncommon, but we both remarked at the violence of the explosion. The recollection of our discussion is more vivid than ordinarily would be the case, because the accompanying event anchored it in my memory.

Mr. Hoover said he had heard that the administration in the Red Cross wished to replace him as chairman of the Council of War Relief Organizations, and he asked me to inquire of Dr. Fred Keppel if this was factual. He also said that Paul Warburg had invited him to join the International Acceptance Bank, just organized by Mr. Warburg, and had offered him any arrangement he cared to make. Mr. Hoover had been much tempted by this proposal, but had concluded to continue in public service. "One thing is fairly certain," he said. "Harding will win and our only hope is to be 'regular' and give the Old Guard as much trouble as possible *from the inside* after we win. If everyone who is progressive goes over to Cox, they still can't possibly elect him, for they are outnumbered by the multitude of voters who don't stop to analyze the main issues. Our only chance is to let the Old Guard swal-

low us and then work to make the Republican party wiser and better in
the years ahead."

On leaving his office and going out of the rear entrance toward Wall
Street, I found myself in a pushing crowd, all headed in that direction.
A wagonload of explosives had been parked in front of the Treasury
just across the street from the Morgan offices. The explosion of its contents was the blast we had heard. The street was still full of injured and
dead people, some prone, others propped against the walls of the buildings, and the pavement was covered with blood. The first police to arrive were trying to keep people away from the shambles. Windows were
broken and the walls of the Morgan building and the Assay Office were
pitted by fragments. They had the appearance of buildings I had seen
in Berlin after the revolution of 1919. Thirty persons had been killed
and over one hundred injured, and to this day the perpetrators of the
outrage are unknown. Had I left Mr. Hoover's office a few minutes
earlier, I would have been at or near the scene of the disaster when it
occurred.

* * *

Mr. Hoover's four years in the White House have been well documented. There are two unpublished incidents which I can add to the
history of a period when one of the ablest men ever called to the presidency, with ideas informed by experience for the betterment of the people, and with the capability of putting those ideas to work, was confronted with a condition so grave that his time and energies were taxed
to the utmost merely to keep the institutions of the nation intact.

Mr. Hoover's appointments to the judiciary were exemplary. He
made four nominations to the Supreme Court. One of them was to
name, as Chief Justice, Charles Evans Hughes, certainly one of the great
jurists the nation has produced. Hughes was a Republican, as was Owen
J. Roberts. Two others, of not inferior merit, were Democrats. One of
them was John J. Parker, a Southerner of long experience on the bench
and an outstanding reputation among men of the law. Judge Parker's
nomination failed of confirmation in the Senate, where he was opposed
by certain special groups in a campaign of personal derogation which
reflected no credit on those who voted against him. The other Democratic appointment was that of Justice Benjamin Nathan Cardozo,
whose opinions ornament and illuminate the most distinguished pages
of American jurisprudence. He was not only a member of the opposition party, but was a devout Jew, and there were those among Presi-

dent Hoover's advisers who, recalling the difficulties attending the confirmation of Justice Brandeis in 1916, did not hesitate to tell the President that it was a political error of judgment to appoint the scholarly Cardozo. Mr. Hoover, guided by his conscience and his conviction that Cardozo was ideally qualified by judicial temperament, experience, and his comprehensive knowledge of the law, never hesitated in his decision.

One particular incident concerns an important though less well-known appointment. For a vacancy existing in a federal judgeship, a lawyer I shall call Smith had been well recommended to the President, but was not personally known to him. President Hoover, aware that I knew Smith, telephoned to ask me to inquire as to his willingness to accept the post if named. In the course of conversation with Smith, he told me that normally much of the litigation in the district involved the General Motors Corporation; and that he was a substantial stockholder in that company, having acquired the stock many years before at prices far below those to which the boiling stock market of the 1920s had carried them. He said that if he took the post he ought to dispose of his holdings and that this would involve him in the payment of a considerable tax. He then asked for time to think it over, and the following day called me to say that he had made the decision to sell his holdings. The stock was disposed of and the appointment duly followed. As it happened, this occurred about two months before the great stock-market collapse of the autumn of 1929. The rewards of virtuous decision are not invariably so prompt as in this case.

The undeniable excellence of President Hoover's appointments to the judiciary and his disregard of partisan considerations stemmed directly from his secure grounding in the Constitution and therefore his respect for the judiciary as a co-ordinate and independent branch of the Government. The second incident was another illustration of the same set of high principles.

Historians are authority for the fact that every president, beginning with Washington, has been the target of mudslingers. It is an occupational hazard associated with tenancy of the White House. Mr. Hoover's experience, however, was probably more of an ordeal than those his predecessors had experienced, if only because his traducers were better financed, and the media for disseminating slander and libel, identical with the channels for the spread of news and truth, have benefited by the technical advances in the art of communication. A lie, which in the days of Lincoln would have traveled slowly, could be heard during Hoover's incumbency instantly over radios in millions of homes.

Years before Mr. Hoover became President, two obscure hack writers produced books about him in which he was charged with various fantastic crimes. Articles appeared picturing him as having absconded with the mineral wealth of China, as having fed poisoned food to the starving people of Europe, and as being a conspirator to deliver the United States back to the British Crown. In the political campaign of 1928, he became the target of more professional character assassins who knew how to plant stories and speeches, initiate whispering campaigns, and doctor photographs. They had almost unlimited resources at their disposal for the purpose of seeing that these calumnies were dinned into the ears of the American people.

When the tide of the great world-wide depression finally reached our shores in 1929 and found a part of our economy highly vulnerable as a result of several years of unbridled speculation, Mr. Hoover, though but eight months in the Presidency, became a convenient scapegoat. He was pictured as indifferent and complacent, heartless and inept. The very opposite of these was true, and the economic excesses against which he had repeatedly warned an unheeding public while serving as Secretary of Commerce culminated in an economic collapse, unjustly and inaccurately called the "Hoover Depression."

During his Presidency, the Constitution of the United States included an amendment—the Eighteenth—which had been proposed during World War I and became law in January of 1920. This was the Prohibition Amendment. Mr. Hoover had not been bigoted on the subject; he regarded alcohol as the occasional and pleasant concomitant of a social meal. But he refused to participate in the popular attitude of the day, which regarded the law as a dead letter. In consequence, no alcoholic beverages were served in the White House or in his other residences.

By 1930 dissatisfaction with the Prohibition amendment had grown to such proportions that it was a lively political issue. It was clear that the majority of the people despised the law, not alone because it appeared to be an infringement of personal liberty, but also because it had generated widespread disrespect for law. Mr. Hoover's most likely opponent in the presidential campaign of 1932, Governor Roosevelt of New York, took a public position in vigorous favor of repeal of the Eighteenth Amendment, and this won him considerable support. Concerned at this condition and at Mr. Hoover's adamant position in support of law enforcement, one of his close friends, Jeremiah Milbank of New York, and I went to see him at the White House. We laid before him what we thought was a politically expedient pronouncement on the issue. We told him that failure to dissociate himself from the Eighteenth Amendment and to espouse the cause of its repeal would endanger his re-election. He listened tolerantly to our earnest adjuration. Then he said:

"The President of the United States takes an oath to preserve, protect and defend the Constitution. If he comes into office with the intention of changing that great instrument, it is a mental reservation which makes hypocrisy of his oath; and if, as President, he acts to advocate a change in the Constitution, it would set the most dangerous precedent I can think of." We were sitting in the conservatory on the second floor of the White House. The weather was hot and each of us had been provided with a refreshing glass of something cool and distinctly nonalcoholic. "There is a constitutional procedure for changing the Constitution," Mr. Hoover continued, "but the President has no part in it, and should not have. Regardless of what you believe will be the effect upon my political fortunes, and however right you may be, that is of no consequence compared with the great principle of our form of government which properly proscribes the Chief Executive from tampering with the Constitution under any circumstances."

Hoover was a president, not only of decision, but of principle.

III
Rebirth of a Nation

The only primary-school textbook large enough to conceal an open copy of *The Liberty Boys of '76, Frank Merriwell,* or other dime novels of my childhood was a worthy work titled Maury's *Manual of Geography.* It was illustrated with singularly unattractive half tones, apparently selected with an eye to discouraging young explorers. One illustration, which accompanied the brief paragraphs describing Finland, pictured a wintry landscape on which stood a little man in a fur parka, holding the bridle of an equally diminutive reindeer. This, presumably, was a typical Finnish scene and what young Americans might expect Finland had to offer.

It took the Olympic games of 1924 to turn the spotlight on Finland. Paavo Nurmi, the "Flying Finn," outdistanced all competition in the 1500-, 5000-, and 10,000-meter races, and many people were surprised to discover that Finland produced things other than fish, fur, and reindeer. The climate, at least during part of the year, must be warm enough for running trunks.

By the winter of 1918–19, however, I had made the acquaintance of the people of this remarkable country. World War I had been over for three weeks and the cargoes of food which had started on their way from the United States even before the Armistice were beginning to arrive at European Atlantic ports. None had been consigned to Finland. The emissaries of small countries were standing in the vestibules and anterooms of the Big Four in Paris, waiting an opportunity to put forward the claims of their countries for self-determination and food.

Finland had been a more or less independent grand duchy, though within the Russian orbit, since 1809. She had managed to have her own currency and to persist in holding stubbornly to her own language (which resembled Hungarian more closely than Russian) and with a tenacity which had frequently cost her dear, she had refused to submit to the absolute rule of the Czars.

Finland's diplomatic representative in Paris was Rudolf Holsti. In those days, when well-turned-out statesmen all affected striped pants with morning coats or cutaways, Holsti would never have been mistaken for a diplomat. He dressed as though clothing was an afterthought and peered at the world through spectacles with lenses so thick that they looked as if cut from the bottoms of beer bottles. He spoke English fluently but with a unique accent. He had instructions from his government to see what could be done about getting American food as a first priority and the recognition of his government second. Accordingly, he presented himself at our offices in the Ritz Hotel in London.

Holsti said that Germany had siphoned off so much of the limited cereal crop of Finland that for nearly two years their bread had been largely an admixture of sawdust, moss, bark, and other adulterant indigestible matter as a stretcher. The loaves he had brought with him were repulsive. One could imagine that even animals would refuse them. He insisted that his people did not want a handout, that they had some eight million pounds sterling on deposit in London and approximately ten million dollars in banks in New York, and that they would insist upon paying for whatever we could let them have. We immediately offered to send food to Finland and to consider its dollar value as a loan, since this was the standard procedure. Holsti as promptly declined this, saying that so long as the Finns had a penny left they preferred to pay rather than go into debt.

In this respect the Finns proved to be singular. When finally, having used up their balances, they were compelled to accept loans from the United States, they were the only country, following World War I, to pay interest and reduce principal without interruption. On the balances in existence when World War II began, they continued to pay interest and installments even after they found themselves under German control. In some manner during those years, they contrived to obtain dollar exchange and to present a check for it to the Secretary of the Treasury in Washington on the due dates. Like the return of the swallows to Capistrano, the interest payment dates always signaled the arrival of the Finns bearing money. My admiration for the honor of these people, which began when I first became acquainted with them in 1918, has never diminished. Admiration for another quality—their courage—was to come later.

It was necessary to make very strong representations to our allies for breaching the blockade to get supplies into Helsingfors (Helsinki), despite the fact that the war was over and that there was no military justification for continuing the blockade. This phenomenon of maintaining blockades affecting civil populations after any military warranty had ceased was general after World War I, and there is no explanation for it beyond the assumption that the illogical decision in each case must have been made by the same set of bureaucrats.

Holsti's personal subsistence allowance in 1918–19 was only a few French francs a day and, as I had a pocket full of ration tickets, he dined with me often during the period. He was interesting company and rewarded me on these occasions by informal lectures on the history of Finland and the aspects of Finnish culture, each lesson ending with a homily on the aspiration of the Finns for complete independence from Russia. The result of this was that, completely indoctrinated, I prepared a paper on the subject and, at Mr. Hoover's direction, transposed it into a letter he wrote to President Wilson:

Paris, 26 April, 1919

My dear Mr. President:

I am wondering if there is not some method by which the recognition of the full independence of Finland could be expedited. They have now had a general election, they have created a responsible ministry; this ministry is of liberal character. There are many reasons why this matter should be undertaken, and at once.

1. The United States has always had a great sentiment for the suffering of the Finnish people, and their struggle of over a century to gain independence.

2. By lack of recognition, they are absolutely isolated from a commercial point of view from the rest of the world. They are unable to market their products except by the sufferance of special arrangements with government at every step. They have ships without flags, and have no right to sail the seas. They are totally unable to establish credits, although they have a great deal of resource, as no bank can loan money to a country of unrecognized government. They are isolated by censorship. Their citizens are not allowed to move as their passports do not run.

3. The most pressing problem is their food supply. In January last the Finns were actually starving in hundreds. Order in the country was preserved by sheer military repression. By one measure and another, and altogether out of Finnish resources, without the cost of a dollar to us, we have for the last three months fed Finland. Order has been restored. The populations are rapidly recovering nutritional conditions. They have begun to take hope of the future. They have prepared large quantities of materials for export. All through these operations,

they have shown the most sturdy independence and have asked for nothing but the facilities to make their own solutions. Their resources are now practically exhausted. Unless they can have immediate recognition, so that they can create further commercial credits and can sell their products, they are either doomed or we must support them on charity.

If ever there was a case for helping a people who are making a sturdy fight to get on a basis of liberal democracy, and are asking no charity of the world whatever, this is the case. I am convinced from our reports that unless Finland is recognized within a very short time that the present government cannot survive the difficulties with which it is faced. One instance would show the utter paralysis under which they are suffering. Their banks have deposits of upwards of ten millions of dollars in the United States, but they can secure no legal assurance that the control and ownership of these banks is the same as that which existed at the time the deposits were made. It is purely a technical question, but it, amongst numerous other instances of this character, threatens absolutely to destroy the Finnish Government.

Nor do I see why any half measures need to be taken in this matter. They have gone through every cycle that the world could demand in political evolution, to the point of an Independent people, and I feel that they would long since have been recognized had it not been for the terrible cloud of other questions that surround the world. I realize that there are a lot of people who consider that General Mannerheim* casts a sinister shadow over the present government, but the very fact that under this same shadow Finland has established democratic institutions should be enough of an answer.

Faithfully yours,
/s/ HERBERT HOOVER

* Mannerheim was a dictator-president at the time whose tenure ended without bloodshed.

Ten days later the subject of Finnish independence was considered at a meeting of the Council of Five, the foreign ministers to the Allies, and on May 7 Secretary of State Lansing wrote to Holsti to say that the United States was recognizing the independence of Finland.

A sentimental letter to me from Holsti at that time recalled the meeting which Mr. Hoover's decision had been taken to come to the aid of Finland. Holsti added, "That was the one really extremely happy day in my life so full of political suffering. Now week after week the Finnish people see their food situation improving and I know very well indeed to what an extent it was due to your kind assistance. May 7th there was another really wonderful day in my life when Finland's independence was in principle recognized by the USA and Great Britain. I know how closely your name is associated with that great event in our history. I feel very deeply that I have never thanked you enough." I have treasured that letter over the years, not only for the unction it contained, but also for a sequence of events.

The Allied foreign ministers had met on May 3 to consider Mr. Hoover's letter to President Wilson. That discussion had ended in general agreement that all the Allies would recognize the independence of Finland, but it was a part of the agreement that the decision should be withheld from the Finns until it could be announced simultaneously by each ally at a date set. Barely hours after this decision had been reached, Holsti came to see me fairly weeping with gratitude. His story was that both his British and French contacts had told him, in strict confidence, of course, what had been done. Each informer modestly indicated that the successful outcome had been the result of *his* country's insistence. Holsti, however, was under no misapprehension, for he had assisted in the preparation of the memorandum which had resulted in the letter to President Wilson.

Holsti later became Minister of Foreign Affairs, an increase in responsibility and status which effected no change whatever in his simplicity. On one occasion when, as Foreign Minister, he visited the United States, I went to meet him at a pier on the East River at which his ship was to dock. I stood at the foot of the gangplank as the passengers disembarked, but he was not among them. It occurred to me that he might be traveling second-class, and I went to that part of the pier where passengers in second-class were gathering their luggage for customs inspection, but he was not there, either. Eventually he was located in third-class, comfortably seated on a carpetbag, his only piece of luggage, smoking his pipe and patiently waiting to be met.

In 1939 Holsti managed to escape from the Nazis and eventually to make his way to the United States. With the assistance of Raymond Fosdick, president of the Rockefeller Foundation, and of President Ray Lyman Wilbur, of Stanford University, we were able to get him a faculty position at Stanford. His wife and sons joined him and he ended his days there after a fruitful period of teaching and writing. I hope that he has left an account of his personal experiences, for they were dramatic. He was not just an interpreter of history, he also made it, and he was a great patriot. It might be of interest to those historians who study the loom of language to observe that a new word has been added to the ancient Finnish tongue. The word is *"Hooveri,"* and its meaning is "benevolence" and "charity."

Finland continued to prosper between the great wars and was not seriously injured in the economic collapse which, beginning in Austria, spread around the world and triggered the Great Depression in the United States. Indeed, when Hitler began World War II in September 1939, the Finns appeared to have read the storm signals correctly and had battened their hatches. Nevertheless, the first blow of war fell on Finland as a complete surprise and from an unguarded sector.

Without any warning or justification, Stalin invaded Finland on November 30, 1939. Division after division of Soviet troops poured across the Russo-Finnish border. The invasion, irrational when it occurred, has never been explained by relating it to any subsequent course of action by the Russians. Even a score of years later, it appears as it did then, an example of savagery, perpetrated without any reason by a large strong nation upon a small, weak neighbor. It did not fit in at all with the image of the Communists as chess players whose every move, supposedly, is calculated—never haphazard.

But the Russians apparently had not calculated upon the quality of the resistance which Finnish fighting men could oppose to the far greater Russian numbers.

With almost no military equipment in the modern sense, the Finns succeeded in annihilating whole regiments of Russians. Finnish troops armed themselves with captured Russian equipment. They were fighting for their homes and firesides, and they were experienced in campaigns in the snows, even more so than the Russian Army. Despite initial successes, however, the overwhelming manpower and resources of the Communist empire beat them down. The American public watched the gallantry of the Finns with admiration while the press editorialized on their bravery and on the treachery of the unprovoked attack, but nothing was done to assist them.

On Sunday morning, December 3, 1939, I was called at my home in New York by Hjalmar Procopé, the Finnish Minister in Washington. Finnish envoys to the United States, evidently upon standing instructions from their Foreign Office, had regularly come to see me after presenting their credentials and thereafter consulted on matters concerning Finnish commerce and financing in the United States. I avoided capitalizing on this relationship and declined any fees for the financial service. Procopé was relatively new to Washington and we had met only a few times. Speaking with great emotion, he said, "I am at the very end of my rope and Finland is near the end of hers. Everywhere I go in Washington—to the State Department, to the Treasury, to the White House, even to the Red Cross—I get sympathy, but nothing more. We can't defend ourselves with sympathy. Can you help me at all?"

There was one idea in my mind that would provide some money for food for Finland. With their own funds for food released, the government might be able to buy some war matériel.

Procopé reacted to this proposal by coming to New York at once. My idea was to ask Mr. Hoover to head a relief operation similar to his Commission for Relief in Belgium. It was clear that the American public would contribute funds to such an enterprise which, while it would not directly help the Finns in a military way, would do so indirectly.

Later that day I sought the advice of an old friend. Ben Cohen was high in the councils of the Administration, an original thinker and one of the most brilliant and self-effacing men I have ever known. He came up with the idea that a corporation might be formed which could borrow money from the Export-Import Bank or from the Reconstruction Finance Corporation, provided that the sympathy of the RFC Chairman, Jesse Jones, could be enlisted. The agency had been created by President Hoover during the world-wide depression and had been continued by his successor. Funds so borrowed by the Finns, Ben thought, could be used to purchase defense items.

When Procopé reached New York that night, both plans were outlined to him and he accepted them with alacrity. Reaching Mr. Hoover at his home in Palo Alto, California, I asked whether he would be willing to serve as chairman of a relief fund for the Finns. If he would, a number of our former associates could come together and incorporate such an organization in the pattern he had set in the case of Belgium. Mr. Hoover that very morning had issued a statement about Finland and had been thinking along similar lines. He authorized me to proceed, and the following day, December 4, calling in another old friend, Donald C. Swatland of the Cravath law firm, I asked him to take the necessary steps to incorporate the "Finnish Relief Fund" and the "Finnish-American Trading Corporation." Both organizations were promptly established.

Mr. Hoover, who was en route by automobile that morning from Palo Alto to Pasadena, stopped at a filling station and telephoned to make two suggestions. They were typically original. The first was that an approach should be made at once through the clearinghouses to national banks all over the United States, to ask them to receive and hold contributions for the Finnish Relief Fund and to make no charge for doing so. The second suggestion was that we should ask the newspapers of the United States to carry our appeal for funds and to receive and transmit gifts to the national banks. This was quickly accomplished through the co-operation of the banks and of the Associated Press and the United Press.

Within forty-eight hours of filing the applications for charters, Ambassador Procopé and Count Folke Bernadotte came to New York for the first meeting of the officers of the Finnish Relief Fund. We had already begun the campaign for funds and more than a thousand newspapers had agreed to receive contributions. James P. Selvage volunteered to direct public relations, and the late John Jay Hopkins gave his full time to the management. (A successful organizer, he later put together the General Dynamics Corporation.) Mr. Hoover was chairman; Edgar Rickard, president; myself vice-president; and the directors included Sidney A. Mitchell, Edwin P. Shattuck, John L. Simpson, Perrin Galpin, Clare Torrey, and Holger Sumelius. With the exception of the last, all were old Hoover men.

Mr. Hoover had dropped all other matters and went about the country speaking for the fund. There were the usual meetings, radio programs, benefits, and other paraphernalia of fund-raising. In this case, however, a new phenomenon was in evidence—for the first time in the United States, strong opposition to a philanthropic activity. Communist demonstrators tried to break up Relief Fund meetings and heckled speakers. When on one such occasion Mr. Hoover reminded the hecklers that he and the same group now working with him had organized relief for Russia during the great famine of 1920–23, they hooted.

Nevertheless, the drive raised what was for those days a considerable sum. It was conducted actively by volunteers and the proceeds were expended for food, medical supplies, and transportation without deductions for expenses.

While I had pursued the course prompted by my sentiments and instincts, I was aware that the activity of a private citizen in such circumstances must not embarrass our government.

When Ambassador Procopé urged me to advise on the contracts which his military attachés were making with American manufacturers, I communicated with the State Department in order to be sure that what was requested was compatible with our national objectives. A letter to

George S. Messersmith, Assistant Secretary of State, outlined the situation. Two days later Secretary Messersmith replied that he had discussed my letter in the department:

> It is my opinion that in writing me as you have, you have performed the only act which is necessary, so far as this Government is concerned, in connection with this service which you are performing for . . . the Finnish Government.

The military aspect of our assistance of Finland was insulated from the relief operations. Mr. Swatland had drawn up papers for the Finnish-American Trading Corporation. I enlisted Dr. Julius Klein to head this. He once had served as chief of the Bureau of Foreign and Domestic Commerce and, with Julien Saks, had been successful as a partner in their firm of industrial engineers. My partners at Kuhn, Loeb & Co. contributed offices in our building, and these were quickly staffed. Eric Warburg, an able young scion of the old Hamburg banking firm, who had friends in Finland, abandoned his business and gave his full time to this operation. The Government lending agencies were duly approached. Warren Pierson, of the Export-Import Bank, and Jesse Jones promptly agreed to lend funds to the corporation. These were used to finance the purchase of fighter planes and other equipment. Quickly shipped, they were soon in action in defense of Finland.

There were contributions from foreigners as well as Americans. Dr. Niels Bohr, the great Danish physicist, had already given the gold medal received with his Nobel prize to be sold for the relief of Finnish refugees in Denmark. He now wrote from Copenhagen to say that he wanted to contribute to the fund which he had learned we were raising. The Franklin Institute had just announced the award to him of its gold medal, and Bohr said that if they would not object he would like to contribute that medal to the fund for whatever intrinsic value it might have.

He concluded his generous message by noting that, "in Denmark, Franklin is the symbol of liberty. It would make me extremely happy if my modest contribution can be of any help in your endeavors. I need hardly add that everyone in this country is ready in any possible way to assist, in particular in offering hospitality to Finnish women and children, a large number of whom have already arrived here." Morris Wolf, a distinguished member of the Philadelphia bar, made appropriate soundings and sent word that the institute would not take Dr.

Bohr's gesture amiss, but, unfortunately, the medal had already been sent to Copenhagen.

Weeks passed, and one morning the Danish Ambassador, Henrik de Kauffmann, his faced lined with worry over the fate of his country, showed up at my office in New York. He brought a letter and a parcel from Dr. Bohr which had been long en route. The parcel contained the Franklin Institute Gold Medal. The Finns, however, had concluded an armistice with the Russians, and even as the Ambassador and I talked, the tanks of the German Wehrmacht were rolling through the pleasant country lanes of Denmark and the streets of Copenhagen.*

Since it would have been folly to send the medal back to Bohr, it was placed in my dispatch box with a note to the effect that it was Bohr's property and, if found by my executors, should be returned to Bohr or his heirs. Years later, the war over, Bohr came to New York to a lunch which I arranged for him to meet Mr. Hoover and Mr. Baruch. Both of the latter had suffered some dimunition of hearing and both used hearing aids. Bohr habitually speaks in tones so low that a man with acute hearing is hard put to follow him. The resulting meeting was not a triumph of communication, though the three men expressed genuine pleasure with the experience. After lunch, Dr. Bohr came to my office and retrieved his gold medal in its leather box, leaving in a taxi bound for the station and his train to Washington.

An hour later, the taxi driver was at the door. He did not know my name, but had been able to describe my *necktie* to the elevator starter in the building. He was bearing a pipe, a tobacco pouch, and the leather box containing the gold medal. Dr. Bohr evidently had been thinking of something more important and had left these items in his cab. I have been necktie-conscious ever since. The medal was later put into the hands of Dr. Bohr's son and is safe at Carlsburg.

During the time we were raising funds privately, Finland also applied for direct loans from the United States. But it was not until late March 1940, following Hoover's vigorous representations with his friends in the Congress, that a loan of twenty million dollars was finally voted. Mr. Hoover wrote to Holsti on March 19, "Lewis Strauss has forwarded to me your letter of March 7th. I have steadily been advocating

* The King and the people of Denmark were outstandingly represented in Washington during the war and for years afterward by Ambassador de Kauffmann. The Danes sheltered many refugees from Hitler's tyranny and saved the lives of thousands. It was not long after the incident that Niels Bohr himself was forced to flee for his life and with the help of friends escaped to Sweden.

more help to Finland. It was my hope that the British having somewhat relaxed the blockade on your country, there should be a loan from our Government to Finland. We sought that it should be taken up in the United States Senate and yesterday the loan was granted. I think it probably covers the food question for the present. What may arise later on no one of us can tell."

It is idle to speculate on what the results might have been had vigorous measures been undertaken by the Administration at an earlier date. Too much time had been lost. The flower of the Finnish Army had been sacrificed in the early weeks of the war. On March 12, 1940, the Finns had asked for terms of peace. These were severe—a large part of their best land had to be ceded to Russia, and, in consequence, half a million people were dispossessed of their homes. Thereafter, the attention of the world was focused on the Low Countries, into which Hitler's armies were pouring. The war that had been called "phony" had become very real indeed.

IV

Twentieth-Century Anabasis

They could not sleep for sorrow, longing for home and parents, for wives and children, which they never expected to see again.

XENOPHON

In the year 401 B.C., ten thousand Greek survivors of an ill-fated expedition into Asia Minor, their leader slain, began a long retreat through wild and hostile country to find a way back to their beloved Hellas. The direct route was blocked by the victorious armies of Artaxerxes, and their alternate course lay over snow-covered mountain passes and barren deserts. In their extremity, they elected as their leader a young knight who had joined the expedition more as reporter than as soldier. He wrote an account of their hardships and the return which became a classic. A twentieth-century parallel of that epic "long march up country" did not have the benefit of a Xenophon.

In the early months of World War I, the Russian armies sliced into the Austro-Hungarian forces. Many prisoners were taken and, though no reliable figures are available, the numbers were in the scores of thousands. The troops of Emperor Franz Joseph were not professional soldiers for the most part, but citizens who had been called to the colors during the mobilization which followed the assassination at Sarajevo. These troops—shopkeepers, artisans, and farmers—had no heart for a war in which the chestnuts to be pulled from the fire by the Hapsburg armies were so obviously intended for the appetite of the Hohenzollern Emperor. They surrendered individually and in groups and were herded to the rear by the armies of the Czar.

Large prison camps were established for them in Siberia, where a minimum of guarding was necessary. The Ural Mountains and the battle front lay between the prisoners and their homeland if any should escape and attempt to go westward. It was unthinkable to go east, for eastward lay the uncounted miles of steppe and tundra, an area uninhabited and forbidding, its farthest margin washed by the Pacific, a strange ocean thousands of miles from the Danube.

The amenities of model prison camps were lacking—no Red Cross parcels, no letters from home—resulting not so much from cruelty as from lack of organization, which, by 1917 when the revolution toppled the Romanoffs, became total disorganization. At the news from Moscow, Petrograd, and Odessa, the camp guards piled into their lorries and drove away. The prisoners were confined thereafter only by the barriers of geography. The gates of the prison camps were wide open.

Thousands streamed out and headed home in bands of from a few to some hundreds. Those who survived the snows of the Urals and starvation were obliterated in crossing the front, which was then miles in depth, with every man's hand against these bedraggled strangers. They disappeared into the vastness of Russia, just as had the stragglers of Napoleon's legions a hundred years before.

Back at the camps, a wiser few took more deliberate council. The perils of the longer route were obvious, but if they remained together and were fortunate, there was at least a map to eventual safety—the tracks of the Trans-Siberian Railroad. This single-track line stretched eastward across the wastelands, boring into the rising sun, finally branching to reach termini at Harbin and Vladivostock. If they could walk the crossties and live on the country, they might survive to see their homes and loved ones once more.

Some twenty-five thousand set out on this march. Fewer than half lived to complete it. The bodies of the rest lay scattered along the route, their enemies not man but ice, wolves, and starvation. By comparison with this journey, the last hundreds of miles of it barefooted, the long march of Xenophon's companions could have made no greater demand on stamina and fortitude.

Singly and in small groups, the vanguard began to stagger into the outskirts of Vladivostok and of Harbin, Manchuria. As the number of emaciated scarecrows increased, ragged, frostbitten, lame, and diseased by nutritional deficiencies, the people of the two cities barred them entry. They were provided with shacks and stockades in the outskirts, less from humanity than from fear of them. But these men, though desperate, had but one desire—to return to wives and children from whom they had been cut off for six years.

By 1920 their numbers had been reduced by death to about eight thousand. Dr. Fridtjof Nansen, following his introduction to relief operations after World War I, had been given responsibility by the League of Nations for the repatriation of all prisoners of war, but the responsibility had not been matched by money. He had no funds to transport over so great a distance these miserable Austrians and Hungarians marooned in Siberia. The Austrian government was too poverty-stricken to help, and the Hungarian government, though in little better case, had passed through the bloody Communist regime of Béla Kun and was indulging in a "regency" under Admiral Horthy, spending every spare krone on a gold-braided and futile military establishment. An indifferent or uninformed world ignored the plight of the eight thousand prisoners.

Early in 1920 I had met a young Tennesseean, George A. Sloan, then assistant to Dr. Frederick P. Keppel, vice-chairman of the American Red Cross. Sloan was the heir to a prosperous mercantile business, but had left home imbued with an ambition to serve his fellow men, an objective from which he never deviated during his life. (In later years his ability resulted in his election to directorships of great corporations, but to the untimely end of a useful life, he was happiest when engaged in some project for the general good.)

The plight of the prisoners in Siberia offered such a project. One afternoon in 1920 George accompanied me to an afternoon meeting with Alan Fox, Royal Victor, Joe Cotton and others working to obtain a voice in the Republican convention to nominate Herbert Hoover for President. When the meeting was over, George and I went to dinner and the subject of the prisoners in Siberia came up, as I had received a letter from Nansen deploring the fact that he could do nothing for them. Then and there we brashly decided that, since no one else was doing anything to repatriate these unfortunate men, we would try to take on the task.

Though we had no personal fortunes, and neither authority nor responsibility, the decision never struck us as unreasonable. We figured that George had some influence with the American Red Cross and that I might have some with the American Jewish Joint Distribution Committee, of which I was a director and Felix Warburg was chairman.

Both Warburg and Keppel gave our project their blessing, and, what was more substantial, each organization agreed to contribute some money. But the aggregate thus committed was far short of what George and I estimated would be required. We set about organizing an "American United Effort for the Repatriation of War Prisoners from Siberia" and raising the funds for it. The first meeting took place in April 1920, and the means proved hard to get. On an inspiration, we approached a Hungarian countess who had been born a Vanderbilt. She proved to be our most generous single contributor.

Only the fact that, besides having money, we were also able to enlist the services of two quite extraordinary men made the enterprise successful. Indeed, in all the undertakings with which I have ever been connected, I have never encountered two more unusual people. One of them, Daniel O'Connell Lively, was a Texan who had been a farmer, cowboy, reporter, editor, and successful oil operator. In middle life, financial success palled on him and he made a decision to devote his life to helping others live theirs more happily. Later in his career, and until his death in 1933, he was national director of China Famine Relief and of Flood Relief in China, but in 1920, fortunately, he was on a business trip in Harbin, and that was where we signed him up.

The other man was Captain Robert Rosenbluth, a tough, resourceful Army officer. These two men chartered ships for us at a fraction of the cost we had any right to expect. They fitted out the ships with racks of bunks to carry the maximum number of men; found supplies and provisions in unlikely places and at bargain prices; supervised the loading and clearing, and worked for nothing but bare expenses.

The dollars Sloan and I succeeded in raising in the midst of the 1920 depression would have been quickly exhausted but for Lively and Rosenbluth. They made the cashbox as miraculous as the "widow's cruse." As a matter of fact, when we had finished, a surplus of a few hundred dollars was left with which the accounting of the enterprise was paid. Samuel Welldon of the First National Bank of New York, acted as our treasurer, and his institution accepted no compensation. Aside from the accounting, there was not a penny of overhead of any kind in the enterprise.

The names of the decrepit steamers that we chartered for the operation—*Scharnhorst, Meinam, Stiegerwald, Frankfurt,* and *Pierre Benoit* —linger in memory, as well as how we prayed that they would stay afloat from Vladivostok through the Indian Ocean, the Red Sea, the Suez Canal, and the Mediterranean. At about that time, I was reading Joseph Conrad and suffered from troubled dreams of leaky ships, overcrowded with men and foundering in tropic seas. The five ships were far from being passenger liners, but rusted, slow, aged vessels better suited to be scrapped than to carry human cargo. So close was the space tolerance on these vessels as they were loaded that there was no room for baggage, and each man was allowed only a small sack of personal belongings. When the first ship left, numbers of stowaways were found aboard, since it was believed that there would be no second sailing and that this was the last chance to get home.

"One man," Lively wrote me, "came up the gangplank with an extra large sack over his shoulders. When he was told that it was too big, he mournfully said, 'Captain, all I have in the world is in that bundle.' He was so convincing and sorrowful that he was allowed aboard with it. After the ship had weighed anchor, we learned that the bundle contained his buddy, another prisoner, all trussed up like a chicken so that he could be carried aboard in the sack."

When the first contingent of men which had been embarked by Lively and Rosenbluth reached Budapest on November 18, 1920, an enormous celebration was staged. The repatriates were lined up behind a military cordon, their arms filled with flowers. Their wives and children, faint with eagerness, were held back behind a barrier and there, for two hours, they were compelled to listen to orations delivered from a velvet- and gold-draped rostrum by Nicholas de Horthy, Archduke Joseph, and other notables. They told their truly captive audience how grateful they should be that the patriotic speakers had preserved their fatherland and had brought them back to it. The Hungarian Government had done precisely nothing, financial or otherwise, to bring about their home-coming, nor did it ever acknowledge by word or letter what had been done. The final tally was 7296 men brought home.

I never saw Lively after the repatriation was completed, although he survived it about a dozen years, all of them filled with relief tasks of various sorts. When he died, we learned that he had willed his body to science and, after a brief service, it was turned over to the New York Post-Graduate Medical School. He died as he had lived, with the welfare of other people, unknown to him, his chief concern.

Captain Rosenbluth at one point in his career during World War I had been an Army instructor stationed at a military camp in the West. While on a training march, a group of officers were some distance ahead of the column and amusing themselves by "plinking" at tin cans and other chance targets with their service revolvers. One of the officers was killed. The inquest found that his pistol had accidentally discharged and that he had killed himself. His father, however, an army general, was unwilling to accept a coroner's verdict which reflected upon his son's ability to handle firearms. Rosenbluth was accused of murder by an enlisted man who was with the group and who later changed his testimony a number of times. Though eventually cleared, the case dragged out for years and Rosenbluth's career was permanently damaged. I have not heard from him in a long time and do not know whether he is living, but if he is, I hope that he derives the satisfaction to which he is entitled for the important role he played in an enterprise which saved many lives.

I had developed some qualms about the future of the refugees during the operation, and on October 4, 1920, wrote to Dr. Keppel to say that it would be the greatest pity if, after all that these men had endured, they would be impressed into military service directly and sacrificed in one or another of the small wars then being waged. It occurred to me that we might ask Nansen to present the issue to the League of Nations and try to obtain a firm undertaking from the countries concerned that no returned prisoner of war should be liable to compulsory military service for a period of three years from the date of his return. I made it clear to Keppel that, even if we were refused, we would complete the project, but I hoped that we might secure the adherence of the two countries to the proposal. The greater part of the movement was yet to take place and he might make the governments feel that if they refused to give the assurance we might be too discouraged to continue. A cable was drafted for Nansen:

Extremely bitter feeling here among individuals and organizations who have contributed to the fund for Repatriation of Prisoners in Siberia over the now apparent fact that some of these men will be returned to their homes only to be immediately impressed into military service. Collection of further money which absolutely needed for completion of the task almost entirely depends upon settlement of this issue, therefore urge you approach League of Nations to secure quickest possible action on following proposition: That in consideration for work which Siberian War Prisoners Repatriation Fund is doing and because of condition of men being repatriated, each country shall undertake to exempt from any call for military duty during a period of three years from date of repatriation each prisoner so repatriated. We cannot too strongly emphasize necessity for making this representation promptly and in as strong terms as possible and feel that each country for moral effect of recovering its Nationals will be quick to accede this agreement as otherwise we will feel obliged to give preference to the Nationals of those countries which do so. Please take action and advise.

The proposal never reached the agenda of the League of Nations. Almost surely, some of the returned prisoners were young enough to have been swept into World War II and, in such event, to have faced the Russian armies once again.

For what would be a salutary effect upon popular sentiment in Austria and Hungary, I also attempted to have the widest publicity in both countries to the fact that the funds to repatriate the exiles had been contributed by American private individuals. However, the entire credit for the operation was arrogated by the then governments of Austria and Hungary, and I failed in this purpose.

V

Decisions about Money

The month was May, in the year 1929, and the partners of Kuhn, Loeb & Co. were gathered for the brief meeting which regularly was held in the first hour of the business day. The great stock-market collapse and the deep depression, only months in the future, were not even discernible as a cloud the size of a man's hand. Admitted to partnership only the preceding year, I held my peace while wiser men spoke. The question before the firm was what should be done about an issue of bonds that were to be offered the next day by the City of New York. The amount was fifty-two million dollars and the coupon rate 5¼ per cent. Ordinarily the rate would be attractive (now it would be considered a fantastically high return for tax-exempt municipal securities), but in May of 1929 the great stock-market boom of the decade was in full career. Prices were rising, optimism was unlimited, and forecasts for uninterrupted growth of the economy were announced by the "experts" and believed, almost as an article of faith, by the great majority of people.

Thousands of men and women in all walks of life were borrowing money to buy stocks and pledging stocks as collateral for their loans. The loans made on the collateral of stocks listed on the great exchanges were generally regarded as sound. The interest rate was adjusted each day, based upon the demand for money and its availability. At about the time of which I write the interest rate for such loans was in excess of 14 per cent. The question before us was whether the firm should continue to lend its capital at the "call rate," as it was known, or invest in the New York City bonds.

In the paneled office in downtown Manhattan where I had come to work for the firm ten years before, Mortimer Schiff, the senior partner and grandson of the founder, an elegant, brilliant, and precise man, was first to speak. He sensed danger in the condition of the stock market, he said, and had come to the conclusion that he would rather forgo the high interest and see more of the firm's capital in safe, fixed-interest-bearing obligations. Otto H. Kahn, the Lorenzo de' Medici of his day, a fresh rosebud in his lapel, and with an air of detachment from anything as plebian as money-making, spoke with a marked German accent but in splendidly chosen words—he commanded an amazing vocabulary—to express confidence in the market for equities and his feeling that New York City would find its bonds hard to sell. Jerome Hanauer, who had been the youngest partner until my admission to the firm, said that he intended to buy the bonds for his own account from whatever firm was lucky enough to be awarded the issue. He stated his reasons with what seemed to me convincing logic.

The other partners concurred, the decision was taken, and we were successful bidders for the issue. As there was somewhat more than enough for the partners' portfolios, I went to see Bertram Cutler, in the office of John D. Rockefeller, Sr., and a part of the issue found a place in Mr. Rockefeller's portfolio. Twenty-one years later I was to become associated with Mr. Cutler again, when I made my office with the Rockefeller family in New York.

With these and other high-grade bonds in their vaults, Kuhn, Loeb & Co. were on high ground when the stock market came apart only six months later. Billions of dollars of market value evaporated into thin air and thousands of men and businesses were ruined. The call-money rate, incidentally, had dropped from 14 per cent to 4.88 per cent by December.

* * *

Ten years before, when I had written to Justice Brandeis from Paris to let him know that I had accepted the offer from Mortimer Schiff to become an employee of Kuhn, Loeb & Co. in New York, the Justice was displeased. He sent word that he had "expected better things" of me and that in his opinion I had taken a wrong turning. "You are sacrificing a promising career in public service," he wrote. "You will no doubt go on to become a member of that firm but no man can go from a partnership in Morgan's or Kuhn, Loeb's to any position of public trust." A few years later, however, Dwight Morrow, a Morgan partner, became a member of the United States Senate and also served as Ambassador to Mexico. The rule could have exceptions.

My decision to join Kuhn, Loeb & Co. had not been hard to reach, for the attraction of an association with a famous banking firm in New York was, if anything, greater in 1919 than it is today. There were then fewer great houses and far fewer partners in those firms. The rewards were large, taxes were low, and the difficulties which brought the Securities and Exchange Commission into existence were not then in the lexicon.

The profession of investment banking in the years before the New Deal was different in a great many respects from the business as it is conducted today. The men engaged in it generally commanded large personal fortunes and many of them lived and conducted themselves like princes. They generally took a personal responsibility for the financial well-being of their clients and were rewarded with the confidence and the loyalty of these clients. There was an unwritten code which respected the banker-client relationship between firms which otherwise competed vigorously for new business. A well-defined seniority order existed for the names of firms on contract and prospectus where securities were issued by more than one banking house. Thus J. P. Morgan & Co. never appeared other than in first position and Kuhn, Loeb & Co. was never second except where the Morgan name was first and then only on the same line to the right. The protocol was as formal as a minuet.

A client, let us say the X Y & Z Railroad Company, represented by its president or financial vice-president, would call at the office of its bankers with the information that the acquisition of an amount of rolling stock or the construction of a new line or the purchase of the shares of another company was under consideration and that a certain number of millions of dollars would be required for the purpose. The bankers would offer their appraisal of the market, its receptivity to an issue of bonds of a certain maturity with a certain coupon rate and to be sold at a premium or a discount, as the case might be, to yield a desired return. Other features such as callability, sinking funds, etc., might be suggested. The client railroad, through long familiarity with the bankers and relying upon their acquaintance with the money market and their judgment, would then indicate whether or not the cost was satisfactory. There was no haggling. An agreement having been reached, counsel were called in, a mortgage prepared, and not infrequently an issue of securities was made within a matter of a day or two. The bankers underwrote (i.e., guaranteed) the public acceptance of the issue and in the event of their misjudgment purchased any securities which were unsold. In exchange for this reliance upon their judgment the banking houses as a matter of course would provide their clients with funds when they were needed in times when market conditions made securities unsalable. For this purpose, firms utilized their capital and not infrequently their credit as well. This aspect of investment banking has almost disappeared with the institution of competitive bidding for railroad and utility financing, a competition which severed the traditionally close and mutually beneficial relationship between the borrower and the banker.

On arrival in New York in September 1919 following the Peace Conference, I knew only two of the partners of Kuhn, Loeb & Co. and them only slightly. I had become acquainted with one of them, Felix Warburg, in connection with a charitable matter which had brought him to Washington three years previously, and I had met Mortimer Schiff when he had come to Paris during the war representing the American Red Cross. That chance meeting had resulted in his offer. The other three partners of the firm—there were but five—were Jacob H. Schiff, the senior partner, who had been only a revered name to me and who died in 1920; Otto H. Kahn, known to me only as a patron of the arts; and Jerome J. Hanauer I did not know at all.

The leading and legendary figure in the American banking community in those days was J. Pierpont Morgan. He had visited my home town of Richmond, Virginia, many years before to attend an annual convention of the laymen of his church. For that brief visit, he had taken one of the stately houses of the city, staffed it, brought down his own transportation—a barouche and horses, complete with top-hatted coachman and footman on the box. I remember standing goggle-eyed with a crowd of other small boys along the curb across Franklin Street to see the great man arrive and depart, with the footman hopping down to open the carriage door for him and unfold the little iron steps. Years later, as the very junior representative of Kuhn, Loeb & Co., I was to see him again on a number of occasions before his death, and I recall his courtesy and unpatronizing consideration of a young person who was very unsure of himself.

The only other early contact with the rich and mighty was on an occasion when traveling south with Mr. Hoover during World War I. Looking through the train for an empty compartment where I could type, I intruded on a man who was sitting bundled up in an over coat, wearing a golf cap and dark glasses. The only other occupants of the drawing room were two elderly ladies. He was easily recognizable as John D. Rockefeller, Sr. Use of private railroad cars had been forbidden by the railroad administrator, William McAdoo, and Mr. Rockefeller had simply taken all the compartments on a car. I don't know who was more surprised at the invasion. He graciously allowed me the use of a drawing room until we reached Richmond. I never saw him again.

Kuhn, Loeb & Co., as I have indicated, was second in standing and perhaps in resources to J. P. Morgan & Co., although no one in our organization would have conceded either differential. The offices of our firm were in its own building at the intersection of William and Pine, and the firm's letterheads immodestly bore no name or other identification than the words "William and Pine Streets." In those days every letter was signed either by a partner or by an employee who held a power of attorney. Before the letters were dispatched, they were placed between the blank tissue pages of a copybook next to a dampened square of cloth. The book was then squeezed in a "letter press" and by this means the text was reproduced on the tissue and a permanent record in time and place was thus kept of each signed letter. A result of this practice was that the outgoing mail was generally a watery affair, looking as though it had been retrieved by deep-sea divers from a shipwreck. The firm rather prided itself on this and other archaic business procedures, and I reflected that each of them must at some time in the distant past have been a revolutionary innovation.

For more than twenty years from September 1919 until I was called to active duty as a Naval Reservist in March 1941, I was with the firm. In 1922 the partners gave me a joint power of attorney, which authorized me—together with another—to obligate the firm's name and credit and entitled me to a microscopic participation in profits, a *tantième*, as it was called. I still remember the sense of euphoria it gave me. The event occurred just as I was about to write a letter of resignation because I was sure that I had not been pulling my weight in the boat.

The years that closely followed were without disappointment. I found my wife in 1923, and was admitted to full partnership in the firm in 1929.

In the interval I visited Japan and other countries, representing the firm. Kuhn, Loeb & Co. had financed the Japanese Government during the Russo-Japanese War, and a friendly tie bound the Japanese Government and the firm. No Japanese official of any consequence came to New York without taking the long ride to Salem Fields Cemetery, to make a respectful and ceremonial bow at the grave of Jacob Schiff. Mr. Schiff had visited Japan after the Treaty of Portsmouth, which ended the Russo-Japanese War, and my visit in 1926 was the first that had been made by anyone connected with the firm in the score of years which had elapsed. In consequence, my wife and I received a princely welcome and were entertained by the Prime Minister, Baron Wakatsuki, and other officials. The present Emperor was then Regent for his father, who was in poor health, and I had an audience with him at which the interpreter was a young naval officer, Commander Isoroku Yamamoto, who fifteen years later, as admiral in command of the Japanese forces, ordered the attack on Pearl Harbor.

The audience with the Prince Regent was conducted with great formality, the expected things being said by both parties. I remember the occasion chiefly because of an incident which preceded it. A few days earlier my wife and I were on our way to Kyoto by rail, and, the ride being hot and dusty, I had asked the car porter for a bottle of Tan San. This was a brand of mineral water we had used in Tokyo and which was not carbonated. The porter gave me the bottle unopened, so I pulled the cap off. Alas, there are two kinds of Tan San, one of them very much carbonated and this was it. The contents of the bottle blew out, and across the aisle, where sat an elderly and very dignified gentleman, richly dressed in Japanese style. The unexpected shower drenched him. Two young men who were his aides or servants descended on me, awaiting only his gesture to give me my just deserts for this impiety. I explained in the best English, French, and German at my command that I was humiliated by what had happened and that it was all an accident. I did not appear to register in any language. The old gentleman disdained to notice me and said nothing.

Ten days later at the Imperial Palace in Tokyo, I entered an anteroom with Commander Yamamoto. A group of Japanese gentlemen in frock coats and striped trousers—Japanese court dress—were gathered at one end of the room. "Would you like to meet the Emperor's Privy Council?" asked Yamamoto. "They have an appointment with the Regent after yours." As we came up to the group, one stepped forward and shook my hand. "I'm glad to see you again," he said in impeccable English, and, seeing by my expression that I was at a loss to identify him, he added, "I am Baron Iwasaki. You gave me a shower bath on the train last week. Sorry I didn't know who you were."

The twenty-seven years with Kuhn, Loeb & Co. were fortunate ones for me, as I came under tutelage of men who were among the wisest and most respected financial experts of their day. Jacob Schiff, a founding partner, whose name was known and honored around the world, had passed the peak of his business activity and was primarily interested in his many philanthropies. He died after I had been with the firm a year and a day. I have mentioned Otto H. Kahn. He was a character of fable. In the public mind his sponsorship of the Muses overshadowed his reputation as a banker, but he was a wise and experienced financier. Working with him, I helped reorganize the Denver, Rio Grande and Western and other railroads. As soon as he had taught me the ropes, he was content to delegate the details. He would have been a success as a corporation executive.

With Felix Warburg, a partner who was the son-in-law of Jacob Schiff, I enjoyed a close working relationship, but almost wholly in the field of philanthropy. Mr. Warburg was a man of cultivated taste in music and the graphic arts. Generously, and frequently anonymously, he supported individual talent, and gave large sums and most of his time to charities.

Shortly before I joined the firm, his brother, Paul M. Warburg had resigned. He had been made a governor of the first Federal Reserve Board and had written the fundamental charter for that institution. It was, in fact, basically his idea. I had the good luck to come to know him well and believed that he had the most lucid grasp of finance, as applied to the affairs of governments, of anyone I have ever met. It was more than the possession of a disciplined mind, for he combined a European banking training with extraordinary imagination.

Hardest working of the partners was Jerome J. Hanauer. Unrelated to either of the founding families, he had reached partnership without benefit of nepotism. I worked as his assistant in the reorganization of the Chicago, Milwaukee and St. Paul Railroad and other carriers, and soon learned why he was regarded as the most knowledgeable authority of his day in the field of railroad finance. Railroad presidents, bond-holders, and insurance companies regularly sought his advice and all received it, impartially. Of all the financiers I have ever known he is the only one who was never wrong on any business question where he was willing to state a judgment. It was his, the boss's, daughter whom I married. All my experience in salesmanship barely sufficed to effect this decision on her part.

My early experience in the banking business had been reasonably successful, thanks to friends. Not long after I had begun work, friends in Richmond came to me with the problem of building and financing a new Union Station in that city. I have always taken a paternal pride in that structure, which, to me, still looks monumental as well as functional. Another friend, Robert A. Taft, directed the financing of the Cincinnati Union Terminal my way. I came to know Leopold and Philip

1. "All men are equal before fishes," said former President Herbert Hoover, who also liked to quote a Babylonian inscription: "The Gods do not deduct from man's allotted span the hours spent in fishing."

The UNITED STATES of AMERICA

UNITED STATES
FOOD ADMINISTRATION

TO ALL TO WHOM THESE PRESENTS SHALL COME, GREETING:

The bearer hereof——— LEWIS L. STRAUSS, Private Secretary to Director General of European Relief Administration and United States Food Administrator,

a citizen of the United States, whose photograph is affixed hereto, is traveling in behalf of the United States Food Administration for the sole purpose of food relief.

I therefore request that he be permitted to pass freely, with all property under his control, and that there be extended to him all friendly aid, protection and information which may forward the purposes of his Mission.

IN TESTIMONY WHEREOF, I, Herbert Hoover, United States Food Administrator, have hereunto set my hand this twenty-eighth ———

day of——— January ———, 191 9.

Herbert Hoover

Lewis L. Strauss
Signature of Bearer

United States
Food Administration

2. Before transatlantic flying it was impossible to secure passports from Washington in time to equip the large number of Army and Navy officers recruited into the Hoover organization in 1918–19. Knowing that European bureaucracy was conditioned to respect documents accompanied by seals, photographs, and formal language, the relief group improvised its own passports. The "Nansen Passport" was natural heir to this successful system.

Dr. The United States ... in ac

1775		Penns.a			Lawful		
July	To amount bro.t forward	£ 466. 2. 10					
No 7	To Sundry Sums paid by my self in the aforesaid Journey – amount g. to				34	8	3
no 8 5	To N. Sparhawks acc.t				2	8	
" 9	To Sam.l Griffin Esq.r	1. 15. 4					
" 10	To the Expences of myself & party reconnoit.g the Sea Coast East of Boston Harbor				18	13	2
11 15	To 333⅓ Dollars given to ———— * to induce him to go into the Town of Boston; to establish a secret Correspondence for the purpose of conveying intelligence of the Enemys movements & designs				100	—	
12	To Cash paid for cleaning the House which was provided for my Quarters & w.ch had been occupied by the Marblehead Regm.				2	10	9
13 19	To Ditto to M.r Eben.r Austin the Steward for House hold Expences †				10	—	
14 24	To Ditto – paid a French Cook				2	5	—
15	To Ditto – paid M.r Austin for Household Expence				2		
	Am. carr.d forw.d – £	467. 18. 2		£	172	5	2

* The names of Persons
who are employ.d within
the Enemys Lines, or who
may fall within their
power cannot be inserted

3. A page from General Washington's account of expenses during the Revolutionary War. Dated July 15, 1775, the entry shows $100 paid to secret agents for security information.

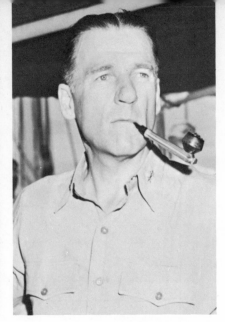

Blackstone-Shelburne, N. Y.

4. "I am convinced there is but one way permanently to settle this [refugee] question..." wrote Bernard M. Baruch, who in 1939 was prepared to tithe himself in connection with a plan discussed in London shortly before the outbreak of World War II.

6. A confessed "battleship admiral," William Henry Purnell Blandy was restive when desk-bound. Later he led a successful task force against the Japanese and commanded at Operation Crossroads, the first atomic tests at Bikini Atoll, in 1946.

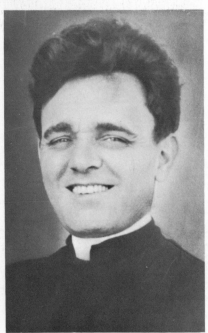

Anne Donahue Studio

5. Rev. James Drought, S.J., Vicar General of the Maryknoll Fathers at about the time of his trip to Japan in 1941. His purpose, to prevent a war, very nearly succeeded.

7. Fleet Admiral Ernest J. King, the Navy's tough and effective commanding officer from the dark hours following Pearl Harbor to the final victory. Caring nothing for popularity, he had but one objective: to win the war.

Block of Chicago, Ernest Weir of Pittsburgh, George Humphrey, George Fink, Tom Girdler, Frank Purnell, and other powerful figures in the world of steelmaking. Eventually, I handled the banking for their companies, Inland, National, Great Lakes, Youngstown, Republic, and other steel companies. At one point, all but two of the large independent steel manufacturers were my clients.

I recall, with some vestiges of the apprehension of long ago, negotiating the purchase of seventy-five million dollars of bonds from the Youngstown Sheet and Tube Company. At that time it was the largest issue ever made by an independent steel producer. There was a question of whether we should take the commitment and carry it over a weekend, thus incurring the risk of some unforeseen international incident adversely affecting the money market in the interval. Although I was not then a partner, the decision had been left to me, and I signed the contract on a Friday, intending the bonds to be offered for sale on the succeeding Monday. After I had committed the firm, I repented my boldness in risking millions which were not mine, and I spent a lost weekend, relieved only by aspirin tablets. Happily, there was no crisis, international or domestic, and the issue was an outstanding success. I walked on air, and still keep the canceled check of that transaction as a paperweight.

In the early thirties, Henry Ford, founder of the Ford Motor Company, decided to sell an affiliate, the Universal Credit Corporation, and to get out of the business of financing the retail sales of his automobiles. I negotiated the transaction by which that enterprise was bought from Mr. Ford through the intermediation of Ernest Kanzler. The purchaser was the Commercial Investment Trust, and the price made Mr. Ford happy and yielded a large profit to the purchasers and to my firm. Henry Ittleson, who was then living and who had founded the Commercial Investment Trust, asked me to obtain an assurance from Mr. Ford in writing to the effect that he would continue to direct his business to the organization which he had sold and that he would not start a competing business. Mr. Ford declined to put such a commitment in written form, but pledged his word. I assured Mr. Ittleson that he might rely upon that statement.

The aggregate of public and private financing in which I was involved totals many hundreds of millions of dollars and included adventurous projects such as building a steel plant near Detroit on an area where literally an entire forest of piling had to be sunk in order to make a foundation for the mills; the laying of a new transatlantic cable on a new course; financing the ideas of inventors; and other enterprises that were off the beaten course of banking. But most of the banking was standard procedure, which is to say, in simplest form, the issuance of bonds secured by fixed assets such as plants, railroads, rolling stock, or other property on behalf of companies with a record of earnings adequate to provide the interest on the bonds and repayment of principal.

What stand out in my memory are not so much the successful transactions as those which did not come off well or which failed to materialize at all, by reason of a financial decision. The banking business was not without its romantic hazards and these were sometimes odd. One of the strangest of these concerned an international swindler.

* * *

At the beginning of the New Year in 1932, my diary entry of January 4 records a visitor, Mr. Edward B. R., who had been a friend since World War I. Edward had been connected with several of the Hoover relief and reconstruction organizations and at one time had represented them in Sweden. Later he had become a member of an investment banking firm in an Eastern city. He came to see me as other friends had done during the depression, friends who had been hurt by the collapse in the stock market, which in 1932 had not yet run its full and disastrous course. I had been able to help him earlier in a very modest way.

On this visit, he began by assuring me that he had not come for "more of the same," but added that he desperately needed a sum in seven figures. "I know that I cannot ask such an amount from you," he continued, "yet if you can help me in a very significant way, I can get the help I need. During the time that I was in Sweden fourteen years ago," he explained, "I made the acquaintance of Ivar Kreuger. I have seen him occasionally since and I am sure that he remains my devoted friend. He disposes of enormous amounts of money and a million dollars from him as a personal accommodation to me would be a drop in the bucket. Now here is where you come in. The one thing Kreuger wants very badly only you can provide. If you do, I feel that I could ask him for help and that he would almost certainly extend it."

What Ivar Kreuger wanted was to be able to meet President Hoover. I replied that such an appointment should be simple for a man of Kreuger's importance and that all he needed to do was to go to the Swedish Ambassador and request an appointment with the President, which I was sure would be accorded when the President's schedule would permit.

"But that is just the point," said my friend. "Kreuger doesn't want to take the Ambassador along, which he would have to do. There must be something on his mind which is too sensitive for the Ambassador to hear." To this I replied that, under the circumstances, there wasn't anything I could do, for protocol was strict. At that a look of such despair settled on the face of my friend that I placed a call to Lawrence Richey, who was the President's confidential secretary. When I told Richey the circumstances, he replied, "For an old friend like Edward I guess we can afford to wink at protocol. Have him come to the East entrance of the White House on the seventh at eleven in the morning, and if he wants privacy, that will avoid the press."

Edward went back to his office and wrote me to say that, "As Kreuger's interests in this country are now very considerable, and as his companies have interests in almost every other country, the recovery in business means a great deal to him. It is on account of this his intimate touch with business in Europe, South America and here, and on account of his important contacts he has developed *certain definite ideas* which he is most anxious to talk to the President about, so I am hopeful that the conference may be helpful and result in good."

The afternoon of the interview it was reported that Kreuger had left the President's office through the Executive Wing of the White House (therefore surely and intentionally meeting the news correspondents) and that, questioned as to what he and the President had discussed, he had replied, "Nothing. I simply came to pay my respects." This, of course, could hardly have been calculated to give any other impression than that he was being secretive about some discussion of transcendent importance.

Puzzled when I read the report, I called Richey, who confirmed that Kreuger had been with the President for less than a minute and had raised no subject at all. It was not until nearly two months later that I recognized this as part of the "act" to add to Kreuger's public image the air of mystery he was at such great pains to cultivate. Some ten days after the appointment, my friend from Philadelphia called on me again. His whole demeanor had changed, and, though I did not inquire, I assumed that his financial pressures had been relieved.

He said he had come because Kreuger was anxious to make my acquaintance, and inquired whether it would interest me to have dinner with him at an apartment which Kreuger maintained in New York. An engagement was made then and there, as I was most curious to see this fabulous character. At the time appointed, I arrived at Kreuger's penthouse apartment at the northeast corner of Seventy-fourth Street and Park Avenue, just three blocks from my house, and a tall blond Scandinavian maidservant who looked like a stand-in for one of the most popular movie stars of the period answered the doorbell. Kreuger addressed her as "Hilda," and I later learned that she was his housekeeper, a Miss Aberg. Kreuger received me in the gallery and I regarded him with curiosity. He resembled his photographs, tall, spare, aquiline, and a little sallow, but it seemed to me that his eyes were unusually closely set, and my first impression was uncomfortable. I have never placed much store, however, on character-reading by the features, and my first uneasy impression soon faded.

As we entered the living room, Kreuger said that he had heard that afternoon from Edward, who had asked him to express his regrets. He had been unavoidably compelled to cancel out. Kreuger added that he hoped that I would not mind if we dined alone. While having cocktails, he showed me the treasures in his living room. There were some items that I shall not soon forget. On the wall on either side of the fireplace hung a Rubens, unusually small for a master who habitually favored canvases of enormous size. The paintings appeared to be on copper panels and were, I judged, about twenty inches square. Even smaller, was a Rembrandt self-portrait on another wall, and on the stand beneath it were six large leather portfolios filled with engravings by the same master. I had become slightly familiar with Rembrandt's engravings as a result of seeing the exceptional collection owned by Felix Warburg. But Kreuger's collection certainly surpassed it in numbers, and he proudly showed me several familiar subjects claiming that he had earliest impressions of every known alteration, or "state," which Rembrandt had made in his plates.

When dinner was announced the dining-room table was set with a handsome service of Jensen silver. I had not previously seen the work of this Danish craftsman, but it was not the last time I was to see these particular objects. With dinner over, Kreuger took me back into the living room and we had coffee before the fire. After a few minutes of silence, while he appeared to be making up his mind how to begin, he said, "Mr. Strauss, I have a confession to make to you. Our friend Edward did not come tonight not because he was ill, but simply because I did not want him here. I wanted to talk to you alone and in confidence." He then told me that he had become apprehensive that his

American bankers (Lee, Higginson & Co.) had allowed their capital to become, as he put it, "so frozen in German credits" that they would be unable to provide the new money requirements for the "Kreuger and Toll Companies" in the months ahead. He explained that he would be needing between a hundred and a hundred and fifty million dollars that year and perhaps twice as much the following year. Then: "Would your firm, Mr. Strauss, be interested in becoming my bankers?"

I replied that there was only one reason why my firm might not be able to act for him. "That," I explained, "is because of a rule we have. We do not invade the business relationships of our friends and we have a long-standing business association with Lee, Higginson & Company." On a personal basis, I added, that one of the Higginson partners, Donald Durant, was an old friend of mine. "Greatly as I should like to do business with you," I continued, "both for the constructive side as well as the profit, these two considerations make it impossible."

"But that is easily taken care of," he said, "for in any case I will want to look out for Lee, Higginson & Co. I want them to have a substantial percentage of any business that you do with me—as much as they can safely handle. You will be glad to have them along and they understand your rule about first appearance. I will have Durant come to see you and assure you that it will be most satisfactory to him and to his partners. But meanwhile and until I have arranged everything you must promise to say nothing about this to him or to anyone." I promised, of course, feeling that the evening could be the beginning of a very rewarding business connection.

He then asked me how much I knew about his companies, to which I recall that I replied, quoting Will Rogers, " 'All I know is just what I read in the papers.' I understand that you have financed the Spanish, Italian, and Turkish governments recently, and perhaps other countries. I would like to know how you do it and as much about you as I can. Your story must be most interesting."

"Yes," he said, "but of course you know that I do not lend to these governments in dollars. You see, in the course of my match monopolies and other businesses, I accumulate very large amounts of the *valuta* of other countries. I was practically compelled to go into the banking business in order to employ these large accumulations of foreign currencies." Then, as though it were an afterthought, he asked, "Do you know much about the Boliden gold mine?" I did not and indeed had never heard the name.

"Well," he said, "it may interest you. Boliden is an area in Sweden which is highly mineralized but it is also overlaid by many hundreds of feet of alluvial deposit. Two young mining engineers, the sons of old classmates of mine at Upsala University, asked me to stake them to make explorations in this area with core drills. As a result of their enterprise and extraordinary good luck, they struck a gold deposit which is the richest in the world. The only drawback is that the ore is very refractory, so much so that we have to send it all the way to the United States, to Seattle, to a plant owned by the Guggenheims to have it refined. They control the only process by which this difficult ore can be handled. But the ore is so rich that it has rewarded us to ship it to Seattle, even paying five dollars a ton for ocean freight. An ore that would even assay as much as five dollars per ton would be rich. I recently arranged to build a smelter at the mine head in Boliden and to pay the Guggenheims fifty cents a ton royalty for the use of their process and thus save shipping costs of four dollars and fifty cents on each ton of ore, which saving is added to the gold value of the ore."

I had never heard of this mine, and the story seemed so unlikely that the next morning I called a good friend, Roger Straus, who was at that time a senior officer of the American Smelting and Refining Company, controlled by the Guggenheim family. I asked Roger whether he had ever heard of the Boliden gold mine, and he said that he knew it well. He then confirmed every detail in the story which Kreuger had told me excepting one fact. I did not mention the source of my information, and, therefore, Roger did not tell me then nor did I discover until long afterwards that Kreuger no more had title to the Boliden gold mine than to the Brooklyn Bridge. It belonged to a Swedish bank.

Besides having imposed a serious hurdle for Kreuger by letting him know that we would not pirate clients from their traditional bankers, I was saved from disaster by one other decision. There was no question of my eagerness to acquire a client whose operations would offer so large an opportunity for financing over the years. Kreuger had mentioned that he expected to need three hundred million in the next five years. That would represent the largest volume of private financing in prospect up to that time and a considerable banking profit in which I would participate. This was still no justification for waiving established standards. In going through the statements Kreuger provided for me over the next several days, I looked in vain for an independent auditor's certification. When I asked Kreuger for it at lunch in my office on March 1, 1932, he laughed and said, "Why, Mr. Strauss, I have my own firm of auditors. There is no accounting firm in New York which has a large enough staff to audit the books of all my companies. I've never employed outside auditors—Lee, Higginson understood that very well—and, as you can see, I do not need them."

I will say for Kreuger that when, after a brief discussion, he saw that there was to be no surrender on this requirement, he never by so much as the flicker of an eyelash indicated that this had pulled the rug from under his hopes of obtaining financing from my firm. He said that he had spoken to Donald Durant, who was relieved and pleased that his firm was not to be dropped as Kreuger's bankers and that they would be associated with my firm. He said that Durant would not come to say this to me, however, until he had informed all of his partners, some of whom were away on winter holiday. Durant later told me that this was wholly false and that Kreuger had never mentioned to him that he was conferring with me.

Kreuger went through all the motions, and an appointment was made for him to meet during the following week with the Paris resident partners of the American accounting firm which was our auditor. He sailed with Mr. Durant on the S.S. *Ile de France* on March 4, and I wrote to Jerome J. Hanauer, who was vacationing in Italy, requesting him to interrupt his holiday and come to Paris to meet Kreuger and Price Waterhouse representatives, our auditors, at a time and place that had been agreed upon.

During this period, as Durant and others subsequently testified, in their meetings with Kreuger he was distraught and beside himself with worry. In his dealings with me Kreuger exhibited no such signs, but conversed in a relaxed manner and produced quantities of detailed statements of assets and liabilities and earnings of his parent company and its subsidiaries. These, to judge from later evidence, had their foundation solely in his imagination. The fact that during these very days Kreuger's creditors were losing confidence in his veracity was a well-guarded secret, while some of them were unloading their match-company stock on the open market. The further fact that a large part of his stated assets, that is to say, the bonds of European governments, were forgeries was not known to his creditors until long afterwards.

The S.S. *Ile de France* with Kreuger aboard reached Le Havre on the morning of March 11, 1932, and within hours he was in Paris. On the twelfth of March, the late-afternoon papers headlined the shocking intelligence that the "Match King" had killed himself in his Paris apartment. In view of the circumstances, his body was cremated with what appears to have been almost unseemly haste. Added to the elements of mystery in connection with Kreuger's demise is the circumstance that he went to Paris at all. I have never seen a reason advanced for this that was wholly satisfactory, nor have I seen it denied that before sailing he drew substantial amounts, in cash, from accounts that were still available to him in New York, amounts so large that, as cash, their actual physical bulk must have posed something of a disposal problem.

A trust company in New Jersey became agent for the disposal of the furnishing of Kreuger's Park Avenue apartment. Impelled by curiosity and accompanied by my friend Lawrence Richey, we attended the auction. There were no portfolios of Rembrandt etchings; there were no paintings by Rubens on copper panels; there was no Rembrandt self-portrait. There were the remembered picture frames, but they enclosed cheap illustrations which appeared as though they had been cut from calendars. Of Kreuger's possessions which I had seen in his apartment, only the Jensen table silver remained. It must have been worth at most a few thousand dollars and was probably too heavy and clumsy to remove. There were many bidders, among them some who had seen their match stock tumble from the heights into the gutter. The competition was keen.

In the aggregate the silver must have brought several times its intrinsic value, and on impulse I bought two silver vases. Occasionally when they are placed on my dinner table I am reminded that, but for a kindly Providence and a decision or two, my firm and I might have been among the unfortunate holders of a very large bag.

Partly because it has always annoyed a number of my friends, among them the lawyers representing some aspect of the Kreuger case, and partly because the fancy intrigues me, I have contended over the years with simulated conviction that Kreuger did not shoot himself on that March day in Paris, but that it was from Paris that this financial fox had planned to go to ground if the hounds ever finally got too close for comfort. At that, I would be the least surprised of men if some enterprising reporter should eventually discover an aging Kreuger sunning himself on some tropical terrace in the kind of company he always found most congenial.

*   *   *

Decisions not to do business can be as important as affirmative conclusions. One in the former category involved a situation in which a leading firm of independent auditors and accountants was hoodwinked.

In 1923, I had purchased a residence on East Seventy-sixth Street in New York. The seller was a Mr. McKesson, of the old and reputable firm of McKesson & Robbins, drug manufacturers. Because of the way the transaction was handled, the name of McKesson became associated in my mind with fair dealing. About 1936 a friend brought to my office F. Donald Coster, who had become chairman of the board and president of McKesson & Robbins. If ever there was a man whose appearance bespoke reliability and respectability it was his. A student of physiognomy who might have faulted Kreuger on his features—his eyes too closely set and his lips too thin—would have been able to detect only stodgy rectitude in the image presented by Coster, with his thinning gray hair, steel-rimmed spectacles, and a well-established paunch. He was the picture of a merchant whose recognized success entitled him to feel at ease in the temples of finance. He relaxed in the chair of my office and stretched out his feet.

Coster told me that he had some financing to negotiate for his company and that he had concluded that his bankers were no longer people he cared to have represent him in the capital market. The interlocutor had been his friend for some years and had told him, he said, that my firm looked after its clients in good times and bad, and *that,* he added, was the kind of banker he wanted. His business was good, he said, and he passed across the desk his latest balance sheets and earning statements, all certified by accountants who were the auditors for my own firm.

I looked at his annual report and noted that one of my friends, a partner in a Wall Street firm, was listed as a director of the drug company, and I remarked on the fact that we could not violate principle by invading the business of a friend. Coster replied that he and the man in question had come to a parting of the ways on policy and that he did not intend to do business with him any longer whether or not he succeeded in interesting us.

When he left the office, I called the friend, who confirmed that McKesson & Robbins was indeed a good company, apparently well run, but there was something about Coster personally he did not like, although he could not put his finger on it specifically. He added that he would not take it amiss if Coster changed his bankers and that the field was open as far as he was concerned. I decided that I was not interested and sent word to Coster by the mutual friend who had brought him in that, in the words attributed to Sam Goldwyn, he should "include me out." This was not an easy decision, but was based upon the feeling that in spite of what had been said we would be interlopers.

This was just a fortunate decision. Shortly there was a sensational revelation. Coster was discovered to be an impostor, a man whose real name was Musica. Over the years, he had systematically robbed Mc-Kesson & Robbins of millions of dollars. He and his family and other confederates had falsified the books and shifted inventories from one warehouse to another so skillfully that the experienced independent auditors had counted the same merchandise more than once, thus certifying to assets that were nonexistent.

My education in the financial decision-making process was advanced during a visit to London. I had visited London in October and November of 1933 and on November 1 had lunch at New Court, the impressive and venerable Rothschild banking establishment. In the high-ceilinged dining room I was seated where I faced a painting showing the original British Rothschild being introduced on the floor of the House of Lords in July 1885 at the time he became Lord Rothschild and a peer of the realm. At the table, with my Rothschild hosts, Anthony and Lionel, were Sir Robert Waley Cohen, Lord Melchett, and other figures who seemed to me to be Victorian or, at the very least, Edwardian. Mr. Lionel, turning, said, "Mr. Strauss, I suppose you know that since you left the United States, your government has been buying gold and this morning your President Roosevelt has set a price of $32.28 per ounce for it. Can you tell us why the President would suddenly jump the price to that particular figure?" To this I replied, "Maybe he just pulled the figure out of a hat." The distinguished gentlemen at the table looked properly shocked, not so much, I gathered, that I should so characterize the judgment of a President of the United States, but that I could be jocular on a matter as important, in those surroundings, as the price of gold bullion.

Many years later, I learned that on October 25, 1933, the then Secretary of the Treasury, Henry Morgenthau, Jr., Dr. George F. Warren, the President's oracle on money matters, and Mr. Jesse Jones, Chairman of the Reconstruction Finance Corporation, held the first of a series of morning meetings with the President for the purpose of setting the price of gold for the day. These meetings were held in the President's bedroom. Mr. Morgenthau records that the President "would lie comfortably on his old-fashioned three-quarter Mahogany bed" and eat his breakfast eggs while engaged on these financial deliberations. On one occasion the President decided that the rise in the price of gold for that morning would be twenty-one cents. "It is a lucky number," the President said with a laugh, "because it is three times seven."[1] Mr.

Morgenthau was a conscientious Secretary of the Treasury and took his responsibilities with unsmiling gravity. Whether or not the President was pulling his leg, it is of record that the price of gold was set by this system. It might as well have been drawn out of a hat, as I had so lightly advised the Rothschilds and their friends.

I have often wished that some of those with whom I had lunched at New Court a quarter of a century ago were alive today in order that I might redeem myself in their opinions for what must have seemed in 1933 an irreverent reflection upon the profound economic scholarship concerned in the decisions on the price set by the United States for gold.

Kuhn, Loeb & Co. occasionally imported gold from England and sold it to the Treasury Department. In the 1930s, when I suspected that its origin, despite the mint stamp, might be from mines expropriated by the Communists, the firm discontinued the practice of importing gold. This was a decision I never regretted.

At some early date after I had begun to work as a banker, I resolved that I would never refuse to listen to anyone needing help who had a proposal which involved a new idea. This decision has afforded me pleasure, considerable profit, occasional small losses, and a number of unusual experiences. Because of a few spectacularly rewarding enterprises, friends have assumed that everything I touched in this area was successful. Of course, that was far from true, and the failures were well interspersed with the successes. One of the former, indeed the first, was the Kowarsky wheel.

Early in 1921, I met two gentlemen by the name of Kowarsky, a father and son. They were refugees but had been prosperous steel manufacturers in Russia under the Czars. The senior Kowarsky was a very distinguished-looking man with a gray beard cut square across the bottom in the fashion popularized by King Leopold of Belgium. Neither Kowarsky spoke English, and their story, as interpreted to me, was to this effect: The elder Kowarsky, on ceding the management of his steel mills to his son, had indulged a flair for invention and his company as a matter of course, but without thinking very highly of his inventive ability had nevertheless patented his ideas in other countries including the United States. Among other things he had invented a method for making steel railroad-car wheels by taking an I-beam, splitting it longitudinally into halves, bending each half around a mandrel, and welding the ends together, thus forming two flanged steel wheels.

When the Bolshevik revolution occurred, the Kowarskys fled before the Communists and settled in Berlin. There they had been approached

by a represenative of an American steel company who offered to purchase the car-wheel patent. The offer was a price in Russian Czarist
rubles, which the steel company needed to dispose of. This seemed to
the Kowarskys a poor transaction, since if the Romanoff ruble were to
be worth anything in the future they might expect by that same event
that their properties would be restored to them. Therefore, they declined the offer and were surprised upon finally emigrating to the
United States to discover that the American steel company had infringed their patent and had built a plant and was making the wheels
by their system. They had visited the company, which denied the infringement but offered them a few thousand dollars for their "nuisance
value."

The story made me indignant. Accordingly I offered to introduce
them to a lawyer so that they could seek the protection of the courts.
They explained that they were destitute and could not afford to retain
counsel, that as a matter of fact they had no money on which to live.
I went to see Joseph P. Cotton, who was then the senior partner of a
leading law firm. I asked him to take the case on a "contingent basis,"
which meant that no fee would be payable unless the case was won, and
he, out of friendship, and sharing my feeling of outrage, broke a rule
of his practice to do so. For the fun of doing it, we organized the
S.P.I.I.—the Society for the Protection of Indigent Inventors.

Cotton thereupon served notice on the corporation that he intended
to bring suit. In order that the plaintiff should be an American, he
had me acquire the patent from the Kowarskys, paying them the same
amount that the steel company had offered them for the "nuisance
value," but the contract stipulated that they would be paid whatever
was recovered above that sum. The steel company asked for time to
reply, this was arranged. The steel company immediately instituted a
painstakingly thorough search of the art and, to our dismay, discovered
that a British ship captain had been inspired by the same idea and had
obtained a patent. This had happened in 1853. The patent, of course,
had long since expired and the whole method was in the public do-
main.

This was very bad news, since it appeared that the Kowarskys really
had nothing now besides nuisance value and I was now out of pocket
the amount I had paid them for their patent. The only thing I could
do was to salvage some of it by writing a story for a magazine, which
I tried to do in a humorous vein.

The president of the steel company learned that this composition was in prospect. With the record clear that his junior officers had decided to disregard the Kowarsky patent when they had failed to buy it, and had deliberately infringed it, the article, however amusing, put his company in a poor light. He felt that it was becoming to make amends. He approached Mr. Cotton with this and negotiated a settlement which took me out whole, provided the Cotton firm with a proper fee and the Kowarskys with something more than their value as nuisances.

A few years later, Colonel Lewis, famous as the inventor of the machine gun, came to me with a project that not only seemed entirely novel but was also covered by patents in good standing. This time it was a method to produce spiral bevel gears for automobiles by an apparatus which, generating great pressure, squeezed a steel die against a hot steel blank, thus impressing the tooth contour of the die into the blank. All spiral bevel gears in those days were made by the time-consuming and expensive process of cutting the teeth into a steel blank. A respectable sum of money was necessary to build the Lewis machine, but there was the prospect that it would hot-roll, in seconds, the complicated spiral bevel gears that ordinarily took hours to cut. The project was examined by an engineering firm of experience and repute. They endorsed it enthusiastically and even asked to share in the financing. So I went ahead with it.

The machine was built and gears were produced, beautiful to look at as they came out like giant beaten biscuits on a bakery production line. But alas, the gears were completely unusable. The engineers had overlooked the simple fact that when the steel cooled there were stresses which were relieved by small malformations in the shape of the teeth. These malformations were only on the order of a few thousandths of an inch, but this was at the time when the style of automobiles changed from open cars to closed bodies and noise in the gearbox caused by imperfect gears reverbrated intolerably within the thin metal walls of these vehicles. The investment was lost. The fruit of this experience was the conclusion that even famous engineers can make mistakes. Fortunately, these early experiences failed to dampen my enthusiasm for new ideas.

Certain aspects of the new ideas which have appealed to me in the past might be described as romantic, but the successful ones have been associated in one way or another with very early interests. An innovation is more immediately appealing when applied to a field with which one has an amateur's familiarity.

As a boy, photography had been a major interest, and I had pursued it as far as the cumbersome color processes of the period. These required multiple exposures on plates sensitive to different colors or exposed through separate filters and their careful superimposition and registration for that use as transparencies. The photographic printing of color commonplace today was simply unknown.

In 1922, Everett Somers, who as an army sergeant had been assigned to our office in France, introduced two young musicians, Leopold Mannes and Leopold Godowsky. They were in their teens when as the result of a mutual interest in photography they conceived a method of making photographs in color with one exposure on a single film or plate using an ordinary camera. The process seemed uncomplicated enough for amateur use. I was persuaded to go to the laboratory of Mannes and Godowsky, which was the kitchen in an apartment, and there with a Brownie box camera I was permitted to photograph some strips of colored crepe paper fastened to the wall with thumbtacks. The plate was then developed, and there, to my astonishment and admiration, the primary colors, though muddy, unquestionably had been reproduced.

Convinced, I arranged for the necessary money to pay for patent applications and attorney fees and to rent and staff a small laboratory. The Eastman Kodak Company co-operated by furnishing required sensitizers, dyes, and other material, but brushed the process itself aside as of no practical interest. Some years later the results were so outstanding that I decided to go over the head of the officers with whom we had been dealing unsuccessfully and traveled to Rochester with Sir William Wiseman, one of my associates, to show examples of the results which had been achieved to George Eastman himself. The upshot of that and subsequent meetings with Mr. Eastman and his director of research, Dr. Kenneth Mees, was an agreement which resulted in marketing the product called Kodachrome. Annually it earns many millions for the Kodak Company and until the patents finally expired in 1952 was highly profitable to the young inventors and to all concerned. Color photography has become part of our daily living, and it is hard to recall that the days of "black and white" were only twenty-five years ago.

Another decision was to back a young inventor, Edwin H. Land, who was introduced to me some twenty years ago by his camp counselor, Julius Silver. Land had made a radical discovery. He had found that he could incorporate certain crystals of microscopic size in a transparent plastic medium and could altar the random arrangement of the crystals so that they were all parallel. One result was that the transparent plastic would then transmit light waves in one plane only. Light so transmitted is "polarized." Light vibrating in any other plane would be blocked in varying degree, and at right angles to the axes of the crystals was shut out almost completely. This property had been observed in nature in a substance, familiar to first-year physics students, as a Nicol prism. Such prisms were not plentiful enough or large enough to be adaptable to Mr. Land's aim, which was to employ the effect for eliminating the hazard of headlight glare in night motoring. He had made enough of his light-polarizing product to demonstrate it convincingly. He called it Polaroid.

The worth of this idea and the true genius of Land impressed me at once, a fact of which I am proud.

After he had been provided with the necessary capital and a company organized, a long period of struggle ensued. The automotive companies resisted the adoption of Polaroid, although they equipped their cars over the years with comical tail fins, useless chromium jewelry, and other nonfunctional impedimenta. There is an intercompany headlight committee in the industry and, of all automotive features, headlights, in consequence, are not competitive among makes of cars. It would appear that this is the primary reason why a system has not been adopted which could have saved the lives of many thousands of persons over the past twenty-five years who have died on the highways at night when drivers have been dazzled by the glare of headlights on approaching vehicles. Thus large application of the principle of polarizing light is still in the future and the existing uses, though smaller in extent, comprise, besides the familiar sunglasses, important components of telescopic, microscopic, photographic, and other scientific instruments in laboratories all over the world.

During World War II, when, at the outset, antiaircraft ammunition was in critically short supply, yet gun crews had to be trained, Land developed a device in which the gunner firing an antiaircraft gun at life-size, three-dimensional motion pictures of planes, heard his gun, felt it vibrate, saw the stream of tracer projectiles leave its muzzle and travel on the way toward the moving targets. Hits and misses were automatically scored, and no ammunition at all was consumed. The effect was achieved by an ingenious application of optical principles.

Land has many inventions to his credit. Quinine, an absolutely essential drug during the war, its molecular structure so complex that it had never been artificially produced, was successfully synthesized in his laboratories. Other useful items, some of them of a classified character, were also conceived and quickly produced by him. He is best known, perhaps for the Polaroid Land Camera, which made the dream of instantaneous finished photographs come true.

There were discoveries and inventions by others which have become a part of daily living and to which I had the excitement of giving a helping hand in the early stages. The general decision to keep an open door and an open mind involves inevitable exposure, and decisions may not be uniformly happy.

In the early 1920s there were still in existence perhaps a dozen of the once very numerous company of American automobile makers. All but a handful of them have long since gone into limbo, and the cars they made are forgotten by all except the older generation and the collectors of highway antiques. One of the most prominent figures of the era was John N. Willys, whose chief product was a popularly priced automobile called the Overland. One morning in early 1922, Mr. Thayer, who was then chairman of the board of the Chase National Bank, invited me to his office. He said that Willys was deeply in debt to merchandise creditors and the banks and that the Chase held the largest block of his notes. Thayer said that Willys' business was so bad and his management so poor that the situation had become critical. The company would have to be reorganized, and Thayer wished to know whether our firm would undertake to draw a plan and be the reorganization managers. I was in my mid twenties and nothing looked impossible. If his bank would pay for an engineering study and report, he would get a prompt answer. Thayer, an experienced banker, said that the *company*—not the bank—would pay for the study.

An engineering firm was retained to make an examination of the company and its prospects. Their report was bleak. At that time the total annual production of automobiles in the United States was about two million cars, and the engineers who wrote the report cautiously observed that it was obvious the country had about reached the saturation point in its ability to absorb new cars. They also pointed to certain practices by Willys which they regarded as extravagant in the highest degree. One of these was the pay scale of his executives. The report cited, as the most horrendous example of this, a vice-president who received a salary of $200,000 a year and who had a ten-year contract.

The upshot of the report was my decision that a reorganization plan would depend upon whether the unsecured creditors would be willing to accept common stock for their notes. While the matter was being debated by a committee of creditors, Willys fired the expensive vice-president, but had to buy his contract with a substantial amount of cash. Very shortly thereafter the sale of automobiles improved with a dramatic upturn in the economy and the year's production for the industry was almost 160 per cent of the previous high mark. The Overland Automobile Company shared in this upturn and was temporarily out of trouble.

The discharged vice-president took his windfall money and bought another and thoroughly defunct automobile business. He immediately launched a new line under his own name with changes so unremarkable that some competitors said that he had only added a radiator cap with rabbit ears. Nevertheless, by superior promotion and with a good product, he shortly moved into the third place in the industry. His name was Walter P. Chrysler. Years later he told me that in procuring the engineering report which had resulted in his discharge by Willys, I had made him rich. That conversation occurred on an occasion when I was soliciting a contribution from him to the campaign fund for Herbert Hoover. He wrote a liberal check.

Early in 1940 I had a business visitor who was a stranger in Wall Street. He was a former United States Senator, Smith W. Brookhart. In addition to other claims to fame, Senator Brookhart was a recognized authority on marksmanship and on small arms, particularly rifles. His experience had begun in the Spanish-American War, and he had later trained riflemen for the Olympic championships. The purpose of his visit had not been announced. He came into the office with an assistant who carried a long case of polished walnut with brass trimmings. Opening it, Brookhart produced a rifle which came apart at his touch and was as quickly reassembled. The Senator explained that the War Department had replaced the obsolete Springfield rifle of World War I with a new arm on which a large amount of money had been spent but few rifles had been delivered. My recollection is that he said fewer than forty thousand. A young officer, he continued, the son of the dean of a leading law school, had invented a completely new rifle, a semiautomatic, for which he claimed immense superiority in every respect— lightness, durability, accuracy, rapidity of fire—and this was the ultimate. Further, it could be manufactured quickly and cheaply.

Senator Brookhart's proposal was that I should join with him and the inventor in the financing and manufacture of the rifle for sale to the United States Government and certain governments in Latin America and China. He told me that the Chairman of the Senate Naval Affairs Committee had a high opinion of the arm and that the

Chairman of the Committee on Military Affairs was so convinced of its merits that he had introduced a bill to adopt the rifle as standard for both services. Senator Brookhart conceded that the military of both services were opposed to it on what he called "purely technical grounds," but he was sure from his senatorial experience that the bill would become law. The profits from the enterprise would run into very large figures.

On May 28, 1940, I wrote to the Senator to say, "I must stand on my statement that I will only be willing to help provided the Government decides to go forward with the project and in that connection I should not personally care to have any interest in any profits. On the other hand, I would not be interested to help with it at all based upon sales to Central American Governments, China or others as referred to by you. I have explained my motives to you sufficiently so that you will understand that the only basis upon which I would be inclined to assist in the production of a piece of armament designed to take human life would be in defense of the United States." The Senator took his rifle elsewhere and I believe was moderately successful in its production.

It was a turn of fate, indeed, that within sixteen years I should be engaged in the manufacture of the most lethal weapon men have ever devised.

* * *

It was a hard personal decision when in 1946, after twenty-five years of association with partners and friends at Kuhn, Loeb & Co., resignation was in order to comply with the law upon accepting appointment to the first Atomic Energy Commission. It is not easy to sever personal ties of long standing and abruptly change the work habits of a quarter of a century. Friends, estimating the simple financial cost of that decision, have occasionally asked whether it is not regretted. I truly believe not. Business was a less demanding and far more agreeable way of life and the material rewards of public service are not comparable, but there is satisfaction of a unique kind in public service if the inevitable disappointments are foreseen and, to lapse into banking parlance, discounted.

VI

De Profundis

ממעמקים קראתיך יי

(Out of the depths I cry unto Thee, O Lord.)
PSALMS CXXX:1

In our own time millions of people have lost their lives as a result of catastrophic earthquakes, tidal waves, and floods, inescapable epidemics and famines. These were indiscriminate disasters in which whole communities frequently suffered a common fate. But our century is stained with a tragedy of a different sort.

Six million human beings, of all ages and conditions, from old people already at the grave's edge down to the youngest and most innocent, were dragged out of their homes and massacred in parts of "civilized" Europe during the years 1933–45 because they were Jews by faith or because they had a Jewish parent or grandparent. These murders, organized in cold blood and accompanied by torture of every description, made unbelievable reading when the reports first began to leak out of Germany.

With the end of the war in 1945, the dimensions of this gigantic tragedy at last became apparent. The German-Jewish industrial and merchant class, the schoolteachers and university professors, the Budapest lawyers, the Viennese physicians were dead. The Jewish poor who lived in the ghettos of Poland and the villages of the Crimea were dead. In many little Polish towns, like Brzeziny, which had been 98 per cent Jewish, no Jew was left alive. Six million Jews—the figure bears repetition because it is such an incomprehensible figure—were dead. They died in the concentration camps, in the camouflaged showers which were gas chambers, in the automobile vans which picked them up in the villages and asphyxiated them with carbon monoxide as they traveled, in the boxcars whose floors were covered with searing quick-lime, and in the bombed cellars and sewers which became their last, desperate refuge.

The years from 1933 to the outbreak of World War II will ever be a nightmare to me, and the puny efforts I made to alleviate the tragedies were utter failures, save in a few individual cases—pitifully few.

For such solace as I can draw from the fact—and it is not much—I did commit myself to the support of a small number of individuals and paid their passage to Palestine or Australia or to the United States, helping them to escape from the doom which befell so very many others. I signed a score or more of affidavits pledging my assets to guarantee that a Mr. A or a Mrs. B would not become a public charge in the United States. None of these people were personally known to me and in no single instance has my pledge ever required fulfillment in the twenty years that have since elapsed. The refugees have made useful lives for themselves. But I might have done so much more than I did. I risked only what I thought I could afford. That was not the test which should have been applied, and it is my eternal regret. Also, I crossed the ocean and negotiated again and again, but to no effect. This is that story.

History will always associate the rise to power of Adolf Hitler with persecution of Jews. They suffered the first onslaught of the Nazi attack on civilized values probably because they represented the ideals which "National Socialism" had to destroy in order to prevail. Also they were conveniently at hand to be robbed and murdered and they were defenseless. Among ignorant or vicious people, there seems to survive, under whatever veneer, some vestige of the calumnies concerning Jews which, since the Dark Ages, have been the penalty of loyalty to their faith.

The German masses did not resist the Nazi anti-Semitic propaganda. With notable exceptions, it was swallowed without question. Jews had lived in Germany for centuries, served her with distinction in war and contributed to her glories in peace—in science, music, literature, and all the arts. But no part of the Jewish role in German life or greatness was remembered when Hitler decided that his road to glory would have to be financed by the property of the Jews and paved, literally, with their corpses.

Almost immediately after Hitler succeeded the senile Von Hindenburg, a program of discriminatory legislative and administrative action was instituted. This proscribed for Jews the right to public service, to practice certain professions, or to enter the universities and higher schools. In practice, the action went much further, for they were also deprived of the protection of life and property by police and the courts. This was followed by the imposition of enormous fines without cause, by boycotts, midnight arrests and deportations, vandalism in cemeteries and defilement in houses of worship, by beatings and personal outrages perpetrated upon the persons of women and children as well as men.

But these early reports were as promptly denied. Karl K. Kitchen, a well-known and "responsible" American journalist, returned from a visit and stated that "Germany is absolutely normal" and that it was "the crassest nonsense to speak of the persecution of Jews in Germany." Other writers were persuaded or deceived to the same effect. But across the borders, at night, terrified people with the few belongings they could carry began to seek refuge in Holland and Denmark and France. They told of a nightmare of horror left behind.

The Poles, whose association with their fellow citizens of Jewish faith also spanned centuries, began to exhibit infection by the virus from Berlin, and gangs of hoodlums modeled on the Nazi pattern terrorized the ghettos in the large Polish industrial centers.

President Hoover was within six weeks of the end of his term when I wrote to him on January 13, 1933, to say:

You may recall that in the Spring of 1919 a series of disorders occurred in Poland during which the population of Jewish Faith suffered seriously at the hands of the military and of organized anti-Semitic groups. There was destruction of property and considerable loss of life. When word of this reached you in Paris you sent word for Mr. Paderewski and made representations to him both orally and by letter as a result of which the Polish Government took energetic measures to suppress the disorders and bring to justice those guilty of inciting them. An era of better feeling resulted which lasted for more than a decade.

In recent months trouble had broken out again. Whether it has come about as a result of the economic hardships of the times or has been deliberately incited I do not know and it is immaterial but the result has been that numbers of innocent people have been harried to death and a reign of fear prevails in a number of communities.

If it would be compatible to include in your remarks to the new Polish Ambassador who will shortly call on you to present his cre-

dentials, some expression of your views and those of several millions
of Americans who hope for internal peace among the racial and religious groups in Poland, it would go far to allay the present troubles
and promote amity.
Should you require information concerning such events as are mentioned I would be glad to furnish it.

Mr. Hoover replied the following day to thank me for the letter and
to say, "I will do what I can." The new Ambassador of Poland called
on the afternoon of January 17, and Mr. Hoover expressed himself on
the subject in strong terms. The fact, however, that he was to be President for only a few more weeks could hardly have been lost on his
diplomatic visitor.

As the news trickled out of Germany, Jews in other countries became
deeply concerned with the predicament of their coreligionists. The Jews
of Germany for several generations had been a prosperous and correspondingly generous community to those less fortunate in other lands.
A number of Jewish communal organizations, therefore, arranged to
meet in London to discuss the plight of these miserable people and to
see what might be accomplished to sustain them in their time of trial.

The American Jewish Committee, which, after the pogrom at Kishi-
nev, had been formed in 1906 to defend the civil and religious rights
of Jews, concluded that it should be represented at the meeting in London, and I was asked to attend for that purpose. I was loath to leave
my business affairs, but Dr. Cyrus Adler, Judge Joseph Proskauer,
Felix Warburg, Albert Lasker, Sol Stroock, and other men who were
my seniors in years and experience, and for whom I had much respect,
represented it to me as a duty. I sailed on October 20, 1933, and
reached London six days later.

On arrival I met with Dr. Chaim Weizmann, to whom I had been
introduced by Justice Brandeis sixteen years before. Dr. Weizmann
was represented to me to be less concerned with the condition of the
Jews in Germany than with the birth pains of the autonomous state
in Palestine. Dr. Weizmann had devoted himself for years to that cause
with a complete intensity. By arrangement with the British authorities,
the Jewish Agency for Palestine, which Weizmann directed, controlled
the issue of permits to enter Palestine for those who would settle there.
Without such a permit, no refugee could enter Palestine legally. The
agency, under Dr. Weizmann's policy, was interested certainly to see
that those who were admitted to Palestine were men and women who

came, primarily, to build the new state. A hard, pragmatic decision had been made.

In that connection, the late Otto Schiff of London (who was giving all of his time to assist those refugees who had managed to get to England) complained to me that "Weizmann is allotting his scant allowance of entry permits for months ahead to people who are Zionists but who are under no pressure of any sort, whereas we are swamped by poor souls who have no place to go and who can't get one of his permits." I can recall my feeling of bewilderment and indignation at the time. As the years have passed, however, Weizmann's resolution has become clearer. For him, it was not a question limited to compassion. He was founding a state in which, at the very best, the living would be difficult. He believed that its pioneer settlers, to the extent that he could control the issue, should be no less dedicated than he was if it were to succeed at all. The wisdom of his course will be determined only long after this is written. He had made his choice long before.*

When the German persecution of the Jews under Hitler began, an effort had been made in England to induce some member government to bring the issue before the Council of the League of Nations. This was to be done on the basis of the fact that the matter lay within the scope of the Second Paragraph of Article II of the Covenant. That language made it the friendly right of any member state of the League of Nations to bring before the Council a subject which imperiled "peace and good understanding between nations." The case was built on the representation that Germany's brutal persecution of the Jews had forced the flight of many thousands of persons into neighboring countries already suffering serious economic depression and that this was a factor which threatened good relations among the states in Europe. It is a sad circumstance that no member government of that day was unwilling to take action under this article of the Covenant. As Hitler was then far from the strength he developed six years later, in either war matériel or alliances, it is interesting to speculate that a prompt, humanitarian response to the conditions which prevailed might have influenced the subsequent course of events. Nazism would have received a body blow.

The meeting of Jewish organizations which began in London on October 29, 1933, was attended by representatives of communities from many parts of the world and of almost every conceivable shade of opinion and pigmentation. One had only to see the diversity of stature,

* But many thousands of refugees did finally reach sanctuary in Israel without benefit of permit. The figure has been estimated as high as six hundred thousand.

physiognomy, and color to realize that the Jews, sharing a common religion, were certainly not a distinctive race. The impotence of the conference could never have been deduced from its trappings, which were those of an important international conference with committees and subcommittees, agendas, and *rapporteurs*. Among the committees which had been set up was one composed of "academicians" (scientists, educators, philosophers, mathematicians) and on that committee was a young Hungarian physicist, Dr. Leo Szilard, who I did not meet but whose name I remembered some years later when we met under far different circumstances. (See Chapter IX, "A Thousand Years of Regret.")

All that the gathering could accomplish was agreement on the conclusion that the refugee problem would continue to grow; that, though it had begun as a Jewish problem, it was increasingly involving many Christians who were leaving Germany from choice or under duress; that the cost to transport, re-educate, and resettle the numbers involved would be an astronomical sum; and, finally, that it must come only from the rich United States. This last would have been a unanimous conclusion but for one not very helpful dissent—my own.

I pointed out that the United States had just suffered the severest economic depression in our history—one which had its roots in Europe; that we had large numbers of unemployed; that all our banks had been closed within the year; and that notwithstanding, we had received nearly fifty thousand refugees and had raised through private charity a number of millions of dollars for the relief of refugees. These escapees were sheltered temporarily in the countries contiguous to Germany and were largely supported by our contributions. They had been put up in camps and barracks where the barest subsistence was all that could be provided. Even this put a great economic strain on these friendly neighbors, chiefly the Dutch, Belgians, Danes, and French. I said that I thought that further private help would undoubtedly be forthcoming from the United States, but that the size of the problem required the co-operation of several governments.

Asked to speak to the opening session of the conference, I said that we in America, though far from the scene, felt the "same deep sympathy which moves your hearts, and our sense of justice is outraged by the same acts which do violence to your own ideals. We are not motivated by rage or hatred toward the German people, millions of whom must be appalled at the realization of the role in history to which a handful of misanthropic leaders have compelled them. And though we are met to deal with the Jewish aspects of this unhappy situation made necessary by the particular discrimination against the Jews of Germany, we see the issue as affecting not only our brother Jews—but, more darkly, as a crisis in the advance of civilization toward Freedom." Despite a certain sense of futility, the nagging feeling that we could protest, but that an oppressed minority could do little more than cry out while it sought to bind up its wounds I went on: "What we may be able to accomplish here lies in the lap of that Providence which has redeemed us throughout so many generations from so many tyrants and oppressors. I do not despair that justice will again prevail. I am confident that it will. Meanwhile it may be permitted to us, as in the past, to alleviate some human misery and to play our part in defending human freedom."

The conference broke up with a series of resolutions and all eyes were turned to the United States. Nazi Germany, by Hitler's pronouncement, was to have "endured for a thousand years." It would have required faith in miracles to believe that in little more than a decade it would crumble to the earth in smoke and ruin. But miracles are the stuff of history.

Sums of money were indeed raised by private subscription in the United States, dwarfing amounts previously collected by private charity, but while a great many lives were saved and much good accomplished, the size of the problem swamped the individual response to its demands. As a result of the cumulative effect of accounts in the press, governments began to awaken to the responsibility so long ignored.

By the spring of 1937, the pressure of public opinion at all levels had become widespread to find some solution to the misery of the refugees and of those as well who had been unable to escape from Hitler. An international conference was called, as a result of which a high commissioner of the League of Nations was appointed with the specific charge: "to solve the problem of transporting and resettling refugees." This organization, under the leadership of the late George Rublee (later succeeded by Sir Herbert Emerson), though it was late on the scene, expressed the conscience of the free world.

There was established also an intergovernmental committee composed of representatives of ambassadorial rank from thirty-two countries under the chairmanship of Lord Winterton, and another body in the United States known as the President's Advisory Committee on Political Refugees, of which the first chairman was James G. McDonald, an experienced and dedicated administrator of worthy international causes. Acting in an advisory capacity to all these bodies and, in effect, steering them was the late Myron C. Taylor, who had been chairman of the board of the U. S. Steel Corporation and was then President Roosevelt's personal representative at the Vatican. The plight of the helpless had finally enlisted men of talent and influence, but the hour was late.

By the end of 1938, some four hundred thousand persons had managed to escape over the frontiers of Germany and Poland and rather more than half of these, largely on their own initiative or aided by individuals, had found homes for themselves in various parts of the world. Then, a series of pogroms, begun in the fall of 1938, struck terror to the hearts of people of even the remotest Jewish extraction in both Germany and Austria. The technique of intimidation and terrorization became official, intensified, and bloody.

Shortly after the appointment of Rublee as League of Nations High Commissioner for Refugees, that great gentleman, whom I recall with respect and gratitude, undertook a series of negotiations with the German authorities to obtain some sort of an agreement to allow for orderly emigration. He was finally able to secure from a certain Herr Wohlthat, a subordinate of Field Marshal Goering, "a statement of intentions." This was sometimes referred to as an agreement and was believed a workable arrangement by Myron Taylor and others who were still under some illusions as to Hitler's intentions. As a matter of fact, the "agreement" was a scheme concocted by Hjalmar Schacht, a clever, cold-blooded German banker who contributed his financial genius to the Nazi regime.

The Hitler government previously had seized practically all of the realizable assets of the Jews in Germany through the imposition of confiscatory fines and by outright extortion for various privileges, including the privilege of permitting the escape of children or parents. It occurred to Schacht that it might now be possible for Hitler to get his hands on the capital of Jews who were citizens of other countries by compelling them to pay ransom. Accordingly, his scheme, the so-called agreement, provided that the remaining capital of the Jews in Germany would be impounded by the Nazi government in a trust fund (to be administered by two Nazis and one other person) and that this loot— no other word would describe it—would be the collateral for a large loan to Germany to which Jews in the free world would be expected to subscribe. The proceeds of the loan would be used to finance exports of German manufactured goods and the transportation of the refugees who would then be allowed to leave Germany.

Commenting on this satanic brain child of Schacht's, Montague Norman, then governor of the Bank of England, sent me a message by Max Warburg. "Tell Mr. Strauss," he wrote, "that in my opinion seized Jewish property in Germany as security for foreign investment is not worth a penny." I was reassured to have my own views thus confirmed by an authority whose emotions were not involved, as were mine. It was apparent that the plan was an enormous and sadistic hoax, a moneyed traffic in lives beyond any historic precedent.

When the German proposal was cabled in detail to the United States, I was shocked by its malevolence and I prepared (and sent to Paul Baerwald and Harold Linder, who were in London for the Joint Distribution Committee) a message in which the difficulties of securing any acceptance of the agreement were detailed. It was impossible to conceive of investment in the Schacht "bonds" without restitution of the property the Germans had already stolen, and other guarantees:

First: Restitution should be made of the billion mark fine either directly to those on whom it was levied or, if that is not feasible—some have already been killed or committed suicide—it should be used to finance emigrants.

Second: Adequate assurance should be given that the Jews in Germany and those who are awaiting emigration may be permitted to live in peace and to be free from further terror or discriminatory laws.

Third: The existing flight tax should be abolished and those who are emigrating should be permitted to take with them their personal property.

Fourth: No foreign exchange should accrue to Germany from the proceeds of the sale of those exports which are allocated against the transfer of emigrant capital.

Fifth: The trustees who are to hold the Jewish capital in Germany, if they invest in goods for export purposes, must be required to do so at fair market prices in order that there may be no charge of dumping to hurt other countries.

Sixth: The German exports which arise in this fashion must be so labelled or marked that they may be definitely identifiable by consumers in other countries and this should be supervised by some authority in a free port.

Mr. Taylor was informed by Wohlthat in the spring of 1939 that unless the Schacht "agreement" were implemented and an Anglo-American corporation formed for the purpose of co-operating with the German Government, and to sell the bonds secured by the "Trust Fund," even more drastic steps against the Jews would be taken. This was undisguised blackmail, but Wohlthat represented himself as a moderate. Hitler was surrounded by others, said Wohlthat, who were for immediate "liquidation" of the Jewish problem. He left no doubt as to what was meant by that word.

Even with contributions from the United States, the British and French Jewish communities were under great financial strain to support the thousands of refugees within their own borders. Our Congress took no action to increase the German immigration quota; for that matter our visa system was so administered that it did not even fill the existing quota. This was the state of affairs when I was asked to go to England again in the early summer of 1939.

Baerwald and Linder were humanitarians and businessmen of great experience and in London had devoted themselves completely to the problem. They had been in almost continuous session with Taylor and Rublee and had gone through the heartbreaking negotiations with Wohlthat. When I joined them in July, though the clouds of war were gathering, we went ahead nevertheless to organize an Anglo-American body in order that at least the free-world part of the "agreement" would have been fulfilled and that the liquidation threatened might be prevented. Those who might criticize us for going even that far in so heinous a program should not forget that there were the scores of thousands of innocent people held for ransom by a government of desperate and criminal misanthropes. This decision to take one preliminary step to payment of outrageous blackmail was one of the most agonizing decisions ever faced.

The Anglo-American corporation was formed. There has probably never been an organization with so unusual a board. The American trustees included the Honorable John W. Davis, who had been a candidate for President of the United States; Dr. Rufus M. Jones, the outstanding Quaker of his day and president of Swarthmore College; Nathan L. Miller, a former governor of the State of New York; Dave Hennen Morris, a former ambassador; Judge Joseph M. Proskauer, a former justice of the Supreme Court of the State of New York; Lessing J. Rosenwald, a prominent American industrialist; Rabbi Stephen S. Wise; and Owen D. Young, chairman of the board of the General Electric Company. The British members were the Earl of Bessborough, a former governor-general of Canada; Viscount Bearsted, head of the Shell Oil Company; Harold Butler, warden of Nuffield College, Oxford; Lionel L. Cohen, a leader of the British Bar; Simon Marks, a successful and charitable merchant; Lionel de Rothschild, of the Rothschild banking firm; Sir Horace Rumbold, former British Ambassador to Berlin; and Sir John Hope Simpson, of the Royal Institute of International Affairs, who was the chairman. Mr. Baerwald and I were also members.

We looked about for a managing director or a president, and the directors agreed that I might offer the post to Dr. Paul van Zeeland, who had but lately been Prime Minister of Belgium. I had known Dr. van Zeeland as a wise statesman and a skillful negotiator. Furthermore, Belgium then seemed like a neutral country. The probability that she would so soon be overrun by German armies did not occur to us. I sent word to Dr. van Zeeland through a mutual friend and companion of World War I, Hallam Tuck, and received his acceptance. The board promptly met and voted him an appropriate salary, which he as promptly declined.

The Coordinating Foundation, as it was called, removed the last excuse of the German authorities for delaying the introduction of the program which Wohlthat had put forward to Rublee. No one will ever know what the German intentions were, for the war began within days of the establishment of the foundation and ended all communication. The capital of the foundation, which had been subscribed, primarily in the United States, was returned to be subscribers when the foundation was liquidated in the early war years.

Concurrently, there was another project, which, unlike Schacht's scheme, had a respectable background. Before leaving for Europe in July 1939, I had received certain assurances from Bernard Baruch, Henry Ittleson, Albert Lasker, Mr. Rosenwald, and a number of other men of considerable means and varying creeds. These assurances were that if the British Government could be persuaded to devote a sufficiently large area in Kenya, Tanganyika, or Northern Rhodesia for settlement by refugees from European countries so that, in effect, a new colony under British sovereignty could be established, these men were willing to tithe their capital to assist it. They had in mind the subscription of a number of millions of dollars to the capital of a central bank to be located in the new country. The bank would be the bank of issue for a local currency to be based on sterling, and it would also issue loans in the United States, England, France, and elsewhere. The proceeds of financing would be used to develop the roads, utilities, and other services of the new country.

Ex-President Hoover was interested and stated that he would be willing to visit the new country and organize its communications, its transport, and the development of its resources. The plan looked to the possibility that in a temperate climate with good soil a new country which would absorb the surplus manufactured goods of the world for a period of a generation or more might be the answer, not only to the refugee problem, but to the general economic distress and widespread unemployment which had begun in Europe in the mid-1920s, had reached us in 1929, and from which the world had not yet recovered. It could do for the world in the generation ahead what the United States had done in its period of development before 1860, when it offered a constructive opportunity for investment to open it to growth and settlement.

Mr. Baruch gave me a letter which I carried to London. In it he had written:

I am convinced there is but one way permanently to settle this question and that is as follows:

That a large part of Africa . . . be converted into one country and called, for want of a better name, the United States of Africa. It would be under the sovereignty and protectorate of Great Britain. The reason it should be under the sovereign control or protectorate of England is because England will not have anything but a democratic government.

Every man 18 years of age who goes there should serve in the military for at least one year and should be trained and commanded by British officers. As time passes, that will build up a large body of trained men and reserves who would make that country safe from the domination of any influence other than that of England.

Great engineers, like Herbert Hoover, should study the country for drainage, power, cultivation, mining minerals and oil. The country can be cleaned up with modern equipment. The world has not always been as clean as it is now. Our own country was full of morasses. Panama and Cuba were cleaned up, and Africa can be cleaned up too. The country should be for all refugees who could pass the tests set up by the English protectorate. I want to make one thing clear and that is that this country should not be a Jewish state but one for all refugees. How many non-Jewish people in Russia, Germany and Italy do you think would be glad to get out of those countries if there was some place to which they could go? Now even an Aryan cannot get out and if he does, they will shove him back.

But in this new land there would be a place for tens of millions and they would be the best, the strongest and the most courageous people because they are anxious to get away from these over-regulated, goose-stepping civilians of Russia, Germany and Italy.

It will cost a lot of money, yes, but the money is to be raised principally by the Jews of the world by assessing themselves at least 10% of their total capital. I do not doubt that a sum far exceeding $300 million would be raised. This money should be given, not loaned, it should be spent for cleaning up the country under the engineers. Some of it might be reserved to help immigrants. After the country is partly settled, they can raise money under the watchful care of the English protectorate for other purposes and for continued cleaning up. Mind you, I want to repeat—this is for all kinds of people, Catholics, Jews, Protestants, and unbelievers who want to get away from totalitarian forms of government.

It would not be long before so many people will have left Central Europe that there would be a stoppage of emigration. No sooner would this start in Africa than the rest of the world would be bidding for these people. Remember they would be a pioneering people who may perhaps build in Africa a new country like America.

Another thing, the activity of these men in a remade country would undoubtedly start an economic revival. Indeed, it would start a rebirth of freedom and liberty that might start that whole world going again.

The greatest difficulty is going to be with the British Government. All the people in Kenya, Tanganyika and Rhodesia will not want refugees to go there. But if Mr. Chamberlain and Mr. Baldwin want to fully solve the problem, there it is. . . . While one's heart is naturally deeply touched by the distress of these people, we must think of the future before settling them in the various sections of the world that are now being suggested. Would they be safe there?

If this plan or one similar to it shows promise, then those refugees who are under pressure could be moved in maybe to special cantons in France, Holland and Switzerland and housed there temporarily while arrangements are completed to take them to their sanctuary. Each would be bonded while enjoying temporary asylum and guaranteed against becoming a charge or even taking a job in those countries. It would mean the expenditure of large sums to take care of these travellers and would have a gradual increasing affect on world trade in which all would share.

In general, the broad plan here outlined would be a solution of the over-population question of all of Europe.

Mr. Hoover prepared a memorandum for me to take to London:

I have looked over the report on British Guiana* as a possible area for large settlement of Jewish refugees. It would seem abundantly

* The reference to British Guiana is explained further in the text.

clear that the fundamental of fertile soil is not present in sufficient quantities in the upland area. . . .

It has long seemed to me that there is but one unoccupied area in the world upon which a new and sound civilization could be builded. That is the uplands of Central-East Africa, embracing parts of Northern Rhodesia, Tanganyika, Kenya, and Belgian Congo. The adaptability of this area from this view point of course needs further examination. But from reports available it does seem to have the soil, climate, and resources upon which 10 to 20 millions of white civilization could be builded.

And the world greatly needs such an outlet for population pressures as well as refugees of all races. Since the best parts of the Western Hemisphere were closed to population movement, these pressures have been growing steadily.

Nothing could contribute so much to peace and stability of the world as to systematically open such an outlet.

To do so and do it rapidly, a large *gift* of capital would be necessary. If 500 millions of dollars could be provided and certain economic rights secured there is hope for a great relief to a troubled world. Further finance could be found by secured loans, but there must be a large foundation of capital from which no return was sought. Mr. Baruch feels that this foundation capital could be secured if

   (a)   The project proved sound on examination.

   (b)   The necessary governmental arrangements could be made.

   (c)   It were conducted under the highest auspices.

In view of the pressing world situation it certainly should be explored further.

Herbert Hoover.

Let me say at once that I failed completely to make any headway on this proposal with the members of the British Cabinet with whom I talked. All agreed that a recommendation would have to come from Malcolm MacDonald, Secretary of State for Colonies. Mr. MacDonald received me kindly. We talked about the visit of Prime Minister Mac-Donald to President Hoover's camp on the Rapidan a decade earlier, and other subjects remote from my objective. He then took me to lunch at the Athenaeum to meet Lord Haley and others of his advisers, but it was apparent after the second interview that I was getting nowhere. There were two apparent reasons. One was that, among the British white population in the African areas in question, although it was extremely sparse (about one man to five square miles), those who had been consulted took a dim view of civilization crowding in upon them. Their objections must have been overriding as far as the Colonial Office was concerned. The second reason may have been that the British Cabinet had a resettlement area of its own which it favored. This was the British Guiana project to which the first paragraph of Mr. Hoover's memorandum refers. It was a land of swamp and jungle where the white community hung on at the coastal fringe and where the back country was not only largely uninhabited but uninhabitable. The possibilities for settlement in this area had been canvassed by a League of Nations mission four years earlier in the interest of finding a new home for the Assyrians of Iraq, and with totally discouraging results. The soil was so unproductive that after one or two crops it was exhausted and required massive fertilization. Insect-borne animal diseases made cattle raising prohibitive.

In spite of this, pressure from British sources to proceed with a settlement project in Guiana was intense. Our ambassador informed the Secretary of State in June that he had learned from the Secretary of State for Colonies that, if American individuals were not prepared to subscribe to the Guiana project, the British Government might find itself obliged to reconsider its position with regard to the whole refugee question. With this choice of alternatives, there was nothing else we could do but subscribe, whatever our misgivings and despite the fact that it would provide an initial haven for fewer than five hundred people while the emergency involved hundreds of thousands.

Following a meeting between Malcolm MacDonald and Anthony de Rothschild, Mr. de Rothschild wrote me to say that the Secretary of State for Colonies was "most anxious to learn what the prospects were of our being able to undertake the experiment in Guiana and assured us of the earnest wish of His Majesty's Government that the experiment should be conducted under the most favorable auspices. . . . We impressed upon the Secretary of State [for Colonies] the great advantage that would follow if it were possible to obtain a grant of money in aid of the scheme. To this he replied that he obviously could not answer at this stage, but the whole question was under the most careful consideration and he certainly gave us every encouragement to think that the Government was seeking for some way in which it could further help."

We committed our participation to this enterprise, which was the only definite proposal to come out of all the conversations and negotiations, and it was far too late. One month to the day after the war had begun, Mr. de Rothschild found it necessary to cable me: "Committee cannot continue Guiana."

* * *

There were other projects of even less promise than Guiana. While I was in London a Mr. Bedeaux called on me with such a plan. He was a personality of the period who had achieved considerable success and an equal measure of unpopularity with a procedure to increase the output of industrial workers by what was known as the "speed-up." He had an area which he described as ideal for colonization and he added that, satisfied of the potential of the region, he had already acquired the necessary concessions or rights there. The area turned out to be the so-called "Suds" where the waters of the White Nile spread out over an enormous acreage of bottomless swamps. No native population lives in this steaming and mosquito-infested inferno; it is populated solely by serpents and crocodiles.

After the Coordinating Foundation had been agreed upon, I left England for the Continent. My family was with me. Feeling that war was coming and that it might destroy many of the monuments of European culture, my wife and I wished to see them once again and to show them to our son.

Before leaving London for Paris, I talked with Ambassador Joseph P. Kennedy. He said that he thought there was sufficient intelligence in Germany to avoid a mistake which would be as terrible as a second World War, and that he allowed himself the optimistic belief that it would not occur. On arriving in Paris, I had lunch with an old friend, William C. Bullitt, who was the American Ambassador to France. To the same question, Ambassador Bullitt said that he felt that war was inevitable, but not imminent. His best guess was that it would start in eight to ten months, "as soon as the roads are dry enough for tanks and artillery to move."

The following evening I had dinner with M. Paul Reynaud, who had served his country in many posts. He took a much less optimistic view. "Do you have your family here?" he asked. I said that my wife and son were with me and were then in the château country. "When are you planning to leave?" I said that we had reservations on both the *Ile de France* and on the *Normandie*. "If I were you," said M. Reynaud, "I would take the earlier sailing. There may be a scramble to leave in late August."

Hitler invaded Poland on September 1.

There were meetings of an Intergovernmental Committee on Refugees in the autumn of 1939 while the "phony war" was being fought in Europe. The Coordinating Foundation hopefully opened offices in

New York. A small colony of refugees was settled in the Dominican Republic, thanks to the efforts of James N. Rosenberg and of Messrs. Linder and Baerwald. But soon a curtain of fire separated the rest of the world from the millions left behind to the mercies of the gas chambers and firing squads in Germany and Austria, Czechoslovakia and Poland. The sound of their cries did not penetrate this barrier. Disaster piled upon disaster and with the invasion of the Low Countries in 1940 even people who had given refuge to others, unhappier than themselves, also became lost to sight.

There was no place to apply leverage, and postponement was the order of the day. On July 13, 1940, the Under Secretary of State, Sumner Welles, wrote to say:

> Your letter of July 8th, 1940, raises the fundamental question whether, in the light of the present chaotic situation in Europe, the President will wish to continue with plans prepared by M. Van Zeeland and the Coordinating Foundation earlier in the year.
>
> I can assure you that the President maintains unabated his interest in a practical solution of the refugee problem. . . .
>
> Specifically with regard to the proposed meeting at the White House mentioned in your letter, I suggest that the decision be postponed. . . .

The tidal wave of war swept over the continents and across the oceans and a world in shock closed its eyes, figuratively and literally, to the plight of the unfortunate beings who were engulfed.

VII

Sidelight on a Decision in Tokyo

"Niitaka Yama Nobore." These three words, which in English mean "Climb Mount Niitaka," carried a different imperative in December of 1941. They were a message in code flashed by Admiral Isoroku Yamamoto from his flagship, *Nagato,* at the Japanese Naval Base at Kure to the fleet, until then hidden in the Kuril fogs. Thereupon, the ships turned southeastward toward the Hawaiian Islands and the United States Naval Base at Pearl Harbor.

The three words launched the best advertised and yet, for reasons still unresolved, the most complete surprise attack in history. If our radio monitors caught and translated the message, its words were meaningless. They had been chosen arbitrarily to convey a specific directive, and when received by Admiral Nagumo, who commanded the Japanese task force from his flagship, the aircraft carrier *Akagi,* they were completely clear. They meant that negotiations for a peaceful settlement of Japan's differences with the United States had failed. They were the signal for an attack long planned.

In more ways than one, the signal was Admiral Yamamoto's personal message. The surprise assault on our Pacific base, and the destruction of our ships at anchor there, was a strategy of which he appears to have been the author and of which he felt so confident that, when it was first opposed, he had offered "to turn in his suit." I had something more than a passing acquaintance with the Admiral. As a promising young commander, he had served as one of the aides to the Prince Regent, now Emperor, Hirohito, and had been assigned as interpreter for me during a visit to Japan in 1926.

Our ability to crack the codes in which the Japanese military sent their operational messages later in the war eventually cost Yamamoto his life. The plane carrying him to his flagship was shot down by our airmen, who were literally able to ambush him as a result of our air combat intelligence.*

* Public revelation that this had been due to successful cryptanalysis by the Navy leaked shortly after the formal act of Japanese surrender on the deck of the

I had not seen Admiral Yamamoto in the intervening years, although many of my old contacts with other Japanese in industrial and banking circles had been maintained. Among these there were a number who were good friends. Nine months before "Pearl Harbor," in March 1941, I had been ordered to report for active duty as a member of the Naval Reserve. Even in March, it was clear that war with the Fascist powers in Europe could be avoided only with difficulty. War with Japan seemed less likely.

There were others also who thought that war was coming, and from the East, unless affirmative steps were taken to head off the cataclysm. Diplomacy seemed in the grip of paralysis. One man in the Diplomatic Service emerges from the period with vision and great stature, Joseph C. Grew, our experienced Ambassador to Tokyo. His advice seems to have been largely unheeded.

Two American priests, Father James M. Drought, vicar-general of the Maryknoll Fathers, and Bishop James E. Walsh, took an initiative as concerned citizens. Bishop Walsh is today held prisoner, and incommunicado, by the Communist Chinese Government, and I have not been able to consult him concerning his recollection of the details of the incident I am about to relate. Father Drought is dead. During his lifetime, he was my close friend.

Our association began when he had asked me to review his order's financial investments, which had suffered during the depression of 1929-32. Thereafter I had acted as a part-time adviser to Maryknoll. Father Drought was a young priest of good education, personal charm, humor, and a genuine dedication to his fellow men. He had been of comfort and practical assistance during the months when Father Coughlin, a demagogue of the 1930s, was spreading religious and racial hate over the radio. Father Drought had played an important role in bringing that disgraceful episode to a close.*

U.S.S. *Missouri* in Tokyo Bay on September 2. Almost immediately, an anguished message arrived in the Navy Department from Tokyo to say that the story was causing great embarrassment. Naval officers engaged in interrogating Japanese officer prisoners had been getting from them valuable information on Japanese codes and channels of communication. Some of these officer prisoners, humiliated on hearing this report, felt that no course was open to them but immediate hara-kiri.

* In that connection there is a message from him sending to me an excerpt from a letter addressed to the Catholic clergy in America by Pope Pius XII. The reference to Father Coughlin is oblique, but Father Drought suggested that I note that results would follow, as indeed they did.

"We have learned with no little joy that your press is a sturdy champion of

Early in November 1940, Father Drought came to see me with Bishop Walsh to say that they proposed to go to Japan. The Maryknoll Mission had long been engaged in the Far East, and such a journey was not in itself unusual. However, on this occasion they planned to visit and, if possible, to persuade highly placed persons in the Japanese Government that the course upon which they were embarked would lead to war with us, and a war in which their defeat would be inevitable. They had only a few acquaintances in Japan, but they had made a contact with Foreign Minister Matsuoka. This had given them some encouragement to believe that Japan might abandon the pact with Germany and Italy, restore the territory which had been seized from China, and withdraw Japanese military forces from occupied Chinese territory. The two priests asked if I would be willing to give them letters of introduction to friends in Japan.

Thirty-five years earlier, the banking partnership of which I later became a member had supported Japan in the Russo-Japanese War. One of the founding partners of the firm, the great philanthropist Jacob Schiff, had visited Japan in 1906 as the guest of the Japanese Government, and twenty years later, in 1926, I had retraced his steps, as told earlier. The then Prime Minister, Baron Wakatsuki, the former Prime Minister and Minister of Finance, Baron Takahashi, and other gentlemen of Japan in positions of importance in the financial and diplomatic communities had been very hospitable. I had continued a correspondence with most of these men and felt that they would be glad to receive my two friends. There were also a number of other Japanese I had known prior to my visit, mainly young bankers who had been stationed in Washington or in New York in charge of the financial interests of Japan in the United States, the negotiation of government and industrial loans, etc.

To these men I addressed letters introducing Father Drought and Bishop Walsh. The addressees included, besides Wakatsuki, Mr. Yamagata, in the Ministry of Foreign Affairs, who had been assigned as an

---

Catholic principles, that the radio—eloquent image of the apostolic faith that embraces all mankind—is frequently and advantageously put to use in order to insure the widest possible promulgation of all that concerns the church. We commend the good accomplished. *But let those who fulfill this ministry be careful to adhere to the directives of the Teaching Church even when they explain and promote what pertains to the social problem; forgetful of personal gain, despising popularity, impartial, let them speak 'as from God, before God, in Christ',* (II Corinthians, 2nd Chapter, 17th Verse).

aide and adviser in 1926; Tadeo Wikawa, who had been Japanese Financial High Commissioner in New York in the 1920s and who was then in charge of the Bureau of Banking of the Department of Finance; Juichi Tsushima, of the Bank of Japan; Baron Mitsui, of the banking and industrial family; Eigo Fukai, of the Bank of Japan; H. Kashiwagi, of the Yokohama Specie Bank; and T. Okubo, the son-in-law of my old friend Baron Takahashi, who had been assassinated by war-party fanatics in 1936.

On Armistice Day, 1940, Father Drought and Bishop Walsh sailed for Yokohama on a Japanese liner and arrived in Tokyo on November 24. They began their conversations with Japanese personalities immediately. Early in 1941 they returned to the United States with a result considered by both of them to be highly encouraging. They had conferred with many influential Japanese whose friendship for the United States was apparently genuine and who seemed confident that the steps necessary to restore good relations could be taken by Japan. When they telephoned upon landing, I suggested that before coming to Washington they might call to see Mr. Hoover and get his advice. The former President was then living in Palo Alto, California, only a few miles from San Francisco. Mr. Hoover heard their story and suggested that it was of sufficient importance to be related to President Roosevelt at once. However, by reason of the barriers to communication which existed between him and the President, Mr. Hoover did not feel that he could provide them with an entree. Therefore, he proposed that they should first call on the Postmaster General, Frank C. Walker, for that purpose. Mr. Walker was a Catholic, and the two priests met with him promptly. Walker was likewise impressed and arranged an interview with President Roosevelt, at which the volunteer peacemakers laid before him the results of their conversations. Both the Postmaster General and Secretary of State Cordell Hull were present at this meeting in the White House.

At this point, perhaps, the amateurs should have been thanked for their trouble and dismissed, but apparently the President and Secretary Hull decided that the two priests should continue their personal contacts with the Japanese on an informal basis and attempt to codify just what they understood the Japanese were willing to concede. The result was that in April a paper upon which they had collaborated and which they called a "Draft Understanding" was delivered to the Secretary of State by the Postmaster General. It seems to have been the combined work of Father Drought; Bishop Walsh; a military attaché of the Japanese Embassy, Colonel Hideo Iwakuro (who had been introduced to Father Drought by my friend Wikawa); and Wikawa himself. Wikawa was a friend of the United States and by faith a Christian. His wife was an Anglo-Saxon and his daughter was living in the United States.

The hazard of amateurism in this negotiation was compounded shortly afterwards when the Japanese Government sent Admiral Kichisaburo Nomura to Washington as a special envoy. Nomura was an officer of highest rank and outstanding reputation in his field, but with limited practical experience in other areas and none apparently in foreign affairs.

Notwithstanding the availability of interpreters for conferences between Nomura and Hull, they seem to have seen each other, most frequently, alone. This may have been due to the unfortunate fact that Admiral Nomura spoke a smattering of English, enough to enable him to carry on a polite dinner-table conversation, but inadequate for a negotiation in depth. As is not infrequently the case in such instances, he gave the impression of comprehension by a smile and nod of the head, when in fact he was substantially unable to follow what had been said. Thus, the two men had a number of meetings in person, but it would appear almost no meeting of minds. The interviews invariably took place in Secretary Hull's hotel apartment and in the evenings. Various documents which Secretary Hull assumed that Admiral Nomura had agreed to dispatch to Tokyo were never sent, because Nomura did not understand that dispatch was intended. Others, which he did transmit, arrived in Tokyo with confused explanatory texts, some mistakenly indicating United States agreement. There appears to have been no attempt at deception.

Secretary Hull records that on March 14 he took Admiral Nomura to see the President. The Admiral told the President that Japan desired but three things in China: "Good will, economic cooperation and defense against Communism." And then, "picking up Nomura's reference to Communism in China, the President remarked that the people of China were constituted very differently from those of Russia and had a philosophy that stablized and guided them along much broader lines. China, he said, was not really communistic in the same sense as Russia, and Japan had an undue fear of Communism in China."[1]

In a meeting at Secretary Hull's apartment in the Wardman-Park Hotel a month later, Hull handed to Admiral Nomura a document containing "four principles" which were stipulations that the United

States would insist upon before negotiating an agreement with Japan. These were: respect for the territorial integrity and the sovereignty of all nations; support of the principle of noninterference in the internal affairs of other countries; support of the principle of equality, including equality of commercial opportunity; and, finally, the principle that the *status quo* in the Pacific should not be altered other than by peaceful means.

Admiral Nomura did not cable these four principles to the Japanese Foreign Office for nearly a month, and when he did, he was apparently under the impression that he had been able to mollify the American stand and that these points might all be set aside for discussion at a later date.

Typical of the failure of minds to meet, the Drought-Walsh-Iwakuro-Wikawa "Draft Understanding" reached Japan in a dispatch from Nomura under circumstances which led the Japanese to assume that it was a wholly American composition. Its arrival overjoyed those in Japan who hoped for uninterrupted good relations with the United States, and it is said that my friend, former Premier Wakatsuki, "wept with joy" upon being informed "of the proposal received from Washington." This misunderstanding persisted in Japanese circles until after the end of the war. There has probably been no sadder indictment of unprofessional diplomacy than the Nomura mission. It is difficult to understand how a government in a time of supreme crisis should have entrusted its relations with a powerful possible adversary to a man of such limited practical experience in negotiation. There is an awesome lesson in this for foreign offices and state departments.

The ineptness of Admiral Nomura is also illustrated by an episode which is said to have occurred during one of his late-evening conferences with Secretary Hull. By some inadvertence Nomura had taken with him on a visit to Hull the secret text of an agreement between Tokyo and the Chinese puppet-Emperor, Pu Yi, who was being supported by Japanese bayonets. Nomura left this revealing paper in Hull's apartment. The next day, in consternation, he visited Hull again to repossess the telltale document.

Hull finally met the two Japanese negotiators who were assisting Bishop Walsh and Father Drought. Colonel Iwakuro made a good impression, and Hull found him "a fine type, honest, calmly poised, very sure of himself without being annoyingly self-confident." My friend Wikawa, on the other hand, struck him as being the "slick politician type." Wikawa was not in politics, had been educated as a banker, and for years had been stationed in New York as the Financial High Commissioner of the Japanese Government. His English was perfect. At the time that Wikawa and Iwakuro were negotiating with Bishop Walsh and Father Drought, he was a high official of the Cooperative Bank of Japan. (He did not survive the war.)

On June 21, Secretary Hull presented Ambassador Nomura with a note in which he asked for some concrete evidence that the constantly reiterated Japanese desire for peace was real. By then the Japanese were already in the midst of a cabinet upheaval and the note went without answer while the Japanese Army in Indochina continued to push forward to locations from which it threatened both Singapore and the Dutch East Indies.

To refresh himself, Hull went to White Sulphur Springs in July. On July 13, Nomura traveled from Washington to that resort to see the Secretary. He had been so confident of the importance of his errand and of his friendship with the Secretary that he had not made an appointment. Hull refused to see him. It was reported that some of Hull's advisers thought it might be good "to put the Admiral in his place" and not to see him at any and every time he sought an appointment.

In this state of affairs, President Roosevelt issued the order on July 26 freezing all Japanese assets in the United States. The Navy regarded that action as tantamount to a trigger,[2] and Admiral Harold Stark, Chief of Naval Operations, was sufficiently concerned by it to warn Admiral Thomas C. Hart, in command of the Asiatic Fleet, that he should take appropriate precautions against eventualities.

The door which had been opened by Father Drought and Bishop Walsh was about to be slammed. The Japanese war party took advantage of every diplomatic fumble to press its own suicidal policy.

I was not among those who were able to predict the beginning of the war and the hemisphere in which it would start. Although the entire atmosphere was charged with the electricity of the approaching storm, its imminence was no more apparent to me than to those in the Navy Department beside whom I was working. There were indications on my desk, however, had I been able to understand them. I had received a letter dated December 4 from S. Kitadai, of the Bank of Japan, written from his office in the Equitable Building in New York:

Dear Friend:
This is to inform you that my office, the Bank of Japan, will be closed on and after December 5th, 1941, pursuant to instructions from the head office in Tokyo.

At this time I wish to say that I am deeply grateful for the many kindnesses you have shown to me, and I hope that a favorable situation between your country and mine will be agreed upon under which conditions we shall reopen this office in the nearest future.

I shall leave New York within several days to go to Los Angeles where I shall sail aboard the Tatsuta Maru. Please accept my best wishes for a happy prosperous life and I hope we shall meet again.

Like many others, I did not read anything between the lines. Yet closing the office of that great financial institution, which had not taken place when Japanese assets were frozen in July, could not have been ordered except in the gravest extremity. The procession of dates was significant.

In retrospect, it is difficult to explain the peculiar and general obtuseness during those last months before the war. In an age of fable, when antic gods capriciously deceived men and intervened actively in their affairs, it would have been natural for warnings to be ignored and important steps taken in defiance of facts; but this was A.D. 1941. Ambassador Grew had reported to Washington, ten months before the fact, that he had heard rumors of plans for a *surprise attack on Pearl Harbor*.[3] It is interesting to speculate how such a leak could have occurred in a nation as security-conscious as Japan. Grew also noted in his diary, "I rather guess that the boys in Pearl Harbor are not precisely asleep."

Admiral Nomura presented one note which proposed a sort of summit conference (the term, of course, was not yet in fashion), a meeting between President Roosevelt and the Prime Minister, Prince Konoye. This in its original form had been a suggestion of Father Drought. It was not rejected out of hand by Secretary Hull, but was answered with the stipulation that a solution of the existing differences of view between the governments would have to be a precondition. In other words, the negotiation and settlement would have to precede the conference. The Japanese war party was well satisfied with that response, while our Japanese friends, holding it to be a rebuff, were correspondingly disheartened.

The volunteer intermediaries, Bishop Walsh and Father Drought, now passed completely from the picture, but the negotiations they had begun in February 1941 continued up to the last hours. The Prime Minister, Prince Konoye, who had become their friend, favored friendship with the United States to the last, and evidence at the Japanese war trials five years later confirmed that attitude, but the efforts of men of good will were completely thwarted.[4]

The penultimate and fateful step was the formulation in Japan of a set of "maximum concessions" and "minimum demands." These figured in further exchanges of notes, but failed to impress Secretary Hull other than as constituting appeasement if we should accept them. He also saw them as representing humiliation and loss of territory for our friends in the Pacific. Prince Konoye, seeing his efforts fruitless, was unable to resist the pressure of the war party and resigned on October 16, an event which again caused enough uneasiness in the Navy Department for Admiral Stark to warn his commanders, both at Pearl Harbor and in Asiatic waters, to take "due precautions." Perhaps these warnings cried wolf too frequently, yet in a classic demonstration of the confusion of disunified command, the Army, at the same time, was advising its commanders in the Pacific that "no abrupt change in Japanese foreign policy" was anticipated. Pearl Harbor was less than sixty days in the onrushing future.

A Japanese imperial conference, with the Emperor himself presiding, formulated new proposals in early November which Admiral Nomura transmitted to Secretary Hull on November 7. These also were rejected by us as being too indefinite and uncertain where they dealt with the withdrawal of the Japanese armies from China and Indochina.

The belief that a war could come with catastrophic suddenness now became a conviction in the minds of a number of military leaders. Admiral Stark (whose distinguished career became one of the first casualties after December 7), had prophetically chosen *November 7* to write to Admiral Kimmel at Pearl Harbor: "A month may see literally most anything . . . It doesn't look good." It was to be a month, precisely to the day from that message, that would, literally, see everything.

We were intercepting and decoding Japanese cable exchanges at this time, and Secretary Hull and the President were aware from the texts that the proposals of November 7 were regarded by the Japanese Cabinet as their final word.

The Navy now contributed another in the series of warnings. On November 24 a signal was sent from Washington to the Pacific Fleet to say that there was little likelihood of agreement with the Japanese and that a *"surprise* aggressive movement in any direction" was now possible. The warning was to be passed along to the Army commanders in the area. There was another alert three days later from the headquarters of both services. The Navy dispatch significantly styled itself "A War Warning."

On the previous day, November 26, our final word had been handed to the Japanese Ambassador. It effectively put an end to negotiations, although Admiral Nomura and Saburo Kurusu remained in Washington. (The latter, an experienced diplomat, had been sent to help Nomura, but far too late.)

The ultimate Japanese note, in no sense a document of negotiation, was delivered by the two envoys to an "icily furious" Secretary of State. He had read it well before their arrival at his office, perhaps even before it had been received and decoded in the Japanese Embassy.

General George C. Marshall, Chief of Staff of the Army, composed a warning to his commanding general in Hawaii to let him know that cable and wireless intelligence had revealed that the Japanese were presenting an ultimatum and that a specific hour had been set for its delivery. "Just what significance the hour may have, we do not know, but be on the alert accordingly," Marshall cautioned. That message, certainly as urgent as any ever sent to an American military outpost, for some reason was sent over a commercial communication system. Delayed in transit and still in code, it was carried by a messenger boy on his bicycle between Honolulu and Fort Shafter. As he pedaled along, our great battle fleet, shrouded in the billowing smoke of its death agonies, settled into the mud of Pearl Harbor a few miles away.

* * *

Six days before, there had been a top-level conference at the Imperial Palace in Tokyo. The Emperor attended, but it was later testified that he did not speak. The issues were discussed and a vote was taken. It was unanimous. Across the international date line, war would begin at Pearl Harbor in the early morning of December 7—the day that would "live in infamy." Shortly, the message "Climb Mount Niitaka" pulsed upward to the Heaviside layer and back to the waiting antenna of the Japanese flagship. It climaxed a decision that eventually took the lives of nearly 300,000 Americans* and an uncertain but vastly greater number of Japanese.

In consequence, the December 1 decision in Tokyo started a chain reaction of events whose end, nearly a score of years later, is not even dimly visible. More significantly, it precipitated the first use of a new weapon which, not yet completed before the defeat of Germany, might

* In all theaters of World War II.

otherwise never have been used or even tested. The series of decisions which constantly reinforced one another give the appearance more of fate that of free will. Forty-three months later, in July 1945, at Potsdam, the next fateful decision would be taken—a decision that would round out the flaming disaster at Pearl Harbor by a searing holocaust over Japan herself.

On Friday, December 5, 1941, I left the Navy Department and flew up to New York for the weekend. Everything was business as usual there. A friend twitted me for wasting time in Washington. At lunch on Saturday, however, a former business associate, noting that I had now been away from the world of finance for nearly a year, observed, prophetically, that I might never come back to it. On Sunday, after a family dinner, I walked down Madison Avenue. Washington seemed more remote than 250 miles, and the activities there took on the slow-motion quality of a dream. Perhaps the time had come to resign from the Navy. A small group of Sunday strollers were clustered around a parked automobile. Its radio was turned to so much gain that all it emitted was noise.

"What's going on?" I asked a man on the fringe of the group.

"Big news!" he shouted. "The Japs have just bombed Honolulu but we shot down all their planes and sank all their ships."

VIII

A View of the Navy from the Beach

James Forrestal, our first Secretary of Defense, once remarked to me, "The hell of public service is that it isn't enough to do the job well— you have got to convince the country of it." (It was his failure, or so he mistakenly thought, to accomplish the last half of that charge which took his life.)

For an administrator in our government with one of the major responsibilities, there is little time to devote to public relations; an occasional press conference, a dinner now and then with friendly members of the press are about all. The pressure of work; an endless succession of reports to read; subordinates to see, hear, and encourage; colleagues to meet, to convince, or by them to be convinced; Congress to cajole for support and to resist when it invades the Executive function; and day after day the making of decisions, small and great—these things and more. There is precious little time either to convince the country that a good job is being done or even to stand back and look at it objectively long enough to satisfy yourself of that fact.

* * *

The banking years were years of constructive work, of friendships, of laying by some savings. They were not years of decision such as those which preceded them or those which were to follow. There were decisions, but they affected primarily my own capital or that of my friends and partners. As I look back upon them, they were part of a golden age in more ways than one. The years ended suddenly.

I had held a commission in the Naval Reserve since 1925, and in March 1941 orders had arrived to report for duty. This was nearly ten months before Pearl Harbor, and I seriously considered asking to be released, as I was then forty-five and had been a lieutenant commander for fourteen years and would soon have been dropped for age in grade. My commission, issued thirty-five years ago, bears the signature of Calvin Coolidge. But it seemed inevitable that war would be the result of Hitler's outrages, and I wanted to be useful in any way possible. While continuing to be a member of Kuhn, Loeb & Co. during my Navy service, I took no part in business until demobilized in May of 1946 and by November of that year had resigned from the firm.

The orders assigned me to duty with the Bureau of Ordnance. I reported first to a building known as Tempo 1. It seemed familiar and with good reason: twenty-two years before, it had been built to house the temporary wartime Food Administration. My office had been in it and I was familiar with every detail of its construction. The temporary character of the building resembled my temporary active duty, which, initially to cover a few weeks of training, became five years.

I had become acquainted with Admiral W. R. Furlong, chief of the bureau, but just as these orders arrived, he was transferred to a command in the Pacific. The new chief of bureau, who, by reason of outstanding ability, had been promoted over officers senior to him, was Rear Admiral William Henry Purnell Blandy. Blandy had graduated with the highest marks in his Annapolis class. By professional specialty, he was a gunner—a "battleship admiral"—and proud of that tag although it was already beginning to be used as a term to indicate obsolescent naval thinking. Years before, he had commanded the battleship *Utah* when she was used as a target for aerial bombing experiments and, as a result, he was convinced that a battleship could be designed which would be essentially immune to damage from the bombs of that era.

Blandy's first action was to reorganize completely the Bureau of Ordnance. His new setup was on a functional basis, and the staff of only eighty regular officers allotted to him spread experience very thin. In consequence, the reserve officers had great opportunities. Some of us (myself in particular) were assigned to responsibilities for which we were unprepared. After a few weeks of duty in various divisions, I was placed in charge of ordnance inspection with the astonishing designation General Inspector of Ordnance.

The number of inspectors at plants manufacturing armor plate, guns, mounts, explosives, shells, depth charges, optics, mines, torpedoes, and other ordnance matériel was even then insufficient to cope with the increased procurement. Vastly greater procurement was programmed for which appropriations were being obtained, but the Navy was not permitted to accept and make payment until each item had been inspected and approved. Scores of millions of dollars' worth of material was backing up in the factories and warehouses of the manufacturers. As William Knudsen, the production expert of the period, said to my wife at that time, "We have a shortage of everything, including a place to store it." Later, when production was at full tilt but still encountering local difficulties, Knudsen, by then a lieutenant general, observed that "We have a surplus of one thing—we have bottlenecks running out of our ears." Manufacturers suffered both from lack of storage space and from delayed payments, which used up working capital and forced many to decline further orders until paid for what they had made.

Searching bureau records, I found World War I statistics and, using them as a yardstick, made a rough calculation that each million dollars' value of manufactured ordnance in specific categories, in gun-mount production, for example, had required a certain number of inspectors. The numbers varied with the category. The total number of inspectors needed, therefore, might be a factor of the appropriated funds. The actual numbers worked out somewhat differently due to the higher costs for material compared with 1917–18. As we had only a handful of qualified men, the first step was to train more immediately. I arranged for a school for inspectors to be set up at the Naval Gun Factory and, by dragooning civilian friends and acquaintances, recruited some hundreds of men of all ages. Others were procured through regular Navy enlistment channels, and by the time hostilities began, nine months later, there was a trained staff of "INOs" (Inspectors of Naval Ordnance) at all the major centers of manufacturing.

There were also in many of these plants inspectors for the Bureau of Ships, the Bureau of Aeronautics, and other Navy bureaus and offices. These bureaus regularly maintained offices independent of one another, even in the same plant. There were a number of instances of three separate crews of Navy inspectors in a single plant. This led to the obvious conclusion that there should be one naval inspection service. It also led to a tragicomedy.

At dinner one evening at the home of the Secretary of the Navy, Mr. Knox asked whether I had observed anything in the naval organization which could be improved. Since inspection was uppermost in my mind, I expounded on the value of consolidating all naval inspection activities, thus simplifying the problems of the contractors, also saving manpower and some millions of dollars annually for the Navy. The Secretary was impressed and asked me to give him a memorandum on the subject, which I did the next morning. He had the memorandum reproduced and sent to all the chiefs of bureau with a request for comment as to why the proposal should not be put into effect immediately. Having no idea that he would do this, I was totally unprepared when summoned to the office of the Chief of the Bureau of Ordnance, whom I had not even seen since reporting for duty.

Admiral Blandy, whose nickname was "Spike," was a man, rock-visaged, the picture of stern authority and command. As I entered, the memorandum from the Secretary of the Navy was the only paper on his desk in the large office, whose walls were ornamented with pikes, cutlasses, and other reminders of the days when ordnance was largely composed of weapons for close combat.

"Have you ever seen this before?" he asked, indicating the paper before him. I acknowledged authorship (months later, I would have added, in officialese, of the "referenced memorandum").

"Well," he said, "you may be interested to know that I have just received this from the Secretary of the Navy and I find that it is written by *you*, a lieutenant commander in *my* bureau. Haven't you had the word that you may not communicate with anyone senior to me other than through me? What have you to say for yourself?"

Well, I had very little to say for myself, because I recognized, too late, that I had been guilty of a serious breach of discipline. The fact that it had occurred in the unofficial atmosphere of the Secretary's dinner table was, I reflected (but did not say), no excuse. I began to feel, right then, that I had been in the Navy long enough, and so volunteered the observation that it would be a good thing for discipline in the bureau if the chief of the bureau would make an example of this issue and send me back to private life, where, obviously, I belonged. At this, Blandy could contain himself no longer. His scowl disappeared and he threw back his head and laughed. "I happen to agree with everything you have written," he said, "but I wish I had known of it before you wrote it. I could have improved your case." Captain Albert G. (Chuck) Noble, my immediate senior, who was present during the interview, appeared as relieved as I was. Later I learned that he had tried to shoulder the blame by saying that I had told him of my ideas and might therefore have assumed that he had reported to Blandy.*

Navy material inspection was duly consolidated for the remainder of the war, but only after a pitched battle with the bureau chiefs. As it had the blessing of James Forrestal, Under Secretary of the Navy, and

* Noble had a distinguished combat career and on his return served as chief of the bureau.

was also favored by Admiral Nimitz, it was finally adopted and it did result in increased efficiency and savings.

The next morning my assignment was changed and I was ordered to report as executive assistant to the chief of the bureau—Admiral Blandy. We soon became friends. Blandy, like other graduates of the Naval Academy, had been imbued with love of country more strongly than with any other sentiment, and I think he sincerely believed in the doctrine that the Navy was the one indispensable service which could defend and preserve the nation against all aggression. He had that rare quality of leadership which elicited respect and absolute confidence from those who served under him. I have heard many junior officers who were with him in the Pacific say that they had rather go into battle with Blandy on the bridge than any other commander. I never heard him critical of those senior to him, except in their presence, and then on some matter he regarded as important and when a mistake in judgment was about to be made. On such an occasion, he spoke out with a frankness that spared no feelings.

During his tenure as Chief of the Bureau of Ordnance, he succeeded in "putting the prod into production"—a slogan he coined.

Blandy's record as an administrator and later as a great combat officer was not destined to be crowned with his ultimate ambition, appointment as Chief of Naval Operations. With the retirement of Admiral Nimitz, it appeared that his goal was about to be reached. There were two other officers of high rank, however, whose qualifications had to be considered along with him, Admirals Ramsey and Denfeld. In this instance, President Truman appears to have found decision difficult, and Forrestal, who admired Blandy personally, resisted an impulse to urge his selection, because the three men were of such ability that he could not choose between them on grounds of merit. In November 1947, the President finally made his decision on the safe grounds "of age and position on the lineal list," selecting Denfeld, who not only turned out to be able, but by his display of stamina and personal courage in the subsequent B-36-versus-carriers controversy, surprised some who thought he would be an easygoing timeserver. The President had Blandy come to his office, told him the reasons for his decision, indicated that Blandy would be next in line, but as things turned out, naval advancement was ended for him. He never seemed more admirable than by his conduct in the face of this crushing disappointment.

During Blandy's administration of the Bureau of Ordnance there was a Research Division under the capable command of Captain Garrett L.

Schuyler and later Captain Samuel Shumaker. This division was particularly alert to new developments and free from the affliction known as "NIH" ("not invented here"), which was widely believed to prejudice the Armed Services against developments dreamed up by inventors outside the military establishment. Blandy himself was on the lookout for new weapons, and it was due to his personal success in bringing back to the United States, some months before the war, detailed drawings of the Oerlikon and Bofors quick-firing antiaircraft guns that the fleet was equipped with these revolutionary new weapons. The only antiaircraft machine guns prior to that time had been two of lesser caliber with neither adequate range nor ammunition large enough to contain a bursting charge, firing only solid bullets. It was rumored that, in the best cloak-and-dagger tradition, Blandy obtained the detailed drawings of the two new guns overseas and concealed them in reduced form under postage stamps. I never persuaded him to confirm this, or deny it, either.

* * *

One of the most original and effective military developments in World War II was the proximity, or "VT," fuse. It was of incalculable value to both the Army and Navy and it helped save London from obliteration. While no one invention won the war, the proximity fuse must be listed among the very small group of developments, such as radar, upon which victory very largely depended.

Prior to the invention of the fuse, projectiles and bombs were detonated by fuses which operated essentially upon impact or were "timed," either by a powder train or by clockwork, to explode within a predetermined time after leaving the muzzle of a gun or the bomb bay of a plane. Such time fuses required presetting. A calculation had to be made, manually or mechanically, after observation of the speed and range of the target, speed of the ship or plane from which the projectile or bomb was launched, windage, and other variables. For a long time, ordnance specialists had dreamed of a fuse which would be activated by the target itself, that is to say, a fuse which would tell the shell or bomb to explode just when it came within that distance of the target where fragmentation and blast would be most effective. Such a fuse would turn near-misses into hits. In effect, it would increase the size of the target. Only a small percentage of rounds fired under combat conditions actually hit targets.

There were several ways, in theory, of realizing this dream, but in practice none had been made to work. The Office of Scientific Research and Development, a civilian agency doing remarkable work on other projects, had been engaged on the fuse problem since early in the war but had about concluded to abandon it for more promising enterprises. The Navy Bureau of Ordnance, however, was loath to see the project dropped. The bane of the surface Navy was attack by aircraft. Even as far back as 1938, three years before the war, during a meeting of the Battleship Advisory Board, Admiral King (later to command the Navy) estimated that perhaps 5 per cent of hits could be obtained by aircraft flying at 15,000 feet. The discussion was in terms of 500-pound bombs.[1] Based upon allied experience in Europe in the early months of the war, even good antiaircraft fire from the ground (i.e., from a fixed platform) brought down only one plane for about every 2500 rounds fired. At 2500 or more rounds per plane downed, ships could not carry enough ammunition for long cruises and many attacks.

Blandy's interest was of long standing. One of his first acts on becoming chief of ordnance was to contract with the Carnegie Institution of Washington "for preliminary experimental studies on new ordnance devices," cover language for the attempt to develop a proximity fuse.

Dr. Merle A. Tuve, a brilliant young scientist in the Terrestrial Magnetism Laboratory of the institution, was put in charge of the work. He proved to be a miraculously good choice. Heading research in the Bureau of Ordnance was Captain G. L. Schuyler. He was familiar with the work which had been attempted in other countries on such fuses. Photoelectric effect, acoustic, and other means all had been experimented with, but none had been successful. A pragmatist, Schuyler insisted that no proximity fuse would be of any value unless the target were within the fragmentation pattern when the shell exploded. Otherwise, as he put it, the fuse would not be a weapon but "the world's most complicated form of self-destroying ammunition."

It was finally decided that the best hope lay in designing a fuse to be activated by an electronic pulse reflected from the target. In order to accomplish this, it was necessary to design a fuse which could contain a radio transmitting station, a receiver, and a power supply to operate both. The transmitter would have to be designed so that it did not start to operate until a certain time after the projectile on which the fuse was riding had been fired. This was necessary to prevent the projectile from mistaking as its target the ship or plane which had fired it. The signals reflected by the target would be picked up by the receiver in the fuse and then, at the precise point where the signal and its echo

indicated the desired nearness to the target, the projectile would be instructed to explode.

In this oversimplification, an elegant device is shorn of the multitude
of difficulties which confronted its inventors. The power source, the
sending and receiving equipment, and all other components had to be
contained within a space somewhat smaller than a hundred-watt light
bulb. The vacuum tubes—this being before the age of transistors—and
all the other components would have to be not only miniatures but unbelievably rugged. They would have to withstand an initial force—"set-
back"—experienced in firing a five-inch antiaircraft shell, approximately
twenty thousand times the force of gravity. After this enormous sudden
acceleration, all the components in the fuse would have to function perfectly. It is no wonder that many technical men considered the attempt
to make such a fuse as a waste of time. Indeed, it looked so unpromising
in comparison with other projects on which the Office of Scientific
Research and Development was working that it was about to be "put
on the back burner" and its emphasis reduced. Blandy's judgment at
this juncture that the goal was worth the gamble of almost any amount
of money and talent was one of the fortunate decisions of the period.

For Tuve and his co-workers, among whom most notably was Lawrence Hafstad,* eventually succeeded brilliantly. Many of the tests of
fuse models were conducted at the Naval Proving Ground at Dahlgren,
Virginia, where with Admiral Blandy we would go down to see the
fuses in dummy bombs dropped from planes and then dug out of the
earth and examined anxiously for the functioning of their components.

Following the success of the Japanese air-borne torpedo attack on our
fleet at Pearl Harbor, from which most of the Japanese planes returned
unscathed, and the sinking a few days later of the great British battleships *Prince of Wales* and *Repulse,* the Navy eagerly desired that development of the fuse should be hastened. Ordnance funds were put at
the disposal of the Office of Scientific Research and Development, and
Commander William S. Parsons (later to figure prominently in the development and initial use of the atomic bomb) was assigned by Blandy
as a special assistant to Dr. Vannevar Bush and in charge of what was
known as Section T. Tuve, Hafstad, Henry H. Porter, and D. Luke
Hopkins of Baltimore, the last mentioned representing Johns Hopkins
University (which replaced the Carnegie Institution as contractor to

* Dr. Hafstad later came to the Atomic Energy Commission, where he brought
atomic electric power from the experimental stage into actual use.

the Navy), were now full time on the project with a large staff. A laboratory to be known as the Applied Physics Laboratory of Johns Hopkins was organized and housed in a garage building in Silver Spring, a Washington suburb convenient to the Bureau of Ordnance. Externally, the garage appeared unchanged, and many of its neighbors never suspected that protecting their homes and lives, rather than their transportation, was the purpose of the work being carried on inside.

When rugged and miniaturized electronic components were finally perfected—vacuum tubes as small as beans which could be dropped from the top of the Washington Monument without injury—fuses were assembled and fired at a variety of targets. Batteries were developed which were inert until the projectile was fired. By September 1942 we were in quantity production of fuses, and they were tested against drone planes, radio-controlled. With Secretary Knox and Admiral Blandy on a visit to the proving grounds, we saw drones brought down in flames, one after another, with a minimum of rounds fired.

It was reassuring to know that the development had first been made by the United States. The earliest use of the fuse in action occurred in the South Pacific in January 1943. From that time on, proximity-fused shells became more and more lethal for the Japanese attackers.

The details of construction of the fuse and even its existence were most secret. Originally it was not issued to the Army for fear that if an ammunition dump were captured or a dud should fall into enemy hands the device might be copied and turned against us. Even contractors who made components were not informed of the use of the assemblies. Stocks of fuses were kept under constant military guard, and when a ship with fuses aboard returned to port, all were accounted for before any of the crew were allowed to come ashore.

The interest of the Army increased, naturally, since it was realized that fuses could be set to burst at a predetermined height above the earth or buildings and therefore could be used effectively against enemy troops out of sight behind hills or in trenches or in streets or towns. A mechanical fuse could not be timed precisely enough to accomplish regularly what the proximity fuse would always do. The proximity fuse could be depended upon to burst at the same height above a hill as above the floor of a valley and, in that manner, a barrage as it moved forward could actually follow the contour of a terrain.

The Navy finally released the fuse to the Army. It had been difficult to secure the consent of Fleet Admiral King, Chief of Naval Operations, who had feared its accidental compromise if used over land. Near the end of the war, a number of shells equipped with VT fuses were reported to have fallen into the hands of the Germans when they overran one of our ammunition dumps in the Battle of the Bulge. The plastic nose cones in which the tops of the fuses were contained, being black and opaque, looked like a conventional metal fuse and did not excite German curiosity. The ammunition dump was recovered intact when our lines moved ahead not long thereafter.

The fuse was used by the Army with great effect against the Germans under Von Rundstedt on December 16, 1944, and not only brought down numbers of German planes, but, used in howitzer ammunition, stemmed the German advance toward the River Meuse. German prisoners described our artillery fire as completely demoralizing, and General Patton on December 29 wrote to General Levin Campbell (a graduate of the Naval Academy), Chief of Army Ordnance and a friend and classmate of Admiral Blandy: "The new shell with the funny fuse is devastating. The other night we caught a German battalion, which was trying to get across the Sauer River, with a battalion concentration and killed by actual count 702. I think that when all armies get this shell, we will have to devise some new method of warfare. I am glad that you all thought of it first."[2]

The most spectacular success of the proximity fuse, however, was against the German V-1, the "buzz bomb." Early in 1943, Admiral Wilson Brown, who was an aide to President Roosevelt, had sent Blandy a message which the President had received from Churchill. British intelligence, the Prime Minister said, had heard of a project called "Athodyd," reported to be a rocket powered by an "aerodynamic thermal duct" (from which presumably the term Athodyd was derived) and that it was to be used as a pilotless aircraft to bomb Britain. "What do your people," the Prime Minister inquired, "think of its feasibility and the likelihood that it could be made operational?"

Admiral Blandy read the message at a staff meeting of his division heads, and it was the concensus of opinion that this was most likely more of the "secret weapon" propaganda—weapons invented by Goebbels for psychological warfare. Captain Sam Shumaker and I, however, felt that there was a possibility that a self-propelled bomb could be flown across the Channel, riding a radio beam rather than taking a ballistic course. Given the short distance of England from the Continent, this beam could be kept narrow enough for hits on targets as large as cities. Blandy said that he had no objection if we wanted to express our conjectures, but "definitely not as the opinion of 'BuOrd.'" This, in some detail, we did. Shumaker even dreamed up a device which nearly paralleled the actual weapon. Intelligence subsequently confirmed the prospective construction of the V-1 bomb, and even pin-pointed launching sites.

As a result, we had a supply of proximity fuses in England three months before the first "buzz bomb" appeared. The VT-fused antiaircraft shells were distributed to batteries along the channel coast with the expectation that if any of the rounds were duds they would fall into the water and could not be recovered by the Germans. The V-1 buzz bombs came over at about 350 miles per hour, were tracked by radar, and the batteries which fired shells with proximity fuses were aimed by means of Army and Navy fire-control systems. The results were spectacular. During the last four weeks of the buzz-bomb campaign 24 per cent of the bombs were destroyed in the first week; 46 per cent the second; 67 per cent the third week; and in the final week 79 per cent were knocked down. On the last day the Germans used buzz bombs 104 of them were picked up on the radar screen, of which number only four reached London.

* * *

My friendly relations with Admiral Blandy and with the Vice-Chief of Naval Operations, Admiral Frederick J. Horne, were in marked contrast with my standing with the man who became the highest officer of the Navy, Fleet Admiral Ernest J. King, Chief of Naval Operations. King was a character and he lived up to a reputation for saltiness. Able, hard, fearless, and to some domineering, he ran the Navy as a taut ship. King was not on duty in Washington when war began, but soon was sent for. When the orders to report as CNO reached him, he is quoted as saying, "I expected this. When they get in trouble back there, they always send for the S.O.B.s."

He took command with vigor. The Navy was his, every ship and man. He knew their capacities and trusted them. He and his Chief of Naval Personnel, Admiral Jacobs, however, held their rapidly increasing complement of Reserve officers in something less than enthusiastic regard. There was undoubtedly plenty of justification for this. Many Reserve officers were inadequately trained and undisciplined. I was a prime example. With time we overcame both defects. The hostility of a few regular officers was not characteristic, and generally they helped the Reserves to learn. I recall an occasion when, after his initial successes in the Pacific, Admiral Halsey had returned to Washington for medical attention. Secretary Knox invited the press to his office to interview the Admiral. A reporter asked, "Admiral, what is your general impression of your Reserve officers?" to which Halsey, without a split second of hesitation, replied, "I haven't any idea which of my officers are Reserves."

The great increase in the number of ships meant, of course, that there were not enough Regular officers available even for command, and many of the smaller craft were of necessity skippered by Reserves. Reserves also became executive officers, gunnery officers, damage control officers, and heads of other departments on many of the large ships. They turned in a noteworthy record and many were cited for outstanding performance, devotion to duty, and gallantry in action.

My difficulties with Admiral King, however, had nothing to do with my being a reservist and were strictly my own fault. Secretary Knox had flown to Pearl Harbor after the disaster on December 7 and, upon his return to the department, all officers were mustered in the dining hall on what was nautically called the top deck of the old Navy building. Seated on a platform at one end of the hall were the Secretary, Assistant Secretary Bard, and Admiral King. When King arose to speak he referred to an ALNAV he had signed. King's name was signed to a number of ALNAVs (directives broadcast to the entire naval establishment). Some, which had been issued in the days after Pearl Harbor, seemed almost comic under the circumstances. One, for instance, stipulated that in future the eagle on the cap ornament must face the sword arm instead of to the left, as previously. The ALNAV which Admiral King now read, addressed to all the naval establishment at sea and ashore, directed that "paper work" should be drastically curtailed and, to this end, half of all the typewriters should be impounded. The objective was admirable but the means were so unusual that I turned to a friend standing behind me, H. Struve Hensel,* and observed (*sotto voce,* I thought) that this would be like inhibiting pickpockets by doing away with pockets. Actually, I employed a somewhat earthier metaphor. I was to regret my poor idea of humor. Unfortunately, a period of absolute silence had followed King's words and my voice carried beyond my intended audience. The doughty Admiral's face changed color, and as he turned to Secretary Bard I could almost see his lips frame his question, *"Who* is that officer?" and Bard's response, "A Reserve lieutenant commander named Strauss."

* Later General Counsel of the Department of Defense.

I was to regret my sense of the ridiculous because this was the beginning of my private war with Fleet Admiral King, which survived both V-E and V-J days. It was very gracefully terminated by Admiral King himself, who invited me to lunch in 1946. He said somewhat gruffly that during the war he had misjudged me. "You rated a well done," he added. This enabled me to clear my conscience and I told him some of the things I had thought about him, and that I had once said that he was the equivalent of two Japanese task forces. To my immense relief, he laughed. We remained good friends to the end of his life, and on an occasion when he with General Vandegrift (former Commandant of the Marine Corps), Admirals Halsey, Spruance, Joy, and Mitscher decided to make a statement to the nation in defense of aircraft carriers, appropriations for which were then under attack, King, as informal chairman of the group, called me in to draft the paper.

There was, however, and to my regret, no truce with Admiral Jacobs, who never was able to understand my representation on behalf of Reserve officers as a member of the Reserve Policy Board, to which Knox had named me. On one occasion in November 1943, meeting in a corridor of the Navy Department, Jacobs stopped to say that at the direction of Secretary Knox he had that morning prepared the papers promoting me to rear admiral, skipping the rank of captain (I was by that time wearing the three stripes of a commander). He added that he took a very dim view of this act on the part of the Secretary. It was the first I had heard of it and I took a dim view of it likewise, but for somewhat different reasons. I returned to my desk and wrote a letter[3] to the Secretary, requesting that he withdraw the proposal for my promotion on the ground that, if a Reserve were to be selected for flag rank, there were Reserve officers serving at sea who should be considered first. Secretary Knox sent for me and told me that he had telephoned to the White House and recalled the recommendation. In due course, I was promoted to captain, later to commodore, and finally in 1945 to rear admiral.

* * *

In the spring of 1942, Forrestal, Blandy, Forrestal's aide, Captain John Gingrich,* and Frank Folsom, of the War Production Board

* Gingrich was well known among navigators as the author of *H.O. 214*, a publication of the Hydrographic Office with tables of computed altitude and azimuth for every latitude. He later distinguished himself in combat as captain of the U.S.S. *Pittsburgh*, and joined me in work with the Atomic Energy Commission.

(later president of the Radio Corporation of America), flew to the South Pacific by way of Pearl Harbor, stopping at Palmyra, Canton Island, Johnston Island, Midway, the Fijis, and New Caledonia. There had been loud complaints and bitter criticism by the Submarine Command, under Admiral Lockwood, about the malfunction of our torpedoes, and I was taken along for that reason. I had visited the torpedo factories at Newport and Alexandria and had some acquaintance with torpedo mechanisms. I arranged for two real experts to be along.

Our submarine skippers, who were taking extreme hazards to put themselves in the lanes of Japanese shipping, reported that after firing a spread of torpedoes they could hear them through their hydrophones as they struck the hulls of Japanese ships without exploding. This defect was traced to an exploder which was of a type that should have been far more effective than the World War I contact exploders. The only trouble was that it did not function at all. The reason explained to me by Blandy was that torpedoes cost about twelve thousand dollars apiece and, because of the pittance available to Navy Ordnance for proof-testing during the period between the two World Wars, no torpedo had been fired with a live warhead, since that would have destroyed it. Torpedoes fired at proving grounds were recovered intact, if possible, and used again and again. The new type exploder, insufficiently tested, had to be inactivated by order as the result of our survey on the trip and for months we relied upon a design which was essentially more than twenty years old.

At Pearl Harbor, Admiral Furlong, who was in command of the Navy Yard there, told me of the experience on the morning of the attack. His command then was the Mine Laying Squadron, and he was having breakfast on the deck of his flagship, the *Ogalala,* when the explosion from the first near-miss toppled the eggs and coffee into his lap. He took me aboard the battleship *West Virginia,* which was burned out and resting on the bottom but with her deck awash. Her commander had been Captain Merwin S. Bennion, with whom I had served in the Bureau of Ordnance. Bennion had impressed me as one of the kindliest and most considerate men I had ever met. Realizing how green I was, he and his assistant, Captain Zimmerman, had spent hours helping me on my assignments. He wrote me when taking command of the *West Virginia* that it was the realization of his ambition. In the attack on December 7, Bennion was on the bridge directing the fire of his batteries. A fragment from a Japanese bomb struck him in the stomach, inflicting a wound that was obviously fatal. He refused to leave the bridge and, propped against the rail, continued to fight his ship until he died. He was a member of the Mormon Church, and we had often discussed religious subjects; I know that his faith was equal to his courage. I asked Admiral Furlong for a brass direction marker pried from a fire-blackened bulkhead of the *West Virginia*. On it are the words *"Forward and Up."* I often look at it.

Our fortunes in the Pacific were at the ebb. Supplies and equipment had not yet begun to build up. On occasion, Japanese submarines had been able to lay offshore at night and shell our garrisons at Johnston and Canton islands. In all such places, complete blackout was obligatory. On one fearfully hot night on Johnston Island, Blandy and I went for a walk on the beach after supper. The Admiral lit a cigarette. Instantly from somewhere in the thick darkness, an indignant Marine voice called out, "Hey, you S.O.B., put out that —— —— cigarette."

"Mind your language, soldier," Blandy responded. "You happen to be addressing a rear admiral of the U. S. Navy."

"O.K.," came the reply, "you put out that —— —— cigarette or you'll be a dead rear admiral." Under the circumstances, Blandy made the quick decision that discretion at this point was more important than discipline. He ground out his cigarette in the sand.

One evening as we sat at supper on Admiral Ghormley's flagship in the harbor of Nouméa, New Caledonia, we discussed military research, its neglect in peacetime, its feverish resumption after war began, and the pittance for testing and "proving" ordnance between wars to ensure that stockpiles would be in "ready" condition. In the old days, this aim had been expressed by the simple admonition to "keep your powder dry."

We were all of a mind in thinking that the surprise factor in warfare would be developed to the point where it could become absolutely decisive and that a third World War, if it should ever occur, would not afford the United States days of grace necessary for the development of countermeasures against enemy weapons and for perfecting new weapons of our own. These days of grace in World War II had provided the time within which the Office of Scientific Research and Development, under Dr. Bush and Dr. Conant, performed so significantly.

This supper was four years before an atomic chain reaction had been demonstrated and before most of those in the wardroom had ever heard the words "atomic bomb." We also agreed that in all likelihood the end of World War II would witness as a first effect a reduction of interest and support for purely military research. When we returned to

Washington, the subject was discussed with Under Secretary of War Patterson, who agreed. It was apparent that research other than the military would not languish for support after the war. Aeronautical research would be sustained by the requirements of the aviation industry. Electronic research would prosper due to the development of the communication and entertainment industries, etc. But it was apparent also that, without some special stimulus, research on weapons and countermeasures would become unpopular with scientists and businessmen alike, since it would be widely assumed that the end of the Nazi and Fascist dictatorships would be the end of war itself.

In early 1944 I proposed to Forrestal that we should make an effort to obtain a sizable appropriation from the Congress for *postwar* research in military areas and to get this while the war was going on. We should request a billion dollars (at that time a good deal more could be done with such a sum), with the understanding that the principal would be left with the Treasury Department for investment and reinvestment in U. S. Government obligations, the idea being that military research would be able to subsist upon the income. The main feature of this arrangement was that it would enable long-range research programs to be undertaken without dependence upon annual appropriations. It is obviously impossible to produce results from research on the arbitrary schedule of a fiscal year, and legislative attitudes are not reliably consistent over the time span required for most research.

Forrestal invited Under Secretary Patterson, Charles E. Wilson, of the General Electric Company, Frank B. Jewett, president of the National Academy of Sciences, to meet with us in early June 1944, and, as a result, a Committee on Post-War Research was named under Wilson as chairman. It had among its members the military chiefs of the Army Technical Corps, and the chiefs of naval ordnance, ships, and aeronautics. Science was represented by Jewett and by Karl T. Compton, J. C. Hunsaker, and Merle Tuve. The committee regarded itself as temporary and recommended a permanent body to be called the Research Board for National Security. That board was organized but never became effective and was given the *coup de grâce* by the Secretaries of War and Navy the following year.

Others in the Navy Department were concerned with the problem of research in the postwar period. A group of able young officer technicians who had been brought into the work by Dr. Hunsaker (especially Commander Bruce S. Old) were pushing a project to have an Assistant Secretary for Research added to the Navy top echelon. Forrestal, who abhorred increasing staff, took a jaundiced view of the suggestion and it made no headway at that time, although the idea is now represented in all three service departments and again in the Office of the Secretary of Defense.

A year earlier, in October 1943, Forrestal, then Under Secretary, had asked R. J. Dearborn, who was Chairman of the Committee on Patents of the National Association of Manufacturers, to survey the situation in the Navy with respect to patents, inventions, and research. The Dearborn report was completed by March 1944, and its conclusions were so sound that, though the Office of Naval Research did not come into existence until later, Mr. Dearborn deserves credit for the basic concept. Admiral Bowen, first Chief of Naval Research, has too generously ascribed its establishment to me.[4]

When the war in Europe had ended and the war in the Pacific was clearly near its end, Struve Hensel and I joined forces to convince Forrestal that, if any research organization of a permanent nature were to be established before the expected letdown at the end of hostilities, no further time could be lost. A directive for a new "office"—the Office of Research and Inventions—was prepared, and the Naval Research Laboratory near Washington and the Special Devices Center of the Bureau of Aeronautics, among others, were to be assigned to it. The last-mentioned organization was the particular empire of Rear Admiral Luis de Florez, a reservist of unusual qualities. Aviator, gadgeteer, and sometime professional joker, he was also a first-class administrator and a fruitful generator of new ideas. A day with him was an exhausting and nerve-racking experience especially if it included being a passenger in his plane, which he piloted, talking and gesticulating all the while. It was a tossup whether his passenger was more stimulated by the ideas or the hazards.

The office later became the Office of Naval Research, and Admiral Bowen, an "engineering duty only" officer, thereafter had as much trouble in his day as Admiral Rickover was to experience twenty years later and for some of the same reasons. Bowen was a highly competent engineer, original, pioneering, and fearless. His campaign in earlier years to introduce high-temperature and high-pressure steam in naval propulsion ran into the inevitable and almost immovable mossback opposition. At the risk of his future advancement, Bowen lobbied and blasted his project through. The efficiency of the fleet owes him much for that and other innovations. His early realization of the importance of radar (developed at the Naval Research Laboratory when he was in charge) and of atomic energy for ship propulsion was farsighted.[5]

The Office of Naval Research fortunately was able to begin with money. De Florez had some twenty-four million dollars of unexpended appropriations in his Special Devices Center, which became part of Naval Research, and Congress soon gave its confidence to ONR, as the new office came to be called. The crusty Chairman of the House Naval Affairs Committee, Carl Vinson, had known Bowen of old. The men had differed, but Bowen stood up to him, and Vinson respected him. Vinson had seniority and great power in the Congress. The ONR proceeded to work out a program by which contracts were made with universities for basic research under conditions palatable to the scientists and yet reasonable to the Bureau of the Budget. Men who had vowed that they would never do any work after the war for either Armed Service found themselves doing so.

The result was that when the Office of Scientific Research and Development began to liquidate at the end of the war, the Office of Naval Research filled the breach. A Naval Research Advisory Committee, recommended by Bowen, met regularly and included some of the best minds in the country. The timely organization of the Office of Naval Research and the manner in which it has operated during its fifteen years deserve much of the credit for the commanding position of the United States in many fields of research since World War II. The Atomic Energy Commission has shared many projects in nuclear physics with ONR.

NAV-TECH-MIS-EU

As the war in Europe neared its close, it was clear that there was a treasure to be captured from the enemy to which we were entitled as a proper spoil of war. It would not be pillage in the ordinary sense. It was material which, if, by default, we did not possess ourselves of it, might be destroyed or might fall into the hands of the Russians. In our keeping, it might contribute to our future security. Accordingly, I proposed the establishment of a task force to be composed of naval personnel with technical qualifications to be sent to the European Theater at once.[6] Their duty would be to discover and take possession of German military and scientific data.

A related project had been initiated by Manhattan District of the U. S. Army Corps of Engineers, though it was not then known to me. It was secretly conducted because it was designed to uncover any work the Germans might have been doing on atomic weapons. Under the code name "Alsos" (Greek for "Groves") it was skillfully managed by Dr. Sam Goudsmit, who later worked with the Atomic Energy Commission.

Our project, lacking the inspiration of Greek nomenclature, was called more awkwardly in Navyese "Nav-Tech-Mis-Eu"—an abbreviation for Naval Technical Mission—Europe. It had no specific goal like that of Alsos and, in consequence, turned up an astonishingly large and heterogeneous variety of scientific information, material, and people. It located cunningly concealed laboratories and manufacturing installations (by the ingeniously simple expedient of tracking power lines); it found refugee scientists hidden in mines and caves, camouflaged wind tunnels, and rocket plants. It took possession of tons of documents and reports. It was commanded by Commodore H. A. Schade, an officer whom I had known for the high quality of his work in the Navy Department. (His second-in-command was to have been my good friend Captain Festus Foster, who lost his life in a plane accident over Paris en route to his post.)

Fleet Admiral King was proud of the success of Nav-Tech-Mis-Eu. In his final report to the Secretary of the Navy, he noted that the mission was under his "direct operational control"; that it had worked closely with the Army G-2 and with Allied intelligence services. "It has uncovered a vast amount of data," he wrote, "concerning German wartime industrial and scientific developments, the status of experiments on secret weapons, etc. . . ." King was not the only one who had pride in the mission. Among the officers commended was a young J.G. who had entered some occupied cities ahead of the liberating army. He was my son and I was more than pleased.

* * *

Before we were at war, many manufacturers were reluctant to take ordnance contracts from the Navy Department. One reason was that they enjoyed a large volume of business from the British, who were less exacting to deal with. Secretary Knox asked me to devise a project which would overcome this reluctance. "Would it be possible or desirable," he asked in a memorandum, "to publish a black list of concerns which have practically refused to bid for Navy business?" Since black lists seldom accomplish anything good, I suggested that an incentive system—a white list—would accomplish more.

Captain Theodore Ruddock of the bureau called my attention to the awards for gunnery and engineering that had become time-honored in the fleet—the right to paint an "E" on the turret of a ship as an award for gunnery or on the stack of a ship to indicate an award for engineering efficiency. This suggested that "Navy Es" might be awarded to contractors who completed their contracts on schedule, for reducing costs, and for general efficiency. Knox approved the plan and suggested that it be tried out as a Bureau of Ordnance project. I enlisted James P. Selvage of New York, an experienced public relations counsel, who had done a fine job for Finnish Relief; also James Irwin, who was given leave of absence by Edgar Queeny, of the Monsanto Chemical Company. These men, together with J. Handley Wright and several officers from the bureau, especially Commander Dan Armstrong, made up a task force which did such an outstanding job that the project was quickly adopted for the whole Naval Establishment. In the following year the project became the "Army and Navy 'E' Award." It has generally been regarded by those competent to appraise such enterprises as a model for successful industrial and public relations campaigns. Admiral Clark Woodward, Admiral Wat T. Cluverius, and their opposite numbers in the Army who managed the project in its later stages maintained the high standard for the awards which had been set in the Bureau of Ordnance. In consequence, there are many plants today, nearly a score of years later, in which the insignia, a white "E" surrounded by a wreath of laurel on a background of Navy blue and Army crimson, is still proudly displayed.

* * *

In order to survive the pressures of wartime Washington, it was necessary to arrive, if possible, with a sense of humor and to go to any lengths to hang on to it.

During the hot summer months in 1941, a subcommittee of the House Naval Affairs Committee had begun an investigation of the procurement policies of the Navy. Counsel for the subcommittee was a man named Toland, who usually referred to his client committee as the "Toland Committee," although he was not, of course, a member of it. Someone had informed him that I had been instrumental in placing large orders for aircraft with companies in which I had a substantial financial interest. This reason for Toland's particular interest in me did not appear until long afterward, and a simple question from him could have elicited the fact that the Bureau of Ordnance placed no contracts for aircraft; that I had nothing to do with the letting of contracts for such items as the Bureau of Ordnance did place; and that I had never had any financial interest in companies producing aircraft. Instead of inquiring, Toland undertook to obtain evidence by subpoena.

Late one afternoon two young men with credentials identifying them as attachés of the Toland Committee arrived at my office and presented a demand for the contents of my desk and my files. As this was before we were at war and quite late in the afternoon, counsel for the bureau had left for the day and no one was in the office of the Judge Advocate General of the Navy. Under protest, therefore, I surrendered what the subpoena called for, although the only items in my desk were some undeposited Navy salary checks and several letters from my wife. The files were too voluminous for the two agents to carry off, so they were sealed in place.

In the course of conversation while they did this, the two young men mentioned the fact that they were Army Reserve officers who had been borrowed from the War Department by counsel for the Naval Affairs Committee. They were thoroughly disgusted with their assignment. Subsequently, I learned that the Military Affairs Committee borrowed naval officers for similar surveillance of the War Department. The following morning I walked into the office of the Under Secretary of War and expressed my indignation at this practice. Judge Patterson agreed that it was outrageous to have officers of one service used to police the other, and promptly recalled the two officers in question from the Naval Affairs Committee. I heard nothing more of the inquiry. The House committee had found nothing to disturb it. My personal correspondence was returned intact. Captain Noble was then my immediate superior, and when word reached him of the incident he sent me a note. "You should have called me at my home," he wrote. "I would have gotten a few Marines and chucked those fellows out of the window."

During part of the time that I was attached to the Office of the Under Secretary of the Navy, there was assigned to me as an assistant, a young lieutenant commander named Douglas Fairbanks, Jr. Fairbanks was as glamorous in real life as in a Hollywood studio, and in his Navy uniform he was a show-stopper, or, more properly, a work-stopper. The stenographers and young lady clerks bringing messages to our office took an inordinately long time to dispose of their business. Messages that ordinarily would have been sent through the department mail system were personally delivered, and the hallway outside the doors of the office was generally populated with groups of star-struck young ladies. Fairbanks endured this good-humoredly for several months, but finally requested a change of duty, which I sympathetically endorsed. He was clearly miscast in the prosaic duties assigned to him, and his request was for active duty at sea. He was sent to the European Theater, assigned to train with the Commandos, and in subsequent landings and diversionary raids, he conducted himself with great intrepidity, winning medals and citations for valor. My regard for his industry, which had been based upon the most limited acquaintance with the men in it, was very greatly enhanced by his example. Our friendship has continued down the years and we have often laughed at the hazards which beset him early in the Navy under my command.

(The men who worked with me from time to time were an unusual group, and I was most fortunate. They included George Keith Funston, who became president of Trinity College, Hartford, and later president of the New York Stock Exchange; Harold Linder, who became Assistant Secretary of State and afterward president of the Export-Import Bank; John Young, a partner of Morgan Stanley & Co.; Thurmond Chatham, who served his home state of North Carolina in Congress; William T. Golden, mentioned elsewhere; Harry F. Byrd, Jr., who is a Virginia publisher and state senator, and a number of other men of talent, imagination, and devotion.)

Representing the Navy, I once attended a meeting in the office of Secretary of the Treasury at which were representatives of the State and War departments. Although the meeting was informal, Secretary Morgenthau, following his custom, had a stenotypist at his desk making a verbatim record of everything that was said. This particular practice of the Secretary, since it inhibited freedom of expression at informal sessions, had been a source of some annoyance to his friends. (It has resulted in perhaps the richest archive of the period.) At this meeting, John J. McCloy, who was Assistant Secretary of War, took from his pocket a little camera, not much larger than a man's thumb. With this he proceeded, as ostentatiously as possible, to photograph the room and the participants. The Secretary, visibly annoyed, snapped, "McCloy, what are you doing with that thing?"

"I'm taking pictures," replied McCloy.

"Who authorized you to take pictures in my office?" inquired the Secretary.

"Who authorized you, Mr. Secretary, to have my conversation taken down?" said McCloy. The air seemed suddenly charged, but McCloy burst into laughter, as did everyone else, including Morgenthau, who thereupon excused the stenotypist.

One's sense of humor was strained or sustained by various crackpot proposals for conducting the war and for bringing it to a guaranteed conclusion. These included such scientific contributions as that of the man who conceived the idea of trapping large numbers of seals and sea lions, feeding them for months near simulated submarine periscopes and conning towers. Conditioned to seek food, when such things appeared at sea, these herds of innocuous animals would be released, each with an explosive charge (ingeniously fused) fastened around its neck like the casks of brandy carried by the dogs of St. Bernard. Another inventor proposed conditioning sea gulls by feeding them around such structures. By means of small, very light radio transmitters wired to the birds' legs, they would report the whereabouts of the submarines. There were even more subtle schemes afoot.

On one occasion, a young officer came in and seriously declared that, since becoming engaged to be married, he had discovered a faculty he had not known he possessed. This was the ability to project his consciousness to a great distance and to discover what a specific person was doing or thinking at that time. He said that he had been able to experiment with his fiancée, who lived in a distant city. By arrangement with her, they would mentally commune each night at a given hour and he would make a memorandum of where he pictured her to be and what she was thinking or doing. She thereupon would write to him with the required information. In substantiation of his clairvoyance, he was able to offer a large bundle of letters which in one form or another confirmed his visions. Just how he could project himself into the planning of the German and Japanese general staffs and find the same rapport he had with his fiancée was not clear, but, of course, only a detail to be worked out.

On another occasion, a mathematician obtained an appointment with Colonel William J. Donovan, who headed the Office of Strategic Services. With some embarrassment, he began, "I know, General Donovan, that you take a dim view of astrology and at one time, so did I. But I can assure you that it is not a pseudo science, there is something to it, and I am prepared to prove it and to show you how the war can be won with it."

"I want nothing for myself and I think that I can demonstrate with only a small amount of money to cover expenses that very remarkable things can be deduced about the plans and the fate of men whose date and hour of birth can be precisely known. This, of course, would have *very enormous implications with respect to Hitler.*"

Colonel Donovan told me that he had replied, "But look, how would one know the date and hour of Hitler's birth? Even his parentage is in doubt."

To this the mathematician responded, "In the case of Hitler, these time elements can be more precisely ascertained than even in your case or mine. This is true because we know certain events in Hitler's life with great precision. We know the date and hour that he became Chancellor of Germany; we know the hour that he invaded the Ruhr; the moment he invaded the Rhineland; the time he invaded Czechoslovakia, Austria, and Poland. These are fixed points on the chart and by simply extrapolating backward in time, we can arrive not only at the date and hour of his birth, but at the precise instant that he first saw the light. Then having determined the circumstances and the conjunction of the planets at his birth, we extrapolate *forward* and find out every decision he will make in the future."

"This is perfectly wonderful," said Donovan. "How much did you say it would cost?"

"Well," said the mathematician, "only enough to hire an actuary, a second-class astronomer, and maybe two or three clerks for a matter of a month or so. I would think that twenty-five or thirty thousand dollars would cover the bill."

"Fine," said Donovan dryly. "It is precisely what my office should do, but I must observe protocol very strictly or we could not exist, operating as we do between the military and the White House. Put on your hat and coat, sir, and go get the Secretaries of War and Navy to ask me to act on this and my office will take it from there." As his visitor was going out the door, Donovan called, "And be sure to get it in writing." Oddly enough, considering some of the projects of the time, nothing more was heard of this idea.

*   *   *

There was a variety of assignments during the tour of duty in the Navy. Once Forrestal asked me to follow the Navy's interest in a biological warfare project. It was clear that he regarded this as a distasteful assignment. "Just keep an eye on it," he said, "and if necessary, get a couple of keen fellows to follow it up for you. The Army has the direct cognizance, thank God." Fearing recourse to desperate tactics by the Japanese and Germans which might lead them into germ warfare, the Army had asked George Merck of the pharmaceutical firm to prepare serums or antidotes to immunize the armed forces and the general public against biological plagues. German and Japanese biologists who admittedly were more than competent might devise methods to introduce these horrors. It was a surprise to find that Mr. Merck's principal assistant was J. P. Marquand, whose *The Late George Apley* (published in 1937) I had just been reading. The biological warfare unit was clearly aimed at the production of countermeasures. In other words, it was a defensive activity.

On a visit to a laboratory operated by Dr. Merck and his associates, I was provided with a plastic coverall as a precaution. After touring the installation, I found that I had torn a small hole in the garment. "If I have been exposed to anything," I asked, "what symptoms should I expect and how soon?"

"You'd best not worry," was the answer. "If you picked up any of those bugs, it's too late for Herpicide."

Appointed as Navy member of the Munitions Board in 1944, I served for a period of a year as chairman of that body in the absence of a civilian chairman. The Munitions Board at that time, however, had a limited function, primarily the stockpiling of strategic materials.

In 1945 Colonel William Draper (later Under Secretary of the Army) and I wrote a report for the Secretaries of War and Navy, recommending and establishing procedures for unified purchase of materials common to both services, such as petroleum products, clothing, foodstuffs, surgical supplies, blankets, ammunition of common caliber, and many other items among the millions of items bought. At that time no catalogue or comprehensive list existed. The reforms recommended by this report, each specifically approved by the service secretaries, were at once instituted, but with the passage of years most were honored in the breach.

A more permanent result of this effort was the establishment by General Donald Armstrong of a school to instruct military personnel in business procedures for the negotiation and termination of contracts, etc. This survives as the Industrial College of the Armed Services.

* * *

Secretary Knox died suddenly in 1944 and was succeeded by James Forrestal. Blandy achieved his ambition to command a fleet in the combat area and left for the Pacific. Orders arrived for me to report for duty with the Secretary of the Navy. In a way this was an unlikely happening. In private life, Forrestal and I, while acquainted, had not been close friends. Indeed, as bankers we had been brisk competitors. We respected each other but at arm's length.

He first saw me in uniform while he was still Under Secretary during one of the monthly inspection visits he made to each bureau. In Ordnance, these visits were occasions for a summary by the chief of bureau and detailed reports by heads of divisions. After being called upon in my turn to report as "General Inspector of Ordnance," Jim drew me aside. "I didn't know you were here, Lewis," he said. "You know I could have you ordered to Argentia or Recife." Recife and Argentia were almost poles apart geographically but alike in remoteness, and I wondered if by any chance he could be serious, in which case I silently cursed my luck. The next day in fact new orders did arrive for me; they read: "Additional duty as Special Assistant to the Under Secretary of the Navy."

Later when he became Secretary of the Navy, my office was moved at Forrestal's order to one connecting with his. We saw each other several times daily. He would occasionally telephone in the early morning to get me over to start the day's work at breakfast. The friendship between us was marked by candor in discussion of his plans for the management of the Navy and, after the war was clearly won, of his own future. I am convinced that before the end of the war, he had made up his mind not to go back to Wall Street. Politics began to attract him. He had read widely on political economy and had ideas of his own which were arresting and which he could express convincingly. He liked to draw other people out and he was a good listener.

Of those who enjoyed his confidence, there were a number who were older and closer friends than I was, among them such men as Bernard Baruch, Arthur Krock, Ferdinand Eberstadt, and John Cahill. His aide, John Gingrich, and his assistants, Struve Hensel, John Kenney, Eugene Duffield, Charles Detmar, Matt Correa and Wirt Dulles were also admitted to his thoughts. He placed particular reliance upon a young officer, Marx Leva. Leva was a lawyer who had been a destroyer escort commander and was so susceptible to seasickness that during his entire service at sea, which spanned several years, he never passed a day without turning green. Forrestal was impressed by his stamina as well as his ability. He later became Assistant Secretary of Defense, in which capacity he served under each of Forrestal's successors during the Truman Administration. Many of Forrestal's other friends were held at a distance. All were united in admiration for his disciplined mind and respect for the intensity with which he drove himself in his job.

By 1944 he was recognized as the most influential man in the Cabinet. Stimson was the more venerated and by far the most experienced, but was obviously in his final public post. Forrestal was on his way up politically and there was no comparable rival. Under his direction the Navy became the greatest in the world and its morale the highest in its history. He was everywhere with the Fleet. In a Navy work uniform, without identifying insignia, he was a familiar sight on the bridge of a cruiser during an invasion operation or flying in a gunner's seat in carrier-based aircraft. He visited the Army commanders at their headquarters and, as a fighting man himself, was on terms of easy intimacy with them. He especially admired General Eisenhower, regarding him as tough but tactful and, in his own words, "very wise and clever, but too clever to get a reputation for that alone—in Navy parlance we'd call him 'savvy.'"

Had Forrestal lived, there is the possibility that he might have been General Eisenhower's opponent in 1952. He denied ambition for the presidency or even any desire for further Government service in the days when he was considering retirement to private life before the establishment of the Department of Defense. Undoubtedly, he believed that he was correctly describing his aims; yet, having frequently discussed them with him, I am convinced that the same considerations which persuaded him to accept appointment as the first Secretary of Defense would have led him to the nomination had not dark tragedy recognized in him a shining mark.

A decision by Forrestal in 1946 was the forerunner of an important aspect of American foreign policy. In that year we had begun to denude ourselves of our military strength, demobilizing, scrapping armament, moth-balling ships, and bulldozing planes and jeeps and other equipment into deep water in the Pacific. This was given publicity at the time as an earnest of our peaceful intentions in the supposition that we would be rewarded with favorable world opinion. There is nothing more ephemeral than that commodity.

Forrestal felt that the situation in the Middle East would benefit by "a show of the flag" and, accordingly, proposed sending fleet units into the Mediterranean. His idea found no favor with the State Department. Later with Admiral Forrest Sherman, Forrestal contrived an operation to accomplish this. It was based on the happenstance that the body of the Turkish Ambassador to the United States, who had died during the war, had not been taken back to his native land. Such a funeral voyage is usually accorded full military honors.

Forrestal proposed to President Truman that the diplomat's remains should be taken back on the battleship *Missouri*. Either the appropriate-

ness of the diplomatic gesture or the suggestion of the particular battleship, or both, presumably appealed to the President. Mr. Truman was
well known to have a soft spot for the *Missouri*. In any event, he was
convinced. Of course, a battleship could not proceed without its destroyer screen, and therefore the customary number of destroyers accompanied the *Missouri*. After the ambassadorial casket had been duly
delivered to the Turks, it would have been an affront not to pay courtesy calls at some of the ports that had been passed, such as the Piraeus,
and a whole schedule of courtesy calls was worked out. Forrestal drew
the President's attention to the fact that to have so much equipment
in the Mediterranean without any air cover was improvident, and, the
aircraft carrier *Franklin D. Roosevelt* was sent to provide that air cover,
plus *its* escort of other naval vessels. And so, when the British were
compelled to abandon the protection of the Greeks, leaving the sort of
power vacuum which Communism adores, we found ourselves with
naval strength in the Mediterranean, thanks to Forrestal's foresight. Our
flag is still there.

As far back as 1945, Forrestal believed that Communist Russia regarded us as an ally of convenience and that the day would come when
we would need to be not only strong but united in purpose, to survive
the militant design of Communism to rule the world. Forrestal had
made his own assessment of Stalin's future policy and of what our own
should be. It is evidenced by an incident I recall vividly.

President Truman had introduced system into the meetings of his
cabinet and from time to time Cabinet members were provided in advance with an agenda of topics to be discussed. On September 16, 1945,
Forrestal's devoted private secretary, Miss Katherine Foley, called to
say that at the Cabinet meeting scheduled for September 21 there
would be discussion of atomic weapons and of a proposal to release to
other nations, including the Soviet Government, information on atomic
energy including weapons hitherto a most closely guarded secret. The
Secretary wished me to prepare a memorandum which would state the
arguments in opposition to this proposal.

On his return from that session, Forrestal called in his yeoman and,
as was his habit, dictated an entry for his diary. In this entry he re-
counted the discussion in the Cabinet room. As the diary entry concerned a matter in my area, a carbon copy of it was sent to me. It was
illuminating to read the names of those seated around the table and the
arguments that were advanced in favor of making available to the Communist government the advantage we had achieved at such huge cost.

Others who were present supported Forrestal's strong dissent from such a step, and the weight of the President's decision was with them.

When Forrestal's diaries were published, the names of those present (including a number who were not members of the Cabinet) were listed, but their expressions on either side of the issue were censored. An exception was the opinion of Secretary of Commerce Henry Wallace, which was rather fully stated as favoring release of the information. He was not alone. The fact that Russian espionage had penetrated our atomic weapons project at several points was not then known. Likewise unknown was the degree of Soviet interest in rocket development. That it existed was shown by the zeal with which they were carrying off to Russia every German rocket specialist they could lay hands upon. Twelve years later, the Soviets launched their first Sputnik.

Had Forrestal's good health continued, the history of Communist primacy in rocketry and satellites might well have had a different outcome. Few remember that as early as 1947, in Forrestal's annual report, a project to study and develop an earth satellite program was announced. After his death, it fell into an orbit of low priority.

His conviction that militant Communism was the enemy of the Free World induced Forrestal to undertake the task of reorganizing the defense structure in 1947 at the request of the President. No man was better equipped to do it by experience, by the degree of congressional respect he enjoyed, by the support of the press, and by the confidence of the President he served.

Somehow there came into this picture in 1948 a distortion. Forrestal learned that some of his administrative subordinates had begun to undercut him. Forrestal's manner and even his physiognomy being those of a prizefighter, one might have expected that he would chop his opponents down. All he had to do was to ask the men to resign and, if they refused, demand that the President remove them. But Forrestal's tough image was deceptive. Tough he was in his approach to matters of public concern, but he could not deal in the manner warranted by the situation with a man who had been his friend. He temporized and tried persuasion and forbearance. The word went about that he was intimidated. He began to lose face.

On one occasion, he allowed some of his people to convince him that the stockpiles of completed atomic weapons should be delivered to the military establishment for custody. The Atomic Energy Act was specific in establishing that atomic weapons should remain in the keeping of the civilian agency which made them. Only the President could order them to be transferred. Jim called me to his office—I was then a member of the Atomic Energy Commission—to let me know that he intended to request the President to order the transfer of completed atomic weapons to the Department of Defense forthwith.

"Don't do it, Jim," I urged. "The President will decide against you."

"Why should he?" he asked.

"For the same reason," I answered, "that the public still fears the 'trigger-happy Colonel.' Don't get yourself into a position where, for the first time in your dealing with him, the President will overrule you. If he does, the fact can't be kept secret. It's bound to leak. An important element in your authority is that the President has always backed you up in everything concerned with national defense." Searching for a way to convince him, I pointed out that the military had *effective* custody under existing conditions. They guarded every arsenal where weapons were stored.

To this, Forrestal replied that he had already been in public service too long, and that he was entirely prepared to resign if the President overruled him on a matter in his area.

The issue was joined at a meeting around the President's desk. The entire Atomic Energy Commission was present, one of the rare occasions when it met with the President as a body. Forrestal stated his case and David Lilienthal, then Chairman of the Commission, responded, pointing to the specific provision in the law and to the legislative history which had preceded its enactment. He cited the views of Senators who had been Mr. Truman's colleagues. He made a convincing case. The President listened to a brief rebuttal from his Secretary of Defense and then stated his conclusion: custody would be retained in civilian hands until and unless he ordered otherwise. Later he said that "the continual control of all aspects of the atomic energy program . . . including the custody of atomic weapons is a proper function of the civil authorities." The occasion may have been a turning point in Forrestal's relations with the President, and, in looking back, Forrestal's difficulty with the decision may have been an early indication of his failing health.

Preoccupation with my own work in the winter of 1948–49 reduced the frequency of my meetings with Forrestal, but on March 8, 1949, he asked me to lunch in his dining room in the Pentagon, for what was to be the last time. I was shocked by the change in his appearance. He had lost much weight and his eyes were deep-sunken. An unfinished portrait of him stood on an easel covered with a cloth. I had looked at it while waiting for Jim. The artist had caught an expression almost of despair.

He wanted to talk about other days. He discussed his career in the past tense, describing himself as "a failure." "I might have succeeded in combining the three Services," he said, "if I had been able to keep you and Struve here with me." This was surprising, since flattery was out of character for him. I was troubled and remember telling my wife that evening how unlike himself Jim had seemed that day. I assured him that he had succeeded beyond what any other man could have done; and I used the example of the Israelites who had not entered the Holy Land until the generation which had been slaves in Egypt had passed away. Just so, I said, a complete unification of the Services would not be possible while officers were still in command who had been indoctrinated in their school years with strong Service loyalties. I added that this might be good rather than otherwise and that, while unification was the goal of the Administration, to risk losing the *esprit de corps* of the Army, Navy, and Marine Corps was too high a price to pay for the supposed efficiencies of consolidation. They might never be realized. In any case, I assured him, he was not at fault. He was not comforted.

On January 7 (1949) the resignations of both General Marshall and Robert Lovett were announced. The State Department thenceforward would have a new Secretary and Under Secretary. Marshall was a man with whom Forrestal had occasionally but rarely differed and there was an overriding mutual respect and trust in their relationship. Lovett was one of Forrestal's oldest and most intimate friends. The changes would not strengthen Forrestal, and the realization further depressed him. He submitted a resignation to the President four days later, but it was couched in the language customary when a President begins a second term and the members of his cabinet place their *pro forma* resignations in his hands. On January 28, however, it appears that President Truman indicated that he thought Forrestal should retire in favor of Colonel Louis Johnson. This was shattering to Forrestal, and in the words of a close friend it came with the force of a "dismissal under fire."

By that time he was plumbing the depths of a kind of depression with which Navy physicians had become familiar during the war, a condition associated with severe and prolonged operational fatigue. Under prompt and wise treatment, others recovered from such excursions to the brink of despair, but for him there was to be no recovery.

In the early hours of the morning of May 23, 1949, the telephone on my bed table awakened me to shocking news. Through the haze of sleep, I heard that my friend had ended his life a short while before. The fact, in spite of all that had gone before it, found me unprepared.

It has been said of many men who have died since the war ended as a result of some service-incurred disability that they gave their lives for their country as surely as though the sacrifice had been made on the battlefield. In no instance could the evidence be more clear than in the tragic end of this man, one of the most promising figures of our times. He is buried in the National Cemetery among comrades-in-arms of the First World War and those whom he commanded in the Second. For some time his grave was marked simply:

JAMES V. FORRESTAL
Ensign, USNR

which is as he might have wished it, for he had been one of the pioneer Navy aviators. Among the group of men whom he had gathered about him in the eight years of his public service, there were many who wept unashamedly as a single bugle sounded and the last volley echoed in the rolling hills of Arlington.

IX

"A Thousand Years of Regret"

The most powerful weapon we have—indeed the most powerful weapon that any people can have—is Truth. If we ever find ourselves in a position where we cannot tell the truth, or where we feel that the telling will injure us, we will have sacrificed that most powerful weapon.

DWIGHT D. EISENHOWER

Tell us how near is danger that we may arm us to encounter it.

RICHARD II (V. 3)

Ranking, certainly, among the most momentous military and moral decisions in history were the conclusions to make and to use atomic weapons. The decision to develop the atomic bomb was taken in order that we might not find ourselves at the mercy of Hitler. The Germans were believed to be engaged in a like enterprise. The decision to *use* the bomb, however, was made after Germany had been defeated, and to employ it against an enemy unable[1] to develop the weapon and already suing for peace. Preliminary to the first of these events and in the interval between them, there were other and less crucial decisions.

The chain of events began for me in a personal way years earlier. The beginning was under circumstances quite the opposite from the thought of weapons. Following the deaths of both my parents (in 1935 and 1937), I became aware of the inadequate supply of radium for the treatment of cancer in American hospitals. Generally there was none of the rare element except in the largest institutions in the big cities, and in those hospitals the demand was so great that the stock was divided into milligrams. Dr. James Ewing, then the director of Memorial Cancer Hospital in New York, told me that if he had enough radium he would construct a "bomb" holding several grams, which he felt might be the answer to the treatment of deeply located cancers.

The use of the word "bomb" in this connection no doubt followed from the appearance of the lead containers in which radium was stored. Years later, when a radioisotope of cobalt was used for cancer therapy and was likewise contained in such a bomb, the use of the word confused some writers, who asserted that the Atomic Energy Commission was making "cobalt bombs" for military purposes.

Toward the end of 1937, two young nuclear physicists, Dr. Arno Brasch and Dr. Leo Szilard, having learned of my interest, approached me through Francis Rosenbaum, a mutual friend. They asked me to finance them in the construction of a "surge generator" with which they wished to explore nuclear phenomena in high-energy ranges. A surge generator was the name given to an invention which could accumulate an electrical charge in a bank of condensers over a period of time until the charge reached a predetermined point. Then the condenser bank could be discharged instantaneously and focused or aimed by means of a special tube at a given target. The cycle of charge and discharge could be indefinitely repeated.

Brasch and Szilard believed that it would be possible to produce radioactive isotopes of many elements by bombarding selected targets with subatomic particles accelerated by surges of current at very high voltages. An isotope of cobalt thus produced would be radioactive and would emit gamma rays similar to the radiation produced by radium, though with a much shorter half-life than radium. Radioactive cobalt could be made, they calculated, at a cost of a few dollars per gram. Radium was then priced at about fifty thousand dollars per gram. Cobalt had certain advantages over radium besides cheapness. If radium is accidentally set free in the body it remains in the tissues and destroys them, whereas cobalt is rapidly excreted. I foresaw the possibility of producing this isotope in quantity and of giving it to hospitals as a memorial to my parents.

Brasch was a refugee from Germany. Before coming to the United States, he and a colleague, Fritz Lange, had pioneered high-voltage work in Europe, at first by building large lightning attractors on Monte Generoso in the Italian Alps, and later, with the assistance of German industry, constructing a surge generator near Berlin. High voltage discharges had been obtained in the experiments with lightning but this had proved to be an uncontrollable method of research and therefore unsatisfactory. The work had been assisted by the Notgemeinschaft der

Deutschen Wissenschaft, a government-sponsored scientific society. The high-energy device built in Germany was the result of interest by the Allgemeine Electrizitaets Gesellschaft, the large stockholder-owned electrical firm. Its board of directors had concluded that the "artificial transmutation of elements was a field that should be explored." Brasch had invented discharge tubes which stood up under electrical tensions of as much as four million volts. At about that time, his partner, Lange, had been invited to Russia on the representation that the Soviet Government would give him unlimited assistance. He was reported to be building a plant at Kharkov as early as 1937. Szilard was an extraordinarily brilliant young Hungarian.

Impressed by the representations of these young scientists, I decided to help them. Anticipating that the sums required would soon exceed my resources, I sought participation from industry. First I approached the Westinghouse Company, with which I had business connections over many years, but after some consideration they decided that they "would not be justified in committing themselves to additional expenditures in the field of nuclear physics." Later, however, they did consult with the people I had sent to the California Institute of Technology, and made helpful suggestions relating to the design and operation of the equipment constructed there. I then approached my neighbor, John Lee Pratt, of Fredericksburg, Virginia, who was a director of the General Motors Corporation, and, accompanied by him, visited Detroit to see Charles F. Kettering, the engineering genius of that company. Kettering, whom I was later to know well and who in so many other areas was a man of great imagination, likewise did not ignite. At that juncture he was absorbed in developing an antiknock additive for gasoline, and most of the time we spent with him in his laboratory was in watching demonstrations of his experiments in that and other lines. My inadequate presentation failed to interest him in the production of radioactive isotopes.

I then visited two friends, Drs. Irving Langmuir and W. D. Coolidge in Schenectady at the laboratory of the General Electric Company. Both were interested, but the top management of that company in those days felt that nuclear energy was "for the science fiction fans." One could not help contrasting the attitude at that time of American and German industrialists. Dr. Coolidge did me the inestimable favor of providing me an opportunity to meet Ernest Orlando Lawrence, whose friendship for the following twenty years was one of the finest experiences of my life. In Dr. Coolidge's letter of introduction, he wrote:

"Dr. Lawrence, as you will recall, is the man responsible for the wonderful development of the cyclotron. Because of interest which you have shown in radically new scientific fields, I am giving him this letter to you. He will explain much better than I can the importance of this big step which he is now contemplating." (Dr. Coolidge was referring to Lawrence's project for a hundred-million-volt cyclotron.)

Lawrence came to see me with the letter, and some time later wrote to express "gratitude" for my assistance in finding some funds "for the project closest to my heart—crossing the frontier of one hundred million volts." What I did for him must have been miniscule indeed, as I have no recollection of its details, and by 1939 I was already deeply committed to Brasch and Szilard. Most of the cost of the cyclotron was financed by Mr. Rockefeller.

At this point I turned to Mr. Hoover and asked him if he would arrange for me to talk with Robert A. Millikan. I had met Dr. Millikan in Washington during World War I, but was certain that he would not remember me. Mr. Hoover was well acquainted with him and they were co-trustees of the Huntington Library in Pasadena not far from the California Institute of Technology, which Millikan directed. I knew that there was much interest in high-energy physics at that institution on account of Millikan's specialization and because of the presence on the faculty of such outstanding men as Lauritsen, Fowler, and others. It was also likely that they would not be working along the same lines as Lawrence and his group at Berkeley.

Mr. Hoover telegraphed me from Palo Alto on January 11, 1938, to say that Millikan was interested in principle and had asked me to lay the matter before Dr. Goetz, of his faculty, who was passing through New York on his way back to Pasadena from Europe. Millikan wrote me on January 29, 1938, to say that he had received Goetz's report of our conversations and that they were sufficiently interested for me to send Brasch to California. He concluded his letter by saying that the Brasch-Lange method was not under development in any place in the United States so far as he knew and, without expressing an opinion as to whether there would ever be any practical use for radioactive isotopes, nevertheless, "because of its relation in general to artificial transmutation it has large scientific interest . . . and therefore it would be highly desirable at some place to undertake a relatively large-scale experimental program for working out the relative merits of the different methods. . . . It is also true," he added, "that there is no place that I know of in the country where there has been as much done in the high potential lines, of which the Brasch-Lange methods are a variant, as has been done here under the leadership of Dr. C. C. Lauritsen. It was therefore in view of this situation that I thought it would be worth while to at least explore the possibilities with Brasch and then make a further report to you expressing more fully my judgment after these conferences as to the wisdom or unwisdom of pushing along further in these directions."

Brasch had spent only a few days in Pasadena when Millikan wrote me again on February 12 to say, "In its present stage the problem of going to voltages of many million volts . . . is essentially a pure science problem and an extremely interesting one. No one can predict at the present time what kind of values will come out of it. Work which we have already underway here on atomic transmutations, not using potentials higher than one and a half million volts, has kept us so busy with the newer developments in nuclear physics which have been possible, that we have not wanted to divert our energies to efforts to push up the obtainable potentials still higher. . . . If Dr. Brasch were to carry out his projects here, he would add effectively to the group and would undoubtedly be able to reach higher potentials by his method than could be obtained by any other. The so-called Van de Graaff method should be capable of reaching with small energies 10,000,000 volts, and Dr. Brasch thinks he could go to 15 or even 50, but would prefer to start—and I think this is wise—on an attempt at only 12 or 15,000,000. How matter would behave under bombardment of such voltages of electrons, we do not know."

Dr. Millikan prepared me for disappointment concerning my dream of producing gamma-ray-emitting isotopes for cancer treatment, but the hope sustained me nonetheless. He wrote, "The possibility of making radioactive substances artificially which would replace radium is only *one* objective, and from our point of view not the most interesting or the most promising.* . . . The California Institute would be delighted to join with you in making the plans and pushing them forward as rapidly as possible . . . My report then to you is that Dr. Brasch's schemes of obtaining very high potentials *are feasible* and that the field that would be entered by going to such potentials as he can practically

* Dr. Brasch had pointed out in our earliest conversations the possibilities of "the storage of tremendous energies concentrated in light weight and in small space. At least this much can be claimed now is that it probably will be possible to accumulate energies in proportion to equal weight, which will have one million times more intensities than is the case for instance with the lead accumulator [i.e., the storage battery]."

certainly obtain would be *an exceedingly interesting and thrilling* one to open up; that the expense of opening it up would possibly be as much as and probably more than $100,000; and that if you would think this a suitable place for this project, the California Institute would be glad to discuss the problem with you of ways and means and conditions."

A little later, Millikan offered to put at my disposal the facilities of the Kellogg Radiation Laboratory, "a building which was especially designed for very high potential work, with unusually large clearances and with big power facilities needed for this project, and all in place." There then ensued some debate as to whether an apparatus to produce from 12,000,000 to 15,000,000 volts, or an intermediate step to produce 5,000,000 volts, should first be constructed, Brasch advocating the former and Lauritsen supporting my feeling that the 5,000,000 volt surge generator should be first constructed. Millikan had written me in February of 1939 to enclose a letter from Lauritsen to say that "the publicity given to a discovery in Germany" to the effect that "during the bombardment of uranium by neutrons, barium and other elements of median atomic weight are formed, has tended to confuse the situation and led Brasch to want to make unsafe haste in getting to the originally proposed 15,000,000 volt plant.

"I am in complete agreement with Dr. Lauritsen," Millikan continued, "that the information we could get from the 5,000,000 volt plant will certainly more than justify the expense and delay in reaching Dr. Brasch's objective of a 15,000,000 volt plant, and Dr. Lauritsen is very firmly convinced that the procedure of going through a pilot plant is the only safe way to proceed. From both my point of view and that of Dr. Lauritsen, the Hahn discoveries have not in any way changed the reasons which originally induced us to attempt the procedure which we agreed upon last June . . . The main purpose of this letter is to set your mind at rest as to the concensus of informed judgment here that the only possible bearing which the newer developments have upon the program which we agreed upon last June consists in emphasizing the desirability of speeding it up as much as possible, since they show what unexpected possibilities may come out of explorations in this quite new field of nuclear physics . . . With the 1,000,000 volt plant Dr. Lauritsen's group has already brought to light a large number of nuclear reactions in the lighter elements, namely, up to about atomic No. 9. With the 2,000,000 volt plant of the Van de Graaff type, which he has just built, it is possible to explore pretty well the possibilities up to atomic No. 30, and with the 5,000,000 volt plant, using deuterons as the bombarding elements, Dr. Lauritsen thinks that it is possible to produce nuclear reactions in all the elements up to uranium, so that we feel quite sure there are a greater number of new possibilities which can be explored with the 5,000,000 volt plant. The advantage of the Brasch method, not yet utilized in any large way, lies in the fact that we are very hopeful that we can get with it very much larger intensities, though no larger voltages than can be obtained by the other available methods of bringing about nuclear reactions."

In due course the work was begun. Dr. Richard C. Tolman, who was the dean of the graduate school, then acting for Dr. Millikan, regularly billed me for the various expenses with the exception of salaries, which I paid directly. The project continued even after the developments which began in 1939 as a result of the "discovery in Germany" to which Millikan had referred. But in 1940, after the federal government became interested and after projects began to be placed in the universities under Government contracts, it became necessary to exclude aliens from the laboratory at CalTech and to defer the surge generator program.

Work on the surge generator had been well under way when the epic event which so wholly eclipsed it was in the making. Drs. Otto Hahn and F. Strassmann, working in Germany, had discovered that, when uranium was exposed to neutrons under appropriate conditions, an isotope of barium was found in the uranium target, which had not contained any barium to begin with. The results of the experiment were not immediately understood, but their true significance was interpreted shortly thereafter by Dr. Lise Meitner and Dr. O. R. Frisch, to whom they had been communicated. Drs. Meitner and Frisch, at that time, were refugees in Scandinavia from Nazi Germany. Seventeen years later (in December of 1955) Dr. Hahn, then in his seventy-fourth year, was dining at my home and gave us an account of the historic discovery. There were other guests, among them Dr. Vannevar Bush, who paid Dr. Hahn a graceful tribute and called him a "famous and historic character." Dr. Hahn, responding, admitted that he was indeed "famous" and could explain how he had come to be.

"In 1903," he said, "a reporter from the British magazine, *Nature,* wrote an article about Lord Rutherford, the famous physicist, and a photographer came to the laboratory to take Rutherford's picture. This was in the era before sixty second photography. When the photographer had adjusted the usual black cloth over his head and the

camera and saw Rutherford's inverted image on the ground glass, he
noticed for the first time that Rutherford was wearing no cuffs. In England of that day, it was unthinkable that so great a man should be
photographed without his linen exposed and since Rutherford had no
cuffs, I volunteered to lend him mine. In that remote era, cuffs were
detachable and were fastened to a man's shirtsleeves by little metal
gadgets—a man did not even need to wear a shirt to have cuffs," Dr.
Hahn noted parenthetically; "and so, the famous Lord Rutherford was
photographed with Hahn's cuffs. So you see how I became famous."

Dr. Hahn then told of his discovery of protoactinium and mesotho-
rium and described the period when he, Strassmann, and Lise Meitner
were working together.

"Early in 1938," he said, "it became impossible for Meitner to go
out on the streets in Germany. Being Jewish, she had to wear a yellow
badge, and, although she was an elderly woman, she was subjected to
abuse and even to physical violence. She had received an invitation
from Niels Bohr to come to his Institute in Copenhagen. I wrote a letter
to our Minister of Culture to ask that she be permitted to go there but
he refused on the ground that if allowed to leave 'she would probably
not speak well of Germany.'" He smiled at the understatement. "Therefore, Gorter [an associate of Hahn] and I were determined to smuggle
her over the border and we did, by motor car, late one night. Later
she went to Sweden.

"When we had the results of our experiment," Hahn continued, "we
could not understand why we had barium in the stuff. We had not
started with any barium. I wrote to Lise and she replied with a letter,
signed by her and her nephew, Otto Frisch. I still have it, though it is
partly burned. It is one of the few things that remain from the Archives
of the Institute after the bombings. In the letter she pointed out that
what had happened was that we had fissioned the uranium atom. The
use of the word 'fission' in that connection, I think, was made for the
first time. She and Frisch had also computed the energy release and
we were able to confirm it by experiment."

We listened spellbound as Dr. Hahn told more of the details, modestly
disclaiming credit, asserting that it was all due to Lise Meitner. I also
learned for the first time that Hahn and Strassmann were both chemists. Meitner is a physicist. I had been under the impression that all
three were physicists.

Dr. Meitner and Dr. Frisch had reasoned that the phenomenon
could be explained by the absorption of a neutron within the nucleus

of a uranium atom and by the subsequent splitting, or fissioning, of that nucleus into approximately equal parts. These parts proved to be atoms of elements lighter than the original uranium atom.

They also computed that the difference between the mass of the original nucleus and that of the sum of the fragments—the sum was less—had been transformed into energy. When Einstein's thirty-four-year-old formula was then invoked, $E=mc^2$, it became apparent that, although the amount of matter which had been transmuted into energy was very small indeed, the energy released had been truly enormous. The reason for this is that the mass (m) has to be multiplied by the square of the speed of light (c [186,000 miles per second]^2) to find the energy involved (E). That range of energy made the performance of our surge generator in Pasadena insignificant. The device had just been completed.

The news of the discovery, more exciting than anything which had occurred in physical science since the discovery of radioactivity by Becquerel forty-two years earlier, was brought to the attention of American scientists by the great Danish physicist Niels Bohr. He came to Princeton to spend a few months with his friend Albert Einstein, a refugee from Nazi Germany. By the time of his next visit, he himself would be a refugee. Bohr's communication set up a chain reaction in the scientific community, but he was not among those who saw its initial potentialities for evil. A gentle soul and a real humanitarian, to use that overworked term, Bohr naturally saw the peaceful visage of the atomic Janus. In a letter addressed to me after he had returned to Copenhagen he wrote:

> I have the most pleasant remembrance of my visit with you. . . . I wish I could now discuss with you more closely the great prospects and possibilities of mastering the nuclear energy opened by the discovery of uranium fission. As we spoke of, I think that in this respect the recognition of the very different properties of the common and rare isotopes of uranium has not only removed any immediate fear of dangerous use of nuclear energy but has, at the same time, created the hope of beneficial use of this energy for practical, and perhaps specially for medical purposes by obtaining neutron sources of hitherto unknown strength.

But Dr. Bohr's visit had stirred other scientists to darker forebodings. Dr. Szilard on January 25, 1939, wrote to me about it and his letter is historic in its first mention of "atomic bombs."

Hotel King's Crown
420 West 116th Street
New York City
January 25th, 1939

Dear Mr. Strauss:

I feel that I ought to let you know of a very sensational new development in nuclear physics. In a paper in the "Naturwissenschaften" Hahn reports that he finds when bombarding uranium with neutrons the uranium breaking up into two halves giving elements of about half the atomic weight of uranium. This is entirely unexpected and exciting news for the average physicist. The Department of Physics at Princeton, where I spent the last few days, was like a stirred-up ant heap.

Apart from the purely scientific interest there may be another aspect of this discovery, which so far does not seem to have caught the attention of those to whom I spoke. First of all it is obvious that the energy released in this new reaction must be very much higher than in all previously known cases. It may be 200 million volt instead of the usual 3–10 million volt. This in itself might make it possible to produce power by means of nuclear energy, but I do not think that this possibility is very exciting, for if the energy output is only two or three times the energy input, the cost of investment would probably be too high to make the process worth while. Unfortunately, most of the energy is released in the form of heat and not in the form of radioactivity.

I see, however, in connection with this new discovery potential possibilities in another direction. These might lead to a large-scale production of energy and radioactive elements, unfortunately also perhaps to atomic bombs. This new discovery revives all the hopes and fears in this respect which I had in 1934 and 1935, and which I have as good as abandoned in the course of the last two years. At present I am running a high temperature and am therefore confined to my four walls, but perhaps I can tell you more about these new developments some other time. Meanwhile you may look out for a paper in "Nature" by Frisch and Meitner which will soon appear and which might give you some information about this new discovery.

With best wishes.

Yours sincerely,
/s/ Leo Szilard

After receiving this letter, I asked Szilard to meet me in New York, where we spent a day together and then rode as far as Washington in further discussion. On February 13 he wrote again: "After I left the train in Washington I spent a day with Dr. Teller there* and another

* Dr. Edward Teller was on the faculty of the George Washington University in Washington, D.C.

day with Dr. Wigner at Princeton. . . . Dr. Wigner thought that some of the experiments which we discussed could be done at Princeton. . . . On my return to New York I went to see Fermi to tell him of these conversations and also to discuss some of the small scale experiments which might be made in the near future. Since my return almost every day some new information about uranium became available, and whenever I decided to do something one day it appeared foolish in the light of the new information on the next day.

"I found that the Radium Chemical Co. had in stock 200 milligrams of radium mixed with beryllium, which is a nice constant source of fast neutrons. As Fermi thought that he would like to use such a neutron source for his experiment I felt that I ought to get it for him. It did not seem fair to ask you to take any decisions from a distance, and so I thought it might be best that I should advance expenses of this type and to see later whether you could sanction the expenditures afterwards. . . .

"The outlook has changed in some important respects since I last saw you. It is now known that fast neutrons split both uranium and thorium, but slow neutrons do not split thorium, and they probably do not split the bulk of uranium either. If enough neutrons are emitted when fast neutrons split thorium or uranium it will still be necessary to see whether or not the emitted neutrons get slowed down to a velocity at which they are ineffective before they had a chance to split enough nuclei to make the maintenance of a chain reaction* possible.

"On the other hand, slow neutrons seem to split a uranium isotope which is present in an abundance of about 1% in uranium. If this isotope could be used for maintaining chain reactions, it would have to be separated from the bulk of uranium. This, no doubt, would be done if necessary, but it might take five or ten years** before it can be done on a technical scale. Should small scale experiments show that the thorium and the bulk of uranium would not work, but the rare isotope of uranium would, we would have the task immediately to attack the question of concentrating the rare isotope of uranium.

"As you see, the number of possibilities has increased since you left town. Some of the experiments which were devised, in particular the experiment which Fermi first planned, appear now to be much more difficult than before. Other experiments, such as those with photo-

* It was the first time I had seen mention of a chain reaction.
** Szilard hit the mark with the five-year estimate.

neutrons, are not affected, but of course they have somewhat the character of preliminary experiments.

"With best wishes,   /s/ Leo Szilard"

The letter was significant in its identification, at least for me, of the facts that:

(a) It was the "rare" isotope of uranium which fissioned.

(b) That it would have to be separated in some manner from the abundant isotope with which it was mingled.

(c) That neutrons had to be slowed down before they would split a nucleus.

(d) That a "chain reaction" might be realized under proper conditions.

The original experiment was quickly repeated in several university laboratories, and Dr. Enrico Fermi (who had been one of the consultants on our surge generator), together with Dr. John Dunning and Dr. G. B. Pegram of Columbia University, looked to see whether any ionizing radiation accompanied the phenomenon of fission. For, if found to exist, it would tend to confirm a theory of Fermi's that some neutrons might be expelled from a nucleus when it fissioned. In such a case, these neutrons might go on to split other nuclei, which in turn would emit neutrons, and it was thus that a chain reaction might occur.

On Washington's Birthday, Szilard sent me a short bulletin. "There is a fairly good chance now that if we can concentrate the uranium isotope 235 from uranium a chain reaction could be set up in the concentrate. I am therefore beginning to give attention to the process which could be used for concentrating the isotope. . . . Fermi is convinced that the native uranium is no good [for that purpose]."

Fermi and Szilard saw their experiments succeeding and on March 6, Szilard wired:

PERFORMED TODAY PROPOSED EXPERIMENT WITH BERYLLIUM BLOCK WITH STRIKING RESULT. VERY LARGE NEUTRON EMISSION FOUND. ESTIMATE CHANCES FOR REACTION NOW ABOVE 50%.

By early April, during a visit to my farm, Fermi said that it had been arranged to co-operate with the Carnegie Institute of Terrestrial Magnetism and, through Dean Pegram of Columbia University, with the Navy Department. He was absorbed in an endeavor to discover the average number of neutrons emitted upon the fission of uranium nuclei. He held a strong belief that the number was greater than one. He described his preparations for an experiment on what then seemed a very large scale, using a quarter of a ton of uranium oxide. Szilard had first asked me to purchase this material for them, but it was later possible to obtain it as a loan.

In a letter dated April 11, Szilard first referred to the voluntary attempt to control the publication of scientific reports on the subject. This was a security measure. He wrote:

> So far publication of the papers, which were sent to the PHYSICAL REVIEW on March 16th, is being delayed at our request and efforts are made to get similar action in England and France. In the meantime a paper by Joliot* appeared in NATURE which relates to our subject but so far, it did not attract much attention. Now we are trying to get Joliot to cooperate but I do not know whether we will succeed.

> * Frédéric Joliot-Curie

On April 14 he wrote to say that "After an exchange of cables with Joliot in Paris and Blackett* in England, the Physics Department of Columbia University decided to publish our papers which were sent to the *Physical Review* sometime ago. This decision which runs contrary to my personal wishes was largely based on Joliot's unwillingness to delay his papers in connection with his view that the situation has already gotten out of hand."

He enclosed a typescript of a report on the "Instantaneous Emission of Fast Neutrons in the Interaction of Slow Neutrons with Uranium," which was signed by him and Walter H. Zinn. (Dr. Zinn was later to be associated with the Atomic Energy Commission.)

Replying to Szilard on April 17, 1939, I expressed regret that it had not been possible that publication of these developments could be deferred in view of the international situation. The terrible war was still five months distant, but it required no prophetic gift to foresee that a certain amount of care should be exercised.

The experiment with five hundred pounds of uranium oxide was completed, and on June 15 Szilard telegraphed:

> YESTERDAY FERMI AND I HAVE COMPLETED SEMI-LARGE SCALE EXPERIMENT WITH POSITIVE RESULTS.

Szilard and Zinn were finally able to report[2] the finding that, on the average, about 2.3 neutrons are emitted per fission. This confirmed Fermi's hypothesis and became the basis for the portentous development which ensued.

* P. M. S. Blackett

During May and June, Fermi, and Szilard had worked together on a system of uranium and water to see whether it would sustain a chain reaction. A fellow scientist, George Placzek, who had dropped into the laboratory for a visit, pointed out the theoretical shortcomings of the proposed system and suggested helium gas as a better moderator for slowing down the neutrons. Szilard remembers that Fermi thought this impractical and "funny" and used to refer to helium as "Placzek's helium." The suggestion, however, led them to consider graphite in place of water, and it was graphite which performed that function in Fermi's history-making experimental pile, which three years later proved that a chain reaction could be sustained and controlled.

It was an event of enormous historical importance when, on December 2, 1942, Fermi and his group of pioneer scientists achieved the world's first controlled, self-sustaining, chain reaction in the famous "pile" of uranium and graphite courses under the spectators' stands of the athletic field at the University of Chicago. One of my prized possessions is a block from a graphite layer in that pile. The historic structure has been demolished.

Fermi's experiments at Columbia University were carried on in the basement at Schermerhorn Hall. During this period Szilard and Zinn were engaged in an experiment on one of the upper floors. They were using thorium metal powder and there was an accidental chemical explosion. Billows of smoke poured out of the laboratory windows. Firemen promptly responded and everything was soon under control. A reporter called to ask what had happened and was told by the switchboard operator that it was "nothing of any importance at all, just an atomic explosion." And, so downgraded, the story did not get printed.

Szilard was gravely worried by the possibility of an early German success in producing a new weapon based on nuclear fission. The liberation of vast energy from a quite small amount of material had suggested to him the feasibility of making a weapon which would utterly dwarf any chemical bomb and with which, should Hitler be the first to achieve it, the conquest of Europe would be quickly accomplished. It was assumed that heavy water would be useful in the process. Heavy water had been discovered by an American, Harold Urey. In it, the normal hydrogen molecules were represented by an isotope of hydrogen (deuterium) with twice the weight of normal hydrogen.

The significance of heavy water was its usefulness as a moderator or decelerator of fast neutrons. The eagerness shown by the Germans to capture a Norwegian plant producing heavy water gave color to the apprehension that the German military establishment was vigorously engaged in some kind of atomic weapon project. We knew that several kilograms of heavy water were being produced daily at Trondheim and that orders had been placed for a large quantity of paraffin, incorporating deuterium instead of hydrogen in its structure. The initial paper by Hahn and Strassmann having appeared in *Naturwissenschaften* in January 1939 (the same publication, incidentally, which had carried Einstein's famous communication over thirty years earlier), German scientists were naturally presumed to have been alerted to the possibilities at least as early as we were.

Szilard discussed the alternatives with Wigner. They agreed that something had to be done. One thing that could be attempted would be to prevent the Germans from acquiring uranium. At that time, nearly all of the world's supply came from one uniquely rich deposit, the great Shinkolobwe mine in the Belgian Congo. The mine was owned by the Union Minière du Haut Katanga, a Belgian corporation. Einstein enjoyed the friendship of Elisabeth, the Belgian Queen Mother, and the two young men suggested that he should write a letter to her apprising her of the circumstances and urging that she use her influence with the Belgian mining interests to pre-empt the supply. A copy of the letter was to be addressed to the Secretary of State so that the Administration would have notice of what was contemplated. This letter was never sent for the reason that Szilard felt an approach should be made directly to President Roosevelt about the entire concept.

Szilard knew that I could provide him with no entree, since the President identified me with Herbert Hoover. A mutual friend, Gustav Stolper, a German publisher and former member of the Reichstag who was living as a refugee in New York, had told Szilard that Dr. Alexander Sachs of New York, a scholarly economist, had the confidence of the President. It was arranged for Szilard and Sachs to meet. Out of their meeting grew the plan to have a letter written by Einstein to the President. Recollections are at variance as to the precise circumstances of its drafting—Sachs recalling that it was prepared in his office and Szilard that it was written by him in two versions, a longer and a shorter ("I wondered how many words we could expect the President to read?" Szilard says. "How many words does the fission of uranium rate?"). There is no conflict as to the sequence of events which followed. This divergence in recollection of the details of a distant event by two meticulous participants gives emphasis to the importance of history recorded as close to the event in time as possible.

On a morning in late July, Szilard set out for Einstein's summer retreat on Peconic Bay, Long Island. Einstein had been loaned the cottage of Dr. Moore, a friend. On a previous visit, Szilard and Wigner had driven about for half an hour, without being able to locate Dr. Moore's home. No one they asked seemed to know Dr. Moore. Stopping a boy of about seven or eight, Szilard finally put the inquiry differently. "Do you know where Dr. Einstein lives?" The boy offered to guide them at once.

Certainly Dr. Einstein's unique scientific eminence and his relationship to the concept of equating energy and mass, upon which everything that was going on was based, made his participation essential. The great mathematician was vacationing where he could indulge his favorite hobby of small-boat sailing. Szilard did not have a driver's license, and as Wigner was unable to make this trip, another young physicist, also a native of Hungary, drove the car. He was already well known in scientific circles and, later, to be known to a wider public— Dr. Edward Teller.

The three scientists discussed the letter. Einstein selected the longer version and it was sent to him for signature, signed, and dated August 2. It was handed by Szilard to Sachs for delivery to the President.

A suitable occasion for an interview with the President did not develop during the next two months and the letter remained in the keeping of Sachs. An appointment having been arranged, the President read the letter.

Albert Einstein
Old Grove Road
Peconic, Long Island
August 2nd, 1939

F. D. Roosevelt
President of the United States
White House
Washington, D.C.
Sir:

Some recent work by E. Fermi and L. Szilard, which has been communicated to me in manuscript, leads me to expect that the element uranium may be turned into a new and important source of energy in the immediate future. Certain aspects of the situation which has arisen seem to call for watchfulness and, if necessary, quick action on the part of the Administration. I believe therefore that it is my duty to bring to your attention the following facts and recommendation.

In the course of the last four months it has been made probable through the work of Joliot in France as well as Fermi and Szilard in America—that it may become possible to set up a nuclear chain reaction in a large mass of uranium, by which vast amounts of power and large quantities of new radium-like elements would be generated. Now it appears almost certain that this could be achieved in the immediate future.

This new phenomenon would also lead to the construction of bombs, and it is conceivable—though much less certain—that extremely powerful bombs of a new type may thus be constructed. A single bomb of this type, carried by boat and exploded in a port, might very well destroy the whole port together with some of the surrounding territory. However, such bombs might very well prove to be too heavy for transportation by air.

The United States has only very poor ores of uranium in moderate quantities. There is some good ore in Canada and the former Czechoslovakia, while the most important source of uranium is Belgian Congo.

In view of this situation you may think it desirable to have some permanent contact maintained between the Administration and the group of physicists working on chain reactions in America. One possible way of achieving this might be for you to entrust with this task a person who has your confidence and who could perhaps serve in an inofficial capacity. His task might comprise the following:

a) to approach Government Departments, keep them informed of the further development, and put forward recommendations for Government action, giving particular attention to the problem of securing a supply of uranium ore for the United States.

b) to speed up the experimental work, which is at present being carried on within the limits of the budgets of University laboratories, by providing funds, if such funds be required, through his contacts with private persons who are willing to make contributions for this cause, and perhaps also by obtaining the co-operation of industrial laboratories which have the necessary equipment.

I understand that Germany has actually stopped the sale of uranium from the Czechoslovakian mines which she has taken over. That she should have taken such early action might perhaps be understood on the ground that the son of the German Under-Secretary of State, von Weizsacker, is attached to the Kaiser-Wilhelm-Institut in Berlin where some of the American work on uranium is now being repeated.

Yours very truly,
/s/ Albert Einstein

The President listened to a detailed exposition by Sachs in amplification of its several points and was impressed. Shortly afterwards, Roosevelt referred the technical questions to Dr. Lyman Briggs, Director of the National Bureau of Standards, with a request for advice. Later a small study committee was established under Dr. Briggs as chairman.

This was not the first time that atomic energy had come to the attention of the Government. The earlier approach was concerned with its potential for generating power as well as its use as a weapon. As Szilard's letter of January 25, 1939, indicates, initial reactions to the power potentialities of atomic energy were dim. Too little was then known. The Navy is entitled to whatever palms for imagination and initiative are due to the first department of government to become seriously interested on both counts. They had reason.*

In the prenuclear era, submarines were limited in operational radius when submerged. The limiting factor was the capacity of their storage batteries. Internal-combustion engines could not be used when running totally submerged, because they competed with the crew for the oxygen contained in the hull. Batteries could not be recharged unless the submarine was on the surface or near enough to the surface to raise an air-breathing device. (In either case, detection was risked.) A further limitation on submarine operational radius was fuel capacity. Obviously, if a source of power could be found which would occupy little space, would last for long cruises, and which required no oxygen, it would be the answer to the submariners' dream. Naval officers and Navy civilian scientists grasped the possibilities of atomic energy for this application at a very early date. Dr. Ross Gunn, of the Naval Research Laboratory, on June 1, 1939 (two months before the Einstein letter), had written to the director of the laboratory to explain the possibilities and importance of atomic energy for submarine propulsion.[3]

Gunn and P. H. Abelson, of the Naval Research Laboratory, first took steps to separate the active isotope U-235 from normal uranium. Separation defied ordinary procedures, as U-235 and U-238 are so nearly of the same weight and their chemical properties are identical. The Navy scientists successfully developed a process in which the isotopes were separated by the difference in their location in a liquid column when heated—a process known as thermal diffusion. Other methods later tried out by the Manhattan Engineer District were even more successful.[4]

* How the Navy learned about the potentials of the atom is explained in Chapter XII, under "Fermi."

8. Enrico Fermi in his laboratory.

9. "The new shell with the funny fuse is devastating," wrote General Patton. "I'm glad you all thought of it first." This was the pint-sized, variable-time, or proximity, fuse which produced a revolution in tactics and helped to save London from total destruction by the V-1 bomb.

Photo by Bob Wheeler for Time *magazine*

10. To discuss the initial task of assembling a staff, the first Atomic Energy Commission met in temporary quarters, November 1946. Left to right: Sumner T. Pike, Robert F. Bacher, David E. Lilienthal (chairman), the author, and the late William W. Waymack.

Hotel King's Crown
420 West 116th Street
New York City

January 25th, 1939.

Mr. Lewis L. Strauss
c/o Kuhn, Loeb & Co.
52 William Street
New York City

Dear Mr. Strauss:

I feel that I ought to let you know of a very sensational new development in nuclear physics. In a paper in the "Natur-wissenschaften" Hahn reports that he finds when bombarding uranium with neutrons the uranium breaking up into two halves giving elements of about half the atomic weight of uranium. This is entirely unexpected and exciting news for the average physicist. The Department of Physics at Princeton, where I spent the last few days, was like a stirred-up ant heap.

Apart from the purely scientific interest there may be another aspect of this discovery, which so far does not seem to have caught the attention of those to whom I spoke. First of all it is obvious that the energy released in this new re-action must be very much higher than in all previously known cases. It may be 200 million volt instead of the usual 3-10 million volt. This in itself might make it possible to produce power by means of nuclear energy, but I do not think that this possibility is very exciting, for if the energy output is only two or three times the energy input, the cost of investment would probably be too high to make the process worth while. Unfortunately, most of the energy is released in the form of heat and not in the form of radioactivity.

I see, however, in connection with this new discovery potential possibilities in another direction. These might lead to a large-scale production of energy and radioactive elements, unfortunately also perhaps to atomic bombs. This new discovery revives all the hopes and fears in this respect which I had in 1934 and 1935, and which I have as good as abandoned in the course of the last two years. At present I am running a high temperature and am therefore confined to my four walls, but perhaps I can tell you more about these new developments some other time. Meanwhile you may look out for a paper in "Nature" by Frisch and Meitner which will soon appear and which might give you some information about this new discovery.

With best wishes,

yours sincerely

Leo Szilard

(Leo Szilard)

11. Prelude to decision: facsimile of the letter from Leo Szilard, dated January 25, 1939, forecasting the atom bomb.

12. Word to reach the United States concerning fission of the uranium atom was brought by Dr. Niels Bohr of Copenhagen.

13. Edgar Sengier, the Belgian mining engineer whose foresight and co-operation were invaluable to the U.S. atomic enterprise—a slip of paper secured for the U.S. a major uranium supply.

14. Six weeks before Hiroshima, Ralph A. Bard, Under Secretary of the Navy, advised, "I have had a feeling that before the bomb is actually used against Japan that Japan should have some preliminary warning."

15. "For whatever it is worth, therefore, my judgment is that we should proceed with this phase of atomic weapon development. . . ." With these words to the President, the late Dr. Karl T. Compton, president of the Massachusetts Institute of Technology, became one of the few prominent scientists of the day supporting development of the hydrogen bomb by the United States.

The Navy was not selected to conduct the great scientific and engineering enterprise which the President decided should be undertaken,
nor was the Secretary of the Navy made a member of the top policy
group established in 1941 to give it over-all guidance. Under Secretary
Forrestal told me that he felt this was a mistake, but did not know
whether Secretary Knox had ever made any representations to that
effect. The subject at one time was considered too secret to discuss unless one was personally connected with it. The top policy group, besides the President, comprised Vice President Henry Wallace, Secretary of War Stimson, Chief of Staff General George C. Marshall, Dr.
Vannevar Bush, and Dr. James B. Conant.

The Navy had arranged for the first approach to the Union Minière
du Haut Katanga to obtain a supply of uranium. In June 1940, Dr.
Briggs, Dr. Harold Urey, and Dr. Sachs conferred with Admiral Bowen
at the Naval Research Laboratory on the amounts of the ore believed to
be needed. After the meeting, at Bowen's request, Sachs made a contact with the company and a small quantity of uranium ore was secured. Nearly two years elapsed before the Government sought significant quantities of the unique material.

Edgar Sengier, who represented the Congo mining interests, had
concluded, with extraordinary prescience, that uranium eventually
would become important to the war effort and he had managed to
divert to the United States some two thousand steel drums containing
about twelve hundred tons of ore. These were stacked in the open at
Port Richmond, Staten Island, New York, and plainly marked "Uranium Ore, product of the Belgian Congo." They apparently excited no
interest.

Sengier communicated with Thomas K. Finletter, who was then
Special Assistant to the Secretary of State, to let him know that the ore
was available. Finletter passed the word to Colonel Kenneth D. Nichols,
of the Corps of Engineers, and Nichols purchased it from Sengier. The
transaction between the two men was written on a scrap of yellow
scratch paper in which all the terms were stated including the retention by the sellers of whatever radium might be in the ore. In spite of
the informality of that contract, no question has ever arisen as to its
clarity or comprehensiveness, and it served for all of the many succeeding shipments. In 1942, radium would have been the only constituent
of the ore with much worth. Radium, of course, has subsequently declined drastically in importance. Sengier's co-operation, not only in this
instance but throughout the war, was beyond value. It was recognized

by the award of the Legion of Merit by the United States and a knight-hood by the British Crown.

The atomic weapon project, having been assigned by the President to the Corps of Engineers of the Army, was placed under the command of General Leslie R. Groves. The Corps of Engineers is organized by districts, and the Groves assignment was named the "Manhattan District" to cover its purpose. While the account of the successful accomplishment of its mission is known, it is not realized everywhere that it required a feat of organization which dwarfed the construction of the Panama Canal, the building of the Pyramids, or any other enterprise previously accomplished by men. The work may be fully appreciated only from the perspective of history. It was even disparaged by some at the time as a job of "cement-pouring." But the goal called for the highest degree of engineering skill, combined with qualities as diplomats and negotiators. Groves and his top staff had to flatter and cajole and bully and inspire and produce. Production was the pay-off.

General Groves, primarily, and his deputy, Colonel (later Major General) Kenneth D. Nichols, have handsomely deserved every mark of commendation which has come to them.

There was some friction between the civilian and military people, but remarkably little with such things considered as the pressures to meet schedules, the different institutional values, and the security measures. The last-mentioned were routine to men in uniform, but novel and frequently irksome to the civilians. With the end of the war, latent differences were to erupt, and civilian scientists engaged in a well-organized and successful lobby to persuade the Congress to take the direction of the project out of the hands of the Army. Its vast empire of land, production plants, and laboratories should be transferred, it was argued, to the administration of a commission of civilians. No professional military person should be eligible for appointment to it. The public image of the "trigger-happy colonel" was invoked, and the danger of an impulsive and unauthorized use of the weapon was pictured.

Two proposals finally resulted—the May-Johnson bill, providing essentially for continued Army supervision, and the McMahon bill, which would transfer the enterprise to civilian control. The War Department was inclined to support the former, while the Navy favored the latter. By this time Forrestal had become Secretary of the Navy, and the naval officers who testified before congressional committees represented his beliefs. The President's position at first was not known, though he was said to favor the May-Johnson bill. On October 31,

1945, I was able to write Forrestal concerning a memorandum from the President to the Director of the Budget instructing him to advise the Secretary of War that the May-Johnson bill did not necessarily correspond with his view and that its representation as "administration favored" legislation must be carefully avoided. "This affords an opportunity," I added, "to raise the points which we have been foreclosed from making" and actively to endorse the McMahon bill.

The McMahon Act was not passed until July of 1946. It was essentially acceptable to the Navy and, since it established a liaison committee between the Atomic Energy Commission and the Armed Services, was palatable to the Army. In practice, the Military Liaison Committee (MLC) has operated very successfully. During testimony before the Senate side of the Atomic Energy Committee in 1947, one of the Senators inquired how I thought the AEC and the MLC ought to function. I had replied that it would be well if they "could wear the same suit of clothes." We did arrange to share offices, and in fourteen years of continuous association no friction has developed between the AEC and the MLC.

The fears in 1941 and later that the Germans would be first with an atomic bomb were reinforced by Hitler's frequent and cryptic references to devastating "secret weapons." These proved to be the V-1 and V-2 missiles, which, though not the weapon we feared, were powerful threats. As the war with Germany drew to a close, it became more and more clear that the apprehensions as to what the Germans were doing in atomic energy had been exaggerated. German scientists have since denied that there was ever any attempt to make atomic weapons. There is considerable evidence that these statements were self-serving, but there is no doubt that very little was accomplished. This may have been because Germany was severely handicapped by the death or flight of her first-rank scientists from the program of the Nazi party.

V-E Day came and Germany's unconditional surrender was signed in U. S. Army Headquarters at Rheims at 8:41 P.M. Eastern Standard Time on May 6, 1945. President Roosevelt had not lived to see it, and President Truman, when he took office just twenty-four days earlier, had virtually no information about the Manhattan District and its awesome product.[5]

However, an odd assortment of people had been admitted to confidence. Among them were Joseph P. Clark of the International Brotherhood of Firemen and Oilers, and Al Wegner, of the International Brotherhood of Electrical Workers. They had been told about it in considerable detail as early as December 5, 1944, in an effort to avert labor difficulties at Oak Ridge.[6] Even though Vice President of the United States, Mr. Truman had been kept in the dark. The doctrine of "need to know" had been rigidly observed, and it must have been reasoned that the Vice President was not in the category of officials whose duties required them to be informed on this most secret subject. While in the Senate, Mr. Truman had been chairman of a committee on the conduct of the war and at one point was about to investigate the huge and unexplained sums which disappeared into the Manhattan Engineer District, from which no visible results were emerging. Secretary of War Stimson talked him out of doing so. The matter was too secret to be exposed to an investigation. So secret indeed that General George Marshall, Chief of Staff, operated in person the valve which controlled the flow of money from military appropriations to General Groves.*

The new President had received an intimation of fate from Secretary of War Stimson immediately after taking the oath of office on the evening of April 12. There had been a short cabinet session, and Stimson had remained for that purpose after the others had left. There was a more complete briefing session the next day by Dr. Vannevar Bush, Chairman of the OSRD. One wonders how the new President must have felt to discover how many were familiar with what he had not been permitted to know though he had been but a heartbeat away from the great responsibility he had so suddenly inherited.

On April 25 Secretary Stimson called at the White House to brief the new President on other aspects of the atomic project. No bomb had yet been tested, but the timetable indicated that the first one would be ready for a test about mid-July. Mr. Stimson carried a memorandum[7] with him from which the President learned in detail what all the

---

* Years afterwards, General Marshall told me with obvious enjoyment that one morning during the war General Groves had called at his office and when admitted stood at attention before his desk while Marshall finished something that he was writing. Preoccupied, he kept Groves waiting for perhaps a couple of minutes. When Marshall looked up, Groves quickly came to the point, which was that the project needed "another two hundred million dollars" at once. Would General Marshall please sign the authorizing documents Groves had brought with him? Marshall did so, whereupon Groves turned to leave the room. Marshall called him back and said, "General, I have just kept you waiting for that two hundred million and I am sorry. You might like to know what I was writing while you waited. I was making out a check to my seed store for a dollar and sixty cents worth of grass seed."

mystery had been about; that bombs would be ready in a matter of four months or less; that "one bomb could destroy a whole city"; and a personal opinion to the effect that the "development of this weapon had placed *a certain moral responsibility upon us* which we cannot shirk without very serious responsibility for any disaster to civilization which it would further." (Italics supplied.)

There was more. The President heard from General Groves, who stood before his desk, and with diagrams and charts gave him the proportions and possibilities of the new weapon. Finally, on July 16, the estimates were replaced with observed facts. But by this time the President, accompanied by his advisers, was in Potsdam and the evidence was flown across the Atlantic and placed before him in his temporary headquarters.

This, in brief, was that evidence. At Los Alamos, New Mexico, where the main atomic weapon laboratory had been established atop a remote mesa in sight of the Sangre de Cristo Mountains, the first atomic bomb had been finally assembled. Then it had been taken apart and carefully shipped to a location in the desert near Alamogordo, New Mexico. Reassembled, it was hoisted to the top of a steel tower and, in the moment before dawn on that sixteenth of July, it was detonated.

There have been many weapons tests since, but those who witnessed that first demonstration of an atomic explosion and since have seen others far larger were more overwhelmed by the first. It was spectacular and awe-inspiring. The force of the explosion (measured in terms of the TNT equivalent) was of the order of fifteen to twenty thousand tons. This meant that it would have required thousands of bombing planes carrying conventional bomb loads such as had been used over Germany and Japan to have equaled the force of that one blast. The men who made it and the military who were with them were profoundly impressed with the fact that this was not just another, bigger weapon. As one of them described it, "It was a force of nature."

The report to the President was long and emotional. It described the test as "successful beyond the most optimistic expectations of anyone." It depicted the visual impressions of the explosion with eloquence and its physical results in awesome detail. One observer, General Thomas F. Farrell, was quoted at length. He concluded by saying that the sight and sound "warned of Doomsday and made us feel that we puny things were blasphemous to dare tamper with the forces heretofore reserved to the Almighty."

Secretary of War Stimson, to whom the report was addressed, conveyed it to the President and Prime Minister Churchill. Stimson's diary records that the President "was tremendously pepped up by it." Harvey H. Bundy, who was present when Churchill heard it, has recorded that the elder statesman waved his cigar and said, "Stimson, what was gunpowder? Trivial. What was electricity? Meaningless. This atomic bomb is the Second Coming in Wrath."[8]

But weeks before the date of the Alamogordo test, the war in the Pacific was already in its final stages, and the Japanese Government knew that they faced defeat. The Japanese High Command had been aware of it for months. It was not a secret in Washington, either. Two weeks earlier than the Alamogordo test the Secretary of War had informed the President that the Japanese Navy "is nearly destroyed and she is vulnerable to surface and underwater blockade which can deprive her of sufficient food and supplies for her population. She is terribly vulnerable to our concentrated air attack upon her crowded cities, industrial and food resources." He was inclined to think that it would be well worth while to give the Japanese warning of what was to come and definite opportunity to capitulate.

Fleet Admiral Ernest J. King, Commander in Chief of the United States Fleet and Chief of Naval Operations, in his final report to Secretary Forrestal noted:

. . . when she [Japan] surrendered . . . her Navy had been destroyed and her Merchant Fleet had been fatally crippled. Dependent upon imported food and raw materials and relying upon sea transport to support her Armies at home and overseas, Japan lost the war because she lost command of the sea, and in doing so lost—to us—the island bases from which her factories and cities could be destroyed by air.
. . . of twelve [Japanese] battleships, eleven were sunk; of twenty-six carriers, twenty were sunk; of forty-three cruisers, thirty-eight were destroyed; etc. throughout the various types of ships which collectively constituted a fleet considerably larger than ours was before the war. The few ships that remained afloat were for the most part so heavily damaged as to be of no military value.
. . . After Okinawa was in our hands, the Japanese were in a desperate situation, which could be alleviated only if they could strike a counterblow either by damaging our fleet or by driving us from our advanced island position. The inability of the Japanese to do either was strong evidence of their increasing impotence and indicated that the end could not be long delayed.

Between July 10 and August 6, the forces under Admiral Halsey's command had destroyed or damaged 2804 enemy planes and sunk or damaged 148 Japanese combat ships and 1598 merchant ships. "This impressive record," Admiral King observed, "speaks for itself and helps to explain the sudden collapse of Japan's will to resist.

> . . . While the damage to their cities and production centers by strategic bombing was fully as great as photographic reconnaissance had indicated, the strangulation from our less obvious, but relentlessly effective surface and submarine blockade and from our carrier-based air attacks had been a decisive factor in the enemy's collapse. Their Merchant Marine had been reduced to a fraction of its former size; of the few remaining ships, mostly small ones, only half were still operable. Their food situation was critical, and their remaining resources in fuel and all strategic materials were not less so. It had been known that their few remaining carriers and heavy Navy vessels had been damaged, but it appeared that the fury of our carrier strikes had forced them to withdraw all but a handful of men from these ships, practically abandoning them.

There were plans, well advanced, for landing our troops on the main Japanese islands in the autumn. Nevertheless, the Secretary of War also informed the President that if we were to effect a landing on one of the main islands and begin a forceful occupation of Japan, we should probably find that we had cast the die of last-ditch resistance. Fleet Admiral Nimitz was confident that *neither invasion nor atomic bombing* was required to produce surrender. He commented that our Pacific fleet was pounding Japan "with complete immunity." Japan was out of fuel. The battered remnant of her Navy had taken refuge of sorts in the Inland Sea. Secretary Stimson wrote that the attempt to exterminate Japan's armies and her population by gunfire *"or other means"* (the bomb was seldom mentioned in a memorandum except obliquely) would tend to produce a fusion of race solidity and antipathy.[9]

At a far lower echelon, but as an indication of the state of opinion in the Navy Department on the end of the war, this is from a memorandum I addressed to the Secretary of the Navy on May 7, 1945:

> Dear Jim:
> . . . there is the possibility that V-J Day will follow V-E Day rather earlier than it is conservative to predict from the point of view of conducting the war. However, it would be conservative to plan on a rather prompt termination. You might find it useful therefore to ask the Bureaus now for a prompt report on steps to be taken with respect to

(a) contracts under negotiation, (b) work in progress, (c) personnel;
—on the assumption that V-J Day will occur on, say, August 1 or at
the latest by December 31 of this year.

The United States had, beside these individual judgments, one clear
open window on Japan—our ability to intercept and rapidly decipher
practically every communication between the Japanese Foreign Office
and the Emperor's ambassadors overseas. We knew, accordingly, that
the Japanese not only believed that they were beaten, they wanted to
get out of the war as quickly as possible.

Admiral Joseph R. Redman, Chief of Naval Communications, brought
to my office on July 13 an intercepted and decoded message from the
Gaimusho (the Japanese Foreign Office) to Ambassador Sato in Moscow. It was signed by Togo, the Foreign Minister, and it instructed the
Ambassador to call on Molotov at once before the Russians took off
for Potsdam, where the Big Three, President Truman, Prime Minister
Churchill, and Marshal Stalin were to meet. Sato was directed to lay
before Molotov the earnest wish of the Emperor to see the end of the
war. There were some pious expressions about the cessation of bloodshed, followed by a statement that Japan was prepared to forgo retention of territories she had conquered.

Later intercepts grew more desperate as Sato reported that he could
not get to Molotov and had to content himself with interviews with a
deputy, Lozovsky, who continually put him off with diplomatic double
talk. On July 15, Sato's dispatch made it clear how well aware he was
that Japan was utterly and completely defeated.

Forrestal, of course, saw the intercepts as they were received. We
frequently read them together. He noted in his diary that Russian intervention to end the war was being sought even before there could
have been much effect from the thousand-plane bombing raids of the
Third Fleet and the naval bombardment of Kamaishi. As rapidly as
they were received, Forrestal sent the intercepts to Admiral Leahy, the
President's Chief of Staff, and later took the whole collection with him
to Potsdam. He had not been invited to attend the Potsdam Conference,
but he shared the view of former Ambassador Joseph C. Grew, our
wisest and most experienced Far Eastern diplomat, that if permitted to
retain the Emperor the Japanese would agree to what, in every other
respect, would be the "unconditional" surrender we sought.

Having decided that his responsibilities warranted him to "kibitz"
(as he put it), Forrestal went to Potsdam without the grace of an invita-

tion. He did not fly there directly. Wishing his appearance to appear
casual and in the course of other business, he stopped over in Paris on
July 27, calling on Ambassador Jefferson Caffery and attending to
certain Navy business and did not reach Potsdam until the twenty-
eighth. An irreversible entropy of events had occurred before his plane
touched down.

Immediately on arrival he took the file of intercepted messages to
Secretary Byrnes, who then saw them "in detail" for the first time. The
Secretary of State had only been sworn in on July 3. On July 6 he had
left for Potsdam, and the intervening day of briefing was almost entirely
devoted to the issues on the Potsdam agenda. These related to the
Allied positions on the defeat of Germany. He had not previously seen
the texts of the messages.[10]

One message carried by Forrestal had been intercepted as recently as
July 25. It was an instruction from the Japanese Foreign Minister to
the Japanese Ambassador in Moscow. He was to go to any place that
Molotov might designate and while still maintaining "unconditional
surrender" to be unacceptable, to state that Japan had "no objection to
a peace based on the Atlantic Charter" and that the terms requested by
Japan were only those necessary to "secure and maintain our nation's
existence and honor." The message mentioned the imminence of "complete collapse" and could only be read as having been prepared in an
atmosphere of desperation.

Forrestal was too late by forty-eight hours. The Potsdam Declaration
—the ultimatum to Japan—had been dispatched on the twenty-sixth,
and events were now in the saddle, riding the decision makers.

On August 2, there was another intercept. "The battle situation has
become acute," it understated. "There are only a few days left in which
to make arrangements to end the war. . . . Since the loss of one day
relative to this present matter may result in a thousand years of regret,
it is requested that you immediately have a talk with Molotov."

About the only relief in this tense period is a curious picture of
President Truman and Premier Stalin trading intelligence.

The problem had arisen as to what if anything should be disclosed
to Stalin about the coming A-bomb attack. Churchill agreed that it
would be appropriate that the President might offhandedly tell Stalin
that the U.S. had perfected "an entirely novel form of bomb, something
quite out of the ordinary." And Stalin for his part had some intelligence to impart to the President. He had evidently decided to treat it

"offhandedly" also. There had been some sort of a message from the Japanese Emperor, he indicated, which had been delivered by the Japanese Ambassador in Moscow. The message stated that, while unconditional surrender was unacceptable, the Japanese were ready to come to terms. Stalin played it down.

President Truman could not compromise his intelligence sources by saying he had known of the messages well before Stalin ever saw them, and Stalin, for his part, when the President spoke so calmly of the new bomb, gave to Mr. Churchill (who observed the colloquy from the other side of the room) the impression "that he had no idea of the significance of what he was being told." Stalin's espionage organization, as we now have reason to know, had been able to keep him informed. Secretary Byrnes thought that Stalin's lack of eagerness to know anything about the bomb was due to the fact that "The Russians kept secret their development in military weapons" and "thought it improper to ask about ours."[11] Unfortunately, there is no photograph of the two highest-level poker-faces at that moment in history.

On July 25 the President had made his decision. His orders had gone out to the Pacific, and on the little island of Tinian the special bomber group which long had trained to handle the bombs made its final preparations. Some months earlier a few officers especially cleared for the purpose had reviewed the maps of Japanese cities and selected a number of them as prospective targets. A committee of officers had been sent out to Los Alamos, where they conferred with Dr. J. Robert Oppenheimer, the director of the laboratory, and some of his associates. Dr. Oppenheimer was to testify nine years later that "Hiroshima was of course very successful partly for reasons unanticipated by us. We had been over the targets with a committee that was sent to consult us and to consider them, and the targets that were bombed were among the list that seemed bright to us."[12]

One individual had a negative voice in the choice of targets for the bomb. Among the cities initially selected for the bombing had been Kyoto. Secretary Stimson, when he learned of it, interposed his personal veto. I had visited Kyoto in 1926 and could appreciate his reasons. Kyoto was the cultural and religious center of old Japan. There were located the delicately beautiful palaces of the former emperors who held court in exile while the country was governed by the warlike shoguns in Tokyo. There were the hundreds of ancient temples and shrines fashioned of carved and gilded wood. Destruction of Kyoto would have added vandalism to whatever charge might be leveled against the target selections.

About a recommendation which had been made that instead of exploding the bomb over an inhabited city it should be demonstrated over some unpopulated area, the laboratory group said that they "did not think exploding one of these things as a firecracker over a desert was likely to be very impressive."[13]

Einstein and Szilard sought unsuccessfully to arrest the course of events initiated by the famous letter of six years earlier. A second letter to President Roosevelt was written by Dr. Einstein and is reported to have been found unopened among the President's mail in Warm Springs, Georgia, at the time of his death in April 1945.[14]

The letter requested an appointment for Dr. Szilard to propose certain considerations and recommendations which "unusual circumstances" persuaded Einstein should be brought to the attention of the President in spite of the fact that he did not know the substance of the considerations and recommendations which Szilard proposed to submit. This was due to the fact that security prevented Szilard from any disclosures to Einstein. Einstein concluded with the statement that he understood Szilard was greatly concerned about the lack of adequate contact between the scientists who were working on the project and the members of the President's cabinet who were responsible for formulating policy.

When President Truman received the letter, he referred it to Secretary Byrnes with the request that the Secretary see Dr. Szilard, who, in company with Drs. Urey and Walter Bartky, called on him at his home in Spartanburg, South Carolina, on May 28. When they left, Secretary Byrnes gave them Dr. Einstein's letter, which Szilard duly returned to the President's secretary. Secretary Byrnes has recorded that, as Dr. Einstein's letter had forecast, Szilard "complained that he and some of his associates did not know enough about the policy of the Government with regard to the use of the bomb." Secretary Byrnes did not react favorably to the suggestion that discussion between the scientists and the policy-makers at Cabinet level should be initiated. In the course of his presentation, Byrnes recalled that Szilard had said that the younger scientists were very critical of Drs. Bush, Compton, and Conant, who were among the senior scientific advisers to the President. Byrnes told the delegation that Dr. Oppenheimer would be consulted about the use of the bomb, which assurance appeared to satisfy them.[15]

Under Secretary Ralph Bard represented the Navy Department on the Interdepartmental Committee on Atomic Energy (Army, Navy, State) and forthrightly committed his views to the record at the time:

27 June 1945

MEMORANDUM ON THE USE OF S-1 BOMB

Ever since I have been in touch with this program I have had a feeling that before the bomb is actually used against Japan that Japan should have some preliminary warning for say two or three days in advance of use. The position of the United States as a great humanitarian nation and the fair play attitude of our people generally is responsible in the main for this feeling.

During recent weeks I have also had the feeling very definitely that the Japanese Government may be searching for some opportunity which they could use as a medium of surrender. Following the three-power conference emissaries from this country could contact representatives from Japan somewhere on the China Coast and make representations with regard to Russia's position and at the same time give them some information regarding the proposed use of atomic power, together with whatever assurances the President might care to make with regard to the Emperor of Japan and the treatment of the Japanese nation following unconditional surrender. It seems quite possible to me that this presents the opportunity which the Japanese are looking for.

I don't see that we have anything in particular to lose in following such a program. The stakes are so tremendous that it is my opinion very real consideration should be given to some plan of this kind. I do not believe under present circumstances existing that there is anyone in this country whose evaluation of the chances of the success of such a program is worth a great deal. The only way to find out is to try it out.

/s/ Ralph A. Bard

Dr. Arthur H. Compton, the Nobel laureate in physics, who had contributed so outstandingly to the war effort, also raised the question of whether it might not be possible to arrange a demonstration of the bomb, "in such a manner that the Japanese will be so impressed that they would see the uselessness of continuing the war."[16]

I had made a suggestion to Secretary Forrestal that the power of the bomb be displayed as a warning in an uninhabited area. It seemed to me that a demonstration over a forest would offer impressive evidence to show the terrible effect of enormous blast and heat. A meteor which fell near Lake Baikal in Siberia in 1908 had knocked down forests for miles around its point of impact and the trees lay in windrows radiating like the spokes of a wheel from the center. I recalled a grove of crypto-meria trees near the little village of Nikko on the main Japanese island. This seemed to me a place where an impressive demonstration could be made. The inhabitants, priests, and shrine servants could be warned to evacuate beforehand. It troubled me to think of using what might turn out to be a cataclysmic weapon over a crowded Japanese metropo-lis of wood-and-paper houses and multitudes of women and children in a defeated nation.

In justification for the rejection of these proposals it has since been argued that even the first test in New Mexico was not sufficient to assure that the weapon would explode when dropped from an airplane. This was because the system for detonating the bomb at a predeter-mined altitude had not been proved at Alamogordo, where the bomb was fixed on the top of a steel tower. This argument was furnished to Secretary Stimson, who restated it in a magazine article in 1947. The fusing system had been repeatedly and successfully tested, however. This specific justification against a demonstration seemed to me of little va-lidity.

Secretary Forrestal recorded a conversation which he had with John J. McCloy in March of 1947. McCloy had recalled a meeting with President Truman in the summer of 1945, before Potsdam. Mc-Cloy had volunteered his views, which were that the Japanese should be told that we had perfected a terrifyingly destructive weapon which we would have to use if they did not surrender. He had said that some of the Japanese who had been in Germany during our bombing raids were now back in Japan and could testify to the devastation they had seen produced by conventional weapons. We should add, McCloy said, that the Japanese would be permitted to retain the Emperor and a form of government of their own choosing. Forrestal noted that McCloy ob-served that the military leaders were somewhat annoyed at his inter-ference but that the President welcomed it. At the conclusion of Mc-Cloy's comments, the President had "ordered such a political offensive to be set in motion."[17] The offensive greatly strengthened the hands of the peace party in Japan but was eclipsed.

General Eisenhower was in Potsdam at this period, but, the war in Europe being over, he had not been invited as a participant in the conference. Secretary Stimson told him, however, about the test at Ala-mogordo and described his relief that it had been successful. He indicated his keen sense of personal responsibility. General Eisenhower expressed the hope that we would never have to use such a weapon against an enemy because he disliked seeing the United States "initiate the use" of anything so horrible and destructive.[18]

The voices recommending restraint were crying in the wilderness. First doubts and then opposition had developed in the weapon laboratories themselves. There had been round robins and petitions. One of the latter, the so-called Franck report, was prepared at the University of Chicago and addressed to the Secretary of War on June 11, 1945. It bore a distinguished group of names besides that of James Franck, a Nobel prize winner, the first to sign it—among them Leo Szilard, Glenn T. Seaborg, D. Hughes, T. Hogness, E. Rabinowitch, and C. J. Nickson. I have seen no indication that it reached the President and am inclined to think that it did not. The document made the point that a demonstration of the new weapon might be made before the eyes of representatives of all United Nations on a desert or a barren island.

A petition to the President had been prepared in the Metallurgical Laboratory (the Atomic Weapons Project) at the University of Chicago and signed by a large number of scientists. It read in part:

> Until recently we have had to fear that the United States might be attacked by atomic bombs during this war and that her only defense might lie in a counterattack by the same means. Today, with the defeat of Germany, this danger is averted and we feel impelled to say what follows:
> The war has to be brought speedily to a successful conclusion and attacks by atomic bombs may very well be an effective method of warfare. We feel, however, that such attacks on Japan could not be justified, at least not unless the terms which will be imposed after the war on Japan were made public in detail and Japan were given an opportunity to surrender.

The text of the petition apparently reached the White House as a copy provided by Szilard to Presidential Secretary Connolly eleven days after Hiroshima.

The Hyde Park Agreement of September 19, 1944, which is later described and which for many years was thought to exist only in the original possessed by Sir Winston Churchill, until another signed original was found ten years later at Hyde Park, states a conclusion reached between the President and the Prime Minister at that time: ". . . when a bomb is finally available, it *might perhaps, after mature consideration,* be used against the Japanese. . . ." (Italics supplied.)

Mr. Churchill recalls that at Potsdam, however, "there never was a moment's discussion as to whether the atomic bomb should be used or not," adding, "The historic fact remains, and must be judged in the aftertime, that the *decision whether or not to use the atomic bomb to compel the surrender of Japan was never an issue. . . .* There was unanimous, automatic, unquestioned agreement around our table; nor did I ever hear the slightest suggestion that we should do otherwise." (Italics supplied.)[19]

A declaration, in effect an ultimatum, was issued over the names of President Truman, Clement Attlee, and Chiang Kai-shek on July 26. Stalin was not a signatory, since Russia had not yet declared war on Japan and was not to do so for another thirteen days. Indeed the Japanese and the Russians had a mutual nonaggression pact which was to be violated by Soviet aggression. An article of the Charter of the United Nations could be conveniently construed that, if a conflict should develop between the previous understandings of a member nation and its obligations under the U.N. Charter, the latter would prevail. Churchill was not a signatory as the tally of votes in the British elections had unhorsed him on that very day. Though he had expected victory and was surprised by the Labor-party landslide, he had brought Attlee to Potsdam with true statesmanship in order that continuity would be provided in the remote possibility of defeat.

The declaration contained no warning that anything as radically different from conventional weapons as the atomic bomb would be used against Japan if she resisted surrender. Four days before the President had left for Potsdam, Secretary Stimson brought him a memorandum which had been prepared in collaboration with Forrestal, McCloy, and Grew. It urged the issuance of a warning proclamation which would make it clear that the maintenance of a constitutional monarchy under the ruling dynasty was not excluded. It is also clear from Stimson's covering letter that inclusion of a specific warning about the new weapon was implicit. He called the President's attention to the fact that the draft proclamation made no specific mention of the employment of any new weapon and that it would "have to be revamped to conform to the efficacy of such a weapon if the warning were to be delivered, as would almost certainly be the case, in conjunction with its use."[20] But the declaration contained no mention of willingness to concede the continuation of a constitutional monarchy. (We volunteered this concession, of course, *after* surrender in order to facilitate the procedures of occupation.) How that essential and apparently settled feature disappeared from the drafting is not entirely clear, though there were those who opposed it, including former Secretary of State Hull, who believed that it would be regarded as a form of appeasement. In a pre-Potsdam conversation with Forrestal, Grew had expressed his satisfaction with the draft of the proposed message to the Japanese which had been finally "whipped into shape." Although its aim was to make the phrase "unconditional surrender" more specific, Grew said he was afraid that it would be "ditched on the way over" to Potsdam by people who were accompanying the President and "who reflect the view that we cannot hold out any clarification of terms to Japan which could be construed as a desire to get the Japanese war over with before Russia has an opportunity to enter."[21]

In the Stimson memoir a point is made of the possibility, in the light of the final surrender, "that a clearer and earlier exposition of American willingness to retain the Emperor would have produced an earlier ending of the war," though both President Truman and his military advisers had to weigh the alternative possibility that it might have been construed by the Japanese as an indication of weakness. This is difficult to reconcile with a nation suing for peace and our knowledge of the state of Japanese morale.* The decision to omit this one point from the Potsdam Declaration had consequences from which the world will be long in recovering. It was indeed the ultimate decision which precipitated the use of the bomb.

Ambassador Grew later wrote that the surrender of the Japanese could have been obtained had the President issued a categorical statement that surrender would not mean the elimination of the Japanese imperial dynasty. Such a statement, Grew felt, would have afforded the "surrender-minded elements in the government . . . a valid reason and the necessary strength to come to an early clear-cut decision."

Flashed across the Pacific, the ultimatum reached the hands of the divided and panicky body of men who in various official capacities surrounded Emperor Hirohito. It was closely examined for some indication of protection for his person. Finding none, they let it be known on July 28 that the declaration would be "received in silence." This indecisive expression, an effort at temporizing, was interpreted or paraphrased to the Allies in Potsdam even more negatively as "rejected." The fatal word was *"mokusatsu."* This has been variously rendered as

* The term "suing for peace" may be questioned, but the intercepted messages exchanged between Foreign Minister Togo in Tokyo and Ambassador Sato in Moscow in July 1945 are scarcely open to any other interpretation.

meaning "to disregard it," "to take no notice of it," "to treat it with silent contempt," "to ignore it." Never perhaps in history has so much depended upon the decision to select from alternative translations one destined to stand forever under the blight of disaster. The men in Potsdam fully understood that it was not in any sense a formal reply.[22]

On the same day Stalin appears to have informed President Truman and Prime Minister Attlee of the Japanese proposal to send a mission headed by Prince Konoye to negotiate a cessation of hostilities. While we knew by way of intercepts of this Japanese attempt to approach us by way of the Russians and that it had been delayed by Moscow with apparent deliberation, nothing appears to have been done thereafter to encourage any other contact, direct or otherwise, with the Japanese.

Meanwhile, fate, moving on the tiny island of Tinian, gathered momentum.*

Although the orders to General Spaatz in the Pacific had been dispatched before the July 26 ultimatum, the President had an understanding with his Secretary of War which included the possibility of a countermand if the Japanese reply proved to be acceptable.[23] There was no countermand. Accordingly, at two forty-five in the morning of August 6, weather conditions being favorable, the bomber *Enola Gay* was air-borne. Soon afterward, Captain W. S. Parsons inserted the fissionable charge into the lethal cargo. He performed the feat of arming the bomb barehanded (for a more secure "feel" of the parts), in freezing temperatures, in the bomb bay of the aircraft. This was done in the air to protect the personnel on the base at Tinian if the plane had failed on take-off.[24] Six and a half hours later the bomb was released over Hiroshima, set to explode as soon as the plane had reached a safe distance. Seconds later the city and most of its inhabitants ceased to exist. Three days later Nagasaki, another of the targets that had "seemed bright to us," became literally bright in the more-than-sun-like brilliance of the second bomb's explosion. Neither had been "a firecracker exploded over a desert": 152,000 people were dead.

Only three days elapsed between the first bomb and the second, but our ally, Stalin, was quick to act. The Soviet declaration of war was

* Eloquently expressed by Dr. Herbert Feis in his *Japan Subdued.* "Two measures, long in preparation, were about to be taken: dropping the atomic bomb and the entry into the war of a great new antagonist, the Soviet Union. By this time in fact the impetus of both was so great, and the plans for their execution were so complete, that only a most resolute and courageous act of will—of a kind rarely recorded in history—could have stayed them."

promptly handed to Sato by Molotov on the afternoon of the eighth of August. It was so phrased as to convey the impression that it was mandatory upon the Soviet Government under the Charter of the United Nations. This was, of course, a convenient sophistry. By the following day, August 9, Soviet tank divisions were rolling into Manchuria, and on the next day Japan sued for peace—formally. In the general rejoicing over that event and its association in time with the atomic bombings, the weight of Russia's action on the Japanese decision has been largely overlooked. Expert opinions differed.

General Arnold, the Army Air Force Chief of Staff, believed that it was air bombardment by conventional means which had brought Japan to her knees.[25] Major General Claire L. Chennault, who had commanded our air forces in China, was convinced that it was the entrance of Russia into the war which produced the collapse of Japan. In an interview in the New York *Times* on August 15, he was quoted as stating that Japan would have surrendered whether or not atomic bombs had been dropped. A few years later the United States Strategic Bombing Survey, with all the facts before it, was to confirm that Japan was ready to surrender in 1945 without the atomic bomb and without an American invasion.

The survey found that "It is apparent that the effect of the atomic bombings on the confidence of the Japanese civilian population was remarkably localized. Outside of the target cities, it was subordinate to other demoralizing experiences."

The report also said that the atomic bomb alone had not convinced the Japanese leaders of the necessity of surrender. The decision to seek ways and means to end the war, influenced in part by the low state of popular morale had already been taken in May of 1945 by what was known as the Supreme War Guidance Council. Prior to July 1, doubts about a Japanese victory were shared by 74 per cent of the population, and some 47 per cent had become certain that a Japanese victory was impossible. With regard to the bombing, the Strategic Bombing Survey concluded that the reaction of the Japanese population at some distance from the target cities was blunted by their direct experience with other misfortunes and hardships, and that in Japan as a whole military losses and failures, such as those at Saipan, the Philippines, and Okinawa, "were twice as important as the atomic bomb in inducing certainty of defeat. Other raids over Japan as a whole were more than three times as important in this respect. Consumer deprivations, such as food shortages and the attendant malnutrition, were also more important in bringing people to the point where they felt that they could not go on with the war."

The war was over. Our inscrutable Eastern ally, with his concealed plans looking far ahead into the future and to world conquest, had come in, in time for the kill. The Russians knew from the desperate approaches made by the Japanese Ambassador in Moscow that the Japanese craved to end the war. They had known this from the last days in May, yet they had told us nothing of it until Stalin's offhand reference in Potsdam.

President Truman did not shirk responsibility for the decision. As he put it in his memoirs:

> The final decision of when and where to use the atomic bomb was up to me. Let there be no mistake about it. I regarded the bomb as a military weapon and never had any doubt that it should be used: The top military advisers to the President recommended its use, and *when I talked to Churchill* he unhesitatingly told me that he favored the use of the atomic bomb if it might aid to end the war. (Italics supplied.)

But it was not that unilateral. All of us, the President's fellow countrymen, shared in varying degrees in that responsibility. His principal adviser, Secretary Stimson, was a man who had been a lifelong champion of international law. He had repeatedly argued that war itself must be restrained within the bounds of humanity, and as recently as sixty days before the atomic bombings had asked General Arnold whether the apparently indiscriminate fire-bombings of Tokyo were absolutely necessary.[26] Yet he had made a decision he later described as "stern and heart-rending," in the advice he gave to the President. Other advisers must have been similarly torn. Against Mr. Churchill's recollection that there was never a moment's discussion as to whether the bomb should be used or not, the President recalls "unhesitating" agreement from him. Both men and their counselors appear trapped in the path of the avalanche of events.

Historians would do well to disregard an observation recorded by one of the President's close advisers "that the scientists and others wanted to make this test because of the vast sums that had been spent on this project." No such sentiment was ever expressed by any of the many scientists with whom I have discussed the subject at length and over the years.

General Eisenhower, reflecting on the holocausts of August 6 and 9, wrote while yet in Germany that "with the evidence of the most destructive war yet waged by the peoples of the earth about me, I gained increased hope that this development of what appeared to be the ultimate in destruction would drive men, in self-preservation, to find a way of eliminating war . . . that fear, universal fear, might possibly succeed where statesmanship and religion had not yet won success."[27]

The decision to use the atomic bomb to accelerate the end of a war already won was not the same as the one five years earlier when a decision had been taken to make the bomb. Yet both were decisions by compassionate men within the finite limits of human judgment. Both were decisions made by our chosen representatives. All of us in some degree shared an inescapable responsibility which will be judged, as Churchill has said, "in the after-time."

X

The Decision to Detect

Make strong the watch—establish watchmen—prepare . . .
JEREMIAH 51:12

But if the watchman see the sword come, and blow not the trumpet, and the people be not warned . . .
EZEKIEL 33:6

In 1946 the Soviet delegate to the United Nations let it be known that in peace-loving Communist Russia the facts about atomic energy were "very well understood." But atomic energy was being employed by his country for peaceful purposes only—to change the courses of rivers and to remove mountains. This was welcome news to a world, bone-weary after six years of the most devastating war in history.

To a surprising degree the world has maintained its wide-eyed and childlike credulity about Soviet pronouncements. It is a state of mind that, astonishingly, survives periods of disillusionment when the actions of the Soviets expose their insincerity and untruthfulness. The phenomenon is unexplained. Not everyone, however, accepted Soviet assurance in 1946 that the development of atomic energy in Russia was solely pacific and humanitarian. The first Atomic Energy Commissioners did not.

The several Commissioners were confirmed by the Senate in April 1947. At a meeting shortly thereafter we discussed a memorandum I had addressed to my colleagues. The memorandum noted that we had no information as to whether the intelligence arrangements of the Manhattan Engineer District had made provision in the past for continuous monitoring of radioactivity in the atmosphere. "This," it said, "would be perhaps the best means we would have for discovering that a test of an atomic weapon had been made by any other nation. It is to be presumed that any other country going into a large-scale manufacture of atomic weapons would be under the necessity of conducting at least one test to 'prove' the weapon. If there is no such monitoring system in effect, it is incumbent upon us to bring up the desirability of such an immediate step and, in default of action, to initiate it ourselves, at once." There was unanimous agreement, and the Chairman suggested that, having raised the subject, I might like to push it.

Following this, there were meetings with General Hoyt Vandenberg, then Director of the Combined Intelligence Group, before whom I urged the appointment of an interservice committee to make an immediate study of the problem. General Vandenberg acted promptly, addressing identical letters to the Secretaries of War and Navy and the Chairman of the Joint Research and Development Board. He recommended that each of these agencies appoint representatives to a "long-range detection committee" which would formulate a general plan. After the early meetings, the Commission was represented at subsequent sessions by Commander William T. Golden, to whom great credit is due. (Mr. Golden had come to work with me in the Navy during the war and left his business again to join us in Government service in the AEC. His originality and initiative made him singularly valuable as an officer in the Navy and on the staff of the Commission.)

Golden had a quality of perseverance which he demonstrated with great effect in these sessions. At that time there was a general disinclination to engage in any monitoring based upon the feeling that it would be a waste of time, personnel, and money. The experts for the most part believed that the construction of an atomic bomb was simply beyond the immediate competence of Russian science or the capability of existing industrial organization in the Soviet Union. The earliest date any of us had seen estimated for Russian achievement of nuclear weapon capability was five years. Intelligence reports to President Truman varied in estimates of the date when Russian achievement of an atomic weapon could occur, but in general none expected the Soviets to detonate any atomic device before 1952.[1] The majority opinion set the time substantially further in the future,[2] while not a few believed it beyond Soviet capacity in *any* time scale likely to be of much concern to us.

By May of 1947, being satisfied that we had no monitoring program in being, we found it necessary not only to devise adequate technical methods but to fix a responsibility at some point in the operating organization of the Government. Divided responsibility could invite the same circumstances as prevailed at Pearl Harbor. But there were an unusually large number of organizations which seemed to have a special interest in such a monitoring service—the Joint Chiefs of Staff, the Army, the Army Air Force, the Navy, Central Intelligence, the Joint Research and Development Board, the Department of State, and the Atomic Energy Commission. Obviously, all could not operate the project. Operation by committee would guarantee failure. Responsibility had to be firmly fixed.

Some months earlier, in order to have an experienced man on the Security Panel of the commission, I had suggested to my colleagues the name of Rear Admiral Sidney W. Souers. Souers, an industrialist and insurance executive, had served, when a reserve officer, as Assistant Chief of Naval Intelligence during World War II, and I knew him to be a wise man with a judicial temperament. My colleagues agreeing, I located Souers in Mexico City and persuaded him to return to Washington. He was not with us long, however, before he was drafted from our work by President Truman, who designated him to be his Special Assistant for National Security Matters. It was in this capacity that I asked Admiral Souers to review my conclusions on long-range detection, and he agreed with them wholeheartedly. From that time he became of the greatest assistance in helping launch the program and in steering it around the roadblocks which, oddly, were put in its way.

The next step had been to call on Secretary of the Navy Forrestal. His response when he heard that we had no round-the-clock monitoring to see whether the Russians were testing atomic weapons could be reasonably anticipated. It was, in fact, "Hell! We must be doing it!"

"Well," I answered, "you can be sure it isn't going on in the Navy or you would know it. Why not call Ken Royall and see if the Army or the Army Air Force is?"

Forrestal lifted his phone and called Secretary Royall, who returned the call a few minutes later to say that there was no such project in the War Department and some question as to whether it was necessary. "Jim," I said, "if neither of the Armed Services takes on this responsibility, the Commission will. If we do it, we'll have to buy planes and hire pilots. We'll have to get an appropriation for that. When we ask for the money, that will be the first time Congress will know that monitoring hasn't been going on all this time." Forrestal saw the point immediately. We went together to lunch with Secretary Royall for further discussion.

There was a second meeting on September 15, and on the next day General Dwight D. Eisenhower, as Chief of Staff, placed the authority in the hands of General Carl A. Spaatz and the Air Force. The order called for establishing and operating a system to have as its objective "the determination of the time and place of all large explosions which might occur anywhere in the world and to ascertain in a manner which would leave no question, whether or not they were of nuclear origin."

Details of the system were closely guarded as a matter of security for nearly ten years—until the scientific conference with the Soviets on the cessation of testing atomic weapons was begun in 1958. In 1947 we had the accumulated experience both from the original test at Alamogordo in 1945 and the two tests on naval structures at Bikini in 1946. There had been recordings at varying distances from the site of these explosions, but the results were inconclusive. It was important that the tests which the Commission was planning to conduct in the vicinity of Eniwetok in the spring of 1948 should be monitored in order that a system for a reliable detection might be perfected.

During the New Year's holiday in 1948, two officers from General Spaatz's command called on me to say that the Air Force found itself short of funds to procure instrumentation for the monitoring program and that about a million dollars would be required to complete it; that certain contracts had to be let at once if the instruments were to be ready in time. Since every day counted and no Commission meeting could be held until the Commissioners returned from the holiday, I volunteered to obligate myself for the amount so that the contracts could be made firm immediately. The Commission met on January 6, and we undertook to supply the shortage from our own appropriation —to my very immense relief.

Our forthcoming test series, with the code name Sandstone, was staged at the Pacific Proving Grounds, which included several atolls in the group known as the Marshall Islands. As it turned out, the series was efficiently monitored and the principle established that an atomic detonation above the surface of the earth and within the atmosphere, under given conditions, could be detected without difficulty.

Even after this event, however, there continued to be an important body of opinion which regarded the operation as unnecessary. As late as June of 1949, a Subcommittee on Atomic Energy of the Joint Research and Development Board of the Department of Defense was reported as expressing the opinion that the amount which the detection program was estimated to cost might be spent more wisely in other fields.[3]

But in that same year, on September 3, not only the cost of the operation but the apprehensions of those responsible for it became chillingly justified. As former President Truman described what had happened:

> ... one of the planes operating in the long-range detection system collected an air sample that was decidedly radioactive, and the entire detection machinery at once went into high gear. The cloud containing the suspicious matter was tracked by the United States Air Force from the North Pacific to the vicinity of the British Isles, where it was also picked up by the Royal Air Force, and from the first these developments were reported to me by the CIA as rapidly as they became known.[4]

It was hard to convince a number of people who had been skeptical of Soviet success at so early a date that some mistake had not been made by our monitoring system. The findings were carefully reviewed, however, and on September 21 it was reported to the President that there was no room for doubt that an atomic explosion had occurred somewhere on the Asiatic mainland and at some date between August 26 and 29. On the morning of September 23, the President gave the news to his cabinet and issued a statement to the public:

> I believe that the American people, to the fullest extent consistent with national security, are entitled to be informed of all developments in the atomic energy field.
> We have evidence that within recent weeks an atomic explosion occurred in the U.S.S.R.
> Ever since atomic energy was first released by man, the eventual development of this new force by other nations was to be expected. This probability has always been taken into account by us.
> Nearly four years ago I pointed out that "scientific opinion appears to be practically unanimous that the essential theoretical knowledge upon which the discovery is based is already widely known. There is also substantial agreement that foreign research can come abreast of our present theoretical knowledge in time. . . ."
> This recent development emphasizes once again, if indeed such emphasis were needed, the necessity for that truly effective enforceable international control of atomic energy which this government and the large majority of the United Nations support.[5]

Even after the successful detection of the first Soviet atomic test (or more properly, as I tried repeatedly to emphasize, the first Soviet atomic test *we detected*), there were those who believed that it was not the test of a weapon at all, that what had probably happened was some sort of an accident in Russia during an experiment with this highly sensitive process. These views may have been responsible for the second paragraph in the President's statement, in which he referred to an atomic "explosion" rather than a test of an atomic weapon.

And even after this, there were recommendations to cancel the research and development program concerned with long-range detection. "Stop orders" were issued to cancel contracts for instruments. These orders actually had to be changed so that our analysis of the debris from the first Soviet test could be completed.

The precedent for the announcement of Russian atomic weapon tests following their detection has been continued. When a sequence of weapons tests in fairly close order was recorded, however, the fact that a series had been detected was announced, although the individual shots were not separately specified.

It has been stated that the United Kingdom initiated the long-range detection of Russian nuclear explosions, but this is not factual.[6] The British authorities, however, co-operated fully with our detection system.

The assignment of responsibility on an individual basis ran into considerable difficulty. Dr. Ellis Johnson, of the Carnegie Institution, was first selected because of his contribution to mine detection during the war, his experience in geophysics, and other relevant disciplines. He obtained a leave of absence from his academic post and began his work in early 1948. Though only a few months were available between the date of his arrival and the scheduled date of the Sandstone series, he accomplished the almost impossible task of getting the necessary apparatus designed, procured, tested, and installed in good season to be effective. So far as I know, his work has never been adequately recognized.

He was succeeded by General W. M. Canterbury and Dr. Doyle Northrup, two men who put the enterprise on a continuing basis and made notable improvements in the system.

One of the most dramatic demonstrations of long-range detection was the recording as far away as Washington of the greatly attenuated shock waves originated by the Pacific tests in 1954. The signals initiated by one of these tests were picked up at the National Bureau of Standards, amplified, and the distance between the crest and trough of the waves electronically compressed and recorded. This enabled me to take a recording to the President. The explosion had occurred many thousands of miles away at Bikini, but the unbelievably faint signals had been caught by the most delicate of instruments and were impressively re-created. The Bureau of Standards is an agency of which little is known by the general public, but it is one of the most useful adjuncts of our government. Dr. Allen Astin, its director, and his staff are self-effacing men of the highest competence in their several scientific fields, and the work they do rates excellent.

It is sobering to speculate on the course of events had there been no monitoring system in operation in 1949. Russian success in that summer would have been unknown to us. In consequence, we would have made no attempt to develop a thermonuclear weapon. It was our positive knowledge of Russian attainment of fission bomb capabilities which generated the recommendation to develop a qualitatively superior weapon—thus to maintain our military superiority. And *that* recommendation nearly failed because of determined opposition to it. The Russian success in developing thermonuclear weapon capability in 1953 would have found the United States hopelessly outdistanced and the Soviet military would have been in possession of weapons vastly more powerful and devastating than those in our stockpile.

The course which events would then have taken can be only conjecture. But to assume that Communism would have used such overwhelming power benignly is belied by history. The effect on the so-called neutral and uncommitted nations almost certainly would have been demoralizing. Hard decisions would have been before us—to compromise, appease, surrender or fight. The decision in 1947 to undertake the long-range detection of nuclear weapons tests was a fortunate one and far more crucial than we knew.

XI

Decision on the Hydrogen Bomb

The arms are fair when the intent of bearing them is just.
HENRY IV, PART I
ACT V, SCENE II

Yet, in holding scientific research and discovery in respect, as we should, we must also be alert to the equal and opposite danger that public policy could itself become the captive of a scientific-technological elite.
PRESIDENT EISENHOWER'S
FAREWELL ADDRESS TO THE NATION,
JANUARY 17, 1961

On August 16, 1945, a week after the atomic bomb had been exploded over Nagasaki, I sent a memorandum to Forrestal:

Dear Jim:
During the interval between World Wars I and II, there was inadequate testing of large charges (torpedo warheads) against ship structures due to a penurious policy for research and development.
This leads me to the suggestion that we should at once test the ability of ships of present design to withstand the forces generated by the atomic bomb. If such a test is not made there will be loose talk to the effect that the fleet is obsolete in the face of this new weapon and this will militate against appropriations to preserve a postwar Navy of the size now planned. If, on the other hand, the tests should substantiate so radical a contention, the Navy itself would certainly wish to be the first in the field with a revision of its program.
What I have in mind is the selection of a number of the older ships of each type and their assignment to a task force for the purpose of such a test. These ships could be equipped with automatic controls, and could be, without personnel aboard, subjected to both air and *an underwater* explosion of the new type bombs. Suitable instruments

on the ships if they survived could indicate the possible effect on
personnel. By proper spacing of the ships the effect upon them at varying distances from the center of the disturbance could be approxi-
mated.

If this suggestion has merit, it would have to be inaugurated before
the ships in question are laid up or scrapped—that is to say, promptly.
I assume that because of the controls established around the new
weapon this program would require the approval of the President.

On August 25, Senator McMahon, later to become Chairman of the
Senate Special Committee on Atomic Energy, suggested that the sur-
viving ships of the Japanese Navy be used "to test the destructive power
of the atomic bomb against naval vessels," and this was echoed on September 14 by Lieutenant General B. M. Giles in General McArthur's
Tokyo headquarters. Admiral King had previously called for the destruction of all Japanese naval tonnage, and this order was counter-
manded in order that an interservice committee under General Curtis
LeMay's chairmanship might study the composition of a target array
and make necessary plans for a test.

In due course, Operation Crossroads was laid on. The purpose was
to test the effects of weapons air-borne and submerged on a cross-section
of the fleet from battleships to landing craft. Ships of both conquered
navies were also included, the Japanese battleship *Nagato* and the German cruiser *Prince Eugen* among them. Admiral Blandy was put in command of what was known as Joint Task Force One to carry out this test.

Much would depend upon it. Was the fleet now obsolete? What
would be the effects of blast on ships and of radiation on crews? How
much of the fission products would be trapped in the water? Would
they contaminate the ships that survived physical damage? Could they
be washed off? What kind of ship construction (e.g., welded seams or
riveted seams) was best? Are new tactics to be learned? Which ships,
large or small, are more vulnerable? There were scores of other questions all adding up to a major one: Was there a role for the Navy in
the defense of our country in the Atomic Age or was the day of sea
power ended?

In spite of the obvious need for answers, there was widespread opposition to the test. It was asserted that it would kill all fish and whales
for thousands of miles and cripple the fishing industry in the Pacific for
years to come; that the cost of the test would not justify the results;
that a tidal wave might be created which would overwhelm many
Pacific islands with resultant loss of life; that a chain reaction might

propagate in sea water which would wipe out all life on earth; that a crack might be opened in the ocean floor allowing sea water to rush into the white-hot interior and produce subterranean explosions and earthquakes; etc., etc.

None of these dire events came to pass, and most could be demonstrated beforehand as theoretically impossible. They are mentioned here because of their similarity to some of the arguments offered three years later as reasons for avoiding a test of the hydrogen bomb. Among the more imaginative of these latter were that it would "blow a chunk out of the earth the size of the moon," and that a few such detonations would tilt the earth off its axis and permanently alter the seasons and weather.

Blandy gathered a remarkable staff. It included Rear Admiral W. S. Parsons, Generals A. L. McAuliffe and W. E. Kepner, Rear Admirals J. A. Snackenberg and T. A. Solberg, and Captain F. L. Ashworth. My friends Dr. John von Neumann and Dr. Karl T. Compton were present as observers and evaluators, as well as General Albert C. Wedemeyer, General L. H. Brereton, General T. H. Farrell and a group of senators and congressmen. Also, and unobtrusively, on hand were two representatives of our "ally," the Union of Soviet Socialist Republics— a physicist from the University of Leningrad, Dr. A. M. Mescheryakov, and Mr. S. P. Alexandrov, who purportedly represented the Soviet press. What they saw and thought they kept to themselves, except for Alexandrov, who, when asked for his impressions, was quoted as saying the Russian equivalent of "pooh!"[1] I do not know how they happened to have been invited. It was before the AEC was established. If it was with any expectation of reciprocity, we were mistaken. No United States citizen has ever been invited to witness a Russian atomic weapon test.

Blandy had offered me a place on his staff for Crossroads similar to the one I had filled in the Bureau of Ordnance. I declined regretfully in order that a resolution to return to private business might be realized.

During the same week that the underwater, or "Baker," test was scheduled at Bikini atoll, I went to California to be the guest of ex-President Hoover at the annual encampment of the Bohemian Club of San Francisco. The club maintains a fabled out-of-door institution in the sophisticated rusticity of a handsome grove of redwoods, and there is a gathering of kindred spirits in these surroundings for a fortnight in the early summer. Mr. Hoover and a few of his friends maintain a camp there where I had enjoyed a visit some years earlier.

Reaching the camp late in the evening of July 27, I found that all of the other campers had turned in with the exception of Dr. Ray Lyman Wilbur, president of Stanford University. He had waited up in order to be sure that I received a telegram which had arrived in the morning. It was signed by Matthew J. Connelly, private secretary to President Truman. The President regretted interrupting my holiday and requested me to come to see him immediately. The telegram concluded with an injunction that the subject was to be off-the-record and that I should telephone Connelly upon reaching Washington and he would tell me where to report.

One of the informal customs of the club with which I had become acquainted on my previous visit was the staging of elaborate practical jokes. The telegram I had just read was typed informally on yellow paper and I decided that the telegram was a fabrication and that the victim of the joke this year was to be me. Accordingly, I went to bed that evening without replying to the telegram and said nothing about it the following day. In the morning, the solicitude of friends in the camp, wanting to know whether I had received the telegram and hoping it was not bad news, only confirmed my suspicions. Late the next day, however, Western Union sent a messenger to the camp to check on the delivery of the message. It was genuine.

By this time nearly three days had elapsed and, consulting my host, Mr. Hoover, I found he agreed that a request from the President was a command. We speculated on what might be in the President's mind and guessed that it concerned the administration of the United Nations Relief and Rehabilitation Administration or some other relief operation. I prepared my expressions of regret and flew East.

Reaching the White House at the time set in a telephone conversation with Connelly, I was shown into the President's office. He asked me to be comfortable and handed me a portfolio of paper, legal size and ruled around the margins. A glance at the title revealed it to be an act by the Congress. I had not seen an "engrossed bill" before. It still required the President's signature to become law. The President enlightened me by saying that this was the Atomic Energy Bill, which had been passed by both houses of Congress and was now before him for signature. He suggested that I should take it into the Cabinet Room to read and then come back to discuss it further.

Being reasonably familiar with the text, it did not take me long. At the same time it was a reasonable guess now that what the President had in mind concerned the Atomic Energy Commission, which the law would establish. Back in his office, the President came directly to the point and asked whether I would be willing to serve as a member of the body he characterized as "the most important branch of the Government to be created in a hundred years."

"Mr. President," I said, "before attempting to answer, may I ask you why you have chosen me? Do you know that I am a black Hoover Republican?"

"Of course," he answered, "I know your political affiliations, but I am relying on the fact that you are a man who will not allow politics to influence your actions in the discharge of this great responsibility. As for Mr. Hoover—you may not know it, but I hold him in very high regard. I think he is a great American and will someday be so recognized even by people who have defamed him. As to why I have selected you, I will tell you. I asked a number of people in whose judgment I have confidence to give me a slate of names of possible Commissioners and your name did not appear at the top of any list. But you were a common denominator—that is to say, your name appeared on all of the lists."

This was flattering and I said so. I then asked the President who the other members of the Commission would be. He seemed to bridle at the question. "Mr. Strauss," he said, "the members of this Commission will be people satisfactory to me." Seeing that he had misunderstood, I quickly explained that my question was prompted by the fact that there were some persons with whom I felt that I could work usefully and others with whom it might be difficult because of their views on government and security. It seemed desirable that he should know that in advance. The President laughed, said that he had indeed misunderstood me, that there were people with whom he couldn't work either, and then gave me the names of four individuals. They were not, however, members of the Commission as finally announced. I judge that for one reason or another they were not invited or were unable to accept.

I must have appeared puzzled at the names mentioned, for he said, "Do you know any better men?" Offhand, I replied that Dr. Karl T. Compton, the president of the Massachusetts Institute of Technology, by experience, disposition, and public standing, was the sort of man who would make an ideal commissioner and chairman. The President did not register approval or the contrary. I took my leave, saying that I would consult my wife and give him my answer promptly.

When I left the White House, I called my wife, who, as has always been her habit, responded that if it were something I wanted to do, she would conform her plans to mine. She knew the subject was one which had interested me for many years, but added that she hoped we had reached the point where we could enjoy life in retirement on our farm in Virginia. I also consulted two friends. I called Robert A. Taft. Bob was in Salt Lake City at the time and his voice over the long-distance telephone was unequivocal. "Lewis," he said, "under ordinary circumstances, I would not be happy to see you become a part of the Democratic Administration, but this is a very special post and I will feel better about it if you are in it." The other friend was Arthur Krock, the dean of American journalism. I went to his home and talked it over with him. His advice was, "Accept it."

That afternoon I sent word to the President. A message came back through his secretary to the effect that I was to say nothing of it to anyone until the President announced the full membership of the Commission.

There was no other word from the White House until the end of August, and then on one Sunday afternoon, while at my farm near Brandy Station in Virginia, a long-distance call came through from the President. He was on his yacht, the *Williamsburg*, somewhere on Chesapeake Bay. He asked if I remembered talking to him about Dr. Compton. I replied that I did. "Do you still feel that he is the best man to become chairman of the organization of which you will be a member?" he asked. I said that I believed he was. "Well, then," concluded the President, "will you get hold of him and see whether he will accept it?"

Dr. Compton was vacationing somewhere deep in the Michigan forests, where he and his two brothers maintained a lodge, and I did not know whether I could find him. "Well," said the President, "take my plane and go get him."

I was able to communicate with Dr. Compton, who came to meet me the following afternoon in Detroit. He was accompanied by Mrs. Compton and we discussed the subject at length. He told me that he had suffered a mild heart attack and that this had necessitated a leave of absence from the presidency of his institution. I urged him to give favorable consideration to the President's offer, which he said he would try to do. A few days later, he sent me a telegram of regret, followed by a letter in which his reasons for declining were set forth at some length.

They were interesting as bearing upon the McMahon Act, which had been signed into law the day after I had seen the President. Dr.

Compton wrote that in his testimony before the McMahon Committee he had favored provisions in the rejected May-Johnson Bill "which would have led to a stronger Commission." Then he added, "Both the President and the Congress have taken a contrary point of view which of course settles the matter. Feeling as I do, I would not be happy on the job and probably would not make a success of it." Dr. Compton believed that the restrictions imposed on the Commissioners by law would be "a continual aggravation and a limit on effective operation. . . . In your very potent presentation of the case," he concluded, "you emphasized the fact that whether we like the present legislation or not, the job must be done, and this, of course, is true. I do not see how you could have stated the case more strongly or more understandingly than you did."

A provision of the Atomic Energy Act to which Dr. Compton took particular exception was the stipulation that the members of the Commission would serve full time and could have no other interests. I believe that the Atomic Energy Act of 1946 was the first U.S. law to require that appointees to the commission it established should engage in no other "business, vocation or employment." It may be unique in that respect. If its purpose was to eliminate any possible conflict of interest, it also required an unusual sacrifice on the part of the appointees. The men who framed the law are not themselves subject to such a requirement.

In my own case, I construed this provision to mean that I had to resign from my partnership in the banking firm with which I had been connected since 1919, and from directorships in the business concerns with which I was connected. There were a number of these and they were both rewarding and pleasant associations. Also, following the counsel of General Donald C. Swatland, who had been my adviser for many years, I sold or disposed by gift of all my shares in businesses which by any stretch of the imagination could deal with the Atomic Energy Commission. I did not feel that the continued ownership and operation of my farm would be in violation of the law, and the Attorney General confirmed this with a written opinion.

In late October, the President announced the members of the Commission, and they were called to a meeting in the office of the Secretary of State. On the appointed day, and for the first time, I met the four men with whom I was to serve. They were David E. Lilienthal, the Chairman, who had headed the Tennessee Valley Authority and had established a reputation as an able administrator; there were also William W. Waymack, who had been an editor of the Des Moines *Register;* Sumner T. Pike, an engineer and former associate of a Wall Street firm; and Dr. Robert Fox Bacher, a distinguished physicist on the faculty of the California Institute of Technology. With these men, the composition of the Commission was complete and we served together for varying periods. Of the original Commission only Mr. Pike remained as a member at the time of my resignation in 1950.

During the Commission's first three years there were occasions upon which I found myself at odds with a majority of my colleagues. These occasions were not many (in more than five hundred formal Commission decisions during the period, I cast a dissenting vote only twelve times), as, in the main, having stated my position, I was inclined to go along with the majority if I could not bring them to see justice in my point of view. The dissenting votes were registered only in those cases where I felt that it was required as a matter of record. The Joint Congressional Committee on Atomic Energy in a report to the Congress in 1949 stated:

> The evidence shows that in more than 500 formal Commission decisions a dissenting vote was cast 12 times. In each of these dozen ballots the minority consisted of one Commissioner who was throughout, the same individual, Mr. Strauss. The framers of the McMahon Act deliberately established a 5-man directorate, rather than a single administrator, to control our atomic enterprise, for the very purpose of assuring that diverse viewpoints would be brought to bear upon issues so far reaching as those here involved. The possibility of split votes was not only anticipated, but regarded as wholesome. The fact that one Commissioner had demonstrated the courage and independence to dissent upon occasion lends added validity to decisions in which he concurred."[2]

The committee also reported:

> The presence of dissent . . . implies that democratic methods underly Commission Management and, not incidentally, that the dissenting Commissioner contributes keen and independent thinking to policy formation."[3]

The fact that two or three of these dissents were closely spaced in time resulted in some speculation in newspaper columns that I was on the point of resigning. I sent word to the President through his special assistant, Admiral Souers, to say that my resignation was indeed ready if he disapproved of the course I was pursuing. He replied that he was "in accord" with my statements and that he was "perfectly satisfied with your work on the Commission."

"When I appointed a five-man Commission," he later told me, "I did not expect a Chairman and four yes-men and I won't have it that way." He confirmed this at a news conference on June 16, in answer to a reporter's question.

Shortly after the Commission took over the conduct of atomic energy operations, I looked for some indication that the intelligence agencies of the Government were equipped to detect a possible test of an atomic weapon by the Soviets. Finding that we were not prepared, my colleagues were willing for me to see what might be done, as earlier related. (Chapter X, "The Decision to Detect.")

By the time of our test series at the Pacific Proving Grounds in 1948, the system was ready to demonstrate, and by the summer of 1949, vigilance was rewarded. The President's statement which followed this detection described the event as an "atomic explosion." The use of this term instead of flatly characterizing the event as a "test of an atomic weapon" was a concession to a body of opinion which, holding to the fallacy of Soviet scientific inferiority, persisted in regarding the incident as more probably the result of an accident in a Russian atomic experiment than a bomb. This speculation, however, was not compatible with other evidence, and I was completely convinced that a weapon or an explosive device had been tested, purposefully, on or about August 29. Furthermore, I felt that there was a possibility, since our monitoring had begun only a year and a half earlier, that it might not have been the first such test by the Soviets.

Accordingly, a few days after the President's announcement, I wrote to my colleagues:

October 5, 1949

Memorandum to the Commissioners:
The purpose of this memorandum is to raise a question for immediate consideration in the light of the information as to progress which has been apparently made in Russia.
In the days since the President's announcement, I have found a tendency in my own thinking to resort to the prospect of increased production of fissionable material and weapons as the logical procedure. Although this is very important, I feel strongly that it is not enough. The frequently expressed thought that we must "maintain our lead" is generally taken to mean that we must have a larger stockpile of weapons than the Russians because we began sooner and can make

them faster. Of these considerations, however, only the fact that we began sooner can be relied upon absolutely. And, in any case, we can only maintain our lead in some arithmetical difference since our relative lead is most likely to decrease.

It seems to me that the time has now come for a quantum jump in our planning (to borrow a metaphor from our scientist friends)— that is to say, that we should now make an intensive effort to get ahead with the super. By intensive effort, I am thinking of a commitment in talent and money comparable, if necessary, to that which produced the first atomic weapon. That is the way to stay ahead.

The "super" to which the memorandum referred was a hypothetical weapon. From quite early days in the Manhattan Project, several of the scientists, notably Dr. Teller, had speculated on the possibilities of producing a bomb which would derive its force not from "fission" —the splitting of the heavy elements (uranium and plutonium)—but from "fusion"—the coalescence of nuclei of light elements at the other end of the atomic table (e.g., hydrogen and its isotope, deuterium). This was well known in theory. An Austrian physicist, Hans Thirring, had actually published a paper on the subject. No requirement for such a weapon existed so long as we had a monopoly of fission weapons. My memorandum was based upon the fact that we had a monopoly no longer. It concluded:

I recommend that we immediately consult the General Advisory Committee to ascertain their views as to how we can proceed with expedition.

My colleagues received the memorandum considerately, and Chairman Lilienthal requested Dr. Oppenheimer and the Commission's General Advisory Committee to meet with us for the purpose of advising us in the circumstances.

The first occasion upon which a meeting could be held was at the end of October, as Dr. Fermi was in Rome, and it was desirable that he should be present. As matters worked out, Dr. Glenn T. Seaborg,* the famous discoverer of several of the transuranic elements and subsequently a Nobel prize winner, was in Sweden and could not attend. His views were embodied in a letter[4] addressed to Dr. Oppenheimer, but did not reach the Commission until four and one-half years later in connection with the hearings on the security clearance of Dr.

* Chairman of the AEC since January 1961.

Oppenheimer. He deplored the prospect of putting a tremendous effort into the hydrogen bomb project but added "I must confess that I have been unable to come to the conclusion that we should not."

The General Advisory Committee met on October 28, 29, and 30, 1949. It carefully considered the questions which were put before it by the Commission. The report of the committee is still classified "Secret," and it would be unfair to its members to attempt to paraphrase language where presumably they had weighed each word with care.

It is no secret, however, that the General Advisory Committee discouraged the suggested effort to develop a thermonuclear weapon at that time. Scientific and political, economic and moral arguments were arrayed against it. The Commission was counseled also that there were no foreseen peaceful possibilities of the thermonuclear reaction.

Before the meeting with the General Advisory Committee took place, Drs. E. O. Lawrence and Luis Alvarez, of the Berkeley Radiation Laboratory, were invited by Senator McMahon of the Joint Congressional Committee on Atomic Energy to meet with him. The two scientists expressed grave concern that Russia might be giving top priority to the development of a thermonuclear bomb. They called the attention of the Senator to the fact that the Russian scientist Dr. Kapitza was one of the world's leading authorities on the physical properties of light elements and that it would be logical to expect that the Soviets would have his help and might perfect a hydrogen bomb before we did.

When the Commission received the recommendation of the General Advisory Committee, I suggested that we should report our recommendation to the President, after consulting the Departments of State and Defense in order that both the diplomatic and the military aspects of the issue, combined with our recommendation as to its feasibility and cost, could be laid before him in one paper. This idea proved unacceptable, however, and the Commission views were placed before the President without prior reference to the State or Defense departments. This led Mr. Truman to write on November 10 that "the question involves consideration not only of the factors presented by the Atomic Energy Commission in its report, but also political and military factors of concern to the Departments of State and Defense."[5]

Initially the Commission was split on the issue—4 to 1. I favored a recommendation to the President that we proceed urgently to undertake the development. My colleagues, for various reasons, opposed it.

Commissioner Dean, who subsequently became Chairman of the Commission, later changed his opinion and concurred with me, making the division 3 to 2. Before this had happened, however, I was more deeply disturbed than I can find words to describe to find myself at odds with four men whose patriotism was unquestionable and a General Advisory Committee for whose scientific competence I had a respect verging on awe. With the issues as clear-cut as they seemed to me, I could not understand how a conclusion was possible other than the one expressed in a letter which later I addressed to the President:

25 November 1949

Dear Mr. President:

As you know, the thermonuclear (super) bomb was suggested by scientists working at Los Alamos during the war. The current consideration of the super bomb was precipitated, I believe, by a memorandum which I addressed to my fellow Commissioners following your announcement on September 23rd of an atomic explosion in Russia. I participated in the discussions which were antecedent to the letter to you from the Commission on November 9th, but did not join in the preparation of the letter as I was then on the Pacific Coast. It was my belief that a comprehensive recommendation should be provided for you, embodying the judgement of the Commission (in the areas where it is competent), together with the views of the Departments of State and Defense. My colleagues, however, felt that you would prefer to obtain these views separately.

Differences on the broad question of policy between my associates as individuals were included in the Commission's letter to you, and it was correctly stated that the views of Commissioner Dean and mine were in substantial accord on the main issue. It is proper, I believe, that I should state them on my own responsibility and in my own words.

I believe that the United States must be as completely armed as any possible enemy. From this, it follows that I believe it unwise to renounce, unilaterally, any weapon which an enemy can reasonably be expected to possess. I recommend that the President direct the Atomic Energy Commission to proceed with the development of the thermonuclear bomb, at highest priority subject only to the judgment of the Department of Defense as to its value as a weapon, and of the advice of the Department of State as to the diplomatic consequences of its unilateral renunciation or its possession. In the event that you may be interested, my reasoning is appended in a memorandum.

/s/ Lewis L. Strauss

25 November 1949

This is a memorandum to accompany a letter of even date to the President to supply the reasoning for my recommendation that he should direct the Atomic Energy Commission to proceed at highest priority with the development of the thermonuclear weapon.

PREMISES

(1) The production of such a weapon appears to be feasible (i.e., better than a 50-50 chance).

(2) Recent accomplishments by the Russians indicate that the production of a thermonuclear weapon is within *their* technical competence.

(3) A government of atheists is not likely to be dissuaded from producing the weapon on "moral" grounds. ("Reason and experience both forbid us to expect that national morality can prevail in exclusion of religious principle." G. Washington, September 17, 1796.)

(4) The possibility of producing the thermonuclear weapon was suggested more than six years ago, and considerable theoretical work has been done which may be known to the Soviets—the principle has certainly been known to them.

(5) The time in which the development of this weapon can be perfected is perhaps of the order of two years, so that a Russian enterprise started some years ago may be well along to completion.

(6) It is the historic policy of the United States not to have its forces less well armed than those of any other country (viz., the 5:5:3 naval ratio, etc. etc.).

(7) Unlike the atomic bomb which has certain limitations, the proposed weapon may be tactically employed against a mobilized army over an area of the size ordinarily occupied by such a force.

(8) The Commission's letter of November 9th to the President mentioned the "possibility that the radioactivity released by a small number (perhaps ten) of these bombs would pollute the earth's atmosphere to a dangerous extent." Studies requested by the Commission have since indicated that the number of such weapons necessary to pollute the earth's atmosphere would run into many hundreds. Atmospheric pollution is a consequence of present atomic bombs if used in quantity.

CONCLUSIONS

(1) The danger in the weapon does not reside in its physical nature but in human behavior. Its unilateral renunciation by the United States could very easily result in its unilateral possession by the

Soviet Government. I am unable to see any satisfaction in that prospect.

(2) The Atomic Energy Commission is competent to advise the President with respect to the feasibility of making the weapon; its economy in fissionable material as compared with atomic bombs; the possible time factor involved; and a description of its characteristics compared to atomic bombs. Judgement, however, as to its strategic or tactical importance for the armed forces should be furnished by the Department of Defense, and views as to the effect on friendly nations of our unilateral renunciation of the weapon is a subject for the Department of State. My opinion as an individual, however, based upon discussions with military experts is to the effect that the weapon may be critically useful against a large enemy force both as a weapon of offense and as a defensive measure to prevent landings on our own shores.

(3) I am impressed with the arguments which have been made to the effect that this is a weapon of mass destruction on an unprecedented scale. So, however, was the atomic bomb when it was first envisaged and when the National Academy of Sciences in its report of November 6, 1941, referred to it as "of superlatively destructive power." Also on June 16, 1945, the Scientific Panel of the Interim Committee on Nuclear Power, comprising some of the present members of the General Advisory Committee, reported to the Secretary of War, "We believe the subject of thermonuclear reactions among light nuclei is one of the most important that needs study. There is a reasonable presumption that with skillful research and development, fission bombs can be used to initiate the reactions of deuterium, tritium, and possibly other light nuclei. If this can be accomplished, the energy release of explosive units can be increased by a factor of 1000 or more over that of presently contemplated fission bombs." This statement was preceded by the recommendation, "Certainly we would wish to see work carried out on the problems mentioned below."

The General Advisory Committee to the Atomic Energy Commission, in its recent communication to the Commission recommending against the development of the super bomb, noted that it "strongly favors" the booster program, which is a progam to increase the explosive power and hence the damage area and deadliness of atomic bombs. These positions and those above appear not to be fully consistent and indicate that the scientific point of view is not unanimous.

(4) Obviously the current atomic bomb as well as the proposed thermonuclear weapon are horrible to contemplate. All war is hor-

rible. Until, however, some means is found of eliminating war, I cannot agree with those of my colleagues who feel that an announcement should be made by the President to the effect that the development of the thermonuclear weapon will not be undertaken by the United States at this time. This is because: (a) I do not think the statement will be credited in the Kremlin; (b) that when and if it should be decided subsequent to such a statement to proceed with the production of the thermonuclear bomb, it might in a delicate situation, be regarded as an affirmative statement of hostile intent; and (c) because primarily until disarmament is universal, our arsenal must be not less well equipped than with the most potent weapons that our technology can devise.

RECOMMENDATION

In sum, I believe that the President should direct the Atomic Energy Commission to proceed with all possible expedition to develop the thermonuclear weapon.

Grieved to find myself entirely alone (as I then thought) on so vital an issue, I decided to get away from Washington and its pressures and to review all my reasoning to find the flaws in it. I went to Beverly Hills, California, and took a room in a hotel there, where I reexamined the decision with which the country was confronted. There, I began to compose the above letter to the President.

On the second afternoon, the telephone rang. Senator McMahon was on the line. I remarked that his voice was so clear it was hard to believe that he was in Washington. "I'm not," he said. "I'm in California. As a matter of fact, I am right in the lobby of this hotel and I have come here to see you."

When we met, he first brought the welcome news that my colleague, Gordon Dean, who was his close friend, had come over to my point of view. He then assured me that at least as far as he was concerned he intended to support my recommendation. He thought that other members of the Joint Congressional Committee—perhaps most of them— felt likewise.

McMahon told me that he had written the President to make the point that there was no moral distinction between the use of a single weapon causing great loss of life and heavy damage and the use of series of smaller weapons with the same aggregate result in death and destruction. He pointed up the fact that the raids on Hamburg reported to have killed over a hundred thousand persons and the fire raids on Tokyo had been no less lethal than the raids on Hiroshima and Nagasaki.

He reasoned that the argument that we should indicate our willingness not to develop a super bomb if the Russians would pledge themselves to refrain was totally meaningless without inspection and control to ensure compliance. The Russian attitude toward the Baruch proposal for the control of atomic energy had indicated how far we would be likely to get with any proposition for foolproof inspection and control. He pictured what in his opinion would be the effect if the Russians were able to develop a thermonuclear weapon before we should succeed in doing so, expressing the apprehension that they might be attempting to leapfrog our development by going directly from their first fission weapon test into the development of thermonuclear weapons.

He concluded, as I recollect, by pointing out that, if the Russians should produce the thermonuclear weapon first, the results would be catastrophic, whereas if we should produce it first, there was at least a chance for protecting ourselves.

The alternatives, therefore, were on the President's desk by the last week in November. No man has ever been faced with a more difficult decision. The choice between courses before him differed in one major respect from that which confronted him four years earlier at Potsdam. There he had the advice from his top-level scientists: Use the bomb; use it on an inhabited city; and use it without warning. The scientists with opposing views did not get through to him.

Now, however, in the winter of 1949–50, both sides of the argument were before him and there were advocates on both. The one element which united their thinking was the hope that the weapon would prove to be impossible to produce—that some physical limitation would be found which thwarted the construction of a device by which such enormous amounts of energy would be released if the nuclei of the light elements could be fused. But from that point, there was the greatest divergence, the majority of the members of the General Advisory Committee comprising many distinguished names counseling against the proposal, while equally distinguished men, including E. O. Lawrence, Edward Teller, and others urged that the step be taken without delay. This position received powerful support also from Dr. K. T. Compton, who was at that time chairman of the Research and Development Board of the Department of Defense.

Dr. Compton went so far as to address a personal letter to the President on November 9 and entrusted it to Under Secretary of Defense Early, who took it to the President the following morning. Dr. Compton made the point that, if a unilateral decision by the United

States not to develop a hydrogen bomb could ensure a similar attitude on the part of all other governments, he would agree with the GAC, but that, failing a strong international agreement backed by adequate inspection, Russia could proceed to develop such a weapon regardless of any altruistic decisions on our part. Dr. Compton felt that there was no scientific hurdle the Russians could not surmount with time, and he deplored the tendency to underrate their ability. Concluding, he gave his judgment that we should proceed to develop a thermo-nuclear weapon.[6] His wisdom and standing undoubtedly had weight with the President.

The President appointed a small committee to consider all the recommendations and to counsel with him. The committee consisted of Secretary of State Dean Acheson, as chairman, with Secretary of Defense Louis Johnson, and AEC Chairman Lilienthal as members. President Truman has recorded that the recommendation of this committee was unanimous for proceeding with development of the new weapon.

Toward the end of December, there was another explosion, this time in security. As a result of a successful joint enterprise by the Federal Bureau of Investigation and Scotland Yard, Dr. Klaus Fuchs, a German native who had become a naturalized British subject, was apprehended as a spy and traitor. Fuchs was a physicist who had been sent to the United States with other British physicists to work at the atomic weapons laboratories during the war. He confessed that he had regularly communicated to Russian agents particulars concerning such work on the hydrogen bomb as had been done at Los Alamos up to the time of his return to England in 1945. Also, as he had revisited the United States and atomic research laboratories in 1947, it was to be presumed that what we had been thinking or had found out up to that time had been compromised to the benefit of the Soviets. The President, of course, was informed as the case broke.

I had made up my mind that when the President reached his decision it would be time for me to resign from the Commission. My reasons were that if his decision should prove to be adverse, I could not continue in good conscience, while on the other hand, if his decision were one of concurrence, it would be less embarrassing to my colleagues to carry out his directive.

On January 31, 1950, (which happened to be my birthday) the President let us know his decision. His directive to the Commission was succinct. At the same time, he issued a public statement concluding with these words:

It is a part of my responsibility as Commander-in-Chief of the Armed Forces to see to it that our country is able to defend itself against any possible aggressor. Accordingly, I have directed the Atomic Energy Commission to continue its work on all forms of atomic weapons including the so-called hydrogen or super bomb. Like all other work in the field of atomic weapons, it is being and will be carried forward on a basis consistent with the over-all objectives of our program for peace and security.

This we shall continue to do until a satisfactory plan for international control of atomic energy is achieved. We shall also continue to examine all those factors that affect our program for peace and this country's security.

Between the date of my memorandum of October 5, 1949, and the President's decision four months later, a great debate had occurred. Those opposed to the development were more numerous and more articulate. A powerful campaign was mounted in the various media of information and it continued even after the decision had been taken and announced by the Commander in Chief.

Some authorities furnished "evidence" to Senator Kefauver which was later used in his campaign for the vice presidency. The New York *Times* of October 17, 1956, quoted the Senator as follows:

"The force from the explosion from a large hydrogen bomb," Senator Kefauver said, "is getting so stupendous and so dangerous that the maximum force available to us right now from a concussion of hydrogen bombs is, according to some information, sufficient to blow the earth off its axis by 16 degrees, which would affect the seasons."

Alarming opinions were voiced that the explosion of just a few such weapons would so poison the atmosphere that life would cease to exist. Other opposing views were rather more worthy of consideration.

Dr. Hans Bethe, of Cornell University, a distinguished physicist, writing in the April 1950 issue of the *Scientific-American* and after the decision had been made, stated his belief that the most important question was a moral one. He wrote:

. . . Can we who have always insisted on morality and human decency between nations as well as inside our own country, introduce this weapon of total annihilation into the world? The unusual argument, heard in the frantic week before the President's decision and frequently since, is that we are fighting against a country which denies all the human values we cherish, and that any weapon, however ter-

rible must be used to prevent that country and its creed from dominat-
ing the world. It is argued that it would be better for us to lose our
lives than our liberty, and with this view I personally agree. But I
believe this is not the choice facing us here; I believe that in a war
fought with hydrogen bombs we would lose not only many lives, but
all our liberties and human values as well.

Whoever wishes to use the hydrogen bomb in our conflict with the
U.S.S.R., either as a threat or in actual warfare, is adhering to the
old fallacy that the ends justify the means . . .

But, say the advocates of the bomb, what if the Russians obtain the
H-bomb first? If the Russians have the bomb, Harold Urey argued in
a speech just before the President's decision, they may confront us
with an ultimatum to surrender. I do not believe we would accept
such an ultimatum even if we did not have the H-bomb, or that we
would need to. I doubt that the hydrogen bomb, dreadful as it would
be, could win a war in one stroke. Though it might devastate our
cities and cripple our ability to conduct a long war with all modern
weapons, it would not seriously affect our power for immediate retaliation. . . .

In an article published in May 1950 issue of the *Scientific-American,*
Dr. Robert F. Bacher, a distinguished physicist and my former associate on the first Atomic Energy Commission, questioned the military
usefulness of the hydrogen bomb. He pointed out that from a military
standpoint the solution of the delivery problem is not less important than
the kind of bombs that would be delivered. He added:

The President's decision to go ahead with the development of the
hydrogen bomb created a tremendous stir in the nation. From the
standpoint of its military effectiveness, there seems to be little reason
to attach such a great significance to the hydrogen bomb. While it is a
terrible weapon, its military importance seems to have been grossly
overrated in the mind of the laymen . . . pumped full of hysteria by
Red scares, aggravated by political mud-slinging, the average citizen
is easily convinced that he can find some security and relief from all
of this in the hydrogen bomb. The most tragic part is that the hydrogen
bomb will not save us and is not even a very good addition to our
military potential.

Here we have the outcome of what can happen in a democracy
when decisions of far-reaching national significance are made without
public scrutiny of pertinent information. While most of the pertinent
information is not at all secret, some of the information the citizen
should have in order to judge whether our national policy is sound is

being kept secret. One of the most important facts the citizen should have, to make a reasonable judgment, is the approximate number of atomic bombs in our stockpile.

I doubt whether the average citizen would be able to judge, on the basis of knowing the number of atomic bombs in our stockpile, whether the quantity were adequate, inadequate, or excessive. Equally important factors would be the number of weapons that would be lost in an attack, the number of aborted sorties with our weapons, the number and size of targets, and the methods of delivery and our war plans if attacked. The number of weapons in our stockpile, however, as I have frequently tried to point out, would be information of incalculable value to an enemy.

At the close of the spring 1950 meeting of the American Physical Society, twelve of the country's prominent physicists commented on the President's decision and were critical of those who had urged the President to so decide. They did not name them directly, but the statement offered the opinion that these men could not have realized the full import of their recommendations, and went on to add:

We believe that no nation has the right to use such a bomb, no matter how righteous its cause.

Presumably, even the defense of life and freedom was not righteous enough. They added:

. . . Russia has received, through indiscretion, the most valuable hint that our experts believe its development possible.

This, of course, did not refer to the treason of Fuchs, which was certainly not an "indiscretion" and was something more than a "hint." The statement ended on an eminently reasonable note:

. . . There can be only one justification for our development of the hydrogen bomb, and that is to prevent its use.[7]

That was surely implicit in the decision of the President.

A contrasting point of view is exemplified by an article published in the *Bulletin of the Atomic Scientists* by Dr. Harold C. Urey, the discoverer of deuterium:

. . . Many would wish that such weapon developments as these should prove physically impossible; but nature does not always behave in the way we desire. I believe we should assume that the bomb can be built.

We should not be complacent about the inability of other countries to develop this weapon, as many people were in connection with the development of the ordinary atomic bomb. To be specific, let us assume that the USSR is developing this bomb; and suppose that she should perfect it first. Then it seems to me that there is nothing in the temperament of the present negotiations between East and West that would lead us to believe that the rulers of the USSR would not reason approximately as follows:

"It is true that the bomb is exceedingly dangerous, and we would not wish to produce so much radioactivity in the world as to endanger ourselves and the people of Russia, but the explosion of a few of these bombs will win us the world. Therefore, we will build these bombs and issue ultimata to the Western countries, and the millenium of communism will be with us immediately. After this the universal government of the USSR will abolish all stocks of bombs, and no more will ever be made in the world."

Then, discussing the state of unstable equilibrium if both Russia and the United States succeed in developing hydrogen bombs, Dr. Urey concluded:

I am very unhappy to conclude that the hydrogen bomb should be developed and built. I do not think we should intentionally lose the armaments race; to do this will be to lose our liberties, and, with Patrick Henry, I value my liberties more than I do my life. It is important that the spirit of independence and liberty should continue to exit in the world. It is much more important that this spirit continue to exist than that I or you or any group should continue this mortal existence for a few more years. Second, there is no constructive solution to the world's problems except eventually a world government capable of establishing law over the entire surface of the earth . . ."

Dr. Teller contributed his thinking through the same journal:

President Truman has announced that we are going to make a hydrogen bomb. No one connected with work on atomic bombs can escape a feeling of grave responsibility . . . but scientists must find a modest way of looking into an uncertain future. The scientist is not responsible for the law of nature. It is his job to find out how these laws operate. It is the scientist's job to find the ways in which these laws can serve the human will. However, it is *not* the scientist's job to determine whether a hydrogen bomb should be constructed, whether it should be used, or how it should be used. This responsibility rests with the American people and with their chosen representatives.

Personally, as a citizen, I do not know in what other way President

Truman could have acted. As a scientist, I am troubled by other questions, more limited, more specific, but not less urgent and not less harassing. Can a hydrogen bomb be built? Can we build it before the Russians succeed in doing so?

I cannot answer these questions. Even the elements which will be used in answering them cannot be mentioned publicly. But the background from which we start in our work can be discussed, and this discussion may be found relevant.

. . . To my mind we are in a situation not less dangerous than the one we were facing in 1939, and it is of the greatest importance that we realize it. We must realize that mere plans are not yet bombs, and we must realize that democracy will not be saved by ideals alone.

Our scientific community has been out on a honeymoon with mesons. The holiday is over. Hydrogen bombs will not produce themselves. Neither will rockets or radar.

. . . Many of our friends are disheartened. They had some hope in the summer of 1945. But if the atom bomb did not help to establish peace, why should the hydrogen bomb? Why should anything else, for that matter? I think we should try again. The situation is not different. We have now a success and a failure behind us: The scientists enjoy the prestige of having successfully made atomic weapons; their advice may have a somewhat greater weight now. We also have had the experience of a dismal failure: We did not have enough realism, courage, and initiative at the time of Hiroshima. We did not, in fact, win the peace. We must try again; there is no other way. Such a new attempt cannot come from the scientist, however strongly he feels about the subject. The primary responsibility for action lies with the groups directing the policy and foreign relations in our country.

With the advantage of high moral ground and the perspective of half a decade, the Archbiship of York in May 1955 stated the case as I wish I might have had the ability to express it:

I agree with my correspondents in detestation of the bomb and with the opinion held by most of them that if war should break out, nuclear weapons would almost certainly be used. With them I agree that we must aim at progressive disarmament and the eventual abolition of war as means of settling international disputes. But we disagree as to the immediate method by which war may be prevented. Violent denunciation of the evils of war does nothing to remove the danger of it breaking out. Strong words and rhetorical resolutions may relieve your own feelings, but they do nothing to promote peace. Many have urged . . . a policy of non-resistance, but this policy if acted on would almost certainly bring war nearer, for it would tempt the strongly armed state to attack an unarmed State whose ideals and way of life it repudiated and whose possessions it coveted. . . . I believe the possession of the bomb by a peace-loving State like our own gives some hope (I do not put it higher than that) that the bomb may never be used against our nation, or against Russia or China or any other people. But without the bomb we should be at the mercy of any powerful State which, possessing it, would be able to blackmail us into yielding to its demands and to surrendering our freedom and heritage.

. . . It is simply not true to say that our possession of the bomb implies warlike intentions against Russia or China. We shall possess it as a deterrent, in the hope that it may never be used. We must pray for the day when the use of all weapons of wholesale destruction is banned, and still more for the day when the folly and madness of war give way to an international rule of justice and peace."[8]

As a result of brilliant invention, accurately attributed to Dr. Teller and by him generously attributed to others who worked with him, we were able to test our first hydrogen bomb in November 1952. The Russians tested their first weapon involving a thermonuclear reaction the following August.

The President's decision was not only sound but in the very nick of time.

By so close a margin did we come to being second in armament, not only in the eyes of the world, but in fact. Had we begun our development after the successful Russian test, there is no reason to believe that we would have been accorded time to equal their accomplishment. Thus the decision, made when it was, provided us with the time and posture which have sustained us to this writing.

* * *

My decision to resign from the Commission, on which I had served for more than three years (following five years of military service), was expressed in a letter to the President immediately following his January 31 directive. The President accepted it effective April 15 with a letter in which he referred to the fact that my personal concern and diligence were reflected especially in the medical and military phases of the program and that the policies in force bore the impress of my efforts to serve the military needs of the nation.

I had no intention of ever again undertaking public service.

XII

Vignettes of Research
and Researchers

By what way is the light parted,
Or the east wind scattered upon the earth?

Canst thou bind the chains of the Pleiades,
Or loose the bands of Orion?

JOB 38

Certain of the men concerned with the decisions in these chapters died
in the prime of life. Of three, Dr. John von Neumann, Dr. Ernest
Orlando Lawrence, and Dr. Enrico Fermi, some brief contemporary
material is presented—and one item of antiquarian interest.

VON NEUMANN

No military commander in antiquity who expected his men to follow
him into battle would have failed to consult some oracle to fix the
most favorable day and hour to initiate the attack. The auspicious day
for imperial decisions is still subject to astrological determination in
parts of the Far East, and when the great American expeditionary
force stood poised in England for the invasion of the Continent in 1944,
a modern variant of this custom was invoked.

Because of the tremendous amounts of supplies and the large number of men to be ferried across the surface of the often treacherous
Channel, it was important that both the tides and the weather should
be propitious. The tides could be predicted. Even the ancient associated
the lunar phases with tidal changes and were able to make fairly good
predictions of the latter from their observation of the former.

Sir Isaac Newton, in his *Principia*, 275 years ago, accounted for
many of the properties of tides, and, followed by the work of Bernoulli,
Euler, Lord Rayleigh, Vannevar Bush, and others, there came to exist

mechanical devices which predict tidal fluctuations with great accuracy. Weather, on the other hand, continued to be capricious and eluded the art of prediction. The best that could then be said with any certainty for weather over the Channel was that it was broadly variable on a seasonal basis and the best long-range prediction which could be made was one based upon calendar records.

In this way, a date was chosen for the Normandy landing. In the long recorded history of Channel weather, it had been generally propitious in June. The critical importance of accurate weather forecasting was never more graphically illustrated. The convoys had to cross the Channel at night so that darkness would conceal the strength and direction of the attacks. The air-borne assaults would profit by moonlight. The attack had to be made on a relatively low tide because of the beach obstacles which had to be removed or destroyed while they were exposed. But everything was subordinate to good weather. As General Eisenhower noted in his memoirs, the statement that "the weather is always neutral" is untrue. "Bad weather," he observed, "is obviously the enemy of the side that seeks to launch projects requiring good weather, or of the side possessing great assets, such as strong air forces, which depend upon good weather for effective operations." His meteorologic staff was severely limited by the state of the art in making their long-range prediction, and, as it developed, they were in error.

A hurricane which struck on June 19, and for a period of four full days put an end to practically all the landing activity on the beaches, was so violent that it made military operations extremely difficult. It became next to impossible to land airplanes on the small strips that had been constructed in the beachhead. The artificial harbor at Omaha Beach was damaged beyond repair. Hundreds of ships and small vessels were grounded or tossed far up on the beach by the force of waves and winds. On the day the storm ended, the commanding general flew from one end of the beach line to the other and counted more than three hundred wrecked vessels, "all larger than small boat size," many so badly damaged they could not be saved.

In the late summer of 1945, after the end of the war in Europe and in Asia, John von Neumann, a great mathematician in his or any era, and Vladimir Zworykin, an authentic electronic genius on the staff of the Radio Corporation of America, called on me at the Navy Department. They laid out an idea they had developed for the construction of a device which, if it proved to be successful, would be the forerunner of apparatus to predict the weather over quite long periods with the same accuracy as the mechanical tide-predicting devices just mentioned. These tide predictors, Von Neumann explained to me, needed to deal with only a few variables. It should be possible, he continued, to assemble electronic memory tubes (which had been developed by Zworykin and Reichman and their associates) in a circuit so that an enormous amount of information could be contained. This information would consist of observations on temperature, humidity, wind direction and force, barometric pressures, and many other meteorological facts at many points on the earth's surface and at selected elevations above it. This information could be stored in the "memories" of these tubes. From the observed results of weather, a pattern or harmonic system might be developed which eventually would enable such a data storage device to predict weather at extremely long range and with accuracy. They proposed that the Institute for Advanced Study, the Radio Corporation of America, and the Navy participate in this development by building the first of these devices, which are now the growing family of computers.

They pointed out the military advantages of accurate long-range weather intelligence, and this seemed to justify the cost of such a venture, estimated at about $200,000. Naturally, there were persons who had to be consulted who felt that the war which had just ended would be the world's last war and that any requirements for such a device had better originate in the Department of Agriculture or the Weather Bureau. Fortunately, that point of view did not prevail.

A decision finally was taken, the Army being primarily interested, and the computer was built adjacent to the campus of the Institute for Advanced Study at Princeton, where Von Neumann was a faculty member. The vision of Herbert Maass, then president of the institute, and of Samuel Leidesdorf, its treasurer, was important to the launching of this enterprise; likewise, the support of Admiral Harold G. Bowen, Director of the Office of Naval Research, who saw its possibilities in other areas. It became one of the prototype of devices that were proved useful far afield from its original purpose, which, incidentally, has yet to be realized. Work on it was begun in 1946, but the problems of constructing a machine so new and of getting it to operate took nearly five years. Interestingly, the first large problem put to it was in the thermonuclear weapon program. Had the decision to make the computer not been taken in 1945, the thermonuclear program might have been delayed long enough for the Soviets to have had the first weapons. This was far from the minds of anyone when Von Neumann initiated the project.

The behavior of nuclear reactors was understood in principle, but when accurate detailed knowledge of reactor characteristics was required, many complex mathematical problems had to be dealt with. A number of these could be solved in any reasonable time only by employing high-speed electronic computing devices. The Argonne National Laboratory constructed such a computer for its own use and another for the Oak Ridge National Laboratory. Both were based on the general design of the first one built by Von Neumann.

There are now many generations of these devices, known as mathematical and numerical integrators and calculators, or, in a new abbreviated terminology, using first letters and syllables, as "Maniacs"— each more sophisticated than its progenitor. Other mathematicians and physicists, notably Drs. Eckert and Mauchly, made vital contributions to this new art. The Eniac, their initial computer, which was established as a calculator for ballistic problems at the Aberdeen Proving Ground, was the pioneer development in high-speed electronic calculation. Specialized designs have come into widespread use in the military establishment, in industry, banking, research laboratories, and many other fields. Von Neumann's original Maniac and Johnniac, at last reports, were still going strong.

Von Neumann had been blessed with one of the most remarkable intellects of our generation, and an engaging personality. He was a mathematical authority, recognized around the world in his field of specialization, but his interests were unusually broad. He was an expert on the subject of Byzantine art and architecture. He was completely current in international politics and followed the stream of history with a deep personal concern for the adverse influences which he believed were eroding the welfare and safety of the country of his adoption. He was passionately devoted to the service of the United States.

Von Neumann also had a spontaneous humor and an inexhaustible fund of anecdote. A memory which seemed to operate with even more speed than his machines enabled him to bring up, from his vast and well-indexed mental filing system, stories appropriate to whatever occasion. There were a number of refugee scientists in the United States who, like Von Neumann, were natives of Hungary. This was extraordinary in that one generation in one country had produced them. It included such men as Wigner, Szilard, Von Karman, Teller, among others. John's anecdotes about them were famous and funny, but when one of them was the butt, he was always at the receiving end also as, for example, his observation: "It takes a Hungarian like———or me to go into a revolving door behind you and come out first."

In October 1954, I had the good fortune to persuade Dr. Willard F. Libby to leave his university chair and accept appointment to the Atomic Energy Commission. The Commission had been organized in 1946 with one scientific member, Dr. Robert F. Bacher, a brilliant physicist from the California Institute of Technology, and the precedent of always having one scientific member had been continued. It seemed to me better to have two scientists among the five members in order that, on issues where a technical decision was required, two informed points of view might be debated. When the next vacancy occurred, I turned to Von Neumann and found him ready to accept. Earlier he had confided that he had made up his mind to leave the professorship in which he was then serving. The fact that he was a naturalized citizen caused some eyebrows to be raised in the Joint Congressional Committee, but he was confirmed and quickly gained the respect of the Congress.

We were not long to benefit from his association. While in Geneva in August 1955, at the first conference on the Peaceful Uses of Atomic Energy, Johnny telephoned from Washington to describe a diagnosis which had just been made of a shoulder ailment. Dr. Shields Warren, the world-famous radiologist, who was a member of our delegation, explained to me the gravity of the diagnosis and volunteered to leave at once for Washington to take Johnny under his care. A few days later Johnny met me at the airport in New York and we flew at once to Boston, where Dr. Warren's hospital is located. A series of operations there and at Walter Reed Hospital in Washington were too late to arrest the spread of the cancer and Johnny entered upon an agonizing decline, ending in his death on February 8, 1957.

Before his death, Johnny received two important awards while he was able to enjoy them—one from the Atomic Energy Commission, the Enrico Fermi Medal and its prize, and from the President, the Medal for Freedom. The latter was given to him in the President's office, where he had been brought in a wheel chair. I took the Fermi Medal to him in the hospital during his last days. He insisted on keeping it within reach as long as he was conscious.

There is a memorandum in his handwriting on the subject of a common-sense view of radiation hazards, about which there was and has been much misunderstanding.[1]

Until the last, he continued to be a member of the Commission and chairman of an important advisory committee to the Defense Department. On one dramatic occasion, I was present at a meeting at Walter Reed Hospital, where, gathered around Johnny's bedside were the Secretary of Defense and his deputies, the Secretaries of the three Armed Services, and all the military Chiefs of Staff. The central figure was a young man who but a few years before had come to the United States as an immigrant.

FERMI

Albert Einstein's famous letter to President Roosevelt is generally believed to have initiated the interest of the United States Government in nuclear energy. This is true in the sense that direct results came from it in a traceable series of events. However, it was not the first approach to the Government in an attempt to arouse interest and enlist support for research into the possibilities for national defense latent in the atom.

News of the sensational interpretation by Meitner of the experiment by Hahn and Strassmann had been brought to the United States by Bohr only a few weeks before Enrico Fermi, the great Italian physicist, came to Washington with Professor George B. Pegram. Both men were working at Columbia University. Fermi lectured before the Technical Division in a ramshackle old board room in the Navy Department on Constitution Avenue. The date was March 17, 1939. Among the listeners there were representatives of other naval bureaus and of the Army, and there were two men at least who were enthralled by what they heard.

One of them, Captain Garrett L. Schuyler, later Chief of the Research Division of Ordnance, wrote a memorandum of his impressions. He had gone to the meeting, as he put it, "in order to have all available information in replying to inventors' letters, a deluge of which may be expected," following the Meitner, Hahn, Strassmann communications. Schuyler came away from the meeting convinced that a new day in naval propulsion and military explosives was at hand. His report on Fermi's talk, originally marked "Secret," has been declassified, and the following paragraphs, though they are notes taken at a lecture on a new subject twenty-two years ago, could serve today as an elementary exposition of nuclear fission. Schuyler must have been both attentive and retentive:

The following is what I got from the [Fermi] talk.

When neutrons pass through a material containing hydrogen (such as wax or water), they rebound from the heavier atoms with little loss of velocity. But whenever they encounter a hydrogen atom, which has about the same mass as the neutron, they are slowed. Slow neutrons are about 1000 times as effective in splitting up uranium atoms. In ordinary materials, their mean free paths are about five or six centimeters. For the splitting-up process to be self-propagating so as to give explosive action, it is an obvious requirement that the splitting up of the uranium atoms must be attended by the release of at least one neutron to carry on the work.

In a tank of water, the number of neutrons observed at distance seems slightly increased by interposing uranium, which is split up by the original bombardment, and it is upon this that all hopes of explosive action are based. The excess in the number of released neutrons is not very great and has not yet been demonstrated *absolutely* beyond the possible limits of experimental error. However, new experiments with an improved set-up are expected within a month or two. If these experiments show more neutrons are released from the uranium atoms than are necessary to split them up, continuous release of energy in a mass of uranium is a theoretical possibility.

In the small samples so far used, however, the released neutrons are possibly not all effective because some will too rapidly escape; but in a sufficiently large mass of uranium, they necessarily will be all trapped and available in time. Roughly, I suppose it is like a mass of pyrotechnics. In a small pile, some will displace the others, but in a sufficiently large mass, this scattering action is not possible, and all will be exploded (compare experience in burning wet gun cotton or even smokeless powder, if one burns too large a pile).

Dr. Fermi says the forthcoming experiments should indicate the critical size of a mass of uranium large enough to permit explosive action.

At this point in Fermi's lecture, Schuyler, I believe, interrupted. "What might be the size of this critical mass?" he asked. "Could it be something small enough to go into the breech of a gun? Or would it be impractically large?"

"Well," Fermi replied with a smile, "it just might turn out to be the size of a small star." One might wish, as Fermi surely did later, that a requirement so "impractically large" might have been found to exist.

Schuyler's memorandum continues by observing that in such event the results became of academic interest. He continues:

But if the critical mass is of practical size, perhaps craters three or four miles in diameter can be blasted out. There then might be military uses of a nature which Dr. Fermi leaves others to predict. Possibly, though, some of the material may always have to be wasted as in the case of low order detonations of various types of explosives.

One kind of uranium has a weight of 235, and another has a weight of 238. The lighter type is only 1/100th as frequent in occurrence, and there is a suspicion that only this lighter type is the "working" kind. If so, only 1% of our present uranium supply is available, but it may be we are working with mixtures from which the inert type of uranium could be removed to better the effect.

In uranium mines there are numerous masses of uranium which (from cosmic rays, etc.,) have presumably had at least an atom or two split up. The question arises, therefore, whether the existence of these uranium mines does not show that mass detonations of that element are impossible. Dr. Fermi thinks, however, that perhaps impurities, or possibly even the presence of too much heavier uranium in these natural deposits, could have prevented mass detonations.

Dr. Fermi's position is that of a scientist who, feeling that it *may* be possible to unlock atomic energy in this way, considers the military services should be informed.

The other enthralled listener was Ross Gunn, a young physicist attached to the Naval Research Laboratory near Washington. Gunn went back to his desk and wrote a memorandum to his chief, Admiral Bowen. It is dated only three days after Fermi's talk and it outlined a project to build a nuclear reactor which would produce steam to operate turbines for *submarine* propulsion. The plant he described in this[2] and later memoranda was much like that which was installed in the *Nautilus*, but not until fifteen years later.

The Naval Research Laboratory, under Bowen, took the situation seriously. It was a fantastic theory, but Bowen risked ridicule and began to spend laboratory appropriations to find a method of separating the uranium isotopes. The sums he could spare from his appropriations were, by later standards, funny. The first allotment was $1500.

Later Gunn was joined by Abelson of the Carnegie Institution and progress began to be made on a system which was finally taken over by the Corps of Engineers when General Groves was placed in charge of the whole project. Although feelings were hurt by this unified direction of research, it was probably one of the wiser decisions that have been made in government administration. Our poor showing relative to the Russians in rocket propulsion at the date this is written may be shown by history to be due to the fragmentation of the development between branches of the Government instead of an early concentration of responsibility and talent, such as was the case in atomic energy.

When the Manhattan District was formed, a laboratory was established at the University of Chicago. Here Fermi climaxed his achievements by building the first pile in which a sustained chain reaction was produced and controlled.

Fermi's many accomplishments will be recorded by writers competent to discuss them with an understanding I cannot claim. There is one which fascinated me because it was the result of pure reason. There is a subatomic particle which interacts so weakly with material that, theoretically, it will pass unresisted through billions of miles of solid matter. Fermi and a friend, Wolfgang Pauli, predicted that this particle would someday be found. Its existence was the only way they could account for the carrying away of certain energy released in a radioactive process known as beta decay. They imagined such a particle and described the properties it would be found to possess if ever it should be identified. The year after Fermi died, two physicists, Reiner and Cowen, detected the particle, confirmed their discovery, and identified it beyond doubt. It is known as the "neutrino."

Enrico Fermi, born in Italy in 1901, was thirty-seven when he came to make his home in the United States. There are many who think he stands first among the great men of science of our generation. In no position to make such a judgment, I can only contribute to an estimate of other qualities. He was certainly the kindliest of men and he demonstrated in the terminal days of his illness that he also ranks with the bravest.

We had been introduced by Szilard and Brasch in 1938, when we were working on the surge generator project. Fermi had left his native Italy to go to Stockholm to receive the Nobel prize. With the medal, citation, and the prize money in hand, he took his family directly to the United States instead of returning to Rome. His lovely wife, Laura, was the daughter of an admiral in the Italian Navy. Even though Italian Fascism was less satanic than its German counterpart, it was vicious enough, and as the Admiral was a Jew, the lives of the Fermis were endangered by that fact. America welcomed the exiles. Shortly after they arrived, there was a memorable evening in my home when at the dinner table were Fermi, Lawrence, Wigner, Szilard, Brasch, and Land, the last a young scientist and inventor of whom much would later be heard.

Fermi performed his early experiments in the United States at Columbia in New York. He was drafted into the bomb project when it began in earnest, and his teaching activities, which were close to his heart, were suspended until the end of the war. By the time the Atomic Energy Commission was established, however, he had arranged to return to teaching (at the University of Chicago), but we were fortunate in obtaining his consent to serve on the General Advisory Committee. At its meetings, he would usually sit quietly, occupied with an odd habit of sighting along the edge of a pencil or a ruler as though in search of the explanation for some phenomenon that eluded him. When he spoke, it was always softly, briefly, and very definitely to the point. When there was some exchange between the scientists which one or all of the four nonscientist Commissioners had been unable to follow, Fermi on request would explain it in lucid lay language. It seemed to give him real delight when he perceived on the faces of his listeners the wide-eyed, lips-parted indication that understanding had suddenly dawned.

Once I was able to return the favor and do some minor interpreting for him. It was on an evening in 1947 when we had dined at the club where I then lived in Washington. As it was fine weather, we walked downtown. The lighted marquee of a motion-picture theater advertised a Walt Disney film—something about *Uncle Remus*. Fermi was curious, so we bought tickets and went in to see it. The folklore of the Old South and its anthropomorphic small animals as told in the stories by Joel Chandler Harris had been familiar to me from childhood, but, of course, totally unfamiliar to Dr. Fermi. Brer Rabbit, Brer B'ar, and Brer Fox were in the cast of characters. Fermi was especially puzzled by the theme song, which, if I remember correctly, was "Zippedy-Do-Dah." When the picture was over, he asked me what that expression meant. I was unequal to the task of literal translation but ventured that it was of the same genre as "Funiculi-funicula." At this, he laughed and said he understood very well.

Fermi's name is written large in the history of basic neutron physics, and he will be remembered as long as civilization endures for his achievement of the first controlled nuclear chain reaction. This feat merits the adjective "Promethean," for it was the bringing of a new energy source to mankind. It is memorialized on the medal given annually by the Atomic Energy Commission, together with a substantial cash prize, to an individual who has made a contribution to knowledge deemed sufficiently important to warrant the bestowal of the award which now bears Fermi's name.

In 1954, when President Eisenhower enthusiastically approved my recommendation to establish the award, Fermi was already on his deathbed. He was in no doubt about the nature of his illness, but he wrote me his pleasure at the award. It was to have been presented on December 2, the twelfth anniversary of the historic occasion when his first atomic pile "went critical," i.e., the chain reaction was allowed to start, but was controlled within prescribed limits. Calm and courageous to the end, he died four days before the medal could be struck.

LAWRENCE

On a visit to the Radiation Laboratory at Berkeley, California, fifteen years ago, I was allowed to look through a microscope at what appeared to be a piece of tarnished metal. With the naked eye it was barely visible as a speck of dust. This was plutonium, which is one of the series of elements heavier than uranium, and which had never been found to exist naturally on earth. The metal, so essential to our military strength, is now made in substantial amounts. The possibility that elements heavier than uranium could be made had been postulated, and eventually were produced, one after another, by an inspired team working under the leadership of Ernest Orlando Lawrence, a young, enthusiastic, friendly giant mind who was the antithesis of the popular image of the reserved, cloistered scientist.

We had first met in 1938. He was still fresh from his triumphs as the inventor of the cyclotron, a device which had grown from its prototype—a few bits of copper, sealing wax, and a flattened glass laboratory flask—to an apparatus filling a huge building, with coils and magnets weighing many tons. His ambition at that moment was to build a larger cyclotron with which new discoveries might be made about the structure of matter. It would require a lot of money. Steel and copper were expensive. (Asked on another occasion just what he expected to discover with a larger cyclotron, he replied, "Why, if we knew that, there wouldn't be any sense in building the damn thing.") Working with him, there had grown an amazing group of younger men, attracted by his brilliance, and all of them exceptionally talented —Glenn Seaborg, principal discoverer of the transuranic elements (and now Chairman of the Atomic Energy Commission), Edward McMillan and Luis Alvarez, among others, who have been recognized by prizes, medals, awards, and other scientific preferments for their individual contributions to knowledge.

Lawrence was enlisted in the Manhattan Project at an early date. His participation turned out to be crucial, for his inventiveness was invariably stimulated by every confrontation with an insuperable problem. The electromagnetic system used at Oak Ridge for the separation of uranium 235 and 238 was his. The heart of it was an amazing device in which the atoms comprising normal uranium in gaseous form were propelled through an electric field which bent the path of the heavier less than the lighter. The atoms were collected at the end of their trajectories in separate compartments so that, somewhat analogous to the manner in which an egg grader separates light from heavy eggs, uranium 238 accumulated in one box and the isotope 235 in another.

A great deal of electricity was necessary for the process, and in order that copper might be spared for other war uses, the large bus bars which conducted current in the electromagnetic plant were made of many tons of silver borrowed from the U. S. Treasury. None the worse for its war service, the silver was returned intact to the Treasury Department when the plant was finally shut down.

Throughout this book there are many references to Lawrence. His personality is woven into the fabric of science in America and especially into the area of high-energy physics. He was deeply concerned about the preservation of free institutions. He believed that the true spirit of scientific inquiry could not long survive in a climate of tyranny and oppression. This not only accounted for the enthusiasm with which he attacked the problem of the atomic bomb in World War II, but it was the reason that he favored the decision to develop the hydrogen bomb when some of his scientific contemporaries opposed it. He believed that international control of atomic energy was both essential and feasible, but that strong international guarantees and inspection are inseparable from any prudent agreement. He strongly opposed any decision on the cessation of developing and testing atomic weapons without such safeguards. Believing this, he went to Geneva in the summer of 1958 to participate with other scientists in a conference preliminary to negotiations with the Soviets on test suspension. He was unhappy at the turn of events there, but he worked until overcome by an illness which forced him to leave for home. He died serving the causes of science and freedom. To him it was one cause.

LINCOLN, DAHLGREN, AND THE TORPEDO

During service in the Bureau of Ordnance, I came upon a record of several men and a decision of long ago, long forgotten. In the early days of the United States Navy, the chief clerks were powerful functionaries who, on occasion, even served as Acting Secretary of the Department. As permanent officials, they knew more than anyone else about the history and archives of the bureaus. The Chief Clerk of the Bureau of Ordnance had in his files a copybook dating from 1861 and, learning of my interest in the "old Navy," brought it to me. In its time-yellowed pages there was a series of eloquent documents.

From some of them, it appeared that President Lincoln had received from a Connecticut inventor a design for a torpedo which could be launched from one ship against another. This was a radical idea, for the device contained its own power and a screw propeller. In 1861, the word "torpedo" did not apply to an automotive device, i.e., an underwater bomb that carried its own propelling mechanism. The torpedo of that day was either fastened to a stake in the bed of a harbor to explode on contact with a ship's hull (we would call it a small mine) or was fixed to the end of a spar extending forward from the bow of a vessel, in which position it would explode when rammed against the enemy ship. In that use, it was successful to the extent that it might damage the enemy more than it did the user.

President Lincoln must have been impressed. He was by way of being an inventor himself. He once said that the American patent system had "added the fuel of interest to the fire of genius." The Patent Office may still possess the model of a device for lifting river boats over shoals. The model had been carefully whittled out of cherry wood. For it a young Lincoln was duly awarded letters patent of the United States. The President's interest was shown by his referral of the inventor's torpedo project to the Secretary of the Navy with request for a prompt evaluation.

The Secretary of the Navy, in turn, "bucked" it to Captain Dahlgren, who commanded the Washington Navy Yard. Reading the aged letters, one could imagine the sniff of disdain with which Dahlgren received this. The exchange concluded with a letter-press copy of his report to the President. As I recall, it read about as follows: "This device has been proposed, obviously, by a landlubber, unfamiliar with the vagaries of wind, tide and current. Why, Sir, with one good ship

of the line, I would gladly confront a fleet armed with such a weapon."
And so the *Cumberland* was defenseless against the *Merrimac,* and
other naval engagements also might have had different endings.

This anecdote appears to support a belief, widely held, that the
military services are generally prejudiced against inventions that are
not the product of indigenous imagination. My observation does not
sustain this. An inventor able to express himself can always get a hearing. It is true, of course, that ideas good, indifferent, and wild rain
down upon the military in a steady fall-out which becomes heavier
in times of international tension. Not infrequently, inventors are escorted to the Navy by their legislative representatives who are convinced, or at any rate hopeful, that a large industrial operation in
their constituency may result. Though the percentage of these ideas
that are of value is minute, the Services have offices qualified to
evaluate them, and the National Inventors Council also has been of
great help in the screening.

Not infrequently, inventors hit upon some area in which work has
already started. Simultaneous invention is a well-recognized pattern.
In these cases when the item is classified, i.e., secret, the inventor
cannot be told that his idea is unacceptable because it is already in
hand. In other cases, some "new proposals" are not new at all, but fall
into familiar approaches to the solution of a problem.

Only a few months before World War II, an inventor approached
the Bureau of Ordnance with a device. He claimed that when planes
bombed ships the percentage of hits could be enormously augmented
by his invention. It would have the effect of converting to sure hits
many drops that would ordinarily be near-misses. The inventor claimed
that he had bad experience in previous years in dealing with a Government agency which had pirated his ideas. He would only reveal his
discovery in this instance if the Navy posted the asking price in escrow
with a well-known bank. If then, upon his revealing the method, the
Navy elected to go forward with it, the bank was to pay over the
money to him at once. It seemed fair enough, but as the Bureau of
Ordnance had no funds to speculate, its chief, Admiral W. R. Furlong,
asked me to see if anything could be done about it from private
sources of funds.

At my suggestion, the inventor consented to submit his idea to an
impartial judgment and we agreed on the president of a national
scientific organization, with the understanding that his report might
greatly influence private individuals to advance the money. The in-

ventor then spent an evening with the academician, who called on me the next day to say that, in his opinion, the device, although unbelievably simple, would perform as the inventor had represented. I had asked whether it would be as effective against fortifications and targets ashore as against ships. The answer was no and that, to be effective, the ships would be presumed to be under way.

What prompted me to ask that question I cannot remember, but when I reported it along with other comments to Admiral Furlong, Captain Schuyler, who was present, said, "Why, all that fellow has is the old notion that you can drop two bombs, connected by a cable, from two planes. Then if they straddle a ship, he thinks the bombs will be warped around to the hull by the forward motion of the ship and detonate against her sides. But he's wrong because from any ordinary bombing altitude, the bombs will fall in tandem one behind the other. They won't straddle the ship. We don't need to pay anything for that idea."

The next day when I asked the inventor if, in fact, that was what he wished to sell to the Navy for a million dollars, he simply got up and left the room. I have never seen him since.

XIII

Decisions on Security

If ye had not plowed with my heifer, ye had not found out my riddle.

SAMSON TO THE PHILISTINES
JUDGES 14:18

It may be right to give the British public this information, but if they choose to have it, they ought to know the price they pay for it and the advantage it gives the enemy in all their operations.

WELLINGTON

He that guardeth his lips keepeth his life; but for him who openeth wide his lips the end is ruin.

PROVERBS 13:3

The fact of spying and that of being spied upon are both repugnant to most Americans. They are associated in the public mind with the present state of world unrest and the existence of a system of government with announced designs aggressively opposed to our way of life. The institution of intelligence-gathering by spying, however, is as old as history and our own history begins with it.

General Washington's meticulous journal of accounts, posted regularly in his own hand, begins within hours after he had taken command of the Continental Army. An entry on July 15, 1775, reads:

To 333½ Dollars given to ———* to induce him to go into the town of Boston to establish a secret Correspondence for the purpose of conveying intelligence of the Enemy's movements and designs.

---

* "The names of Persons who are employed and within the Enemy's lines and who may fall within their power cannot be inserted."

This is a classic example of both intelligence *and* security.

There are at least a dozen further notations of similar disbursements in Washington's accounts, totaling what was for those days a substantial figure. In other ways as well, we were active in efforts to penetrate the "Enemy's designs." They were the prototypes of operations like the U-2 reconnaissance flights over Russia, which among other things created so much unnecessary surprise in the early months of 1960.

In the Revolutionary period we were the objects of penetration by espionage on a number of occasions, including one that, for its day, was a very sophisticated operation. Edward Bancroft, a British agent, was planted with Benjamin Franklin to be his private secretary and, in consequence, our most distinguished Ambassador's negotiations with France and Spain, his correspondence with Congress, even such timely information as the dates of the sailings of our ships and the nature of their cargoes, were duly transmitted to the enemy in London by means of messages written in "invisible ink" between the lines of innocuous letters addressed to a lady "on matters of gallantry."

Spying is not limited to cloak-and-dagger operations, codes, and invisible inks. It is a professional technique assisted, it is true, by the indiscreet, the boastful, and alcohol-lubricated, but its mainstay is the panning of pay dirt—the tiny, almost unseen speck of information in a mass of other material. These are accumulated, and with enough of them together important information is compromised. Witness Takeo Yoshikawa,[1] a former officer of the Imperial Japanese Navy. Yoshikawa was the principal espionage agent of Japan in the Hawaiian Islands before the attack on Pearl Harbor. He regularly made the rounds of our Government offices, gathering up armfuls of pamphlets, magazine articles, and newspapers. He read a vast amount of material. The information he needed was all there. It had only to be dug out and put together by a trained operator.

"Security" is the word given to the procedures for preventing the loss of privacy, initiative, and military advantage which a government must take to protect itself from expert espionage and from almost equally dangerous idle curiosity and loose tongues. Security as practiced by our government has been given a bad name. Admittedly, it has been carried to excess on occasion, but even in such cases, exasperating as they may have been, it was preferable to exposure. Security can be maintained, contrary to the beliefs of some, without infringing the proper and legal rights of individuals.

There are many examples of security made silly. Once during the war, while waiting to see the head of a Government department, I asked a secretary if I might look up a man in "Who's Who." Word came back that the rule stipulated that before releasing the book the librarian was required to know the credentials of the individual who wanted it and for what purpose. Or take the case of a Navy directive, a score of years ago, which, in order to protect the secrecy of the development of radar, forbade even the use of the word "radar" for fear that it would disclose by its orthography that direction and range could be obtained by means of radio signals. In January 1944 the order was relaxed[2]—if that is the word—to provide that "mere mention of the word" was thereafter "permissible," but not in relation to description, operation, use, production schedules, experiments, or any "other matter relating to Radar." Then there are the countless anecdotes, mostly fabricated perhaps, about telephone directories and dictionaries being stamped "Secret—Restricted Data."

Since its beginnings, however, our military establishment has observed strict rules differentiating between information that may be public property and information which, if compromised, would give aid and comfort to an enemy. Such information as pin-pointing the location of ammunition depots and the quantities of ammunition on hand is intelligence which the enemy pay spies handsome amounts to obtain. This kind of knowledge gives the enemy enormous advantage in planning his strategy. Yet not long ago an important consultant to the Government, in an interview in which he defended the security features of certain legislation, saying that some of the information protected by it involves the fate of the whole country, was then asked, "The number of atom bombs for instance?" to which this man replied, "That's the last thing I would want to keep secret."

At a press conference in October 1953, President Eisenhower said, ". . . We do not intend to disclose the details of our strength in atomic weapons of any sort, but it is large and increasing steadily. We have in our atomic arsenals a number of kinds of weapons suited to the special needs of the Army, Navy, and Air Force for the specific tasks assigned to each service." What a military commander may regard as vital to be concealed a person not in the chain of command may feel is an idle or overly zealous exercise of caution. For this reason, if any security whatever is to exist, there must be a recognized authority and a rule to which all must adhere. The opposite of that is a chaotic status greatly favoring the enemy.

This is well evidenced by certain events which began in 1939. In that year a significant instance of civilian awareness of the importance of safeguarding specific information arose spontaneously within the scientific community. There is reproduced elsewhere in this book a letter which was written to me on January 25, 1939, by Dr. Leo Szilard in which he speculated on the possibility that, as a result of experiments confirming the hypothesis of the fission of uranium, it might be possible to make an "atomic bomb." As I have said, it was the first time I had seen these two words in juxtaposition.

Almost immediately thereafter a small group of physicists, including Dr. Szilard, Dr. Teller, Dr. Eugene Wigner, Dr. Victor Weisskopf, and Dr. Fermi, concluded that the weapons potential of the discovery might also be apparent to the scientists working for the Nazi regime and, therefore, in order to afford them no hint nor give them the benefit of any work done in the Free World, all publication on the subject should be deferred. (To the reader who may not be familiar with the fact, it should be said here that publication of scientific hypotheses, proofs, and discoveries is the custom among scientists as a means of diffusing knowledge more widely. It is a practice carrying the sanction of greatest antiquity.) There was complete concurrence with this plan among American and British scientists. Frédéric Joliot, the distinguished French physicist, however, refused to co-operate. In later years Joliot's Communist associations, which may have accounted for his attitude, became known to the French Government, and, despite his scientific eminence, he was separated from the French atomic energy project.*

The arrangement among American and British scientists was voluntary and at first unorganized, but by April of 1940, the war having reached the Low Countries, a "reference committee" was established under the auspices of the National Research Council. This committee functioned as an effective security organization. The editors of scientific journals were asked to refer all communications offered to them for publication, and if they were deemed to be of military significance, their publication was to be withheld. The editors co-operated without exception.

This arrangement worked without any criticism as long as the principal enemy was the Nazi-Fascist axis. Almost immediately after V-J Day, a report was published on the development of atomic energy for military

* This was in 1950, three years before the Oppenheimer hearing in the United States. I am aware of no record that Joliot was accorded a hearing, as is our practice in the United States, although this may have occurred.

purposes. It had been compiled by Dr. Henry D. Smyth (later a member of the Atomic Energy Commission), who had been a consultant to the Manhattan District of the U. S. Corps of Engineers. The report had been written and was published by direction of the commanding officer of the Manhattan Project, General Leslie R. Groves. Widely circulated and known briefly as the "Smyth Report," it was welcomed by the scientific community, which, including many of those who had worked on the bomb project, had been so compartmented for the sake of security that only a few had the complete picture of the total enterprise which the Smyth Report afforded.

There has been much discussion as to the wisdom of revealing what the Smyth Report contained and as to whether or not it was of assistance and, if so, how much, to the Communists.[3] No one on this side of the Iron Curtain is likely to know the answer, but had those who made the decision to publish the report been able to foresee the state of the world today, it is conceivable that they might well have refrained from disclosing any information which could have been of assistance in accelerating the date of atomic weapon production by the Soviets.

The Smyth Report was issued only after substantial objections had been overruled. These were not solely from professional security quarters, but were voiced particularly by some of the British scientists who had collaborated on the atomic weapons project. Some of these expressed themselves to the effect that the publication would be "an effective guide through the labyrinth." Others argued that so complete an account would be of material assistance to foreign scientists and would result in saving them many months of work. As an example, objectors felt that it was highly imprudent to specify the methods by which uranium 235 had been produced and to indicate that there were several different approaches that were successful.

Lord Cherwell, F. A. Lindemann, adviser on scientific matters to Prime Minister Winston Churchill, wrote:[4]

> Since your people insisted on publication our constant endeavor was to eliminate as many as possible of the dangerous items of information . . . as a result a certain amount of information was omitted [but] . . . we would have preferred a great deal less.

Those who favored immediate release of the report argued that the intelligence service of a foreign country could uncover the information in the course of time and that foreign science would discover it eventually. It was also stated that Congress "needed to be shown where the money had been spent." This latter argument was unnecessary, as in any case a report to the Congress would have to be made in due course.

As a practical matter, however, the British were confronted with the choice of agreeing to the publication of the document as it stood or of insisting upon no publication at all. It was urged upon them that the consequences of no publication would be dangerous to security because of the "itch of some individuals to unburden their minds" and because of the pressure to give the proper persons due credit for accomplishments. The report was finally modified to include the names of certain scientists who had not been mentioned, and publication was agreed to. A British version with somewhat more emphasis on the contribution of British scientists was issued in England.

Secretary Stimson recalled that the Smyth Report had been issued in order to offset any possible reckless statements by independent scientists after the bomb was used. He noted in his diary that he would have preferred not to give it out if he and his colleagues could be sure that no such statements would be made.[5]

AEC Chairman Lilienthal, testifying before the Joint Congressional Committee on Atomic Energy on January 28, 1947, described the report as "The principal breach of security since the beginning of the Atomic Energy Project. . . ."[6]

The argument that science flourishes in a climate of unhampered communication is surely correct, though it does not account for the apparent success of Russian science, where it is completely subordinated to the military concept of security and where toward specific goals it has been outstanding. This paradox has not yet been resolved. Scientific freedom to publish and communicate as we enjoy it does not exist in Russia and nothing even remotely resembling the Smyth Report has ever been published with respect to the Soviet atomic weapon enterprise. There has been great reluctance in some quarters to concede that the Soviets benefited either from their espionage or from our disclosures and to ascribe their accomplishments solely to their scientists and engineers. Since they operate under strict security, the situation is, to say the least, contradictory.

In spite of exchange visits, we know relatively little about the Soviet atomic establishment. Until 1961, and their test series with its strong propaganda overtones, they have conceded their atomic weapons tests only after we detected and announced them (with one exception), and not always then. Occasionally, revealing information reaches us by way of exchanges in atomic scientific conferences. For example, we have learned that their first reactor, designated PSR, is almost a carbon copy of the reactor 305 which we built at Hanford, our great plutonium installation on the Columbia River. Here are a few comparisons between them:[7]

	HANFORD 305	SOVIET PSR
Power	10 watts	10 watts
Diameter	18–20 ft.	19 ft.
Lattice Spacing	8½ inches	8 inches
Loading	27 tons uranium	25–50 tons uranium
Road Diameter	1.4 plus inches	1.2 to 1.6 inches

As the Russian reactor was completed before 1955, while the data on our reactor were not made public until 1955, the odds are astronomic against such a series of neat coincidences.

Dr. Charles Allen Thomas, chairman of the board of the Monsanto Chemical Company, who was a key figure in the early years of the Manhattan Project, recalls another of these interesting coincidences. Scientists at that time were intrigued by the ease with which some atoms could stop certain neutrons. "One of them," said Dr. Thomas, "compared the process with the ease of hitting a barn when it presented a broadside target. As a result of this chance remark, the unit of measure for nuclear capture cross-sections became known as the 'barn' and this function of atoms is still measured in 'barns,' just as distance is measured in miles. When we first learned of Soviet nuclear technology some years later, we were surprised to hear *they* were measuring these same cross-sections in terms of 'barns,' even though the closest word to 'barn' in the Russian language is 'bahrahn,' which means mutton. . . . I leave it to you to say who has been whose lamb chop," concludes Dr. Thomas. This incident only suggests that there was a fairly free flow of scientific information—in one direction.

There are a few axioms concerning security. One may be stated: When security is found to be excessive, it can always be cured by relaxing it. There is no cure for inadequate security. Information once compromised is information broadcast forever.

Beginning with the organization of the original Atomic Energy Commission when the law transferred control of the project from military to civilian authority, the Commissioners sought to rationalize the security program. They found themselves between two considerable pressures: one, a representative group which while regarding Soviet intentions with great reserve believed that much greater relaxation of the control of secret data was desirable "in the interest of the spirit of free scientific inquiry"; the other, an unorganized body of opinion which did not share the prevailing state of euphoria as to Stalin's amicable intentions. The latter opinion held that, if the reason for withholding information from Hitler's Germany was valid in 1940, it followed that equal prudence was called for in dealing with Stalin's Russia in 1947. Those who adhered to this point of view, however, had a pretty rough time of it, being stigmatized as security addicts.

Scientists were far from unanimous in their attitude on the handling of security information after the war. A letter addressed to me over the signatures of a number of scientists expressed their deep concern with the problem of maintaining our atomic lead over the Russians and with the treatment accorded to classified information by high-ranking officials. They wrote, "We are all agreed that the ultimate criterion which should govern whether a specific item of information is released, is the gain to be achieved by this nation versus the advantage which will accrue to our enemies. Such a weighing of the scales of advantage is admittedly not a simple matter, but the problem must be faced in each case realizing that the consequences of an error may be most grave. No individual can properly judge the complete meaning of any piece of information because apparently disconnected and useless facts may mean a great deal to an expert in the field. (It follows that the less expert a person is, the less competent he is to make a judgment.) Nor is it necessary to describe the technical details of a bomb design in order to give away the secret. The most important technical fact about the H-bomb, for instance, is that it exists. We do not disagree with the necessity for disclosing *this* fact because it is essential to any realistic view of the world situation on the part of the American people."

They then listed the kind of statements which had been made and the revealing nature of some of them. "This," they concluded, "is the burden of our worry; this pattern has been repeated again and again through the years and there is something suspect with a system of security which allows the Russians to profit by every major gain made by us and with precious little effort on their part. . . . Our present national course seems to be to give away the big secrets and retain the little ones."

There were also many intermediate shades of opinion. Based upon the huge sums which the Manhattan District had expended in order to achieve success; the enormous industrial resources of plant and skills which we were able to draw upon; and the unprecedented galaxy of

British, Canadian, and American scientific talent which had been marshaled, some felt that Russia could not hope to equal our accomplishments in the foreseeable future. Some even said, "Never." Most, however, felt that in ten to fifteen years the Soviets might make a prototype weapon.* There were others, but they were in the minority, who knew that prewar Russian science had been very competent and who suspected that industry, regimented under Communism, could be sharply focused to a single objective. And finally, there were fears, even then, of successful penetration by espionage. The Canadian spy cases, reported in full by a royal commission in 1946 following the confessions of Gouzenko, a Soviet defector in Canada, reinforced this apprehension.

As early as September 18, 1945, with victory over Japan popularly attributed to the bombing of Hiroshima and Nagasaki, President Truman had called a Cabinet meeting to help him decide whether or not to declassify our atomic information and to give to the Russians whatever we had learned. It is certain that, though this course may have been urged upon him, he had not favored it. Indeed, the President in his memoirs makes a sharp distinction between giving the world (and therefore the Soviets) scientific information of a basic character on the one hand and information on the technology, the design, and construction of atomic weapons on the other. The "know-how of putting it [the bomb] together" he did not propose to share. He had decided that "the secret of the manufacture of the weapon would remain a secret with us."[8]

The President announced his decision shortly after the Cabinet members left. He had either already determined to bring the U.N. into the picture or looked favorably upon that part of Forrestal's suggestion. As the meeting ended he said that he did not intend to do anything without concurrence of the Congress, and two weeks later, on October 3, sent a message to Congress recommending the establishment of an administrative body which in due course came into being as the Atomic Energy Commission. It was a farsighted message spelling out most of the provisions of the measure that later became Public Law 585.

There *were* already outstanding two agreements on the subject of

* President Truman at a press conference at Reelfoot Lake, Tennessee, in reply to a reporter, on the subject of declassification: "Well, I don't think it would do any good to let them in on the know-how because I don't think they could do it, anyway. You would have to have the industrial plant and our engineering ability to do the job, as well as the scientific knowledge. . . . If they catch up with us on that they will have to get it on their own hook, just as we did."

controlling atomic energy and sharing information, both of them with the United Kingdom. They had been drafted and signed, one in Quebec and the other at Hyde Park, by President Franklin D. Roosevelt and Prime Minister Winston Churchill. But the Senate had never been informed of either, and their existence was known to very few persons. (They are more specifically dealt with in Chapter XVII, "The Peaceable Atom: Decisions Affecting New Problems and Old Friends.")

The Cabinet discussion on September 21, 1945, is illuminating as an indication that we were faced with a decision of far-reaching consequences, since, as revealed in the Stimson memoirs, we had expended our stockpile of ready atomic weapons in the preceding month. There is now reason to believe that the Russians, even then, must have begun their own atomic weapons project.

President Truman's decision reflected the same conclusion he had expressed over a month earlier when, following his announcement of the new weapon, he had said:

> . . . the atomic bomb is too dangerous to be loose in a lawless world. That is why Great Britain and the United States, who have the secret of its production, do not intend to reveal the secret until means have been found to control the bomb so as to protect ourselves and the rest of the world from the danger of total destruction.[9]

This principle found its way more or less directly into Section 10 of the legislation which established the Atomic Energy Commission. In that section, Congress stipulated that "effective and enforceable safeguards" against the use of atomic energy in war would have to come into being before any "secrets" or information could be exchanged with other nations even for industrial purposes.

In practice, however, the Atomic Energy Act, which was to guide the Commissioners, proved to be ambiguous on matters of security. In most other respects, the law was a model of good draftsmanship. But the ambiguity is evident in Section 10, where, in the space of a few lines, contradictory injunctions are given to the new Commission:

> Sec. 10. (a) POLICY. — It shall be the policy of the Commission to control the dissemination of restricted data in such a manner as to assure the common defense and security. Consistent with such policy, the Commission shall be guided by the following principles:
> (1) That until Congress declares by joint resolution that effective and enforceable international safeguards against the use of atomic energy for destructive purposes have been established, *there shall be*

no exchange of information with other nations with respect to the
use of atomic energy for industrial purposes; and

(2) That the *dissemination of scientific and technical information
relating to atomic energy shall be permitted and encouraged* so as to
provide that free interchange of ideas and criticisms which is essential
to scientific progress. [Italics supplied.]

This attempt to make concessions to two differing legislative objectives developed a difference of viewpoint within the Commission on the
administration of security of information, a difference which was not
cured until the act was amended some four years later. As I adhered to
the letter of the law, the brand of "security obsession" was early burned
upon me, and I still wear it. There were a number of incidents in
which this security consciousness figured and of which three may serve
as illustrations.

1. The Commission adopted many of the procedures of the Army's
Manhattan District, among which was the wearing of identification
badges in restricted areas. This was one of many precautions to exclude
trespassers of all sorts and to restrict admission to such areas only to
those who were cleared to enter on business. A visitor to the headquarters
building, for instance, was required to be announced by telephone
from the entrance and to be escorted to and from the office with which
he had dealings.

In 1948, I learned that an alien was the holder of a permanent pass
to the Commission's headquarters, a pass moreover, which was of a
character that did not require him to be accompanied while in the
building. It developed from the record maintained by the guards at the
building entrances that this particular alien was a frequent visitor in the
evenings after usual work hours. Being concerned, I took the matter up
with my colleagues and found that none of them had been aware of the
situation. The pass was withdrawn at once. The name of the alien was
Donald Maclean, an attaché of the British Embassy. His name made
headlines when he disappeared and later turned up in Moscow with
Guy Burgess in 1951.

2. The second incident was a discovery that an employee in an extremely sensitive position in one of our atomic energy establishments had
been a member of a Communist group. His assignment required him
to have custody of scientific documents and reports of the *utmost* secrecy.
He had been assigned clerical work during the early days of the war
when other men of his age—he was twenty-six—were being drafted for
military service. He was not a scientist himself, but his superiors had
secured his deferment from military duty on grounds of his indispen-

sability almost immediately after his employment began. His record indicated no previous experience in the type of duties assigned to him, and no acquaintance whatever with the work of the establishment in question.

In filling out the question forms for his employment when the Army was in charge of the atomic weapon project and again when the Atomic Energy Commission took it over, this man had concealed the fact that he had been a member of the Communist organization, although the questionnaire called for the disclosure of present or past connections of every sort. When confronted five years later with the evidence of his Communist membership and of his misrepresentations on the two occasions when he had signed the questionnaires, he took the position that he had terminated his Communist connections just prior to his employment in the atomic weapons establishment.

When these facts were brought to my attention by the late Admiral John Gingrich, Chief of the Security Division, I felt that the administrative officer who had acquiesced in the man's continued clearance for secret information had made an error. The employee had access to matter of too great sensitivity to accept the risk that he could be trusted. The officials in the establishment where the employee was engaged disagreed with this conclusion and sent a committee of their number to meet with the Commissioners to voice their protest against a decision to revoke the man's clearance, tantamount to his discharge. The members of the committee which came to Washington to confer with us were important and loyal men.

They argued that, although their associate had now admitted being a Communist prior to the date of his employment, they were absolutely confident that he was a Communist no longer; that they would take upon themselves full responsibility for his future actions; and, finally, that if he were removed, there would be "consternation" in the establishment and morale would be shattered.

My colleagues turned to me and one of them said, "Lewis, look what a piece of flypaper you've gotten us into." I said that if we were the directors of a bank and our responsibility was to depositors who were widows and orphans, and if we had suddenly discovered that one of our cashiers had been an embezzler, who had concealed that fact from us when we had hired him, we would surely have to dismiss him. Our responsibility as Atomic Energy Commissioners was of a far higher order. As bank directors we would be responsible to our stockholders and depositors for nothing more important than money, but as Commissioners, we were fiduciaries of the whole American people for the safety of their lives and the defense of our government; that the offer of our friends to accept responsibility for the man's future actions was a fine gesture but totally unrealistic because the responsibility was *ours,* under the law, and we could not be absolved of it and they could not relieve us of it. And finally I said that if the last point they had made, with respect to morale, were a fact we would be better advised to close the establishment than to operate it.

The Commissioners then excused the committee and we took a secret ballot, which turned out to be unanimous to remove the man at once. There were no resignations from the staff of the institution and it continued its high standard of performance. A few years afterward, however, friends in the establishment told me that my part in the episode was known and was deeply resented. The fierceness of this resentment came into the open a full decade later when a witness charged that I was "antiscientist."

3. The third instance has had some airing. In 1949 a request was received by a laboratory of the Commission for a shipment overseas of a radioactive isotope of iron. The shipment was made to a man in the laboratory of the Ministry of Defense Research in Norway. Word of the shipment reached me only after it had been forwarded and I was concerned that it had violated Section 10 of the Atomic Energy Law.

What was the purpose of the shipment? I asked. The answer was that the request had been transmitted through the State Department and had clearly indicated that the iron isotope was to be used to develop alloys for jet or gas turbines at high temperatures, "particularly above 700° if possible." This to my mind meant that the application must surely be for military purposes, since in 1949 jet engines were used only to power military aircraft. It appeared to me that the law had been flouted, however, for, even had the intended use not been military, the law prohibited the exchange of the information for "industrial purposes" without international safeguards. With the concurrence of my colleagues, I took steps to see that no further shipments should be made without prior Commission approval.

Before this we had been shipping radioactive isotopes abroad for medical purposes, and my stipulations* expressly excepted such consign-

---

* Excerpt from recommendations to Commissioners from Mr. Strauss, October 27, 1947: "That in cases where isotopes are required for therapy, they will be provided . . . where proper supervision can be supplied. . . ." A later memorandum on the subject of requests from foreign countries for radioisotopes and dated August 24, 1949, reads as follows: "If the requests are for medical or

ments. Nevertheless, the fable was published by a columnist that I had objected to a shipment of radioisotopes to Norway to be used *"for medical purposes,"* and this charge was revived ten years later at the hearings on my confirmation to be Secretary of Commerce.[10]

The scientist in Norway who had requested the shipment of the radioactive iron isotope was later "allowed to resign" from his post because of his Communist party connection.

*   *   *

Personnel security is a part of the task of protecting our installations not only from the compromise of information but also from damage by sabotage. Even those who are sincerely convinced that it would be better if all information were "free" do not advocate the indiscriminate employment of every applicant for a job, since this would open the door to enemy saboteurs. In the first months after the Atomic Energy Commission was organized under the chairmanship of Mr. Lilienthal, decisions on personnel security occupied an amount of Commissioners' time which prejudiced the conduct of other aspects of the Commission's work. Voluminous files—in some cases running into hundreds of pages each—had to be read and evaluated. The threat to the security of the country, however, caused natural reluctance at the outset to delegate this responsibility to staff. This finally had to be done.

In the first seven years after the Commission began to operate, over a half a million persons were investigated. Of this number a little over 1 per cent, 5532, had their eligibility questioned. Of these, 1622 were cleared and 3910 were denied clearance, or resigned prior to the completion of their cases, or had the request for their clearance canceled.[11] This should not be construed as a quantitative indication of the extent to which the atomic weapon project was the target of Soviet espionage, but only as an evidence that there was need for the exercise of great caution. (Men were unfit for trust for reasons other than disloyalty.)

Obviously, the Commissioners were unable to deal on a personal basis with such a load, and accordingly, at their request, I obtained the assignment from the Navy for duty with the Commission of an extremely able officer, very well and favorably known to me. He was Rear Admiral John Gingrich, who had been Forrestal's aide during the first years of the war and later had distinguished himself in battle in the Pacific.

---

basic scientific research or instruction purposes I should like to be voted in approval. If for military or industrial use, I should like to be voted against granting the requests."

Admiral Gingrich and his organization relieved the Commissioners of the burden of studying the huge accumulation of files on questionable cases and saw to it that there reached the Commissioners only a minimum of the most difficult decisions.

General Groves had addressed the Commissioners, shortly after we took over from the Manhattan District, to point out that his clearance of various persons for work in laboratories or plants must not be construed as an endorsement of their reliability. He explained that during the war, the responsibility being upon him individually, he had at times taken very great "calculated risks" with persons whose records were highly questionable. He felt he could afford to do this because he had a large organization, which reported directly to him, conducting continuous surveillance of these people. He placed in the Commission's hands files on a number of the dubious cases.

It is difficult, now that fourteen years have elapsed, to recapture the state of mind in which the decisions of that day were made, but, looking to the judgment of the future as to its current actions, the Commission took pains to be scrupulously fair. A Personnel Security Review Board of the highest possible caliber was established. Chairman Lilienthal obtained the services of Owen J. Roberts, a retired Justice of the United States Supreme Court, as its chairman. Recruited by me were Dr. Compton; George M. Humphrey, a prominent industrialist who five years later became Secretary of the Treasury; Henning W. Prentis, Jr., a retired manufacturer; and the Honorable Joseph C. Grew, the dean of our diplomatic corps, a public servant with a most distinguished record. This board considered and made findings for the Commission on a number of conspicuous cases.

When I returned to the Commission in 1953, I was asked by one of the members of this panel, Mr. Humphrey, to furnish him with a copy of the opinion he had written on one of these cases. Mr. Humphrey's report and recommendation, however, along with the other opinions of the Roberts Board on this case, could not be found in the AEC files, having been lost or purloined.

Those who regard this period as one of nothing but witch-hunting, with only innocent people being harassed by federal bureaus and agencies, tend to set aside the fact that people like Maclean, Burgess, May, the Rosenbergs, Greenglass, Slack, Fuchs, Pontecorvo, and a number of others used such positions of trust as they held in the United States, Canada, and the United Kingdom in the interests of the Soviet.

Those who were apprehended were, in all likelihood, but a part of the espionage net which operated and doubtless still operates against us.

One of the first acts of the Commission under Mr. Lilienthal's chairmanship was to set a standard for personnel security hearings which has since become practically uniform throughout the federal government. These rules provided that an individual whose reliability had been brought into question either as an applicant for employment, as an employee, or as a person whose clearance was required for some other reason, had certain affirmative rights. He had first to be fully informed of the charges against him. He could decide whether or not the charges should be heard by an independent panel. In the event of such a hearing, he had unlimited right of challenge as the personnel of the panel was selected. He could appear before the panel in person and with counsel of his own choosing. He could confront and cross-examine adverse witnesses and produce evidence in his own behalf by witnesses and by documents. He could appeal the findings of the panel to the Commission's standing Personnel Review Board and to the Commission. He had the election as to whether the results should or should not be made public. In spite of this it is significant that there was sufficient evidence during the Commission's first seven years to result in Commission action denying clearance to 494 persons.[12] (Others, to a total of nearly four thousand, resigned.)

One of the anomalies of the problem of security turned out to be the fact that action to enforce the law occasionally had to be withheld because further compromise of information would be the result of legal action. There was an example quite early in the history of the Commistion.

In 1947 a former employee of the Manhattan District, and since then a frequent critic of Government atomic policies, took two pieces of uranium to a friend in the Department of Defense and requested that they be kept for him there in a safe place. Amazed at receiving a material, private ownership of which was extraordinary if not forbidden by law, and recognizing that the geometry of the pieces revealed highly secret information, the individual into whose keeping they had been been given took them to his senior officer. That officer in turn took them to General K. D. Nichols, then commanding the Armed Forces Special Weapons Project. General Nichols took possession of them and informed the Atomic Energy Commission, which in turn reported the situation to the Department of Justice.

The former Manhattan District employee was then interviewed. He claimed that he had received the objects as souvenirs from another person, who, however, being no longer alive, could not confirm the statement. Following that interview the former employee turned up with more "souvenirs" of the same description. The Commission had to weigh the alternatives that, although a serious irregularity appeared to have occurred, prosecution in the courts would entail an exposure and description of the exhibits. This would be news, widely reported in the press here and abroad. For that reason no further action could be taken.

This points up the difficulty of enforcing laws protecting the security of information under circumstances where security has to be further breached in order to obtain a conviction. Even a prosecution which did not reveal specifics attests to the importance of the compromised information.

*   *   *

As compared with personnel security, the security of plants and documents presented a less difficult problem. Indeed, on returning to the Commission in 1953, I found that a large backlog of reports had accumulated, many of which did not warrant retention in "Top Secret," "Secret," or even "Confidential" status. Some of them contained information which would be of clear benefit to industry and to the public generally, whereas retention of the information in some classified category was no longer meaningful to our defense. The rate of the accumulation of these documents was greater than the speed with which the existing machinery was able to review them to determine whether or not they should continue classified. The men regularly charged with this determination, in the Office of Classification of the Commission, were an experienced and devoted group of scientists and engineers, but too few in number to cope with the accumulation plus the waves of increment. During the first year of my return to the Commission, therefore, we increased the number of men thus engaged and, making a concerted attack on the backlog of scores of thousands of documents, within three years reduced the classification of some twenty thousand and released over ten thousand from any restriction whatever. Marion Boyer, then the General Manager of the AEC, initiated this program. He was a talented and most successful officer.

Our plants still needed protection from sabotage, but we were able to discontinue round-the-clock patrols by armored cars and tanks around the periphery of huge reservations embracing many hundreds of square miles. In general, we adopted a policy of higher walls around smaller areas; that is to say, we imposed stricter surveillance around the truly sensitive parts of installations.

With the development of electronics, one of the less attractive aspects of the mechanism of security in recent years has been the tapping of telephone conversations and the clandestine monitoring of conferences in offices. These practices have always been repugnant to me as a matter of principle. In July 1953, on my first day in the office as Chairman of the Commission, when I sat at my desk my knee touched a projection which proved to be a toggle switch. The wires connected to it were traced to a tape recorder concealed in an alcove behind the fireplace. The device was dust-covered, showing no signs of recent use, and, in fairness to my predecessor, I must add that no member of the office staff I inherited ever knew it to have been used. I had it taken out immediately. Some eleven months later, a columnist who has been characterized as a liar by former Presidents,[13] wrote of "a recording device installed by Strauss at Commission meetings" and to "phone-tapping on behalf of Strauss." Both statements were false. At the time the installation was discovered, I showed it to two members of the Joint Committee. After the column appeared, Senator Hickenlooper stated on the floor of the Senate on June 9, 1954:

> The facts are that when Admiral Strauss took office as Chairman of the Atomic Energy Commission . . . he found that the offices were wired for recording. Within a few days of that discovery, he had the recording equipment and system ripped out of the office . . . I was in his office about 4 days after he assumed his duties. I saw the place where the secret recording devices had been installed, and I saw the evidence that they had been removed by the order and direction of Chairman Strauss. I have made a further check and I am completely convinced and satisfied that there is no secret tapping of the telephones of the Atomic Energy Commission.

* * *

Security of information can be relatively useless when leaks are occurring at the bottom of the structure, and it is far harder to impose it there than at the top. How simple it is to keep high officers in ignorance of what is taking place can be demonstrated. As related in the chapter on the decision to use the atomic bomb, Mr. Truman, while Vice President, had not been informed of the existence of nuclear weapons because by military criteria he had no "need to know." In his memoirs

Mr. Truman has written, "So strict was the secrecy imposed [in atomic energy matters] that even some of the highest ranking officials in Washington had not the slightest idea of what was going on. I did not." At the same time, two trade union officials were told.

Two years later the Secretaries of War and Navy were still unfamiliar with certain areas of information. The Atomic Energy Act of 1946 required the President periodically to instruct the Commission as to the number of atomic weapons it was to manufacture. The President acted upon recommendations on this subject from the two armed services secretaries—War and Navy. A recommendation was prepared for President Truman to be signed by Secretary of the Navy Forrestal and Secretary of War Patterson early in 1947. At dinner on March 19, Forrestal complained to me that he had before him for his signature a paper addressed to the President containing numbers for which he did not know the justification. It was thus that I discovered that the data on the stockpile and production of atomic weapons had been so very secret that neither the Secretary of the Navy nor the Chief of Naval Operations had been included among those informed. Accordingly, I arranged for a meeting in Forrestal's office on March 26 at which, in the presence of Fleet Admiral Nimitz, the Chief of Naval Operations, Vice Admiral Ramsey and Admiral Forrest Sherman, a briefing was presented by Rear Admiral Parsons, the only naval officer in Washington possessing the information.

Later that day I mentioned the meeting to General Brereton, then Chairman of the Military Liaison Committee. I suggested that he might look into the situation in the War Department. He found that the Secretary of War was likewise uninformed and on March 28 wrote a request that a briefing be arranged for Secretary Patterson and a few officers of the highest rank and responsibility.

The point of this incident is that during the same period that responsible officials at the very top of the defense establishment were uninformed on certain vital defense data, Soviet spies were operating in our establishments, and one of the most dangerous of them, Klaus Fuchs, who had returned to England, was being specifically invited back, to revisit our atomic installations. Of course, he came. It is not a new observation that the barn door can be closed on the wrong side of the horse.

Personnel security, plant security, and security of information are aspects of war whether it be hot or cold. The question of whether we must live with security for as long as we can see ahead is really a question of whether by some affirmative steps we can secure peace. The resolutions passed by organizations of men of good will frequently call upon the President and the Congress "to reach an agreement with the Soviets for mutual disarmament under terms which both governments will respect" or language to the same effect. This seems so reasonable to many reasonable men that they cannot comprehend why such an agreement can be difficult to negotiate. They should read the record on the frustrations of negotiating with the Soviets either at summits or in the valleys.

The Soviet Government has an international policy which is no secret. It is frequently reaffirmed. It is basic to the Marxist program and has been restated by heads of the Russian state from Lenin down to and including its present leader. No one can argue that the Free World is not on adequate notice of the aggressive program of Communism. Hitler's *Mein Kampf* was a similar volunteered insight into his totalitarian world strategy. Revelation of long-range planning appears to be a compulsive weakness of tyrants, and we ought to take advantage of it the better to protect ourselves.

With another war threatening widespread devastation, three courses of action are open. One, of course, is that the Free World can surrender. The decision is usually sugar-coated with semantics. This course of action has been seriously proposed by some who equate a World War III with the destruction of all life and who value survival above freedom. Lord Russell is the best known spokesman for this point of view. In a television interview, in March 1958, he is reported to have said, "If the Communists conquered the world, it would be very complex for a while, but not forever." In a letter quoted in the Washington *Post* on May 9, 1958, he wrote, "I favor negotiations between them for the abolition of nuclear weapons on both sides. I do hold, however, that if all negotiations prove futile and no alternative remains except Communist domination or extinction of the human race, the former alternative is the lesser of two evils." This has since appeared as the slogan "Better Red than dead" —a false limitation on the possible alternatives. These are sentiments which would be intolerable to men who over the ages have been willing to give their lives for freedom, and besmirch the memory of men who have.

It is no doubt true that such a course might secure peace, of a kind. It would be the peace of the police state and slavery for the great majority of men and the peace of the grave for those who held it unacceptable to live other than free.

A second course of action, put forward as a moral alternative, is that we *unilaterally* disarm and attempt by nobility of example to convince the Communists that their world program is wrong. This is something like saving one's life in the jungle by a symbolic attempt to convert tigers to vegetarianism. We have no channel of communication for an attempt to domesticate Communism. We cannot communicate at all with the Russians in the area of divine imperatives, or of morals, or ethics. Honesty, truth, and solemn covenants appear to be abstractions which have existence for them only as bait for those of other nations naïve enough to believe in them. The Ten Commandments and the Sermon on the Mount are "antique dogmas" which Communism heaved into the dustbin in 1917. How does one proceed to convince a government that it is wrong when it exists on the premise that whatever *it* does is right, and that *it* alone defines right and wrong?

Very different from surrender, or from trying to convert the Soviets to peace for the sake of peace, is the third course of action: to try to convince them that war will not profit them—that they cannot succeed with it. We have been engaged on this course for the past fifteen years. Continuing that course means keeping strong militarily, ahead of the Soviets in both military and peaceful technology if possible. This has been described by some as perpetuating an atomic arms race begun by President Truman's decision of January 31, 1950, to initiate work on thermonuclear weapons. But in fact it had begun years earlier—perhaps soon after our atomic project was launched, although we did not discover it until the day in August 1949 when the radioactive debris from a Russian atomic weapons test first reached our monitoring system. We cannot *unilaterally* disengage ourselves from this race without risking the certain loss of our freedom.

Meanwhile we have been living in peace. Certainly it is not an ideal peace. It is uneasy, expensive, and wasteful, but it is infinitely preferable to either war or surrender. On our side in this third course could be—time. We can make time our active ally if we can use it wisely by husbanding our economic strength and by maintaining at peak efficiency our military strength. Security meanwhile will continue to be one of the most essential elements in our defense.

XIV

Decision in the Case of
Dr. J. R. Oppenheimer

In the chill of late afternoon on December 3, 1953, there was a telephone message from the White House. President Eisenhower wished to see me immediately. Ushered into the large oval office dominated by the great desk of the President at its southern end, I found a meeting in session. Gathered about the President were Secretary of Defense Charles E. Wilson, Attorney General Herbert Brownell, Director of Defense Mobilization Dr. Arthur S. Flemming, and Special Assistant to the President for National Security Matters General Robert Cutler. General Wilton B. Persons, Assistant to the President, sat on a couch near the wall on the President's right. He followed the conversation attentively but did not participate in it.

A bulky file of papers lay on the desk blotter. Indicating it, the President asked whether I was familiar with a report which J. Edgar Hoover, Director of the Federal Bureau of Investigation, had prepared on the subject of Dr. J. Robert Oppenheimer.

I was. As Dr. Oppenheimer was then a consultant under contract to the Atomic Energy Commission, I had received a copy of the report from Mr. Hoover directly, had noted it, and had sent it to my fellow Commissioners for their information. Unlike myself, none of them had been a Commissioner in 1947, when Dr. Oppenheimer was appointed to the General Advisory Committee, the body composed mainly of scientists, which was established by law to counsel the Commission.

The report was a review of voluminous data concerning Dr. Oppenheimer, originally collected by the security staff of General Groves and then in the files of the Department of Justice. I had become acquainted with much of it when the Atomic Energy Commission was organized in 1947 and when the question of Dr. Oppenheimer's clearance was considered, affirmatively, by the Commission, of which I was at the time a member.

Director Hoover's decision to review the record was the result of a sensational letter written to him on November 7, 1953, by William L. Borden. Mr. Borden had been a responsible official in the legislative branch of the Government, and his statements could not be brushed aside. He had been engaged by the Joint Congressional Committee on Atomic Energy as the Executive Director of its staff during the administration of President Truman and while Senator Brien McMahon of Connecticut was Chairman of the Committee. By virtue of the position he held, Borden had access to Secret and Top Secret information concerning atomic energy matters, and it was in this capacity that he had become concerned about Dr. Oppenheimer. It was understood that Borden had been an Air Force Pilot for three years, assigned to the 8th Air Force during the war, with an excellent combat record. He had graduated from Yale with an LL.B., and his letter indicated that as a lawyer he was aware of the serious character of the charges it contained.

Borden had begun his service with Senator McMahon just before my resignation from the Commission four years earlier, and I had met him at that time but had not seen him since Senator McMahon's funeral in 1952. He had resigned from his connection with the Joint Congressional Committee after the Republican Congress of 1953 reorganized it.

His letter, as it was later introduced in evidence in the hearing, made most serious charges about Dr. Oppenheimer.[1]

The President indicated that he was very much disturbed by what he had read and asked whether the Atomic Energy Commission, as the responsible organization, had conducted a hearing on the charges as required by Executive Order 10450 (issued in April 1953). I replied that there had been no hearing since the order was promulgated but that the AEC was engaged in applying the directive to all employees. This, I added, would include contract consultants, such as Dr. Oppenheimer, in due course. The President ending the meeting, directed that a "blank wall" should be placed between Dr. Oppenheimer and any further access to Secret or Top Secret information until a hearing had been completed. He added that he wished to make it plain that he was not in any way prejudging the matter. At a later date, the President stated that the action he had taken seemed to him "compulsory" in the light of circumstances.[2]

Shortly after I returned to my office, a messenger arrived bearing an action copy of a memorandum from the President to the Attorney General. It confirmed the President's verbal directive and was worded in the same terms.

At this point, it might be informative to examine events preceding these two documents.

* * *

In the chapter on security, there has been described the procedure instituted by the Atomic Energy Commission in 1947 to deal with cases where the record contained evidence or allegations that an individual should not be hired for, or retained in Government service. The Commission was more liberal in its regulations than the long-established agencies of the Government, most of which operated on the principle that, upon the finding of reasonable doubt as to an individual's fitness, employment could be denied without explanation. Generally, there was no provision for a hearing nor for appeal from an adverse decision such as the Commission had established.

The Employment Security Program must have been well to the fore in the minds of President Eisenhower and his Cabinet in 1953, for it was discussed at one of the first Cabinet meetings after the Inauguration. Some ninety days later there was issued Executive Order 10450, "Security Requirements for Government Employment."

The order set new standards. Its preamble stated that the interests of national security required that all persons "privileged to be employed" by the Government shall be *reliable, trustworthy and of good conduct and character.*" (Italics supplied.) Government service was thus defined as a privilege—a doctrine which brought some criticism almost immediately. The criterion henceforth was not to be loyalty alone. As applied, the yardstick was more comprehensive so that untrustworthiness and personal misconduct were among other factors which, under the provisions of the executive order, might be found not "clearly consistent with the interests of the national security." These conditions, of course, had not been disregarded theretofore, but they were now specifically denominated.

The order standardized procedure among Government agencies and adopted many procedures already in use by the Atomic Energy Commission. The Commission, assured by counsel that its practices were in full accord with the new regulations, continued them without material change.

During his first few months after taking office, the President had learned of serious breaches of security due to a number of causes, including carelessness. One was the case of an individual who traveled to Washington carrying with him a document of the highest sensitivity and Top Secret classification. He inadvertently left it in the lavatory of a Pullman car. By the time he remembered and returned to retrieve it, it had disappeared. The presumption could not be dismissed that he had been followed by foreign agents who knew the nature of his work and took advantage of the opportunity his negligence presented. The President was disturbed and indignant. He was also reported to be concerned by the fact that during the first four months of the security review, begun pursuant to his executive order, a total of 863 persons had been dismissed from Government service and 593 employees had resigned without asking for a hearing when notified of certain information in their records.[3]

Like concern had been evidenced for some time in both England and France. As previously noted, no less a person than Dr. Frédéric Joliot-Curie, one of the most distinguished French physicists, had been separated from the French atomic energy project in April of 1950. It will be recalled that in 1939, when Russia and Germany were allied, he had declined to join the scientists of Great Britain and the United States in the voluntary withholding from publication of scientific reports on uranium fission.[4]

My acquaintance with Dr. Oppenheimer dated from 1945. He was recognized as the genius who had organized the atomic weapons laboratory at Los Alamos and to whom enormous credit was due for the success which had been achieved there. Although many men had participated importantly, none contested attributing to Dr. Oppenheimer's direction the paramount contribution. We first met during a conference in the office of the Secretary of War shortly after I had succeeded Under Secretary Ralph Bard as representative of the Navy on the Interim Committee on Atomic Energy. We did not meet again until 1946, when, after nomination to the Atomic Energy Commission, the Commissioners flew to California to visit the Radiation Laboratory at Berkeley. We were met at the airport by an old friend, Dr. Ernest O. Lawrence, and by Dr. Oppenheimer, who had resigned his position as director of the laboratory at Los Alamos and had returned to teaching.

Several years previously I had been elected a trustee of the Institute for Advanced Study at Princeton and had been appointed chairman of a trustee committee to find a director for the institute to succeed Dr. Frank Aydelotte. I consulted personal friends on the faculty, including

Dr. von Neumann, Dr. Edward Meade Earle, and Dr. Oswald Veblen. Veblen informed me that there had been a faculty committee on the subject some years before, whereupon he opened his safe and took out an envelope containing a list of names. There were five names in all, the first being that of Dr. Oppenheimer.

I also sought the views of Dr. Abraham Flexner, who had been the first director of the institute, and of Dr. Einstein, an early member of its faculty. Dr. Flexner was opposed to the selection of Dr. Oppenheimer for reasons which seemed to me somewhat irrelevant. He wrote me strong letters on the subject both then and later. Dr. Einstein, then suffering from an attack of jaundice, was living in the house of his physician within a few doors of my home on East Seventy-sixth Street in New York. He received me in his familiar costume of tennis sneakers, gray slacks, and sweat shirt. I could not persuade the venerable scientist to comment on any of the names which appeared on the faculty memorandum, nor to propose any candidates of his own. Regretfully I observed that my visit to him would be a "water haul," using the fishing term for a seine brought up empty. Dr. Einstein's eyes brightened. "What is it—a water haul?" he asked. Explaining, I besought him to tell me, at the very least, what ideal qualities the trustees should seek in a director of the institute. "Ah, that I can do gladly," he replied with a smile. "You should look for a very quiet man who will not disturb people who are trying to think."

I communicated with the members of our committee to suggest that under the circumstances we should sound out the availability of those on the list, beginning, in the order of their listing, with Dr. Oppenheimer, and received their approval with the exception of Trustee Lewis Douglas, who was then our Ambassador to Great Britain.

By the time Dr. Oppenheimer met the Commissioners at the airport on the occasion of the visit just mentioned, I had been authorized by the board of the institute to offer him the directorship. We walked apart from the others on the concrete apron in front of one of the hangars. I put the proposal before him. He indicated that his response would probably be affirmative but asked for time to consider it. Following word that he sent to me some time later, he was formally elected. We were to see each other frequently thereafter both in that connection and in his relationship to the Atomic Energy Commission.

Dr. Oppenheimer's influence in the early years of the Atomic Energy Commission was very great. It was understood that he was largely responsible for drafting the report of the panel of consultants to the

Secretary of State on the international control of atomic energy. This document was a forerunner of the McMahon Act. The report stands up well even at this date (except for a section which states, with some qualifications, that U-235 and plutonium can be "denatured" and thus rendered unavailable for bombs with no loss in effectiveness for peaceful applications).

The Atomic Energy Act provided for the organization of a General Advisory Committee of nine men to be appointed by the President. While not specifically limited to scientists as its members, it was to advise the Commission "on scientific and technical matters." The Commissioners submitted a list of names to President Truman, who promptly appointed them, and at their first meeting Dr. Oppenheimer was chosen as first Chairman of what is usually known by its initials as the GAC. He continued to serve in that capacity until 1952.

In recommending Dr. Oppenheimer to the President for appointment to the General Advisory Committee, the Commission reviewed a file of information about him as of that date. The Commission also had before it certain information from General Groves, who, as I have said, commanding the Manhattan District, had maintained his own security organization independently of the Army G-2. Within a few days after the Atomic Energy Commission had assembled for the first time in 1946, General Groves had addressed the Chairman:

November 14, 1946

Dear Mr. Lilienthal:

I desire to bring to your attention that in the past I have considered it in the best interests of the United States to clear certain individuals for work on the Manhattan project despite evidence indicating considerable doubt as to their character, associations, and absolute loyalty.

Such individuals are generally persons whose particular scientific or technical knowledge was vital to the accomplishment of the Manhattan project mission. In some instances, lack of time prevented our completely investigating certain persons prior to their working for the Manhattan project, so that in some cases individuals, on whom it was subsequently determined that derogatory information existed, had access to project information.

With the appointment of the Commission and the legal provisions for investigation of personnel by the Federal Bureau of Investigation, I see no reason why those persons on whom derogatory information exists cannot be eliminated. I unhesitatingly recommend that you give the most careful consideration to the problem.

The FBI is cognizant of all individuals now employed on the Manhattan project on whom derogatory information exists.

Sincerely yours,
L. R. Groves, Major General, USA.

Chairman Lilienthal in his reply remarked that, since the persons referred to in General Groves's letter had been continuously employed beyond the accomplishment of the mission of the Manhattan Project, it was to be inferred that General Groves did not regard their presence as a source of critical hazard. To this, General Groves responded on December 19 that the removal of these individuals was a rather slow process and "whenever possible such removals have been effected by us through administrative means when the individuals could be conveniently relieved of such assignments . . . It would seem to me," he added, "that, with the reinvestigation of all Manhattan project personnel by the Federal Bureau of Investigation, you could find it appropriate to effect the removal of the remaining individuals of questionable character."*

In a memorandum which General Groves wrote to the Secretary of War four months later (on March 24, 1947), he stated that [in 1942] he had concluded it to be in the best interest of the United States to use Dr. Oppenheimer's services despite the fact that "the security organization, then not under my control [he had just taken charge of the project], did not wish to clear Dr. Oppenheimer because of certain of his associations, particularly those of the past." General Groves concluded his memorandum:

In connection with the above statement, it must be remembered that the provisions of the Atomic Energy Act of 1946 did not control my actions prior to the enactment of that law. My decisions in respect to clearance of personnel were based on what I believed to be the best overall interests of the United States under the then existing circumstances. As I have long since informed the Atomic Energy Commission, I do not consider that all persons cleared for employment by

---

* Dr. Oppenheimer, having left the Manhattan project before these letters were written, was not one of those persons whose elimination from the project they suggested, but they became relevant when he returned to government service and his clearance again came under consideration. General Groves testified before the Gray Board that although he did not have Dr. Oppenheimer in mind when he wrote the letters "if he had been a member of the Manhattan project at the time, he would have been one of these about whom I was thinking." (Hearing Transcript, page 170)

the Manhattan District, while under my command, should be automatically cleared by the Atomic Energy Commission, but that that Commission should exercise its own independent judgment based on present circumstances.

The Commission exercised its independent judgment and on the basis of the information then available to it approved the "clearance" of Dr. Oppenheimer.

Elsewhere I have related how the first detection of a Russian atomic test occurred and of the debate which ensued over the wisdom and feasibility of developing a qualitatively superior weapon. The General Advisory Committee, of which Dr. Oppenheimer was then Chairman, was asked for its advice. They counseled against proceeding with the project at that time. This recommendation was reported to the Commission by Dr. Oppenheimer as the unanimous decision of the General Advisory Committee. One member, however, Dr. Glenn T. Seaborg,[5] did not concur, although this was not known to the Commission until some four years later, when a letter from him to Dr. Oppenheimer, written before the Commission meeting, was found in Dr. Oppenheimer's official files, and was put in the record of the security hearing.

The great debate of the winter of 1949–50 on the subject of the "super" was resolved on January 31, 1950, by President Truman's decision to proceed with it as a matter of urgency. Klaus Fuchs had meanwhile been apprehended and confessed that he had given information to the Soviets on all he had learned about our weapons while at work in our laboratories.

Contrary to predictions, the Commission experienced no difficulty in finding dedicated scientists who were willing to work on the H-bomb and who supported the decision of the President. During this period, Dr. Oppenheimer and I were on opposite sides of the debate, but there were no personal animosities. He was a guest in my home and on occasion, when in Princeton, I was his guest at the residence provided for him as director of the Institute for Advanced Study.

My predecessor as Chairman of the Commission, Gordon Dean, had informed me in the spring of 1952 that he felt a change in the composition and the chairmanship of the General Advisory Committee would be beneficial and, accordingly, Dr. Oppenheimer retired both as chairman and as a member, before President Eisenhower's election and a year before my reappointment to the AEC. In 1952, Dean had executed a one-year consultant contract with Dr. Oppenheimer. It was renewed for a further year just prior to the expiration of Dean's term on June 30, 1953. It was this contract which involved the AEC in the clearance of Dr. Oppenheimer and which required that the Commission, rather than some other agency of the Government, was made responsible to hear and resolve the charges against him.

* * *

With the President's directive on my desk, I was troubled as to the next step to be taken, for earlier in the week the President had instructed me to be prepared to leave with him at seven-thirty the following morning for Bermuda, where a meeting had been arranged with Prime Minister Churchill and Premier Laniel of France. Commissioners Murray and Zuckert were out of the city, as was the General Manager of the Commission. I called in the acting General Manager, Walter Williams, and told him of the circumstances. Later I was able to reach Commissioner Smyth, who was confined to his home with a bronchial ailment. I asked Williams to try to assemble the Commissioners on the following day and explain the matter in my absence.

A further meeting on the subject by the Commission was held on December 10 after my return from Bermuda. All the Commissioners were present and I reported the suspension of Dr. Oppenheimer's clearance by the President's order. On December 15, Dr. Smyth, who at a later date was to be the only Commissioner to vote in favor of restoring Dr. Oppenheimer's clearance, sent me a memorandum in which he noted that "Borden's letter of accusation is important not because it brings forward new evidence of any consequence but because of the position he has held as head of the staff of the Joint Congressional Committee on Atomic Energy." He added that to ignore the Borden letter and to continue clearance were obviously unwise.

While these events were transpiring, Dr. Oppenheimer was in Europe. Upon his return, he was asked to come to Washington, and an appointment was arranged for the afternoon of December 21.

On the day before the appointment, a man named Herbert Marks telephoned our farm in Virginia. My wife answered. Mr. Marks told her that he had to see me on a subject of such urgency that it could be called "a matter of life and death." He proposed to drive to the farm, which my wife discouraged, hoping that we might get some rest. She suggested that he call at the AEC office in Washington the following morning. Mr. Marks had been the first General Counsel of the AEC and in that capacity had recommended the initial clearance of Dr. Oppenheimer by the Commission in 1947. Later in that year he had resigned, and subsequently had been counsel to Dr. Oppenheimer in personal matters.

At the appointed time, Marks came in. He began with a statement that what he had to say concerned Dr. Oppenheimer. I interrupted to say that Dr. Oppenheimer was coming to see me in the afternoon, adding, "Since you are his counsel, it's entirely appropriate that you be here with him if he desires it. But I can't discuss the subject with you in advance."

Marks replied that he knew nothing of Dr. Oppenheimer's scheduled visit and that, while at one time he had been the doctor's attorney, he was no longer acting in that capacity. He continued, then, saying that it had just come to his attention from sources that he was not at liberty to identify but which were completely reliable, that a Senate committee chaired by William Jenner was about to investigate Dr. Oppenheimer as its next piece of business. This, observed Marks, would be seriously embarrassing to the AEC and to the Vice President of the United States. Therefore, he pointed out, it should be headed off at once and by me.

"In what way will it embarrass the Vice President and the AEC?" I inquired.

At this, Marks took from his pocket a sheet of paper on which was pasted a clipping from the New York *Times* of May 11, 1950, reporting a speech by Mr. Nixon in California. Nixon, then a member of a congressional committee before which Dr. Oppenheimer had testified, was quoted as endorsing Dr. Oppenheimer. Marks suggested that, because Nixon had since become Vice President of the United States and would probably again be a candidate, he would be interested in having the investigation quashed.

I asked Marks if he had told Dr. Oppenheimer about this, and he said he had not spoken with him at all. He offered to leave the clipping, but I said that I did not intend to follow the matter. (No such proceeding was ever undertaken by the Jenner Committee and as far as I know was not in contemplation.) Marks left.

When Dr. Oppenheimer arrived, we were joined by General Nichols, then General Manager of the AEC, and took seats at a table ordinarily used for executive sessions of the Commissioners. We talked about Admiral Parsons, a mutual friend, whose unexpected death, following a heart attack some two weeks earlier, had been a great shock to all of us. I then mentioned the visit that morning of Herbert Marks but did not pursue the subject when Dr. Oppenheimer indicated that he had

Official U. S. Air Force photo

16. "One of our planes operating in the Long Range Detection System collected an air sample that was decidedly radioactive. . . ." The plane: a WB-29, a type now obsolete. The sample: Russian.

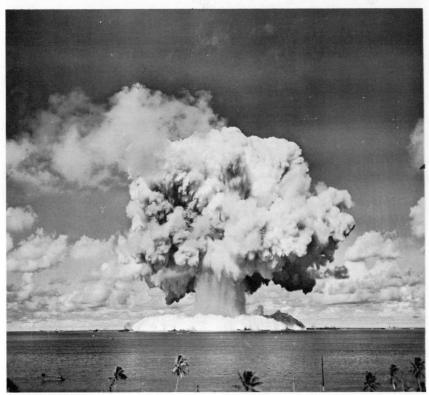

U. S. Navy

17. Was the fleet now obsolete? Small by comparison with later results, this underwater explosion tested the effects on naval vessels (visible at the base of the enormous column of water) at Operation Crossroads, Marshall Islands, 1946.

18. Captain W. S. ("Deke") Parsons, who acted as weaponeer on the flight over Hiroshima.

19. "I have conscientiously weighed the record...Dr. Oppenheimer's clearance should not be reinstated." Major General Kenneth D. Nichols, General Manager of the Atomic Energy Commission; before that, second-in-command of the Manhattan Project from its inception.

20. Robert A. Taft. "Only a few weeks earlier...I brought him the final and terrible verdict."

21. "The Prof," as he was affectionately styled by his Prime Minister, Dr. Frederick A. Lindemann (Lord Cherwell) served, not only as Churchill's chief scientific consultant, but as adviser in matters of broad policy.

22. The great scientist celebrated his seventy-second birthday by presenting the first Albert Einstein Medals and Prizes at a brief ceremony in Princeton, New Jersey. The recipients were Kurt Gödel and Julian Schwinger.

23. "...in early January, he [Secretary of Defense James V. Forrestal] asked me to lunch in his dining room at the Pentagon. I was shocked by the change in his appearance." From the chapter "A View of the Navy from the Beach."

24. The Atomic Energy Commission meets with its new chairman in 1953. By that time, growing opportunities and problems included the development of peaceful uses for atomic power and the manufacture of more sophisticated weapons. Left to right: Eugene M. Zuckert, Harry D. Smyth, the author, Thomas E. Murray, Joseph Campbell, and General Manager Marion Boyer.

not known of it. The conversation turned to the subject for which the meeting had been arranged. Dr. Oppenheimer was informed that under the executive order of the President the files of all Government employees concerning whom there was any derogatory information had to be re-evaluated. Dr. Oppenheimer knew that his file contained much material in this category. Commenting on this, he said that he was aware of Executive Order 10450 of the preceding April, and realized that in due course his case would be reached. He was then told that a former Government official who had occupied a responsible position in the preceding administration had made a statement concerning him which had occasioned a special and detailed report to the President by the Federal Bureau of Investigation. The established Commission procedure (with which Dr. Oppenheimer was familiar) was then outlined, and he was told that the first step would require the suspension of his clearance pending a hearing.

The large octagonal room in which we were seated had been the scene of meetings of the Combined Chiefs of Staff during World War II, and important decisions had been taken there—none more personally difficult than this one. On notice for nearly two weeks that this meeting would be inevitable I had tried unsuccessfully to think of language which would soften the impact of what had to be said.

I outlined, although he knew them, the rights he had. They were the right to challenge the appointees to the Security Panel; the right to testify; to produce his own witnesses; to cross-examine witnesses against him; to be represented by counsel; and, in the event of an unfavorable decision, to appeal it to the Commission.

A letter which the General Manager had prepared but had not yet signed was then handed to Dr. Oppenheimer in draft. He read it carefully, commenting afterwards that there were many statements in it which were correct, and others that were incorrect.

He said that there might be some merit in resigning instead of having a hearing and asked me what I thought of the alternative. I felt unable to advise him. A resignation might carry connotations a hearing might dispel. On the spur of the moment it was not possible to be sure which course of action would have been the most prudent, and I am uncertain even now as to which would have been the wiser. Resignation would have left all the charges on the record. (The charge of disloyalty was settled in his favor by the opinion of the panel.)

Dr. Oppenheimer said he wished to think the subject over and mentioned the fact that the Jenner Committee might be holding public hearings and his resignation prior to such hearings might be poor public relations from his point of view. He seemed to feel that I favored his resignation rather than a hearing, and I took pains to impress upon him that he was not to consider that I had recommended either course of action as against the other and that he ought to seek advice from counsel.

Dr. Oppenheimer asked for time to reach his decision. He said that he intended to consult Herbert Marks.

Some other procedural details were discussed by the General Manager, bearing upon the steps the Commission would take after learning of Dr. Oppenheimer's election of the course he would follow, and it was understood that the entire subject would be classified Confidential by the Commission.

In taking leave, Dr. Oppenheimer asked if the circumstances were known "on the Hill." He was told that so far as the Commission was aware it had not been reported, but that under the Commission's obligations to keep the Joint Congressional Committee informed it could not be withheld from them.

Dr. Oppenheimer said that he saw no option to the Commission but the alternatives which had been discussed and if it came to that he would regret severing his relationship with the Government.

He left the office, saying that he was going to call on Mr. Marks.

When General Nichols returned to his office, he dictated his recollection of the conversation. Since there has been much conjecture and some misrepresentation about the circumstances, his memorandum in full will be found in the Appendix.[6]

Later, at the request of Dr. Oppenheimer's counsel, there were stays and postponements, and the hearing did not begin until mid-April.

As I have stated, the hearing procedures of the Commission provided that an individual whose employment or clearance was questioned could elect to appear before an independent panel of three individuals unconnected with the Commission and whose selection could be challenged by him. He could be represented by his own counsel and confront and cross-examine adverse witnesses and produce witnesses of his own. The finding of the panel could be appealed and would be ruled upon by the Commission itself. It was further stipulated that all hearings would be in closed sessions in order that the reputation of the individual might be protected. It was the policy of the Commission that no statements would be made by the Commission unless the individual made a statement at his own initiative.

In due course, Dr. Oppenheimer notified the Commission that he elected a hearing. General Manager Nichols delivered to him the signed original of the letter which he had read in its draft form on December 21. The full Commission thereupon met on December 23 and concurred with the procedures taken and planned.

In order to secure a panel of unquestioned probity and impartiality, Gordon Gray was requested to serve as its chairman. Mr. Gray was a Democrat with an eminent career in the law and as a newspaper publisher. He had volunteered as an enlisted man in World War II and had risen to the rank of captain in the European Theater of Operations. He later had a fine record under President Truman as Secretary of the Army and retired from public life to become president of the University of North Carolina. The second member was Thomas A. Morgan, also a Democrat, who had but recently retired after a successful business career as president of the Sperry Gyroscope Company. The third was Dr. Ward V. Evans, a Republican, who was professor of chemistry at Loyola University, Chicago. The Commission enlisted the services as counsel for the board of Roger Robb, a successful Washington attorney, whom I had never met.

The panel was duly appointed by the General Manager in accordance with the Commission's regulations and procedures. Before the panel had begun to hold its hearings and while even its existence was known presumably only to Dr. Oppenheimer, his counsel, and to those in the Government who were immediately concerned, a subordinate official in the Defense Department learned of it. One of the members of the panel, Mr. Morgan, received a telephone message from the official requesting an appointment. He then called on Morgan in New York. Morgan said that he had been urged to refuse service on the panel. Morgan reported this approach to the proper authorities. Despite its impropriety, I attributed it to a misdirected excess of zeal and requested that no action with respect to the official should be taken. There was no evidence that Dr. Oppenheimer or his associates had anything to do with the approach.

While the hearing was under way a series of personal attacks upon me, as Chairman of the Commission, began to appear in certain syndicated columns. The Gray panel itself also came under fire. For instance, the Atomic Energy Commissioners had met briefly with the panel for a formal introduction on April 5 before they convened for the hearing. It was the one and only meeting I had with the members of the panel, either together or separately. Yet a columnist asserted that I was meeting with the panel at night during the hearings for the purpose of influencing their decision. This particular writer obtained an appointment with a member of the President's staff and made that charge, thereby not only slandering me but more importantly reflecting on the integrity of the three members of the panel, who were performing a necessary public service.

* * *

As in another prominent security case some years earlier, many important men, as character witnesses, attested to Dr. Oppenheimer's reliability and integrity. They included college presidents, scientists, former members of the Commission, and others who used superlatives to describe their regard for him. Also, taking the stand as a witness was General Groves, who had been his employer. He was asked whether in the light of his experience with security matters and in the light of his knowledge of the file pertaining to Dr. Oppenheimer, he would "clear Dr. Oppenheimer today." The General thereupon read the pertinent section of the Atomic Energy Law and gave his interpretation of the reference to endangering the common defense and security. He said, "I don't care how important the man is, if there is any possibility other than a tortured one that his associations or his loyalty or his character might endanger [sic]. In this case I refer particularly to associations and not to the associations as they exist today but the past record of associations. I would not clear Dr. Oppenheimer today if I were a member of the Commission on the basis of this interpretation.

"If the interpretation is different, then I would have to stand on my interpretation of it."[7]

The findings and recommendation fill twenty-one closely printed pages and the transcript of the hearing nearly a thousand more. Quite early in the course of it, there appeared an unusual colloquy between members of the panel and counsel for Dr. Oppenheimer on the subject of two documents[8] which were a part of the proceedings treated as "Confidential" by the panel but which had been leaked to the press. On the first day, Dr. Oppenheimer and his counsel had informed the panel that their belated arrival at the hearing was due to the fact that they had their "fingers in the dike" to keep the proceedings from leaking. Later the record showed that the material which had appeared in the press had been handed to a reporter by one of counsel for Dr. Oppenheimer. Panel Chairman Gray thereupon observed, "So that you knew when you made the statement here yesterday morning that you were keeping the finger in the dike, that these documents dated December 23 and March 4 were already in the possession of the New York Times." At this point, Herbert Marks's name again came into the story. The panel chairman inquired as to the status of Marks and was told that he was "not counsel of record in this proceeding." Following further questions, however, Marks was identified as "of counsel."

Eventually the hearings were concluded and the panel addressed its findings to General Manager Nichols. By a vote of 2 to 1, they recommended against the reinstatement of Dr. Oppenheimer's clearance for access to secret data.

The General Manager, in summing up and transmitting his recommendations to the Commission on June 12, wrote a strongly worded concurrence with the majority. His published report is a part of the official record.[9]

United States Atomic Energy Commission
Washington 25, D.C.
June 12, 1954

Memorandum for: Mr. Strauss, Dr. Smyth, Mr. Murray,
                         Mr. Zuckert, Mr. Campbell

Subject: Dr. J. Robert Oppenheimer.

On December 23, 1953, Dr. J. Robert Oppenheimer was notified that his security clearance had been suspended, and informed of his right to a hearing under AEC procedures. By telegram dated January 29, 1954, Dr. Oppenheimer requested that he be afforded a hearing and on March 4, 1954, after requesting and receiving three extensions of time, he submitted his answer to my letter of December 23, 1953.

Mr. Gordon Gray, Mr. Thomas A. Morgan and Dr. Ward V. Evans agreed to serve as members of the Personnel Security Board to hear Dr. Oppenheimer's case. The Board submitted its findings and recommendation to me on May 27, 1954. A majority of the Board recommended against reinstatement of clearance, Dr. Evans dissenting.

On May 28, 1954, I notified Dr. Oppenheimer of the recommendation of the Personnel Security Board and forwarded to him a copy of the Board's findings and recommendation. I informed Dr. Oppenheimer of his right to request review of his case by the Personnel Security Review Board and informed him that upon full consideration of the entire record in the case, including the recommendation of the Personnel Security Review Board in the event he requested review by that Board, I would submit to the Commission my recommendation as to whether or not his clearance should be reinstated. I also informed him that the final determination would be made by the Commission.

By letter of June 1, 1954, Dr. Oppenheimer waived his right to a review of his case by the Personnel Security Review Board and requested an immediate consideration of his case by the Commission.

FACTORS CONSIDERED

In making my findings and determination I have considered the question whether a security risk is involved in continued clearance of Dr. Oppenheimer. I have taken into account his contributions to the United States atomic energy program and in addition I have, in accordance with AEC procedures, considered the effect which denial of security clearance would have upon the program.

DR. OPPENHEIMER'S WORLD WAR II CONTRIBUTION

Dr. Oppenheimer has been intimately associated with the atomic energy program virtually from its inception. He participated in early weapons research and was selected as the wartime Director of the Los Alamos Laboratory. As district engineer of the wartime Manhattan Engineer District, I was keenly aware of the contribution he made to the initial development of the atomic bomb. His leadership and direction of the Los Alamos weapons program were outstanding; his contributions leading to a successful atomic weapon have properly received worldwide acknowledgement and acclaim.

WORLD WAR II CLEARANCE 1943

As deputy district engineer of the Manhattan District, I was also aware of the circumstances, which have been brought out in the record, surrounding Dr. Oppenheimer's appointment as head of the Los Alamos Laboratory, and his subsequent clearance. He was selected in spite of the fact that he was considered a "calculated risk." He would not have been chosen had he not been considered virtually indispensable to the atomic bomb program. After he was chosen as General Groves testified before the Board, Dr. Oppenheimer probably would not have been cleared had he not already been thoroughly steeped in knowledge of weapons research and had he not been considered absolutely essential.

Security officers opposed the clearance of Dr. Oppenheimer and it was not until July of 1943, after he had participated in the program for many months, that the decision to clear him was made by General Groves. I personally signed the directive advising the commanding officer at Los Alamos that there was no objection to Dr. Oppenheimer's employment.

The Manhattan District had one mandate—to build an atomic bomb as quickly as possible. Fears that Germany would build an atomic weapon first and possibly win the war thereby spurred the Manhattan District in what was felt to be a race against the German effort. Communist Russia was also fighting Germany at that time.

General Groves testified before the Board that he did not regret having made the decision to clear Dr. Oppenheimer in consideration of all of the circumstances which confronted him in 1943 but that under the present requirements of the Atomic Energy Act, as he interprets them, he would not clear Dr. Oppenheimer today.

BASIS FOR CLEARANCE UNDER ATOMIC ENERGY ACT AND EXECUTIVE ORDER 10450

In this case as well as in all personnel security cases, the AEC in granting or reinstating a clearance must determine that the common defense and security will not be endangered. Under the Atomic Energy Act, such determination must be made on the basis of the character, associations, and loyalty of the individual concerned. Thus, a finding of loyalty in any given case does not suffice; substantial deficiency in any one of the three factors—character, associations, or loyalty— may prevent the determination that permitting such person to have access to restricted data will not endanger the common defense or security.

In addition, the criteria set up by Executive Order 10450 must be considered. This order requires that a program be established to insure that the retention in employment of any employee is clearly consistent with the interests of national security.

SECURITY FINDINGS

I have reviewed the entire record of the case, including the files, the transcript of the hearing, the findings and recommendation of the Personnel Security Board, and the briefs filed by Dr. Oppenheimer's attorneys on May 17, 1954, and June 7, 1954, and have reached the conclusion that to reinstate the security clearance of Dr. Oppenheimer would not be clearly consistent with the interests of national security and would endanger the common defense and security.

I concur with the findings and recommendation of the majority of the Personnel Security Board and submit them in support of this memorandum. In addition, I refer in particular to the following considerations:

1. Dr. Oppenheimer's Communist activities. —The record contains no direct evidence that Dr. Oppenheimer gave secrets to a foreign nation or that he is disloyal to the United States. However, the record does contain substantial evidence of Dr. Oppenheimer's association with Communists, Communist functionaries, and Communists who did engage in espionage. He was not a mere "parlor pink" or student of communism as a result of immaturity and intellec-

tual curiosity, but was deeply and consciously involved with hardened and militant Communists at a time when he was a man of mature judgement.

His relations with these hardened Communists were such that they considered him to be one of their number. He admits that he was a fellow traveler, and that he made substantial cash contributions direct to the Communist Party over a period of 4 years ending in 1942. The record indicates that Dr. Oppenheimer was a Communist in every respect except for the fact that he did not carry a party card.

These facts raise serious questions as to Dr. Oppenheimer's eligibility for clearance reinstatement.

It is suggested that Dr. Oppenheimer has admitted many of the facts concerning his past association with Communists and the Communist Party. Whether this be true or not, it appears to me that Dr. Oppenheimer's admissions in too many cases have followed, rather than preceded, investigation which developed the facts. It appears that he is not inclined to disclose the facts spontaneously, but merely to confirm those already known. I find no great virtue in such a plea of guilt; certainly it does not cause me to dismiss Dr. Oppenheimer's past associations as matters of no consequence simply on the ground that he has admitted them.

2. The Chevalier incident.* —Dr. Oppenheimer's involvement in the Chevalier incident, and his subsequent conduct with respect to it, raise grave questions of security import.

---

* In 1943, while in charge of the Los Alamos Laboratory, Dr. Oppenheimer was interviewed by Colonel Pash, an officer of the U. S. Army Military Intelligence charged with the duty of protecting the atomic weapons project against spies. Dr. Oppenheimer told Colonel Pash, in detail, of an attempt on behalf of Soviet espionage to obtain from him information about the work on the atom bomb. Although he refused to disclose to Colonel Pash the name of the person making the approach, he subsequently identified him as Haakon Chevalier. Chevalier was a professional colleague and, at that time, a friend of Dr. Oppenheimer. The record includes Dr. Oppenheimer's testimony that his conversation with Chevalier about transmitting technical information to Soviet personages was brief and innocuous but that when questioned about it by Colonel Pash, he invented "a cock-and-bull story" involving the Russian Consulate, the use of microfilm, and approaches to three persons in the atom bomb project. The testimony (transcript pages 137 and 149) reads in part as follows:

Q. Now let us go back to your interview with Colonel Pash. Did you tell Pash the truth about this thing?
A. No.
Q. You lied to him?

If in 1943, as he now claims to have done, he knowingly and willfully made false statements to Colonel Pash, a Federal officer, Dr. Oppenheimer violated what was then Section 80, Title 18, of the the United States Code;* in other words if his present story is true then he admits he committed a felony in 1943. On the other hand, as Dr. Oppenheimer admitted on cross-examination, if the story Dr. Oppenheimer told Colonel Pash was true, it not only showed that Chevalier was involved in a criminal espionage conspiracy, but also reflected seriously on Dr. Oppenheimer himself.

After reviewing both the 16-page transcript (as accepted by the Board) of the interview between Dr. Oppenheimer and Colonel Pash on August 26, 1943, and recent testimony before the Board, it is difficult to conclude that the detailed and circumstantial account given by Dr. Oppenheimer to Colonel Pash was false and that the story now told by Dr. Oppenheimer is an honest one. Dr. Oppenheimer's story in 1943 was most damaging to Chevalier. If Chevalier was Dr. Oppenheimer's friend and Dr. Oppenheimer, as he now says, believed Chevalier to be innocent and wanted to protect him, why then would he tell such a complicated false story to Colonel Pash? This story

---

A. Yes.

. . . .

Q. Why did you go into such great circumstantial detail about this thing if you were telling a cock and bull story?

A. I fear that this whole thing is a piece of idiocy. I am afraid I can't explain why there was a consul, why there was microfilm, why there were three people on the project, why two of them were at Los Alamos. All of them seems wholly false to me.

Q. You will agree, would you not, sir, that if the story you told to Colonel Pash was true, it made things look very bad for Mr. Chevalier?

A. For anyone involved in it, yes, sir.

Q. Including you?

A. Right.

Q. Isn't it a fair statement today, Dr. Oppenheimer, that according to your testimony now you told not one lie to Colonel Pash, but a whole fabrication and tissue of lies?

A. Right.

Q. In great circumstantial detail, is that correct?

A. Right.

* 18 U. S. Code, sec. 80, provides in pertinent part: "Whoever *** shall knowingly or willfully falsify or conceal or cover up by any trick, scheme, or device a material fact, or make or cause to be made any false or fraudulent statement or representations *** in any matter within the jurisdiction or agency of the United States *** shall be fined not more than $10,000 or imprisoned not more than 10 years, or both."

showed that Chevalier was not innocent, but on the contrary was deeply involved in an espionage conspiracy. By the same token, why would Dr. Oppenheimer tell a false story to Colonel Pash which showed that he himself was not blameless? Is it reasonable to believe a man will deliberately tell a lie that seriously reflects upon himself and his friend, when he knows that the truth will show them both to be innocent?

It is important to remember also that Dr. Oppenheimer did not give his present version of the story until 1946, shortly after he had learned from Chevalier what Chevalier himself had told the FBI about the incident in question. After learning of this from Chevalier, Dr. Oppenheimer changed his story to conform to that given to the FBI by Chevalier.

From all of these facts and circumstances, it is a fair inference that Dr. Oppenheimer's story to Colonel Pash and other Manhattan District officials was substantially true and that his later statement on the subject to the FBI, and his recent testimony before the Personnel Security Board, were false.

Executive Order 10450, provides:

"Section 8 (a). The investigations conducted pursuant to this order shall be designed to develop information as to whether the employment or retention in employment in the Federal service of the person being investigated is clearly consistent with the interests of the national security. Such information shall relate, but shall not be limited, to the following:

(1) Depending on the relation of the Government employment to the national security:

(i) Any behavior, activities, or associations which tend to show that the individual is not reliable or trustworthy.

(ii) Any deliberate misrepresentations, falsifications, or omission of material facts.

(iii) Any criminal, infamous, dishonest, immoral, or notoriously disgraceful conduct, habitual use of intoxicants to excess, drug addiction, or sexual perversion."

In my opinion, Dr. Oppenheimer's behavior in connection with the Chevalier incident shows that he is not reliable or trustworthy; his own testimony shows that he was guilty of deliberate misrepresentations and falsifications either in his interview with Colonel Pash or in his testimony before the Board; and such misrepresentations and falsifications constituted criminal, *** dishonest *** conduct.

Further, the significance of the Chevalier incident combined with Dr. Oppenheimer's conflicting testimony from 1943 to 1954 in regard to it were not, of course, available in whole to General Groves in 1943, nor was the complete record on the Chevalier incident considered by the Atomic Energy Commission in 1947. Consideration of the complete record plus a cross-examination of Dr. Oppenheimer under oath were not accomplished by anyone prior to the Personnel Security Board hearing in 1954.

3. Dr. Oppenheimer's veracity. —A review of the record reveals other instances which raise a question as to the credibility of Dr. Oppenheimer in his appearance before the Personnel Security Board and as to his character and veracity in general.

(a) The record suggests a lack of frankness on the part of Dr. Oppenheimer in his interview with the FBI. It appears that during this hearing he recollected details concerning Communist meetings in the San Francisco area which he did not report in previous interviews with the FBI.

(b) Dr. Oppenheimer told the FBI in 1950 that he did not know that Joseph Weinberg was a Communist until it became a matter of public knowledge. When confronted with the transcript of his interview with Colonel Lansdale on September 12, 1943, he admitted that he had learned prior to that date that Weinberg was a Communist.

(c) It is clear from the record that Dr. Oppenheimer was a great deal more active in urging the deferment of Rossi Lomanitz and his retention on the atom bomb project than he said he was in his answer to my letter of December 23, 1953. Furthermore, Dr. Oppenheimer testified that if he had known that Lomanitz was a Communist he would not have written the letter to Colonel Lansdale of the Manhattan District on October 19, 1943, supporting Lomanitz' services for the project. However, the record reflects that Dr. Oppenheimer told Colonel Lansdale of the Manhattan District on September 12, 1943, that he had learned that Lomanitz was a Communist.

(d) Dr. Oppenheimer admitted in his testimony before the Board that in 1949 he wrote a letter to a newspaper which might have misled the public concerning his testimony before the House Un-American Activities Committee on Dr. Bernard Peters. He testified that an earlier article in the newspaper which summarized his testimony was accurate, yet the effect of his published letter was to repudiate the earlier article.

(e) Dr. Oppenheimer in his answer to my letter of December 23, 1953, and in his testimony before the Board with respect to the H-bomb program undertook to give the impression that in 1949 he and the GAC merely opposed a so-called "crash" program. It is quite clear from the record, however, that the position of the majority of the GAC, including Dr. Oppenheimer, was that a thermonuclear weapon should never be produced, and that the United States should make an unqualified commitment to this effect. In discussing the building of neutron-producing reactors, a majority of the GAC, including Dr. Oppenheimer, expressed the opinion that "the super program itself should not be undertaken and that the Commission and its contractors understand that construction of neutron-producing reactors is not intended as a step in the super program." The testimony of Dr. Oppenheimer viewed in light of the actual record certainly furnished adequate basis for the majority of the Board not believing that Dr. Oppenheimer was entirely candid with them on this point.

(f) Dr. Oppenheimer testified before the Board that the GAC was unanimous in its basic position on the H-bomb. He specifically said that Dr. Seaborg had not expressed his views and that there was no communication with him. It should be noted that the statement that "there was no communication with him" was volunteered by Dr. Oppenheimer in his testimony on cross-examination before the Board. However, Dr. Oppenheimer received a letter from Dr. Seaborg, expressing his views, prior to the October 29, 1949, GAC meeting.

4. Dr. Oppenheimer's continued associations after World War II. —Dr. Oppenheimer has continued associations which raise a serious question as to his eligibility for clearance. He has associated with Chevalier on a rather intimate basis as recently as December 1953, and at that time lent his name to Chevalier's dealings with the United States Embassy in Paris on a problem which, according to Dr. Oppenheimer, involved Chevalier's clearance. Since the end of World War II he has been in touch with Bernard Peters, Rossi Lomanitz, and David Bohm under circumstances which, to say the least, are disturbing.

5. Obstruction and disregard of security. —Dr. Oppenheimer's actions have shown a consistent disregard of a reasonable security system. In addition to the Chevalier incident, he has refused to answer questions put to him by security officers concerning his relationships and knowledge of particular individuals whom he knew to be Communists; and he has repeatedly exercised an arrogance of his own judgment with respect to the loyalty and reliability of his associates and his own conduct which is wholly inconsistent with the obligations necessarily imposed by an adequate security system on those who occupy high positions of trust and responsibility in the Government.

FINDING OF SECURITY RISK IS NOT BASED ON DR. OPPENHEIMER'S OPINIONS

Upon the foregoing considerations relating to the character and associations of Dr. Oppenheimer, I find that he is a security risk. In making this finding I wish to comment on the item of derogatory information contained in my letter of December 23, 1953 which relates to the hydrogen bomb and, in particular, which alleged that:

"*** It was further reported that even after it was determined, as a matter of national policy, to proceed with development of a hydrogen bomb, you continued to oppose the project and declined to cooperate fully in the project. It was further reported you departed from your proper role as an adviser to the Commission by causing the distribution, separately and in private, to top personnel at Los Alamos of the majority and minority reports of the General Advisory Committee on development of the hydrogen bomb for the purpose of trying to turn such top personnel against the development of the hydrogen bomb. It was further reported that you were instrumental in persuading other outstanding scientists not to work on the hydrogen bomb project, and that the opposition to the hydrogen bomb, of which you are the most experienced, most powerful and most effective member, has definitely slowed down its development."

It should be emphasized that at no time has there been any intention on my part or the Board's to draw in question any honest opinion expressed by Dr. Oppenheimer. Technical opinions have no security implications unless they are reflections of sinister motives. However, in view of Dr. Oppenheimer's record coupled with the preceding allegation concerning him, it was necessary to submit this matter for the consideration of the Personnel Security Board in order that the good faith of his technical opinions might be determined. The Board found that, following the President's decision, Dr. Oppenheimer did not show the enthusiastic support for the program which might have been expected of the chief atomic adviser to the Government under the circumstances; that, had he given his enthusiastic support to the program, a concerted effort would have been initiated at an earlier date, and that, whatever the motivation, the security interests of the United States were affected. In reviewing the record I find that the evidence establishes no sinister motives on the part of Dr. Oppenheimer in his attitude on the hydrogen bomb, either before or after the President's decision. I have considered the testimony and the record on this subject only as evidence bearing upon Dr. Oppenheimer's veracity. In this context I find that such evidence is disturbing.

DR. OPPENHEIMER'S VALUE TO ATOMIC ENERGY OR RELATED PROGRAMS

In addition to determining whether or not Dr. Oppenheimer is a security risk, the General Manager should determine the effect which denial of security clearance would have upon the atomic energy or related programs. In regard to Dr. Oppenheimer's net worth to atomic energy projects, I believe, first, that through World War II he was of tremendous value and absolutely essential. Secondly, I believe that since World War II his value to the Atomic Energy Commission as a scientist or as a consultant has declined because of the rise in competence and skill of other scientists and because of his loss of scientific objectivity probably resulting from the diverison of his efforts to political fields and matters not purely scientific in nature. Further, it should be pointed out that in the past 2 years since he has ceased to be a member of the General Advisory Committee, his services have been utilized by the Atomic Energy Commission on the following occasions only:

October 16 and 17, 1952.
September 1 and 2, 1953.
September 21 and 22, 1953.

I doubt that the Atomic Energy Commission, even if the question of his security clearance had not arisen, would have utilized his services to a markedly greater extent during the next few years. I find, however, that another agency, the Science Advisory Committee, Office of Defense Mobilization, has stated in a letter dated June 4, 1954, signed by Dr. L. A. DuBridge, Chairman, and addressed to Chairman Strauss, that:

"*** It is, therefore, of great importance to us that Dr. Oppenheimer's 'Q' clearance be restored. This is especially true since our Committee is planning to undertake during the coming months an intensive study of important items related to national security on which Dr. Oppenheimer's knowledge and counsel will be of very critical importance."

Dr. DuBridge further stated that:

"*** His value is, it seems to me, so enormous as to completely overbalance and override the relatively trivial risks* which the Personnel Security Board reports. In other words, the net benefits to national security will be far greater if Dr. Oppenheimer's clearance is restored than if it is terminated. Even though he served the Government in no other capacity than as a member of the Science Advisory Committee of the Office of Defense Mobilization, the above statements will, I am confident, be true beyond question."

Other Government agencies may also desire to use Dr. Oppenheimer's services if he were to be cleared. In addition, contractors and study groups involved in atomic power activities undoubtedly will from time to time, as one or two have already indicated, desire to clear Dr. Oppenheimer for consulting work.

---

* "It should be noted that Dr. DuBridge to my knowledge has never had access to the complete file or the transcript of the hearing."

Dr. Oppenheimer could of course make contributions in all these fields, but he is far from being indispensable.

CONCLUSION

I have conscientiously weighed the record of Dr. Oppenheimer's whole life, his past contributions, and his potential future contributions to the Nation against the security risk that is involved in his continued clearance. In addition, I have given consideration to the nature of the cold war in which we are engaged with communism and Communist Russia and the horrible prospects of hydrogen bomb warfare if all-out war should be forced upon us. From these things a need results to eliminate from classified work any individuals who might endanger the common defense or security or whose retention is not clearly consistent with the interests of national security.

Dr. Oppenheimer's clearance should not be reinstated.

K. D. Nichols
General Manager.

* * *

On June 11 one of my fellow Commissioners who had taken a portion of the transcript to study, while traveling by rail to a distant city, fell asleep in the chair car with the transcript in his lap and arrived at his destination to find it missing. He telephoned in great distress to report that the document might have fallen into unauthorized hands and might perhaps be published. The Commission decided to make a general release in advance of a possible unofficial publication. Consent of all witnesses was obtained.

The Public Printer was called in and asked if he could set up and print the complete transcript as a matter of urgency. That typographical feat was accomplished by the Government Printing Office in less than two days, and the result, a document of 992 pages, practically free of misprints, was made available to the press as quickly as the consent of witnesses to the publication of their testimony could be obtained. It was released on June 16. The file which had been lost in the train subsequently turned up in the lost-and-found office of the railroad.

The Commissioners had before them the complete transcript, the majority and minority findings of the Gray Board, the recommendation of the General Manager of the Commission, and a concluding brief in behalf of Dr. Oppenheimer from his counsel. With the exception of Commissioner Smyth, the Commissioners had posted themselves by reading the current transcripts. Commissioner Smyth had preferred to allow them to accumulate, and at the conclusion of the hearings he retired to his home with an attorney supplied by the General Counsel of the Commission, to study the record in its entirety and to prepare his opinion. On June 28, the Commission voted 4 to 1, Commissioner Smyth dissenting, to approve the recommendation of the Gray Board and of the General Manager that Dr. Oppenheimer's clearance not be reinstated. Three of the Commissioners wrote separate, concurring opinions. One, that of Commissioner Murray, while concurring with the conclusion of the majority, differed from the others in that on the basis of his definition of loyalty he had concluded that Dr. Oppenheimer "was disloyal." Commissioner Smyth wrote an eloquent opinion in dissent. The opinion notes that "The Chevalier incident involved temporary concealment of an espionage attempt and admitted lying, and is inexcusable." Commissioner Smyth, nevertheless, did excuse both concealment and lying in order to reach his decision that reinstatement of Dr. Oppenheimer's clearance was "clearly consistent with the interests of the national security."

Widespread discussion ensued. There were many letters and editorials. Some correspondents argued that Dr. Oppenheimer ought not be judged by the same set of standards as ordinary people, that "being superior intellectually, there should be special criteria in his case." Some expressed the opinion that there should be a sort of "scientific license," entitling Dr. Oppenheimer to exemption from liability for certain actions, a privilege which, admittedly, could not be applied generally.

Following the announcement of the decision there was criticism of the procedures and regulations employed by the Commission in handling its security cases. Seven years earlier, when Dr. Oppenheimer was Chairman of the General Advisory Committee, the Commissioners had met with his committee and with him to inform them of plans to establish boards which, at the request of individuals concerned, could hear evidence, examine witnesses, and advise the Commission in the event that the employment of an individual was deemed inconsistent with the interests of national security. The General Advisory Committee at that time commended the proposed regulations as a fair and liberal procedure.

The hearing was unusual in the respect that, although counsel for Dr. Oppenheimer submitted both a lengthy oral argument and a brief to the Gray Board, the rules under which the proceedings were conducted did not provide for counsel to the board to submit either oral argument or a brief. When the proceedings ended, Dr. Oppenheimer's counsel acknowledged the "fairness which the members of the board have displayed in the conduct of these hearings and the sincere and intense effort . . . to come to a just understanding of the issues."[10]

On January 17, 1955, with the hearing procedures in mind, I convened the heads of all the Commission laboratories in Washington to review and recommend improvements in our personnel security regulations. No material changes were suggested and the regulations were commended as eminently fair.

The testimony before the Gray Board by scientists who defended Dr. Oppenheimer and by others whose testimony was damaging resulted in a rift in the scientific community. Some men refused to shake hands with each other at scientific meetings. The review board in the course of its report noted that "the Board has been impressed, and in many ways heartened by the manner in which many scientists have sprung to the defense of one whom many felt was under unfair attack. This is important and encouraging when one is concerned with the vitality of our society. However, the Board feels constrained to express its concern that in this solidarity there have been attitudes so uncompromising in support of science in general, and Dr. Oppenheimer in particular, that some witnesses have, in our judgment, allowed their convictions to supersede what might reasonably have been their recollections." This, in judicial and deliberate language, was a commentary on the quality of some of the testimony.

Two Washington reporters wrote a book, *The Hydrogen Bomb,* which appeared not long after the case ended and generated a minor controversy on its own account. It represented the delay in the hydrogen bomb program in a light unfavorable to Dr. Oppenheimer. The authors were James Shepley, now assistant publisher of *Life,* and Clay Blair, now an editor of the *Saturday Evening Post.* Scores of messages were sent to me after the book appeared, some of them suggesting, and others demanding, that I should issue a statement forthwith, denouncing the authors. Some of the messages were in identical language. What was not generally known was that the authors had presented the manuscript to the Atomic Energy Commission, in accordance with custom, in order that they might be advised if it contained any information which might not be published without violating the law. It passed the AEC review office in that respect.

Informed in this manner of its intended publication, I was concerned lest it exacerbate relations within the scientific community. Impulsively, and ill-advisedly, I made an offer to the authors to buy the manuscript with my own funds in order to defer publication for a period of years during which tempers might cool. The authors explained that they were committed to their publishers, and my proposal could not be considered. The fact of my offer was related by one of the authors in the course of a Sunday-afternoon television program on which he was the guest in September 1954.[11] In consequence, I was criticized on the one hand for allowing the book to be published and on the other for trying to suppress it.

At various times in subsequent years, while Chairman of the Commission, I was asked whether the AEC would be willing to reopen the case. I answered that in the event of significant new evidence the Commission would most probably do so.

I was also asked how I could justify having voted with the Commission to clear Dr. Oppenheimer in 1947, and seven years later in 1954 find him untrustworthy. Generally those who have asked this particular question had not read the full transcript of the hearing. That would have told them that, while it was known to the Commission in 1947 that Dr. Oppenheimer had informed on a professional colleague at the University of California as being involved in an attempt to obtain secret information on the atomic weapon project for the Soviet espionage organization, it did not become known to the Commission until the 1954 hearings that Dr. Oppenheimer had continued his contact with that colleague, Haakon Chevalier, during the intervening years; nor that he had met with him in France as recently as the month in which the proceeding was ordered by the President. This continuing and current association by Dr. Oppenheimer with a man concerning whom Dr. Oppenheimer himself had made a grave accusation came to light only during his examination by counsel for the Gray panel during the hearings.

The hearings also developed Dr. Oppenheimer's admission that he had fabricated a "tissue of lies" to tell to American security officers (the ugly phrase is in the transcript), and this also was not known to the Commissioners in 1947 when they voted to clear him. There was other information not before the Commission or known to it in 1947.

These circumstances, others cited in the finding of the Gray panel and the report of General Manager Nichols, convinced the majority of the Commission that Dr. Oppenheimer's employment was not "clearly consistent with the interests of the national security." I believed so then and do as this is written. This did not mean that I considered him unsuited to continue his academic position as director of the Institute for Advanced Study. His intellectual attainments were his qualifications for that post. I not only voted for his re-election as director of the institute, after the hearings and the decision, but offered that motion myself. It has been said that this was inconsistent with my vote against restoring his security clearance for work on national defense matters. It did not appear inconsistent to me then, nor does it now. The areas are distinct.

Another question occasionally asked is whether Dr. Oppenheimer has not by now been "punished" sufficiently. The decision of the majority of the Gray Board, the decision of the General Manager of the Commission, and the decision of the majority of the Commissioners—seven men out of nine—was not taken to mete out punishment. The Commission had no authority to set penalties. The decision was limited; namely, not to restore to Dr. Oppenheimer clearance for access to defense information vital to the security of the United States. It was a measure taken to safeguard such information, pursuant to an executive order of the President of the United States, the Commander in Chief of the Armed Forces, and for no other purpose. That the decision involved distress for Dr. Oppenheimer was inescapable. It was also the result of his own conduct and free choice. The decision was agonizing also for the men who had to make it, but for them the oath of office, which each had taken solemnly, left no choice.

XV

Decision in the Tennessee Valley

Multitudes, multitudes in the Valley of Decision.
JOEL 3:14

Some time ago the press reported that in Madras a poor Hindu vendor of vegetables, frustrated over the years to the breaking point at having his stall raided by meandering cows, had seized a club and driven one away. Indignant neighbors promptly set upon him and cracked his skull for impiety. Western visitors to India are often astonished at the liberties permitted to these sacred animals, but the institution is not exclusively Hindu. Peoples of other lands have sacred cows of their own and resent interference with their prerogatives.

In the United States we have an institution—the Tennessee Valley Authority. Even a suspicion of unfriendliness to it is about as much of a sacrilege as offense to a cow on the streets of Benares.

The TVA bill became law upon President Roosevelt's signature in May 1933. Originally established to check floods in the valley of the Tennessee River and its tributaries, to preserve farmland, and to improve navigation (with power production as an adjunct), the Tennessee Valley Authority, which has performed outstandingly in these particulars, began selling hydroelectric power generated at its flood-control dam sites.[1] At a later stage, a few coal-fired steam plants were built to produce electricity for such purposes as "stand-by power" in periods of low water. Eventually, however, steam-generated power became a chief concern of the TVA, and now more electricity is produced by its steam plants than by water turbines. Hundreds of millions of dollars of money collected from taxpayers in every state have been invested in power plants serving the Tennessee Valley area (parts of Alabama, Tennessee, West Virginia, Ohio, etc.). Independent utilities which once produced power for the area have been forced to sell out, at a loss, to this powerful, tax-privileged, Government competitor.

Wendell Willkie, once the head of the Commonwealth and Southern system, a stockholder-owned utility group, testified before a congressional committee, giving a dramatic example of TVA's competition. Willkie mentioned Commonwealth properties in Alcorn County, Mississippi, which had been sold to the TVA. It was sell out or face continuing, unfair government competition, he told the committee. "That was the reason I sold Alcorn Company at the price I did," he testified. "It is gently cloaked but the fist is there." The properties he sold had cost $617,000. TVA offered $234,000.

"I say to you," Willkie added, "that I lost more faith in American institutions during that period than I had gained in the previous years of my life. When we are told, 'You sell at this price or Federal money will compete against you,' industry has no alternative."[2]

Since TVA enjoys this great preferential and, until 1960 (when it entered the public market for funds), has financed its expansion by congressional appropriations, it has been able to sell electricity in its area at rates substantially lower than those charged elsewhere by independent companies. Such companies must pay federal and state taxes and also pay interest on borrowed capital and dividends to their stockholders. The lower rates for electricity enjoyed by the people of the TVA area have persuaded most (though not all) of their legislative representatives in Washington to be fiercely zealous to protect the special privileges of their constituents. Furthermore, the influential group which believes, as an article of faith, that *all* electric power generation should be Government-owned and operated guards TVA as a showcase of convincing accomplishment.

TVA is indeed a spectacular show. Official foreign visitors from countries to which we are lending money—loans made possible by taxes collected from our free competitive-enterprise system—are regularly conducted to Tennessee, almost as soon as they reach our shores, there to be shown an untaxed, socialized operation, presumably as an object lesson of something to be imitated when they return to their homelands. Few seem to be aware of the paradox.

When General Groves located the great uranium separation plants at Oak Ridge in Tennessee during the first years of the war, the TVA was the attractive source of electricity for these huge, power-hungry installations, and eventually the AEC became TVA's biggest customer, using about 30 per cent of the power produced.

The Commission on Organization of the Executive Branch of the Government (the Hoover Commission) in its report of June 27, 1955, recommended, "That the Government or its agencies cease the building of steam plants and provide for the equation of their power loads by interconnection with the grids of neighboring power systems."[3] In that section of the report dealing with the Tennessee Valley Authority and other federal power operations, the Commission also stated:

> It is obvious from the financial experience . . . that the Federal tax-payer is subsidizing these projects. The burden, however, is very unequally distributed.
>
> When these present Federal programs are completed, the total population directly benefited will be less than 10% of the whole population.
>
> This subsidy is even more sharply illustrated in the case of the States of New York, New Jersey and Pennsylvania which have 20% of the total population and pay 29% of the taxes and receive no Federal power. . . . The task group estimates that these exemptions from tax charges and other uneconomical rate-making practices caused revenues received from Federal power sales in 1953 to fall about 40% below the value of the power.

The members of the Commission, with ex-President Hoover as Chairman, were Joseph P. Kennedy, Herbert Brownell, Jr., James A. Farley, Arthur S. Flemming, Styles Bridges, John L. McClellan, Robert G. Storey, Clarence J. Brown, Chet Holifield, Sidney A. Mitchell, and Solomon C. Hollister. Farley filed a separate statement. Holifield filed a dissent and separate statement.

During the month before I became part of his administration, President Eisenhower had gone to North Dakota to speak at the closure ceremonies at Garrison Dam on June 11, 1953. In the course of his remarks, he quoted Abraham Lincoln's observation: "The legitimate object of Government is to do for a community of people whatever they need to have done but cannot do at all or cannot do so well. In all that the people can individually do so well for themselves Government ought not to interfere." The President explained that this was his philosophy. He added that the Garrison Dam was the sort of development in which the state had a distinct function, but pointed out that private enterprise also had its function in our system and that if ever the function of private enterprise disappears "then we will be under some other alien form of Government and one that we would not recognize now."

Proponents of public power saw even this mild statement as a direct challenge, with the result that, less than a week later, at his press conference the President was asked to give an example.

He said that not long before he had received an appeal on behalf of the expansion of federal expenditures in the TVA region. It was supported by the argument that more power was needed in that area because of the number of industries moving from New England and other parts of the country, drawn there by cheap power.

He pointed to a curious situation: "Apparently subsidized by taxes from all of us, all over the country," the region thereupon siphons away industries from the rest of the country.

He said that he thought a re-evaluation of this condition was called for and he added, "Now please understand me. I have stated a thousand times, I am not out to destroy TVA."[4]

Like the great majority of taxpayers, I had very little information about TVA, though I was aware that taxes were appropriated to subsidize the cost of electrical energy in the Tennessee Valley, but I was just as indifferent as most other citizens, since I assumed that my share was too small to be beastly about. Even the taxpayers in New England, with their high-rate electric bills, have supported TVA without organized complaint in spite of the fact that over the years New England has been hardest hit by the TVA area's inroads on New England's industries. Much New England labor, stranded among deserted plants and smokeless chimneys, has been left between the pincers of fewer jobs and higher local taxes.

The TVA was very far from my mind indeed when on December 2, 1953, the Director of the Budget, Joseph Dodge, asked me to a meeting on that afternoon in his office. In Washington the Director of the Budget is a very important person. He is often the channel for directives from the President to those agencies of the Government not having the same regular contact with the Chief Executive enjoyed by Cabinet members. Good relations with the Bureau of the Budget and its Director are essential to the smooth functioning of the departments, and the independent agencies as well. Assuming that the subject was the budget, I went to Dodge's office, taking along the AEC's Deputy General Manager, Walter Williams, who would follow up whatever we were to talk about; I was due to leave with the President for Bermuda on the fourth. It was to be a more important meeting than I could have anticipated and its consequences have not yet exhausted themselves.

The AEC's budget was not the subject. Dodge informed me that he had received appeals from the Chairman of TVA, Gordon Clapp, urging that the Administration support his request to the Congress for more funds to construct new steam plants for the production of electricity. Clapp wrote that the Memphis area was becoming short of power and that, unless additional capacity were promptly constructed, the results would be serious within a very short time. In a letter to Dodge three weeks later (December 24, 1953) Clapp wrote that the provision of additional power in Memphis was essential "to prevent a catastrophe in power supply in 1957."

Dodge said that whether or not Clapp's warning was justified the Congress had repeatedly defeated such an appropriation under the Truman Administration as well as the present one. He added that the President wished to see the area supplied with all the power it would require but believed that one way of doing this would be for the Atomic Energy Commission to arrange with private industry for 450,000 kilowatts and to release that much of the power we were buying from the TVA.

In his annual budget message to the Congress the following month, President Eisenhower said that arrangements were being made to reduce by the fall of 1957 existing commitments of the Tennessee Valley Authority to the Atomic Energy Commission by 500,000 to 600,000 kilowatts. "This," he added, "would release the equivalent amount of TVA generating capacity to meet increased load requirements of other consumers on the power system and at the same time eliminate the need for appropriating funds from the Treasury to finance additional generating units. In the event, however, that negotiations for furnishing these load requirements for the AEC from other sources are not consummated as contemplated, or new defense loads develop, the question of starting additional generating units by the TVA will be reconsidered." He made no request for appropriations to construct new power-generating units for the TVA.

During the Truman Administration, the AEC had contracted in various parts of the country for large supplies of power from private utilities. Satisfactory arrangements had been made and were in force with two independent power groups—Electrical Energy Incorporated and the Ohio Valley Electric Corporation. Neither of these companies, however, was in the Memphis area, and they were not interested in building there or in increasing plant capacity in their own areas. We discussed the subject with their principal officers and they put us in touch with the heads of independent utilities situated nearer the point of consumption.

In the conversations which ensued, the AEC first proposed that the simplest solution would be for the TVA to make direct arrangements with independent utility companies. One such company, Middle South Utilities, had proposed to furnish TVA with 450,000 kilowatts directly in the Memphis area, and to supply the power at whatever cost the Federal Power Commission might deem fair. When I read of this proposal, it did not seem that anything could be more reasonable. We also were able to stimulate a similar proposal from the Southern Company. TVA appeared determined to get an appropriation of public money and to build its own plants. It gave no encouragement to either of the independent proposals.

The two utilities then became sponsors of a new company, established expressly to make a proposal and to construct a new power plant close to Memphis. The cost was to be privately financed; the power would be sold to the Government over a twenty-five-year period at rates approved by the Federal Power Commission. Since the AEC was the only agency of Government at that time which could contract for a term as long as twenty-five years and since that period of time was an essential factor in a public financing program, the President on June 16, 1954, directed the AEC, representing the Government, to negotiate a contract.

The Director of the Budget transmitted the President's order:

The President has asked me to instruct the Atomic Energy Commission to proceed with negotiations with the sponsors of the proposal made by Messrs. Dixon and Yates, with a view to signing a definitive contract on a basis generally within the terms of the proposal. He has also requested me to instruct the Commission and the Tennessee Valley Authority to work out necessary contractual, operational, and administrative arrangements between the two agencies so that operations under the contract between AEC and the sponsors will be carried on in the most economical and efficient manner from the standpoint of the Government as a whole. . . .

It is desirable that the Commission proceed as rapidly as possible with the necessary negotiations with the sponsors and with the Tennessee Valley Authority.

For honoring his reasonable instruction of the Chief Executive, the AEC was soon accused of becoming a "power broker"—about the least offensive of the charges leveled against it.

At the time the Commission received the President's directive, the Budget Director stated that he and his staff had fully analyzed the proposal, had compared it with the alternative of providing additional capacity through appropriations of public funds to the TVA, and had reached several conclusions.

The first of these was that the use of privately generated power would avoid an outlay of about a hundred million dollars of federal tax revenue for capital investment over the following three years.

The second conclusion was that the independent proposal was a firm offer with a stated maximum capital cost to be reflected in the demand charges for current, whereas there would be no guarantee as to the ultimate capital cost of a TVA-owned plant.

Third, that the annual costs of the private proposal were reasonable in comparison with those estimated by TVA, when all the factors were considered, and that the significant differences were that the private company must pay state and local taxes, plus a higher cost for money than the federal government was required to pay on its borrowings.

His fourth conclusion was that the private proposal provided cancellation privileges in the event that the AEC operations were reduced or terminated during the life of the contract, whereas under the same circumstances, and if built by public moneys, the Government would be landed permanently with the additional capacity.

The new independent company was named the Mississippi Valley Generating Company. The presidents of the sponsoring companies, whom I had not previously known, were experienced and honorable gentlemen, Eugene A. Yates and Edgar Dixon. The opponents of the proposal immediately dubbed the new company "Dixon-Yates" and, with this catchy handle, began to belabor the project with such zeal that the average newspaper reader soon came to equate "Dixon-Yates" with "Teapot Dome" or the "Mississippi Bubble." The charges were necessarily vague, but the public was led to believe that some big theft of public funds was hidden in fine print. These opponents included friends of TVA who view its expansion and its consequent absorption of the independently owned plants standing in its way as a process which, in time, will spread westward across the country. To such persons the erection of a large, independently financed plant at Memphis was an unacceptable barrier in the path of this advancing front of public ownership.

Two months after the President had issued his order, the opposition had become desperate enough for the Chairman of the Democratic National Committee to say publicly that the President of the United States had given the power contract to advantage a friend.

At his press conference the following day, President Eisenhower was questioned by a reporter:

QUESTION: Mr. President, Stephen Mitchell, the Democratic National Chairman said yesterday you personally ordered the Dixon-Yates Power contract awarded to a firm in which one of your closest friends has an interest, and at $90 million more than a competitor syndicate. His office later identified the friend as Bobby Jones. Do you care to comment on that matter?

THE PRESIDENT: Well, ladies and gentlemen, I knew when I once went into political life that I would be subjected by many types of strange characters to many kinds of innuendoes and allegations.

He said, with some anger, that he was astonished that the innuendo was aimed at a private citizen "of the character and standing of Bob Jones." There was no gentleman, the President said, of whose integrity and probity he was more certain.

Now, as to my own actions, I am not going to defend myself, as I have told you time and again I shall not. I merely say this—of course I approved the recommendations for this action. Every single action I take involving the contractual relationships of the United States with anybody, except only when the question of national security is directly involved, is open to the public. Anyone of you here may, singly or in an investigating group, go to the Bureau of the Budget, to the Chief of the Atomic Energy Commission, and get the complete record from the inception of the idea to this very minute; it is all yours. Now that is all I have to say about it.

This offer of the President resulted in the compilation by staff members of the Bureau of the Budget and the AEC of a "Chronology of Principal Events" and a collection of all the pertinent letters. This was made public. The completed document contained no mention of the name of Adolph Wenzell. Wenzell was a vice-president of the First Boston Corporation, an investment banking firm of the highest standing which, together with Lehman Brothers, another equally reputable house, was subsequently designated as bankers for the sponsoring utility companies. Staff members who had compiled the chronology had not included Wenzell's name or the names of several others who had attended conferences because they were not principals. Wenzell's function was as an expert consultant on the availability of the public market for financing by the sale of securities, and on interest rates for the various types of such securities.

Early in the previous year Wenzell had been engaged as a consultant to the Bureau of the Budget, had attended meetings with the utility companies and with Government representatives but prior to the decision to proceed with contract negotiations. He had invariably registered in and out of the AEC headquarters building as a man representing his banking firm. He was not known to me in any other capacity, and the record indicates that I saw him briefly, twice. After the AEC was instructed by the President to enter into contract negotiations, Wenzell was not consulted by the AEC with respect to any phase of the negotiations. Indeed, before the time that the proposal of contract was made (April 10, 1954), Francis L. Adams, Chief, Bureau of Power, Federal Power Commission, had been called in and was serving as the Bureau of Budget consultant.

Opponents of the contract, on the basis of the fact that Wenzell had been a consultant for both the Budget Bureau and the independent utility companies, called the circumstances "scandalous" although injury or loss to the Government was never specified. It was intimated nevertheless that some gigantic fraud had been practiced on the Government by dishonest men in high places.

Within a week of the President's directive to the AEC to begin negotiations, so much of a storm had blown up that I was visited by Senator Bourke Hickenlooper and Chairman W. Sterling Cole of the Joint Congressional Committee on Atomic Energy. They came to discuss the bill then before the Congress to amend the Atomic Energy Act. It was designed to provide a liberalization of the existing Government monopoly over the atom so that its use for peaceful civil purposes would be facilitated. There was no question in their minds that the bill would pass the House, but considerable apprehension of its fate in the Senate —if the supporters of TVA made good a threat to halt its passage there, with the price of its enactment being the ditching of the Dixon-Yates proposal. Senator Hickenlooper estimated that friends of the TVA might be able to muster a decisive number of votes for that purpose.

Accordingly, on June 23, 1954, I met with Governor Adams, the Assistant to the President, General Persons, his deputy, and the Director of the Budget, by then Rowland Hughes,* to tell them, and through them

* Mr. Hughes, a kindly, even-tempered gentleman, had succeeded Mr. Dodge as Director of the Budget. He habitually wore a black patch to cover an injured eye which gave him a piratical appearance that totally belied his nature. He was a Christian Scientist. The members of that persuasion with whom I have come in contact over the years have all impressed me with their genuine good

the President, what I had been told. General Persons called me the same afternoon to say that the President would not depart in any respect from the course of action he had outlined and that he wished me to inform Senator William Knowland, the Republican leader in the Senate, of that fact.

Forebodings notwithstanding, the Atomic Energy Law of 1954 was successfully steered through both Houses and became effective in August, and when the Dixon-Yates contract itself was executed and sent to the Joint Congressional Committee, the statutory waiting period of thirty days was waived by a majority vote in the committee in order that the contract might become immediately effective. We were faced with Clapp's earlier warning of a catastrophe if the additional power were not available in 1957. Ordinarily, such a plant requires from two to three years to construct and the contract was not signed until November of 1954.

The Dixon-Yates contract, however, continued to be bitterly criticized in the Joint Congressional Committee hearings. The Commission was harassed for days with the charge that negotiation of the contract had diverted the time and energies of staff from more important tasks (such as military matters) to their great detriment. In order to rebut that accusation, statements had to be submitted by the various divisions of the Commission showing the actual number of hours devoted to the power contract. Most of the divisions certified that they had spent no time on the contract at all. Richard Cook, the Deputy General Manager, who had been made chiefly responsible for the negotiation, certified that his time on the job had averaged better than fifty hours a week and that he had spent approximately seven hours per week on the contract.

This left open the question of the time of the Commissioners themselves. I arranged to have brought into the hearing (held in the old Supreme Court chamber in the Capitol) a complete set of the documents the members of the Commission had received during the period covered by the negotiation. These were accompanied by armed guards because they included some material which was "Classified." The files were separated into two groups, one the papers dealing with the contract and the other papers on other subjects considered by the Commission. The former occupied a few small folders. The latter was so voluminous that they filled a number of cases which had to be rolled in on trucks.

The Junior Senator from New Mexico demanded to know who was

---

will and consequent composure. Mr. Hughes was severely and very unjustly criticized during congressional hearings on Dixon-Yates. He died not long thereafter.

responsible for the display. I said that I was and that the relative volume of documents indicated the amount of work required of the Commissioners on the Dixon-Yates contract and other Commission business. It might, I hoped, be convincing to the Committee and settle the charge that the Commission had been spending an excessive amount of its time on the contract. Representative Cole, then ex-Chairman of the Joint Committee, expressed his approval of the graphic manner in which the point had been made.

Among those strongly opposed to the contract was Governor Frank Clement, of Tennessee, who communicated with the President directly. President Eisenhower, replying to him on October 30, 1954, again stated the Administration position:

> It seems to me that all arguments for the construction by the Federal Government of the additional steam plants ignores this one and very important truth: If the Federal Government assumes responsibility in perpetuity for providing the TVA area with all the power it can accept, generated by any means whatsoever, it has a similar responsibility with respect to every area and region and corner of the United States of America.
>
> Logically, every section of the United States should have the same opportunities and the Federal Government cannot discriminate between the several regions in helping provide this type of facility. My own conviction is, that we have not been alert enough in making certain of this equality of treatment. If this is the case then it is high time that other regions were getting the same opportunities.
>
> The directive to the AEC to make arrangements for the purchase of private power—either directly or by finding a new private source to replace available TVA power—was designed to allow time for a thorough examination of this whole vast field without hurting the citizens of the valley.

The details of the contract were resolved, and it was signed, as noted above, on November 11, 1954, following approval of its text by the Bureau of the Budget and of the rate factors by the Federal Power Commission. There had also been a statement by the Acting Comptroller General that he found it legal and unobjectionable. A few months later ground was broken and construction began.

During the month of June 1955 there were repeated indications that the city of Memphis now intended to erect a municipally owned power plant. On the last day in June, the White House issued a release. It referred to the fact that the President had long ago recommended that

Memphis develop its own power plant to supply its needs for electricity and that it was in the absence of any action by the city that the federal government had made the plans to provide power for the general area.

The statement continued that in the light of the notification by the city of Memphis to the TVA of its intentions to build a municipal plant, the President had asked the Budget Bureau, the AEC, and the TVA to determine whether the public interest would be best served by the continuation or cancellation of the Dixon-Yates contract.[5]

Budget Director Hughes asked us to tell him whether the AEC itself could make economical use of all or a part of the power that would be made available through the Dixon-Yates plant if completed, and to provide him with information on the problems that would be encountered if the contract were canceled. Three days later, on July 5, I told him that there would be no economical way for the AEC to use the additional power, and that since the Commission had entered into the contract upon instructions from the President, if a decision to terminate the contract resulted from a review of the data, I assumed the President would so direct.[6]

Next day, the President held a press conference. He was asked: "Mr. President, many Democrats on Capitol Hill are now claiming that your decision to reopen or to restudy the Dixon-Yates matter is a political victory for their side, and claim that it represents a backing-down on your part on this whole matter. Could you discuss that with us, sir?"

"I hadn't heard this particular point," the President replied. "The first group that ever came to my office to urge upon me the building with Federal funds of a new steam plant in the TVA were very insistent that this be done. It was the only way they could get a plant; and they said the city of Memphis is going to be without power in that whole region.

"I recommended to them that the city of Memphis build its plant just like New York City or Abilene, Kansas, would, if they had to have a plant. And they showed me, or attempted to show me, that this was impossible in their area because of the type of contract that TVA had made with all its customers. It is an exclusive sort of contract. If you take any power from TVA then you may not, under your contract, get any power anywhere else. That was the situation at that moment.

"Actually, I am delighted that the city of Memphis or any other local community, when it comes to the simple building of a power station through steam-plant methods, and, with no flood-control or navigation or other factors in it, do it themselves. I believe we should do it ourselves. So I am not really concerned as to who is claiming political victory. This is in accordance with the philosophy in which I believe."

The President's philosophy was consistent and unequivocal.

A few days later the Mayor of Memphis came to see the President to inform him officially that the city had decided to finance and build a power plant of its own, without federal financial assistance. The President, his aim accomplished, ordered the contract to be terminated by the Commission.

Budget Director Hughes wrote to me on July 16:

> The President has accepted the commitment made by the Mayor of Memphis at the White House on Monday last that the City of Memphis will construct a power plant adequate to serve the people of his community, and that the City of Memphis will not request any funds from the Federal Government in any way to apply on the cost of construction of that plant. In this situation, there is no longer any requirement for the arrangement made with the Mississippi Valley Generating Company pursuant to my letter of June 16, 1954, to you. The President has therefore requested me to convey his direction to the Atomic Energy Commission to take immediately the necessary steps to bring to an end the relationship between the Mississippi Valley Generating Company and the United States.

Opponents of the contract charged that the President "repudiated" the contract, an assertion which the record shows to be untrue. A contract which embodies provisions for orderly cancellation is not repudiated where those provisions are invoked for good and foreseen reasons.

The President's directive was carried out. The company then asked for reimbursement to cover costs incurred and cancellation costs, also as provided in the contract. Our General Counsel, William Mitchell, concluded that these should not be paid until there was an answer to the question of whether Wenzell's position had been in conflict of interest. He added that "there is a substantial question as to the validity of the contract which can only be settled in the Courts." Mitchell was a son of an old friend, Attorney General William D. Mitchell, who had served in the Cabinet of President Hoover. My predecessor as AEC Chairman, Gordon Dean, had appointed Mitchell General Counsel of the AEC, and I had retained him out of great respect for his ability and because I trusted his advice. In this instance, his advice made me unhappy, for I believed the parties had acted in complete good faith.

The Mississippi Valley Generating Company was compelled to sue the

Government for recovery and after taking much testimony and on the findings of fact, the U. S. Court of Claims, by a majority of 3 to 2, concluded that as a matter of law the company was entitled to recover on a part of its claim. This was appealed.

On January 9, 1961, the Supreme Court on writ of certiorari to the U. S. Court of Claims found for the Government against the Mississippi Valley Generating Company on the ground that a conflict of interest had in fact existed as a result of Wenzell's functions. The majority opinion written by Mr. Chief Justice Warren, however, specifically exonerated the AEC:

> . . . it is significant, we think, that *no one in the AEC,* which was the governmental contracting agency, and which had expressed reluctance about the contract throughout the negotiations, had knowledge until December 1954 that 'Wenzell, while serving as a consultant to the Budget Bureau, had been meeting with and supplying information to the sponsors regarding the project.'
> [Italics supplied].

The Court of Claims decision, however, was not reached until after the Senate had voted on my appointment to be Secretary of Commerce four years later, and in both the hearings before the Senate Committee and in speeches on the floor of the Senate, "Dixon-Yates" was cited by certain Senators to create the impression that some scandalous wrongdoing had occurred and that the President and I, as his nominee, were implicated. One Senator characterized it as "a shocking example of political corruption," which struck me as a shocking example of political hyperbole.

Senator Wayne Morse of Oregon, speaking on the floor of the Senate, said on June 18, 1959, that in my effort to "foist" the contract upon the country, I was "an enemy of the American people." To make it clear that being an enemy of the American people involved things other than Dixon-Yates, however, the Senator added that, "In his continuing opposition to suggestions and proposals which seek to limit the testing and use of nuclear weapons, Mr. Strauss has been an enemy of the American people." I have often wondered how he felt about this after the flagrant Russian breach of the moratorium in 1961. Senators McGee, O'Mahoney, and Kefauver, among others, echoed Senator Morse's strictures. Morse made a few concessions, by way of laying a wreath on the casket. "I do not deny," he declaimed, "that Mr. Strauss is probably a very intelligent man . . . I do not think he is disloyal to our country or to our form of Government . . . I do not find that Mr. Strauss has used his powers of office or will use them to enrich himself . . . There is no indication of a personal conflict of interest," but "he is an enemy of the people." There is more of this banter in another chapter.

Throughout the Dixon-Yates negotiation, the performance of the AEC staff was outstanding. The General Manager, Major General Nichols, an engineer officer of wide experience who had been second-in-command of the Manhattan District and who knew the TVA area well; the General Counsel, William Mitchell; and, in particular, the Deputy General Manager, Richard Cook, who was primarily charged with the contract, conducted the negotiations with conscientious skill and meticulous attention to detail. They bore the brunt of political bullying without losing their composure or, fortunately, their sense of humor. All of them have left public service. It is a sad fact that a few Senators and Congressmen—not many, but a few—make a practice of abusing public servants, especially those in subordinate echelons, when they appear before committees. No such system could operate in industry since men of spirit would not submit to more than one such experience. It is not generally recognized that there is a large factor of dedication in the attitude of men in public service.

There were consequences in this exercise of decisions in which a political victory over private enterprise was won by the advocates of public power.

The Dixon-Yates contract had called for furnishing electricity by 1957, when, according to the Chairman of the TVA, it had to be available or the "catastrophe" in the area would ensue. But Memphis did not begin to get power from its first unit until late in 1958 and the plant was not in full commercial operation until well into 1959.[7] There was no catastrophe in 1957, nor in the years that followed.*

The Dixon-Yates plant was estimated to cost $107,250,000** (including transmission lines and working capital). The Memphis municipal plant and transmission lines financed by revenue bonds were reported at the end of 1959 to have cost $151,862,000. (Direct comparison

* This is stated without intent to disparage Mr. Clapp's ability as an administrator. He was applying pressure in his letter of December 1953. It is generally conceded that he ran the TVA with devotion and competence.
** The contract stipulated that any increase in actual cost of construction over $107,000,000 and up to $117,000,000 would be shared by the Government. Any increase over $117,000,000 would be borne by the company alone.

is not possible, since the installed kilowatt capacity of the Memphis plant is larger.)[8]

The rates for power to the customers of the Memphis municipal system already have had to be raised since completion of the plant.[9]

Over the years the state and federal governments would have received substantial tax revenues from the Dixon-Yates plant. The Memphis municipal plant does not pay such taxes.

The defeat of the principle of private enterprise in this instance has ill served the people of the area, though few of them probably are aware of that fact.

Not all the sacred cows are in India.

XVI

A New Charter for the Atom: Atoms for Power

Isolation is no longer possible or desirable.
PRESIDENT WILLIAM McKINLEY
IN HIS LAST ADDRESS.

Between 1946, when the Atomic Energy Act became law, and 1953, when the administration changed, decades of technical achievement at a normal rate had been compressed into seven years. Weapons had been very markedly improved—if the word may be used in that context—that is to say, they had been made lighter and smaller and there were many more of them. Atomic energy for submarine propulsion also had become a reality. Industrial power, from atomic energy, however, was still unrealized.

My colleagues and I concluded in the autumn of 1953 that the McMahon Act was overdue for review. There had been a few small amendments in prior years, but no major revision of that statutory charter of the Commission. President Eisenhower being in full accord, we drafted a bill designed to accomplish this.

Under the Atomic Energy Act of 1946, and during the chairmanship of my predecessors, the Commission, while giving first place to the development of atomic weapons, had not neglected the benign uses of atomic energy. The original act recognized that advances in the art would necessitate amendment to the statute, and its text included interesting language disclaiming infallibility:

The effect of the use of atomic energy for civilian purposes upon the social, economic, and political structures of today cannot now be determined. It is a field in which unknown factors are involved. Therefore, any legislation will necessarily be subject to revision from time to time.

There may be similar statutory expressions in our code, but I am un-acquainted with an example of comparable legislative modesty.

The proposed amendments reflected the conclusion that, certain of the "unknown factors" having become resolved, the time had arrived for a number of revisions to be made in the law.

Our suggestions were designed to relax the Government monopoly and accelerate peacetime atomic power development by encouraging private partnership and participation. We planned likewise to terminate federal ownership and operation of the towns of Oak Ridge, Tennessee, and Richland, Washington, so that the citizens of those communities, which had grown large under an extreme paternalism, could manage their own affairs thereafter. Other provisions would widen co-opera-tion with our allies and improve procedures for the control and dis-semination of atomic energy information.

Our draft measure was sent to the Congress in February 1954. The Joint Congressional Committee thereupon made its own redraft and, as the "Cole-Hickenlooper Bill" (so called in the usual manner for its sponsors, Congressman W. Sterling Cole, then Chairman of the Joint Congressional Committee, and Senator Bourke B. Hickenlooper, the ranking Senator on the committee), it was passed. The President signed it on August 30, 1954.

The paramount objective of the Atomic Energy Commission re-mained as it had been: to make the maximum contribution to the common defense and security by continuing to develop and manufac-ture atomic weapons. The amended law, however, placed additional emphasis on the development of peaceful applications of atomic energy and generally provided the Commission with the workable authority it had requested. The Commission's research activities would encourage medical, agricultural, and industrial applications, while inventions and discoveries in such fields by private persons might thereafter benefit their inventors under our patent system. This was a most important improvement. In the immediately preceding years, our patent system had begun to come under increasing attack. During forty-five years in business and Government, it has been my observation that our living standards and military strength owe far more than generally is realized to the incentive which the patent system has afforded. It will be a sad day for the United States if the efforts to abolish, or cripple, the patent system ever succeed.

The new law also provided that agreements might be made between the United States and friendly nations which would allow for an exchange of information on a mutually beneficial basis. Under certain conditions this co-operation could include providing special nuclear material for research and for power reactors. It also made possible the exchange of certain restricted information with friendly nations after security controls had been instituted by them satisfactory to us.

There was determined but unsuccessful opposition to the amendments, much of it from quarters interested in retaining the federal monopoly on power development. Support for this position came from unexpected directions. The Associated Press reported Dr. E. U. Condon, a former chief of the National Bureau of Standards, as stating that if power development should be released to industry, it "would tend to weaken the possibility of effective international control" and would "do little if anything to speed the development of atomic power." The Congress decided otherwise.

In signing the act, the President announced that he was confident the new law would lead to greater national strength and that programs undertaken as a result would help the nation to progress more rapidly to the time when atomic energy would be wholly devoted to constructive purposes. He pointed out that the new law would permit the United States, under proper security safeguards, to give its allies certain information that they must have for effective defense against aggression. "This information," he explained, "includes data needed for training in the use of and defense against atomic weapons and for evaluating the atomic capabilities of a potential aggressor . . . Also reflected in the new law is the fervent desire of our people to proceed with a plan for an International Atomic Energy Agency which would advance the peacetime applications of atomic energy. . . ." This referred to the suggestion which had been made in his speech to the General Assembly in the United Nations some months earlier.

One of the first indirect results of the amended Atomic Energy Act was the endorsement by the General Assembly of the President's proposal and the appointment of a special advisory committee to the Secretary-General to make plans for the international scientific conference we had proposed in April under circumstances elsewhere related.

By the end of 1954, in consequence of the AEC program to encourage prospecting for radioactive minerals, uranium mining had become a major segment of the nonferrous-metal mining industry in the United States. Many long-established mining companies were entering the field. The unique element—uranium—central to the whole atomic project, had been so rare in the beginning that we spent important sums in studies to recover it from low-grade domestic deposits where it was present only to the extent of a few parts per million. The extensive phosphate beds in Florida and some shale deposits in other parts of the country contain uranium, but in such small concentration that its separation, like winnowing needles from haystacks, would have necessitated handling truly heroic amounts of material.

Uranium now began to be discovered in our mountain states in significant amounts. This was the result of a Commission decision under Chairman Dean in 1951, when a bonus system was instituted to encourage prospecting on a wide scale. The discoveries relieved the nation of the fear that we might some day be cut off from overseas sources or of having to resort to the enormously expensive processing of ores of marginal content.

My colleagues and I continued the bonus offer, being agreed that if good fortune continued we might find ourselves with a superabundance. We were advised, however, that the chances, based on geological information of the day, were against such a result. In any case, we reasoned that while an oversupply might be embarrassing a shortage could be embarrassing in a very different and serious degree. The longshot paid off—uranium was found where it had not been known to exist—and by 1955 the United States had moved into the front rank of uranium-producing nations. In this matter, one man deserves particular credit, Jesse C. Johnson, who headed the Raw Materials Division of the AEC and was the brains of the uranium program. It was he whose display of confidence in intensive prospecting proved prophetic.

Uranium: The origin of our supply of the potent element begins with the story, mentioned earlier in passing, and revolves about the granitic figure of an engineer and industrialist, Sir Edgar Sengier. Although a loyal subject of the King of the Belgians, Sengier is proud of the knighthood bestowed by King George VI and a decoration received from the President of the United States. There is probably no other man, alien to both countries, to whom both are similarly indebted.

Sengier is now past eighty and semiretired, but in 1939, as the sixty-year-old chief executive of the Union Minière du Haut Katanga, the huge Belgian mining combine, he controlled a mine in the Congo which was the world's richest producer of uranium ore. Not only was the deposit in this mine extensive, but the concentration of uranium was uniquely high. Despite all the prospecting that has occurred within the past twenty years, no other deposit has ever rivaled the Shinkolobwe mine for richness.

Prior to 1939, of course, there had not been much interest in the ore. Uranium itself had few prewar uses, perhaps the chief one being to make an orange-yellow glaze for ceramics. The Union Minière sold about eighty tons a year for pottery. The world production was only a few tons more. Sengier recalls that in May of 1939, about five months after the news of fission had reached England, he was introduced to Sir Henry Tizard. Tizard led him aside and asked him to give the British Government an option on the entire ore production from the Shinkolobwe mine. Sengier made some excuse, whereupon Tizard took him by the arm and said, "Be careful and never forget that you have in your hands something which may mean a catastrophe to your country and mine if this material falls into the hands of a possible enemy." A few days later Sengier was visited by Joliot-Curie, Perrin, and Halban, three French scientists who suggested to him that the Union Minière should join with them in making an experimental bomb in the Sahara. Sengier accepted this idea in principle and agreed to furnish the preliminary material and to bear part of the cost, but in September 1939 the outbreak of the war ended the project.[1]

On the outbreak of hostilities, Sengier decided to take some steps on his own responsibility. His decision had important results.

He gave orders to send to the United States all the radium and certain uranium ores which were then at plants of the Union Minière in Belgium. At the end of 1940, fearing a German invasion of the Belgian Congo (which did not seem fantastic in view of the ease with which the German Army had invaded North Africa), he arranged for the shipment to New York of *all* the ore on hand at the mine, about one thousand metric tons. The drums containing this raw potential of the new era were stacked, in the open, near the dock at which they had been unloaded, on Staten Island in New York. There they remained unguarded and unnoticed for nearly two years.

It was not until September 18, 1942, that Colonel Nichols, representing General Groves, called at Sengier's office in New York for the purpose of purchasing some uranium. His directness inspired Sengier's confidence.

There had been a number of previous conversations between Sengier and representatives of the State Department having to do with cobalt, rated a "strategic material," which also was produced in the mining operations of the Union Minière. Sengier had hinted during these talks that he had a material to offer of rather greater importance, but did not get a nibble from the men with whom he spoke. He addressed a letter to the department concerning the availability of "ores containing radium and uranium," but that aroused no action. Sengier was puzzled.

The visit from Nichols was, he satisfied himself, unrelated to these approaches. Within an hour, Nichols left his office, taking with him a sheet of yellow paper torn from a scratch pad. On it was a declaration from Sengier that title to the uranium cargo on Staten Island now belonged to the Government of the United States. The conditions of sale were left to a later date. Thirteen years later, when I became Chairman of the Combined Development Agency, the Anglo-American body set up during the war for the purchase and allocation of uranium, it fell to me to complete some of these details with Sengier. We had both been connected with Hoover's Commission for Relief of Belgium in World War I, and our friendship dated from those days. It was agreeable for both of us to negotiate together. Sengier was more than a man of business—he was an effective diplomat representing the interests of his country and a world statesman in the best sense.

In the field of atomic energy, a special relationship thus existed between the United States and Belgium, and the two governments have closely co-operated ever since. The Belgian Government agreed with the governments of the United States and the United Kingdom that all uranium ores ought to be subject to effective control "in the interest of civilization," and undertook to ensure control of ore located in all territories subject to Belgian authority. In consideration of this co-operation, the governments of the U.S. and the U.K. agreed that the Belgian Government should participate on equitable terms in the utilization of these ores as a source of energy for the production of electricity, at such time as the two governments might decide to use the ores for that purpose themselves. No weapon uses were included in the arrangement. The broad-guage attitude of the Belgians and commercial interests in all negotiations resulted in a condition where there was never a moment of friction or tension.*

* Sengier was succeeded by Herman Robiliart, who had been his assistant for many years, and who ably carried on in the tradition of Belgian-American accord.

On the day that Japan surrendered, General Groves took Sengier to the White House and presented him to President Truman as the man "without whose assistance the Manhattan Project would not have been possible." Groves and Sengier then went to lunch at the Army Navy Club, where a procession of officers stopped at the table to extend congratulations. Sengier later philosophized: ". . . *mais aux Etats-Unis, plus qu'ailleurs, la gloire est éphémère.*" In other words, in the United States fame has a short half-life.

Belgium was our mainstay in the beginning. Canada and South Africa later became important suppliers. With the discoveries of our domestic potential, we began to look ahead to a period of atomic plenty. No dangerous cutbacks would need to be considered in the weapons program in order to provide fuel for power reactors for peaceful purposes and for the Atoms for Peace program of the President.

* * *

The development of atomic fission for military purposes was due to its theoretical application as an explosive, but the application of fission to the production of electrical kilowatts was to produce political explosions as well. In 1946 when several standing committees of the Congress were asserting jurisdiction over atomic legislation and considerable pressure had built up, Senator Theodore ("The Man") Bilbo, of Mississippi, made the suggestion that the subject might be handled most appropriately by his committee (the Committee on the District of Columbia) because "most explosions occur in the District anyway."

Senator Vandenberg, the Chairman of the Foreign Relations Committee, was a member of the special committee to which the drafting of the atomic energy law had been referred. He realized that the bill, to which by then he was committed, put all phases of atomic energy development (including its industrial aspects) into a framework he considered socialistic. He was worried by this but he viewed it as a transitional condition. He let it be known that he had brought himself to swallow what he called "totalitarian control of atomic energy" as long as that control was temporary.[2] After the 1947 hearings on the confirmation of the original Commissioners, Vandenberg expressed himself as somewhat reassured by my response to a question. I had said that, after its weapon responsibilities, I regarded the task of the Atomic Energy Commission as a trusteeship of the peaceful applications until we had learned enough about the subject so that the American pattern of free enterprise could be applied to it, as to any other area of science or industry. Thus I was on record in opposition to continuing government monopoly in the civil uses of atomic energy as far back as the beginning of the Commission. (At the very least, this was consistency.)

It seemed to me illogical to treat electrical kilowatts generated by heat from fission differently from the same electrical output generated by burning coal, oil, or gas. In an attempt to see that the law itself recognized this fact, the framers had included specific language in their declaration of policy. Subject at all times to the "paramount objective" of assuring the common defense and security, the law stated that "the people of the United States" declared it to be their policy to develop and use atomic energy to strengthen "free competition in private enterprise." Atomic Energy Commissioners who in later years took this injunction as a serious mandate found the going rough.

It was a dead letter in certain quarters from the moment of its enactment. Those who viewed the development of atomic energy for electrical power as a means of combatting private investment in the power industry construed this language in the law as a pious platitude, having nothing to do with free competition in the utility enterprise. Familiar with the legislative history, I felt that it meant just what it said. Consequently, I did what I could to discourage legislation proposed in 1956 that would have appropriated hundreds of millions of dollars with a mandate to the Commission to build and operate power plants. These were to be plants duplicating existing designs and would not materially have advanced the techniques. Although the bill was passed in the Senate, it was successfully defeated in the House of Representatives.

In the following year, the measure was reintroduced and again defeated. President Eisenhower let it be known that he would oppose the expenditure of public money for large-scale power reactors unless private enterprise received a reasonable opportunity to bear or share the cost. The stated policy of the people of the United States as expressed in the Atomic Energy Act was thus sustained.

Four years earlier, in December 1952, the month before the Eisenhower Administration took office, the Joint Congressional Committee issued a report with the title "Atomic Power and Private Enterprise." The report was critical. It noted that, while in its early days the AEC had undertaken one power development project having no military aspect, a so-called "breeder reactor," it had been abandoned in 1950. The report continued, as described earlier: *"Since Spring, 1950, however, there has been no major project whose purpose is to achieve a reactor directly advancing industrial power."* (Italics supplied.)

The circumstances which produced this criticism were not the fault of my predecessor, Gordon Dean, nor of the Commission, over which he was presiding. The caution which the Commission had exercised was a continuation of a policy of the Commission of 1947–50, of which I had been a member.

All five members of the first Commission had flown out to Berkeley, California, in the winter of 1946 to visit Dr. Ernest Lawrence and see his radiation laboratory. At dinner one evening, Lawrence had said, "If you fellows are going to wait until you dream up the *ideal* power reactor, take it from me, you will never get around to building one. Why not use Daniels'* design and build a reactor now and light a few light bulbs with it? What difference does it make that it won't be economic? The first reactor will be a Model T in any case. The thing to do is to get the lead out of your pants."

We were all enthused that evening, but in the days and months that followed, we were persuaded to caution. Before us had been a report, by a scientific committee under the chairmanship of Dr. R. C. Tolman, which noted that the "Development of fission piles solely for the production of power for ordinary commercial use does not appear economically sound, nor advisable from the point of view of preserving national resources."

A spokesman for our General Advisory Committee, composed predominantly of leading scientists, in a statement released by the office of the United States Representative on the U. N. Atomic Energy Commission some four months after the Commission was organized, had stated, "I think it will take between 30 and 50 years before atomic energy can in any substantial way supplement the general power resources of the world. That is under the assumption that development is pushed, that intelligent and resourceful people work on the job, and that money is available for it."

Eight months later, in a letter to President Truman, the entire General Advisory Committee went on record with respect to atomic reactors: "They may within a time which will probably not be short, and which is difficult to estimate reliably, be developed to provide general industrial power . . . many years will elapse before our work in this field has the robustness and vigor which its importance justifies."[3]

* Dr. Farrington Daniels, professor emeritus, Department of Chemistry, University of Wisconsin.

A leading scientific adviser to the Commission was quoted to the effect that he considered the prospects of civil atomic power extremely remote from any viewpoint, and from any viewpoint extremely unimportant.[4]

Dr. Kenneth S. Pitzer, then dean of the College of Chemistry of the University of California at Berkeley and now Chairman of the General Advisory Committee to the AEC, said on March 7, 1952, ". . . I am sorry to say that some of these [General Advisory] Committee members of long standing seem to have remarkably little enthusiasm for the primary goals of the atomic energy program. Their recommendations on military projects are, of course, secret, and I am not at liberty to discuss these. Concerning useful power, some have spoken publicly." One of them "has stated that he has little hope for useful atomic power and has predicted that in the 1960s the effort in that direction will be abandoned. Certain other members of the Committee have expressed similar opinions."

In this advisory climate, the early Commissioners may be entitled to some sympathy for their disinclination to rush in and spend money on vastly expensive installations in face of the dim view of the enterprise taken by their eminent advisory body.

For their part, executives in private industry believed that there ought to be assurances that the Government was willing to allow a private atomic energy industry to develop; that risk-taking would be compensated by profits for success and financial allowances made for failures; and that regulations would be established with progress and profit in mind as well as safety and security. Amendment of the Atomic Energy Law was, of course, a prerequisite before private industry could own or even lease fissionable material for fuel. As for the Commission itself, it had been fully engrossed in its weapons operations, its submarine reactor, and in a multifaceted research program, which did include *experimental* power reactor concepts. This was the condition when I returned to the AEC in 1953.

That year the Commission asked several teams of independent experts to study the existing technology and design of reactors. Our own studies, supplemented by these surveys, indicated that there were four promising approaches to achieve electric power from nuclear fuel at a cost which might eventually compare with that of power from coal, oil, or gas. These four approaches were: pressurized water, sodium graphite, fast breeder, and homogeneous concepts. We concluded that two of the four (one known as the pressurized-water type, the other the sodium-graphite type) might be explored in a fairly short time, perhaps three to five years being required to complete a full plant. (The nomenclature is based upon the material used to cool and moderate the reactor.)

During my first month in office, the Commission decided to authorize a pressurized-water reactor, and the development, design, and construction were assigned to the Westinghouse Electric Company. No sponsor had been found to put up any money, however, until the Duquesne Light Company of Pittsburgh came on the scene some months later.

The chances for amendment of the Atomic Energy Act had begun to look hopeful in the spring of 1954. Then I met Philip Fleger, president of the Duquesne Company. Fleger was a man of vision, an executive who knew how to take risks courageously and intelligently. He was entirely aware, of course, that the first private money invested in an enterprise to make electrical kilowatts from atomic energy would eventually appear to have been improvidently spent. The plant would be obsolete by comparison with succeeding generations of design. Nevertheless, on behalf of his stockholders and directors, Fleger was willing to make such an investment in the national interest. Someone had to take the first step. If the investment proved bad, only Duquesne would suffer. If it turned out well, the advantage would belong to everyone. The country owes Duquesne a debt of gratitude.

We decided on the pressurized-water design for this plant because its technology had been considerably advanced by the work on the submarine thermal reactor. The plant was designed to have a power level of approximately 300,000 kilowatts of heat and an output of about 60,000 kilowatts of useful electricity. The Duquesne Company's proposal included furnishing the site and the construction and operation of the electric-generating half of the plant. They would also operate the reactor at no cost to the Government. Besides agreeing to bear the labor costs entailed, the company was willing to contribute five million dollars toward the cost of research and development and construction of the reactor; to buy steam from the AEC; and to waive any reimbursement of costs if the Government decided to cancel the contract and call the project off. We estimated that, along with the revenues from the sale of steam to be generated by the reactor, the company's proposal would reduce by at least thirty million dollars the expenditures which the Government otherwise would have had to make during the period of construction and five years of operations. The

Westinghouse Company as a contractor made a contribution of its total estimated profit.

North American Aviation became the second private contractor and elected to explore the sodium-graphite approach, that is to say, a reactor moderated by graphite and cooled by liquid sodium metal. The company agreed to contribute two and a half million dollars of the ten million dollars estimated for the development, construction, and operation of that experiment. Following this, various other types of reactors were also farmed out for initial construction.

The arrangement with Duquesne resulted in a ground-breaking at Shippingport, Pennsylvania. In the usual popular-science manner dear to the heart of public relations men, the President was asked to do this, not by pushing the conventional button, but by using a wand containing a neutron source. By this appropriate device, a signal was sent to Shippingport, where giant bulldozers, unmanned and robot-controlled, roared impressively into view and broke ground for the new plant, literally as well as ceremonially. Construction of the reactor was supervised by Admiral Rickover, since its design was somewhat similar to the reactor in the *Nautilus*.

Finished in record time for a structure so revolutionary, the plant was dedicated on May 26, 1955. It was the world's first large-scale nuclear power plant* for the generation of electricity, and with no military overtones or purposes.

The President had followed construction of the plant with keen interest and had seen monthly photographic progress reports. Again he sent a signal to Shippingport opening the throttle valve on the main turbine whereupon 60,000 kilowatts of electricity derived from the splitting of billions upon billions of invisible atoms, surged over the lines serving homes, stores, and industrial plants in the Pittsburgh area. It was a day to remember.

* Even before the Shippingport plant became operative, the U.S. had been first to demonstrate a pilot-plant reactor designed exclusively for the purpose of producing electric power for civil use. Located at the Argonne National Laboratory near Lemont, Illinois, and designated an "experiment," it yet produced five thousand kilowatts of electricity and served the electrical needs of the laboratory. It was dedicated by Carl Durham, Chairman of the Joint Congressional Committee on Atomic Energy. Durham had been a member of the Joint Committee from its inception. When he became its chairman, he gave the Commission co-operation and encouragement. His voluntary retirement from the Congress in 1960 was a loss to development of atomic energy in the United States, and to me personally.

"It is with pride in what has been accomplished in Shippingport and with equal confidence in the future," he said that he dedicated the power station to the cause of progress and peace. In the course of a brief remark, I ventured a prediction that nuclear power plants of much greater size and more sophisticated technology would soon be built. As the Shippingport plant was far from economic, one of my colleagues remarked, "You stuck your neck out." I could hardly blame him. Although Shippingport made industrial history for America and the world, the news caused little stir—nothing by comparison with the announcement of the first Russian satellite. But the plant is now producing almost double its original power rating.

The Shippingport plant did not encounter serious opposition. In late 1953, we consolidated two advisory committees to the Commission, the Reactor Safeguards Committee and the Industrial Committee on Reactor Location Problems. Combined to form a new entity known as the Advisory Committee on Reactor Safeguards, the group was made up of nuclear scientists, industrial engineers, and others qualified by knowledge and experience. Their responsibility was to review safety studies made by contractors, on proposed reactors and reactor sites, and to advise the Commission as to the safety of projected installations. Continually composed of the best talent in these new fields, the Committee has served the country well.

Nevertheless, its advice was challenged by the United Automobile Workers in the matter of the location of the Enrico Fermi Atomic Power Plant at Monroe, Michigan. This was the first indication that the private development of atomic power would be fought. Union intervention delayed the completion of that enterprise for many months, and a legal battle to prevent it from operating, on the claim that it would be unsafe and hazardous,* was finally carried all the way to the Supreme Court of the United States. The judgment of the Commission was upheld by a 7-to-2 decision.

The atomic power record for the five years 1953–58 was one of great expansion. In 1953 there were in existence only two small power reactor *experiments,* whose electrical output met their own laboratory re-

---

* The case was argued on a more technical issue. AEC procedure is, first, to authorize "construction" of a reactor and, at a later stage, to authorize its "operation." The main contention of the union was that this procedure was not sanctioned by the Atomic Energy Act. The issue of public versus private power did not appear in the case but was central to it.

quirements with no surplus. Five years later, eight civilian power reactors and large reactor experiments rated to produce over 900,000 kw were built or building, and more were planned. Four of those being built, and since completed, were financed entirely by private capital with no taxpayers' money involved in "bricks and mortar" or "hardware." This array[5] did not include the power reactors built for the Armed Services, the submarine propulsion reactors, or the propulsion system for the first nuclear merchant ship, the Nuclear Ship *Savannah*.

The origin of the N.S. *Savannah* warrants mention. She was to bear the name of another *Savannah,* which in 1819, as the first ship to cross the Atlantic using steam, had proudly carried the flag from Savannah, Georgia, to Liverpool. On April 25, 1955, President Eisenhower proposed that the United States should be first to put a merchant-type ship on the high seas to be propelled by nuclear energy and designed solely for peaceful voyages. He saw it as going from port to port about the world, bearing the message of good will everywhere.

The project at once generated political opposition in the Congress, where it was ridiculed as a "showboat." Though few in number, the men who fought it succeeded in delaying it for more than a year. Eventually, Public Law 848 permitted the Commission and the Maritime Administration to proceed, but the delay was costly. The *Savannah* was not ready for launching until July 1959. In the meanwhile, the Soviets were able to put an atomic-powered icebreaker in operation. We had planned that the *Savannah* would be a clipper-type vessel, powered by a pressurized-water reactor, because experience with that design had proved its excellent performance qualities and its inherent safety. Also, we decided that information about the reactor would not be classified so that there would be opportunity for the world to become familiar with nuclear-powered surface ships.

* * *

Under its new charter, the Commission was able to expand its radioisotope program greatly. Radioisotopes are forms of the several elements, chemically identical with them but physically unstable. This instability is manifested by the radiation from the nucleus of alpha and beta particles and of gamma rays. These radiations, which distinguish the radioisotope physically from the atoms of the stable element, are useful in many ways. Radioisotopes have been distributed by the Commission ever since 1946, but between 1953 and 1958, both the number of users and the volume of sales of radioisotopes trebled.

Benefits already obtained from isotopes have been direct and appreciable. Over a million medical patients are being diagnosed or treated with radioisotopes each year. In industry, savings through isotope use were estimated at about a hundred million dollars in 1953. By 1958, they were five times that. This is the first return (other than the great, intangible dividend of security) on our national investment in atomic energy.

Many isotope applications have become standard practice for a whole industry. Over 90 per cent of the tire fabric and 80 per cent of the tin plate made in the United States are controlled in production by radioisotope thickness gauges.

As tracers, radioisotopes have found good use in oil refineries and elsewhere in measuring the mixing of fluid streams and catalysts, precisely locating leaks in pipe lines, determining the wear and corrosion of metals, and evaluating plant operations.

As sources of massive radiation, their uses include sterilization of foods and drugs, vulcanization of rubber, polymerization of plastics, initiation of chemical reactions, and X-raying of castings, welds, etc.

In medicine, prominent among many and growing uses are the location and treatment of certain tumors. Isotopes are also the treatment of choice in polycythemia and in disorders of the thyroid. It has been known for many years that high-energy radiation will destroy living cells. This knowledge has formed the basis for devising suitable sources of high-energy radiation which could be carefully controlled and used for the destruction of tumors. With these points in mind, linear accelerators, cyclotrons, reactors, and radioactive isotopes have been employed. Large numbers of patients have been treated, and investigators have found certain advantages in the use of each device, depending upon the nature of the lesion and its location.

Tumor diagnosis and the precise localization of cancerous lesions are still difficult problems for physicians. Certain radioactive isotopes such as iodine and cobalt have been successfully used to locate brain tumors, and another radioactive isotope, palladium 103, has been used with success to treat advanced tumors of this nature. Yttrium 90 is being used with success on patients who have metastatic carcinoma of the breast. Various organic compounds, labeled with radioactive isotopes (drugs in which radioactive isotopes have been incorporated), are being used in diagnosis of cancer of the liver and other organs in which they accumulate. The fact that they are so located is revealed by their property of exposing photographic plates, thus affording the physician a silhouette of the diseased portion of the organ. Radiation from the 184-inch cyclotron at the Lawrence Radiation Laboratory at Berkeley, California, is presently the only known nonsurgical means available for inhibiting the functions of the pituitary gland and has been used to produce changes similar to those observed following its surgical removal.

In agriculture, the use of radioactive tracers is revealing a wealth of information on plant nutrition and growth with an important bearing upon our immense national outlay for fertilizers. It has long been the custom to apply fertilizers to crops without any knowledge as to at what point in their growth cycle crops require certain elements. This has meant the waste of billions of dollars' worth of fertilizer over the years. It is now possible to furnish plants with the elements required at the time of germination, growth, blossoming, or seed and fruit formation. A plant needs nitrogen at one stage, phosphorus at another. This information was obtained by noting the uptake of radioactive fertilizer by certain parts of the plant at certain times in its life. Rust-resistant oats and wheat have been developed from radiation genetic studies, and other radiation-induced mutations of crops are being found which give greater yields per acre.

The demand for isotopes, both radioactive and stable, has been steadily gaining as new uses are found. It is entirely possible that these by-products of the fission process may have future economic value more important than the application of power. Paul Aebersold, of the Commission staff, made isotopes his particular province and with the enthusiastic backing of Commissioner Libby solid progress was made in bringing these new tools to public awareness.

In 1953, restrictions of law on access to *technical information* made impossible the degree of industrial participation and international cooperation in the peaceful uses of atomic energy which developed under the new legislation. Some declassification actions were taken in 1953, but little could be done in the industrial area until the Atomic Energy Act of 1954 recognized the desirability of bringing industry into a real partnership. In 1955 our classification policies were revised to open up large areas of reactor information, and to reduce from more secret categories to "Confidential" much that remained classified. As of today, in the field of reactors, only data primarily of importance to reactor systems for military applications remain classified.

The record of the Atomic Energy Commission in administrative efficiency during the period 1953–58 was noteworthy and evidenced the excellent condition in which the organization was left by General Manager Marion Boyer and his successors, General Nichols and General Kenneth Fields. One measure of this efficiency is the AEC administrative overhead—the salaries and related costs for the staff engaged in directing and planning the work of contractors. In spite of the added responsibilities due to growth, and of added responsibilities in such fields as international co-operation, licensing, and inspection, which did not exist in 1953, our overhead cost in relation to total operating expenditures was steadily reduced. In the fiscal year 1953 this administrative cost was nearly 5 per cent of AEC total operating cost. In fiscal year 1958 it was 2.1 per cent, a decrease of nearly 60 per cent. It was a good record and I was proud of it.

The Quebec and Hyde Park agreements, referred to elsewhere, were made during the war when no specific legislative authority for them existed. With the new legislative charter of 1954, the Commission had a legal basis for co-operation with friendly nations. The first bilateral agreements under its provisions were negotiated with the assistance of the State Department, and some were concluded within twelve months of the new authority. As of June 30, 1958, agreements for co-operation were in effect with thirty-nine countries (twenty-seven countries having agreements covering atomic research and twelve countries with agreements for both research and power).[6]

Many research reactor projects were "on order." Seven had been exported from the U.S. and were in operation in six countries by 1958.

Grants of $350,000 had been made or committed for research reactors in fifteen countries, and the Commission also instituted grants for equipment and "package" laboratories to advance the interests of training and research. Nearly six hundred foreign nationals received schooling in radioisotope techniques at our Oak Ridge Institute of Nuclear Studies or at Argonne National Laboratory in reactor science and engineering.

In Puerto Rico, where we established a regional nuclear training center for all of Latin America, instruction is conducted in Spanish. This was preparatory to a reactor project which had been first suggested by my son after a volunteer survey of the power needs of the growing economy of the island. In co-operation with the Water Resources Authority of Puerto Rico a so-called "boiling-water, internal nuclear superheat reactor" is being built at Punta Higuera and is expected to produce 16,300 kilowatts of electricity in 1962.

The feature of our international co-operation, or "Atoms for Peace" program, which distinguished it most completely from enterprises by other nations, is that we were both able and willing to allocate quantities of reactor fuel. In 1958 there was a total allocation for peaceful uses of 100,000 kilograms of uranium 235—half for our own country and half for the Atoms for Peace program.

Another part of this program was the two Scientific Conferences on the Peaceful Uses of Atomic Energy, both in Geneva, the first in August 1955, the second in September 1958. The reopening of lines of scientific and technical communication thus begun led to a succession of topical and regional conferences. An outstanding example was the Inter-American Symposium at Brookhaven Laboratory in 1957, which brought together many scientists from Latin America.

Our efforts stimulated multilateral enterprises in international co-operation to develop the peaceful atom. In 1955, during the first conference in Geneva, Jean Monnet, the architect of the Common Market, visited me there and explained an ambitious idea for a European atomic undertaking on a comprehensive scale. We had been friends since World War I. No one man has done so much for the cause of unifying the free nations of Europe. The task of persuading independent European nations to make the concessions of sovereignty required to form an atomic development union seemed insuperable, and the goal too utopian. But Monnet's logic, perseverance, persuasiveness, and capacity for self-effacement succeeded in this instance, just as he had in previous enterprises in the areas of coal, steel, and common markets. The result was an organization known as Euratom. The potential of the agreement among six Western European nations is considerable. The AEC co-operated with it, hoping that it would provide additional impetus toward that unity which will strengthen Western Europe and at the same time free our allies from dependence upon an often threatened fuel supply line to the Near East.

XVII

The Peaceable Atom:
Decisions Affecting New Problems
and Old Friends

Come now and let us reason together.
ISAIAH 1:18

Peace hath her victories no less renown'd than war.
MILTON (TO THE LORD CROMWELL)

Providence has a way of redeeming man from his follies and even from his sins. Since time immemorial, man's inventiveness has been stimulated to produce weapons and engines for use against his enemies, most of which were eventually turned upon the inventors themselves. But finally these devices often were transmuted into peaceful tools.

Perhaps the first employment of metals was to make weapons, more efficient than chipped flints, for the purpose of killing beasts and other men. Industrial civilization may even have begun as a result of man's early successes in metallurgy. If so, the tempering of swords was the precursor-discovery of industrial cutting tools. Gunpowder, a significant Chinese contribution to the art of killing more people more quickly, and its "improved" successors—dynamite and TNT—eventually led to the peaceful uses of explosives in engineering, mining, agriculture, and many other fields. Mine and submarine detectors, first developed for the military, have become the air-borne locators of ore deposits. The modern marvels of electronic computing machines made early appearance as aids in calculating trajectories of shells at military proving grounds. And radar, which now brings aircraft to safer landings, thus saving lives, was developed in wartime to improve fire control that lives might be more efficiently destroyed.

All military inventions of the past paled in the searing glare of the nuclear explosion. Into that weapon, which has been so refined by engineers and physicists and chemists since the first lumbering atomic bombs were carried to Japan in heavy bombers, there now has been packed an explosive charge many times more powerful than all the bombs carried by the largest bombing fleets of World War II. These are the weapons whose production the United States Atomic Energy Commission administers.

Within the week after he became ex-President, Mr. Truman was quoted in a widely published interview, expressing skepticism that the Russians had nuclear weapons. "I am not convinced Russia has the [atomic] bomb," he was quoted as saying. "I am not convinced that Russians have achieved the know-how to put the complicated mechanism together to make an A-bomb work. I am not convinced they have the bomb."

It is most likely that the former President was misquoted. There had been three formal statements from the White House during his administration—one in 1949 and two in 1951—to inform the American public of the detection of atomic test explosions within Soviet territory.

The publication of Mr. Truman's interview on January 27, 1953, caught the Joint Congressional Committee on Atomic Energy before it had been reorganized under the new Congress. Some of its members were alarmed, fearing that if the statement were credited it might result in a reduction of support for the atomic energy program, specifically in the area of appropriations for weapons research and development. Accordingly, some of the ranking members of the committee conferred, and a bipartisan statement was issued. In part, it noted, "The purpose of this joint statement is to clarify history and to point out that the ex-President's statement is highly unfortunate in that it contradicts indisputable evidence. . . ."

The statement continued, quoting a report which the Joint Committee had made on October 19, 1951, citing the interest of the committee in long-range detection. The statement noted that the active intervention of a handful of individuals "may well have meant the difference between failure and success in becoming aware of the . . . Soviet bomb tests announced by the President. Had these . . . tests passed unnoticed in the United States, the consequences to ourselves could have verged upon the disastrous."[1]

I knew neither of former President Truman's interview nor of the congressional statement when they appeared, as my wife and I were cruising with friends in the Windward Islands. Shortly after returning to New York, a message arrived from President Eisenhower inviting me to call upon him in Washington. By then I had caught up on these events.

My acquaintance with the President began after the war, during the period of his service as Chief of Staff, and had been limited to a few social occasions. While sharing the widespread respect and admiration for him, I was a pre-Convention supporter of Senator Taft, who had been a close friend and associate since both of us were young men.

My relationship to the Senator was known to President Eisenhower. It was a surprise, therefore, when the President asked if I would make a study and report on the atomic energy situation. Gordon Dean, Chairman of the Atomic Energy Commission, had tendered his resignation as Chairman. His term of office would expire in June of that year.

Dean was a Democrat who had been a law partner of the late Senator Brien McMahon of Connecticut. My relations with Senator McMahon had been cordial. When considering whether he would propose Dean to President Truman to fill the vacancy on the Commission caused by the resignation of William Waymack, McMahon had invited me to dinner at his home to meet Dean. I was impressed that evening by his keenness, a wry sense of humor, and his penetrating questions. He was appointed and confirmed in 1949, and when I resigned from the Commission in 1950, I spoke to the President, at the request of Senator McMahon, to recommend the nomination of Dean to succeed David Lilienthal, whose resignation had shortly preceded mine. As elsewhere related, Dean had been the only one of the Atomic Energy Commissioners to support me in the recommendation to the President that he should direct the AEC to proceed with the development of thermonuclear weapons. Dean and I found interests in common and in course of time became friends.

At a second session with the President in his office, he asked me to join his administration as chairman of the Atomic Energy Commission. I thanked him for the evidence of his confidence but proposed an alternate course. While looking into the AEC at his request, I said that some facts had been brought to my attention by Chairman Dean and former Commissioner T. Keith Glennan.* These involved security

* Dr. Glennan, president of Case Institute, has on several occasions accepted public office in scientific organizations—most recently as head of the National Space Agency.

infractions, raw material and labor problems, and personnel. Some of the key executives of the Commission had left for higher salaries in industry, and others had given notice. I had also examined the Commission agenda for the preceding three months and had come to the conclusion that there were things to be done which the Commission simply had not had the time to do. The AEC was like a board of directors attempting to operate a business larger than General Motors or DuPont under a procedure requiring daily meetings and debate among five men of equal authority on a constant succession of problems, some important, others trivial, but each of them of importance to one or more Commissioners.

It was clear that whoever became its chairman and responsible for its administrative work would soon be equally flooded by the tide of minutiae and by the statutory responsibility to keep the Congress "fully and currently informed." General Groves had been protected from this avalanche by the military nature of his organization. Nor was he required to give time to testify before congressional committees. The Chairman of the AEC, on the other hand, was expected to spend perhaps a third of his time preparing testimony on the witness stand, and reviewing transcripts thereafter. Therefore, I first suggested to the President that no change be made in the chairmanship. I offered to come to Washington full time as soon as I could conclude a real estate transaction I was then negotiating in New York between Columbia University and Rockefeller Center. As a consultant to the President on atomic energy matters, perhaps I could be helpful.

The President and his advisers, however, felt that the post of AEC Chairman involved a major Administration responsibility where policy would be formulated and where participation in the councils of the Government at cabinet level would be essential. For these reasons it was desirable that a member of the President's own party, with suitable qualifications, be named to the position. Not long afterwards, Dean confided to me that he was anxious to return to private life and I later introduced him to the partners of the banking firm with which he made a mutually happy connection.*

The Commission had been well administered during Dean's chairmanship and both its military and civil programs, despite recurrent

* There was a report to the effect that, as a result of Dean's departure from the Commission, relations between us were strained. Soon after he left, Dean wrote:

serious problems, were in excellent condition. But Congress had been critical, and in December of 1952 the Joint Congressional Committee had found fault with the civilian atomic power program. A report issued by the committee included the following stricture: "Since Spring, 1950, however, there has been no major project whose purpose is to achieve a reactor directly advancing industrial power." (A few members of the Joint Committee were hard to please, as they continued to find fault when, less than five years later, there were numerous civilian power reactors and reactor experiments in operation, under construction and planned.)

The President gave me leave to look about for a Republican qualified to be Chairman. From the beginning, I encountered difficulty in locating a man who combined all the needed qualifications with willingness to make the sacrifices involved in accepting that appointment. These latter were considerable. The Atomic Energy Act stipulated that "No member of the Commission shall engage in any other business, vocation, or employment than that of serving as a member of the Commission." This requirement had always been strictly construed. As I've said, during my period of service as a Commissioner from 1946 to 1950, in order to be free (as I naïvely assumed) from partisan attack I had disposed of all securities of any companies which did any business with the Manhattan District (the predecessor of the Atomic Energy Commission). As the Commission later expended some twenty hundred million dollars annually and dealt with a wide spectrum of suppliers, the only securities that I felt I could retain were government and municipal bonds, bank stocks, and the shares of a company whose principal business was the manufacture of photographic equipment.

As the June 30 date and the end of Dean's term drew near, the President was informed that I had interviewed a number of potential

One William Street
New York 4
July 29, 1953

Dear Lewis:

I think it highly appropriate that the first letter on this stationery should go to you. As you know I am most grateful to you for the efforts on your part to get the Lehmans and myself together. I shall need your guidance in the future, as well, for I have much to learn in order to be effective. . . .

With every good wish to you,

Sincerely,

/s/ Gordon

Mr. Dean lost his life in an airplane accident in 1958.

candidates but that none had been willing to accept the post. He let me know that he was drafting me for the chairmanship. The nomination was sent to the Senate on June 24 and, being approved without objection by the Senate members of the Joint Committee to which such nominations are referred, was confirmed in the Senate without opposition on June 27, 1953.

When first named to the Commission seven years earlier, I had taken the evidence of my appointment down to the District of Columbia Court and, finding an obliging judge whose court was not in session, was duly sworn. But on July 2, 1953, the oath-taking was a ceremony in the office of the President. Chief Justice Vinson administered the oath, and the President stood near as the solemn and time-honored words were spoken. I had placed a marker in my Bible at a familiar passage, Micah 4:3:

> And He shall judge between many peoples, and shall decide concerning mighty nations afar off; and they shall beat their swords into plowshares, and their spears into pruning hooks; nations shall not lift up sword against nation, neither shall they learn war any more.

Friends on the Atomic Energy Commission and from the Joint Congressional Committee on Atomic Energy had come as witnesses. There was a tragic figure in the group. Senator Taft had arrived on crutches. His complexion was ruddy, almost flushed, but it was not the glow of health. He had requested a blood transfusion that morning in order to have the strength to attend.

Only a few weeks earlier, I had sat with him at his home in Georgetown, where, behind doors closed so that his invalid wife might not hear us as we talked, I brought him a final and terrible verdict from Dr. Cornelius Rhoads of Memorial Hospital in New York. It was the diagnosis that multiple metastases of a cancer would take his life in a matter of months. The memory of that hour in the cool living room of the quiet old Georgetown house, with the afternoon summer sunshine bright outside the curtained windows, and of the courage with which Bob accepted the sentence, will remain with me always. After a long silence, he asked if there was anything to be done about it. There were chemotherapeutic approaches which were being explored, I told him, but little was known of their possibilities, and the time odds were very long against them in his case. "Well," he said, "let me be a guinea pig at any rate. They can try them on me as long as I last."

It is hard for me to write about Bob Taft without emotion. Few men have heroic proportions in the eyes of their early contemporaries. The aura of the founding fathers was about Bob, almost as though he had been born out of that generation. His associates sensed it and accorded him unusual respect even when they opposed him. He deeply loved his country but without patriotic exhibitionism—a love so much a part of him that he, certainly, felt no need of its assertion. His aim was to serve the nation by protecting the principles on which it had been founded. He saw and adapted to the need for change, but he made a distinction between the fundamentals which are of immutable substance and the changes of form necessitated by population growth and technological progress. He sought the presidency as a post from which to serve more effectively and with some element of sentiment because his father had been defeated for a second term. When, with victory almost in his grasp, he was defeated in 1952, he did not sulk in his tent, but with his full power campaigned in behalf of the man who had defeated him.

(It happened that I was with him at his headquarters in Chicago when, immediately after the nominating vote on the convention floor, General Eisenhower telephoned and came to call upon him. When the General arrived, I joined the staff in another room. Secretaries were weeping unashamedly and all voices were muted. In a little while Bob entered, a smile on his face, and spoke a few appropriate words of encouragement, of party loyalty, and of gratitude to his staff. I saw this man in triumph, in defeat, and finally in the blackness of despair as he heard the news of his fatal illness. He was completely superior to every circumstance. It was fitting that when his time came he should lie in state in the rotunda of the Capitol flanked with the figures of Washington and Lincoln in bronze and marble, and by the concourse of his contemporaries of both parties who knew that they were in the presence of greatness.)

After the ceremony in the President's office, when the oath had been administered and Bob and other friends were leaving, the President asked me to remain. As the photographers carried the electric cables out of the room, the President led me to the bay window which looks toward the Mall and the Washington Monument, and he said, "Lewis, let us be certain about *this;* my chief concern and your first assignment is to find some new approach to the *dis*arming of atomic energy. Try not to get so involved in the AEC detail you've told me about that you lose sight of that primary objective. The world simply must not go on living in the fear of the terrible consequence of nuclear war."

I pledged him that this would be my concern (as it had long been), but, familiar with the fate of all the thought and effort which had been exerted to that end by Bernard Baruch and his aides seven years earlier, I was not sanguine. These men, experienced in negotiation after nearly two years of trying to reach an understanding, had been frustrated by Soviet tactics. (See p. 354.)

"We had every right to expect that the Russians would accept Barney Baruch's plan," the President continued. "It certainly was in their self-interest, but they killed it. We have got to find out why and then be ingenious enough to make a new proposal that will be safe for the free world and attractive to the Russians, before it gets too late for *any* plan to work. Meanwhile, we have to continue to keep our lead in weapons development. I am counting on you for that, too." I went to my office and, before doing anything else, wrote down these words as nearly as I could remember that they had been spoken.

There were only a few new faces on the staff of the Commission since I had worked there in 1950. One of these was the very effective General Manager, Marion Boyer, a vice-president of the Standard Oil Company of New Jersey. He was on limited leave of absence and could stay for only a few months longer. A former colleague, Professor Henry D. Smyth, was still serving, and the other members, Thomas E. Murray and Eugene Zuckert, had been appointed since my resignation in 1950. I had known both slightly. They were devoted men with strong personalities and convictions. Zuckert was a hard worker and, though of the opposition party, was tolerant, meticulously fair, and co-operative.

There was one vacancy, resulting from the resignation the preceding autumn of the president of Case Institute, Dr. T. Keith Glennan. I had tried to persuade Dr. Glennan to return as Chairman, but he had all the Government service he could afford at that time. The vacancy was filled on my recommendation by the appointment of Joseph Campbell of New York. Campbell was then a vice-president of Columbia University in charge of real estate and finance. We had worked together in New York and I had high regard for his ability. He brought to the Commission an expert knowledge of fiscal management but, to my great regret, resigned the following year to accept appointment as Comptroller General of the United States.*

* Between 1953 and June 30, 1958 (the end of my term), the President appointed Dr. Libby and Dr. von Neumann to fill vacancies resulting from the retirement of Dr. Smyth and Mr. Zuckert. It was the first time that the Com-

One of the early problems which confronted us was a familiar one: security. There had been some breaches. One case had come to the attention of the President in the early spring and had caused him great concern. It had long appeared that criticism of the Commission because of its alleged excessive attention to security was unjustified, and probably uninformed. There were aspects, however, in which criticism might be warranted or improvements made. One was that the area covered by security was too large, not only its physical perimeter, but the too extensive categories of information and documentation. A more reasonable approach to the protection of those things vital to our security would be possible if the physical expanse protected were reduced and the *degree* of vigilance enhanced. For example, as I have indicated, the boundaries of some reservations, covering hundreds of square miles, had been fenced and patrolled by armored cars and tanks. This protection against penetration was more perfunctory than real, not only because of the enormous areas involved, but because espionage had grown more sophisticated than the kind of invasion which patrols of this character were expected to prevent. This system was modified.

We began a review of classified documents, and in the course of three years intense effort found that nearly a third of an enormous accumulation could be declassified completely and that approximately another third could be reduced in classification from "Top Secret" to lower categories. This made it easier and less costly to handle them. In consequence, we were able to provide more care and security for a smaller volume of important principles, reports and facilities. Notwithstanding, we continued to be regarded in some quarters as over-

---

mission had two scientists among its members. They were excellent foils, each for the other, and the work of the Commission benefited very greatly from their influence, though that of Von Neumann was short-lived by reason of his untimely death. Other changes in the Commission resulting from the death of Von Neumann and the expiration of appointments included the naming of Harold S. Vance, an industrialist who had been a friend of many years; John F. Floberg, a lawyer who had seen active sea duty in the Navy during World War II and who had been Under Secretary of the Navy in the Truman Administration; and John Graham, an Assistant Secretary of the Treasury in the previous administration. All three of these men became valuable Commissioners.

The impression that the Commission was rent with dissension during the period 1953–58 is not a fact. The Commissioners were men with convictions and character, but it is significant that during the period in question there were only 70 split votes whereas 1531 votes were unanimous.

zealous in the protection of strategic information, and a few cartoonists, on a quiet day, searching for something to lampoon, could always fall back on a staple image and depict the Atomic Energy Commission presiding over safes and "Top Secret" filing cabinets stuffed with telephone books and back numbers of the *Congressional Record*.

SHERWOOD

One of my first concerns on returning to the Commission was to learn the state of progress in the effort to use the energy of fusion for peaceful purposes. At the time of the great debate on the issue of whether or not the United States should develop a qualitatively superior weapon (on the fusion principle), an argument advanced against the proposal was that, even if such a weapon could be made, there was "no conceivable *peaceful* application of the thermonuclear reaction." Basis for that argument was probably more emotional than scientific. Now that we knew thermonuclear reactions of very brief duration could be produced (e.g., in weapons), it was the duty of the Commission to discover if controllable and peaceful applications of thermonuclear energy could be made.

It was disappointing to find that only a handful of people were at work upon the project and a very small amount of money budgeted for it—less than two hundred thousand dollars during all of the preceding six months. To put this in scale: In the same period, the Commission was spending over seven million dollars every working day on its other responsibilities. The Commissioners unanimously supported my proposal that a more impressive effort should be made and in the course of time twenty million dollars annually was devoted to it. The importance of "Sherwood," as the project was called, now conceded to be at least theoretically feasible, can hardly be overstated. When it becomes possible to control the fusion of the nuclei of light elements, a new source of power will be at the disposal of the human race. We will be independent not only of the dwindling supplies of fossil fuels (the coal, gas, and oil which store the energy poured down upon the earth by the sun in past ages), but independent of uranium as well.

Upon the assumption that eventually a fusion reactor, fueled with an isotope of hydrogen, will be operated successfully, it may be expected to have these advantages: First, the fuel costs will be extremely low. At present, the proposed fuel, deuterium (an isotope of hydrogen), costs about $140 a pound to extract from ordinary water. If its nuclear energy content can be converted completely into electrical energy (a theoretical efficiency unnecessary to be reached), a pound of deuterium could yield forty million kilowatt hours of electricity. The gross fuel cost has been estimated at only three and one half thousandths of a mill per kilowatt hour. This figure, of course, does not consider the capital cost for the reactor, which in all likelihood would be considerable, but which should require a minimum of maintenance.

Second, the fuel supply would be virtually unlimited and easily obtained. Heavy hydrogen, or deuterium, exists in all the waters of the world and the total amount is estimated at one hundred thousand million million pounds. The complete fusion of this amount of deuterium, I am told, would produce one thousand million million million kilowatt years of electricity—represented by a figure of ten followed by twenty zeros. (I am unable to visualize quantities like these.)

Third, a fusion power plant should be safe. All present calculations indicate that a nuclear explosion could not occur, and the risk of an ordinary accident appears to be about the same as for a conventional coal- or oil-fired power plant.

Fourth, radioactive hazards of operations would be extremely low. Radioactivity may be induced in the material surrounding the reactor, but the *fusion* reactor itself is not expected to create quantities of long-lived radioactive by-products that must be disposed of as waste. This is one of the problems with *fission* reactors of present design.

Fifth, the efficiency of such a plant may be quite high. A part of the energy released in fusion reactions in a power plant might be convertible *directly* into electricity without the loss of efficiency which results from interposition of cooling agent, boiler and turbogenerator. Such heat-transfer processes would be used only to put the rest of the energy to work as electricity.

During the early years of the program, the fact that we were engaged in research to develop a controlled thermonuclear reaction was classified as "Restricted Data" under the Atomic Energy Act. We were criticized for this secrecy by those who stated that, if the research were not secret, the problem could be solved more quickly. The results of de-classification four years ago have not yet borne out this supposition, though it may eventually prove true. The chief reason for initial secrecy was the recognition that, if the research were successful, the achievement of controlled fusion would provide an intense source of neutrons which could have great military significance from the point of view of producing fissionable material in substantial amounts. The case for declassification of information in this field was strengthened by the fact that neutrons were becoming more readily available throughout the world, a result of the rapid development of fission reactors. Also, fissionable material has proved to be less rare in nature than once believed.

Just before the first International Conference on the Peaceful Uses of Atomic Energy in Geneva in August of 1955, my colleagues and I, meeting in Washington, determined to announce at that conference that we were conducting research on the controlled thermonuclear reaction. The president of the conference, a distinguished physicist, Dr. Homi Bhabha of Bombay, delivered an opening statement in the course of which he discussed the goals of controlled thermonuclear research and predicted that power from the fusion reaction would be achieved within twenty years. In conformity with the decision of the Commission, I announced that the United States had been supporting a long-range program to this end. It was assumed at the time that the announcement had been the result of Bhabha's address, but disclosure had been formally agreed upon in Washington some weeks earlier.

Public interest was soon focused on the subject, and from time to time, in one laboratory or another, neutrons observed in the course of experiments led those optimistically inclined to the belief that the required conditions of temperature and containment had been achieved.

Three years later at the Second International Scientific Conference in Geneva our exhibit featured a number of working thermonuclear devices in their state of development to that time. Other nations also exhibited their apparatus for this purpose. The Russians described, but did not exhibit, a very much larger device than any of ours, and claimed to have operated it. We were informed by scientists who visited Russia two years later that it had not in fact operated and was not yet operable. The dependability of Russian scientific claims is confusing. That Russian technicians are capable of fine work must be conceded, but it is also true that they do not hesitate, for propaganda purposes, to assert as factual that which is not.

There were press reports (in 1957) that our British friends had achieved a controlled thermonuclear reaction and that its announcement was being withheld at our request, but this, as well as some unsubstantiated reports from our own laboratories, was the result of overoptimism and hyperbole. Success is still ahead, but the rewards are so great and the prospects so attractive that no reasonable effort should be spared to bring the development of one or more of these experimental approaches to a successful conclusion. I hope to live long enough to see the same natural force which powers the hydrogen bomb tamed for peaceful uses. A breakthrough could come tomorrow as well as a decade hence.* Out of our laboratories may come a discovery as important as the Promethean taming of fire.

In the process known as "fission," the nuclei of very heavy atoms such as uranium 235 or plutonium 239, are split when an additional neutron penetrates them. The result is the formation of nuclear fragments lighter than the original nucleus, plus several neutrons. These expelled neutrons can then cause other heavy nuclei to split and a sequence of split nuclei results, called a "chain reaction." In each fission process the sum of the mass of the nuclei produced by the splitting is less than that of the original nucleus. The difference in the mass (m) becomes energy (E) in the course of the reaction, in accordance with Einstein's formula, $E=mc^2$, where c represents the speed of light. A rise in temperature is one result of this kinetic energy, and the heat can be utilized by withdrawing it to produce steam, which in turn revolves conventional turbines and generators to produce electrical energy. The atomic power reactors now built or building operate on this principle. Excluding military installations and large reactor experiments, many of which generate power, there are thirteen in the United States at the present time.

In a good many respects, the "fusion" process is almost the reverse of this. In fusion, the nuclei of two *light* atoms (such as isotopes of hydrogen, for instance) are induced to fuse together to produce a single nucleus of an element which is heavier than either of the two, though not as heavy as their total mass before they fused. This difference in mass also appears as kinetic energy. The energy release in each fusion reaction is appreciably less than that involved in each fission reaction, but the energy release per unit weight is greater.

Very great difficulties block the road to the development of con-

* Among those working on different approaches to this goal are James L. Tuck, Richard F. Post, Stirling A. Colgate, John A. Wheeler, and Lyman Spitzer, Jr. Arthur Ruark of AEC is in over-all supervision of the effort. He and his predecessor, Amasa Bishop, have given wise allocation of support and continuous encouragement to the laboratories.

trolled thermonuclear reactors at the present time. When a hot plasma* is confined and the temperatures are further raised to the order of some millions of degrees, the probability of nuclear collisions becomes correspondingly greater. A primary difficulty is to reach the very high temperatures which are necessary in order that the particles be given sufficient energy for the collisions which will make fusion reactions plentiful.

An associated difficulty is that nuclei of atoms carry positive charges and, being "like" charges, repel each other. To overcome this repulsion so that the nuclei may physically collide and fuse, they must be slammed into one another at very high velocities. The chances that they will bounce away from one another greatly exceed the probabilities that they will fuse. They must, therefore, be confined in some limited space and move at high speeds with respect to one another until fusions occur by brute force. This means raising the nuclei to temperatures probably higher than those in the interior of the sun. This, of course, would instantly vaporize a container of any material substance. The present experimental containers, therefore, are not material at all, but are various configurations of magnetic fields known as "bottles," "mirrors," "pinch machines," etc., in which the magnetic lines of force may be imagined as a cage of invisible rubber bands.

The reason that elements at the extreme low end of the atomic table are considered to be the only possible fuels for the fusion reaction is that the force of nuclear repulsion appears to increase with the atomic number—i.e., the number of positively charged protons in each nucleus. Since the temperature required to overcome the mutual forces of repulsion would increase very rapidly with the atomic number of the element used, it is for this reason that isotopes of hydrogen, the lightest of the elements, seem to have been providentially destined as fuel in fusion reactors. Elements with higher atomic numbers may someday be used, but it would appear at the present time that even higher temperatures will be required for them.

Another difficulty involved in developing a thermonuclear apparatus is to make the reaction self-sustaining, as is the fission chain reaction in a conventional reactor. This means keeping the device at a temperature at which the system will remain in a steady state and not cool off.

---

*A plasma is a gas made up of atomic nuclei which as a result of high temperatures have become stripped of the electrons normally surrounding each nucleus—perhaps in some such configuration as the planets surround the sun, although I am told that this is an idealized, and not a precise, analogy.

None of these major difficulties (nor many minor ones) are regarded as insuperable by the excellent teams now at work on this tremendously important research project. When my term expired, there were in existence a number of different experimental approaches to solving "Sherwood." These research efforts are now carried on in five major locations—Los Alamos Scientific Laboratory, Oak Ridge National Laboratory, the Forrestal Memorial Research Center at Princeton University, and the University of California Radiation Laboratory at Berkeley and Livermore, California. Several other university and industrial sites are also connected with the enterprise.

SHIP PROPULSION

The first months as Chairman were much occupied with trying to catch up on the technological changes which had occurred during the three years that I had been in private life. In a field so rapidly expanding, much information becomes obsolete quickly. It was a surprise to discover how much had become outdated. Among the new events was the success of a tough young naval engineer, Captain Hyman G. Rickover, an officer who combined some of the qualities of Henry Ford, Admiral Farragut, and (if one listened to his detractors) Simon Legree. He had completed building the prototype of a reactor for a nuclear submarine to be called the *Nautilus*. This successful, full-scale nuclear engine, the first ever to be built (other than experimental installations), was erected in a huge tank of sea water at an AEC reservation in the Idaho desert. News writers were quick to christen it "The Ship in the Desert." Rickover and his then chief, Admiral Earle Mills of the Navy's Bureau of Ships, had first approached me with the project when it was a dream of Rickover's in 1948. It sounded fantastic then, when we did not even know how to build a power reactor on land, much less one to drive a submerged vessel. Rickover just never let it drop.

Books have been written about Rickover and more undoubtedly will be. Certainly he is too remarkable and complex to characterize in a paragraph. I used to think of him as a sort of Savonarola in a blue uniform. During the years I worked with him, my respect increased steadily. This did not mean that working with him was fun. His personality was astringent—some even found it abrasive, though I did not—and his job was to him the most important assignment in the whole world, taking precedence over any other enterprise of anyone else whatever. Believing that with all his heart, he convinced his staff of it, and the task, no matter how difficult, was done. Toes trodden in the process were merely necessary casualties in the path of achievement. If ever a man merited the adjective "dedicated," it is Rickover, who long since would have had a man on the moon had that been his assignment.

The ship in the desert began to generate power in August. It was used to train the crews for the *Nautilus* and for the school of nuclear submarines which followed her down to the sea. The *Nautilus* herself was under way on nuclear power by January 17, 1955, having been sponsored by Mrs. Eisenhower. It was followed into the water in short order by the *Seawolf* and the *Skate,* and all three established immediate records. The *Nautilus* was the first craft ever to traverse the top of the world passing under the polar ice west to east across the Arctic Ocean. The *Seawolf* set an underwater cruising record which far outdistanced any previous performance. The *Skate* crossed the Arctic Ocean east to west under the ice of the North Pole.

The prototype *Nautilus* reactor was routinely shut down in August 1956 at the end of the longest full-power run ever completed by any type of propulsion plant. On a single charge of uranium fuel (and using only a part of that charge), the reactor operated at an average power of 100 per cent for 1600 hours, the equivalent of 66 days. Had the *Nautilus* itself made a cruise of this length of time, she could have steamed at top speed submerged, around the world, and many thousands of miles more, without refueling. A similar cruise by conventionally powered submarines would have required about a million six hundred thousand gallons of fuel, or enough to fill a freight train of railroad tank cars over a mile long. Admiral Rickover might be pardoned for a justifiable pride in that record.

ARMS RACE—NEW PHASE

The first weeks in office brought another event and a decision.

On August 7, 1953, a few days over a month after taking office, as a product of a restless and worried night, I wrote a memorandum for the President. The fact that we had not detected a Soviet weapon test in nearly two years was the sleep disturber. Three possible reasons suggested themselves. First, that the Russians were economizing on fissionable material. (That seemed unlikely, with the large land mass available to them for prospecting.) Second, that they might be hiding their tests underwater, in Lake Baikal for instance, or in caverns or mines. Third, it might be that from the beginning they were intent on leapfrogging our development by proceeding directly to hydrogen bombs, about which Fuchs could have given them information. "If that should be so," the memorandum concluded, "their latest test—1951— may have been of an essential component for their H bombs and it may have been satisfactory for that purpose. In that case, the next test they make might very well be a test of an H-bomb." Five days later, we detected an explosion in Soviet territory with thermonuclear reactions positively indicated. Our first test of a thermonuclear bomb had taken place only nine months before.

When doubt had been resolved as to the nature of their test, I telephoned President Eisenhower in his summer office at Lowry Air Force Base near Denver. "You must have a pipe line into the Kremlin," he said. Then, receiving his authorization, we made a public statement: "The Soviet Union conducted an atomic test on the evening of 12 August. Certain information to this effect came into our hands that night. Subsequent information on the subject indicates that this test involved both fission and thermonuclear reaction. It will be recalled that more than three years ago the United States decided to accelerate work on all forms of atomic weapons. Both the 1951 and 1952 Eniwetok test series included tests involving similar reactions." From that time we announced Russian nuclear explosions as a matter of course.

Had the Russians, since the date of President Truman's announcement in 1950, now succeeded in duplicating our research with no outside assistance and in almost the identical time span? I turned to Dr. von Neumann. His judgment: "In the period between our first use of the atomic bomb, to the date of Russia's first test of that kind of weapon, there was a time lag between us of four years in *our* favor. Their technical manpower, though it is reported to be growing rapidly, certainly does not yet exceed ours and their capacity in all the relevant areas—steel, coal, electrical KWs—is, let us say, somewhere between one-quarter and one-half as great as ours. The rapid overtaking of our lead [in this instance] required explanation and the simplest explanation, and probably the correct one, is that they began their thermonuclear program *before* we started ours. We can thank Fuchs and a few like him for that."

The fact that this Soviet success occurred within so short a time after their test of a fission weapon fortified my conjecture that from the beginning they had attempted to leapfrog our weapons by aiming to produce hydrogen bombs at the time they began their nuclear weapon program, while refusing nuclear disarmament and control. In such an enterprise their scientific establishment was certainly assisted—we may never know to what extent—by the defection of Klaus Fuchs, who had worked at Los Alamos and who, when he left the United States in 1947, carried with him such experimental and theoretical information on the "super bomb" as was known to us at that time. Fuchs, of course, was not the only Soviet link to our laboratories.

With both nations in possession of hydrogen bombs, the arms race with Russia had entered a new phase. We had reason to believe that we had more weapons and more sophisticated weapons than the Soviets, but it was also reasonable to suppose that, if they intended to strike us, a time would come when they would have made as many weapons as they required for that purpose. Our possession of more weapons, or more devastating weapons, would not necessarily be a deterrent if the Communists were determined upon aggression by surprise at some future date.

A PRESIDENT'S CONVICTIONS

President Eisenhower's views on Russian-American relations and on nuclear weapons were known. As to the former, he had expressed himself at the end of World War II with restrained optimism, but optimism nevertheless:

> In the past relations of America and Russia, there was no cause to regard the future with pessimism. Historically, the two peoples had maintained an unbroken friendship that dated back to the birth of the United States as an independent republic. Except for a short period, their diplomatic relations had been continuous. Both were free from the stigma of colonial empire building by force. The transfer between them of the rich Alaskan territory was an unmatched international episode, devoid of threat at the time and of any recrimination after the exchange. Twice they had been allies in war. Since 1941 they had been dependent each on the other for ultimate victory over the European axis.

and he had commented upon the philosophical differences of the two systems of government, observing that:

Idealogically, however, they were in diametric opposition; the United States were devoted to a social and political order based upon individual liberty and human dignity; Russia, dedicated to the dictatorship of the proletariat, seemed in Western eyes to be engulfed in a form of statism under the absolute direction of a few men. By the same token, it is probable that to them our adherence to a system based upon personal liberty was actually a political immaturity that permitted exploitation of the masses. Out of this cleavage between the governmental systems of two great powers there might develop in the world two hostile camps whose differences would ultimately provoke another holocaust of war. Should the gulf, however, be bridged practically by effective methods of cooperation, the peace and unity of the world would be assured. No other division among the nations could be considered a menace to world unity and peace, provided mutual confidence and trust could be developed between America and the Soviets.

Obstacles, doubts, fears of failure in American-Soviet relations, there were on every side. But the alternative to success seemed so terrifying to contemplate that all of us on occupation duty sought every possible avenue through which progress might be achieved.[2]

The President's opinions on nuclear weapons were well informed. During his experiences in Europe, he had been kept posted by oral reports brought to him by trusted officer-messengers throughout the war, and at the Potsdam Conference in July 1945 which he attended as an observer, Secretary of War Stimson told him of the test scheduled for Alamogordo. General Eisenhower had expressed the hope that the United States would never have to use such a weapon against any enemy, because he disliked seeing his country take the lead in introducing into warfare anything as destructive as the new weapon was expected to be. "Moreover," he said, "I mistakenly had some faint hope that if we never used the weapon in war, other nations might remain ignorant of the fact that the problem of nuclear fission had been solved. I did not then know, of course, that an army of scientists had been engaged in the production of the weapon and that secrecy in this vital matter could not have been maintained. My views were merely personal and immediate reactions; they were not based upon any analysis of the subject."

After the bombs had been dropped on Hiroshima and Nagasaki, he was profoundly disturbed by the impact of this revolutionary change in warfare. In an instant, as he saw it, the old concepts of war had been swept away. The purpose of an aggressor nation thereafter would be to stock atom bombs in quantity for a devastating surprise attack, while the defending country would in turn launch its store of atom bombs against the attacker's homeland.

As he looked about him, even the bombed ruins of Germany seemed to serve as but a faint forecast of what war in the future would mean. "I gained hope," he wrote, "that this development . . . of the ultimate in destruction would drive man . . . to find a way of eliminating war." He even speculated that, where statesmanship and religion had not been successful, universal fear and the instinct of self-preservation might find a way.

Later, by 1947, when General Eisenhower was Chief of Staff of the Army and stationed in Washington, his views on the necessity of inspection as a precondition of atomic disarmament were recorded by former Under Secretary of the Navy Ralph A. Bard. At that time, Bard represented the United States in the UN's perennial negotiations on conventional weapon disarmament and reported to Secretary Forrestal. Bard had attended a meeting with Under Secretary of State Lovett, General Eisenhower, and General Gruenther. Forrestal noted in his diary that Eisenhower had made the point that it would be dangerous to proceed on the subject of conventional armaments "until the Russians had agreed to a workable plan of inspection." His point was that, if we agreed to a plan for disarmament involving conventional weapons without an agreement for rigid inspection, the Russians could move for the application of the same unsafe formula to atomic weapons. It was General Eisenhower's opinion then that "any agreement about atomic weapons without enforceable methods of inspection would be most dangerous for the United States."[3] This was a position far ahead of his time, but one which, a few years later, was shared by most of his fellow citizens in the United States.

The President flew from Denver to New York to join in celebrating the eighty-third birthday of Bernard Baruch on August 19, 1953. His personal assistant, C. D. Jackson, and I went up to New York to breakfast with him that morning. Among other subjects, we discussed the fact that our relative position in the area of weapons had altered radically, just as was the case in 1949. While our first thermonuclear test had occurred nine months earlier than the Soviets', our clear lead was again threatened.

August passed with no new ideas along the line of the President's insistence on finding a procedure for ending the nuclear stalemate. There was a fairly steady flow of plans and suggestions which, generally, were variants on themes ranging, on the one hand, from those urging that we should simply disarm, unilaterally, and trust that noble example and world opinion would exert an irresistible moral persuasion on the Soviets, to those, on the other hand, who cautioned that there should not be even a negotiation with the Communists—anywhere, at any time. These advisers believed that negotiations could only benefit the Soviet and hurt us. "Just make more bombs," said these counselors, "and be alert for eventualities."

In the middle ground were more hopeful formulae, none however but which in one form or another had been put forward at the United Nations and there either ignored or denounced, or vetoed, by the Communist representatives. It seemed as though we were in a tunnel, increasingly dark and constricted, and without an end.

The nuclear threat had long been on my mind. A little less than four months after the first two atomic bombs had been used in warfare, I was one of the speakers at a Red Cross dinner in New York, and had chosen as a topic the necessity for international control of atomic energy.

A few days earlier Von Neumann had made the semiserious observation that the appearance in the heavens of super-novae—those mysterious stars which suddenly are born in great brilliance and, as quickly, become celestial cinders—could be evidence that sentient beings in other planetary systems had reached the point in their scientific knowledge where we now stand, and, having failed to solve the problem of living together, had at least succeeded in achieving togetherness by cosmic suicide. I told my audience that Van Neumann had pointed out that this piece of science fiction was not very much more fantastic than was the first fission of an atomic nucleus, so minute at its birth and yet becoming the force which, six years later, pulverized Hiroshima and Nagasaki.

In the intervening years, I added, some of us had consoled ourselves with the hopeful doctrine that, historically, new weapons have produced their effective countermeasures. Some were sanguine enough to feel that the solution to the threat posed by atomic weapons would be simply to "outlaw" them.

True, weapons have stimulated countermeasures, but the weapons continue to be deadly. Alfred Nobel, at one time, is said to have nursed the delusion that his discovery of dynamite, so much more powerful than gunpowder, would ultimately bring peace to the world. It is a fact of life, however, that while countermeasures of sorts have been developed for "conventional" weapons, the weapons continue to be used. The only thing that retires a weapon is a superior weapon. Countermeasures developed against aircraft did not prevent numbers of them from reaching their targets in every war in which they have been employed.

Nor, historically, my remarks continued, has the "outlawing" of weapons been effective. When the influence of the Church in temporal affairs was so widely accepted, there had one time been an unsuccessful attempt made to outlaw the crossbow, then a revolutionary new weapon. It would puncture the armor of knights. No instance of successful prohibition of any important weapon is recorded. The proscription of poison gas is occasionally cited, but this weapon of World War I was not used in World War II substantially for the reason that high explosives and incendiary bombs were preferred for tactical reasons. Combatants on both sides had poison gas in their arsenals had it been needed. And the humanity of napalm bombs over poison gas would be hard to explain.

Nor is public conscience dependable. I used the example of how, after the first crossing of the English Channel by heavier-than-air craft in about 1910, an authority of that day speculated on the future of aviation, concluding that planes might be used as scouting aids in warfare but would never be permitted to drop explosives on cities. To readers fifty years ago, the meaning was clear. The bombing of cities would never be "permitted" by the public conscience. Within little more than one generation, the public conscience became unaccountably numbed.

These after-dinner observations closed with the thought that we could not hope to avert the danger of nuclear war by a countermeasure, nor outlaw it by some *unilateral* decision. Only with the consent of all governments could we hope to bring all men to the point where, as far as this newly discovered natural force is concerned, everyone would be under the protection of an international covenant superior to any sovereignty. The destructive applications of atomic energy, I believe, would have to be brought under international control with effective and enforceable safeguards, if the world of free societies could expect to live otherwise than under the cloud of a great and continuing fear. These were my views in the autumn of 1945. There were views by others of considerable influence offered then and later.

SENIOR OPINIONS

In the closing days of his tour of duty in 1945, Secretary of War Stimson prepared a memorandum on the future course of the international relations of the United States, being sole possessors of the atomic bomb. His idea was a proposal to the Soviets that we would be prepared to enter into an arrangement" . . . the general purpose of which would be to control and limit the use of the atomic bomb. . . . Such an approach might more specifically lead to the proposal that we would stop work on . . . the bomb as a military weapon, provided the Russians and the British would agree with us that in no event will they or we use a bomb as an instrument of war unless all three Governments agree to that use . . ."[4]

Senator Vandenberg, in a contemporary letter to his friend Dr. Robert C. Angell of the University of Michigan, noted his opinion on our clear and proper course. "It is our task," he wrote, "to develop through the United Nations organization a system of complete world-wide inspection which shall guarantee to civilization that no nation (including ours) shall use atomic energy for the construction of weapons of war. I know of no other logical answer."

On November 15, 1945, President Truman, with Prime Ministers Attlee and Mackenzie King, after a cruise down the Potomac on the presidential yacht, announced in the form of a "declaration" that the three governments were agreed on the need for international action under the auspices of the United Nations to provide controls over atomic energy to ensure that it would be used only for peaceful purposes. Though my opinions were far from senior, the declaration had disturbed me because it proposed a procedure in stages. The successful completion of each one before the next step was undertaken. The fourth step was listed as "effective safeguards by way of inspection and other means to protect the complying states against the hazards of violations and evasions."[5]

I wrote Forrestal that to exchange information before arriving at a means of safeguarding the results of the exchange would be putting the cart before the horse.[6]

Forrestal told me later that he discussed this aspect of the subject with the President and subsequently with Mr. Baruch. A month later Secretary of State Byrnes and Foreign Secretary Bevin went to Moscow to meet with Foreign Minister Molotov, taking with them a definite proposal based on the Washington declaration. The proposal called for the establishment of a United Nations Commission on Atomic Energy, which would have jurisdiction over all weapons capable of mass destruction.

Secretary Byrnes recalls that in these meetings, just as earlier at

Potsdam, and later at the Council of Foreign Ministers in London, no member of the Soviet delegation expressed any curiosity about atomic energy. At Potsdam neither Stalin nor Molotov ever mentioned the subject again after the President had made his rather veiled revelation to Stalin about our new and powerful weapon. Byrnes had invited President Conant of Harvard to accompany him to Moscow, and, although Conant attended most of the meetings and his presence in Moscow was noted in the Russian press, no Russian scientists made contact with him. Molotov, during the course of a dinner at which he was host, made the suggestion that a great chemist who was also president of a great American university should address the University of Moscow on the subject of atomic energy. It was assumed the suggestion was firm, but on the following day Molotov explained that he was not serious, that he had no authority to extend such an invitation and "had only been trying to be pleasant." There was to be no chance for an inadvertent leak by Russian scientists from which we might learn that they were feverishly at work on atomic bombs. The Soviet aim was to achieve this potential in complete secrecy, a circumstance which would greatly enhance its surprise value.

The proposal to establish a U. N. Commission on Atomic Energy was finally adopted by the three principal governments and presented to the General Assembly of the United Nations, then meeting in London, on behalf of all five permanent members of the Security Council. It was adopted without amendment and by unanimous vote—a significant fact in the light of subsequent Soviet actions.

At about the same time, Secretary Byrnes named a board of consultants which produced a study and a suggested plan. Known as the Acheson-Lilienthal report, it was released in March 1946. It was summarized by Under Secretary Acheson as offering "a plan under which no nation would make atomic bombs or the material for them. All dangerous activities would be carried on—not merely inspected—by a live, functioning, international authority with a real purpose in the world and capable of attracting competent personnel . . . The extremely favored position with regard to atomic devices which the United States enjoys at present is only temporary. It will not last. We must use that advantage now to promote international security and to carry out our policy of building a lasting peace through international agreement. . . ."

On the recommendation of Secretary Byrnes, President Truman then appointed Mr. Baruch, a wise negotiator and statesman whose experience in government had begun under President Wilson, to be chairman of a commission to prepare and implement a definitive plan for the control of atomic energy. Baruch and his assistants, John Hancock and Fredinand Eberstadt, drafted a proposal which was presented to the United Nations Atomic Energy Commission on June 14, 1946. Presenting his proposal, Baruch began with the arresting observation: "We are here to make a choice between the quick and the dead." He advanced the first formal United States plan to control atomic energy.

The plan provided for the creation of an International Atomic Development Authority, which would be entrusted with "everything"—beginning with the raw material and including control or ownership of all atomic energy activities that might be dangerous to world peace. It would have power to control, inspect, and license all other atomic energy activities. It would be charged with the duty of fostering the beneficial uses of atomic energy and with responsibility for research and development to detect any misuse of the new knowledge. The plan also provided that, when an adequate system for control and inspection had been agreed upon and had been put into operation, the manufacture of atomic bombs should cease.* Existing bombs would be disposed of pursuant to the terms of a treaty, and the authority would be given full information by the United States concerning the method of producing atomic energy.

The Baruch Plan also provided that penalties should be established for illegal possession or use of an atomic bomb and that the punishment should be "condign," fitting—in other words the punishment should fit the crime. The resolution proposed by the United States after months of debate was eventually defeated in the Security Council by a surprise veto of the Soviet delegate.

It has been assumed that the basis for Soviet objection was the fear of unlimited mutual inspection and the presumption that this would in some way embarrass the internal affairs of the Soviet Union. It seems plausible, however, that a strong reason why inspection was unacceptable to the Soviets in 1946 was their apprehension that it would expose their work on developing a thermonuclear bomb. They could very well have known from Fuchs and others that we were not working on that weapon. If they could succeed, they would be in a strong position. If this conjecture is correct, President Truman's decision in January 1950 to build the thermonuclear bomb was extraordinarily fortuitous. At this

---

* It will be noted that *inspection* and *control* were to be not only agreed upon but *in operation* before the manufacture of weapons would cease. Our position in that regard was greatly improved over the declaration of November 15, 1945.

writing, Soviet attitude toward inspection has shown no change. Inspection is given lip service in principle when new negotiations begin, but it is thwarted as soon as it becomes the subject of detailed specification.*

In 1947 a group headed by Dr. Compton, of the Massachusetts Institute of Technology, and including President Harold W. Dodds, of Princeton, Rev. Dr. Daniel A. Poling, Father Edmund A. Walsh, and Judge Samuel I. Rosenman, reported to the President that "So long as any great nation has power to stop by veto any proposed United Nations action against it as an aggressor, the United Nations cannot act to protect against such aggression. *So long as there is no operating system of inspection whereby the United Nations can thoroughly check on the atomic energy activities of every nation, there is no guaranty that preparations for atomic war are not going on in secret, and there can be no certain security and no absence of suspicion and fear."*[7] (Italics supplied.)

IDEA

From the beginning of his term, President Eisenhower had been under pressure to talk about the devastation which atomic and hydrogen weapons could produce. Disarmament of the atom was a cause which had been on dead center ever since the Soviet veto. Very shortly after his inauguration, a scientific advisory group had presented him with a report on atomic weapons which the President referred to the National Security Council for study. During the course of this study, he commissioned C. D. Jackson, his special assistant whose particular assignment was cold-war strategy, to try his hand at preparing a candid speech about nuclear weapons. A number of drafts were produced by various writers and submitted to Jackson. All of them were preoccupied with the theme of human destruction, speculations on what damage the

* In a letter to this writer dated September 1, 1961, Mr. Baruch observed, "I do not know whether we can ever reach a meaningful agreement with the Soviets on any of the crucial issues of peace, but I do know that we are courting disaster unless we are as strong as we can make ourselves. . . . I hope this latest Soviet move [resumption of weapon testing in the atmosphere] will impress upon everyone—including the so-called neutrals—once and for all Moscow's consistent record in frustrating meaningful atomic control. . . . back in 1946 . . . the Soviet representatives on our [U.N.] Scientific Committee agreed that our control plan was scientifically and technologically feasible and that agreement was essentially a political problem. . . ."

Russians might do to us and what damage we would do them in retaliation. But beyond reciting the awful consequences of a third world war, there was no expression of hope that the atom might be harnessed to serve man instead of annihilating him. Jackson was dissatisfied with the drafts and so expressed himself to the President.

During that period the President opened a press conference by saying that the Soviet development of the hydrogen bomb had not come to him as a surprise. He had always estimated, he added, that it was within the scientific and technical capabilities of the Soviets to achieve it, and that we had been on notice for some years that their native ingenuity had material assistance from what they had learned of our program through espionage. He continued:

> The Soviets now possess a stockpile of atomic weapons of conventional types and we must furthermore conclude that the powerful explosion of August 12th last was produced by a weapon, or the forerunner of a weapon, of power far in excess of the conventional types.
>
> We therefore conclude that the Soviets have the capability of atomic attack on us, and such capability will increase with the passage of time.
>
> Now a word as to our own situation. *We do not intend to disclose the details of our strength in atomic weapons of any sort,* but it is large and increasing steadily. We have in our arsenals a number of kinds of weapons suited to the special needs of the Army, Navy, and Air Force for the specific tasks assigned to each service.
>
> It is my hope, my earnest prayer, that this country will never again be engaged in war. As I said in Atlantic City this week, with reference to atomic energy, "This titanic force must be reduced to the fruitful service of mankind. . . ."[8]

The President's flat declaration (which I have italicized above) that we would not reveal any details of our strength placed a considerable damper on some who had advocated more "candor" in that direction. The President had been urged to disclose the extent of our weapon stockpiles and be candid in a number of other particulars which would not have advantaged the American public but certainly would have relieved the Soviets of trouble in their espionage activities.

The President came East from Denver again on September 10 to attend the funeral of Chief Justice Vinson. As he traveled, an idea occurred to him about disarmament. It was a subject about which he thought constantly. The next morning he spoke of the idea to General Cutler, with instructions to pass it to Jackson and to me at once. Shortly before noon a messenger brought a memorandum from Cutler:

In discussing with the President this morning the action taken at the Council yesterday . . . the President suggested that you might consider the following proposal which he did not think anyone had yet thought of. . . .

Suppose the United States and the Soviets were to turn over to the United Nations, for peaceful uses, X kilograms of fissionable material. . . .

This was the seed from which the Atoms for Peace program was to grow. Though sown upon the rocky soil of political querulousness and international suspicions, it did germinate and in the course of time struck root.

On reading the President's suggestion, my imagination was slow to take fire, but the more I thought about it in the following days, the more promising it began to appear.

"ATOMS FOR PEACE"

At this time "fissionable material"—uranium—was still an excessively rare commodity and the key to the control of atomic energy. The great reserves of uranium in the United States were scarcely suspected.

The scheme the President had proposed needed a method to safeguard the fissionable material so that, once contributed to the UN and deposited at some point, it would not be "hijacked" by an aggressor nation. A method suggested itself to me for storing fissionable material so that it could not be removed either clandestinely or suddenly. The method was the suspension of the uranium in solution, in very great dilution, in underground tanks, thus making a quick raid impossible. There were other refinements. A memorandum for the President to this effect, which he read during the closing days of September, had, among its other suggestions, the establishment of an International Atomic Energy Agency, to which the contributions of fissionable material, as originally envisaged by the President, would be made by nations subscribing to the plan. At the President's direction, the memorandum was then sent to Secretary of State Dulles and to the Chairman of the Joint Chiefs of Staff, Admiral Radford. Jackson, of course, had read it as soon as I wrote it. It was then referred to a National Security Council working committee, and on September 30 word came that the President desired that the study be completed by October 30 at the latest.

It seemed to most of us who discussed it that, if an initial amount of uranium could be put up by the United States, the Russians, and the

British, it might, as my assistant, William Golden, put it, be like "getting the first olive out of the bottle." In the course of time, larger and larger amounts of the essential but dangerous element would be in the hands of the International Agency and eventually atomic weapon stockpiles themselves would have to be cannibalized to continue the contributions. These stocks of uranium in carefully supervised installations would be used to provide fuel for power plants throughout the world.

The President was pleased as his plan developed. It was simple and uncomplicated. It did not depend upon good faith at this stage. He directed that the draft of a speech be prepared in which the prospect of atomic war would be explored, its consequences described, and his plan then put forward as a hopeful alternative. He assigned Jackson to this task of draftsmanship. While it was in preparation, Jackson and I would meet for breakfast at the Metropolitan Club, a meal which provided the convenient code name for the project in a period when everything carried a pseudonym. Our standing order started with a cereal advertised as "Wheaties." We began to refer to the enterprise as "Wheaties" when necessary to talk about it on the telephone or elsewhere.

On December 4, the President left for Bermuda to meet with Prime Minister Churchill of Great Britain and Premier Laniel of France. We took the last draft of the Wheaties speech along. On arrival, it was discussed with Churchill. Sir Winston had brought with him F. A. Lindemann (Lord Cherwell), the physicist who held the post of Paymaster General in his Cabinet. Cherwell was rather more than a member of Sir Winston's cabinet. Referred to by his chief, with obvious affection, as "The Prof," he was Churchill's most trusted counselor and scientific adviser, and his friend. During the war Cherwell had visited the United States on several occasions and I had come to know him socially. He was the brother of a friend, Brigadier General Charles Lindemann.[9]

Cherwell was extraordinary by any set of standards. A vegetarian, physically huge, he stood about six feet four, his altitude accentuated by a derby with a high crown, a sort of personal trademark. He always reminded me of the Nelson Column in Trafalgar Square, minus the pigeons. People either hated him or were devoted to him, but none doubted either his physical courage or his scientific competence. He had demonstrated the former in World War I when he solved the problem of how to get planes out of tail spins—generally fatal—proving his theory in planes which he put into spins deliberately. As for the latter, he had been made professor of physics at Oxford as a young man.

Line by line, I went over the draft speech with Cherwell. The plan appealed to him, although he sent a note to the Prime Minister on December 6 in which he saw the danger that the project might be wrecked on the rocks of allocating the contributions. He also forecast "interminable arguments" with the Russians. He added that he "agreed, of course, that it would be most desirable to work out. . . ."

I told him that if the plan ever got off the ground we hoped to convene an international scientific conference on the peaceful uses of atomic energy and restore communication among the scientists of the world. He was skeptical of the idea but generously wrote to congratulate on the success of the first conference a year and a half later. In his letter he remembered and mentioned that he had deprecated it earlier.*

During the second day of the Bermuda Conference, arrangements were made that upon the President's return to the United States on December 8, he would accept an invitation to appear before the General Assembly of the United Nations, deliver his speech, and make his plea for atomic disarmament. While Jackson and I thought the speech just about perfect as it read in the last draft, it turned out to be susceptible of great improvement. On the return flight from Bermuda to New York, the President took his pencil and began to edit the text. I have a part of the "last" draft with the changes in his handwriting. Only a small part of the original text survived his critical pencil. The most trenchant language throughout the speech was his own. During the flight, this final draft was transcribed by the President's secretary, Mrs. Ann Whitman. Secretary of State Dulles, Jackson, and the rest of us turned to as mimeograph operators, proofreaders, and staplers. The speech in many copies was completed when the *Columbine* touched the runway at LaGuardia Field.

We whipped across the Triborough Bridge and down the East Side of New York to the headquarters of the United Nations. A hushed gathering filled every seat in the great Hall of Assembly as the President stepped to the lectern to make one of the great speeches of our time. With a few introductory remarks, indicating his respect for the United Nations, he began by saying that he had come to speak of some of the things that had been in his mind and in the minds and hearts of his

* "I have just heard of the tremendous triumph you had at Geneva. I little thought when you proposed it at Bermuda that it would be such a great show and I rather doubt whether you did either. . . ."

associates for a great many months. He said that if danger existed in the world today it was a danger shared by all, and that if there was hope of avoiding it that hope should be shared by all. He felt impelled, he added, to speak in a new language, "the language of atomic warfare." It was a language which he would have preferred not to use.

He then recited the facts, well known to many of the delegates: that the United States had set off the world's first atomic explosion; that since that date in 1945 we had conducted forty-two test explosions; that atomic bombs today were more than twenty-five times as powerful as the weapons with which the Atomic Age had begun; and that hydrogen weapons were equal to millions of tons of TNT. "Today," he said, "the United States' stockpile of atomic weapons . . . exceeds by many times the explosive equivalent of the total of all bombs and all shells that came from every plane and every gun in every theatre of war in all of the years of World War II." He noted that atomic weapons had virtually achieved "conventional status" within our armed services and that the dread secret and the fearful engines of atomic might were not ours alone but were known both to our friends and allies, Great Britain and Canada, and also known to the Soviet Union. The knowledge possessed by several nations, he predicted, would eventually be shared by others—perhaps by all others.

He continued, pointing out that the superiority and numbers of weapons which we possessed were no preventive against the fearful material damage and toll of human lives that a surprise aggression would inflict, and that costly systems of defense could not guarantee safety for the cities and citizens of any nation. "The awful arithmetic of the atomic bomb does not permit of any such easy solution," he warned.

"Should any atomic attack be launched against the United States," he said, "our reactions would be swift and resolute." Terrible damage would be inflicted upon an aggressor. But to pause there, he pointed out, would simply be to confirm the "hopeless finality of a belief that two atomic colossi are doomed malevolently to eye each other indefinitely across a trembling world."

He then approached his proposal. The United States wished to be constructive, not destructive. It desired agreements, not wars. He knew, he said, that in a world divided salvation could not be obtained by one dramatic act; steps would have to be taken; but we must start to take these steps now. The United States, the President announced, "is instantly prepared to meet privately with such other countries as may be principally involved, to seek an acceptable solution to the atomic armaments race which overshadows not only the peace, but the very life, of the world."

"It is not enough to take this weapon out of the hands of the soldiers. It must be put into the hands of those who will know how to strip its military casing and adapt it to the arts of peace . . . To hasten the day when fear of the atom will begin to disappear from the minds of people, and the governments of the East and West, there are certain steps that can be taken now."

The detailed proposals followed: The governments principally involved, "to the extent permitted by elementary prudence," to *begin* now and *continue* to make joint contributions from their stockpiles to an International Atomic Energy Agency under the aegis of the United Nations, the ratios of contributions and all other details to be settled in negotiations, which the United States was prepared to undertake in good faith and in generosity.

He moved into the closing passages saying that he would be prepared to submit to the Congress "with every expectation of approval" a plan which would encourage world-wide investigation into the most effective peacetime uses of atomic energy; that would begin to diminish the potential destructive power of the world's atomic stockpiles; that would show all the peoples of the earth that the great powers of the earth were more interested in human aspirations than in the building up of armaments; and that would open up a "new channel for peaceful discussion, and initiate at least a new approach . . . if the world is to shake off the inertia imposed by fear and is to make positive progress toward peace."

To the audience, which seemed to hang upon every word, he offered, by way of conclusion, a promise: "The United States pledges before you —and therefore before the world—its determination to help solve the fearful atomic dilemma—to devote its entire heart and mind to find the way by which the miraculous inventiveness of man shall not be dedicated to his death, but consecrated to his life."

The speech was received, at first, with an impressive aspiration, a sound of indrawn breaths, followed by a gigantic, collective sigh—then wave after wave of applause. Even the Soviet delegation was caught up in the general enthusiasm. The President, who by then had returned to his seat, received the ovation with surprise, his eyes shining with the emotion evoked by the experience. He is the central figure in a picture which I will never forget.

Within a few days after the speech, private conversations with the Soviet delegates were begun by Secretary Dulles. During the months which followed, the Russians dragged their feet, duplicating many of the tactics employed when the Baruch proposals were presented in 1946.

In November of 1954, the President had named Morehead Patterson as a special ambassador to negotiate a statute for the proposed International Atomic Energy Agency.[10]

It took two years to complete the statute. The original signatory governments were the United States, Belgium, France, the United Kingdom, Portugal, Australia, and the Union of South Africa. In the summer of 1955 the Soviets finally indicated willingness to contribute fissionable material to the Agency conditionally upon its establishment. In consequence, the draft statute was forwarded to Moscow for review. This Soviet gesture proved hollow, although it generated the usual brief period of euphoria in the Free World. The United Nations General Assembly, in a resolution adopted in December, endorsed the progress made. Following this, we issued invitations to the interested nations to meet at a working-group level in Washington to complete the text of the statute. The meeting was set for February 1956.

In preparation we proposed to President Eisenhower, with the concurrence of both Secretary of State Dulles and Secretary of Defense Wilson, that we should announce our willingness to make available for distribution forty thousand kilograms of the rare isotope uranium 235. The President promptly concurred. At the First International Conferences on the Peaceful Uses of Atomic Energy during the preceding August (1955), I had stated our unit price for uranium 235, from which it was clear that the forty thousand kilograms would be the equivalent of a billion dollars.

In announcing the allocation, the President noted that "Mankind's hopes and aspiration for peace and greater well-being are closely linked to the world's progress in developing the peaceful uses of atomic energy . . . At the recommendation of Chairman Strauss of the United States Atomic Energy Commission, in which the Departments of State and Defense concur, I have determined, under Section 41b of the Atomic Energy Act of 1954, that substantial quantities of the special nuclear material uranium 235 may now be designated for research and development purposes and for fueling nuclear power reactors at home and abroad. This material will be available for either sale or lease under conditions prescribed by the United States Government . . . The quantities of uranium 235 which will be made available for distribution . . . under this determination are: a. In the United States 20,000 kilograms. b. Outside the United States . . . 20,000."

The President then explained that nations presently producing uranium 235, which included the Soviet Union and its satellites, were not to share in this distribution. He emphasized that the distribution of special nuclear material would be subject to prudent safeguards against its diversion to military purposes. "This action," he concluded, "demonstrates the confidence of the United States in the possibilities of developing nuclear power for civilian uses. It is an earnest of our faith that the atom can be made a powerful instrument for the promotion of world peace."

The statute for the Agency was finally approved by a conference of representatives of eighty-eight countries, meeting at the headquarters of the United Nations in New York from September 20 to October 20, 1956. At the time it was the largest number of nations ever to take part in an international meeting. This was, of course, before the emergence of a multiplicity of new states in Africa and Asia. More than two and a half years had elapsed since the conversations had begun. Eventually, representatives of seventy-two nations, including our own, signed the Agency statute. At the concluding session, I delivered a message from President Eisenhower in which he announced that the United States would make available to the Agency five thousand kilograms of uranium 235 from the twenty thousand kilograms which had been allocated during the preceding February for distribution under the agreements for co-operation with other governments.

More significantly, the President offered to match allocations of nuclear materials to the Agency of all the other member nations combined.

Pushed through and around the Soviet roadblocks, the International Atomic Energy Agency held its first session in Vienna in October 1957. The delay of three and a half years in getting it launched, during which time it lost some of its bloom, is attributable to Soviet tactics and to nothing else. As a result, the prime purpose of the Agency has not been achieved thus far—a massive reduction of fissionable material available for weapons. The Agency has served, however, in other important matters and is the only forum for the establishment of international standards of health and safety in the field of radiation, which alone would justify its existence. The United Kingdom and the Portuguese have also made amounts of uranium available to the Agency.

At meetings of the Agency in 1957 and 1958, the Russians made all the usual political *démarches,* attempting to get the Communist Chinese recognized and seated, and to secure appointment of officers in the Agency on the basis of representing Communist and Free World philosophies, rather than upon individual qualification for the tasks to be done. These moves we had little difficulty in checkmating.

W. Sterling Cole became the first Director-General of the Agency. To accept the post, Cole resigned from the Congress in which for years he had represented the 37th District of the State of New York. He had served as an original member of the Joint Congressional Committee on Atomic Energy and as its chairman during the first years of the Eisenhower Administration. It was during this period that the Atomic Energy Law had its first major amendment. This amendment liberated atomic energy development for peaceful purposes from government monopoly and made possible a degree of international co-operation. The selection of Cole to head the Agency was appropriate and fortunate. Under his leadership, a foundation had been established for increasing usefulness of the Agency.

The Agency can achieve its intended purpose, given the co-operation of the principal atomic powers. As an organization in being with that aim, it should be supported at all events by the United States in the hope, however remote it may appear at times, that reason will someday bless the councils of nations.

REUNION IN GENEVA

The long delay in establishing the Agency produced one good result. In the spring of 1954, certain political critics of the President took the position that his Atoms for Peace proposals of December 8, 1953, had been stillborn and that nothing would come of them. Accordingly, I asked the President to let me announce that, as a preliminary step until the Agency was functioning, the United States itself would sponsor "an International Scientific Conference on the Peaceful Uses of Atomic Energy." This idea he had approved in principle while we were in Bermuda. The President agreed and, the World Affairs Council of Los Angeles having invited me to speak there on April 19, 1954, the project was announced:

At this point, I am privileged to state that it is the President's intention . . . to arrange an international conference of scientists at a
later date this year. This conference, which it is hoped will be largely
attended and will include the outstanding men in their professions
from all over the world, will be devoted to the exploration of the
benign and peaceful uses of atomic energy. It will be the first time that
such a body has been convened, and its purpose . . . in the words of
the President, will be "to hasten the day when the fear of the atom will
begin to disappear from the minds of people and the governments
of the East and of the West."

The proposal found general favor in scientific communities all over
the world. Scientists had been even more effectively separated by the Iron
Curtain than had men of other callings. Almost immediately the idea
was adopted by the United Nations, and the scientific reunion was set
for Geneva. This was a good choice, as a conference in the United States
would have posed difficulties at that time in the matter of admitting
large delegations from behind the Iron Curtain.

The idea of an international conference of scientists on the peaceful
uses of atomic energy had been in my mind for some months before
exploring it with Cherwell in December 1953. The idea had occurred
to others as well, however, and two friends subsequently spoke to me
about it. On April 5, 1954, in a conversation with Dr. Alan T. Waterman, of the National Science Foundation, he suggested a conference
and offered the services of his organization, and on April 16, Dr.
I. I. Rabi made a similar suggestion. Dr. Rabi later agreed to undertake
the exacting assignment of detailed planning for the conference and
was outstandingly successful. He was a member of our delegation and
was elected vice-chairman of the conference.

The conference was the first occasion when men of science from both
sides of the Iron Curtain had met together for many years. There were
more than 3600 participants from all over the world. In preparation for
it, an atomic reactor had been built under the supervision of Dr. Alvin
Weinberg at Oak Ridge, Tennessee. It was flown to Geneva and
assembled there in a temporary structure. Designed to resemble a chalet,
the building was located on the grounds of the Palace of Nations (the
old headquarters of the League of Nations). The reactor was of the
swimming-pool type, so called because the uranium fuel elements are
immersed in a tank of water which acts both as a shield against radiation
and as a moderator.

This was not only the first operating reactor in Europe, but the first ever seen by the vast majority of scientists attending the conference. In the two weeks that the exhibit was open, the reactor was the center of interest. It was visited by sixty thousand people, many of whom were permitted to operate its controls. When our exhibit was dismantled, we sold the reactor to the Swiss Government at a figure well below its value, and at last account it was still operating and instructing students of physics.

There were many other exhibits dealing with nuclear power, radiation, applications in medicine, agriculture, chemistry, industry, and scores of other fields. We suspected that this might be the last time that a United States exhibit would be so obviously superior. It was clear from the character of the attendance that an enormous reservoir of talent was available to other countries and that the effect of this would become apparent with time. Among the distinguished scientists who attended the conference were Bohr from Denmark, Cockcroft from England, Perrin and Goldschmidt from France, Giordani from Italy, Bhabha from India, Emelyanov from Russia, to name but a few of the hundreds.

Laura Fermi, the widow of Enrico Fermi, accepted my invitation to accompany our delegation as its historian.* The first "Summit" meeting took place in Geneva while our exhibit was being readied, and President Eisenhower, accompanied by one of his special assistants, Nelson Rockefeller, visited the reactor and operated its controls—the first time a head of state had ever done so.

The Joint Congressional Committee sent a delegation of its members to evidence support and they expressed themselves as highly satisfied.

*   *   *

Three years later, in 1958, the Second International Scientific Conference on the Peaceful Uses of Atomic Energy was held, again in Geneva. It was a dramatic demonstration of the progress made by the world at large and by the United States in particular since the first conference.

The second conference nearly doubled the size of the first. Over 6000 persons participated, a number which included 2700 accredited delegates from 69 nations and 9 international agencies. As an indication

---

* Her entertaining book, *Atoms for the World* (University of Chicago Press, 1957), is the best nontechnical account of the conference, its program and accomplishments. The conference proceedings and the papers which were presented fill many volumes.

of the hold that it had taken upon the public interest, there were 911 accredited members of world news media from 36 countries. There were technical displays presented by 20 nations; only 6 nations had been exhibitors at the first conference. The number of scientific and technical papers presented also roughly doubled the previous record.

On behalf of our respective countries, Sir John Cockcroft and I had announced that information on research to control thermonuclear reactions had been largely declassified. Accordingly the United States exhibit featured our several approaches to the solution of this outstanding problem. We took our chief devices, and the men who had built them reassembled them in Geneva. Huge amounts of water were pumped from Lake Geneva through an eight-inch pipe line especially laid for the purpose in order that these great machines could be cooled when they were in operation. They were certainly among the hottest things in the world at that date.

At the second conference, as at the first in 1955, our contribution in numbers of papers presented (700) and in exhibits (72) was dominant, but progress in the interval by other participating nations was so marked that it was apparent the lead which World War II had afforded us would not last indefinitely. The Russian exhibit was especially impressive. Its principal feature was a full-scale model of Sputnik I, their first orbited space vehicle, launched a year earlier, which of course had no bearing on the theme of the conference. It was a bare bid for prestige and interest, without apology, and it succeeded—at least as far as the general public was concerned. The conference also served to bring into balance world estimates of the time scale within which power generation from atomic energy might become economically competitive with other energy sources. This we hoped would correct the overoptimism current in 1955 which would have had discouraging effects.

While I chaired the U.S. delegation to this September 1958 conference, my term with the Atomic Energy Commission had expired on June 30, and the new Chairman of the AEC, John McCone, who was present, impressed the delegates with his grasp of the matters to which he had so recently succeeded. The United States delegation and staff numbered 372 persons, the delegation being composed of AEC Commissioner Willard F. Libby; Dr. James R. Killian, Jr., Special Assistant to the President for Science and Technology; Mr. Robert McKinney, the United States member of the Board of Governors of the International Atomic Energy Agency; Dr. Isador Rabi, and Dr. Shields Warren, representative on the United Nations Scientific Committee on the

Effects of Atomic Radiation, as alternate United States representative. Seven members of the Joint Congressional Committee on Atomic Energy attended as advisers to the delegation. As in 1955, they expressed enthusiasm for our efforts.

The United States exhibit was divided into sections on physical sciences, reactor science, the life sciences, and a commercial exhibit, and the crowds were so great that guards were necessary to control those seeking admission. We had trained a number of personable young people, proficient in languages, to act as guides, and they made an enormous and instantaneous hit. The most exciting of the exhibits was the fusion research area, where, as mentioned, our principal research tools in our quest for a method of achieving the controlled thermonuclear reaction were brought together for the first time.

Many of the pieces in the exhibit were parts of the working equipment used in research laboratories in the United States for the containment of plasmas and were known by various names. The Forrestal Memorial Research Laboratory at Princeton University was represented by its "stellarator." The University of California Radiation Laboratory exhibited different approaches, including the so-called "magnetic mirror." There were other devices, known as the "astron" and the "ion magnetron," both developed at that laboratory. Oak Ridge National Laboratory featured its direct-current arc experiment for the production of thermonuclear temperatures, and the Los Alamos Scientific Laboratory exhibited a number of devices, the most promising at that time called "Scylla," in which it was then believed that fusion had already been achieved. Other machines exhibited by Los Alamos were a "perhapsatron" and other plasma "pinches" and accelerators. Large crowds of visiting scientists spent all day every day watching the demonstration of these experimental devices and were outspoken in their praise of the work of their American colleagues.

The AEC scientists who designed our exhibits arranged for an entrance hall which featured an acknowledgment of the fundamental contributions of Einstein, Fermi, Wigner, Teller, Von Neumann, and others who had chosen to make their homes in the United States but who were natives of other lands. Our recognition of the universality of science was thus emphasized.

As these lines are written, Atoms for Peace is an established tenet of American policy.*

* A great deal of scientific and technical information of nonmilitary nature has been published, as the law authorizes. In connection with the 1958 conference,

OLD COMMITMENTS COME TO ROOST

Our weapons projects have continued to be, and should remain, highly classified—that is to say, "Secret" or "Top Secret." This distinction between the peaceful and the military uses of atomic energy has extended to relationships with our wartime atomic partners, Great Britain and Canada. Prior to the passage of the McMahon Act in 1946, there was the closest co-operation between the scientists and the military establishments of the three countries in the development of the fission bomb. Under the terms of that law, however, all exchange of information on the subject ceased, even in matters which had no readily perceptible military bearing. This was the condition which prevailed during my first period of service on the Commission, 1946 to 1950.

In spite of a *modus vivendi* negotiated in January of 1948 to get rid of the embarrassment of two agreements dating from the war years, the condition was still in effect at the time of my reappointment in 1953. The situation was without precedent. The two agreements just mentioned were solemn undertakings between President Roosevelt and Prime Minister Churchill, one at Quebec in August 1943, the other at Hyde Park in September 1944. Both dealt with the employment of atomic energy by the two governments. The Senate had not been informed at the time that either agreement was executed. Members of the Senate Foreign Relations Committee did not learn of them until 1947. Senator Vandenberg, as Chairman of the Committee, was startled to discover the commitments involved. He found them "astounding" and "unthinkable."[11]

The Hyde Park Agreement was clouded in its own private mystery. Apparently prepared and executed at the President's country estate on the Hudson River and signed by him and Prime Minister Churchill, it resembled the Quebec Agreement in that undertakings were exchanged which were intended to bind the respective governments. But for years after President Roosevelt's death, though our British friends often referred to the Hyde Park Agreement, their copy of it seemed to be unique. At the Bermuda Conference in December 1953, Churchill had brought with him a photograph of the original signed instrument.

thirteen volumes of reports were published for the delegations. The contents, of course, were strictly concerned with the pacific uses of atomic energy and were screened by a board of responsible reviewers to be sure that no military information was included.

Nine years after it had been executed, the other signed copy was, as earlier mentioned, found at Hyde Park. The Senate, of course, had never ratified it.

The Quebec Agreement established principles and mechanism for co-operation between the United States and Great Britain and provided for the organization of a Combined Policy Committee. That committee made recommendations to the two governments on the division of program in the atomic energy field and the assignment of British scientists to various United States laboratories and facilities. Although the Canadians were not signatories to the Quebec Agreement, the Canadian Government was included in the joint effort, and this was recognized by the appointment of C. D. Howe, the Canadian Minister of Munitions and Supply, to the Policy Committee.

The Hyde Park document formalized the agreement for full collaboration between the United States and the British governments in developing fissionable material for military and commercial purposes after the defeat of Japan, unless terminated by joint agreement. It had, of course, been effectively breached by the McMahon Act, whose congressional draftsmen were unaware of the existence of such a contract. This must also have been the situation of President Truman when he signed the bill into law. The documents taken together imposed restrictions on British use of atomic energy for commerical purposes and on United States use of atomic weapons without British consent.

When, as members of the AEC in 1947, we inherited the atomic project's files and records, we became aware for the first time of the existence of the two agreements. We were surprised to discover that the Senate did not know of them, and since they were in conflict with the law, it was clear that something had to be done by way of reconciling the contradiction. The issue was solved by the *modus vivendi* known as the "Blair House Agreement," so named because the British and American negotiators met in the President's guesthouse. Chief author of the agreement was Under Secretary of State Robert A. Lovett, who saw the impasse which would result from any attempt to reconcile the text of the two earlier agreements with the law, and wisely concluded that they should be swept into the discard and replaced by a new instrument. He also arranged that members of the Senate Foreign Relations Committee and of the Joint Congressional Committee should participate in the conversations. That proved to be a mark of practical statesmanship. The new agreement established nine areas in which information would be exchanged by the wartime allies. None of these had any relation to the field of weapons.

The publication of the text of the Quebec Agreement by the British Government in the spring of 1954 generated a parliamentary attack on the Prime Minister from the left, but it was of brief duration. Lord Cherwell wrote me on April 7:

> The Prime Minister has been very much attacked by the Socialists who say he ought to have been able to demand information from you, and almost suggest he ought to be able to prevent your tests. In the circumstances, it does seem to me he was justified in publishing the Quebec Agreement and pointing out that any charge of impotence must be leveled against those who agreed to its being cancelled, rather than against him. Unfortunately there was so much noise and shouting on the Socialists side that the point was not brought home. Still, in time, no doubt people will realize how unfair it is to attack him on this score.

and again on May 6:

> The excitement from the Quebec Agreement is dying down but it is a pity, at any rate from our Conservative point of view, that we do not seem to be able to state officially that any veto we may have had under the Agreement was given up by the Socialists. It is not for me to say whether or not they had very good reasons for doing so.

The Blair House Agreement had been the guideline for five years when the Eisenhower Administration took office. Prime Minister Churchill had begun to press the new President, however, very shortly after his inauguration, to restore Anglo-American co-operation in all atomic energy matters. The Prime Minister's aim appeared to be to resume the relationship which had existed prior to the passage of the McMahon Act and in every respect. England wished to have an atomic weapon capability, and held it wasteful to spend hundreds of millions to achieve what their allies already knew—knowledge which had been partly won with British help. The Blair House Agreement, though much more orderly than the two documents it replaced, was nevertheless increasingly frustrating to our British friends.

The President sympathized with this point of view—up to a point. He felt that it was unrealistic to expect the British as our allies to be content to remain so much less effectively armed than we were. As he once expressed it to me, "If we are forced to do battle with an enemy equipped with modern weapons, it would not make much sense to expect allies covering our flanks to be limited to the use of bows and arrows." It was, of course, legally impossible for the President to accede to the Prime Minister.

In October 1953, Cherwell was sent to Washington by Churchill for a series of conversations on the subject. The British negotiators included Ambassador Sir Roger Makins and Sir John Cockcroft, while we were represented by the Chairman of the Military Liaison Committee Robert LeBaron, Frank Nash, General Alvin Luedecke, and myself. The McMahon Act had not yet been amended to permit exchange of military information, so our British friends viewed the problem as one of obtaining more liberal interpretation of the areas in which information could be exchanged under the Blair House paper. England had made vitally important contributions to our pool of scientific information in atomic energy and many other fields. The information the British already possessed could not be erased from their knowledge, and they were making further advances and discoveries. It seemed to me to make very little sense that we should withhold from our allies information on the *effects* of radiation resulting from atomic explosions, for example. We could give this information without compromising the secret characteristics of weapons. We had been able to measure these radiation effects with considerable success incident to our weapons tests. Familiarity with them would make our allies better able to protect themselves in the event that atomic weapons were used against them by the Communists. This was in the days before the intercontinental ballistic missile, and the British were physically closer to the danger than we.

Accordingly, some days before the conference, I had obtained the approval of the President to rectify this situation to the extent that the law would then permit. I told our British friends that, while the law forbade realization of their hopes for restoration of the partnership which existed before the McMahon Act, we were now prepared to consider including a new "area" to the information we might exchange, to be defined as "the effects on human beings and their environment from the blast, heat and radiation resulting from atomic explosions." It was to be plain that this did not include any data that might permit the determination of the design of a weapon.

When those present agreed that this would be at least a satisfactory gain, I then cleared the proposal by telephone and telegram with the members of the Joint Congressional Committee, most of whom were then away from Washington. No objections were interposed and the proposal therefore became a first step in the restoration of constructive relations

25. One bomb can now "take out a city"—this was the burden of the report on the Castle test series made to the President and the press by the author on March 31, 1954. In those days, West Executive Avenue was crossed periodically by a somber president en route to and from the old State Department Building, site of most press conferences.

U.P.I.

26. Secretary of the Treasury George M. Humphrey, President Eisenhower, Secretary of State John Foster Dulles, Special Assistant Dillon Anderson, the author, and Secretary of Defense Charles E. Wilson gather at the President's desk following a Security Council session in the Cabinet Room.

27. The long hours of testimony before the Congress are often exceeded by the time required for preparation and later review of the transcripts. A tiring, at times arduous, and essential democratic institution. Here the author testifies before the Joint Congressional Committee on Atomic Energy, Dr. Harry Smyth at his left.

28. An impressive example of photographic reporting. President Dwight D. Eisenhower is pictured only seconds after he had completed his great Atoms for Peace
speech to the General Assembly of the United Nations, December 8, 1953. Not
having anticipated the delegates' reaction, he was clearly moved by the unprecedented ovation.

29. "Books have been written about Rickover and more undoubtedly will be....
I used to think of him as a sort of Savonarola in a blue uniform." (From the text.)
Surrounded by the activity of the control room of the *Nautilus* during a trial
run are the author, Admiral Hyman G. Rickover, Dr. Kenneth Davis (Chief, Reactor Division of the AEC), and Secretary of the Navy Charles Thomas.

U. S. Atomic Energy Commission photo

30. The author and Dag Hammarskjold opening the United States exhibit at the
Geneva Conference on the Peaceful Uses of Atomic Energy in 1958.

with our British allies in the development of atomic energy for mutual defense against Communism—thus opening a door which had been sealed shut in August 1946.

Two months later, in Bermuda, Prime Minister Churchill voiced continuing concern at the cessation of the full-scale co-operation between the two countries and made an eloquent case for its resumption. President Eisenhower indicated his sympathy in principle with the Prime Minister's views and expressed his hope for useful amendments to the McMahon Act at the next session of the Congress. He referred with satisfaction to the exchanges which had followed the recent conversations with Cherwell and explained that this was as far as we could go under existing legislative authority.

The Prime Minister remarked that Congress must sorely realize that in the event the Russians began a war, British planes would almost certainly be expected by us to take part in retaliatory action, along with our own planes. If so, they should carry atomic weapons, yet without information on such rudimentary matters as the weight of these objects, their dimensions, and their ballistics, there was no way of knowing whether the bomb bays of British planes would be big enough or whether the bomb-release mechanisms would be compatible with the weapons.

Sir Winston then asked me if this was basic data which could not be disclosed under the terms of the existing statute and I told him that in my opinion it was. The Prime Minister expressed himself as gratified by what had been accomplished in clearing the exchange of information about atomic weapons "effects," but added that from a practical point of view it did not go far enough. "We will have to spend millions we poor Britons can ill afford," he said, "to learn what you chaps already know and could tell us if you would. We will learn it, of course, but at what an unnecessary cost. It makes no sense whatever to go at it like that. The enemy will be our common one. The means to stop him should be common means."

When the Congress amended the Atomic Energy Act in 1954, it became possible for us to exchange information with the United Kingdom specifically assisting them in their naval reactor development. They exchanged valuable information with us in return. It was not a one-way street.

I believed in the importance of having allies and was happy to have taken part in ending the estrangement in technology between ourselves and a people with whom we have made common cause in two wars for freedom and human rights. It will be argued that the alliance has been costly at times in terms of secret information compromised by a few British citizens who defected to the Communists. The fact that our own record also contains the names of spies and traitors should not be forgotten when we see a mote in the eye of our old friends.

XVIII

Decision in the Senate

In Washington it was in the small hours of the morning of June 19, 1959. A wearing night had climaxed twelve unpleasant weeks. My wife and I were walking down a long hotel corridor to our apartment. We could hear our telephone ringing. Two hours earlier the Senate had voted to reject the President's nomination of a Secretary of Commerce who was *persona non grata* to several powerful Senators. When the tally had been announced—49 against to 46 for confirmation—it was already past midnight.

I had remained at my desk in the Commerce Department throughout that evening to be available if there were last-minute questions in the course of the debate on the floor of the Senate. Three Senators were speeding to Washington in an endeavor to get back before the vote. Until they could arrive other friendly Senators were attempting to hold the Senate in session. When, finally, the roll was called, the Vice President and a number of Senators of both parties telephoned to express regret at the outcome, and I remained to write a few letters of appreciation to those who had voted for me. Then I went home with my wife. She had been superb throughout the contest, maintaining her perspective and sense of humor, and encouraging mine.

The telephone continued ringing as we entered the apartment. It was my old chief, ex-President Hoover, calling from New York.

"How are you?" he inquired.

"Tired but well," I answered.

"Good," he said, "I have been listening to this awful business on the radio and did not want to go to bed until I talked with you to be sure that you are taking it in the right way."

I thanked him, adding that I had his good example before me, and we said, "Good Night." Mr. Hoover was then in his eighty-fifth year. The hour was two in the morning and his regular bedtime was ten o'clock. I reflected that there indeed was a man who had no "ex-friends," and with good reason. I went to sleep, proud and not unhappy.

The Constitution empowers the President of the United States to appoint members of his cabinet, but with the "advice and consent" of the Senate. In the past one hundred and twenty years I knew of but nine occasions of which the Senate had refused its consent. Several of these rejections were during one administration, that of President Tyler. Tyler was an opponent of the "spoils system" and, for that and other reasons, waged a running battle with the Senate during his term of office. He nominated Caleb Cushing three times to be Secretary of the Treasury, and the Senate rejected him by progressively larger votes. Years later the Senate confirmed Cushing to be Attorney General in the cabinet of President Pierce. The rejections of President Tyler's nominees were patently political reprisals and the results would probably have been the same had he nominated the Archangel Michael. He was an upright man who when he believed that the time had come to retire to private life had informed the Senate:

> I shall carry with me into retirement the principles which I brought with me into public life, and, by the surrender of the high station to which I was called by the voice of the people of Virginia, I shall set an example to my children which shall teach them to regard as nothing any position or office which must be attained or held at the sacrifice of honor.

President Andrew Jackson nominated Roger B. Taney to be his Secretary of the Treasury in 1834, but the Senate turned its thumbs down to him also. Taney survived that defeat by thirty years and served most of them as Chief Justice of the United States Supreme Court— with the Senate's blessing. Another rejection, the seventh, that of Henry Stanbery, occurred in the administration of Andrew Johnson, who had succeeded to the Presidency after the assassination of Abraham Lincoln. The eighth, and most recent, had been the rejection of President Coolidge's nomination of Charles B. Warren to be Attorney General. Warren had been black-balled because of an alleged, but unproven, conflict-of-interest. The ninth was myself.

I had long been interested in the case of Henry Stanbery. He had been appointed twice by President Andrew Johnson to be Attorney General, and the Senate confirmed him the first time without question. The relationship between the President and the Attorney General in those days must have been particularly close. There was then no Department of Justice, as that agency of the Executive was not established until 1870, so that the Attorney General also performed services which are today assigned to the Counsel to the President. This resulted in daily and intimate contact between the Chief Executive and his principal legal officer.

It was natural, therefore, for the President, upon his impeachment by the Congress, to turn to his Attorney General for help. The impeachment was the sequel to a series of events—a presidential amnesty to individual Confederates; congressional action which sought to re-establish military control over the defeated South, opposed by the President; and, finally, the President's summary removal of his Secretary of War, Edwin M. Stanton, who he believed had been personally disloyal to him on numerous occasions. The President had dismissed Mr. Stanton without notifying the Senate, allegedly violating the Tenure of Office Act in so doing. The act was repealed twenty years later and finally was found unconstitutional by the Supreme Court, but its "violation" at the time was one of the most impressive counts in the indictment of the President.

In the only proceeding of its kind in history, President Johnson was thereupon tried before a Senate which was presided over by the Chief Justice. Attorney General Stanbery resigned from the Cabinet in order to defend his chief, and conducted the defense with such success that even in the hostile Senate the vote to convict the President failed of the necessary two-thirds majority. Nearly a century later a Senator, later to become President himself, was to study that trial and, characterize Stanbery as "able and learned."

A grateful President promptly reappointed Stanbery to his cabinet, but this time the Senate as promptly rejected him. The drama presented by that conflict between a body of men who had once approved a man for public office and then, when he had succeeded in the performance of his duty to his chief, turned him out had a certain fascination for me which only later became personal.

The Senate had confirmed me on three previous occasions for appointments made by both Democratic and Republican Presidents; in a routine manner when I had been promoted to flag rank during World War II; when I had been appointed to the Atomic Energy Commission by President Truman; and when President Eisenhower recalled me from private life and named me Chairman of the AEC. In 1952 as a private citizen, I had also been Chairman of a panel on "Incentive, Hazardous Duty and Special Pays" for the purpose of a report[1] to the Senate Committee on the Armed Services and had served as Chairman of the Atomic Plant Expansion Advisory Panel for the Joint Congressional Committee on Atomic Energy in 1951. Neither of these latter assignments required Senate confirmation, but no criticism was voiced of me in the Senate at that time so far as I knew. Indeed there was commendation on both occasions.

When my five-year term as Chairman of the AEC neared expiration in 1958, I reminded the President of that fact and submitted a slate of men qualified to succeed to the responsibility. He urged me to accept reappointment. I told him that under ordinary circumstances I would have acceded gladly, but, as he knew, I had long been the target of the Junior Senator from New Mexico who was a member of the congressional committee to which the Atomic Energy Commission reported. In the rotation of the chairmanship of that committee between the Senate and the House of Representatives, this Senator would become chairman of the committee for 1959 and 1960, which would be for as long as the Eisenhower Administration would hold office. It seemed to me clearly in the interest of the Atomic Energy Commission that I should withdraw from the scene. The President had seen enough of the Senator's activity to accept the force of this reasoning and accordingly authorized me to sound out the availability of the first name on my list. This resulted in the appointment of Mr. John McCone, a dedicated and experienced executive who was favorably known to the President.

My responsibilities were turned over on June 30, 1958, and at a brief ceremony in the White House the President awarded me the Medal of Freedom with a most generous citation.[2]

The President then designated me as his special assistant with specific attention to the program of Atoms-for-Peace. In August I left for Geneva as head of the U.S. delegation to the Second International Conference on the Peaceful Uses of Atomic Energy. I also attended the second annual meeting of the International Atomic Energy Agency in Vienna, toward which I felt a parental relationship.

On my return to Washington, the President sent for me and told me that the Secretary of Commerce, Sinclair Weeks, had notified him that personal matters would compel him to retire as soon as his relief could be found. The President added that he wished to have me in his cabinet and offered me the appointment. Besides expressing gratitude for his confidence, I replied that I would be glad to undertake the assignment for several reasons. The Soviet economic challenge to the Free World was beginning to become more and more apparent, and the Commerce Department seemed to me the place at which countermeasures might well be developed. The Commerce Department had reached its greatest period of service under Herbert Hoover, and had suffered in its effectiveness afterward when shorn of a number of its opportunities to contribute to American prosperity. It would be a challenge to try to restore to the Department some of its former functions and usefulness.* And finally, that it would be personally gratifying to continue in the President's Administration and to go into retirement along with him.

Congress being in recess, the President appointed me following Mr. Weeks's resignation, and on November 13, 1958, I took the oath of office on a family Bible which had been used on previous occasions when undertaking public service. Because it seemed appropriate for a Secretary of Commerce, one of whose legal responsibilities is the maintenance of standard weights and measures, I had marked the Bible at the 19th Chapter of Leviticus. Verses 35 and 36 read, "Ye shall do no unrighteousness in judgement, in meteyard, in weight, or in measure. Just balances, just weights, a just ephah, and a just hin shall ye have." The nomination was sent to the Senate when it reconvened in January and was referred, in the usual course, to the Committee on Interstate and Foreign Commerce.

The chairman of that committee was Senator Warren Magnuson of the State of Washington. We had been on friendly terms for many years and had first become acquainted when he was in the House of Representatives. As a junior officer representing the Bureau of Ordnance of the Navy, I testified before the committee on which he sat on a number of occasions. On October 25, 1945, he had taken the trouble to write to the Secretary of the Navy to commend me for advocating the establishment of a National Science Foundation.[3] When the Senate was considering my nomination to the Atomic Energy Commission on June 27, 1953, Senator Magnuson had risen to say, "Mr. President, I merely wish to say that I do not know of any finer statesman in the United States than is Lewis L. Strauss. He is my personal friend." I was happy, therefore, when, following the President's announcement of my appointment to the Cabinet, the Senator telegraphed from Seattle:

* Examples: Commercial attachés in our embassies no longer reported to the Secretary of Commerce and their usefulness had suffered. Transportation was under Commerce, but air transport, of growing importance to the whole problem of transportation, had been placed in an independent agency. The State Department had many overlapping responsibilities with Commerce. Etc.

CONGRATULATIONS ON YOUR NEW APPOINTMENT. I HOPE THIS WILL BE
A RESUMPTION OF OUR FORMER PLEASANT RELATIONSHIP.
                              WARREN G. MAGNUSON, U.S.S.

Weeks passed after Congress reconvened with no call to come before his committee, and not until speculation began to appear in the press as to who might be occasioning the delay was I finally directed to appear in mid-March. On March 17, at nine-thirty, I entered the Senate Commerce Committee Room in the New Senate Office Building for the first time. A large part of the succeeding two months was to be spent there. It is a handsome chamber of blond paneling and massive bronze ornamentation, but I had little occasion to appreciate its décor. At the opening session, the two Republican Senators from New York, Senator Jacob Javits and Senator Kenneth Keating and the two Democratic Senators from Virginia, Senator Harry F. Byrd and Senator Willis Robertson, offered statements supporting the nomination.

On the surface all seemed routine at the outset in spite of Senator Magnuson's unexplained delay and an embarrassed coolness. Ominous overtones were more apparent at succeeding sessions. Seated beside the Chairman, Senator Magnuson, there appeared a stranger. Ordinarily, regular committee counsel would occupy this position, but here was now a lawyer, a special counsel, who had been brought on from the State of Washington to conduct the hearings. I was informed that at home he enjoyed the reputation of being a successful prosecuting attorney. In that role, however, he was superfluous, for the Junior Senator from New Mexico, though not a member of the Committee, attended its sessions by virtue of "senatorial courtesy," whispered to a member of the Committee questions, following which I would be questioned, later sat on the rostrum with the Committee, and later testified against me himself.

His testimony opened with a number of charges on atomic energy issues over which he and I had long disagreed. In one of them the Senator referred to the export of a radioisotope of iron, which had been requested by a scientist in the Norwegian Military Establishment ten years before—in 1949. I had strongly objected to this shipment. The Senator asserted that I had stated that "this isotope was to be used for research in the development of more heat resistant alloys for jet engines. I say to you," he continued, "that that is an unqualified falsehood and if any member of the Committee wants it I ask that you summon the records of the Atomic Energy Commission and the State Department and you will find that it does not so state."[4]

The records of 1949 were not easily available to me, but I did succeed in obtaining from the State Department and introducing into the record the 1949 cable to the State Department from the American Embassy in Oslo, Norway. It described the request for the isotope and included the following sentence: "It is desired to develop alloy for jet or gas turbine use at a temperature as high as possible, i.e., particularly above 700 degrees centigrade if possible."[5]

When I read the cable to the Committee, I asked whether the Senator's description of my statement as an "unqualified falsehood" was just or warranted. That charge was a fair sample of what was to follow.

In the course of the hearings, the Junior Senator from New Mexico even impugned the regularity of the proceeding six years earlier, when I had been confirmed as a member of the Atomic Energy Commission. The *Congressional Record* for June 27, 1953, quotes Senator Hickenlooper, addressing the presiding officer, as follows: "The nomination [of Mr. Strauss] has met with the unanimous approval of all of the members of the Senate Committee and of the Joint Committee on Atomic Energy." The Junior Senator from New Mexico was a member of the Joint Committee at that time.

The Special Counsel for the Committee made Senate history on his own account. During one of the sessions, a witness read a long statement opposing confirmation. It was a document containing many assertions at second hand by persons who were not identified and also a number of untrue statements. The language of the document was that of a lawyer. During his testimony, this witness was asked by Senator Hugh Scott (a member of the Committee) to give the Committee the names of the individuals with whom he had discussed the preparation of his statement. The witness circumnavigated the questions with an unresponsive reply running into some hundreds of words.[6]

But the Senator was not to be put off. Finally he asked, ". . . would the witness be willing to testify whether he has consulted as to the form and tenor and context of his statement *with anyone connected with the Senate or with any Senate staff members?*" (Italics supplied.) The Committee's Special Counsel, who up to this point had remained silent during the exchange, but who had been displaying signs of increasing distress, then interposed, "The witness discussed several matters with me, Senator Scott."

"That is what I am getting at, Counsel," the Senator observed. "If Committee Counsel has been assisting witnesses in the preparation of statements, it is in the interest of the public to know what is going on here because we are not, on this side of the bench, benefitting from Committee Counsel's activities. . . ."

Reporters who covered the event said that, in the course of a normal confirmation, so shocking a disclosure would have blown the proceedings out of the water. It was now clear that this was to be not a hearing so much as an inquisition, with the attorney for the prosecution brought in by the chief judge.

The hearings continued over the period from March 17 to May 14. I was charged with various offenses, among them failure to co-operate with the Joint Congressional Committee on Atomic Energy. Yet three of the five men who had served as chairmen of that committee either made statements or volunteered to testify in my behalf. The fourth, Senator Brien McMahon, was deceased, but the fact of our friendship up to the time of his death was well known. He had appointed me consultant to his committee after my retirement from the AEC in 1950, and in 1951 had made me chairman of a panel to examine into the causes of labor and construction difficulties at AEC facilities.

The report of the majority of the Senate Committee noted in this connection that:

> During the time that the nominee has served on the Atomic Energy Commission the Joint Committee on Atomic Energy had five chairmen. The first of them, Senator Brian McMahon is dead, but a letter which he wrote to the nominee in 1950 in behalf of the Joint Committee praised Mr. Strauss' service during his first term on the AEC and invited him to become a consultant to the Joint Committee. The second Chairman, Senator Bourke B. Hickenlooper, submitted a statement supporting the nominee and testifying to his fine cooperation. The third Chairman, former Congressman W. Sterling Cole, by May 5th, 1959, cablegram to the nominee, introduced into the record, confirmed 'Existence cordial relationship with you as Chairman, AEC, and I, Chairman, Joint Committee.' . . . The fourth Chairman, Congressman Carl T. Durham, who immediately preceded Senator Clinton P. Anderson as Chairman of the Joint Committee, was reported in the hearing on May 6th, 1959, as willing to appear and testify if our Committee wished to hear him. We are authorized by Congressman Durham to say that had he appeared he would have testified to a cordial and cooperative relationship with the nominee reaching back

more than 20 years. . . . The nominee showed great diligence in keeping the Congress informed.*

* The total number of communications and reports to the Joint Committee from the Commission from January 1, 1950, to June 1954 averaged 540 per annum. In the years of my incumbency as Chairman they more than doubled in number.

The hollowness of the charge of nonco-operation is best evidenced by the fact that in the vote on June 18, of the nine Senators on the Joint Committee—four Republicans and five Democrats—only two out of the nine voted against me. One of them, of course, was the Junior Senator from New Mexico. The charge of incompatibility with the Joint Congressional Committee on Atomic Energy was truly without foundation.

I was charged also with the offense of resisting the transmission to the Congress of certain information to which the Congress believed it was properly entitled. In substantiation of this, a former chairman of the Joint Committee, Congressman Cole, was quoted from a 1954 transcript. Addressing me at a hearing he had said:

It may not be in your memory but it certainly is within mine that for the first time within the history of this Committee it was necessary for this Committee to adopt a formal resolution to get information from the Commission.[7]

The Junior Senator from New Mexico, who introduced this "evidence," carefully refrained from telling the full story, which, as a member of the Joint Committee, he must have known. The law requires that Commission decisions be taken by majority vote. I had favored sending the information to the Congress, but since the majority of the Commission held otherwise the Commission initially had declined to comply. My position was known. It is best stated by Mr. Cole himself. In response to comment on the incident at the time it occurred, Mr. Cole had written to a newspaper as follows:

Let me emphasize that my criticism was directed to the *Commission as an agency* since the information at issue was withheld from the Joint Committee until a resolution was formally adopted and transmitted to the Commission.

I believe it is only fair to point out that the Commission vote in this case was a "split vote." *Mr. Strauss was in the minority and did not favor withholding the information from the Joint Committee.*[8] [Italics supplied].

Citing this incident as an attempt to show that I had personally withheld information from the Congress may well have misled some members of the Senate Commerce Committee. In the closing hours, the "evidence" was repeated on the floor of the Senate, but, of course, without Chairman Cole's clarification that his comment had not applied to me at all.

There was other alleged evidence on the charge of withholding information from the Congress. During the hearings, Senator Kefauver appeared as a witness and, referring to the Mississippi Valley Generating Company (the Dixon-Yates) contract, which was executed on November 11, *1954*, testified: "The Joint Committee asked to try to get a copy of the contract on several occasions, as did the Committee that had jurisdiction, the Anti-Trust and Monopoly Committee. We were never able to get the contract until after it was printed in the St. Louis Post-Dispatch in August of *1955*."[9]

This was an astonishing statement, for it is a matter of record that the Atomic Energy Commission testified concerning the contract while it was in negotiation, and sent to the Joint Congressional Committee on Atomic Energy drafts of the "proposed contract." When the contract was finally signed on November 11, *1954*, a copy of the executed document was sent to the Joint Committee within minutes of its signature. Moreover, its terms were made public at the time. The several letters of transmittal to the Joint Committee, the AEC press release on the terms of the contract, and a press release of the Joint Committee itself two days later (November 13, 1954) are in the record of the hearing.[10] Senator Kefauver of course had been seriously misinformed by someone, for I am satisfied that he would not have deliberately misrepresented the facts. Nevertheless, on the day before the vote, while Senator Norris Cotton was pressing Senator Kefauver to admit that he had been in error, the Junior Senator from New Mexico rose and stated, "The one great point is that the contract was not available to the Committee until after it was printed in the St. Louis Post-Dispatch. That is the essential charge. It is true."[11]

A little later Senator Kefauver stated, "Both the Senators from North Dakota and I asked the Senator from New Mexico to give us information about the contract. The Senator from New Mexico said he did not have the contract and could not get it."[12]

As the record is clear that the contract had been in the hands of the Joint Committee of the Congress from the day it was signed, the quality of some of the information which was before the Senate as it prepared to vote on the nomination is apparent.

Senator Kefauver's zeal in lending a helping hand to the Junior Senator from New Mexico was not limited to errors of fact in connection with the Dixon-Yates contract. He had come into possession of an anonymous memorandum to the effect that when I was a captain in the Navy (which would place the event as some fourteen or more years earlier) I had been appointed by the Secretary of the Navy to investigate the reliability of the purchasers of a plant—the York Safe and Lock Company. The burden of the memorandum was to the effect that my duty had been performed in a superficial and perfunctory manner and that later "a low-salaried Navy clerk and a young Navy Lieutenant resigned from the Navy to become Comptroller and President" of the company. My connection with these unnamed individuals was not specified in the anonymous memorandum, but the inference appeared to be that it was in some respect reprehensible. The Senator sent this unsigned paper to the Secretary of the Navy on March 2 with a letter reading as follows:

March 2, 1959

Dear Mr. Gates:

In connection with the Hearings which are currently being held regarding the confirmation of Admiral Lewis L. Strauss as Secretary of Commerce, I am very anxious to have you inform me at the earliest possible time as to who was appointed as investigator for the sale of the York Safe and Lock Company.

Sincerely,
/s/ Estes Kefauver

Secretary Gates replied to say that he had had the files for that period searched and that there was no indication that anyone was appointed or directed to investigate the proposed sale.

There is likewise no record of it in my Navy file of orders or assignments.

Having drawn a blank on this, Senator Kefauver evidently decided not to include this charge in his testimony.

As the hearing progressed, much was made of the fact that I was unable to recollect the details of a letter dated some three and a half years previously. It had not been written for me or to me. It had been written by the Attorney General to the Secretary of Defense. It dealt with an interpretation of a section of the law. A copy had been sent to the Atomic Energy Commission "for information." I had not informed the Joint Committee of the existence of the letter and it was asserted that the letter had been discussed at a Commission meeting which I had attended. When it was found that I had not in fact attended that meeting but had been out of the country at the time, it was then asserted that it had been discussed at a subsequent meeting at which I had been present.

In that period, the Commission kept verbatim transcripts of its sessions and the transcript of this session, when examined, showed that the letter in question had been mentioned only in passing and that my knowledge of it had been at best tangential. However, as the Commission wished to preserve the precedent of keeping its minutes privileged, the transcript was not made available to me to rebut the charge that the letter had been "discussed" in my presence. One member of the Atomic Energy Commission, Dr. W. F. Libby, was so outraged that the minutes were not released to me that he made a special trip to my farm in Virginia to show the entry to me and to offer the use of it on his own responsibility. I could not accept this generous gesture. The circumstance that I could not recall all the details of such a letter three years after it had been exchanged between its writer and its addressee (neither being myself) was characterized as "a shocking lack of truthfulness." Senator Pastore, Chairman of the Subcommittee of the Joint Committee which was charged with this matter and before whom the AEC had testified, disposed of this charge during the hearing[13] but it reappeared in the minority report.

There were other charges by the Junior Senator from New Mexico along the line that I had failed to keep the Joint Committee informed.* Among them was the allegation that a policy decision with respect to uranium procurement had been made by the Commission and announced by Jesse Johnson, Director of the Commission's Division of Raw Materials, on October 28, 1957, without prior notification to the Joint Committee. As a matter of fact, a copy of the speech had been delivered by hand to the Joint Committee on October 25. The Junior Senator from New Mexico contended that the fact that the matter had been under consideration by the Commission was "pending matter of sufficient significance that the Joint Committee should have been informed" even prior to the Commission's action. This would have extended our responsibility to keeping the Joint Committee informed as to our thoughts as well as our actions.

* Since the organization of the Joint Committee, there have been four staff directors, each of them, with the exception of the one appointed by the Junior Senator from New Mexico, either volunteered to testify for me or submitted a written statement to that effect.

In a study made by Green and Rosenthal for the National Law Center of George Washington University, the authors state, "There is considerable reason to believe that the JCAE's running attack on Chairman Strauss for not keeping the Committee 'currently and fully informed' was primarily a device for harassing the Commission and keeping it off balance."[14] For instance, during hearings in 1958 on the nuclear power program, I introduced into the record a telegram I had received that morning from the Pacific Gas and Electric Company. The telegram was to advise me of the decision of the company to build an atomic reactor with their own funds and without Government subvention. The Junior Senator from New Mexico, who was present, assailed me at the time for informing the Committee of this telegram, asserting that it was a device "to show that here stands private industry just itching to build these power plants." I pointed out that this left the Commission on the horns of a dilemma. I had received the telegram that morning and believed I should present it as current and useful information. Had I not done so and the material in the telegram appeared in the press, he would have been in position to castigate me for withholding it.

Communications from the Atomic Energy Commission to the Joint Committee sharply increased in number during my tenure. Exclusive of testimony which covered many days of hearings, there were letters and reports to the Joint Committee at an average of more than two per working day, and this number steadily increased. The Junior Senator from New Mexico alleged that the purpose was "to deluge the Committee with considerable numbers of individual letters and reports" while withholding important information. The line between the significant and the trivial was difficult to draw. For example, I was criticized for not reporting a confidential conversation with the General Manager, who had told me that he wanted to resign in the months ahead.

One further instance may give some additional color to the general subject of the charge of my unwillingness to co-operate with the Congress. In June 1956, the Joint Committee requested a copy of a study which had been made for the Commission on the safety aspects of the Fermi reactor then under construction by the Detroit Edison Company. The Commission demurred on the ground that the report was one element in the evidence being considered by the Commission before acting upon the award of a license to Detroit Edison. But upon insistence by the Joint Committee, the Commission furnished the report with a covering letter which asked that it not be regarded as a precedent and that it be treated as "administratively confidential," as it had been received by the Commission in its quasi-judicial capacity. The Joint Committee returned the report unread, saying that it would not receive it under those conditions, rejecting the Commission's contention that the report was privileged. The Commission capitulated and withdrew its stipulation.

In these instances where failure to provide information was alleged, whether the assertion was true or false, the point was slurred that these were actions of the Commission on which my vote was one in five. The Commission itself, of course, was a part of the Executive Branch doing the best job it knew how in accordance with its legal responsibilities.

One of the charges most often repeated was to the effect that the atomic energy enterprise of the Government had become "involved in politics" for the *first time* during my chairmanship. This was very far from factual. The Atomic Energy Act was born in an atmosphere of politics. When as a bill it reached the floor of the House in 1946 there were charges of "partisan politics," and when President Truman signed the act into law he stated: "I consider that this bill is not in the best public interest since it invests the atomic energy program with an aura of uncertainty and of partisan politics." Partisan politics thus attended the Commission at its birth, and, despite the efforts of its members to escape from politics, the importance of the task of the Commission, the vast sums expended by it, and the geographical distribution of its facilities inevitably embroiled it in the political controversies of the time.

One of these was the Mississippi Valley Generating Company contract—Dixon-Yates—in which connection I was charged with "gross corruption." The United States Court of Claims and later the Supreme Court of the United States disposed of the charge as detailed in the chapter on that contract, but unfortunately for me, this happened long after the Senate had voted. The Washington *Post,* which editorially applauded the Senate rejection in 1959, stated editorially nineteen months later (*after* the Supreme Court decision was announced):

> The Atomic Energy Commission, which came into the proceedings at a late date, was not to blame for the details. That is a point made repeatedly by this newspaper. It is a substantial vindication of former AEC Chairman Lewis Strauss, even though Mr. Strauss complicated his own position by his dogged defense of the contract.

Further to determine my fitness for public office, the Magnuson Committee accepted testimony from witnesses of such credibility as a columnist who has been the object of expressed contempt by Presidents of the United States. That witness and his leg-man, one or another of whom arranged to sit directly behind me during some sessions of the hearing, had written in one of his columns that among the papers in front of me was a certain "neatly typed" document marked "Top Secret," concerning one of the men who had testified against me; that "All the investigative resources of the United States Government had gone into the preparation of that report on his [the witness's] entire life, and it was made available to the man he criticised—Strauss."

As it happens, "Top Secret" documents are individually catalogued and I am informed that no such document ever existed. Certainly I never brought any "Top Secret" document to the hearing. In a session of the hearing after the column had been printed, the witness whose over-my-shoulder inspection of the document had been so comprehensive that he was able to describe its alleged contents then testified to an "error."[15] The document, he said, was actually marked "Confidential" and not "Top Secret." I took no confidential papers to the hearing, either.

A witness testified against me at considerable length with a prepared statement containing allegations, many introduced by such expressions as "It is believed," "It is reported," "It is generally credited," "The impression was" and an assortment of innuendoes.

Another witness, a Mr. Garonzik, was brought on. His testimony must rank with the most irrelevant-matter-to-the-subject ever printed at taxpayers expense, and there are forty pages of it. Near the end of his testimony, this witness was asked if he had ever received a letter from me. He could not recall any. Had he ever had any dealings with me? He had not. Had he ever met me? He had not.

The nightmarish quality of the proceedings was further exemplified when at one session of the hearing a woman arose behind my chair and screamed, "That man Strauss financed Lenin, Trotsky and the Bolshevik revolution." Guards gently led her out into the corridor. One of the Senators observed, off the record, that the nominee was precocious—"Must have been in knee pants when he did all that financing."

There was another comic incident, although it did not seem very amusing to me at the time. Toward the end of the hearings, Senator Smathers had let it be known that he had received a considerable number of telegrams from his state asking him to vote in my favor and that they had all come to him in one or two days. He had checked with some of the persons whose names were signed to them and had found that the telegrams had been sent without the signers' knowledge.

This news was telephoned to me while I was meeting with the Business Advisory Council at Hot Springs, Virginia. With the help of a good friend, an officer of the Western Union Telegraph Company, Edwin Chinlund, I was able to trace the messages. They had all been filed in West Palm Beach by one individual, a retired businessman whom I had never known. It developed that he had been reading the newspaper accounts of the hearing and out of the goodness of his heart felt impelled to do something to help me. Unfortunately, what he decided to do was to send a number of telegrams to Senator Smathers, each over the name of a friend or acquaintance and then, after the fact, to go about to obtain their consent. Persuaded of the possible harm he had done to me, he telegraphed a confession to the Senator.

The incident reminded me of a somewhat similar episode. During the Republican National Convention in Chicago in 1952, a telegram was received by the Republican National Committee which strongly denounced the Committee for barring reporters and television cameras from meetings of subcommittees. The telegram produced something of a sensation because it was signed "Herbert Hoover." It was traced, however, to a young lady in Wellesley who blithely admitted that she had written it and had signed Mr. Hoover's name. The telegraph office had accepted it without question. Endless possibilities for confusion are open, apparently, to eager persons.*

Witness after witness having testified against me for several weeks, I requested and was accorded an opportunity to make a statement. Addressing the Chairman, I said:

"Certain witnesses demand that your committee drive me from my present position as Secretary of Commerce, to which new duty the President appointed me last November. Their criticism, as I have listened to it, is two fold. First they differ with me on public policy; mostly in connections other than in the field of the Department of Commerce; and second, they attack my integrity.

"It would be a human impulse to strike back in anger when a man's record of a lifetime is distorted and defiled. Instead, when you permit me to do so, I shall answer in detail from the record, with truth, but without rancor. I shall present facts to refute the false charges.

"So far in the several weeks since the hearing started, except for the

* In December 1961, the Secretary of State received a telegram signed with the name of Mrs. Franklin D. Roosevelt and which was disowned by her as a forgery. A spokesman for the telegraph company was quoted as explaining that the message had been telephoned by a person who "had spoken in a self-assured voice." The circumstances were reported in the New York *Times* of December 20, 1961.

opening day, and my own testimony, only witnesses known in advance to be hostile to me have been called for statements and questioning. "I greatly appreciate the fact that members of the committee of both parties . . . questioned the testimony. And I trust that, eventually, witnesses in my favor may be permitted to add their evidence.

"Hearing both sides is the fair American method of inquiry . . . With deep sincerity, Mr. Chairman and Gentlemen, I declare that if the cruel accusations as to my character made in these hearings, and there- after reported in the press, were accurate, I would never have accepted President Eisenhower's appointment last November. I would not have betrayed his trust, nor would I come before this committee knowingly with unclean hands.

"Those of you have been long associated with me in public life know I speak the truth. Some who have testified against me, or who have given notice of their intention to do so, have never even met me; a most extraordinary procedure.

"I am proud to have had the opportunity of serving my country earnestly, and in my own view, uprightly, in the administration of several Presidents. Indeed, the better word would be to say that I am grateful that I have had the opportunity. . . .

"Recognition of that public service has come to me in awards by my Government, in honors by universities, and in communications from associates in many walks of life who know me best, but who *do* know me. A continuing stream of editorials, not planted,* not inspired, re- veals the people's support of the President's right to a Cabinet of his choice, even papers which regularly have disagreed with me on public policy.

"I believe the American people in these critical days of national security, threats from the Communist bloc, Soviet trade war, and grave economic problems, want something better from Washington than what appears to be the pattern of persecution through long drawn-out attempts at defamation of a plain man who has done his best as he sees it for his country over many years. And I might add that as a young man, I little thought I would ever be called upon for such a statement as this."

* This was said because Chairman Magnuson at an earlier session (April 21) had indicated his belief that editorial comment on the "dilatory tactics" of the Committee had been "inspired." "I don't know where they were inspired, but I have my own opinion about that," he had stated.

Ex-Senator Bricker, who had been a member of the Joint Con- gressional Committee, came from his home in Ohio to testify in my behalf. Dr. Detlev Bronk, President of the National Academy of

Sciences, came from New York for the same purpose, and over thirty other men of science appeared in person or authorized statements which they had written to be offered for the record.[16]

Dr. Edward Teller left a hospital bed in California to come to Washington to testify. The day after his testimony, the Committee Chairman communicated with a company for which Dr. Teller was a salaried consultant. He wanted to know if Dr. Teller had ever been employed, if so his periods of service, and *the amount the corporation paid him.* Whether this procedure was practiced in the case of other witnesses, I do not know.

To my gratification, ex-President Hoover wrote a most generous letter to the Committee. I learned of it under unusual circumstances. Near the close of the session on May 11, the Chairman, Senator Magnuson, said:

> There are a lot of letters which have been sent to the Committee . . . and they range from Herbert Hoover on down to Joe Smith . . . I don't want to put them all in the Record. If you put one in, you have to put all in, and we would have a record this high [indicating]. So I am going to have them all in the file. I am going to incorporate them in the record now by reference. The files are open to anyone who wants to look at them.[17]

Several Senators (including Senator Monroney, who was otherwise hostile) suggested that a letter from a former President of the United States ought to be admitted to the Record. Senator Magnuson disposed of the issue by saying that the opinion of the former President of the United States regarding the nominee was favorable. The letter was not read into the record. It must have been considered prudent to include it when the Record was printed, and it appears, not as an appendix, but as though it had been read at that point in the proceedings, which it was not.

New York, N.Y., May 9, 1959.

Hon. Warren G. Magnuson,
Chairman, Interstate and Foreign Commerce Committee,
U. S. Senate
Washington, D.C.

My dear Senator:

I believe it is my duty to present to the Committee my knowledge of Secretary Lewis Strauss, whose confirmation is before your committee.

I have known Mr. Strauss intimately for more than 42 years—ever since he was 19 years of age. During most of my service under President Wilson, Mr. Strauss served as my secretary. He served in Washington during almost the entire period of American participation in World War I and in Paris during and after the peace negotiations. He won the respect and admiration of the men with whom he had need to deal during that time. President Wilson often spoke highly of him to me.

Upon the completion of his service, he entered business life in New York where he rose to a high position and respect in the business world from his ability and integrity. And during these years he took part in the direction of the great American enterprises in compassion by relief of famine and pestilence in many countries.

At the coming of the Second World War, he was called for active duty in the Department of the Navy in February 1941. He served for 4 years under President Roosevelt, and the following year under President Truman. His service in this period was so highly valued that he received the unique distinction for a civilian—the rank of rear admiral, an appointment which required the approval of President Truman and the Senate.

In October 1946 Mr. Strauss was called back into public service by President Truman as a member of the Atomic Energy Commission. To take on this assignment he sacrificed his high business positions. Upon his resignation in early 1950, he was publicly commended by the President for his service.

And in June 1953 he was again called into public service by President Eisenhower as Chairman of the Atomic Energy Commission. He was confirmed by the Senate. He served the Commission until his completion of the statutory 5-year term. Upon completion of that work in 1958, he received the highest of public commendation by President Eisenhower and was awarded the Medal of Freedom. President Eisenhower's confidence in Mr. Strauss' abilities and integrity, after 5 years of association with him, is further attested by his appointment as Secretary of Commerce.

Here is a man who has served with unvarying commendation under both Democratic and Republican Presidents.

There has never been in our public service a man so unpolitical, so dedicated, and so able in his tasks, as to command such approvals and commendations upon the completion of every task assigned him.

I served 8 years as Secretary of Commerce. I can say without reservation that Lewis Strauss is the best man who could be selected for that position.

But over all other qualifications, he is a deeply religious man whose integrity is fixed in conscience and religious faith.

Yours faithfully,
HERBERT HOOVER

Eventually the hearing exhausted the participants. The Dixon-Yates case had been tried and retried.* Finally at the close of the hearing on May 14 the Committee adjourned, subject to the call of the chair.

On June 4 a majority of the Committee reported the nomination favorably. All of the six Republican Senators had so voted: Andrew F. Schoeppel of Kansas, John Marshall Butler of Maryland, Norris Cotton of New Hampshire, Clifford P. Case of New Jersey, Thruston B. Morton of Kentucky and Hugh Scott of Pennsylvania. They were joined by three of the eleven Democrats. They were Senators John O. Pastore of Rhode Island, Strom Thurmond of South Carolina, and Frank J. Lausche of Ohio. Senator Pastore knew me better than any member of the Magnuson Committee, as he was also a member of the Joint Congressional Committee on Atomic Energy. I had appeared before him on many occasions. His position was difficult and the pressure upon him severe. As always, however, he followed his conscience. He submitted his "Individual Views" as an appendix to the majority opinion. Reciting the events in which we had been associated he wrote, "In all of these dealings, I found Mr. Strauss to be patriotic, honorable and competent. We did not always agree and I did not expect perfection. I would not trespass on the divine to say, 'There is no fault in this man.' . . ."

I was deeply gratified by the majority support of these nine men. It was a measure of reward.

The Minority Report was extremely critical. It cited the alleged failure to co-operate with the Joint Congressional Committee on Atomic Energy and many other charges. A special emphasis was put upon my *"deliberate use of public office for improper aid to private business"* (italics supplied) in the "notorious Dixon-Yates case." The report stated that "When the details of this abortive attempt to cripple TVA was [sic] finally brought to the attention of the public through the efforts of Members of Congress and some of our great newspapers, *the President was forced to repudiate the contract."* (Italics supplied.)

---

* Senator Kefauver had opened his testimony with the statement, "It is not my purpose to retry the Dixon-Yates deal before this Committee." He then filled more than two hundred pages of the record with its retrial.

Whoever drafted the report did a disservice to those Senators who signed their names to it, for the statement that the President had repudiated the contract to supply power to the Memphis area was untrue. The President ordered the contract to be terminated in the orderly manner which its language provided, and emphatically not for the reason alleged in the Minority Report, but, solely because the City of Memphis, represented by its Mayor, had notified him that the City had concluded to build its own power plant. The President had urged such a course in 1953 and 1954. This is documented in the chapter dealing with the contract.

The Minority Report stated that "from the record it is clear that the nominee time after time has resisted furnishing the appropriate Committee of the Congress with information needed in order for Congress to properly perform its legislative functions." Yet from the report it is also clear that this statement must be based on three parts of the testimony: First, the remark of Chairman Cole quoted above, but which he was at pains to explain did *not* relate to me at all; or second, the assertion by Senator Kefauver that I withheld the Dixon-Yates contract from the Congress, an assertion in which he was factually wrong, and obviously misinformed, as documented in the hearings (pages 315–17); or third, upon my refusal to violate the doctrine of the separation of powers by revealing in response to questions, over the five-year period, the substance of conversations with the President and his personal staff.

The Minority Report also charged that I had been "guilty of an outright misrepresentation" in testifying about my refusal as Secretary of Commerce to allow large-diameter steel pipe to be shipped to Communist Russia. That charge was based upon my testimony that the Department of State and the Department of Commerce were in agreement on the issue. My testimony was accurate. The position of the Department of State had been given to me by the Under Secretary of State, Mr. Douglas Dillon. At a much lower level in the State Department, approval of the export license had been favored, but the policy of the State Department was not established at subordinate echelons. The Senate Committee Investigator in a report to Senator Magnuson admitted that the information on which the charge was based had been "ferreted out from fairly low level officials."[18] The implication that I had ridden roughshod over the State Department and misrepresented that I had done so would not only be without possible motive, but also was not in accordance with the facts.[19]

My views on trading with Communist countries, however, were no secret from the Committee. In reply to a question I had told them that I believed if we could trade with the Russian people and sell them the things the Russian people want and need—not necessarily the things that the government wishes to buy—such trade might tend in the long run to increase the pressure from the people on their government for the domestic supply of such goods. But, I added, "The sale to the Russians, on the other hand, of items which would find their way into their military effort and which would relieve the pressure on their manufacturing capacity of such goods, I think is *not* in the public interest." I said I would prevent such shipments if I were confirmed.

I had little patience with those who argued that we might as well sell strategic items to hostile governments "because they can purchase them elsewhere." This resembled the defense put forward by purveyors of switch-blade knives to juvenile delinquents—that "they can buy them on the other side of town anyway." In the matter of the large-diameter pipe, the Senate Committee's Special Counsel, apparently operating on that philosophy, undertook to find out whether the Soviets could buy elsewhere the size pipe that I had refused to allow to be exported. He obtained information that it was available in Germany and England and a memorandum to that effect was put into the Record. My information was that this was incorrect. But even if it had been accurate it was a bad case—for the Communist government can doubtless buy military end items from other countries, which is a poor argument for selling such material to the Soviets ourselves.

The Minority Report also stated that I had "challenged the integrity of the official transcript of a hearing before a Committee of the House, thus impugning the integrity of those responsible for its preparation." During my defense, I cited for the record, a formal statement by fifteen members of the House Appropriations Committee. In that statement these men had impugned the integrity of the transcript of a meeting of *their own committee*. They had the right to do so and they asserted and proved that the transcript had been tampered with after the meeting.[20]

One Senator made attempts to induce me to voice the same charges which had been written by members of the Appropriations Committee. Weary with the badgering, I was finally compelled to say, "Senator . . . I will not permit you to put words in my mouth—which you have been trying to do since the beginning of this hearing. I will simply read to you again, the statement of 15 of your Congressional colleagues and I will rest my case on that. *They* said material matters were omitted from the record and the record had been moulded."[21]

The Senator persisted and Senator Cotton finally interrupted to say, "Mr. Chairman, I am compelled to protest at this line of questioning when the Senator from Wyoming insists on putting into the words of the witness the words of the 15 Congressmen. They challenged this report and said it was doctored and he [the Senator] persists in trying to say that no one did except Admiral Strauss and I resist that as unfair."

The tactic of the Senator from Wyoming was explained later. Had he been able to confuse me sufficiently that I would personally make the charge that the fifteen congressmen had made, I would have been in contempt of Congress. By good fortune I did not fall into his trap.

In this connection another episode entered the record of the hearings.[22] Three years earlier (on July 26, 1956) the Washington *Post* had published an unfriendly editorial which in part stated:

Defeat in the House of the Gore-Holifield Bill for the construction of atomic power reactors is a tribute to the obstructionism of Lewis Strauss . . . His begging of the essential question on the status of atomic power development so infuriated the House Appropriations Subcommittee that it accused him of "duplicity" and "fraud."

After the editorial appeared the *Post's* editors learned that the House Appropriations Committee had done nothing of the sort, and a disavowal was published noting that:

Mr. Strauss' summary is correct. The testimony before the Subcommittee did indeed concern a dispute about differing views of an involved legal question. The charge that the Atomic Energy Commission's legal argument was "fraudulent" and "duplicitous" appeared in a draft report submitted by the Subcommittee Chairman. The word "fraudulent" was removed in the final report of the full Committee. This report did not accuse Mr. Strauss of "fraud" and we disavow any intention of doing so in our editorial. We are happy to make the record entirely clear on this.

The *Post* had disavowed "fraudulent" but not "duplicitous," for whatever such a disavowal was worth.

The Junior Senator from New Mexico arranged to have the first editorial printed in the *Congressional Record*. When the editorial disavowal appeared, I wrote requesting him in fairness to have it printed in the *Record* also. This he refused to do. (A congressman, T. James Tumulty of New Jersey, put the editorial apology in the *Congressional*

Record on his own initiative. I have never met Mr. Tumulty, but his act was evidence that there are men of good will everywhere.)

The Minority Report further charged that I had "suppressed an important letter from the Attorney General concerning the legality of the 1956 amendments to the Agreement for Cooperation with England." This was the letter earlier mentioned which had been written by the Attorney General to the Secretary of Defense in 1956. Since both the originator of the letter and its recipient were officials both independent of me, and senior to me, how I could have "suppressed" it is not explained, nor was any motive suggested for a charge so extraordinary.

There were other interesting, almost bizarre, features of the Minority Report. It conceded that the nominee's activities "have been impressive in some aspects" and even stated that "we recognize that Mr. Strauss has sought to serve the best interests of the country, as he sees them, and has made real contributions as to its welfare." But, brushing these aside, the report concluded, "mostly on the basis of his conduct and demeanor before us" he is "lacking in the degree of integrity and competence essential to proper performance of the duties of the office to which he had been nominated." With a parting saurian tear the report added, "We regret that this is so. . . ."

Two weeks then elapsed with no indication of when the decision would be taken. Finally on Wednesday, June 17, the Majority Leader, Senator Lyndon Johnson, whose opposition to the nomination, though not publicly expressed was known to his colleagues said on the floor:

> If I can, I should like to assure any members of the Senate who desire to be away on Thursday, Friday and Saturday—so far as I know, I will say, they are not members of my own party—that we shall have a definite agreement as to when to vote *so no one will be taken advantage of*.[23] [Italics supplied.]

The Senator disavowed trying to put over anything.[24] In the same session he proposed a unanimous resolution which would have set the date for the vote for the following Monday, June 22, but this was objected to by the Junior Senator from New Mexico. Before the session ended, Senator Johnson stated: "Under the circumstances, the only thing I could do was to make the other proposal; and if that was not agreeable then to have the Senate remain in session until a rather late hour tomorrow, Friday and Saturday, if we can by that time reach a vote on the nomination; and that is what the leadership hopes to do."[25]

Three Republican Senators had speaking engagements as far away as

North Dakota, Colorado, and Utah. Each of them has written that he left Washington under the impression that he had been assured that no vote on confirmation would be taken during his absence. They were many hundreds of miles away when, on the next day, June 18, it was agreed that the vote would be taken before the close of business. Heroic efforts were made to bring the absent Senators back in time to vote. The White House obtained the use of fast planes from the Air Force. Two Senators made it back in time, the third, while still aloft, was "paired" (his vote counterbalanced by one opposing).

Fourteen Democratic Senators crossed party lines that night and voted for confirmation. Among them was the *Senior* Senator from New Mexico. Their number also included all but two of the Senate Democratic members of the Joint Congressional Committee on Atomic Energy. Of the thirty-four Republicans, there were but two voting against confirmation, but those two were enough to ensure defeat.

In the days that immediately preceded and followed there were hundreds of editorials and thousands of letters on the subject, most of the latter from correspondents I did not know. Oddly, many gifts arrived. A bus driver in Chicago who had read that I was a collector of Washingtoniana, offered a Washington item that he had inherited; another letter accompanied an ancient Bible. The Medical College of Virginia announced a new surgical laboratory to bear my name, clubs extended honorary membership, and George Washington University elected me a trustee. General David Sarnoff, chairman of the Radio Corporation of America, and a few other steadfast friends invited me to return to the boards of companies on which I had served many years before. Editorial comment* was generally critical of the vote. The letters were

---

* The editorial in the New York *Times* of June 20 was captioned:
"POLITICS DEFEATS MR. STRAUSS"

The President, under the Constitution, has the right to appoint the members of his Cabinet subject to the approval of the Senate. This approval is not usually withheld and should not be, for the Chief Executive must be free to choose the members of his official family.

In the case of Lewis L. Strauss, however, forty-nine members of the Senate saw fit to refuse the President's request and voted against the nominee. It seems fitting to inquire into their reasons. Some did it for personal pique, some—and very few, we should judge—because they thought he was unfit, a number to support the pique of their fellow Democrats, the vast majority to go along with their party plan and reduce the prestige of their President.

Thus for an assortment of causes a splendid public figure was cast aside

friendly and brought healing. Some of them enclosed copies of replies that the writers had received from their Senators to whom they had written either before or after the vote was taken. In this way there have been collected the stated reasons of a number of those who voted to reject. They make curious reading.

A public opinion poll was published by the Trendex organization. A "scientifically selected cross-section" of public opinion had been questioned, those approached having been asked whether they had followed the Senate hearings as reported in the press. Those who answered affirmatively were then asked whether they approved or disapproved the action of the Senate. Seventy per cent of those who expressed an opinion disapproved. The answers from women were 83.3 per cent in disapproval of the Senate's action. A happy conclusion to be drawn from this is that it contradicts the popular notion that the female vote is swayed by photogenic considerations.

Other reactions soon began to arrive. The Soviet press was unrestrainedly jubilant. Moscow Radio broadcast a Tass comment from the Soviet official newspaper, *Pravda,* to the effect that: "Long before the discussion of his candidature in the Capitol, Lewis Strauss aroused the hatred of all honorable Americans. The United States Senate has torn the down and feathers from Strauss and he has appeared before the public stark naked as a dyed-in-the-wool reactionary and an inveterate enemy of peace." The Associated Press, reporting from Vienna, noted that Communist broadcasts had informed their listeners that "This was a blow at Eisenhower's prestige the like of which no President had suffered in three decades. . . . Strauss was a big banker who got his Admiral's rank from producing atom bombs."

Most of the Senators who voted against me did so, I feel sure, for political reasons and without personal malice. For most of them, I had and continue to have respect. I was likewise confident that the activity of a few professional anti-Semites was not effective. One such enterprise had obtained access to the papers of the late Justice Brandeis and had reproduced a letter that I had written to that distinguished jurist

---

and the Democratic majority, satisfied with this blow it has delivered to the Republican occupant of the White House, wears a grin of satisfaction.

Tribute should be paid to those Democrats who did not follow the party line and voted to confirm. The real tribute, however, should go to Mr. Strauss himself for his service during the war and as head of the Atomic Energy Commission when the hydrogen bomb, our greatest source of security, was developed under his leadership.

forty years before (when I was twenty-two years old). At that time I was engaged on relief work in Europe with Mr. Hoover. I had written to the Justice about riots and murders in Poland and what I was trying to do to help restore order. On the basis of that letter the attempt was made to depict me as more concerned with the fate of my persecuted co-religionists in Central Europe than with my responsibilities for the American Relief Administration.

In packets of documents which were distributed to Senators there were quotations from anti-Semitic libels, long ago exposed as forgeries. One of these was to the effect that the banking firm with which I had been connected until 1946, had "financed the Bolshevik Revolution in Russia." Also included was a partial list of philanthropic and educational organizations on the boards of which I have served. The list, however, had been edited to include mainly those which were Jewish, and they were so described. Included, however, was Hampton Institute, and in order that the significance of that connection should not be missed, it is followed by the underscored words, *"a Negro College."*

The whole undertaking was not very subtle and I have not the slightest reason to believe that the fact of the faith to which I was born or my affiliations influenced the vote of any Senator. Several Senators sent me the smear documents, which had come to their offices by hand rather than through the mails.

The same columnist who had testified against me at the hearing wrote in a column which appeared after the vote: "Senator Dodd of Connecticut—announced his vote for Strauss as induced by the Admiral's 'courage, competence, intellectual power.' Actually, however, it was pressure from Governor Abe Ribicoff of Connecticut which influenced his vote. Ribicoff advised Dodd that a vote for Strauss was the way to clinch the Jewish vote in that state." This was in character with many of the columnist's exclusives. Governor Ribicoff had never spoken to Senator Dodd concerning me. A letter of flat denial from Governor Ribicoff to Senator Dodd will be found in the appendix.[26]

Cyrus Eaton, the financier whose friendship with Communist leaders has brought him a certain kind of fame, wrote to Senators (improperly using, for that purpose, the official letterhead of a common carrier, the Chesapeake and Ohio Railway Company), urging his addressees to vote against confirmation. One of those so addressed was Senator Dodd, with whom I was not then acquainted. A copy of his reply to Eaton read in part as follows:

. . . I take it from your letter that you are opposed to the confirmation of Mr. Strauss, and this in itself will be taken with the utmost seriousness by me in favor of Mr. Strauss.

Within hours of the vote Eaton and his friend, Menshikov, the Soviet Ambassador, were exulting over the result mistakenly attributed to Eaton's influence with Senators.

After the vote, on the morning of the nineteenth, I breakfasted with an old friend, Senator Harry F. Byrd of Virginia, a man who has done so much over the years to keep us a solvent and a strong nation. Some photographers invaded the breakfast room. One asked what we were talking about that had made us so jolly. The topic at the time was grandchildren. After breakfast I went to the White House and handed my resignation to an angry President. The President showed me a statement he had just given to the press, and later in the day his secretary, Mr. James Hagerty, sent me the page on which it was drafted. It is written in characters nearly an inch tall, which display the pressure exerted on his pencil as the President wrote:

Last night the Senate refused to confirm the nomination as Secretary of Commerce of Lewis Strauss—a man who in war and in peace has served his nation loyally, honorably and effectively, under four different Presidents.

I am losing a truly valuable associate in the business of government. More than this—if the nation is to be denied the right to have as public servants in responsible positions men of his proven character, ability and integrity, then indeed it is the American people who are the losers through this sad episode.

White House news correspondents stopped me at the door of the Executive Offices and asked for a statement. My feelings were too close to the surface to venture much. The taped record indicates that I managed to express gratitude to the President for his support and for the privilege of serving with him since 1953. I also thanked the Senators of both parties who had voted for me, adding that I had done the best I knew how to protect and defend the national security. Concluding, I expressed confidence that history would be just.

* * *

What had brought this to pass?

As I review it, several elements of opposition converged at the vote and augmented one another. Anti-Semitism was certainly the least of these, and negligible. But there was the punitive opposition by the advocates of government development of electric power; the animosity engendered by the Oppenheimer case; the personal animus of a Senator; my strong belief in the paramount importance of maintaining the constitutional principle of the separation of powers and my defense of the Executive Branch in that regard; my unfortunate trait of stubbornness in refusing to conciliate by conceding error where error had not occurred; for following orders and honoring the oath of office; and the opportunity for a numerically superior political opposition to strike a blow at a popular President, at one remove from an attack upon him personally.

When the day arrived for leaving the Commerce Department, I packed my certificate of appointment and took leave of a wonderfully effective and devoted staff. This chapter should not end without acknowledging my indebtedness to them: in my office, my efficient and intensely loyal secretary who had served with me in the Atomic Energy Commission beginning in 1947, Mrs. Virginia Walker; my assistant, Arthur Arundel, a young ex-Marine officer and Korean war veteran who maintained a properly respectful demeanor toward hostile Senators on the Committee, but on the occasion when he was put on the stand, to be given a working over, showed that he could be neither overawed nor confused; Robert Dodds, who had come from Pittsburgh to be General Counsel for the Department of Commerce and who advised me intelligently and dealt restrainedly with the "prosecuting attorney"; Albert Leman, a veteran editor who had served my predecessor, Secretary Weeks, and whose wisdom and humor were a constant blessing; Fritz Mueller, the Under Secretary and my able successor; Under and Assistant Secretaries John Allen, George Moore, Carl Oechsle; Philip Evans, George Becker, Bradley Nash, and all the rest of the staff of the Department of Commerce who carried on, competently and loyally, during my extended absences while on the witness stand. All are fine people and I am grateful to them.

* * *

The decision of the Senate on June 18, 1959, is still too close in time as this is written for me to view it with detachment. It does not fall into the classification of events which were in mind when this book was begun, since the decision was of importance primarily to me. This chapter has been written in the hope of providing a footnote for those who, in the years to come, may deal, more objectively than will ever be possible for me, with the subject of the separation of powers in a representative government.

XIX

Nuclear Tests, Fall-out,
and World Opinion

> *So long as there is no operating system of inspection whereby the United Nations can thoroughly check on the atomic energy activities of every nation, there is no guaranty that preparations for atomic war are not going on in secret, and there can be no certain security and no absence of suspicion and fear. Without such safeguards the United States must not only retain the atomic bomb, but must proceed actively with its further development and production.*
>
> FROM "A PROGRAM FOR NATIONAL SECURITY"
> REPORTED TO THE PRESIDENT, MAY 29, 1947,
> KARL T. COMPTON, CHAIRMAN*

> *If it [democracy] keeps and enhances its strength, no great war need come again. Yet there is chance and change, a great war may come in ways we do not see, and free men must be ready.*
>
> VANNEVAR BUSH (1949)

This is a chapter about a subject which many people find repulsive. It offends reason to think that, at this point in human development, experience should not be overwhelmingly convincing that war is the most witless of human enterprises. It is a fact of life, however, that experience frequently fails to convince. Wars have occurred in our lifetime because some men have deliberately desired them. In this con-

---

* Other signatories were Joseph E. Davies, Harold W. Dodds, Truman K. Gibson, Jr., Daniel A. Poling, Anna M. Rosenberg, Samuel I. Rosenman, Edmund A. Walsh, and Charles E. Wilson.

nection, it is usual to think of Hitler and concede that it may still be possible for war to be caused by a megalomaniac who has come to power. But it is not that simple. War was the choice, not of one satanic individual, but of a large and influential group of men, in Japan, in 1941. The issue was debated there for months before the decision was made. The peace lovers and the moderates were allowed their say, listened to, and voted down. War was the preferred alternative to what the militarists regarded as an otherwise unavoidable economic subjugation to the United States. It was a decision by human beings who, by every standard, were rational, however wrong.

Also, it is interesting to read in the voluminous literature which followed the proceedings of the International Military Tribunal that the Japanese military were confident that war with the United States could be contained—that it could be a "limited war"—and that at its end a "settlement" could be reached, advantageous to Japan. They never planned to subdue the United States mainland, or even to attack it. Admiral Yamamoto, it is true, was quoted in the testimony (he had been killed during the war) to the effect that the peace treaty would have to be dictated by Japan and signed in Washington—but he was atypical.

The Japanese did not count on the effect which Pearl Harbor had upon the American public, nor on the grimness with which the policy of unconditional surrender was clasped and pursued by us. There is a lesson in this for those who believe that wars between great powers can be limited wars. I greatly doubt that events and the nature of man will confirm that thesis, and I pray that it may never be put to test.

In the minds of many people who never considered themselves to be pacifists, the era of nuclear weapons produced a revulsion against war for any cause which they had not consciously entertained in the era of conventional weapons.

Do we feel guilty that we were the first to produce atomic weapons and the first to use them in a war? Many do, and many more do not. The argument will go on for a very long time, but it is beside the point. A feeling of guilt ought not determine a future course of our national policy in a world in which atomic energy and atomic weapons are facts of life. Furthermore, the generation which made the original decisions to develop and to use the weapon is rapidly passing away.

Pacifists, and persons who are not pacifists but who want atomic disarmament, even if it has to be unilateral, are generally the most estimable of people. They have chosen an easy, *personal* escape from the dilemma, but it is not one which a government can follow and survive. The true pacifist abhors any weapon, while the atomic pacifist often is tolerant of conventional weapons for "limited wars" but opposes the nuclear weapon on the ground that it is so much more devastating than conventional weapons. It is devastating, true enough, but TNT bombs and napalm bombs are not more discriminating in their death-dealing. Fire bombs actually took a greater toll in Tokyo than the atomic bomb at Hiroshima.

A distinction between conventional weapons and nuclear weapons is something more than the area and the number of casualties they compass. This difference lies in the fact that the existence of powerful conventional weapons did not prevent two world wars, while nuclear weapons, at this writing at any rate, seem to have been a deterrent to world war. It is their awesome violence which has imparted to them this quality.

For four years, 1945–49, we were the trustees of this potential of violence. We may lay to our souls the unction that at least we tried to use those years to internationalize the control of atomic energy and to share the advantages we alone then possessed for the common good and the safety of all men. But the world was divided and our efforts failed —the reason for failure being less significant than the fact of it. We have the weapon. Do we now put it aside? That is the question which so relentlessly racks the conscience of so many.

In the use of force wrong when it is in defense of freedom and justice? Is the defense of the weak against the strong wrong? If the answer to these questions be "No," then there is no consistent argument against weapons designed to deter assaults against freedom and justice, or aggression against weak populations by brutal governments, simply because they are weapons with force of a new magnitude. For if justice and the oppressed are to be defended, but cannot be successfully defended with the sword, is the cannon a permissible weapon? And where, after that, is the line—and who may draw it?

The Atomic Energy Law defines the "paramount objective" of the policy of the people of the United States to be assurance of "the common defense and security." This is not only common sense, but is in keeping with our tradition since the days of Washington. In 1946 when the law was drafted and our monopoly of atomic bombs was apparently uncontested, even small numbers of this "ultimate weapon" were a reliable assurance of the common defense. The numbers were small indeed, as President Truman has revealed in his memoirs.

This condition, with the complete co-operation of the Military Establishment, the AEC set about to improve. In addition to numbers, which would be greatly increased, it was desirable to find means whereby the fissionable material could be more economically employed and, if possible, the size and weight of the weapon reduced. Achievement of the latter objective would facilitate storage, transport, and combat use of the bomb.

As for numbers, the law required the President to direct the Commission from time to time how many weapons to produce, and there is related in an earlier chapter how this had worked in practice.

Prior to 1953, the Commission had been in the position of tacitly accepting the requirements presented to it. For the first six years the Commission could not question the assumptions upon which requirements were based, because it did not know them in any detail. One of President Eisenhower's early acts was to open that aspect of military planning to the Chairman of the Commission so that the reasonableness of the demands which the Commission was called upon to meet could be viewed and accepted or appealed to the President.

On the second point—size and weight of weapons—the Commission regarded its responsibility as very great, and its laboratories worked diligently and successfully to reduce both. As is public knowledge, the first two bombs used over Japan were different in their design, and it was recognized that, if variety were possible at so early a stage, much unexplored area lay ahead of the research teams in the laboratories. As new ideas occurred to the scientists, they were debated and checked for their practicability in so far as the known properties of materials and calculations based on previous experience could go. If the idea survived this screening, it could be made practical only by testing to prove it.

The difference between theoretical calculations, on the one hand, and the phenomena actually experienced in a nuclear explosion, on the other, may be so great that without an experiment it is impossible to be certain of the result. Before the Alamogordo test, some of the scientists who worked on the bomb had a pool on the yield (explosive force) of the weapon and, except for one or two wild guesses, most were far from the mark. The first thermonuclear test at Eniwetok in the Castle series was substantially more powerful than estimated. Changes in design may be promising on paper but may not work at all at the proving ground. Effects also develop from tests and often lead to new information and new ideas of value not only for military use but for civil defense and peaceful applications as well.

A vast expenditure on hardware and a large commitment of fissionable material could not be risked to create an arsenal of new weapons whose actual performance is unknown; nor can national security be risked upon an untried weapon no matter how plausible the theory upon which its design was based.

This was the reason for the first tests conducted by the Atomic Energy Commission in 1948 at Eniwetok Atoll in the Marshall Islands. The tests at nearby Bikini Atoll in 1946 were not intended as weapon tests so much as experiments with atomic weapons against ship design and construction, and the bombs employed there were substantially weapons such as had been used in 1945.

The 1948 tests, while greatly improving weapon design, incidentally provided the occasion to prove our monitoring system. This was the detecting network which later caught the Russians testing weapons and exposed the sham of their profession of interest only in the peaceful uses of atomic energy. This has been treated in more detail in a preceding chapter. The weapons in that test series at Eniwetok were fission devices and produced yields of the order of thousands of tons of TNT equivalent. Before the next test series, however, three significant events had occurred. We discovered that Russia was producing nuclear weapons; we learned of the penetration of our own laboratories by espionage (e.g., the Klaus Fuchs confession); and the decision was taken to develop the hydrogen bomb. It required more than a decision, however, for an idea had to be born.

The discovery of the principle upon which our hydrogen weapons function was the contribution of the brilliant physicist Dr. Edward Teller and a group which worked with him. Without tests, however, to prove the feasibility of his idea, the weapon would have remained in a "Top Secret" report as a series of drawings and calculations. The Soviet test of a hydrogen bomb would have been our first intimation that the secret of how such a bomb could be made had been found—by them, not by us. The consequences are not pleasant to contemplate.

The test at Alamogordo in July of 1945 had demonstrated the possibility of radioactive fall-out. Cattle grazing near the test site suffered skin burns and subsequent graying of hair on their backs as a result of fall-out from this detonation. Ten years later there had been no detectible change in the health of their cattle or in their reproductive ability as a result of the radiation they had received. A report[1] in 1961 on cattle grazed on the Nevada test site and elsewhere in Nevada, showed that there had been "no evidence of biological damage to date, histologically or grossly." Some benign skin growths on aged cattle were reported in 1961.[2]

Just what was this fall-out?

The fission products of the components of a nuclear weapon are vaporized by heat and become part of a fire-ball after the detonation. As it rises, an updraft sucks dust from the ground. Some of this dust may be made radioactive by the neutrons released in the fission re-action. The radioactive fission products form part of a cloud which originates from the fire-ball. The initial radioactivity in the cloud de-creases rapidly, since many of the fission products have short "half-lives."[*] At the end of one hour, the radiation emitted is only about 5 per cent of the radiation level five minutes after detonation, and at the end of one day, the level drops to .1 per cent. Some radioactivity, however, remains for many years.

The heavier particles fall to the earth around the location of the test or explosion within a few hours, while lighter particles may be blown into the upper atmosphere, where they float, and, depending upon how high they are blown, are delayed in reaching the surface of the earth. If the explosion is small and the wind is light, they fall nearby. If the particles are light, they may be carried to great distances. If the ex-plosion is very large, a portion of the fall-out may be blown above the troposphere and into the stratosphere. Light particles may remain for months or years in the stratosphere before they settle to the earth. Meanwhile, their radioactivity decays at the fixed rates for the vari-ous isotopes of which they are composed.

Radioactive fall-out is not the only source of radiation to which men are exposed. As the detection and measurement of nuclear radiation became perfected, it was learned that we are being exposed con-stantly to radiation from a variety of sources in the air, water, and the earth. A number of radioactive substances occur naturally, and they are widely distributed in the earth's crust.[**] In addition, cosmic rays, originating somewhere in space, constantly bombard the earth. Cosmic

---

[*] Radioactive materials decay at a fixed rate, depending upon the specific elements involved. The length of time required for one half of the activity to expend itself is called the half-life of the radioactive substance.

[**] "It has been estimated . . . that . . . a foot of topsoil from a square mile . . . in midwestern United States . . . would contain about 3 tons of uranium and about one twenty-eighth of an ounce of radium," U. S. Atomic Energy Commission "Questions & Answers About Radiation," 1960.

rays, plus the nuclear radiation from uranium, thorium, radium, and other radioactive materials in the earth's crust and in the air, constitute what is called "background radiation."

Background radiation can vary in its intensity depending upon the time of day, the altitude, the geology of the area, and, to a minor extent, the latitude. For example, at sea level in the northeastern part of the United States, about 6.5 cosmic ray particles per minute cross a horizontal surface 1 square inch in area. But if you go up 15,000 feet in elevation the rate is about 75 times that at sea level.

Rainfall also may increase background radiation. The exact mechanism causing this increase is not precisely known, but it is believed that either the falling rain droplets absorb the minute radioactive particles naturally occurring in the air, or the downdraft air-flow accompanying the rainfall blows these particles toward the earth surface. Natural background radiation may increase as much as tenfold as a result of a rain or snow. Human beings receive between 80 and 800 millirems per year of exposure from natural background sources. (A chest X-ray would be equivalent to from 100 to 1000 millirems; a dental X-ray to the jaw about 5000 millirems.)

On my return from Eniwetok on March 29, 1954, I reported to President Eisenhower on the Castle atomic test series. The President had been greatly concerned over the reports of the first Castle shot, the fall-out having been observed on the atolls of Rongelap, Rongerik, and Uterik and on a Japanese fishing vessel which had sailed too close to the atoll. The next morning, having his regular press conference in the Indian Treaty Room at the old State Department, the President took me with him and asked me to tell the press substantially what I had reported to him.

It was the first time, so far as I am aware, that public attention had been called to the subject of fall-out and the effect described.

The part of my statement which apparently made the greatest impression on the reporters was the observation that the large weapon we had tested could destroy a whole city. The next morning this made the headlines, which was surprising, because seven years earlier almost identical language had been used by Secretary Stimson without any such reaction. In an article published in 1947 he wrote that he had informed President Truman in April 1945 that "within four months we shall in all probability have completed the most terrible weapon ever known in human history, one bomb of which could destroy a whole city.[3]

Pointing out that the first shot, which had been wrongly described as "out of control," was a very large blast about double the estimated yield—a margin of error not incompatible with a totally new weapon—I then explained the nature of fall-out. I told how the Marshall Islands had been selected as the proving ground for nuclear tests because of the meteorological conditions and the long miles of normally empty ocean which lay to the northeast in the direction toward which the prevailing winds blew. Each of the two atolls, Bikini and Eniwetok, was composed of coral reef surrounding a lagoon, and at various points on this reef, like beads on a string, there was a multitude of little islets some a few score acres in extent, others no more than sand-spits. It was one of these small, uninhabited, treeless sandbars which was used for the experiment. The impression that an entire atoll or even a large island had been destroyed in the test was erroneous. It would be more accurate to say that a large sand-spit or portion of a reef had been blown up.

Next, the warning area was described as an area surrounding the proving ground within which it is determined that a hazard to shipping or aviation existed. The United States has established many such areas, as have other governments. We have a large one off the Pacific Coast at Point Mugu, another off the Hawaiian Islands, and the guided-missile warning area from Florida east across the Bahamas. Including our continental warning areas, we have established a total of four hundred forty-seven such warning or danger areas. The warning area around Bikini and Eniwetok was established in 1947, the United Nations was advised, and appropriate notices were carried, then and subsequently, in marine and aviation navigational manuals.

In spite of these notices, there are always instances where accidents, or near accidents, have resulted from trespass on warning areas. The very size of them makes it impossible to fence or police them. Fleet units attached to the task force launched aircraft which carefully searched the area from north to south and east to west and reported no shipping. The shot was fired, the wind failed to follow the predictions, shifting south of that line, and the little islands of Rongelap, Rongerik and Uterik were in the path of the fall-out. The Japanese fishing trawler *Fortunate Dragon* appears to have been missed by the aerial search, but in view of a statement attributed to her skipper to the effect that he saw the flash of the explosion and heard the concussion six minutes later, he must have been well inside the danger area. This has been denied. I do not know the truth of the matter.

The task-force commander promptly evacuated all the natives from the two inhabited islands. They were taken to Kwajalein, where we had naval medical facilities, and they were placed under continuous and competent supervision. I visited them there. A month after the event, the medical staff on Kwajalein advised me that they anticipated no illnesses. One child had been born in the group and others were expected.*

There were reports of radioactive fish in the area following the test, but the United States Food and Drug Administration had advised us that their inspectors found no instance of unusual radioactivity in any shipments of fish from Pacific waters. The press was promised a further and more detailed report when all of the studies had been collected and organized.

As soon as the scores of scientific reports had been submitted and studied, a comprehensive report was issued the following February under the caption "A Report on the Effects of High Yield Nuclear Explosions." In an introduction, attention was called to the fact that "If we had not conducted the full-scale thermonuclear tests in question, we would have been in ignorance of the extent of the effects of radioactive fall-out and, therefore, we would have been much more vulnerable to the dangers from fall-out in the event an enemy should resort to radiological warfare against us. . . ." Also, "In the event of war involving the use of atomic weapons, the fall-out from large nuclear bombs exploded on or near the surface of the earth would create serious hazards to civilian populations in large areas outside the target zones. The Atomic Energy Commission hopes that these dangers will never be experienced by mankind. However, until the possibility of an atomic attack against us is eliminated by a *workable international plan for general disarmament,* the study and evaluation of the effects of weapons which might be used against us and the improvement of our means of self-defense are a paramount duty of our government."

Before the end of 1954, we had conducted medical follow-ups on the Marshallese natives. They had continued in excellent health, their blood counts were approximately normal, and a few skin lesions had healed. A check made three years later (1957) indicated that no deaths had occurred among the Rongelap people except for one stillbirth resulting from an infection and a forty-six-year-old man whose death was at-

---

* The infant, a girl, was named Alice, after my wife, whereupon I presented her with a dowry which in the culture of the Marshall Islanders was a pen of pigs.

tributed to hypertension. Neither was in any way related to radiation effects. The persons who were originally exposed on the island of Uterik were examined and found to be in good health, with no illnesses or clinical conditions that could be related to radiation effects.

But starting in 1954 a crescendo of attack on the United States weapon program began and grew each year in its intensity. In 1958, a large group of pickets, including a number of women, moved into the ground floor of AEC headquarters near Germantown, Maryland, and camped there. They announced that they would neither eat nor depart until they had received assurances of abandonment of atomic weapons by the United States. It was suggested that we should call the county or state police and have them evicted. It seemed to me, however, that, as citizens they had some sort of right to enter a public building peaceably so long as they did not commit a nuisance. Talking with them, I found them respectable, terribly earnest, and completely impractical. I had cots and blankets provided, assigned washrooms for their convenience, and smuggled coffee and sandwiches to some of them at night. During the day, in the presence of the press, they maintained their hunger strike. Their numbers gradually dwindled. At the end of a week they asked to see me again, said some friendly words, admonished me to beat swords into plowshares, and departed.

Others were not so artless. Every time the U.S. conducted a series of tests there were loud outcries. Russian tests which we detected and announced did not produce this reaction. The difference at first was puzzling. A famous chemist, Dr. Linus Pauling, who was very active in the anti-test propaganda was quoted: "I see no reason whatever for the United States to continue to test bombs. Even if Russia continues to test, it is pointless for the United States to carry on. There is absolutely nothing to be gained by it."[4] Pauling was not an authority on weapons.

Pauling was also reported in the New York *Times* on April 29, 1958, as asserting that carbon-14 produced in nuclear explosions was "a far more serious long-term menace than all other radioactive byproducts of an atomic explosion," and that "The earth's content of carbon-14 has been increased by ten per cent." Pauling was shortly answered by Drs. Kulp, Broecker, and Schulert, of the Lamont Geological Observatory at Columbia University. These men demonstrated that Pauling's figures were off by a factor of 50 and then the increase was not 10 per cent but .2 per cent. They pointed out that the final results in exposure to the human body "will be only .002 per cent of the total natural background radiation dose. This would be considerably less than that received from a luminous-dial wrist watch worn for about two hours a year." The other inaccurate figures are deeply imbedded in the popular literature.

Very little evidence being available as to the effect of small doses of radiation on human genetics, it was desirable to conduct as much research as possible with animals and to extrapolate as far as possible from those results. I proposed to double the size of the laboratory and the effort of this phase of the study at Oak Ridge. At that center, under the supervision of Dr. Alexander Hollaender, one of the leading biologists of our generation, a team on mammalian genetics, headed by W. L. and Liane B. Russell and Elizabeth Kelly, run what is locally called "the mouse factory." By the end of 1958, their studies had convinced them that repeated exposure to small doses of radioactivity over long periods did not produce the same effect as single massive doses and that the previous doctrine that it did not matter whether doses of radiation are "acute" or "chronic," if the total dosage is the same, was probably wrong.

The most disquieting opposition to the test program, however, was based upon statements of a very distinguished geneticist, who contended that damage caused by even the smallest increase in radiation could result in an accumulation of undesirable mutations in the human race over a long period of years. Many people accepted this and were frightened, although the statement had been carefully qualified by its author to indicate the lack of solid evidence.

A few years later (1960) the same authority predicted that great damage will result, and in a shorter period, from the accumulation of the undesirable genetic mutations which normally occur, i.e., irrespective of nuclear weapons tests. This he attributed to the fact that medical research now enables people to live and to reproduce who ordinarily would not survive to produce offspring. This theory, if correct, would mean that our hospitals and medical laboratories are more dangerous than atomic fall-out, for, in eight generations, according to such computations, the effect would be just the same as if all parents of one entire generation had been subject to the gamma radiation experienced at Hiroshima.

My former colleague, Dr. Libby, has a long and constructive familiarity with radioactivity. He originated the procedure for dating certain archaeological material by its carbon-14 content and later received a Nobel prize for this contribution to science. He assured me that in the clamor there was much that was scientifically unsound and much that was stated as factual which had not been proven.

Dr. Shields Warren of New England Deaconess Hospital, Boston, who had been director of the Division of Biology and Medicine of the Atomic Energy Commission, preserved a judicial calm under the barrage of charges. He recommended that I get a composite opinion at the highest scientific level. I turned to my friend Detlev Bronk, then president of the National Academy of Sciences, and Dr. Bronk agreed that such a study was within the proper area of concern of the academy. Accordingly, with funds provided by the Rockefeller Foundation so that both the men and the means were equally independent of government, the study was undertaken. It occupied the time of more than a hundred scientists in the fields of genetics, pathology, meteorology, oceanography and fisheries, agriculture and food supplies, and radioactive waste disposal. Titled "The Biological Effects of Atomic Radiation," it was completed by June 1956 and released to the public. It is a straightforward study written in lay language, and it contained what was at the time rather surprising information.

For example, the present dangers from ionizing radiation were found to be due much more to the excessive use of medical and dental X-rays than from fall-out. "Thus, ironically, the public anxiety about nuclear weapons has resulted in reports which emphasize long neglected dangers in medical practices," wrote Dr. C. Auerbach in the British scientific weekly *Nature*.[5] Dr. Auerbach was particularly concerned with a report by the Medical Research Council of Great Britain, which though contemporary with our study was independent of it, and reached the same findings.*

The National Academy of Sciences issued its report in two sections, one titled "A Report to the Public," the other "Summary Reports." On page 2 of the first, the report states:

> Thus far except for some tragic accidents affecting small numbers of people, the biological damage from peacetime activities (including the testing of atomic weapons) has been essentially negligible.

* In a letter from Lord Cherwell to the author written from Christ Church, Oxford, June 26, 1956: "I must say I read the Medical Research Council report with a great deal of satisfaction. How ignorant people are is illustrated by the fact that a man at the press conference was seen surreptitiously removing his radium dial wrist watch though how he hoped to gain safety by putting it in his trouser pocket, I find hard to understand."

The second section, on pages 22 and 30, reads in part as follows:

With these understandings it may be stated that U.S. residents have, on the average, been receiving from fall-out over the past five years a dose which, if weapons testing were continued at the same rate, is estimated to produce a total 30-year dose of about 1-tenth of a roentgen;* and since the accuracy involved is probably not better than a factor of five, one could better say that the 30-year dose from weapons testing if maintained at the past level would probably be larger than 0.02 roentgens and smaller than 0.50 roentgens.

The fall-out from weapons testing has, so far, led to considerably less irradiation of the population than have the medical uses—and has therefore been less detrimental. So long as the present level is not increased this will continue to be true; but there remains the proper concern to see to it that the fall-out does not increase to more serious levels.

* This is less than 10 per cent of the dose which would be received in the same period from naturally occurring rocks and cosmic rays, not including medical exposure.

The reports were summarized in the metropolitan press, but the agitation to ban tests because of fall-out did not abate. When later we were able to test underground without producing any fall-out the agitation continued from some quarters. This suggested that fall-out hazard had been just a convenient hook upon which to hang the argument that the United States should cease testing.

During those years also the Soviets were busy in the dual activity of both testing and denouncing our tests. In the midst of our national election campaign in 1956, the Soviet Premier wrote a letter to President Eisenhower and released it to the press before it could be translated and delivered. It was a blatant attempt to interfere in our elections both in its timing, being three weeks before election day, and in its content. "We fully share the opinion," wrote Bulganin, "presently expressed by certain prominent figures* in the United States, concerning the necessity and the possibility of concluding an agreement on the matter of prohibiting atomic weapon tests. . . ."

In his acknowledgment, the President was understandably caustic: ". . . the sending of your note in the midst of a national election campaign of which you take cognizance, expressing your support of

* The reference appeared to be to the position publicly taken by the President's Democratic opponent, Adlai Stevenson.

the opinions of 'certain prominent public figures in the United States' constitutes an interference by a foreign nation in our internal affairs of a kind which, if indulged in by your Ambassador, would lead to his being declared persona non grata in accordance with long established custom."

Elsewhere in his letter the Soviet Premier charged that the United States renounced its own disarmament proposals as rapidly as the Soviet Union accepted them. This reads ironically in the light of the facts. Consider, for example, what occurred in Geneva in 1960–61, where the Soviets acted precisely in the manner ascribed by them to us. Bulganin had asserted in his letter, *"It is our deep conviction that the solution of the problem of testing atomic weapons should not be made contingent on an agreement concerning the problem of disarmament as a whole."* (Italics supplied.) The collapse of the test-suspension negotiation in Geneva in March of 1961 was accompanied by a Soviet declaration of their deep conviction that test suspension and nuclear disarmament could be dealt with only in the context of disarmament *as a whole*. This diplomatic exercise of blowing hot and cold leads to the inescapable conclusion that the Soviets never desired a test-suspension agreement involving assurance of compliance by genuine inspection. The protracted negotiations were, on their side, clearly a ruse to hold our armament static while they improved their weapons. In a speech at the United Nations, a Soviet spokesman, S. K. Tsarapkin, who had headed their Geneva delegation, scored the U.S.-U.K. position as unacceptable because it was not part of a general disarmament agreement.[6]

The test-ban advocates were also active in England. Prime Minister Churchill and later Prime Minister Macmillan were personally attacked for the British test program. Lord Cherwell noted that, "The ring leaders in the campaign are certainly a very curious collection. Oddly enough, none of them seems to worry very much about the Russian tests. These they seemed to assume will do no harm to anyone. It is *our* tests they insist will poison the world. The Daily Worker, of course, has been in the forefront of the movement."

Speaking in the House of Lords in May 1957, Cherwell told the peers:

For the first time, thanks to the hydrogen bomb the West is in a position to inflict mortal injury on Russia, whose vast distances have swallowed up so many armies in the past. That is why the Kremlin is so anxious that we should not use them. . . . Over 5,500 people were killed on the roads in 1955 in Britain alone and over 250,000 were injured. This could all be avoided if we stopped all the motoring. But nobody proposes that. Why? Because we think the convenience and economy of motor transport justifies the risk . . . The statistical evidence for a connection between cancer of the lung and smoking is much stronger than exists for a connection between radioactivity and bone cancer. But nobody suggests that we should ban smoking, though this would do very little harm to anyone except the chancellor of exchequers. But the excitable, sometimes almost hysterical, people who rush forward ordering us to stop our bomb tests, leave out of account altogether that to do so would prevent our having a deterrent which would probably save us from a war costing millions of lives.

A Senator's statement that the "maximum force available to us right now from a concussion of hydrogen bombs is, according to some information, sufficient to blow the earth off its axis by 16 degrees, which would affect the seasons" was part of the mythology of the period. Allowances may be made for this statement which appeared during a political campaign, but testing was blamed widely for weather (too much or too little rainfall, too high or too low temperatures and the like), in spite of the fact that such abnormalities had been experienced long before the nuclear era. It is interesting to note that the energy released by an atomic weapon of the largest size tested to that time was substantially less than the energy content of a summer thunderstorm. The meteorological effect of an atomic explosion is occasionally the production of local showers which also frequently follow other kinds of explosions. No distant effects could be attributed by our Weather Bureau experts.

On returning to Washington in 1954 after witnessing part of the Castle test series, I had communicated with our laboratories to request that urgent attention be given to the problem of designing weapons with reduced fall-out. Two years later considerable progress had been made in that direction. The Joint Congressional Committee took advantage of an opportunity to hear about it at first hand when Dr. Teller and the late Drs. Ernest O. Lawrence and Mark Mills were testifying before them on other matters.

In the course of their exposition the three scientists so greatly impressed those members of the committee present that Congressman Cole telephoned to the White House and suggested that the President might like to hear the scientists. The following morning, I took them to call on the President. They explained to him the means by which they had achieved the great reduction in the amount of radioactive fission products formed by the explosion of bombs of new design. They said that it was feasible to have a design ready by the next test series from which the fall-out would be less than 4 per cent of that which would result from a current weapon of similar yield. Dr. Lawrence stated his belief that, with three to five years of research and tests, it should be possible to reduce fall-out still further and perhaps to eliminate it entirely. The President believed that this information should be given to the public and called in his press secretary, Mr. Hagerty, who arranged for the three scientists to meet the White House correspondents at once.

The interview resulted in an account in the press the following morning. Unfortunately, it infuriated some members of Congress. In the course of a speech on the Senate floor referring to that event, the *Congressional Record* reported the Junior Senator from New Mexico as follows: "Not only that, but the day on which the Chairman of the Atomic Energy Commission paraded Dr. Teller and Dr. Lawrence to the White House to talk about a cleaner bomb, they had come to Washington to testify before the subcommittee on Military Applications of the Joint Committee on Atomic Energy headed by the able Senator from Washington. In their testimony they said that this country needed more plutonium production. In the course of that testimony, those witnesses made some voluntary observations about how to get a slightly cleaner hydrogen bomb. When word of that testimony leaked out, Dr. Teller and Dr. Lawrence were rushed to the White House in order that a press release could be given out, in which they were labeled as great geniuses who were going to produce a vastly cleaner bomb."

In spite of criticism, work on the weapon design with reduced fall-out continued. It was given the sobriquet "clean bomb" initially as a mark of disparagement. The New York *Post* of October 24, 1956, quoted Senator Kefauver: ". . . this clean bomb nonsense . . ." And there were quips about how we could be certain that Russians would use "clean" bombs on us.

Our aim, of course, was to produce weapons which would be usable over our own or friendly territory for defense against enemy aircraft and missiles. Our intention never to begin a nuclear war necessitates an especial emphasis on defensive measures. Therefore, development of nuclear warheads with greatly reduced fall-out or with fall-out totally eliminated was greatly to be desired. Great strides have been made and more are possible if testing can be continued.

Devices with greatly reduced fall-out have also opened up a new vista of peaceful uses to which the name "Plowshare" has been given. Originally suggested derisively also, Plowshare holds great promise. A number of peaceful and extremely useful applications of nuclear explosions are now possible.

Large volumes of earth and rock can be moved or broken with nuclear explosives at costs far below those of conventional civil engineering projects. The digging of harbors and canals, the removal of large obstructions from navigation, and the creation of water storage facilities both on the surface and underground are projects which can be accomplished cheaply with nuclear explosives. A study has been made in Northwest Alaska to determine the feasibility of the excavation of a harbor, between Cape Steppings and Cape Thompson, where none exists and where access to substantial mineral resources will be facilitated.

Nuclear explosives can be used in the recovery of oil. They can be placed so as to fracture and heat large masses of oil-bearing shale. The oil, thus released, can be conventionally pumped. Some engineers believe that the oil-shale deposits in Colorado, Utah, and Wyoming may be the largest untapped oil reserves in the world. There are also large deposits of tar sands, a mixture of sand and crude oil, where the oil cannot be extracted by conventional methods. It is believed that the heat released by nuclear explosives will reduce the viscosity of the oil so that it will flow and that it may then be recovered by conventional pumping. There is the third method, which results from the fact that oil fields depleted by conventional recovery techniques are known to contain appreciable amounts of oil which may be recoverable following a nuclear detonation.

The energy released and trapped by fully contained nuclear explosions underground could also result in the production of both power and radioactive isotopes. The energy which is stored as heat following such an explosion is in effect in a great thermos bottle, and it could be released in a controlled manner by water or some other medium and produce electric power industrially. It could also be arranged that the neutrons which result from such an explosion be trapped in appropriate substances placed around the device and this would result in the very large-scale production of isotopes less expensively than by other techniques.

Nuclear explosives might also be used in the mining industry to crush enormous amounts of low-grade and otherwise inaccessible minerals or deposits whose hardness makes the use of ordinary explosives inefficient.

Following such an explosion conventional mining methods or leaching by water or other agents could recover minerals pulverized by nuclear explosions.

And finally, in the fields of seismology, geology, and other sciences, highly significant data which are not procurable by laboratory techniques could be studied by means of underground nuclear explosions.

It has also been proposed that the future launching into space of large loads may be accomplished by nuclear explosions and that nuclear motors of a different sort will provide directional mobility after such a vehicle has been orbited. This is not entirely science fiction.

In 1957 we conducted the test known as Rainier at the Nevada test site of the Commission. It was a "small" explosion by nuclear weapons standards (1.7 kilotons of TNT equivalent), but it was a historic one. For the first time in the Atomic Age, a nuclear explosion was produced which added no radioactivity to the atmosphere. This was accomplished by detonating the device in a chamber at the end of a tunnel driven horizontally into the side of a mesa. The tunnel was blocked and the device was fired. A shock was felt nearby, and the mesa appeared to heave upwards a few inches and settle back. There was no mushroom cloud, no fall-out radioactive or otherwise. We had discovered that we could test without producing fall-out. The cease-test agitation continued unabated, however, though it was no longer possible to base it upon the evils of fall-out. Test cessation and nuclear disarmament became equated in this propaganda. The fact that during a test moratorium atomic weapons would continue to be made and stockpiled was ignored. To "ban the tests" became a fixation, and part of the American public was persuaded that the good opinion of the world was ours if we would cease our weapon improvement program (which necessarily included tests) and would condemn us if we held out for genuine guarantees of similar compliance by the Soviets.

There was a hearing[7] before a subcommittee of the Senate Committee on Foreign Relations in April of 1958 on the subject of "Control and Reduction of Armaments." Eminent scientists spoke of their belief, that, based upon nothing more than the spotty seismographic records made by the Rainier shot, that nuclear detonations underground could be detected with practical reliability if there were enough seismic stations. Evidence was submitted to the effect that about 2500 earthquakes of a magnitude of 3.9 (producing a seismic signal equal to the detonation of 1 kiloton of TNT) or larger occur in the U.S.S.R. and China each year. Of this number, about 210 would fall within a range between 5 and 10 kilotons; about 120 within a range between 10 and 50 kilotons; and the remainder of a magnitude of 50 kilotons or larger. It would be necessary to have ground teams free to make unimpeded inspections after any of these seismic signals in order to be sure that they were not clandestine tests.

Dr. Edward Teller testified to his belief that a country which was insistent on violating a test agreement could defeat an inspection system by conducting underground tests in surroundings which would reduce the seismic signal. Dr. Hans Bethe stated his opinion "that this will be true only to a very limited extent, and if a country is intent on defeating a test cessation agreement and violating it, then it will have to conduct a lot of experiments underground with low-yield weapons to find out whether seismic signals from these are detectable."

Teller made no secret of his opinion that an agreement to refrain from testing nuclear weapons would be likely to benefit the Communist position and weaken ours. He was sharply attacked for it. One of his scientific colleagues was reported as stating:

> Dr. Teller believes that any such agreements [to cease the testing of nuclear weapons] would work to our disadvantage because we could not be certain that the Soviet Union might not "bootleg" tests. I challenge this view, and in doing so I do not stand alone in the scientific world. I believe Dr. Teller is willfully distorting the realities of the situation.[8]

There can be no question of the fact that the Soviet Union "bootlegged" its preparations for the most extensive test series of nuclear weapons ever conducted.

The following year, Dr. Bethe, who meanwhile had become a principal scientific adviser to the U.S. team which was negotiating with the Soviets in Geneva, was under the necessity of informing the Russians that definite conclusion had been reached in the U.S. that weapons could be detonated underground in a cavity of suitable size and the seismic signal thereby decoupled or reduced by a factor of 300. Writing of this later, Dr. Bethe stated: "I had the doubtful honor of presenting the theory of the big hole to the Russians in Geneva in November, 1959. I felt deeply embarrassed in so doing, because it implied that we considered the Russians capable of cheating on a massive scale. I think that they would have been quite justified if they had considered this an insult and had walked out of the negotiations in disgust."[9]

We were plagued by naïveté.

Further in the 1958 hearing, Dr. Bethe gave his opinion that a test-suspension agreement would be to U.S. advantage, adding, "I feel that if testing continues, then they [the Soviets] will surely attain the same level of capability as we, and I feel that it is just a matter of simple logic that for the relative standing it is more advantageous to stop when you know that you are still ahead." Senator Symington interposed: "But, if we are ahead and we stop testing and they are behind and agree to stop testing, but do not, then of course they would rapidly overtake and pass us with respect to the development of weapons?" This may have been stated as a rhetorical question. The results have proved too close for comfort.

When my turn came to testify, I pointed out that we were in a transition period in nuclear weapon design; weapon systems were no longer dependent upon large aircraft which required substantial time to launch and substantial time to reach their targets. Instead, systems were possible for very rapid delivery of bombs of various sizes and yields and that the Soviets had demonstrated that they then had or could have in the future an ability to deliver a very heavy attack in this manner. Our position had to be to make sure that such an aggression would be deterred not only by the assurance of retaliation but blunted if it should eventuate.

"We have made substantial strides in developing the weapons systems we need," I stated. "Yet with regard to some, particularly those of extremely severe design characteristics, we still need further development and test. This is particularly true with regard to weapons of greatly reduced radioactive fall-out. In the interest of civil populations, we are convinced that such weapons are a necessity in all types of both strategic and tactical use." I added that it would require more development and more tests before we would have that comprehensive arsenal and that the interruption of our test programs would directly affect our development since there was no substitute for tests in determining whether a weapon, nuclear or conventional, would or would not perform as anticipated.

Here I tried to emphasize what seemed to me a vital point. "A cessation or moratorium on testing will not in itself be a step toward reducing existing armaments. On the contrary, in our case, it is a step which will interrupt the development of *defensive* systems, which we know can be developed in time and which we need. It is a very fateful step, therefore, and one which . . . should only be taken in conjunction with other and more significant disarmament arrangements. . . . It is a

424   MEN AND DECISIONS

step to be taken only when we can have assurance acceptable to prudent men, that the Soviet will not violate the agreement. It is a step to be taken, therefore, only if both parties are willing to allow the inspection necessary to reduce to the utmost the possibility of clandestine violation. . . . A test cessation does nothing to reduce the existing weapon stockpiles. . . . It does nothing to curtail the improvement of an aggressor's delivery system."

Commenting further on the inspection system, I pointed out that if seismic signals were to be identified as earthquakes and not as nuclear detonations, "the right of immediate access to any suspected area must be allowed. Even then, there will be no assurance that all nuclear detonations can be identified as such . . . for with an elaborate inspection system including the right to visit suspected underground explosion sites, there still remains a real possibility that successful clandestine tests . . . could be carried out by a determined violator.

"My belief is that the emphasis on the cessation of testing is a great mistake . . . a spurious argument from the point of view of its effect on disarmament or the security of the world."

"The real danger to the human race is not the continuance of weapons tests. The real danger is a nuclear war. Our weapons tests to perfect our stockpile of nuclear weapons have as their purpose the deterrence of a nuclear war. . . . Since we are a defendant nation and cast in that role by the fact that we are a democracy and are not aggressors, it would be a tragic mistake in my opinion to cease the development of our defenses unless the whole threat of a surprise attack with atomic weapons were cancelled at the same time."

The Chairman, Senator Humphrey, asked, "Do you believe that a cessation of tests would be more advantageous to the United States or to the Union of Soviet Socialist Republics?"

"At the moment," I answered, "I believe it would be more advantageous to the Russians," but I added that I supported the President's proposal that we negotiate a test suspension and a cutoff of nuclear materials production accompanied by inspection. I had testified to my belief "that a cessation of testing alone would result in an improvement of the aggressor's system and a freezing of the defender's system."

To others I expressed apprehension that, if we entered into a negotiation with the Russians on a test moratorium, and suspended our tests while the negotiations were in progress, they would employ the same delaying tactics as they had successfully used in the armistice negotiation at Panmunjom in the Korean War. I feared that negotiations thus might be protracted for as long as a year. As matters developed, the Soviets were able to stretch them out for three years and they ended with an impossible condition completely negating free inspection. Following this, the moratorium was violated by a large number of Russian tests conducted in the atmosphere. Clandestine underground tests most probably had been conducted by them right along as there were a number of significant events recorded by seismographs during the three years for which, of course, no inspection was permitted by the Russians.[10]

The Soviets have undoubtedly increased their fire power. Whether they have equaled us in one aspect or another is not known to me, but the fact remains that, after they had improved their position relative to ours while we were static, their game had been successfully played. It is also clear that those experts who advised our authorities that there was little or nothing more to be learned by us from testing were as wrong as they had been in 1949, when they opposed our development of a weapon qualitatively more effective than the fission weapon of 1945.[11]

The test-moratorium negotiations began within a few months of the Senate committee hearing. A conference of scientists met in Geneva from July 1 to August 21, 1958, following which our government announced that, taking account of the conclusions reached in Geneva, we were prepared to proceed to negotiate an agreement with other nations for the complete suspension of nuclear weapons tests and the establishment of an international inspection and control system.

Negotiations of a test-ban treaty began at the end of October that year, and the expected minuet ensued. By December of the following year (1959) President Eisenhower, having noted that the negotiations had been in progress for fourteen months and that no satisfactory agreement was in sight, announced that the existing voluntary moratorium would end on December 31 of that year and that we would consider ourselves free to resume our nuclear weapons tests but would not do so without announcing our intentions in advance. In any case we would not test in the atmosphere.

In February of the following year, we proposed a phased treaty which would have immediately ended all nuclear weapons tests in environments in which controls could be established, that is to say, all tests aboveground and tests underground over a certain size. This proposal was rejected by the Soviets, though they later changed their position and accepted it, subject to an agreement among the scientists. The scientists met and reached what appeared to be a wide area of agreement in early

May of 1960, but on May 27 the Russian political delegate overruled the views of the Russian experts.

We had proposed to conduct experiments in both countries on detection of small underground tests in order to perfect the instruments useful for that purpose. The Russians countered by stating that they would not consider any such research program in Russia and that it might be conducted only in the United States, *provided it was open to Russian participation and that the devices to be used by us be subject to internal inspection by the Soviet technicians.* By any standard, this was an egregious condition.

A further reinforcement of the conviction that tests could be clandestinely conducted was our determination that, by the use of large underground cavities for nuclear tests, the seismic effects of a detonation could be reduced by a factor as great as 300. The Soviet last-minute insistence on a veto on any test inspection was introduced into the negotiations in the spring of 1961. Prior to that, President Eisenhower, his patience worn thin, had reached the decision that, our freedom to test having been resumed, we should no longer delay actual testing, though not in the atmosphere. Had the result of the 1960 election been otherwise, we would have done so at once, since Mr. Nixon was in accord with this policy. In the circumstances, however, the President did not feel it appropriate to confront his successor with a decision which would have tied his hands after he took office.

The long and elaborate series of Soviet weapon tests in the atmosphere which began in the late summer of 1961 were in cynical disdain of many of their earlier protestations. By knowing something of the degree of preparation incident to tests, the installations required, the elaborate instrumentation necessary to obtain information from the shots, and the complex logistic support, it was obvious that so huge an operation had been long in course of preparation. The Soviets displayed their complete disregard for that decent respect to the opinions of mankind, a concept that for 185 years has guided our actions.

World opinion has shown no evidence of approval for our forbearance in the matter of test suspension any more than it had evidenced even vestigial memory of the gesture we made in 1946 when we volunteered to renounce our atomic primacy, conditioned only on reliable inspection and control. It is a fair question as to whether world opinion exists and if it does, whether it is fundamentally concerned with justice and fairness, or is merely an amalgam of considerations most of which are temporary, political, and basically uninformed. One thing appears certain: such opinion as there may be has a short memory. Among other events, it has forgotten the massacres in Budapest, the blockade of Berlin, the brutal assault on Finland, the cynical alliance with Hitler, and the seizure of Czechoslovakia. Esthonia, Lithuania and Latvia, whose independence once was guaranteed by the U.S.S.R. are now only names in geography books—old ones.

There is an argument for ending the development of nuclear weapons from which the ceasing of tests would naturally follow. It is a case for nuclear disarmament even in the face of danger and a pleading which it is difficult for a layman to answer. It is the argument on the moral plane. For those who say we should possess no weapons whatever may seem to have the angels on their side. Unable here to speak with any authority, I would quote the scholarly Archdeacon of London, the Reverend O. K. Gibbs-Smith, explaining why a God-fearing man can support the fact of nuclear defense: "It is," he says, "because in fact it does deter; because it is the lesser of evils, which in any imperfect world Christians have often to choose; because by a sheer paradox the possession of the deterrent is almost certainly, for the time being, the best possible guarantee against its use."

Conclusion

The fault, dear Brutus, is not in our stars,
But in ourselves . . .

There's a divinity that shapes our ends,
Rough-hew them how we will. . . .

These chapters have been my remembrances of decisions by men, sometimes acting together, sometimes in solitary searching of the soul. Like the conflicting philosophies represented by the familiar lines from *Julius Caesar* and *Hamlet,* there have been occasions when the exercise of free will appeared clear, others when men seemed to be prisoners of approaching and ineluctable fate.

The question of whether decisions are really free long has troubled the minds of men. One might infer from ancient literature that men preferred to believe their destinies shaped by the conjunction of the planets or other forces external to their wills.

And while historic acts of choice, independent of the controlling stars, have been based upon a variety of considerations—patriotism, duty, justice, even love; while in others the weights have been expediency and avarice, fear and hatred—epic decisions also have been made by men avoiding the responsibility of choice altogether, leaving the turn of events to supernatural intervention or to chance. Thus, men have decided to fight or to run away by the casting of lots or the toss of a coin. Others have journeyed to Delphi or to Cumae in the hope of hearing the voice of fate itself.

Often, as in certain events related in these chapters (for example, the decision which brought the onset of war in the Pacific in 1941 or the decision to use the atomic bomb in 1945) destiny seems to have seized the wheel, the decision-makers mere passengers on a vehicle careening too fast to control. Appearing to reinforce this concept is the doctrine that, since the Creator of all things must know the future as well as the past, events which are foreknown are, in effect, foreordained. From this it would follow that action which is foreordained cannot come from free choice.

In ancient literature it is not until we reach the Old Testament that we find a clear statement of man's responsibility for his fate. In the last of the Five Books (Deuteronomy 30:19) the scribe records the words of Moses, in his last hours, declaring to the people that a choice is set before them—on the one hand, life and good, on the other, death and evil. There is an option for man.

The conflict between the assurance of the independence of human decision and the seemingly incompatible doctrine of predetermination has divided theologians from the earliest days.

Flavius Josephus, who studied with each of the three schools in Palestine in the first century, recorded* that the Sadducees denied predestination, regarding good and evil as entirely a matter of man's decision; the Pharisees, while recognizing free choice, laid greater emphasis on fate; the Essenes insisting on absolute predestiny. The same argument was also the subject of historic controversies in the Christian church, the earliest between St. Augustine and Pelagius, and later the Calvinist-Arminian debates. Within the Church of Rome itself, I am told, the issue has continued as a distinction between the Dominican and Jesuit orders.

The problem of reconciling divine foreknowledge with man's freedom of decision troubled the Hebrew philosophers of the Middle Ages. Most learned and revered among them was, of course, Maimonides. His inquiring mind was like that of Da Vinci, whom he preceded by three hundred years, ranging over a spectrum of extraordinary breadth. The issue of free will and determinism confronted him as it had those before him. In his monumental work *Guide for the Perplexed*, he characterized the assertion that man's behavior is completely foreordained as in equal error with the assumption that the position of the stars was responsible for it. In that event, he pointed out, the Commandments and all ethics would be in vain and all reward and all punishment would be unjust whether administered by God or man.

Maimonides reasoned that, while man cannot know a future event, it is an arrogance of man to assume that God cannot do so; for man's

* *Antiquities*, XIII and XVIII.

knowledge and God's knowledge are not comparable, God's "essence" being qualified by attributes not even imaginable to his creatures.

The most potent denial in reasonably modern times of the doctrine of man's free decision was voiced by the famous colonial preacher and metaphysician Jonathan Edwards. He preached eloquently against freedom of will, at the same time and with some inconsistency exhorting his listeners to mend their ways.

In the first century, Rabbi Akiba made the classic formulation of the paradox. He said simply, "Everything is foreseen and yet man has free will." Therefore, though I have been deeply interested in the process of decision-making for fifty years, and while that has been long enough to confirm me in the belief that man does have freedom of choice, it nevertheless remains for me more a matter of faith rather than of proof.

* * *

Now, we are told, we stand at the threshold of an era when it will be possible for man to abdicate both the right and responsibility of free decision and to delegate it to the machine. With all of human frailty notwithstanding, that prospect, if it were real, would be less than alluring. Complex circuits of transistors, diodes, and assemblies as yet uninvented and nameless are to scan coded questions, weigh all the contingencies on the basis of facts and assumptions which the machine has previously ingested, and thereupon decisions will emerge which are to send us to war or lull us to sleep. They will be decisions for which no man will bear responsibility—decisions as coldly impersonal as the crystals and circuits of which the device is constructed.

May that day be far distant. Without doubt, machines will be able to determine the means and avenues to goals, but men will continue to set the goals themselves. For what machine can ever apply the considerations of compassion and justice which, as man's enlightenment spreads and his awareness of brotherhood awakens, will enter ever more often into the decisions that affect his future in the world and in the universe?

Acknowledgments

Though concerned to involve none of my friends in responsibility for what is written in this book, I would like to acknowledge my obligation for help from many of them, both in government service and private life. Civil servants, as bureaucrats, are frequent targets for lampoon and cartoon. I have found the great majority able and devoted. Those who have assisted me with this book I may not name without subjecting them to some risks, but they will understand. Some friends appear in the text itself, and if, in describing them, I have worn a few superlatives threadbare, it is because of my inadequacy in finding alternate expressions of my admiration.

I am grateful to Virginia Walker who, with inexhaustible patience and an encyclopedic memory, shepherded the manuscript through many drafts. Samuel S. Vaughan, a senior editor at Doubleday, was generous with perceptive and experienced advice. My son and daughter-in-law and my wife read the manuscript with constructive criticism—tempered by affection.

The conclusions and errors are my own.

Appendix

The institution of "footnote" and "appendix" is a weariness of the flesh. There is no way to avoid their use, however, since the full story of any event cannot be told in one book or by one author. The ancient scribes who set down for posterity what we know today in Scriptures as the book of First and Second Samuel and First and Second Kings frequently interrupt their narration with expressions such as "But is this not all to be found in the Book of the Kings of Israel"—of the Book of the Kings of Judah—or the Book of the Wars of the Lord. These tantalizing references have alas long been lost forever, unless they turn up someday in the caves of the Negev, but at least there is venerable precedent for the employment of notes such as these which follow.

THE AUTHOR

CHAPTER I. FIRST DECISIONS

1. The remainder of the inscription was gratifying but not pertinent to this record.

CHAPTER II. A MAN OF DECISION

1. House Papers, Yale University.
2. Letter from ex-President Herbert Hoover to Senator Warren Magnuson, May 9, 1959. From Hearings Before the Committee on Interstate and Foreign Commerce, United States Senate, Eighty-sixth Congress, First Session, on the Nomination of Lewis L. Strauss to be Secretary of Commerce, 1959, pages 830–31.

CHAPTER V. DECISIONS ABOUT MONEY

1. Blum, John M., *From the Morgenthau Diaries,* Houghton Mifflin Company, 1959, Vol. I, page 70.

CHAPTER VII. SIDELIGHT ON A DECISION IN TOKYO

1. Hull, Cordell, *The Memoirs of Cordell Hull,* The Macmillan Company 1948, page 990.

2. Admiral Stark had advised against the action. See *Japan's Decision for War*, by Louis Morton, Harcourt Brace, 1959.

3. Grew, Joseph C., *Turbulent Era,* Houghton Mifflin Company. 1952, Vol. II, page 1283.

4. Father Drought suffered internal injuries as a result of an airplane accident, and these so weakened him that he died in 1943. In my file I have a few words of his written to me in the nature of a political testament:

> Seldom in history have the opponents in a conflict been equally prepared. The aggressor conceives well his purposes and methods of execution; the defendant gropes for weapons and fights an emergency defense long, often years, before he has realized the full impact of the conflict.
>
> It is folly to affirm the efficacy of a defense unless it has been organized with a clear perception of the nature and character of the attack. This is true in all fields of operation, whether military, diplomatic, economic or cultural. The Maginot Line and the Munich appeasement are monuments to a defense delusion; the one bled France and the other bled South Central Europe; and made of each a pallid mockery to stupidity.
>
> It requires courage to anticipate and to prompt a radical revelation that exposes truth in such terms that its acceptance or rejection involves a life struggle.
>
> Man now, as throughout the ages past, will exercise more energy in avoiding an issue than in facing it. Men embalm their complacency of indecision in the protective custody of superficial and emotional concerns. Weakened by such ineptitude they can become the pathetic victims of an aggressor who has what they lack—the courage to decide upon issues of fundamental consequences.
>
> So long as we can be kept, or keep ourselves, distracted by secondary and conflicting issues, defense will be impossible and we will assume progressively the character of supine victims. Greater than our need of arms, of wealth, or of anything else is the urgent and compelling necessity of *realizing the nature of the threat* to the world today and of communicating that realization to others.
>
> Communism is the terminal and volcanic explosion of the forces of spiritual disbelief and philosophical negation that have been agitating for years as an underground. Communists are religiously determined to attain a managed utopia. They are able to persuade their people to die in the attempt to attain their utopia and for it they will corrupt the humanity in which we believe and to whose perfection we aspire. They do not believe in hope; they do not believe in free will; and they will destroy ruthlessly without a twinge of regret, the millions who insist on so believing. They are consumed with the compelling urgency of leveling all humanity and of reducing it to dimensions which they can manage.

Chapter VIII. A View of the Navy from the Beach

1. Bowen, Harold G., *Ships, Machinery & Mossbacks,* Princeton University Press, page 368.

2. Baxter, James Phinney, *Scientists Against Time,* Little, Brown & Company, 1946.

3. This letter was prepared with the advice of Vice Admiral Paul F. Foster, under whom I had served in 1926, and a constant friend.

12 November 1943

Dear Mr. Secretary:

Admiral Horne informed me this morning that you are planning to send, or have already proposed, my name to the President to be nominated to the Senate for promotion to Rear Admiral; and to be assigned responsibility for the termination of Navy contracts, the disposal of surplus property and facilities, and related matters. I very sincerely appreciated the expression of confidence which this action evidences on your part and on the part of those officers of the Navy who have recommended this step to you. In the nearly seventeen years of my service in the Naval Reserve, and particularly in the past three years of active duty, there have been gratifying opportunities for the exercise of such abilities as I possess. I have enjoyed the most agreeable personal associations with the Chief of the Bureau of Ordnance and with brother officers in that Bureau and in other parts of the Naval Establishment.

Nevertheless, I must request you not to transmit my name to the President, or, in the event that you have already acted, request you to permit me to decline the promotion. My reasons follow:

My business background, as one of the partners of a large banking firm and as a director of a number of businesses, has resulted in contacts in the industrial world which might conceivably be cited as a disqualification at some future time by persons hostile to the Service, who wished to find some point of supposed vulnerability. With this in mind, when I was ordered to active duty almost a year before Pearl Harbor, I wrote a memorandum to the Chief of the Bureau of Ordnance, where I was detailed, enumerating the companies of which I had been a director or for which my firm had acted as bankers, requesting to be assigned no duty involving any of them. Admiral Blandy respected my wishes; and I have not been involved in the placement of contracts with any firms whatsoever. While I do not anticipate that I shall be called upon personally to negotiate terminations, grant loans, or dispose of property, I would be determining general policy and consulted in complex cases. Were former clients concerned, I should, of course, have to disqualify myself, which, in view of the number of companies involved, would not seem to make me a wise selection from the Navy's point of view.

There is another element of equal—if not greater—weight with me in reaching my decision, and which derives from the policies of the Navy Department in respect of reserve officer personnel. I have long observed how the Navy has suffered in comparison with the Army by restricting the rank upon initial commissioning of Naval Reserve personnel, and by limiting promotion of Reserve Officers, especially in the senior grades. Entertaining this view as strongly as I do, I am most reluctant to be promoted to flag rank while other and better qualified reserve captains are not similarly considered. To be selected as the only reserve officer for flag rank could impair morale in the Establishment, and might diminish the effectiveness of my work for the Navy. If, at some future date, the policy should change and a representative number of competent reserve officers should be selected in the ordinary course, and if then my name should be found worthy of consideration, I would naturally esteem it an honor to be promoted in such company.

I would like to conclude by repeating my sense of deep appreciation that you should have considered me worthy of this preferment.

Sincerely yours,

/ s / Lewis L. Strauss

Honorable Frank Knox
Secretary of the Navy

4. Letter from Vice-Admiral H. G. Bowen to Burt Nanus, dated 8 April 1959. "Admiral Strauss, then a Commander in the Naval Reserve, arrived in Washington when I was Director of the Naval Research Laboratory. . . . He did more to establish the Office of Naval Research than anyone else."

5. Associated with him, besides De Florez, were a group of unusually able men, among whom were Captain Robert D. Conrad, Dr. Alan T. Waterman, and Dr. Emanuel Piore.

6. Vice-Admiral Louis Denfeld, USN, Chief of Personnel, in a memorandum dated December 28, 1945, wrote: "The Naval Technical Mission to Europe was Rear Admiral Strauss' conception. He promoted it and selected the officers who successfully headed it."

CHAPTER IX.   "A THOUSAND YEARS OF REGRET"

1. ". . . most of us [the scientists] are certain that the Japanese cannot develop and use this weapon effectively." From "A General Account of the Development of Methods of Using Atomic Energy for Military Purposes . . ." by Henry D. Smyth, July 1, 1945, 13.3.

2. *Physical Review,* Vol. LVI, No. 7, October 1, 1939.

3.

1 June 1939

MEMORANDUM FOR THE DIRECTOR

Subject: Submarine Submerged Propulsion—Uranium Power Source—Status of as of this date.

1. Under certain special circumstances of bombardment by neutrons, the heavy element uranium dissociates into two other elements with the evolution of tremendous amounts of energy which may be converted directly into heat and used in a flash boiler steam plant. Such a source of energy does not depend on the oxidation of organic material and therefore does not require that oxygen be carried down in the submarine if uranium is used as a power source. This is a tremendous military advantage and would increase enormously increase the range and military effectiveness of a submarine.

2. . . . The next point of importance has been to learn if this reaction can be made to proceed more or less spontaneously. . . .

3. The Carnegie Institution was approached in regard to carrying on tests on this problem. The institution refused to accept a contract to give us this information but did release funds to the Department of Terrestrial Magnetism which permitted them to carry on the required experiments. Dr. Merle Tuve of the Carnegie Institution has been most helpful in keeping this Laboratory informed of all the developments in this field.

4. It has been established that uranium alone will not dissociate spontane-

ously, but the concensus of opinion at this time is that the isotope of uranium 235 is likely to dissociate in a manner which will be most useful in Naval problems. . . . The next step in an understanding of this problem is to secure an adequate supply of the uranium isotope so that final tests may be conducted.

5. The separation of the isotope 235 is best accomplished by a centrifugal method worked on and developed by Dr. J. W. Beams of the University of Virginia. . . .

6. If it is possible for Dr. Beams to separate the isotope to the necessary extent, Dr. Tuve of the Carnegie Institution has agreed to carry on the final tests at his laboratory. . . .

7. . . . If the method will work, it is of outstanding importance. . . . If it will not work, it is of the utmost importance to determine this fact at the earliest practicable date. In view of the willing cooperation of the many scientists in this country to carry on these investigations at practically no cost to the Laboratory, it is recommended that a small appropriation be made available to buy an adequate supply of uranium to carry on these preliminary tests to their logical conclusion.

Ross Gunn
Technical Adviser

4. Smyth Report, 1945.

5. Truman, Harry S., *Year of Decisions,* Doubleday & Company, Inc., 1955.

6. Byrnes, James F., *Speaking Frankly,* Harper & Brothers, 1947, page 258.

7. Stimson, Henry L., and Bundy, McGeorge, *On Active Service in Peace and War,* Harper & Brothers, 1949, page 635.

8. Mr. Bundy served with Robert A. Taft in the legal division of Mr. Hoover's Food Administration in 1917-18. He was one of Secretary Stimson's principal assistants and accompanied him to Potsdam. See "Remembered Words," by Harvey H. Bundy, *Atlantic Monthly,* March 1957.

9. Stimson and Bundy, *op. cit.,* page 622.

10. Byrnes, James F., *All in One Lifetime,* Harper & Brothers, 1958, page 297.

Forrestal, James V., *Diaries,* Viking Press, 1951, page 78.

Secretary Byrnes in a letter to the writer states, "It is understandable that at that time I did not know all the details, because I had only become Secretary on July 3, 1945. The following day was a holiday and we left Washington the evening of the 6th. I was in the Department only two working days, July 5th and 6th. We anticipated little discussion at Potsdam about the Japanese phase of the war and in those two days we concentrated on the subjects incident to winding up the European conflict, which were on the agenda."

According to Herbert Feis . . . "the State Department historians who collected and edited the Potsdam papers have not found it possible to establish precisely which of the messages (in translation) were read by Stimson and other members of the American civilian and military groups while they were in Potsdam, nor precisely when they were informed of the contents of particular messages." Feis, Herbert, *Japan Subdued,* Princeton University Press, 1961, page 57, footnote.

11. Byrnes, James F., *Speaking Frankly,* page 263.

12. In the Matter of J. Robert Oppenheimer, Texts of Principal Documents and Letters of the Personnel Security Board, General Manager, and Commissioners, Washington, D.C., May 27, 1954, through June 29, 1954, page 33, United States Government Printing Office, Washington, D.C., 1954.

13. *Ibid.,* page 34.

14. Letter from Albert Einstein to President Roosevelt, dated March 25, 1945.

112 Mercer Street
Princeton, New Jersey
March 25, 1945

The Honorable Franklin Delano Roosevelt
The President of the United States
The White House
Washington, D.C.

Sir:

I am writing you to introduce Dr. L. Szilard who proposes to submit to you certain considerations and recommendations. Unusual circumstances which I shall describe further below induce me to take this action in spite of the fact that I do not know the substance of the considerations and recommendations which Dr. Szilard proposes to submit to you.

In the summer of 1939 Dr. Szilard put before me his views concerning the potential importance of uranium for national defense. He was greatly disturbed by the potentialities involved and anxious that the United States Government be advised of them as soon as possible. Dr. Szilard, who is one of the discoverers of the neutron emission of uranium on which all present work on uranium is based, described to me a specific system which he devised and which he thought would make it possible to set up a chain reaction in unseparated uranium in the immediate future. Having known him for over twenty years both from his scientific work and personally, I have much confidence in his judgment and it was on the basis of his judgment as well as my own that I took the liberty to approach you in connection with this subject. You responded to my letter dated August 2, 1939 by the appointment of a committee under the chairmanship of Dr. Briggs and thus started the Government's activity in this field.

The terms of secrecy under which Dr. Szilard is working at present do not permit him to give me information about his work; however, I understand that he now is greatly concerned about the lack of adequate contact between scientists who are doing this work and those members of your Cabinet who are responsible for formulating policy. In the circumstances I consider it my duty to give Dr. Szilard this introduction and I wish to express the hope that you will be able to give his presentation of the case your personal attention.

Very truly yours,
A. Einstein

15. Byrnes, James F., *All in One Lifetime,* page 284.

16. Compton, Arthur H., *Atomic Quest; a Personal Narrative,* Oxford University Press, 1956, pages 238–39.

17. Forrestal, *op. cit.,* page 71.

18. Eisenhower, Dwight D., *Crusade in Europe,* Doubleday & Company, Inc., 1948, page 443.

19. Churchill, Sir Winston, *Triumph and Tragedy,* Doubleday & Company, Inc., 1953, page 639.

20. Potsdam Papers, Document 592.

21. Forrestal, *op. cit.,* page 73.

22. Truman, *Year of Decisions,* page 421.

23. Truman, *loc. cit.*

24. No man in the entire project was more widely respected for his intelligence or more admired for personal qualities. He died suddenly, in mid-career, on December 5, 1953. I was at an allied "summit" conference in Bermuda when the news of his death, arrived. President Eisenhower and the Prime Minister were discussing the President's speech on Atoms for Peace, on which Admiral Parsons had collaborated only a few days earlier.

25. Arnold, Henry H., *Global Mission,* Harper & Brothers, 1949, page 598.

26. Stimson and Bundy, *op. cit.,* page 632.

27. Eisenhower, *op. cit.,* page 456.

CHAPTER X.   THE DECISION TO DETECT

1. Truman, Harry S., *Years of Trial and Hope,* Doubleday & Co., Inc. 1956, page 306.

The closest estimate was made by Dr. Vannevar Bush. Secretary Forrestal, who talked with Bush at the Cabinet meeting on September 21, 1945, quoted him to the author as believing that, if the Russians concentrated their scientific and industrial resources upon that one objective, they might equal our 1945 position by 1950. The first Russian test was announced from the White House four years later to the month.

2. The Joint Committee in a report to Congress on October 13, 1949, referred to "Russia's ownership of the bomb, years ahead of the anticipated date. . . ."

3. From a report to the writer.

4. Truman, page 306.

5. *Op. cit.,* page 307.

6. Letter from General W. M. Canterbury to the writer.

CHAPTER XI.   DECISION ON THE HYDROGEN BOMB

1. "Results at Bikini" by Ernest K. Lindley, 22 July 1946.

2. Report of the Joint Congressional Committee on Atomic Energy, Eighty-first Congress, First Session, October 13, 1949, page 81.

3. *Ibid.,* page 47.

4. His letter appears in full in the transcript of the Oppenheimer Hearing: In the Matter of J. Robert Oppenheimer, Texts of Principal Documents and letters of the Personnel Security Board, General Manager, and Com-

missioners, Washington, D.C., May 27, 1954, through June 29, 1954, page 238, United States Government Printing Office, Washington, D.C., 1954.

5. Truman, Harry S., *Years of Trial and Hope,* Doubleday & Company, Inc., 1956, page 309.

6.

RESEARCH AND DEVELOPMENT BOARD
Washington 25, D.C.

9 November 1949

Dear Mr. President:

Just before leaving I feel that I should set down for your consideration certain thoughts with reference to the super atom bomb proposal. These thoughts are my reactions to the situation which led to a recent report by the General Advisory Committee of the Atomic Energy Commission and are the ideas which I expressed at an executive session of the Armed Forces Policy Council on yesterday.

I am taking the liberty of leaving this letter with Under Secretary Early in order that you may not be bothered with it unless the situation develops to a point requiring some decision on your part.

If renunciation of this objective by the United States could ensure its abandonment or failure everywhere else in the world, I could agree with the recommendation of the GAC.

In the absence of a strong international agreement, backed by adequate inspection, it is clear that Russia could proceed with the development of this type of weapon quite irrespective of any high-minded decisions and announcements on our part. There is no basic scientific secret standing in the way and there are some brilliant atomic scientists among the Russians and collaborating Germans.

While I should hope that we can keep well ahead of Russia, I think we are more likely to underestimate than to overestimate their capacity. Certainly we will not keep ahead of them in this particular project if we renounce it and they work on it.

Therefore, until an adequate international solution is worked out, it seems to me that our own national security and the protection of the type of civilization which we value, require us to proceed with the development of the most powerful atomic weapons which may be in sight. We can "hope to God they won't work", but so long as there is a reasonable possibility that they may work, it seems to me essential that we proceed with research and development on such projects as long as possible enemies may be doing the same thing.

For whatever it is worth, therefore, my judgment is that we should proceed with this phase of atomic weapon development, with increased activity and support, but that we should do so without fanfare or publicity.

Respectfully yours,
/s/ Karl T. Compton
Karl T. Compton
Chairman

The President
The White House
Washington, D.C.

7. *Bulletin of the Atomic Scientists,* March 1950, page 75.
8. Diocesan Letter of the Archbishop of York for May 1955.

Chapter XII. Vignettes of Research and Researchers

1. Memorandum to L. L. Strauss.

Sept. 1955

This is a restatement of the remarks that I made during our conversation today, regarding the probable consequence of a UN sponsored study of world-wide radiation effects.

I think that such a study is, in the long run, neither undesirable nor avoidable *per se,* but that it contains considerable elements of danger, unless certain points that we must insist on, are understood *a priori.* If these points are not appreciated, the study would be worse than nothing—even worse than a good deal of international unpopularity.

The points that I have in mind are the following ones.

The present vague fear and vague talk regarding the adverse world-wide effects of general radioactive contamination are all geared to the concept that any general damage to life must be excluded, and at least with certainty. However, it is quite certain, that no realistic and operable approach to these problems will be found, until and unless it is realised that this approach is absurd. No industry, no human effort, no progress has ever been achieved on such terms. Every worth while activity has a price, both in terms of certain damage and of potential damage—of risks—and the only relevant question is, whether the price is worth paying.

No progress in medicine was ever achieved without incurring physiological and biological risks, sometimes of even only very vaguely foreseeable orders of magnitude. The history of the introduction of X-rays is an eloquent example of this, and no one can tell whether our present practices with antibiotics and hormones may not repeat some phases of that experience.

The chemical industry has affected local climate in some important cases in unforeseen—and sometimes still unexplained—ways. Every industry, every new means of transportation improves its quota in casualties and fatalities.

It is characteristic, that we willingly pay at the rate of 30,000–40,000 additional fatalities per year—about 2% of our total death-rate!—for the advantages of individual transportation by automobile.

It is also characteristic that the safety standards of the nuclear industry are a good deal higher than those of the established industries. Two examples: All our Pacific tests had casualties—all, except the Castle fallouts, were due to non-nuclear activities, like automobile accidents, accidents involving the operation of ships, etc. The Castle fallout had one fatality and endangered to varying degrees about two hundred people—within a few weeks of it the capsizing of ferry in northern Japan, in the course of its normal operation, killed about [*sic*] thousand people, including twenty Americans—yet the Castle fallout was what attracted worldwide attention.

The really relevant point is: Is the price worth paying? For the U.S. it is. For an other country, with no nuclear industry and a neutralistic attitude in world politics it may not be. In a UN discussion we must not concede ahead of time, that we may not concur with other countries' evaluations in this regard. The evaluation itself may involve questions of national interest, and ours may differ from that of other countries.

This is particularly true, since the majority of the UN countries is in fact not productive in the atomic energy industry and any proposal to minimize, to eliminate danger, risks, etc. will be per se popular.

A certain amount of international unpopularity is therefore unavoidable for us, and we will have to accept it is part-payment for our more advanced industrial position.

2. It is an interesting coincidence that the young lady who typed the first official document on the possibilities of nuclear propulsion was Virginia H. Walker, who has been my loyal assistant for fifteen years and has typed this manuscript.

CHAPTER XIII. DECISION ON SECURITY

1. *Naval Institute Proceedings,* December 1960.
2. By ALNAV 27.
3. The Deputy Commissar of Foreign Affairs S. Lozovski invited the Canadian Chargé d'Affaires to his office in Moscow on February 20, 1946, and read to him a response from the Soviet Government to a statement made by the Canadian Prime Minister on the fifteenth of the same month. The Soviet statement admitted that the Soviet Military Attaché in Ottawa had received information of a secret character from Canadian nationals but disparaged its importance because, he said, "this information referred to technical data of which the Soviet organization had no need in view of more advanced technical attainments in the USSR; the information could be found in published works . . . and also in the well known brochure of the American Smyth. . . ."

Report of the Royal Commission, Ottawa, 1946, pages 627-28.

4. In a letter to the author.
5. Stimson, Henry L., and Bundy, McGeorge, *On Active Service,* Harper & Brothers, 1949.
6. Eightieth Congress, First Session. Hearings before the Joint Congressional Committee on Atomic Energy. January 28, 1947, page 32.

MR. LILIENTHAL: But there has been a relaxation, which is inevitable in peacetime perhaps, and there have been some serious *authorized* breaches of security—the authorized publication of information—which raises the question in many people's minds: If that information may be spoken about, why may I not discuss such and such a subject?

SENATOR MCMAHON: Mr. Lilienthal, I suppose the Smyth Report is the biggest giving out of information that we have had in the whole history of the project, is it not?

MR. LILIENTHAL: Yes, the Smyth Report is the principal breach of security since the beginning of the Atomic Energy Project, and it may well have been necessary, although many parts of it seemed to me very questionable indeed. But in any case, that has made our present chore a very, very difficult one. I call your attention, for example, to the fact that in that report four different ways of separating were generally described, and then the statement was made that all of them had succeeded.

Now, things like that just make our chore a really heart-rending one.

SENATOR MCMAHON: It has been estimated that that has brought other countries from one and a half to two years closer to the achievement of our own knowledge of atomic secrets. Have you any estimate of that?

MR. LILIENTHAL: No, I have not, Senator. It is hard for me to be temperate in my feeling as to how difficult some of those things have made the present situation.

SENATOR MCMAHON: Who authorized the release of that Smyth Report?

MR. LILIENTHAL: I know it was recommended for release by the Committee; and authorized by General Groves; and authorized by the President, I have no doubt, I still say that this disclosure of information in some respects makes our chore of shoring up this security system a terribly hard one.

7. Kramish, Arnold, *Atomic Energy in the Soviet Union,* Stanford University Press, 1959.

8. Truman, Harry S., *Year of Decisions,* Doubleday & Company, Inc., 1955, pages 525–34.

9. *Ibid.,* page 423.

10. Reference "Hearings before the Committee on Interstate and Foreign Commerce, United States Senate, Eighty-sixth Congress, First Session," May 13, 1959, pages 854–55.

11. From the testimony of John A. Waters, Director, Division of Security, AEC, Hearings before Subcommittee on Reorganization of the Committee on Government Operations, United States Senate, on Joint Resolution 21, Eighty-fourth Congress, First Session, 1955.

12. *Ibid.*

13. The New York *Times,* September 1, 1943; *ibid.,* March 12, 1948.

CHAPTER XIV.   DECISION IN THE CASE OF DR. J. ROBERT OPPENHEIMER

1. In the Matter of J. Robert Oppenheimer, Texts of Principal Documents and Letters of the Personnel Security Board, General Manager, and Commissioners, Washington, D.C., April 12, 1954, through May 6, 1954, pages 837–38, United States Government Printing Office, Washington, D.C., 1954.

2. White House news conference, June 30, 1954.

3. White House news release, October 23, 1953.

4. Smyth Report, III. 2.

5. His letter appears in the transcript of the Oppenheimer Hearing, page 238.

6. Subject: Meeting with Dr. J. Robert Oppenheimer on 21 December 1953 in the office of the Chairman, Atomic Energy Commission.

Representing the Commission: Lewis L. Strauss, Chairman, and Kenneth D. Nichols, General Manager (the writer).

After exchanging amenities, discussing the sudden death of Admiral Parsons, etc., Mr. Strauss told Dr. Oppenheimer of the visit he had had this morning with Mr. Herbert Marks. (Refer to LLS' memorandum of conversation with Mr. Marks.) Dr. Oppenheimer indicated surprise and said that he had not heard of the subject. Mr. Strauss said that he had told Mr. Marks that he expected a visit from Dr. Oppenheimer this afternoon and that he would suggest that Dr. Oppenheimer give Mr. Marks a ring.

Mr. Strauss then told Dr. Oppenheimer that we were faced with a very difficult problem pertaining to his continued clearance. Mr. Strauss informed

Dr. Oppenheimer that the President issued an Executive Order that requires the re-evaluation of the files of Government employees (including consultants) concerning whom there is derogatory data. Mr. Strauss informed Dr. Oppenheimer that his file contains a great deal of derogatory information. Dr. Oppenheimer admitted that he recognized this and that in due course his case would have been reached in accordance with the Executive Order.

Further, Mr. Strauss informed Dr. Oppenheimer that quite recently a former Government official, who had occupied a responsible position in the preceding Administration, had drawn attention to the record, which had resulted in a review of Dr. Oppenheimer's file and a report to the President by the Federal Bureau of Investigation.

Mr. Strauss then outlined the established Commission procedure which Dr. Oppenheimer stated that he had read at one time. Mr. Strauss reviewed the procedure, indicating that the first step would be to suspend clearance by tender of a letter informing Dr. Oppenheimer of his rights and of the nature of the derogatory information. He further outlined to Dr. Oppenheimer that the rights included the right to challenge the appointees to the Security Board, his right to testify, to produce witnesses, to be represented by counsel, and to appeal to a Personnel Security Review Board.

Mr. Strauss then informed Dr. Oppenheimer that such a letter had been prepared in his case by me but had not yet been signed. At this point Dr. Oppenheimer read the letter and, while reading it, commented that there were many items that could be denied, some were incorrect, but that many were correct. He further questioned Mr. Strauss concerning his opinion on whether anyone had ever been cleared by a Board with a comparable record. Mr. Strauss indicated that he did not believe a comparable case had ever been heard before and he did not venture an opinion of what the outcome would be.

Dr. Oppenheimer then discussed with Mr. Strauss the relative merits of resigning versus having a hearing. Dr. Oppenheimer raised the question of resigning prior to Mr. Strauss discussing this alternative. Dr. Oppenheimer stated that he wanted to think over this matter and indicated that the fact that the Jenner Committee might be about to hold a public hearing would have some bearing on his decision to resign but he expressed the opinion that a resignation just before a hearing by the Jenner Committee might not be too good from a public relations point of view. In the discussion, Dr. Oppenheimer indicated that he believed that Mr. Strauss felt that resignation was the better course to follow, but Mr. Strauss indicated that he was not trying to prevail upon Dr. Oppenheimer to accept any prescribed course of action but that Dr. Oppenheimer should make his own choice. Dr. Oppenheimer asked how long he would have to think the matter over and Mr. Strauss indicated to him that he would be available at his home this evening from 8 o'clock on to receive his answer. Mr. Strauss stated that the following day he felt would be the latest that the Commission should be expected to defer action. He said that on his own responsibility, in view of the fact that Dr. Oppenheimer was abroad, he had delayed the procedure for nearly three weeks. Dr. Oppenheimer indicated that he was going to consult Herbert Marks on the matter. Dr. Oppenheimer asked if he could have a copy of the letter, but Mr. Strauss indicated to him that it would be unwise to give it to him prior to signature and that he would send it to him as soon as he had decided whether he desired to request termination of his contract to go through the normal procedure. In this regard, it was indicated to Dr. Oppenheimer that if he requested his contract be cancelled, we would inform the various laboratories that we had taken such action at his request and that clearance was cancelled as a result. Further, Mr. Strauss discussed with Dr. Oppenheimer that if Dr. Oppenheimer did cancel his contract in such a manner and his clearance was cancelled, that he was then in the same status as any other individual and if at some future time he desired to renew his work with the Government, he could request clearance and a hearing in accordance with procedures prevailing at that time.

We also discussed with Dr. Oppenheimer the means for notifying the laboratory directors in case Dr. Oppenheimer selected suspension of clearance and hearing. Mr. Strauss read the memorandum which I had prepared for this purpose and I specifically cleared with him that we would like his consent to include the sentence, "This classification (Confidential) has been discussed with Dr. J. Robert Oppenheimer and he presently desires that it be maintained."

Dr. Oppenheimer asked if the Hill knew about this, Mr. Strauss indicated that he believed they did not, but that he doubted if such a thing could be kept from the Hill indefinitely.

Dr. Oppenheimer indicated that he would regret severing his relationship with the Government under either alternative but felt that we had very little recourse except to confront him with the two alternatives suggested.

Dr. Oppenheimer gave no indication that he was aware of this proposed action prior to his coming into the office. Upon leaving the office, he indicated that he was going to call Herbert Marks and then proceed to see him. Dr. Oppenheimer left the Commission at approximately 3:35 p.m.

Kenneth D. Nichols
General Manager

7. "In the Matter of J. Robert Oppenheimer," U. S. Gov't. Printing Office, 1954, Transcript of Hearing, *op. cit.*, page 171.

8. *Ibid.*, pages 53–55.

9. "In the Matter of J. Robert Oppenheimer," Text of Principal Letters and Documents of Personnel Security Board, pages 43–48, 1954.

10. "In the Matter of J. Robert Oppenheimer," U. S. Gov't. Printing Office, 1954, Transcript of Hearing, page 972.

11. Perhaps it might be well to let the story be told by one of the authors, Mr. Shepley, who during a television program on Sunday, September 26, 1954, said:

In an accident that was almost miraculous, the U.S. learned just a little more than five years ago this month that the Soviets had mastered the secret of the atomic bomb. Thus began the second round of what is now referred to as the hidden struggle over the H-bomb. With my associate Clay Blair, Jr., I wrote a book about this struggle which has attracted some notice this past week. The hidden struggle over the H-bomb was a remarkable chain of events. Almost as remarkable was the hidden struggle over the H-bomb book. I am going to tell this story now because I think it has important bearing on the vital subject of how the American people shall be informed on their atomic security.

In my 15 years experience as a Washington and overseas newsman, I have never seen such elaborate attempts for a mixture of motives to kill a book or suppress an important news story. When the book was submitted to the

Atomic Energy Commission for security clearance, I expected some immediate reaction. The AEC staff in Washington has been largely untouched by the new Administration, which is as it should be. The AEC should be above politics. So when the book was put in for clearance it was in effect being delivered over to many of the people who would fall under its implied criticism. I expected a reaction, but I was in no way prepared for what actually happened.

A week passed and I received a call from Mr. Lewis Strauss, Chairman of the AEC, whose role in the great H-bomb struggle is treated favorably by the book. He desired that I come to his office immediately. When I arrived, he was seated behind an enormous pile of paper work and at least three United States Senators were trying to talk to him on the telephone. Amidst these interruptions, we had a short, even-voiced conversation. Some of his associates at the AEC were badgering him almost to distraction to stop the book. 'Why stir up the animals?' they demanded. The weapons laboratory at Los Alamos was now working smoothly and the weapons program was progressing satisfactorily. Why should anyone be criticized for past mistakes. Strauss then turned suddenly from his desk and said in a soft voice: 'Jim, I want to buy your manuscript, put it in the safe for 25 years, or at least until the animals are no longer alive and kicking, and then publish it as an historical document.'

I replied that I assumed Mr. Strauss was kidding. Strauss' motives were, of course, of the highest. Certainly he had nothing to conceal. In fact, without him the Soviets would have had the H-bomb and the U.S. would not. I could only surmise, therefore, that he was under great pressure and that he wished to shield his scientists from public controversy, even though he must have known that a savage attack on himself, in connection with the H-bomb struggle, was even then in preparation. I added that Mr. Strauss had already conceded the book had important information for the American people about their atomic security. Things happened too quickly in the atomic era to wait 25 years for a report on how this most vital of all the functions of government had been, and was being, handled.

CHAPTER XV.   DECISION IN THE TENNESSEE VALLEY

1. Commission on Organization of the Executive Branch of the Government (generally known as the Hoover Commission), United States Government Printing Office, 1955, Vol. V, "Water Resources and Power," Vol. One, page 111.

2. Testimony of Wendell Willkie before congressional committees quoted in *Wendell Willkie,* by Mary E. Dillon, J. B. Lippincott Company, 1953, page 44 *et seq.*

3. Commission on Organization of the Executive Branch of the Government (generally known as the Hoover Commission), United States Government Printing Office, 1955, Vol. V, "Water Resources and Power," Vol. One, pages 109–10.

4. Public Papers of the President (U. S. Government Printing Office), 1953.

5. U. S. Court of Claims #479–55, page 149.

6. U. S. Court of Claims #479–55, page 163.

7. Memphis Light Gas and Water Division: progress report of 1959—
"The target date for putting Unit No. 1 on the line was October 1958 . . .
the first of the three turbine-generators was 'phased in' with TVA at 7:49
p.m. on November 21, just 36 days after the original target date. . . ."
Page 10.

1960 Progress report of 1960—"The Divisions' former power purchase
contract with its then only supplier, Tennessee Valley Authority (TVA),
expired May 31, 1958; however, TVA continued to furnish as much of
the Division's power requirements as necessary until two of the three units
at the Thos. H. Allen electric generating station were in commercial
operation (May, 1959). . . ." Page 28.

8. Memphis Light Gas and Water Division: progress report of 1960.

9. Electric Light and Power Industry Report, issue October 1, 1956,
reporting interview with Major Thomas H. Allen, President of the Memphis
Light, Gas and Water Division.

Memphis Light, Gas and Water Division 1960 Progress Report—"New
electric rates, designed to increase electric operating revenues by 18.5 per
cent, became effective December 29, 1959. The need for the increase was
mainly due to (a) annual interest cost for financing the Thomas H.
Allen Electric Generating Station being higher than estimated in the
generating station Feasibility Report, and (b) the future financial efforts
caused by less-than-expected sales and revenues during the business reces-
sion." Page 13.

CHAPTER XVI. A NEW CHARTER FOR THE ATOM: ATOMS FOR POWER

1. From an unpublished memoir by Edgar Sengier.
2. Vandenberg's letter to L. T. Gardler, July 20, 1946.
3. Truman, Harry S., *Year of Decisions*, Doubleday & Company, Inc.,
1955, page 300.
4. Report of the Joint Congressional Committee on Atomic Energy, 1952,
page 265.
5. The following reactors and their output in electrical kilowatts were
built, building, or planned in the United States and Puerto Rico:

Shippingport Atomic Power Station	60,000 kw
Dresden Nuclear Electric Company	182,000 kw
Yankee Atomic Electric Company	110,000 kw
Consolidated Edison Thorium Reactor	255,000 kw
Enrico Fermi Atomic Power Plant	94,000 kw
Hallam Nuclear Power Facility	75,000 kw
Northern States Power Company	62,000 kw
Consumers Power Company	50,000 kw
Humboldt Bay Power Plant	48,000 kw
Rural Cooperative Plant of Elk River	22,000 kw
Carolinas-Virginia Tube Reactor	17,000 kw
City of Piqua	11,000 kw
Puerto Rico Water Authority	20,000 kw

APPENDIX

A total of more than a million kilowatts. In addition, more than ninety other reactors for peaceful purposes such as experiment, teaching, materials testing, etc. were either operable or building. Eighty-two reactors were operable or being built for military purposes.

6. The countries (and one municipality) with which we negotiated research agreements were:

Argentina	Ecuador	Nicaragua
Austria	Germany (City of	Pakistan
Brazil	West Berlin)	Peru
Chile	Greece	Philippines
China (Republic of)	Guatemala	Portugal
Colombia	Israel	Sweden
Cuba	Japan	Thailand
Denmark	Korea (Republic of)	Uruguay
Dominican Republic	Lebanon	Venezuela
	New Zealand	

Power and research agreements were in effect with the following:

Australia	Germany (Federal	South Africa
Belgium	Republic)	Spain
Canada	Italy	Switzerland
France	Netherlands	United Kingdom
	Norway	

CHAPTER XVII. THE PEACEABLE ATOM: DECISIONS AFFECTING NEW PROBLEMS AND OLD FRIENDS

1. The statement continued:

One individual is largely responsible for successful United States detection of the three Soviet atomic bomb test explosions thus far announced from the White House. This individual is former AEC Commissioner Lewis L. Strauss. Mr. Strauss found that inadequate measures were being taken to inform the United States about any successful Russian weapon test. He, therefore, went to Mr. Forrestal and Mr. Patterson and other high-ranking military and civilian officials and insisted that the necessary measures be undertaken. In this effort he had the powerful backing of Senator Hickenlooper, then Chairman of the Joint Committee on Atomic Energy; Representative Cole, ranking majority member on the House side; and Senator McMahon and Representative Durham, ranking minority members. It was Mr. Strauss' foresight, relentlessly endorsed by the Joint Committee—and assisted on the technical side by Dr. Lawrence R. Hafstad, now director of AEC Reactor Development—that brought into being many of the vital measures which averted the disaster that might have ensued had the United States remained ignorant of Russia's success in achieving the atomic weapon.

2. Eisenhower, Dwight D., *Crusade in Europe,* Doubleday & Company, Inc., 1948, pages 457, 458.

3. Forrestal, James V., *Diaries*, Viking Press, 1951, page 327.

4. Stimson, Henry L., and Bundy, McGeorge, *On Active Service in Peace and War*, Harper & Brothers, 1949, pages 642–46.

5. The declaration proposed a United Nations Commission to formulate specific proposals. One of these was "effective safeguards by way of inspection and other means to protect the complying states against the hazards of violations and evasions." But this was the fourth step of a procedure which was to be achieved "in separate stages," each to be completed before the next stage was undertaken. The first stage was the exchange of scientific information, the second control for peaceful purposes, the third the elimination of atomic weapons from existing armaments, and inspection was the last.

6. In a memorandum addressed to the Secretary of the Navy on November 16, the day the declaration was published, I called to his attention the fact that effective safeguards, which should have had first priority, were last: "I have read with some puzzlement the text of the declaration which appeared this morning. It notes that the work of the proposed International Commission which is to make recommendations to the governments on the control of the atomic bomb is to 'proceed by separate stages, the successful completion of each one of which will develop the necessary confidence of the world *before* the next step is undertaken.' [Italics supplied.] These successive stages appear to refer to the preceding paragraph which lists four stages. The first of these reads 'for extending between all nations the exchange of basic scientific information for peaceful ends,' and not until the fourth is there provision 'for effective safeguards by way of inspection and other means to protect the complying states against the hazards of violations and evasions.' It seems to me that the cart is before the horse if we are to exchange information before we have arrived at a means of safeguarding the results of the exchange. Although some other purpose may have been intended, that is the way the declaration now reads. In fact, the declaration further states, 'specifically, it is considered that the Commission might well devote its attention *first* [italics supplied] to the wide exchange of scientists and scientific information and as a second stage to the development of full knowledge concerning the natural resources of raw materials.' Clearly, effective safeguards is at least third, if not fourth, in the order of priority."

7. Report to the President by the Advisory Commission on Universal Training, "A Program for National Security," May 29, 1947.

8. October 8, 1953.

9. While I did not become acquainted with Cherwell, or F. A. Lindemann, as he was then known, until World War II, I had formed an opinion of him at an earlier date. As a fellow guest at the country home of Justice Irving Lehman of New York in the mid-thirties, I had met Dr. Albert Einstein for the first time. In the course of conversation, we discussed the fate of those scientists who were still in Nazi Germany and refugees whose academic placement in the United States had enlisted Einstein's

concern. He also told me of the emigration of a number of his friends to England and of some who had managed to find sanctuary at Oxford and Cambridge. It was in this connection that Einstein mentioned Lindemann's successful efforts in arranging for men such as Kurti, Kuhn, and Mendelssohn to get to England. A number of these recruits added to the glories of the Clarendon Laboratory.

I cannot remember how or even whether Einstein characterized Lindemann as a scientist. This is a source of regret since, a word of appraisal from such an authority would go far to settle the controversy as to Lindemann's professional stature which has been raised since his death. Of this I am sure, however, that Einstein spoke of him with gratitude and respect.

10. Great credit for the completed instrument is due to him, his assistant, Bernhard G. Bechhoefer, and other members of his staff. The Atomic Energy Commission was very capably represented in the negotiations by two of its young officers, John Hall and Algie Wells.

11. Vandenberg, Arthur Hendrick, *Private Papers*, Houghton Mifflin Company, 1952.

CHAPTER XVIII.   DECISION IN THE SENATE

1. Report of the Strauss Commission on Incentive, Hazardous Duty and Special Pays, March 1953, Eighty-third Congress, First Session, printed for the Committee on Armed Services, U. S. Government Printing Office.

2. To LEWIS L. STRAUSS for exceptionally meritorious service in the interests of the security of the United States.

During a crucial period, he has provided leadership, resourcefulness, judgement and courage equal to the immense demands and promise of the atomic age.

His direct contribution to the security of the United States and other free world nations has been outstanding. He was an effective supporter of the development of thermonuclear technology at a time when a less determined and imaginative course might have resulted in severe damage to our security and that of the free world. He initiated a long-range detection system for atomic explosions which adds both to our safety and to our hopes for successful disarmament negotiations.

Equally significant has been his work in helping build the long-term security that comes of devoting the Atom to works of peace. Under his guidance, peaceful use of atomic energy for power, research, healing, agriculture, and production has made remarkable progress. He has played a great part in bringing to reality the International Scientific Conference on Peaceful Uses, and the Atoms for Peace program, now being put into effect through the International Atomic Energy Agency.

Through his wisdom and foresight, his country enjoys greater security today and greater hopes of genuine peace in the years ahead. In recognition of his distinguished service, I take pleasure in awarding the Medal of Freedom to Lewis L. Strauss.

/s/ Dwight D. Eisenhower

3. The effort was premature. The National Science Foundation did not come into existence until 1950.

4. Hearings Before the Committee on Interstate and Foreign Commerce, United States Senate, Eighty-sixth Congress, First Session, on the Nomination of Lewis L. Strauss to be Secretary of Commerce, 1959, page 502.

5. The complete cable will be found in the hearings, pages 854–55.

6. Hearings Before the Committee on Interstate and Foreign Commerce . . . , pages 748–50.

7. Hearings Before the Committee on Interstate and Foreign Commerce . . . , page 509.

8. Letter to the editor, Richmond *News Leader* from Representative W. S. Cole, June 15, 1954.

9. Hearings Before the Committee on Interstate and Foreign Commerce . . . , page 173.

10. Hearings Before the Committee on Interstate and Foreign Commerce . . . , page 315 ff.

11. Congressional Record for June 17, 1959, page 10066.

12. Congressional Record for June 17, 1959, page 10067.

13. Hearings Before the Committee on Interstate and Foreign Commerce . . . , page 602 ff.

14. Green, Arnold P., and Rosenthal, Alan, "The Joint Committee on Atomic Energy: A Study in Fusion of Governmental Power," George Washington University, 1961, page 121.

15. Hearings Before the Committee on Interstate and Foreign Commerce . . . , page 836ff.

16. Dr. Warren C. Johnson, Chairman, General Advisory Committee to the AEC

Dr. John A. Wheeler, Palmer Physical Laboratory, Princeton University

Dr. Eugene N. Beesley, President, Eli Lilly & Co.

Dr. Alan T. Waterman, Director, National Science Foundation

Dr. Niels Bohr, Atomic Energy Commission, Copenhagen, Denmark

Dr. Mervin J. Kelly, past President, Bell Telephone Laboratories

Dr. Shields Warren, New England Deaconess Hospital, Boston

Dr. Alvin M. Weinberg, Director, Oak Ridge National Laboratory

Lord Cherwell, scientific adviser to Prime Minister Winston Churchill

Dr. Eugene P. Wigner, physicist, Princeton University

Dr. Alexander Hollaender, Chief, Biology Division, Oak Ridge National Laboratory

Dr. Carl H. Holm, head, Torpedo Countermeasures Division, U. S. Navy Mine Defense Laboratory

Dr. Lawrence Hafstad, head of research for General Motors, formerly Chief of the Reactor Development Division of the Atomic Energy Commission, and co-inventor of the proximity fuse.

Dr. Norris E. Bradbury, physicist, Director, Los Alamos Scientific Laboratory

Dr. T. Keith Glennan, President, Case Institute of Technology, Administrator, National Aeronautics and Space Administration

Dr. Jaime Benítez, Chancellor, University of Puerto Rico

Dr. John C. Bugher, Rockefeller Foundation
Dr. Gunnar Randers, physicist, International Atomic Energy Agency
Dr. Charles L. Dunham, Director, Division of Biology and Medicine, Atomic Energy Commission
Dr. Paul B. Pearson, Division of Biology and Medicine, Atomic Energy Commission
Mr. Samuel Untermyer, II, physicist, General Electric Co.
Dr. Richard Courant, mathematician, New York University
Dr. Jesse W. Beams, physicist, University of Virginia
Dr. Carson Mark, physicist, Los Alamos Scientific Laboratory
Dr. Seeley Mudd, Los Angeles
Dr. H. W. Jones, President, Youngstown University
Dr. Allan C. Johnson, Manager, Idaho Operations Office, Atomic Energy Commission
Dr. E. D. Harrison, President, Georgia Institute of Technology
Dr. Lawrence A. Kimpton, Chancellor, University of Chicago, and Director, Argonne National Laboratory
Dr. Kenneth S. Pitzer, chemist, University of California, Berkeley
Dr. Paul S. Larson, professor of pharmacology, Medical College of Virginia
Dr. Raymond Allen, University of California, Los Angeles
Dr. Leland J. Haworth, Director, Brookhaven National Laboratory
17. Hearings Before the Committee on Interstate and Foreign Commerce . . . , page 830.
18. Hearings Before the Committee on Interstate and Foreign Commerce . . . , page 1068.
19. Hearings Before the Committee on Interstate and Foreign Commerce . . . , page 1067 ff.
20. Hearings Before the Committee on Interstate and Foreign Commerce . . . , letters from Congressman Taber and other members of the Appropriations Committee of the House of Representatives, page 1010.
21. Hearings Before the Committee on Interstate and Foreign Commerce . . . , page 978.
22. Hearings Before the Committee on Interstate and Foreign Commerce . . . , 977–1012, 1013–14.
23. Congressional Record, Vol. 105, No. 100, Page 10094.
24. Congressional Record, Vol. 105, No. 100, Page 10095.
25. Congressional Record, Vol. 105, No. 100, Page 10100.
26.

STATE OF CONNECTICUT
EXECUTIVE CHAMBERS
HARTFORD

June 29, 1959

The Honorable Thomas J. Dodd
United States Senate
Washington, D.C.

Dear Tom:
On my return from California, my attention was called to a column of last week. I share your surprise and chagrin.

There is absolutely no basis to the item. I have never talked with you concerning Strauss. As I have mentioned to you frequently, there has never been any question in my mind but that your action in all matters, as I am certain it was in the Strauss case, has been taken on strong personal conviction based on conscientious study. To say that I pressured you to vote and assign that reason just is not so.

If you so desire, you can make whatever use you want of this letter.

Sincerely,
/s/ Abe [Ribicoff]
Governor

Chapter XIX.   Nuclear Tests, Fall-out, and World Opinion

1. *Science*, Vol. 133, April 7, 1961, pages 1075-77.

2. *Archives of Pathology*, Tessmer, Carl F., August 1961, Vol. 72, page 175.

3. *Harper's* magazine, February 1947.

4. An interview with *Redbook* magazine, November 1959, page 106.

5. September 1, 1956.

6. New York *Times*, November 7, 1961.

7. Hearing Before Subcommittee of the Senate Committee on Foreign Relations, Eighty-fifth Congress, Second Session, page 1539.

8. *The New Leader*, March 31, 1958, in an adaptation of an address at the University of Minnesota by Dr. Harrison Brown.

9. *The Atlantic Monthly*, August 1960.

10. There have been in recent months indications of some explosions in Russia which they have ascribed to unusually large shots of conventional high explosives.

Commissioner Robert E. Wilson
Atomic Energy Commission
Proceedings of the American Philosophical Society
Vol. 105, No. 2, April 1961.

11. The Los Alamos Laboratory, our chief laboratory in the development of nuclear weapons, which has to its credit most of the weapons which have been developed up till now, is generally of the opinion that not much more can be obtained in the way of weapons improvement.

Hans A. Bethe, Atlantic Monthly, August 1960.

. . . we have already gone far enough so that very little we can do in the future will be of great military significance.

Ibid.

Index